salt in the
spine

FENYXMAERIE

COVER DESIGN SMC
PRINTED IN THE ~~UNITED~~ STATES OF AMERICA

SECOND EDITION
2025 AUGUST

ISBN: 979-89991724-8-8

The power of the people

| 86 - 47 |

Is greater than the people in power.

READER DISCRETION ADVISED

Physical, emotional, sexual abuse; gun violence, grief, & suicide ideation; coercion & consent ethics

This is not self-help.

The scenes are **not veiled.**
And this is **not recommended**
if seeking comfort or kink.

This is to witness, and to wonder.
You will not be told how to feel.
You will be asked to feel something
and to live with what that reveals.
Not all POV's are safe
because not all people are.

If you need to step away—
step away.
But protect your peace,
We don't all get the happy endings.

~ Be well. jm.

for the ones
twisted up by the world,
and then blamed for the
shape they became —

you were **never crazy**
for craving tenderness,
or for lashing out when
it finally came

but the war doesn't end,
until you **stop carrying it.**

COMPA'
Friend

CARIÑO / AMOR / MOY
Darling, love

HOMBRE / VATO
Man, dude

'MANO / CARNAL
Bro, blood (brotherhood)

PÚCHICA / CARAJO
Shit, damn it (mild)

PINCHE / JODIDO
Fucking (intensifier)

NO SÉ
I don't know

¿ENTIENDES?
Understand?

NO PREOCUPA / DISCULPEN
No worries / Excuse me

ESO NO ME IMPORTA
That doesn't matter to me

ATRÁS / BAJA LA VOZ
Get back / Lower your voice

¿CÓMO VOY A VIVIR CON ESO?
How do I live with that?

ME MIENTES OTRA VEZ Y SE ACABÓ
Lie to me again, and it's over

TE VEO
I see you

TÚ DIME
You tell me

¿QUÉ PASA?
What happened?

QUE LO INTENTE
Let him try

SIÉNTATE Y CÁLLATE
Sit down and shut up

Y LO MÁS IMPORTANTE...
And most important...

EL BARRIO TE CRIÓ
The block raised you

¿DÓNDE ESTÁ ELLA?
Where is she?

Y LA DIFERENCIA...
And the difference...

¿NO ERA ASÍ?
Wasn't it like that?

¿QUIÉN VERGA LE HIZO ESTO?
Who the fuck did this?

AÚN TE NECESITAMOS
We still need you

NO SOY TU PERRITO
I'm not your little dog

Salt in the Spine

Birds of Prey

DALY CITY, CALIFORNIA
PRECINCT | 00:00:00:00

|∞|

Dante's ears thrummed slowly, his temper too, pushing into the room with Jeb hot on his heels. It didn't help Dante's mood or his control that Jeb was already prepped to talk over him. Opposite actually; it made the room feel suffocatingly dry.

"I in for another shitty round with you now?" Dante blurted it as if first to talk took the lead.

"Beg—your pardon?" Leti bit back.

Not thrilled, Dante thought. But Dante? *Not surprised.* Safe to say his tone did it but hey, blame the punk in the previous room. The one bordering on betrayal and leaving Dante in a mess with this one here in front of him. *Leti.*

"Make it any better if I say it was an honest question?" Dante scratched his pinky to his ear; the weird space between hairline and hole as he and Jeb pulled out the seats and adjusted into the table like sediment.

It still itched though. The ear. Made Dante sigh as his hand dropped back to the table and Leti nodded slowly from across it.

Her braid was pulled forward, stuffed together with sloppy and thick dark hair; sand or dirt still wedged within it. A dramatic and unfortunate change to go from s'mores on the beach to cuffs on the pavement.

Jeb cleared his throat and both Dante and Leti looked. "Alrighty kids, done flirtin' yet?" Jeb slapped his hands down on the table, body hogging most of the space between Dante and him. Made Dante shift to a subtle side-lean, casually like he was unbothered. *Almost* unbothered.

"Just about," Dante yawned.

Jeb slapped a skinny folder down onto the desk and the thing cracked like it had more information inside it than it did.

"Let's see here." Jeb began with a loud and thick voice.

Dante couldn't help but watch. Jeb was a man that was built like a distraction; sharp eyes. But not sharp like knowing, just sharp with distrust pointed at everyone in the room but the mirror.

Even now, Jeb, eyeing Dante up from down as if he didn't have enough space at the table. As if Dante was a rookie. As if the file wasn't from Dante's fucking desk and his caseload...

Dante eyed him right back. Half his age but twice Jeb's skill. Maybe a third of Jeb's arrogance though, which is saying a lot.

Dante sighed again but cut it off halfway through. The night—*nah, the week*—was starting to feel like shanking roadkill. Pointless, and cruel. Particularly with Leti.

Dante's mouth opened to speak—sitting tall, rigid—but Jeb's voice came out first.

"I mean, this is serious shit, kid...Make ya' way all the way from Washington for a little trouble?" Jeb sighed this time. "Where are your parents anyhow, kiddo?"

Dante smiled—but his head shook.

"Dead." Leti smirked too, but not with humor; with venom.

There was a reason Dante wanted to take the lead. He didn't know her well but he knew her better, and the condescension wasn't going to cut it.

"And you took my ID," Leti went on, "so you should know my age. I'm not a minor; *don't* call me a kid."

"Right," Jeb laughed, but Dante's eyes stayed on the paperwork, flipping through her file aimlessly while pretending to ignore them.

There was names, notes, a sister, a dead dad, family services—

Death, death, investigation...

Maybe Dante'd seen enough. Or maybe he'd seen nothing at all. But what felt less like a "maybe" was the idea of getting Jeb out and getting Leti alone. Felt more like a necessity actually... Dante cleared his throat but Jeb pretended not to hear.

"You know him?" Jeb pushed photos toward Leti before Dante's hand blocked and scooped them up calmly. Casually, even.

Dante shook his head when Jeb made a face of displeasure and they shared an awkward two seconds together—like a car stalling before Jeb realized Dante was dead, giving in.

So Jeb went back to the folder for another picture; a less-dead picture.

"Never seen him." Leti was colder than Dante preferred—watching the men's exchanges the way they watched her—but still refused to show interest. Everyone playing a game of masquerade and emotion.

Dante flipped the crime scene photos to face down, uninterested in another look at a dead minor. The first look he had was enough to scar—pretending an old black-and-white TV spit up a foggy-blue, bloated bag of bones and called it a character instead of what it was; *a boy.*

"Leti-Leti, hunny," Jeb clicked his tongue while the room warmed a degree.

"Is there a reason I'm here?" Leti whispered snidely as she leaned forward, hand rubbing her wrist like they still hurt.

"Boy's dead." Jeb blurted with intrusively spread legs. "*Executed.*"

Executed normally hits different, Dante thought, eying her cool, calm, and collected mask as if that would confirm something for him. But Jeb pulled attention—*again*—adjusting the table as if it was off balance. He made it impossible to ignore him. The metal top peeling from under Dante's arm with each *wiggle;* a *sensation that* probably shouldn't have bothered Dante as much as it did but—

"I said," Leti enunciated harshly which snapped Dante back to front and center. "I. Don't. Know. *Him.*"

"Think harder." Jeb again. "Because your friends do."

But does Dante tell him it wasn't her friends? Does Dante cut her the benefit of the doubt despite being the perfect strangers'? He couldn't say.

And so began the stare down. All three in a potential stalemate; Jeb's fat-fingertips echoing against the desk; Leti's foot bouncing so fast it shook the floor; Dante churning with impatience.

After a moment longer Leti turned her focus to Dante; maybe wondering if he was going to do something, maybe thinking nothing and using him as a place to glare.

But the longer she looked, the less confident Dante felt. Despite six or seven years on her, feeling fit, doing fine in life—under too much scrutiny he was made to wonder: *what exactly do you see?*

The file, the badge—*the man?*

He was supposed to be good at this shit though; finding the softest parts, working around them, or working *with*. But Leti's hardened gaze remained focused, and when Dante's eyebrow slid up, she took it like a challenge to a fight she didn't want to have; turned her chest to the wall—shoulders high, chin neutral—and hugged herself tighter.

She didn't look back at Dante for awhile after that. Not that Dante did much, but maybe it was the fact that he saw her. People like Jeb—the loud ones, the ones that don't notice—they can't judge you when they can't see you.

"Should I try it in another language?"

Dante blinked at the break in silence as Leti followed Jeb's lead, listing off "I don't knows" in a few different languages. Dante was going to let her continue, see how many she got, but Jeb—*good ol' Jeb*—had other ideas.

After her third, *I don't know,* Jeb hacked together a wad of snot and spit. Wet enough that it stopped Leti dead in her tracks, and the words instead became a wretch; chills racing across her skin.

"Sorry," Jeb chortled, gurgling and clearing his throat.

Even Dante chilled with disgust. Went to look at Jeb with betrayal but stopped last minute in the name of a united front. Dante took a deep breath instead because, it's sleep—

It's just the lack of sleep, he repeated.

Dante reached out, tapping on the dead boy's file between them once before he pulled it back in and slid her file out in its place.

Slid her file out *further* when Jeb went for it.

"You're not detained, Leti," Dante began, "but maybe we can help each other out, *eh?*"

The writing on the side tab; the name... She wouldn't look away. She leaned in, pausing, leaning again; battling whether she showed interest or kept cold.

It gave Dante some edge back, cocking his head and clearing his throat at Jeb.

Leti was hypnotized by the closed file. Sneering or thinking but settled on motionless, as if the folder would see her gaze and lock itself up. So Dante used the silence while he had it; pointed a thumb towards the two-way mirror—one quick jab as if he and Jeb had some plan—and nodded his head once, confidently. A one-man act as Jeb stared confused.

Jeb opened his mouth, but *this time*, it was Dante cutting in: "You alright if he steps out?"

Leti looked more surprised than anything; the way her gaze loaded, softened, and then masked itself again.

"Uh," nodding slowly; breathing slower, "Ye—yeah," she mumbled.

A beat of time passed where no one moved; where Dante could feel Jeb glaring into the side of his head before shuffling about with a minor objection, and making his exit.

Left them with a simple, "whatever, kids" as Dante's fingers now tapped the table. Slow, and off beat.

Dante waited to hear the resistant thud of yanking the old, jammed door closed, then gave Leti half a smile.

"Let's have us a chat, ya?"

Even the walls lowered to listen as Leti slowly—*finally*—reached to the folder and spun it carefully.

"You're not supposed to have that," she told him. Eyes hardened like a hawk that's unsure whether it's circling, or the one being circled. But Dante heard another thud then.

A small beat, maybe.

"Millie?" Leti pressed him.

He didn't know who Millie was.

"How do you have that?"

Dante heard another beat and said nothing. *The clock?*

Maybe.

Leti's finger hovered near the tab but didn't touch it. "Cool, cool, cool," she muttered sarcastically instead.

Dante's head rolled sideways, peeking under the table when he felt the ground moving again.

Impatience or fear?

He was about to ask, but the thud. Not the clock, not the precinct.

Her heart?

Another until all sound stopped and time between them froze.

Because she recognized the folder. *The names.* The deaths, the truth—and he had her undivided attention now.

"So," he finally said. "The beginning then?"

Because whatever she and the little fire-bird were running from—

Well, it was here now.

—they just haven't met yet...

Sometimes—

healing
hurts
more
than
the
injury
ever
could.

THE DEMOLITION

Echoes Between the Mountains

DALY CITY, CALIFORNIA
13 DAYS EARLIER

|I|

Afternoon heat waned in with sweat, regret, and a thin layer of comradery clouding the station. And a smell. A smell pungent with *Fabuloso* that came too late and piss in the tank that sat too long.

Dante leaned back.

The coffee burned through his palm as the steam lifted, ghosting toward the ceiling. But his mood? Down low where his shoes felt too tight, the ground too still, and the morning—*too quiet.*

File on his desk was open, pages already yellowing; mugshots too familiar to flinch at and just the same bad decisions in the same shady places; letting the wounds bleed instead of finding a stitch.

Like Kayden.

Dante wasn't sure if he was supposed to call him back because if Kayden called acting casual, how does Dante say, "*this can't be this, brother.*"

Like that, maybe?

Dante let his legs stretch and feet lift—gave himself a little spin but sat up quick when a face appeared as a flash in the turn.

Akira.

Grinning in his door, Dante wasn't bothered to see her. It saved him from turning his free time and folders into his monologues and mission statements.

"...Having fun?" Playful and flirty most times, but serious?

Never.

It felt too weird to call her a friend, yet weirder to say she wasn't.

"Anybody—home?" Still from the outside she gave a gentle knock.

"Yeah, hey, sorry," Dante chuckled. "Been here all night."

Last checked the clock around three AM; not sure how it got to twelve.

Akira pursed her lips and nodded slowly, eyes rolling around his desk curiously. Dante watched her and when it went too long, took up space with his arms over the desk.

"We need something?" he chided.

"Nothing," she shrugged, reversing through the door as suddenly as she came. "But he's out-front waiting for you," she hollered back.

"Ira!" Dante called.

There was a hree second delay before her head popped in again and Dante's face softened. "Who?"

"The younger one—the really cute one."

Dante looked back at his coffee. Brought it to his lips and breathed on it.

"Not man-bun, if that helps. *Obvi* not blondie." She watched, hugging the door frame, finger tapping like a clock.

"Thanks." Dante exhaled.

So Cachí then, he'd thought. But she'd vanished before he could say more.

Dante stood with a grumble and a stretch, yawning before his steps echoed on the concrete, paced, even, and *quick*. Couldn't risk going slow—fat chance Cachí would change his mind and book it before Dante'd even made it out.

Another rookie nodded, got all eager as Dante came closer and then calmed when Dante didn't nod back but pushed through the front doors instead. He was hit by the kind of sunlight that slapped: bright, blunt, and on its way up before he'd even been down.

"Well say it ain't so, Princessa!" Dante hollered across the lot when he saw Cachí leaned against his car; one ankle hooked over the other and a comfortable lean.

"Detective." All drawl, mischief, and boyish smirks.

Dante looked over the car on approach and Cachí stretched his arms overhead until his spine cracked and tussled his dark hair.

Dante doesn't intend to notice shit but he still does, eyeing the round little love-tap on the side of Cachí's bumper. It hadn't been there the last time.

Though *'the last time'* had been a minute back.

"What happened to—"

"*Whoa*—think fast," Cachí interjected, white T creasing as he wound up and tossed something across what was left of the way.

"Careful!" he added.

The smirk put Dante at ease, but the bag coming for his face didn't. Hands went up quick and words stumbled out: "*Que—?" The fuck.*

Drugs, weapons, cash...? But when it hit Dante's hand, it was warm.

...Body part?

But the big round sticker sealing it in said otherwise. Dante's thumb dug into it with a firm squeeze—

"*Cuídate, compa'!*" Cachí, grinning even wider now. "Don't smash that premium romaine, boo. Enjoy that expensive extra crunch."

"Shut the fuck up, *vato.*"

Their hands slapped together twice before they pulled in for a quick pat on the others' back and Cachí whistled at the sky.

"Fiesty then?" Cachí spoke while checking past Dante, behind himself— eyes wandering the same way his feet do while Dante picked at the $12.99 sticker.

"Lemme hit ch'you back for it," Dante lazily waved the sandwich pointing to the building too, but Cachí looked disappointed.

Drawled, "*Hermano,*" out long. "You really think I'm that strapped?"

A push in Dante's brows and squint in his eyes had Cachí copying it, but standing straighter. And taller too.

"*Dependente.*" Dante started to regret broaching the topic about here, but continued regardless; mouth its own monster. "You still taking money from Kayden?"

Landed it as soft as he could but that wasn't one that landed easy.

"Never was."

Cachí wiped at the smudged ink on his hands like he was drawing again, despite the sleeplessness caked into the hollows under his eyes. Dante continued to look him over—eyes about as dark as the shit tattoo on his arm that Cachí just *had* to have when he finally could...

Couldn't help but chuckle at that, making Cachí look up confused.

"You ever get that shit fixed?" Dante pinched the hem of Cachí's sleeve, attempting to peek at his shoulder but Cachí ducked like Dante was coming for blood.

"*Let me see*" and "*leave me alone*" followed like a whip, quick and sharp, But Cachí tugged at the hem, yanking it further down and shoved at Dante's final attempt.

"I just didn't think it could get uglier, *vato.*"

"Shut up..." Cachí grumbled.

Dante knew Cachí wasn't the unsure, copy-cattin' little shit anymore, but he certainly sounded like him then. That whiney twelve-year-old from back in the day who carried his sketchpad and spray cans like a prayer and had a way of slipping places the older kids couldn't; curiosity too wild and handcuffs always too damn big.

Dante's nervous system softened; comfort in the memories despite reality there in front of him.

"So," Dante sighed and pushed back at the comfort. "Not money, no warrants...Favor then?"

"Nah," Cachí shook his head. "First time for everything, I guess."

"Yeah, guess so." Dante shifted the bag in his hand.

The kid was taller than in memory and had a solid inch on Dante now. Maybe two, but he can round down. Skinnier, too.

"You eatin' bro?"

It felt weird even asking—*motherly*—but Cachí looked sharp. And not in a way that said discipline, a way that said stressed and starved and Dante didn't even need to ask. He knew.

"It's my hot-girl-era." Cachí shrugged with half a shoulder.

The joke tickled the nose, but it wasn't enough to laugh. Not when they both knew they were just beating around a thorn bush. So Dante crossed his arms, tucking the sandwich—cutting Cachí off as Cachí, watching the sandwich, looked up in a panic—

"I know," Dante cooed, "*premium* lettuce."

Kid was desperate to change the topic or act a fool. They'd used to have been able to talk about Kayden without much issue but as Kayden was getting worse, as Dante and Mikki were pulling away, Cachí was leaning more into the wrong side and tearing down the center.

It'd been a few months since the last blow out about Kayden, but this shit has been coming for years. And whether it makes Dante a pessimist or not, he knew patterns. And there was something about taunting susceptibility by playing in the street with guys like Kayden.

"Keepin' your nose clean?"

Because statistics weren't in any of their favors, Dante thought.

"From?" Cachí plucked a toothpick from his pocket and rolled it a few times to free the lint.

"Cute." Dante, staring at a stubborn piece of lint that clung to the opposite end, watched the toothpick go into Cachí's mouth.

Dante watched incredulously. He could *never*.

But Cachí's long, "Sooo—" intertwined with Dante's, "Well Mik—" and they both stopped only to entangle again:

"My bad—" "Go ahead—" "Go—a—fuck."

They awkwardly laughed and stalled before Dante shook his head, moving his hands to his pockets. "Fun little dance, but what were you tryin' say?"

"Oh-uh... was just about to dip but was passing through. Maybe grab some lunch soon—beer?"

"Yeah alright," Dante swapped the bag to his other hand as Cachí pushed off the car and checked the time.

"Headed downtown?" Dante guessed.

Cachí nodded, the ice between them thinning, but not from around them; from directly below. "Quick errand is all." Cachí said quieter. "Anyway, *yo voy*. Just figured it'd been a minute."

Cachí reached; Dante reached too. Distinctly clapping skin against skin but not like a general greeting or goodbye, this one was theirs. Teenage smiles and secret handshakes—them, Kayden, Matías too—with that *slap, slap, slide, knuckles* type shit. Couldn't recite it but could do it without thinking.

"Im'ma catch you later," Cachí likely lost in his own memories didn't meet Dante's eyes.

Dante slid from Cachí and nodded once. "Hey—lunch. Call Mikki, fool. She's been trying to set something up, and with the bonfire coming soon..."

Cachí began nodding.

"Willin' to bet that's the end game," Dante laughed, adding more seriously: "Call her."

"*Vale—*"

"*Before* Mouse really drags me into it."

"*Vale, carnal,*"

...*Carnal.*

Dante almost didn't recognize the word. Almost didn't hear it under Cachí's playful exasperation because he hadn't heard it in years. It was a cold shock—his nervous system remembering it before he did—as Cachí threw back a half peace and a nod.

Maybe unaware, but more than likely choosing not to acknowledge Dante's freeze. But looking back one final time with a stupid cheesey grin on his face—he looked the realest Dante had seen in a long, long while.

He looked like Matías.

Salt in the Spine

The Ones We Leave Behind

KALALOCH, WASHINGTON
13:00:00·⁰⁰

|II|

West of the cliffs, a rainbow tried to land but had no legs and had no ground. West, wet, and worn down—only the Sound of the Pacific as they lowered a mahogany casket into the earth.

The Elder rose his hand to the Spirit: "And may we lay his uneasy soul to rest, joining with the steady presence of brother Mountain and sister Sky; blessing his transition into what we hope to be an everlasting peace beside Ava.

"There are many triumphs. But there are also many tragedies. We mourn for the end now, but we thank the Spirit for time spent."

He took the candle from behind him and placed it in front. Slid the match—and slid it again until a gentle light grew against the wind.

Kaia's mouth tightened, but the man's softened.

"We offer fire, not for warmth, but to protect you through the dark and guide you on your journey home."

And as if he was speaking to Kaia and Leti alone:

"Light—not only for the dead. But for the ones left behind."

Kaia's eyes rolled and head shook. The places, the speeches; they begin to feel the same.

That one though...? That didn't feel like anything at all. Nothing did. And were it not for Leti beside Kaia holding her to this earth she might have already flew away.

Beside Kaia like a root, despite Leti's eyes were faded like maybe she wasn't here either.

Kaia blinked—for the first time in what felt like an hour. Around her was only the salt-thick air and a silence too wide to hold.

Kaia could hear a different time around them, a different place as the Elder's voice dropped away behind sounds of memory and haze.

The further back in time Kaia's mind went, the quieter the man in front of her got—memory not whispering but intruding. Violently.

Aluminum crunching; metal bending in unnatural ways; memory thrumming; anxiety climbing; and with just the right amount of pressure in the wrong place—breaks more than just metal—

Leti's hand gently looped through Kaia's there at the funeral like she knew. No cars; no panic. Just the dirt, the sky, and their hold to each other.

Leti squeezed tight to say, '*I'm still here.*'

Waited for Kaia to squeeze back; to promise her, "I'm still trying."

So Kaia squeezed twice because Kaia knows, too. Knows that the handholds and the false comforts were the only thing left, because even the tears had run dry.

Somebody else will need to come by to water the graves.

The procession came to an end sometime later—but that'd blurred. The apologies, the condolences, the blisters on the back of their heels, the walk home.

And a walk, not because they were close, but because Kaia needed to move.

And Leti—Leti needed Kaia, so she'd watched as Kaia jerked her flats off her feet and trudged forward on the rocks. Wasn't sure why until Kaia stubbed her toe and hissed in pain.

Maybe even enough pain to shock her back to life. Rocks on her feet, feet on the edge, running where told to walk, and flying when asked to stay—

Leti wanted to say something aloud but got so wrapped up about what to say and feeling like she couldn't until she literally couldn't. So they shuffled along next to each other with wordless conversations and silent decisions. Neither of them kept track of the amount of time, but eventually, the house crept into view. First time since the incident, too.

Maybe they'd gotten there too fast. Kaia's mouth parted and closed.

Lawn brittle, patio cluttered, garage door streaked with age; and a single bulb above the entryway—also dead.

"Welcome home, right?" Kaia cleared her throat after.

Home.

Still tasted dirty to say.

Jagged tree limbs cast shadows across the front and the beginnings of fall had dead leaves across the yard, crunching as they approached.

Looking around and taking it all in—the house wasn't haunted. It was embodied with history and shadow.

"You alright?" Leti eventually asked.

"*Mmhm*, and you—*you* good?" Kaia countered, forcing a smile they both knew was fake but ignored.

It was one of those things you pretend isn't real for a bit longer, secretly hoping everyone forgets before it comes back around. Because if it's not killing them, it's not a priority with too many other landmines popping off to worry about.

Angry ones. Guilty ones. *Imagined* ones.

A breeze stirred the heat and Kaia shifted uncomfortably, head pounding.

Because grass grew under shadows but within the sun.

Spanning across the porch and into the garage—not where any of it should be. Not *when* it should be.

Kaia blinked, confused. Because Leti was still there at her side where she was supposed to be—

But Kaia?

She looked behind her and Leti was there, too, blades of grass between her toes; braid surfing the wind as sh e ran.

Kaia heard herself shouting but her mouth didn't move. Only the sound of a countdown echoed in a child's voice somewhere between where Kaia's eyes closed and her memory opened.

Three, two...go!

Both sprinting harder, faster—shoulders squared like they had something to prove because maybe then they did. Cheap shots and laughter; aging out; another life crashing in...

Maybe, losing started to mean more than just a loss. Kaia felt Leti's fingers curl into hers then. Tethering, but loose enough to still feel free.

Most days Kaia was just checking to see if anyone noticed because sometimes—as hard as it was to recognize and admit—being sought felt more alive than being found. Especially in moments like these.

Kaia looked at the door again.

The chipped paint, the way the wood bowed. And from the corner of her eye, Leti watched Kaia. Gentle eyes waiting for the smallest signal or refusal as Leti stepped forward, and Kaia reluctantly followed.

Not necessarily because they were ready, but because forward was the only direction offering any light.

The house creaked with every step in; acted and looked abandoned but had life three weeks ago.

Kaia's breath was shaking; Leti's hand was clammy. But at the very least, they knew they were suffering through it together.

They walked further in, stopping to look down the empty hall at some cracked open rooms—took a couple more steps in to see further, and then, *nothing.*

They stood. Like they did at the burial. House too quiet and too loud all the same.

Eventually Leti pointed at the couch and mouthed "let's sit" on burdened breath. So, they sat. And they sat some more. Sat until the day burned off and the dawn threatened to rise leaving only a flat gray light slipping in the kitchen.

Neither Kaia or Leti tried for small talk. Instead, they watched the clock on the TV click through entire rotations of the hours, sometimes motionless.

Kaia's eyes were glazed; but she still blinked and eventually, Leti broke the silence first.

"You good?"

"Just wiped," Kaia admitted, rubbing the back of her neck.

"Me too..." Leti nodded, standing slow. "I'm gonna go to sleep, but if—if you need anything or want to sleep in there, doors open, okay?"

"Yeah. Thanks." Kaia said, eyes on the TV like it left her on a cliff hanger.

And that was it.

Kaia watched Leti go as she disappeared toward their old room and changed into shorts and a T-shirt before chucking some out to Kaia too. She didn't even get the chance to ask but thanked Leti tirelessly.

Pillow came next. Clocking Kaia in the side of the head exactly as she called, "*Can I get a pi*—"And normally it would have made them laugh.

It *was* funny. But they just stared at each other from across the hall, knowing they both wanted to laugh—hell even smile—but *knowing* it just wouldn't be real.

Leti dropped onto the mattress heavily as Kaia tugged a hoodie she found crammed in the couch free. Pulled it over her head as quickly as she found it and settled back into the baggy cotton hood.

"Love you, Lee." she said. But not loud, and not quiet. Words ridden out on breath, only loud enough to be heard.

"I love you too, Kaia-Raye." Said louder. And clearer.

Kaia stretched out while pulling the blanket to her chin and hugged the pillow tight across her chest. She thought she closed her eyes, but at some point, they opened again, pointlessly staring at the ceiling

Moonlight slipped in and crept around the room as the world turned and she watched; unblinking once more.

The walls felt too close. And she might have been crying.

Or maybe it was Leti—? Because Kaia's feelings were gone—like their family. Like everything.

Kaia pictured the dirt tapping against the casket—the sounds it made competing with the sniffling from the other room and she fell into it. She let the sound grow loud as the memory and dreams grew real. Drifting off and afar only to be disturbed and awoke sometime later.

What time—was anybody's guess, but it hardly felt like a minute of sleep. Woken to the sound of a phone vibrating not once but again and again for a minute.

Calls.

Else it'd be a hell of a lot of messages, Kaia figured. Couldn't sleep any after that—the dirt pile from her dreams grew legs and chased her through her mind. Kaia slapped her hands down by her sides before stubbornly getting up and checking the call logs.

Millie.

And something about houses, college, and goodbyes. *Or whatever.*

Kaia went to replay it but hung up quick as Leti turned in her sleep. Not that Kaia was doing anything wrong, but she told herself it was. Maybe in fear of replaying the voice message back with focused ears; unsure what she'd hear or how she'd take it...

Kaia stared at the phone but eagerness to know and panic at being alone took over. She moved quietly to the edge of Leti's bed, touching her arm carefully.

"Lee...? Sorry..."

"You...?" Looking around, scrubbing at her face until her eye was red. "Okay? Wanna lay down?"

Kaia shook her head and Leti began to sit up while wearing worry.

"Millie called," Kaia told her quickly.

It eased the worry, but Leti still had questions. Head swiveled around looking for her phone as Kaia clicked into her voicemail.

"Why you?" Leti's eyebrows pushed together but she didn't have to say more. The reason was clear if you'd ever been around Kaia and Millie since their mom died years back.

Millie used to be the fun aunt—the only aunt they knew, really—but something changed too drastically when Kaia and Leti lost their mom, and Millie, her older sister.

Kaia shrugged and typed in her code before the voicemail welcomed them in. Message intro came first, and then the familiar but terse and restrained voice. Leti watched Kaia carefully as it played back.

"Kiraia, it's me..."

Kaia's jaw flexed and Leti's eyes rolled.

"So formal," Kaia spit mockingly. But they had stopped using those names when they stopped being those people. Those kids.

"Yeah so..." Their aunt sighed in the message. "I told you I needed to talk to you two and you dipped."

Kaia's finger bumped up the volume.

"And I'm not doing this with you. Frankly I have a plane to catch so, whatever, Kiraia. I spoke to the attorneys and there is good news and bad. 'Cuse me, jesus!" She snapped, shuffling around what the girls could only assume was the airport.

"So good news—Yay, college funds. Maybe you actually can change, Kaia Hows about it?"

Leti's nose twitched with rage. "Are you f—"

"It's fine, shhh," Kaia waved a hand at Leti.

"Bad news, depending how you look at it, is house is sold. Six months to pack and shit so don't freak out or do anything crazy-Kaia would, you know?"

Kaia's face scrunched when Leti fell back onto the bed with a grunt.

"Bitch." Leti again.

"Goddamn it, where the hell is my card?" Millie growled.

Kaia chuckled like she enjoyed it because she honestly did.

Karma, she thought.

"Goddamn it, this is ridiculous. The house was sold," the voicemail continued, "some kind of reverse mortgage thing to developers. So. Yeah, I'll reach out to Leti, too or—Im sure you're together, so—stay out of trouble, or whatever. Goodbye, Kiraia. Try to make my sister proud, will you?"

The last of her sentence was barely audible as loudspeakers hollered in the background... But it was loud enough to burn.

Kaia stared at the phone screen again; minute-twenty-seven flashing as the message cut out and the machine cut in. Stuck somewhere between delete and save, Kaia hit the "End" button instead.

Leti's eye twitched, then squinted like she was reading off the roof and the movement caught Kaia's attention.

"That little '*crazy*' dig," Leti growled. "*That*—was not fucking cool."

Didn't phase Kaia really; maybe because she already considered them *all* crazy where Leti denied it.

"Why aren't you wiggin' about the house?" Kaia asked.

Leti laughed sharply. And then more. Bit of a hyena cackle ending in a yawn—the *real* emotion—as Kaia waited.

"I dunno, Kai. Guess I thought we'd have a few weeks. Six months? Shit—we'll be fine."

Kaia, watching Leti twist a corner of the fabric. Waited for another cackle or sign but none came. Instead, halfheartedly and staring to the window, Kaia said:

"Yeah, true." Then chuckling Kaia added, "We'll take a vacation or something then. Because with our family's luck, we won't need six months."

"That's not fucking funny." Leti's breath was sharp then. Wide awake too as Kaia whipped her head back grinning. Not because it was funny, but because it made it harder for Leti to be pissed.

"I know, I know—my b, boo." Kaia grabbed her on the sides of the head and kissed the top. Pushing her sideways to make it *edgier*. Or something.

And maybe it was respecting space, maybe it was lack of energy for a fight, but Kaia didn't say another word. Simply trailed out the door and back to the couch; rooms length away but constantly in sight.

And maybe it was Millie, maybe it was the ghosts, or maybe it was the house and the guilt, but something within—replaying the sound of loudspeakers and *movement*—made Kaia want to leave too.

Just like everyone else.

The Inferno

| III |

The salt air pushed into Dante's lungs as he ran and the city peeled away behind him. Golden Gate Park stretching across the pavement— where the trees bend to the wind like they knew better than to stand straight; where the kites dance; and where Mikki followed just a few strides behind.

Sweat glinted off her skin like the grit crunched under her soles, and Dante kept her far enough behind she couldn't pass, but close enough that he could hear her breathing.

They'd hoped Cachí would show but he also knew he wouldn't reply.

Should have asked to his face when Cachí mentioned downtown.

Say, *hey! Us too.*

Meet you there, *hermanito.*

Then watch him try and say no.

Dante breathed deep; controlled the panting while waiting for Mikki and watched Alcatraz next. A speck of stone tucked between the long arms of the bridges; too far to touch, but too close to forget.

Dante tried to pull in another heavy breath but felt it tightening instead, and it wasn't from the run. *Nah*—he just had this de je vu sitting heavy on his heart. Like he couldn't remember the movie but knows how it ends... And he didn't like it.

So—like he did when he went away, like he did every week, and like he did now—he ran. With or without them.

Keeping the noise exhausted at bay, his friends close behind, and a hope that the ghosts won't take this too.

Sometime later, day or night—*month, year even*—Kaia found herself hovering in the hallway, unsure. Leti on her left, peacefully asleep the way she'd left her, and Kaia there—headed to, or from, the bathroom. Couldn't say. Just felt the sharp throb in her thumb, her index finger blindly picking at a hangnail. Kaia didn't notice until her hand bumped her thigh, hissing as the skin shred and her focus pulled.

"Ow..." she whispered.

But it still didn't hurt enough.

Kaia shifted, peeking at her room and debating whether she'd allow herself there, or if she'd give into the sensation pulling her towards the room where it happened.

But why would she want to go in there?

She challenged her thoughts but only got challenged back—

Dad had a safe in there.

And secrets could be interesting.

So maybe there was more reason than only fear that she had to go into her parents' bedroom. Maybe there was something within the safe that'd answer questions she knew she'd never get the answers too—but would desperately search for anyway. The idea of a mission and a focus greater than any fear she had shadowing inside.

Besides.

Couldn't sleep. And it wasn't like they had much else to do anyway.

Kaia knew he was dead. She knew what was in the room—mostly—and knew Leti would run out of patience and space for Kaia to breathe eventually. They were going to have to talk about it. Unless Kaia could find something bigger to talk about instead.

Though what could possibly be any bigger? She wondered, feet silent against the hardwood as she moved to Leti's door.

Kaia was hovering over Leti now, slipping the blanket further over her sister's shoulders.

Couldn't call her "little" sister anymore, technically.

Or—which end of the story would be the technical side?

They'd only been ten months apart and life took eleven from Kaia.

So, was age defined as eleven months of lived experience, or as a heartbeat?

Kaia watched Leti's lungs fill and then empty twice over before she shut the door and crossed the hall with two big steps. Two even bigger breaths.

No one had been inside since the death. Obvious when she reached to twist the knob only to be met with a flimsy lock.

".... Damn it..." Kaia picked at the skin on her thumb again.

"Okay," cracking her knuckles, then her neck. "Challenge, accepted." Her voice was barely a whisper, but her body was a fist already in the air.

Pressed her palm to the handle, tossed her hip to the wood—the door popped with one of the most grotesque sounds she'd ever heard and her mind bounced between present and past.

Hollow lock—   —*Red rover, red rover*—
    letting her in.   *convince me it's over*—

Kaia swung the door open slowly, noting the way it felt heavier now. Nose assaulted by something rancid and drenched in the stench of old pennies and—*vinegar*.

Spoiled milk. *Flesh? Rotten meat and—and—carcasses and bullet holes look the same. Animal, animal, animal—it was never human—*

Kaia's hands slapped against her face hard, covering her eyes as if it'd take away the thoughts. Flashbacks only becoming more vivid the closer Kaia got.

Though still... She stepped in.

And with her hand on the door, her body twitched, demanding to slam it shut while she pushed it closed slow. Not because she wanted to be on this side of it, but because she wanted to stop herself from running out.

The ramble of past, present, and made up futures went on and on and up the walls where the blood stain loomed. It made Kaia cover her eyes again—the red mark on the wall very real and very *there*. Watching her.

Screaming at her...Kaia wanted to scream back. Sometimes she even thought she did—told it to go—to *get out*! But also ask it, why couldn't the morgue take the mess, too? Scrub the blood from the walls and—

She couldn't think further. She couldn't identify what else was there because her mind wouldn't let her.

Kaia's instincts chose survival, and that involved editing reality to something survivable, so Kaia looked everywhere but there. Which didn't stop her stomach from turning or the floor from swaying— surrounded by the energy.

Metal crashing—sirens wailing—

Leti screamed but only once there in the car with them. Her mom too—the last time she'd heard her voice, it broke. Sharp panic and fear and then—*nothing*. Nothing until waking up in a big room, no better, no worse than where ever she was. Though more intimidating; more *heavy* on her bones and skin like weight was holding her to this planet.

People, nurses, doctors...they asked questions, but memory wasn't a thing where ever Kaia was. No dreams, no thoughts. Only nothing.

And Death even took that too. Scythe sharp across her back again and again until she woke to bright lights overhead and monitors screeching out for attention.

It'd only been five minutes of meditation, to Kaia. Until they told her it'd really been eleven months. Her eyes went to Leti first but thoughts lagged far behind the sleep.

Skin stitched back together wrong and muscles weak, fighting to stay.

Or fighting to go but forced to stay? Five years later and Kaia's still not always sure. But that only felt like an admission of defeat. To life, death—*this goddamn room.*

Denver left everything exactly as Ava had it. And that made it worse. Better or worse though, Kaia was married to reliving it until even the screams sounded polite.

Until the smell—sterile, thick—the glaring lights, the pins and needles all just felt like a bad cartoon. Halfway there now, living in a reality often times unsure which was a dream and which was real.

Kaia swallowed there in the middle of the room watching the morning sun crest against the window. It sliced clean through the Strangler-Fig encroaching on the window—stump like vines.

Kaia's head cocked sideways. It was much smaller before; strange thing her mother planted and not from here. Like their mother, unique and special.

She stood there staring at the tree until her joints ached and felt weak; until knuckles rasped against the door and echoed again in her head.

Kaia turned sharply to see Leti crossing the threshold and paused.

"Hi..." Kaia offered meekly, not daring to turn away as they locked eyes in mutual partnership. Leti, bridging Kaia back to reality the way Kaia bridged Leti close enough to reach.

"Hi." Leti's face was guarded but not cold. "We did it then, I guess?"

Kaia laughed awkwardly but her eyes welled and Leti met her at the window pulling her in tight. And they cried. Not upset, but *unsure*. Dropped in a very big world and left with pieces but no rules.

Sometime later, the tears came to a halt, but their words didn't return until awhile later. They sat on the edge of the bed, back to the bloodstain, eyes to the window, and just waited. Waited in the silence of simply being next to someone who could understand. A silence that holds just long enough to breathe.

Eventually, the afternoon leaned in through the windows, slow and golden. The sun had risen and fallen—some number of times they hadn't tracked—and still, Kaia kept at the lock. Not with brute force this time, but with patience.

Precision.

She'd scoured the house for scraps of numbers with birthdays, death dates, old addresses, phone digits long disconnected—anything code-*like*.

And Leti watched most of the time though she slept a lot more then Kaia. Didn't bother telling her to give it up or quit because Leti knew it wasn't about the safe. Wasn't even about what was inside. It never was. Simply a puzzle to fill the hours.

And when it finally clicked open—soft and anticlimactic—Kaia grinned like it meant something. Though maybe it did, because for a split second, excitement and joy cracked through the room.

So they celebrated like maybe it *could* mean something.

Counted cash; found pot; and skipped quickly through the letters and handwritten cards from their mom. Then everything else? Nothing new or groundbreaking.

Paperwork, dates, accounts, possibilities.

Or just another something to find, just to keep them busy and looking a bit longer.

Kaia had it all spread out—paperwork, pot, and bundles of cash across the coffee table. Even on the couch she'd claimed as hers.

Legs over the armrest, joint hot between her fingers like she was more used to it than she was. Even tried a Godfather accent and—as stupid and terrible as it was, it made Leti laugh. Not hard, but enough; allowing for the room to exhale and the weight to lift.

Then Leti's voice disturbed it:

"Millie? If she comes by again?"

Kaia scrolled the round bit on the Bic and watched it ignite. "Pretend we're not home, I dunno. Why do you care so much?"

"Why don't you care at all?" Leti quipped back.

Kaia zoned out onto the ceiling. More exchanges of the joint before she finally added back in. "He wrote the note... he left. Right?"

But the confidence, the anger was lacking...

"Left doesn't mean didn't love," Leti offered. But in response, Kaia pushed the joint at her and changed topic.

"You think they've always smoked?"

Easy topic change.

"No," Leti rolled with it—else Kaia would roll away completely. "Wha—oh. Dad started after Mom died and y—you..."

Kaia turned toward the pause, already giggling before the joke. "Tooook a cat nap...? Tapped out when the squad was in need?"

"Kaia..."

It wasn't funny, but Leti stayed against Kaia's shoulder anyway. "Don't."

So Kaia leaned her head on top of Leti's too. And instead, offered one of her favorites:

"Would you rather—" ignoring the familiar groan from her sister. "Live in space, or the sea?"

Leti sighed heavily but leaned into it, like the sigh was at her question, not her habit. Had to force herself to think about it, but the longer they sat in the smoke, the more her mind began to melt.

Forget.

"Don't be technical," Leti tried. "But what would even be the difference?"

The truth was: space, sea, safe, house—it all felt the same. They weren't going to find answers here. Not in the couch cushions, not in the safe, and not in each other's silence. Kaia already knew. And by the time morning came, with a bit of help and nagging from Kaia, Leti knew it, too.

She hovered over her empty suitcase, eyes scanning the list she'd created in her head: Clothes. Toothbrush. Deodorant. Camera.

The joint haze of the night before still lingered, but the excuses had thinned with no school, no job, and no real reason to stay.

Kaia had pulled out every trick the night before—needling, joking, bargaining—until Leti finally caved.

Six months, they said.

So... *Why—the—hell—not?*

Give herself a little break while daring someone to tell Leti she doesn't deserve it. She packed her bag with a little more force than necessary, working through her list as Kaia packed her own way from down the hall.

Frantically, if even packing at all; music on, window open, light beaming in, and the countdown to leaving—? *Set.*

They averaged around five-k from the safe and the piggy banks; maybe a bit over. And somehow, Kaia not only rationalized it was enough to live on while they figured it out, but convinced Leti of the same while ignoring all effort to plan.

To figure it out...

Leti scoffed to herself like the idea was some toxic thought to Kaia, but it was received better than Leti's first idea; asking if five-thousand was enough to throw down on the house; put that whole ordeal on pause.

But then that turned into whether they could even stay in a haunted place— Kaia calling them more haunted than the house—and they argued and squabbled until eventually they settled not on a plan, but a direction.

South.

Following the coastline down, turning off wherever looked interesting enough to spend the miles. By that point, Leti was over the argument and simply along for the ride because going with was far better than being left behind.

"What else?" Kaia called, scrolling through her phone while thrumming down the hall and bounding into Leti's room.

"Are you bringing that nicer dress—or beachy looking one?" Leti asked.

Kaia looked at her like she was crazy and twisted back out of the room for her bag.

"Tell me you're not packing a ton of shit," Kaia tested as she dragged her own big bag into the hall.

"What if we end up somewhere nice?" Leti challenged.

But Kaia zipped her bag in one solid motion, popped her hip, and rested her hands against her sides: "Like where? An Outback—Red Lobster?"

Leti glared. *Or a concert.*

Gallery.

Museum...

"Imma load this puppy up," Kaia kicked the bag through the hall as if that was less effort.

Leti watched her struggle until safely out of sight and then marched to her closet and yanked out two more outfits than she'd originally planned.

Why? Because she could. Otherwise—

Essentials only.

Before the Street Lights

|IV|

Cachí leaned back in the battered Nissan. Joint lit, morning heavy, phone pinging and harder to ignore each time. Mikki had reached out—third time now since Dante.

Coincidence—? Cachí thinks not.

Cachí took another drag in, marked them as unread; as if tagging messages for later would work; would prevent him from forgetting and never getting back to them. But he'd already seen Mikki's from the preview; Dante's too actually.

First, something about a bonfire this weekend and Mikki. Didn't want to say it, but Dante was right. Lunch too.

Then Dante's—on about running and pressing Cachí to come. Gently, but consistently when the last thing Cachí wanted to do right now was run. For Dante, Mikki, or Kayden.

Especially not Kayden.   *Fuck.*

Yet there Cachí was. Downtown. *Again.*

Stalling. Letting the car idle a little longer just to keep the silence busy and the time slow. Anything to avoid being where you're going next.

Cachí was supposed to be meeting a few of the guys a couple blocks over for some follow up shit. Didn't know what and didn't ask. *Idiot.*

Assumed it'd be another, *go-run-this-here-and-grab-that-there* shit.

The lighter flicked once in his hand and he lit the joint until the tip bloomed red, soft, and angry. Hand to mouth; like muscle memory and stubbornness—Cachí let smoke fill the car like it was trying to press the Bay out. The fog wasn't the weather; it was the point. Else he'll be able to see through the past; see the five of them in the backseat. Younger versions that weren't afraid to play with Ouija boards because, back then, ghosts didn't answer back. Now though—layer by layer, blood and then flesh—they did more than just answer.

Cachí exhaled slow. He hadn't realized it then, but he needed Dante to stay. He'd forget why he was angry, see him, and be reminded just to feel flustered all over again. *Jealous?*

Probably.

Maybe resentful because he got out. Built new brotherhoods and went so far Dante forgot what he'd been running from when he got back. And Cachí? Closer to Kayden. Because Matías was gone. And Mikki—? She wasn't even close to okay.

Cachí tossed his fist on the wheel. Minimal effort. A pulled punch. Another drag. Because what was the point in even having to think about shit if we couldn't change it?

The phone buzzed against his thigh and Cachí's eyes closed; joint balanced between his lips. Knowing he probably shouldn't, he still adjusted himself as he reached for his phone, shifting his hips up to get into his pocket.

Knew exactly who it was going to be. *Why?* Because it's always an expected, predictable disappointment.

```
KAYDEN
> 850M @ ALDIS P/U
```

Cachí scoffed. Exactly like he'd expected. Smoke bleeding out of his nose in a steady, bitter breath.

Kayden's promises of, '*do this for me, won't ask again.*' The back half of that sentence always misremembered or negated.

Misplaced a pistol like a fuckin' vape and Cachí sorted it for him. Not even a week ago and here we are. Nothing pissed Cachí off more; stepping on your word like you don't know when the promises are made.

This rift between them wasn't fear or running or history, it was primal.

Cachí checked the time; it was almost time to head that way. Made his face get hotter, stuffing the phone back into his jeans and pressing the joint to his lips to drag again.

Feet kicked out under the pedals; legs too long and position too awkward for any real sleep but weariness rolled through the city like the smoke on his windows and the traffic on the street and everything slowly began to get quiet. Peaceful even.

And that's how he knew it was a dream.

Cachí's phone jerked him awake, disorienting and gripping—but still in the car, air warmed by body and breath; joint burnt up, burnt out, and nothing but ash.

The phone vibrated once, beeped twice, then silent before repeating. He let it until it disconnected and went again.

Cachí groaned. Probably one of those assholes he had to meet soon—though maybe it'd be them calling it off.

He was hopeful as he pushed his spine back; pulled his hips up, but closed off when he saw the unsaved digits.

```
INCOMING CALL
> UNKNOWN
```

"Ya?"

The voice on the other end was ragged. *Running.*

"I fucked up! Bro, I fucked up!"

Cachí wasn't sure but he thought he recognized the voice. Twisting the key, cracking the windows, and throttling the resistant engine awake at the first panicked, "*fucked.*"

"Where you at?" he barked, drifting into traffic on the green and tossing the roach to the floor before blasting the AC. "Send me the location."

The traffic slowed Cachí's arrival but thirty minutes later he was cruising the fire lane on some side street in some ritzy hood. Cachí's eyes were wide for trouble; gut nervous with regret; refreshing the fool's location over and fucking over! And when Cachí found him—he wished he hadn't.

Cody smiled wide between a bush and a bus stop like a naked rat. Cachí was dumbstruck and stoned and flinched like he'd been shot when Cody bodied the car. Not so much for himself or the kid, but for the damn car.

Fists to window, mouth open, voice shrill. "Let me in, let me in!"

Cachí turned behind him slow, checking for a pursuit but panicked as the windows continued to rattle. "

Stop," Cachí mouthed. Waiting for them to still before regretfully unlocking the car.

"Lemme—in!" Cody ripped the door open as soon as it gave up the lock and he slid in. Teeth flashing, skin sweaty—somewhere between old enough to drive but too young to vote.

He slapped the dash then the lock and Cachí only stared.

"¡ *Vámonos!*"

Cachí stared harder. Maybe waiting for the story, maybe hoping they were already somewhere Cody'd get out. Watching the reflection; expecting a brother or father racing down the street but seeing neither.

Cachí whacked the rearview sideways and it almost came full circle. Felt like an idiot for jumping into a full-on sprint at Cody's beckon call as Cody was digging into his phone hard.

Multiple messages, not even a greeting to his driver.

"Bro," Cachí barked.

Cody looked up, glossy with adrenaline.

"Where the fuck are your clothes, *chele*?" But Cachí immediately regretted it. Kid was just waiting for him to ask, and despite bordering on *high-as-fuck*, Cachí went digging for more smokes at Cody's first, "*Okay so!*"

Rambling in the background catching partial sentences as if Cachí jammed his ears full of bobby pins. He popped open the center console first, searching.

Nada.

Checked the glove box next, slapping Cody's hand away as he reached past.

Not in there either.

"Cachíflin, dude!" Cody threw both arms forward like it was some joyride.

"Don't." Cachí killed the engine and Cody whimpered.

At first, he was just trying to get a grasp on what was going on but now, honestly, the more Cody bugged the more Cachí'd wait. Same way the other kids used to make Cachí. Deadpanned and staring forward, glaring at traffic while *trying* to get lost in thought.

Anything to burn time.

First, wondering where his smokes went. Then a tirade of why Cody was here crushing Cachí's space, because the kid was damn near louder than Cachí's own fuckin' thoughts right there in his head. Couldn't decide if he was more mad at Cody, or mad at himself for letting him in.

The car was the only place that ever really belonged to Cachí; that felt comfortable. Smoke, music, closed doors—it built its own perimeter through a soft escape in a hard shell, and Cody, was inside staining it.

He glared at the kid. Probably sitting on Cachí's smokes now—*in his jodido boxers.*

Cachí slung himself out of the car to pop the trunk. Knocked the latch to the left when he reached it; gave it a wiggle and a push then lifted on the second release. He grabbed the first t-shirt and bottoms from the pile in the back, and when he dropped back to the seat, Cody was still going at it. Muttering, texts—sweaty thigh restlessly buttering the leather seat.

"Cachíflin," All volume and zero sense. "Guess what...? Man—don't get mad or be jealous or whatever," he whacked Cachí's arm.

Cachí wasn't sure if he imagined it or not. Almost decked him but Cody was already onto the next successfully distracting sentence.

"It's Jaylin!"

Faster than Cachí would have been able to interrupt, too.

Cody hopped a leg onto the seat, turned to face and poke at Cachí, but thought wiser of the poking.

Cachí's face puckered. "Wait, who?" He heard but was loading slow. And wishing he hadn't and wasn't.

Cody nodded slow too, but big. And grand. "That's right! Bro! You ever—"

"*¡Siéntate y cállate!*"

Cachí locked in place to reign in his temper, but Cody didn't stop—couldn't even think around him, let alone question him further on *Jaylin*. Then spitting out words that slapped Cachí with nostalgia:

"¡*Púchica*!" Cody shouted.

Cachí couldn't remember the last him he'd heard, '*púchica*'.

Kid was home grown and Cachí usually forgot, but Cody had that same city in his veins. Just lighter skin under the street dirt. The kind that's fair enough to forget why he sprints with them while the rest only had to jog; not a local but not quite a foreigner either.

"Cody," Cachí muttered, trying to reel him in with a calm, familial tone.

"Come on—*Jaylin*?!"

Idiot.

A Berkeley-Brat playing gangster for a summer.

Cody put hands on Cachí's arm, running along it while tapping his fingers and whistling—the second move came so quick neither of them knew where from: An open handed pop cracked the side of Cody's head. Cody tossed back. Stomped his feet, rubbing his face.

"¿*Y*? Not even a good job...?"

Cachí cut him a look. "That one will eat you alive, *amigito*."

"*What*?" Cody's pitch had a whine.

"I dunno," Cachí appraised him. "She's using you for something, *vato*. No idea what, but I promise you, it's something."

"Maybe I'm using her." Kid smirked, burying a laugh.

"But uh. Bad time to say we gotta' swing back for something? I left the bag...that's why I needed some help. PJ and Darcy are there."

Cachí stared.

Bag.

That crossed from annoying to dangerous, but Cody kept on chirping.

"Bro—yelling at me in front of Darcy like she didn't bring me in and—"

"The fuck you just say, *vato?*" Cachí was still on '*bag*,' but Cody was laughing now.

"Hell of a story for later—tell you that. Wanna know something else?"

"Nah, 'cause this isn't what you think it is, so Im'ma need you to shut the fuck up, or get the fuck out. *¿Entiendo?*"

Cachí turned the key, eyes closed and head shaking. More a prayer for the car than the kid.

Tha-tha-than-thunnnmm—

Pumped the gas. And again, until the old beast coughed awake like it hated them both. Cody waited, gauging the definition of Cachí's words.

"*Entonces,*" Cachí kept on, his voice flat. "You wanna roll to the airport or bus station?"

Cody barked another laugh, drier now. Rubbed the side of his head where he got popped. "Yo' just take me over there to get it. Ya'll tight."

"The fuck I am," Cachí snapped back.

Cody looked over shocked and Cachí kissed his teeth.

Fair enough though.

Cachí knew them a lot better than anyone else, so—whatever that meant. Stories too complicated to understand, or too long to explain. Cachí still shook his head though, because it wasn't just Kayden now. Whole other ball game with whole other players on a varsity squad.

The car thrummed under them quietly, Cody muttering under his breath, going on about Jaylin again, inviting Cachí to watch. First red they rolled into, Cachí twisted and socked Cody in the arm. No warning, and fuckin' hard too.

"Slug-bug," Then Cachí shrugged and nodded towards the street before pushing Cody into the passenger door enough that his ass came off the seat some.

Cachí looked under him, shoving his hand into the crevice of the seat. "Been sittin' on the damn smokes, *chele.*"

Lighter. Stick. Flame—plumed like a firefly in the gloom. Cachí took a long look at Cody as they were stopped. Too small in a city too big, swallowed by hand-me-downs and adrenaline.

On the exhale, calmer, Cachí finally started dialogue again.

"Bags gone, kid. That shit—I'm not touching. And you need to get gone," he waited for eye contact, but the light was turning green. "Or someone is gonna' gone you. ¿*Entiendo*?"

Only to turn red seconds later.

Cody rolled the window down, "Nah." Hands in his lap, legs still. "Jaylin's in on all this shit, just take me back to go get it, dude. Before she sees Kayden. Please."

Something in Cachí twinged when he heard '*please*.' Still. Whether for himself, for seeing Dante recently, or seeing Mikki soon—Cachí didn't touch that side of things.

"You picked the wrong one," Cachí warned. Then looked at Cody again—from head to seat. A little sorry, too. "Well...*Picked* by the wrong one."

Cody stared at him.

Not angry, not laughing. Just playing a game by the rules as if the losers don't rot and the winners don't cheat.

"Ay, you know Jaylin's last name?" Cachí asked, traffic still stop and go.

Cody shook his head—dare to say—*calmly*. Adjusting the oversized shorts on his body, not for size, but for distraction.

Cachí prompted again. "Mkay, right. So not sure who her Pops is then?"

Accelerated as the light turned green; one hand on the wheel while Cody shook his head again, twirling the string. Then colder than a warning shot and old enough to have teeth, Cachí dropped it bare.

"Apollo."

The alerts chiming in Cody's phone—the '*tell me mores and show me the proofs*'—unanswered now. Unchecked.

Cody twirled the phone between his fingers for a while instead.

Kid knows the name of the guy he's running drugs for. Maybe he just didn't expect his daughter—his *house*—to be that accessible.

Cody swallowed so hard it echoed and Cachí wasn't sure where he was going, but it didn't really matter. Traffic, lights; one-ways, back-to-back.

Even with his car he prefers taking the BART around the city. Can't get anywhere any time fast in these cars and this town.

And don't even ask him to parallel park; he'll keep the bitch running and just wait it out from the car.

Cody cleared his throat.

Cachí glanced, then back to the car in front.

"What are you gonna tell Kayden?"

"*Eso no es mi problema, hermanito.*"Cachí's tone was still nicer than the words.

Pity, maybe.

"You don't think he's gonna do anything?" Cody pulled the drawstrings again and twisted hem into a knot.... *As if they were his.*

"*Que lo intente,*"Cachí sighed, "I'll be right here."

No challenge, no shit talk. Only truth.

And Kayden knows exactly where to look.

Cachí tapped the wheel once, the amber edge between his fingers drawing closer to his skin.

Cody swallowed hard, "fuck, *maje,*"turned back to Cachí and plucked the joint from his fingers like a ballsy SOB.

Dead man walking or whatever.

Cachí let it play out and watched the kid pull smoke into a nasty cough tearing through his chest. Choking, smoke and spit.

Cachí's face dropped when Cody kept at it like a baby. Reached to rip back the joint at the same time Cody burped a horrendously deep and smoky sound. Felt it ripple in the air; made Cachí jolt and yank his arm back like Cody was coming for a bite.

"Sh—what the fuck, *perro.*"

Cody caught his breath then burped again. Eyes glossed over, but Cachí would bet it wasn't from the weed but the realization.

"*Perrito,*" Cachí grumbled. "I want you out of my car." For his own realizations.

And his own safety.

Cody picked at his nails before crawling into the hoodie and leaving the baggy cotton over his head.

"My mom's gonna be so pissed..."

Cachí waited, ignoring the sniffle and staring forward for the kid.

Cachí thought about shit talking; thought about getting on him for playing big games but when Cachí looked at him he couldn't help but see himself.

Running around just trying to find somewhere to belong.

Cody sighed and leaned into the door hard, face to the window and breath leaving a fog.

"Bus station, I guess."

in open your eyes please. Not the blood pooling,
making of a man. growing Or deep forc

TEETH TOO SMALL, TOO SHARP AND ROTTED
OUGH. FALLING OUT, BIRDS AND TEETH
WE. BLOOD ON THE FLOOR, BIRDS DIE.

GROWS TALLER EVERY DAY

axies cry, black holes in the sky—
iding with super novas & the co
at happens when the
n finally goes dark?
it's pretty be redrum
only a dream—
their demons

t happens when you die in dreams
ning in place, can't get to the
n of seven feet tall here
k of dead men, arms folded, eyes closed; veins of mahogan
fall. But the ground rocks and the skies fall. Lightening s
Leti—mirages, fading, ghost. REDRUM redrum for thee a
t bent, fading Leti watching in the doorway doorway
can't move fly away if you can't run
don't go, BECAUSE THE WALLS ARE MOVING OUT
eth on the floor blood man throw
D LEANING. ATTICS OF SUNSHINE, DEVOURING EV
the mask bent like plastic. He
flipping the latch to look it down.
olver in one hand. bullet etched in blood. Walls be
shadow man pulling at her legs. Blood smearing.
th clattering. Like quick sand she can't escape. Stu

with sneakers, limp. Souls g
but she wants her feet. Fallin
little
you've not safe
They were dead birds.
The bodies down
Drowning
teeth loose in he
A WHISPER, CAUGHT S
BETWEEN red
SILENCED bulle
& SILENCE.

Salt Wind & Cedar Bone

PORT ORFORD, OREGON
10:00:00:00

|V|

Kaia jolted awake. Head slammed against the car window, fists tight like she'd hit brick, and Leti flinched so hard her arms nearly swung.

"*Jee-zus!*" Leti hollered, hands tight against the wheel and heart racing. Leti looked to Kaia but kept turning back to the road, curving downhill along coastal cliffs; too dark and too foggy to look away long.

On top of the edges was the exhaustion; before the jolt awake, anyway. Long hours on open roads with nothing but the hum of the car and the heat. Suddenly Leti was appreciative of the wake up.

Kaia however—mouth gapped open, eyes blinking rapidly, still fought her way back from somewhere dark.

"Hey—you good?" Leti breathed.

Sweat slicked Kaia's forehead and her arms pushed against the console and door. Eventually her lungs compressed.

Leti probed again, voice soft. "*Kaia?*"

"Yeah, yeah. I'm..." Kaia took a deep breath in. "Wow, sorry."

Kicked her foot up under herself and onto the seat; stare fixated on the dashboard, not blinking. Not moving.

"That was a bad one..."

Sounded flat too.

Leti watched Kaia try to force a laugh they both knew was shit but ignored anyway.

"You're telling me," Leti added into the lingering silence. "Lucky, I uh, didn't jerk the wheel."

One of those *I'm kidding*—but not really. Fog hugging the car; rain slicking roads; beautiful, breathtaking cliff drops and landscapes.

Beautiful, from the top.

"Yeah, that would uh, suck," Kaia groaned, stretching her back and bending towards the rear seats, across the console as she nodded in agreement. They both averted their eyes when LEDs blew around the corner and Leti sucked in a small breath before a big yawn.

"You good-good?" Kaia popped forward and rubbed Leti's forearm aggressively.

"Mmm," Leti nodded but utterly unconvincingly. Eyes heavy, nerves shot, and reach on its way to a Dreamland as Kaia watched her round a corner slowly, exposing the ocean salt and graphite edge dropping fifty-below.

No guard rail, no room for error—

"Hey..." Kaia trembled. "Hey, switch with me, ya'?"

Leti's head bobbed the longer the comment went unanswered, but anytime she attempted to speak, she'd forget the topic before she could complete a sentence. Foot on and off the gas, dragging slower and slower with each minute.

"Pull off," Kaia's voice came through the haze but was coiled as tight as her pretzeled legs. "You're done."

Leti's eyes were open though. *Now.* Only held shut for a second but scanning for an exit too. "I know, I'm trying—"

"Dude, just use the dirt there—right there—*stop.*"

"No," Leti growled. "How stupid would you look if we got hit?"

"I wouldn't care—I'd be dead..." Kaia exhaled heavily on Leti but Leti didn't even have the energy to feel clustered or crowded.

Been at it since Kelso, with a few loops East and West again for the views. Her wrists buzzed, ass was numb, vision was blurry—Leti had no problem giving over the wheel.

"There." Kaia pointed aggressively. "Orchard? Orford?"

Leti leaned forward to read it too, to correct her, but Kaia spoke again first.

"Orford," she confirmed.

The off-ramp dipped down and the pavement changed abruptly. Few moments later the road did it again. Dramatic change: gravel and dirt scattering as the Bronco slowed to a crawl.

Looked like a ghost town in the cliff sitting just above the fog. Two massive cranes tucked themselves over the side; boats strung up like forgotten kites.

Leti was leaning forward, looking for a place to swap drivers but not so sure she liked the way *anywhere* looked.

Just them. Lost in the smell of cedar, diesel mist, and the night.

Kaia sniffed at the dash. Leti noticed a smell now, too. Faint scent of brake pads and wet basalt—but the whole place smelt worked over.

No signs, no people, no open stores. Even the streetlights were halfway to given up. Brown and soiled. Bugs fossilized inside.

"Damn," Leti scoffed. "Roll the window up." Their laugh had an awkward tension as the glass slowly rolled into place.

"How long was I asleep...?" Kaia yawned, slipping into her hoodie.

"Like five hours...? Where..."

"Nice, cool," nodding in approval, not concerned with questions while digging for her phone. Blue light illuminated the corner of Leti's vision and Kaia groaned.

"*Annnnnd,* no signal..."

Kaia reached behind her, in front, out what was left of the crack in the window—hunting signal as Leti pulled into what appeared to be an overflow lot. But overflow to what, she wondered, scanning the backseat. Assessing the console to climb through the center, visions of an abduction the moment doors unlocked.

"I can crawl through the center—"

"Oh, don't be ridiculous."

Kaia was already out, cold creepy air seeping in as she whipped around and slapped the butt of her seat. Aimed the phone at Leti and flashed the camera off real bright.

"Beautiful," Kaia taunted.

Leti maintained an annoyed but unphased look; best option with Kaia.

"Dude—actually?" Kaia backed up and turned her face to the stars. Arms wide, spinning, hoodie catching the wind.

Leti pulled the key, counting the engine ticks as they died. Headlights off long enough for the shadows to open their eyes and begin to lurk.

She didn't like the way the wind moved either but opened the door despite her body telling her to collapse into the seat.

Just walking around though—to the passenger side. *Nothing more,* she promised herself. But when Leti made it around the car, Kaia pounced.

"So, are you gonna' look?" Hands slapped her sides as they dropped from the sky and if Kaia was any more sideways, the girl would fold into the night. Laughing and distracted; *joyful even.*

Leti could see it now: hearing Kaia's laughing getting further as she spun her way straight off the cliff.

"Not like they're going to disappear," but Leti tipped her head back to partake.

"Not like they're going to disappear," Kaia mocked with her lips smashed together and ugly. "Come on. Isn't it beautiful?" She pressed, pointing up and cocking her head next. "There's um, *shoot.* Hang on I totally know that one..."

Kaia stomped her foot like the stars argued back and Leti couldn't help but to mentally quip: *probably just the voices.* Something that didn't seem important at the time, but resonated with Leti—made her feel *unsure.* Sorry, but jealous.

Or worried but proud. When Kaia'd told Leti it was like seven different fonts spoke and wrote to her at once. All of them Kaia. But all of them different.

Somedays, maybe even like now, Leti was jealous because Leti was the opposite. Most days she couldn't find a single guiding voice, let alone multiple. And even her nightmares were lonely.

Leti's eyes closed and she counted the stars behind her lids as they disappeared.

Seven, eight, nine— Despite that, not one version or *font* of Kaia dares to open up. Not unless words escape her dreams in some kind of half logic, half lobotomy.

Leti's eyes opened in time to see a trail tracking behind a falling star and she closed her eyes tight, nodding at it once.

"Kai, make a wish."

Silence crawled between them briefly—the ocean waves echoing louder before Leti wished upon the star and cracked her eyes in time to see Kaia doing the same.

They both could guess what Leti wanted, but Kaia was a mystery. Kaia was a mood. But Leti has actively tried to coax truth—or simply, just any *words*—from Kaia's nightmares before; sat beside her on a more talkative night, asking questions.

What happened in the room?
Who are you apologizing to?   *How'd you know?*

What did he say right before?

Kaia knew Leti had them—Kaia *had* to know. And Leti had a right to not just ask but be answered, because she isn't a curious person asking questions— she's Kaia's sister. And Kaia distracts or dodges the topic any time it comes up.

If Leti had a wish—a single one—she'd make Kaia talk to her about it. Chain her down so she can't run. Running as if the truth didn't have the stamina to follow. And not even chasing, not in a rush, just a steady, unavoidable, forward motion.

"Albireo! "Kaia shouted pointing to the sky and Leti flinched, caught off guard. "And it's with—something to do with a swan, I can't...remember. But the name is Albireo."

She laughed then, real and accomplished and Leti shook her head, but laughed too. Just tiredly.

Kaia came with lows that sizzled like brimstone and had highs that radiated; waterfall-chasing, red-planet-spotting, firefly-field camping—

"Oh and there is Mm-Mizar, I think, and Alcor."

Highs so bright Leti could live on the borrowed light alone.

"You know I have no idea, right?"

Kaia laughed again, "That's why I'm telling you, right?"

But the drops were steep. And sometimes, Leti feared Kaia's lows had the potential to kill them both.

The wind hit then; basalt and cedar twisting tight. The cranes shook, boats too, and Leti leaned on Kaia's door with a yawn. She eyed downwind, down the cliffside, and saw red lights despite her vision slurring like it was drunk.

"Hey," Leti nodded to the deceptively honest, dark, downhill. "I think that's a vacancy sign."

Kaia shrugged, which didn't surprise either of them. She didn't mind sleeping in the SUV; seats off the tracks and removed for extra space. Made shuffling around easy and Denver had pulled the back for a graduation camping trip. They never made it, though.

"Vacancy then," Kaia repeated absent mindedly walking forward.

She stopped short of the edge, but leaned further toward the cliffside to look and Leti stepped once, but couldn't go further. Worried, even her aura could crowd Kaia and push her off.

"Bottom looks the same everywhere!" Leti was higher pitched than she meant, but Kaia didn't turn. Just chuckled low and Leti waited. Watched. Biting back ruthless anxiety while wary the whole cliff might crumble.

And what would she—what *could* she do?

"Hey," Kaia chirped, spinning way too fast. "Think fast, answer fast. K?"

Leti took a breath, "mhm."

"Essay answers this time; let's get into the details, mkay?"

"*Mkay*," Leti mimicked.

"What would you do if the car started rolling off the side? Slow, but E-break is busted. Starts from—ehhhh, little further back."

Leti imagined it—tires sliding, the crunch when the car hit bottom—flinched then. Kaia too after a delay; maybe only then visualizing the scenario, but Leti buried it like they were normal. Considered it without the *bang*. Not because it mattered, not because she wanted, but because Kaia loved it. And because it was familiar. Which makes it comfortable.

Filling the space with dreamy or dreary hypotheticals, some often philosophically fascinating or morally challenging, but all—used as a buffer between uncomfortable silence and avoided themes.

"Yeah, nothing," Leti was dumbfounded. Not much of an essay answer, but Kaia looked even more shocked the more Leti spoke.

"Watch it roll with all our stuff? That one sucks. Gimme another scenario."

Kaia shook her head like she disagreed, like she'd shimmy inside and save it; like she was confident she *could* save it. Save the babies, break up the fights, make a scene so it gives a show; intentions were genuinely always pure. So much so that sometimes it felt like life and law came second best.

They lingered a little while after that. Leti got closer to the edge, Kaia stepped back meeting her somewhere in the middle, and they exchanged a few old jokes, a few made-up words, before a few more stubborn steps back to the Bronco.

They crept back to the car, no reason to rush until human noises peeped from the other side of the mist. Not coming closer, not leaving—just out there.

Probably an average-Joe, but one with a shadow of monsters.

Kaia and Leti exchanged worried looks and casually, if not quickly, returned to the SUV, both hitting the lock simultaneously.

Kaia's face changed over to fury—dramatically angry and without cause. Leti looked around but realized as Kaia adjusted the chair and mirrors like Leti's height—or lack thereof—destroyed them.

"Itsy-bitsy spi—"

"Shut up," Leti barked, thudding Kaia's arm with her hand.

Snickering, the seat slid back and snapped into place. Side mirrors next— small commentary and taunting continued, expertly ignored by Leti who had shoes mostly off and sleep halfway on.

The car hummed, then the heat bumped up and Kaia eased the car forward. Whispering before they even turned for the freeway. "Leti...?"

Leti's head lolled; eyes pried enough to look open; but not see.

"You *need* the hotel? Or care if I drive? I'm wired."

Leti shrugged. Or nodded. Or both. But lids sank low again.

"Wake me whenever."

"K, wait," Kaia chuckled, poking her side and getting Leti to swat again. "Anything you wanna see before California? Else I might drive straight through." Kaia shuffled into the console for a notebook they'd thrown together last minute. "Did I put anything down for this section of the state?"

Eyes didn't even try, only Leti's mouth. "There's some kinda—natural bridge. Rock, hole, thing... Before California. And well—you, we wanna see the red woods. Not the stupid car-thing, but the red—"

"Yep, yep, *yep,*" Kaia bounced.

Leti could feel the car shake, but the tires were still. Peeking at Kaia again, the smile was still there. Thumb refreshing the map over and over impatiently—*and again—*

Leti cleared her throat. "Make me a deal?"

Kaia's head popped up and turned instantly. "Okay?"

"Every hundred miles," Leti's words dropped lower and slower with each one. A losing battle, but still, Leti went on: "Here, 'til we're empty or done. Mkay?"

Kaia waited but Leti stopped there. "Empty...Leti?"

Cranes faded in the mirror as the car pushed onto pavement again and Leti cleared her throat at the jostling.

"I said, one hard thing, every hundred miles. One hard thing," she echoed.

The atmosphere wasn't heavy yet, but it was adding up so Kaia fiddled with the music dial, twisting the knob around the radio like she wasn't about to use a Bluetooth.

"One secret, Kai."

Leti quiet and music loud, not hearing was believable now. Kaia waited.

"I'll tell you the hard stuff too. One v. one, Kaia-Raye."

Kaia faded into the seat as she drove; pretending she wasn't there or maybe just couldn't hear.

"One..."

A heavier song came on louder and Kaia jerked to crank it down but really only touched it.

"You want me to put headphones in?"

Leti shook her head, jacket over her face, body rotating to the window.

"You sound better when the song hides your voice."

Kaia's head leaned.

Bridge divots clicked, passing over gaps in the mountainside:

> *kclm, kclm, kclm, kclm...*

Smooth again. Curvy.

"Right," Kaia smiled. Thumb no longer on the maps, but on the music now. "Love you," she grinned.

Scrolling, scrolling—and loading *James Brown, 'I Got You.'*

Five seconds. Opening only. Kaia peaked at Leti—"Sleep tight, babe..."

She saw the next short bridge approach and waited for the silence after it.

> *kclimk, kclumk, kclimk, kclumk.*

Waterfalls and mountainside, and stereo volume set to full.

Now let it rip.

The fog was thicker in the city than Cachí remembered. It clung to his hoodie, soaked into his jacket, and coiled down his throat while footsteps echoed around them. Laughter too loud and unfazed.

Cachí looked behind him—Darcy, couple others and more up front. Newer guys, but all of them fired up. Poppin' off and shootin' the shit like being witness or accomplice doesn't bother them anymore.

He couldn't help but wonder when that all changed. Watching the newbs in the front but thinking of a couple in the back that he'd known through school. *Sure.* They'd always done dumb shit, but at least they felt something about it.

Kept hearing, '*he deserves it*' and '*you'd hate him*' floatin' around before their group jumped some guy. Cachí couldn't help but to challenge Kayden a bit:

"Yeah, but would you walk away if he didn't?"

No better than a pack of animals that smelt blood.

Kayden slowed down to fall in line with Cachí, probably cuss him out or tell him off, but Cachí went forward. Then before Cachí knew it, Kayden had dipped after they beat that guy. Probably for the best, too. Cachí wasn't sure he wouldn't swing being that hyped up.

Theres still time though.

Always time for a battle with Kayden. On days like today, specifically, it made Cachí wonder why he ever defended Kade and kept their friendship.

Even when he hides it, Cachí respects the hell out of both Mikki and Dante. And if they both walked away and cut Kayden out, there is more weight to it that Cachí should maybe consider.

So Cachí should walk away.

Or did Dante and Mik get too close, get to talking, and turn each other against Kayden?

Cachí knew it wasn't like that really, but his guilt and shame prevented him from believing it fully. From turning his back on one of their own. He wasn't mad at Dante and Mick for doing it—which should have told him something too, maybe—but he just couldn't.

Though maybe it was about more than just Kayden. About life, and direction.

Directionless.

Cachí scoffed and kicked a rock.

Acting sad and pathetic like it made a difference; like being lost excused him for being a—didn't want to think it, but the word *"criminal"* came to mind.

But he wasn't... But he still went; but he still swung.

Cachí followed the rock and kicked it again. *And hey*—maybe it's better to be an animal than just a pretender. Riding the guys about whether they'll have the spine to walk away while standing there pulling punches and softening blows...?

Who didn't have the spine to walk?

Just watched. Wondering what happens if someone rats; what happens if someone hits a little too hard and it escalates six feet down?

Cachí's seeing more and more into this side Kayden's been calling home, and he wants less. He just wants Kayden to come get less of this shit, too. While also wanting to deck his fuckin', fat head.

Kayden's surprise *errand. Lying piece of shit.*

Cachí kept his head down in the hoodie; watched his feet; didn't even want to be seen in the neighborhood terrified Dante would catch wind if the guy called the cops.

But he was fine. He wouldn't be that stupid...

Hands kept switching from his jean pockets to his jacket. Fidgeting. Checked his phone, too. Couple people had asked each other where Cody was 'cause the kid never missed shit. But Cachí hadn't seen him, hadn't *heard* from him; and definitely didn't take him somewhere or see him anywhere... Waiting for the blowback and praying maybe Jaylin did the right thing.

He scoffed again. *No fucking way.* Cachí didn't say shit or show shit but did text Cody subtly a few minutes later. And that was maybe two hours ago. Dumbass should have answered by now with the damn phone glued to his palm and a mouth like a megaphone.

Cachí and them been around the city and in a brawl since he sent it and no one else heard a thing?

Right foot—breath. No thoughts. Because Cachí didn't have the space to create more panic when he was admittedly, a negative person. Trying to train his mind to stop—meditating without ever calling it that—but not having the strength to silence his worries.

Jaylin and a drug supply just....

That's bad; that's so bad. Cachí was starting to tell himself why it was dangerous too but kept hushing at the warnings. Too scared to let himself consider it fully, because then he'd have to consider how picking him up will look if Jaylin doesn't return that shit immediately.

Cachí started counting steps; a weak effort to control the urge to have a full-on panic attack, 'cause that thought rabbit trails into the next, and so on: *like what if he crosses Dante's desk not as a crook, but as a body?*

"Yo, Cachí!"

Almost swung on Darcy when the guy's arm landed around Cachí hard, his voice loud. Another oversized fuckin' bear like Kayden; very specific type to shadow Jaylin.

Cachí rolled his shoulders to free himself. "Come on, don't touch me," Cachí squirmed, counting louder in his head while trying to be normal.

Whatever the fuck that meant anymore.

"You hear me?" Darcy brushed off Cachí's shoulder sarcastically and Cachí swatted at his hand.

"No," he pouted. Nodding at the BART station ahead like it'd send Darcy away.

"Yeah, you comin'?"

"I dunno, maybe," Cachí was quiet. "Gonna walk, though" Because they ran for empty bottles, smoked-out rooms, and pallet beds.

The fuck is the rush for...? Slinking back to the same hole with blood on their hands and dirt under their nails.

Darcy frowned, but didn't seem to really care while scrolling through his phone. "You pissed?"

When Cachí didn't say anything, Darcy—probably trying to sound sincere—added: "Don't be so hard on everyone."

Probably even meant to sound reassuring. But he *sounded* like a prick, Cachí thought, pulling at his hoodie so he could slide deeper within it.

"Right." He muttered, stretching the neckline from his throat.

Cachí didn't want the confrontation or the battle. Right now at least. He was just—*here*. Because Kayden said they just had to have Cachí come too. Why? Wouldn't say—because Kayden fucking knew what the answer would be. And Cachí was just there—*trusting him like an idiot.*

Like this wasn't the first time Kayden snapped old pacts like twigs; promising to keep Cachí out of the bullshit and especially the felonies. Cachí, Kade, and Mick too—swore they'd never pass through his precinct in trouble; Dante promised never to abuse the power on them; and Mick...

is just stuck with them no matter what she does. Far enough to be safe, but close enough to connect. For him and Dante at least.

No one's told Cachí, but he hears. And watches. He knows they've told Kayden to get out of his life; knows they've fought about him—

Cachí.

He didn't like it, and it made him uncomfortable. Probably what subconsciously pushed both him and Kayden closer. Plus—Cachí already lost one from that core group—fat chance he was willing to lose another. And Kayden probably felt the same.

Dante too. Mikki. Hell, fuckin' *all* of them. Treating an old wound in their own ways.

"Hello?"

Cachí gave Darcy his attention but saw the phone to his ear and watched the first couple guys disappear down into the BART station instead. Darcy pulled his attention back though. Didn't mean to, but the slight stutter, the stiff stance, slower step...? That all said, *bad news.*

That was a bad news call, and it made Cachí walk faster; curious, but not curious enough for Darcy-drama. Pit in his stomach warning him otherwise, desperate for a bit of stillness somewhere safe—Cachí didn't turn. He kept walking with his hands in his pockets and his shoulders hunched.

"Hey!"

"I'm good," Cachí mumbled, waving like Darcy would take the hint.

"Bro, hold up," looking down at his phone when Cachí turned and then to Cachí as if surprised. "You know why Miles is in town? That's gotta' be why Kayden dipped, right?"

Cachí's head lolled to the side and he recognized the name but couldn't place it. "Which one's Miles again?"

"Wish I could say the same," Darcy chuckled. But it lacked ease as he looked at the station, then the direction Cachí was going, and back to his phone.

"Not so sure I wanna rush back now," he admitted.

And that shit was probably the most relatable Cachí has felt with those people. Unsure how they got there, but there, just trying to get through.

Valley of the Little Hills

SONOMA COUNTY, CALIFORNIA
07:00:00:00

|VI|

Eight gas stations, two days, and six-hundred circular miles later, Leti and Kaia rumbled into a California town. *Petaluma.*

Having spent the past few nights beach hopping and car snoozing—a shower, a motel? Sounded like a nice idea soon.

Though with the sun still high and the day young, it was moving time. And currently, *refuel* time. The car and the girls.

Leti bumped open the door to a corner mart with her hip, shoulder shifting to hold it long enough for Kaia to slide through and make a beeline for the glass-front coolers and the caffeine in the back.

Her sneakers squeaked once but then went quiet, so Leti kept an eye on her as they passed through alternate rows. Despite the noise, Kaia could move softly when she wanted. Like she could vanish if she tried hard enough and whenever she got too far, Leti got nervous.

So Leti shifted towards the back too, cutting through the canned aisle with a hundred identical labels in neat rows and mostly consisting of beans. Something about it bothered her; shoving some of the beans back, and a couple sideways so the rows were no longer present.

But worse than that? The sound of a coke bottle hissing as Kaia cracked it open against the doorframe, swigging from it like she was dehydrated.

Leti looked around like they'd both be thrown out and shuffled over to Kaia guiltily.

"You're not supposed to do that yet." Leti's braid slid over her shoulder as she looked around again, but Kaia just shrugged.

Pulled a couple other energy drinks while grumbling, "I don't like this town."

"Why?" Leti reached into the neighboring cooler for her own drinks and juice and they cut through the chip aisle to pluck from there, too.

"Feels like a brochure," Kaia answered.

Flat. Glossy. And maybe reasons to visit, but likely none to stay.

After pulling snacks, the clerk rang them up without speaking; bored for decades and part of the pamphlet. They awkwardly butted elbows and helped with the bagging until the girls could slip back into the lot where at least there was the sounds of nature.

Dull heat rose off painted parking lines, bees swarmed around shrubs, humming like a machine, and the wind rustled the trees within the boundaries of historic districts and tiny home communities.

Like the peas and carrots in the store; same homes, same families, same lives; where secrets are currency and divergences stay in the closet.

Leti loaded the bag into the back seat. Chips. Drinks. Maybe a lighter Kaia didn't need but sorely wanted. Grabbed the receipt too. Dumb luck. Eyes scanning as she shut the back and worked towards the driver's seat. Rolling over each line again like a second look would change what she read.

"Kaia," Leti smiled charmingly, crawling up into the seat and turning to face her. "Why do you have Millie's goddamn credit card?"

The name sitting plainly at the bottom.

Kaia's door hung half-open, and she took another long pull of the coke. Wiped her mouth with her wrist as the bottle clinked against her rings and shrugged.

"She shouldn't have touched me."

"You called her a—"

"She shouldn't have started shit," Kaia reiterated. "Had the thing two weeks dude."

"Doesn't help your case, Kaia." Leti slammed the door behind her but Kaia only made her angrier.

Laughing, "Case? Oh shudd'up Leelee."

A few more hours down the road, Kaia went for the radio and Leti flicked it off quickly.

Kaia had told her to shut up, and Leti could shut the fuck up. A war tactic of hers, not even giving the radio the time to load; allowing the sound of the road to fatten and weigh on Kaia.

Leti had always been better with the silence. and wouldn't speak this time until Kaia gave up the card.

But on principle, Leti wasn't going to tell her. Make her figure it out herself.

Action. Consequence.

Kaia sighed heavily. A couple times. And each more dramatic than the first.

She shook her leg, hogged the console, put her feet in the center of the dash, and even into Leti's side. Toes bending and cracking and widening and flexing—

because to hell with traffic apparently.

Desperate for a rise but not getting one.

To their surprise though, Kaia made it another hour. Didn't figure out what Leti wanted, but was first to speak. Softly too, like it was an apology.

"You think they're looking for us?"

Her voice and the question caught Leti off guard.

They...?

She didn't answer right away because, who's *they*?

Leti considered it, almost caught in the distraction but remembered the war and but looped it around to the point.

"You know... A stolen credit card; someone might," adjusting the rearview like she believed what she said.

Kaia rolled her eyes. "Back to that huh."

"Never left," Leti quipped,

But the chip bag crinkling was the last to respond as it settled between them. Kaia pulled a handful out and offered one to Leti. Not so much for Leti to take, but for Kaia to signal:

This is my white flag.

Leti snagged it with her window-side arm and crumbled it into the air.

Couldn't imagine Kaia had many white flags left. And even fewer people left to take them.

The Kids Aren't Alright

DALY CITY
BRISBANE BARRIO | EARLY 2000s

||VI||

The summer heat pressed down on the city like a hand that wouldn't lift, turning the pavement into a skillet beneath their sneakers.

Rubber softening, socks soaked, every step a reminder that even joy could blister.

Cachí trailed a half-step behind the pack, wiry and restless, his hand-me-down shirt stuck to his back like a second skin.

It still smelled like the older cousin who gave it to him—cologne, smoke, something sharper underneath.

Matías out front, always. Leading like instinct, not choice. Curls tucked under a backward cap; grin stretched across his face like it was made to pull you in.

You didn't follow Matías because he asked. You followed because something in you said you'd be less without him.

Kayden was all noise—arms and legs flailing, voice echoing too loud down the alley. Everything about him looked cartoon until you saw his eyes; those were real.

Wild and unbothered as he shoulder-checked Dante; both laughing like boys who'd never seen a body hit the pavement.

And while Dante laughed too, his grin rarely reached the surface. Even then there was something sharp behind it; always clocking the exits; the weight of each laugh; the silence in between.

And Cachí—the youngest—wanted in so bad it itched. Every laugh that didn't include him scraped against his ribs. Every inside joke he walked the outside of was another bruise he wore like armor.

"Matí!" Kayden shouted, winded but glowing, breath and sweat and light. "Tell the little shit to quit riding my ass, brah!"

"I'm not!" Cachí snapped, cheeks burning. "I'm faster than you, gordo."

"You wish," Kayden snorted, faking a stumble. Just long enough for Matías to sneak up and hook an arm around Cachí's neck.

It was the quiet kind of love that didn't speak; but was warmth, strength, and weight. The kind of love you can trust.

"He's just pissed cause you're about to beat him," Matías said, all but riding Cachí's back and throwing a wink over his shoulder.

Kayden milked it. Stumbled again, spun in place, threw his head back in a fake collapse. A big ham—nothing too serious.

And even Dante couldn't help but smile. Brief and crooked and real because they could.

Because the city was in their hands. The city that stunk of fish, burnt rubber, and street food left too long in the sun.

Streetcars screamed; base lines spilled from open windows. Voices climbed fire escapes built out of rust and rot. And the five of them, they could name it all.

Remove five things within the city walls—they'd feel it like losing a game of Operation—a shock to the system—taking the wild from their homes. Because that was their block. Their world.

Scorched and humming and alive.

Dare anyone to take a swing because five would swing right back. Untouchable. And built from the cracked concrete, childhood loyalty, and dreams. Dreams that—at the time—kinda felt a lot like plans.

The abandoned substation door opened. Not with a creak, but with the slow, grinding drag of inevitability. One no one ever hears with planes overhead and traffic outside. Sometimes it was comforting, but today, during Miles' presence...it wasn't.

He came dragging in some guy—*fuckin' Cody?* And Darcy damn near dragging behind, too. Kayden unsure if he was helping or hurting.

"What the fuck?" Kayden sighed but knew it was bad. Couldn't say he wasn't a little relieved though, having been convincing himself it was his life on the line while he'd waited.

Cody'd just started working that side of things, and *now?* Bloodied face; one sneaker gone; t-shirt hanging off his neck like it didn't belong...?

"What the *fuck* happened, enough!" Kayden growled, refusing to cower when Miles looked at him amused.

Daring him—*say it again.*

Kayden swallowed but allowed himself to get angrier the longer they ignored him. Cigarette lit and loose between Kayden's fingers the way the kid hung loose between Miles and D. But tightened fast.

Cody was—hanging loose between them. Miles shoved him forward hard enough to send him to hands and knees on the concrete between the three of them. Kayden didn't get a chance to look at Cody long what with Miles' light coming up and blinding the absolute fuck out of Kayden.

"Been awhile, mate. How's it?" Miles *inquired.* A neutral tone, neutral face. But nothing natural, only controlled.

Kayden on the other hand struggled with it while half panicked a bullet would slice through that white light and into him.

Cody broke the eerie calm though, crying: "Kayden I—I didn't mean to—I"

"Hold on, shut up," Miles waved his hand at the floor dismissively.

"Why the fuck are you here?" Kayden barked before Miles could taunt. But Cody hogged the space in the air. He was loud:

"I didn't know—oh my god man, please, I'm—sorry," grunting when Miles pushed him over further with his foot.

"This the one you two sent me, right?"

Kayden didn't answer. And Darcy wouldn't look.

But Cody *wailed*; calming only when Miles bent down beside him and whispered what Kayden only assumed was a threat. The way Cody's mouth closed and eyes opened said all he needed.

"Right then," Miles flattened his shirt, backing enough to see them both.

"Imagine when I hear my bag didn't make it from the airport."

"I'm—s-sorry, really, it was stupid but it—it's safe, we—can go get it, please?" Cody's voice was small and shaky.

No idea he was buying in for life when he wandered through for a gig.

"Yes, remind me where you told me it was again?"

"It's at their mansion—Jay's got it, it's her stuff too? Please! It's good."

Kayden sighed heavily. Better chance getting it back from a stranger, honestly. Jaylin collects her favors and power like fine China on display.

"Exactly; so the house..."

"Aye man," Darcy didn't sound half as confident as usual. "Whatever Jay said—ain't worth really hurtin' him, she's a liar, and everything was accounted for, I'm sorry but—"

"Shut the fuck up." Miles waited an extra second, maybe testing to make sure Darcy did. Continued, "I haven't spoke to Jaylin yet."

When they looked confused, he added, "Cameras," and then included Cody again. "So, Berkeley, huh? No goodbyes?"

Rhetorically, anyway.

"That where you're from, right?"

Cody went to speak right before the hook landed on his cheek. Miles swung and Cody shouted first at the fist and then the floor. It wasn't that loud or shrill, but it was wet.

And scared. And Kayden didn't like it—he didn't want it. He wanted it over with because he knew it was going to get worse .

"What are we doing here?" he didn't mean to ask, but it wanted out.

"You're cleaning up your messes."

Cody coughed and spat out. Seemed more surprised than the others when a tooth hit to floor and a puddle of blood, but being called a mess had him hysterical again.

"I didn't—I didn't know, okay?!"

Kayden's foot slid back a fraction of an inch as both he and Cody recoiled *And for what?* Seventeen, eighteen years—that's all he gets?

Kayden looked into the dark and around like there'd be some answer or rescue, but it was just Cody's echo and Matías' shadow, because even he lasted longer.

They'll leave behind a couple pictures, some voice notes maybe, but they all have end dates too. Played one final time and then like they never even were. Few years of noise and not even an echo left. But the wailing echoed now. It made the station feel bigger—deeper somehow with many crevices to fold into.

Because that's what they were doing. He was running excuses and denials in his head but he fuckin' knew: Cody was dead the minute Miles decided to search. Stalling, racking his thought for an answer...

Pointless.

"I didn't mean to!" But that didn't make it better, it made it worse.

"She led it, she said it was okay and she knew you!"

Miles frowned, but shrugged. "One of those is true."

"I was delivering them! I didn't even leave Apollo's property technically!"

"Brings me to strike two. Didn't bring the drugs where they were supposed to go, but stuck your dick where it shouldn't have been?"

Felt less like a dire task and more like a game then; Kayden got pissed. "This about business, or *her*?" Louder now. "D's being too nice, she's bein' a whore, and Apollo's locked and doesn't know. What the fuck we really doin' here?"

"She came onto me and she has it I didn't steal it I swear! I didn't have a single one!"

Cody was still easier to look at than Miles. Made Kayden feel secure where Miles had him scared. And stupid when Miles spoke slowly for Kayden:

"I just told you. Cleaning. Getting up to speed, per Apollo."

Still not able to look at Miles, Kayden crouched to Cody and grumbled, "I hope you soiled that man's house."

Stalling? Trying to be good ol' joker.

Or just finding a way to make it worse while trying to right it again?

"I don't think we got a way out of this one, bud." Kayden shook his head, unsure who even heard but not caring either way.

Apollo wanted them up to speed?

Well, even if Kayden didn't pull the trigger today—he's been a killer long before now. Maybe was just never willing to face it.

"Get out...your gun," Miles enunciated.

Might has well have been a fuckin' bot; human-like, but just *off.* Too calm, too controlled, too...

Empty.

Kayden pictured playing hero; shooting Miles, but then what?

Retribution swings through and skins someone like Mikki or their mom. Nah, he may be a lot of things, but the one thing he's not is a danger to them. Never.

They just didn't understand. Cody and Kayden, two cogs in a broken machine; tirelessly twisting until the whole damn thing combusts. But Cody was already on fire—Kayden only prolonging the inevitable while his own flame caught up faster.

Kayden refocused as Cody worked to his knees and faced away from them. Maybe he could fight for it. Not that he stood a chance against any one of them, but better death than on his knees?

Or try hard enough long enough to cool Miles down.

"Cody..." Kayden warned.

Scurrying away slow, shoulders to his ears like he was expecting to get swung on from behind, and Kayden there, watching.

Being watched.

His own gun not steady in his hand—his *mind* unsteady *Remembering.* Feeling the cool concrete; the skin being pulled and torn when Kayden suddenly tossed back onto his ass at a *pop.*

A gunshot rang through the concrete tunnel; slapped Kayden so hard he partially fell out of his mind and into an entirely different flashback, clawing away from that memory with Matias—that place that told him maybe he's always been evil.

A razor sharp cry cut out somewhere too, but the only sound Kayden had was from memory. When Kayden landed back into sense and out of shock, he saw Cody was shot in the back of the thigh, Darcy had a foot partially in front of Miles and his hands were up but muscles were tight.

Never knew if Darcy was trying to calm a situation down or rile it up another beat, but then Kayden saw the gun in Miles' hand. Sent Kayden scrambling to his feet, ignoring Cody while he writhed in pain until Kayden himself was no longer down range.

Kayden looked toward the corner out—or in. No one was coming, because no one good ever does. Buried under the city and a mile of 'see nothing, say nothing' pavement. Maybe everyone down there deserved a bullet with their name engraved.

Himself included, watching Cody curl in on himself. Not quite the way Matías had, but he dropped the same. The kid held his thigh—tried to block the plume of blood—the way Mikki had held Matias—Dante, too.

Desperate and futile.

Miles kicked a piece of trash at Cody and Kayden. "You hear me?"

But Kayden didn't. He looked at Darcy again, like he'd ever been helpful before, down at Cody, and back to Miles who was stepping forward.

"You like options, control." Miles wiggled the so-bright-it-was-blue light across Kayden's face, dropping the light with a smile when Kayden scowled. "I get it."

Kayden didn't trust him. The more ease, the worse it'd be.

"So here's the second choice: either you or Darcy get bagged, and the kid can go. I even got one more. I'll have one or both sent home to Apollo. Either you boys missing the cage?"

Kayden visibly flinched at option three, but he couldn't tell if he was more angry at himself or the ultimatum.

"Why not send Cody in? The fuckin' shit's with Jaylin, right?!"

Bile rose in Kayden's throat to his own weakness. He knew what Miles—*what Apollo*—would say. And as he thought it, Miles said it:

"Not this time. It's a respect thing, come on, let's go."

From behind Miles, Darcy actually stepped forward, determination on his face but otherwise silent, and Miles sensed it. Turned sharp and cocked his head.

"Got something you wanna say? Because you're lucky you're not buried down here with him."

Kayden confused; Cody crying... Darcy didn't regress the entire step, but it was far enough back to submit which offended Kayden too. And he let it. Even beginning to wonder if he was just trying to work himself up into doing what Miles' says.

Letting his fury come out knowing it's ruthless. But the worst part was Cody looking at him.

Kayden wanted to point at them—say it's Miles' fault—but his fists tightened instead. Not sure why the nightmares were coming, only that they dialed in from every direction.

Kayden tried to hold up his gun but it didn't aim straight; it shook too hard and could even bounce. *Right?* Concrete walls all around; shoot the wrong person. Mind bending for reasons or excuses, so disillusioned and self-involved that when the second shot cracked out, a part of Kayden thought it burrowed into him. But Kayden watched Cody still. Thought about the energy and defiance he came in with, and while it made Kayden sad, he felt relief.

Or release, maybe? No longer afraid he'd be shot down there, and no longer under a pleading, crying gaze.

Miles caught his attention with a gentle toss and a holler. "Think fast." Tossing Kayden the still-warm gun he'd just used on Cody and stepping back like this was a drill.

Kayden dropped his cigarette and fumbled with the two weapons.

"As far as anyone's concerned—that's all you." Miles told him.

Kayden's fingers curled around the grip before his brain even caught up, but then he looked at Miles like he was diseased.

"The fuck is wrong with you?!"

Darcy stayed quiet, arms crossed and back. Watching with tension in his neck that said he didn't love it, but he wasn't intervening either.

Miles lit his own cigarette, too. Calm as ever, and said, "Apollo wants everyone on the same page. Let him know it wasn't you and he'll send me right back. You understand?"

Kayden's jaw clenched. He looked at Darcy, hoping for some kind of pushback but Darcy just shifted his weight and looked back like he expected the same.

"Summer's coming to an end, boys," Miles said, flicking ash. "Darcy—you're up bud, where's your car?"

Darcy stepped closer. "What do we—"

"Kayden, gun. Now." But Miles didn't care what Darcy had to say either.

Darcy and Kayden's feet shuffled, bodies turned slightly out.

"You're fuckin' dreamin'," Kayden chuckled, finding both guns a spot under his belt.

"We gettin' rid of two bodies then?" Miles taunted back.

Kayden thought about winding up a swing; saying *anything*. But what could he possibly say that hadn't already bled out with the kid on the floor? There were no apologies in the world, no do overs. Just silence, and roles that they had to play at the cost of staying alive.

But prison? That wasn't a cost Kayden was willing to pay; he wasn't ever going back.

Instead, he smirked confidently, suicidally maybe, and tugged his shirt to assess the two guns on his hip.

"You uh, gonna' shoot me?"

"Might have another one on me, Kayden."

Fair.

Kayden didn't change face, but his swallow was loud. Then to both his and Darcy's surprise, Miles laughed. Which scared Kayden more than the threats.

"Was gonna get rid of it with your boy down there," Miles said, "But suit—"

"Shut the fuck up, no you weren't." Kayden grumbled, annoyed.

Even he was starting to sound a bit too casual, raking his long hair back between his fingers and Kayden looked down at Cody. Still as death.

Only the blood moved now, sticky and black beneath him. Apollo wanted it done, so Apollo got it. But not Cody. Kayden doubted the man gave two shits about any of those kids, but Kayden? *Darcy?*

They belonged to Apollo first, and Jayline second. Because even outside the prison, you either become the monster or you become the meal.

As far as anyone's concerned, you did it, Kayden replayed again.

Well, as far as Kayden's concerned, he might as well have. Chest tight and uncomfortable. No longer a boy, no longer a person, but demolished into a task.

"Go on now," Miles approached, close enough Kayden's back foot slid further the opposite direction, subtly taking a proper stance.

"Go," he said again, ushering Kayden towards the corner. "Else you're participating in this, too."

Without thought, Kayden flicked the ash at Miles and said, "fuck you," as he turned lazily. Head not down—too proud while Miles is still here—but not quite high either.

For Cody. Walking out to the beat of skin dragging against cement and two men folding some poor kid out of existence.

And somewhere—somewhere else in this town and every town like it— there's another shirt, on another kid it doesn't belong. And it still smells like smoke, gunpowder, and milk cartons.

YEARLY, IN THE U.S.—

2.8 MILLION CHILDREN RUN AWAY:
APRX 100,000 ARE SEX TRAFFICKED.
600-800 DIE IN STATE CUSTODY.
7,000-8,000 DIE BY UNINTENTIONAL INJURY.
2,000-2,200 DIE BY SUICIDE.
[NEARLY **50%** LGBTQ+ YOUTH]
1,000-1,200 ARE MURDERED.
[30-60 WHILE AT SCHOOL]
400,000 GO MISSING.
1 IN 5 NEVER RETURN.

How many is too many?

THE FAULTLINE

you
don't
break
chains
by
whispering
at
them

the Boy We Called Sam

| VIII |

The sticky glow of the fast-food chain's neon lights made everything look too sharp while inside. Leti and Kaia sat across from each other, their burgers already halfway dismantled as Kaia slid her tomato across the tray and Leti passed over her pickles. Exchanges coded into the bone because old rituals die hard; harder when you think you've had your last one.

The cafe wasn't anything special though. Another West Coast staple where the nostalgia was thin, the fries were decent, and the grease was dependable.

Leti tore the paper from her straw; jabbed it into her drink and took a long sip while watching Kaia from behind the lid. Her leg bounced and eyes rolled around the place as Kaia took it all in, oblivious Leti stared.

Once they settled, Leti held her hand out, palm side up, and waited. It made Kaia freeze, piecing together the clues as her head went further to the side the longer it took.

"What...?" Face squished at first, but Kaia gave zero resistance when it clicked. Reached into her back pocket and pulled Millie's card, giving it to Leti with a slight curve in the plastic.

Leti's anger lifted when plastic touched her palm and she tucked Millie's credit card into her wallet with her own debit.

"So..." Leti had no further words on the matter, no sass in the hand offf, and no thank you either. Only forward momentum and how it was before.

"You sleep at all?" Leti asked.

Kaia nodded around bite of food; "a bit."

But even the bags under her eyes looked tired. Restless nights leaving a permanent feature across Kaia's face that told people: *I don't care, leave me alone.* Leti used to be able to coax her out of hiding, but Kaia turned in on herself after the incident. Trusted herself less and didn't trust the world at all.

"How far are we?" Leti muttered around a bite—shredded lettuce and leaking sauce.

Kaia didn't answer right away, studying the wall clock like it was a map and watching the world move past the window.

"Hmm? Mmhm." Kaia said eventually, leading Leti to toss a sideways glance.

"To the city...?" she prompted again.

Kaia took a fat bite of the burger, ketchup sliding out the back and into the wrap as she tapped a greasy finger against her phone.

"Maybe an hour or two." She looked back at the window and Leti turned that way, too.

The sun was still high in the sky, but it dragged its bones across the horizon, settling somewhere past noon and before dark. Meaning the sun would set soon. *Ish.* Leti had come to hate sunsets.

"Hey. Leti?" Eyes still to the skies.

"Hmmm?" Another fry and another dunk.

But Leti wasn't listening. She swirled in memory, and anxiety--asking herself why the idea of orange and red skies made her anxious, but she knew. It wasn't the sunset, it wasn't a lack of beauty. It was closing visitor hours and foreshadowing to another evening alone.

"You hear me?"

Leti scrunched her face, but Kaia was already grazing across the table—sweeping crumbs and repackaging her burger like it was to be returned.

"Come on," Kaia encouraged with a small smile on her face.

"What?" Leti—drink in one hand and crumpling the bag with the other.

"We're so close! Don't you want to see the Pier and stuff?"

"I mean, ye—"

"Oh and there's a hill before the bridge. The photo on Mom's nightstand--I'm pretty sure its where I'm thinking!"

Leti hesitated but kicked back into motion slowly. She didn't want to abide, but she didn't have a good reason not to. Besides, she wanted to see the city. She just didn't want to get up, because Kaia said, "get up."

So the bathroom first was Leti's internal compromise. A long wash in the sink, picking at her nails and picturing Kaia pacing on the other side of the door. But on cue—sink turning off, reaching for the door—Kaia burst in. "Let's go" and "come on" on her lips before changing direction:

"Actually wait, hold on—me, too" as Kaia skipped inside.

Leti rolled her eyes and took the food bag and soda Kaia handed off on the go before Leti slid back out. She didn't wait this time because something said to walk. Whether it was trust or habit, she wasn't sure, but the fob was pulled, the unlock pushed—air con, music, and a small delay in the star before the car rolled out and waited curbside like a getaway.

Kaia came bounding out and made her way straight to the driver's door before Leti slapped her hand down on her door's lock and shook her head. She was already settled; she wasn't moving. And Leti wanted to drive, so she waited for Kaia to curl back into the passenger seat before they rolled on.

Windows down, ocean salt tickling the air with moist and electric tendrils, they climbed higher and dropped lower through rolling hills playing more music than they spoke. And before Kaia or Leti could ask twice, a tunnel came barreling before them; just on the other side the city waited, skyline spilling out like a dropped deck of cards.

"Leti!" Kaia whacked Leti's arm with the back of her hand. "Look!"

But Leti'd seen it already; off in the distance, blazing like a threaded flame across the sky was the bridge. Thick, round cables made of smaller ones bundled tight—as if the weight of the whole thing depended on how well it was wound.

Kaia's legs dropped to the floor. She sat up straighter—eyes wide.

"That's where we took that picture," pointing—not just to the bridge but to the far side of it. Up a hill that didn't immediately look accessible.

"Shit—shit—turn! Turn, turn!" Her voice cracked on the second turn, hands hit the window like she could fly through, but Leti shook her head profusely.

Not because she didn't want to go, but because they were running the curves cliffside again: four lanes deep; nature versus neighborhood; and a golden battle line bridging the center.

"Sorry dude—we can flip around... After the toll," Leti added as the little buildings began to come into view across the bridge. She reached back for her bag, nervously fondling it for the cash while the traffic began to slow and build around them.

"Will you pull money out for me?"

"Mhm," Kaia nodded. And then, "Oh! Hey!" Nearly jumping Leti's seat as she turned to reach.

Another bridge across the way, a park under the bridge they were on—both their heads were on a swivel as they encroached the pay-zone.

Kaia popped off the radio and poked her head through the window to see through to the other side.

The toll booths guarded the gates and kept them out but the city was creeping in close; where streets climbed like they're on the run and houses leaned like drunken friends sharing tales through SOMA. Mission made the way to Dolores under the authority of the Chicanos' touch and the streets dripped with culture and art and life. As if the Tenderloin of the city sliced itself open to bleed out the center.

Kaia's eyes were greedy for more.

Monopolies on abnormality. A *home*—except this time it didn't taste so dirty. One for the homeless, the dreamers, the unsure. Other people like them bleeding into the salt-stung city too; where it smiles and makes room for you to stay only to demand you earn it with everything you have. And the bridge—showing not red, but rot.

The kind of rot they find in the city and rename Golden until the world believes it too.

"Oh my, god—look!" Kaia; head leaning over like their childhood dog gaping at something else along the street.

Leti smiled at the toll-man and handed over two-fifty but she couldn't hide the surprise when he stuck his hand back towards her expecting seven more. Her face flushed red—hands scrambled for change—embarrassed to inconvenience the lives' around her.

But when the city let them in—when they got through—Leti's anxiety dried out and her heart began to thrum too. As if Kaia could sense it, she nudged Leti eagerly and clapped twice before they both were forced to calm by the whiplash into heavy traffic, lights, signs, and people.

Leti turned the radio back on low and pinched Kaia's thigh lightly.

"Ow, hey—d"

"So...the pier?" Leti asked; closest to the same wavelength she'd been on with Kaia all month.

"Duh," she grinned, cheeks cheesing from ear to ear. But the smile drooped, and the excitement halted as their slow speed and constant braking dulled the city-shine.

Leti sighed and waited for Kaia to pop in with her usual round of questions, but whether hyper-focused or uninterested, Kaia was quiet. And while Leti could handle the quiet, that was just that for the first time, she didn't want to.

"Why do you think they call it golden?"

"I don't know. Marketing?" Kaia leaned in closer, uninterested, but craning into Leti's space to peek through her window again.

"Hey—Alcatraz. They do this Escape from Alcatraz swim I want to do."

Leti chuckled but nodded along with the idea that'd soon be forgotten. She looked though; and sure enough, beat down and bobbing somewhere under the bridge in a sea of shark teeth and suicide.

Alcatraz.

Leti's neck chilled. They weren't in the Pacific Northwest anymore.

04:00:00:⁰⁰ || VII ||DOWNTOWN, SF

The next morning, Kaia and Leti leaned over the open deck of the tour bus, hair whipping in the salt-thick wind, backpacks they'd packed at their feet, and car stashed in a pay-per-hour slot.

The city sprawled wide and reckless in front of them, stitched together by bridges and broken sidewalks as they were carted through on a double decker.

A voice spoke over the intercom, but neither girl cared about the guide's crackling spiel on earthquakes and gold mines. Leti leaned against the rail at the top-back of the tram instead, smiling despite the wind stinging her cheeks pink and Kaia's arms spread wide—

"No hands?"

Leti copied her sister, laughing and unguarded, clutching the rail tight again as the bus swung around a sharp corner and pulled itself uphill. Kaia's grip slapped onto the railings only a moment after; her stance spreading and feet planting.

They shot past Chinatown next. The scent of roasting pork and cheap incense thick in the air where something new imitated ancient and mighty. A caricature made in porcelain, donning silk robes, a Buddha belly, and cat eyes, waving Leti and Kaia on, and on and on again as they barreled through.

When the next trolly dropped them at the pier, they tumbled off in unison and vendors lined the walk with faux and fabulous. Spray-paint galaxies of the bridge, knockoff sunglasses, greasy paper boats of shrimp and fries.

Kaia spotted a battered easel, grabbed Leti's hand and started pulling that way. "Let's get our portrait done."

"Proof we came?"

Leti scooted onto the stool as Kaia shook the artist's hand. "Won't need proof if we never leave."

Leti went to glare but froze when the man barked out an, "Uh-uh, hold," one pencil in his mouth and one in his hand. He sketched without looking much, exaggerating Kaia's mouth and Leti's eyes.

Leti pictured herself there, drawing strangers and working the tourism and she didn't hate it. Before she knew, he turned the pad around and they both warmed with laughter at the bloated cheeks, big noses, fat heads, and shrunken shoulders.

Kaia paid and waved the rolled portrait like a sword until Leti tucked it into her bag with care; more precious than she'd ever admit.

They wandered the pier after that; buying knockoff sunglasses, beaded things to stack their wrists, sharing fried greasy paper boats and talking about nothing important; just the air in their lungs, the sun on their backs, and each other. The newer version.

As the hours passed, the sun was starting to dip, softening the glare on the sidewalks and turning every window into a mirror. They walked without talking for a bit; the way full days make you quiet with satisfaction under the surface. And introspection.

The background music set the tone, too. A man and his baggy jean jacket holding down the corner with a busted sax, mic, and speaker. Man next to him with the bass playing something lazy, low, and half-mournful.

Beautiful, simple things.

Kaia and Leti had been sitting on a bench with eyes to the horizon and it was simply *stillness*. Deeply earned and needed stillness that Leti never expected to have with Kaia.

"Hey, Kai?" Leti leaned her head on Kaia's shoulder.

"What's up Lee?" Kaia gave a gentle head knock in response and Leti breathed deep like she was pulling air to a bruise at her heart.

"So..." Leti didn't necessarily have something to say, but debated talking her thoughts aloud. Asking Kaia:

Was this peace? Or simply a moment without pain? And was there really even a difference?

Or is it that maybe we don't find peace? We just lose the meaning and build something quieter; something we can try to live inside.

"You ever think about talking to someone?"

Leti blurted it before senses could press pause. She brushed the runaway hair behind her ear, using it like an excuse to look away.

"And I mean a professional, I don't count..."

Kaia sat with it. *Still.* Muelling it over in her head—more unsaid words and unfinished sentences as she watched the water glisten. Like maybe if she didn't have an answer, the sea did.

And by the time Leti blinked, the mask slid back into place—the laziest of shrugs and non-chalance.

"Don't really have any reason to say no," Kaia admitted, to Leti's utter shock and aw.

Always expecting resistance, Leti wasn't entirely sure what to do with Kaia's forfeiting.

"Yeah...cool. We should, you know. Just...there's a lot there is all," Leti tried.

"You're tellin' me, small-fry." Kaia's breath chopped but she covered it with a cough, kicking her feet out when tourists allowed the space, and throwing her arm over Leti. Kaia pulled her back into her side and squeezed the only way bigger siblings knew how.

"But you should know by now—you'll *always* count, Leelee. You're my emotional support snack-pack."

Leti squirmed out from under the bear hug with a couple grunts and a shove, but it was good. And it was real.

And it was Kaia.

"Okay," Leti grumbled, patting hair down back to smooth. "Thanks a lot."

"Oh!" Kaia shouted. "I got a good one," she smiled, staring past Leti—maybe eager to change the topic or maybe—if Leti could allow herself to trust it—Kaia was just relaxing into herself.

Leti turned when Kaia kept focus behind her—but—*nothing.*

"Okay, so—come on, get up." Kaia pulled Leti to her feet, bumping and apologizing as they shuffled back into skin-covered traffic; breath like sewage steam and movement like fleas.

"Alright. Take your time, but...! "

"Here we go..." Muttered while falling into step beside Kaia.

"*But,*" Kaia barked. "Would you rather have more time, or more energy?"

Leti wondered if Kaia had assumptions when she asked or if she dove in, asking questions she really did wonder. Because Leti didn't need to wonder. As always, she knew:

Leti'd want energy; Kaia'd want time.

But the "*whys*"? Maybe next time she'd be the one to ask.

04:00:00:⁰⁰ || VII ||DOWNTOWN, SF

Eventually, they made it back to the car, free of the gridlock, and somewhat on the road deeper into the city. They'd actually crossed into Daly City by mistake but stuck around when they saw direct access to a calm beach and bathrooms.

Leti pulled the Bronco into the half-paved half-rock lot, engine ticking as it cooled and leaving the air thick with burnt metal. Scrunching her nose, Leti figured the car might break down before Kaia ever does, but at least the beach gave the motor a windy place to cool down.

It was a stark contrast from the city to the bare sand, weathered volleyball nets, and golden locks on the surfer-kids. But the beach was still like the city in a way; worn, holding a kind of stubborn, quiet beauty.

Leti climbed out slowly, her backpack slung over one shoulder, eyes tired, but the tension in her jaw softer.

There was small talk here or there; commentary on the people or their surroundings mostly, but what else could be said? Twenty-four-seven, most of it spent in the confinements of a busted up, family Bronco... ?

The small talk was talked out. *And the heavy stuff?*

Leti stole a glance at Kaia, then another at her feet; dark and cold sand slipping between the cracks of her toes, caught between wanting to ask something and the words being stuck, because the heavy stuff was blistering above them.

But the more enjoyment Leti found, the less reason she had to press Kaia on what happened in that room. Because. What was the point in blowing up the few good moments that were left? And who was stopping Leti from just pretending too? Other than the stranger in the mirror.

Leti swallowed as voices cawed somewhere down the beach.

It's not like Leti wanted the thoughts, questions, and hesitations though. Her eyes flicked to Kaia—Kaia watching the waves; Leti watching Kaia—wondering if anything even could change back. Or—*what if*—a type of self-destruction was part of the self-renovation?

What if it had to come first and this was Kaia's process? Like—sometimes the rot is one brick, sure. But other times it's the entire foundation. And on that note—if the cracks are what shaped you:

What does that say about the house?

"So...now what?"

Leti didn't like what it would say about the house. Leti didn't like what it'd say about her, or Kaia.

Especially Kaia.

"I dunno." Kaia's mouth shrugged in place of her shoulders. "Pretend it's fine until it is, I guess"

"Thought that's what we've been doing."

"Then stop asking about a plan."

Leti's eyes slid sideways in a glare but Kaia didn't reciprocate it.

"That's the plan right there," she laughed.

The laughter wanted to be contagious—people sparse, but present—so Leti chuckled, too. Forced at first, then coming to life like something in the world was bending just enough for them to exist within it.

"We are getting a hotel tonight," Leti demanded as the laugh sizzled and the sand sank.

"After this." Reiterating when Kaia didn't answer fast enough.

"Yeah, game. So—"

"Heads up!"

Both turned quick; alert. Greeted by the thud of a very sad volleyball that was held together by duct tape and a dream.

Kaia nodded at it like she approved and saw a man working his way closer, one hand in the air, from her peripheral.

"Think I can hit him?" she teased, snagging it from the sand and tossing it back with a grunt and a heave. Made it most the way too.

Sort of.

The man curved a little left for it. Laughing and shaking his head in the distance as his friends, further back, stuck to the "court" they'd played in. Were they not there, the boundary lines and net posts looked like they might slip back into the sand and disappear completely; old, raggedy thing.

They watched him quietly as he bent for the ball and they stared more intently when he stood there staring right back.

Just as it got awkward, he tossed the ball back, but not at his friends, at the girls; smiling as it approached.

"Hi."

The ball bumped Kaia's shin, and then Leti's foot. Maybe like a gentle nudge of encouragement from its deflated soul.

Kaia bent and snapped back up with the ball in hand, glancing at Leti first when the California-Kid waved again from the side. It was less like a '*hey how's it going?*' and more a—'*get your ass over here*' while cheesing ear-to-ear; pearly whites were visible in the distance and long legs pointed right to them.

"You think it's an invite?" Leti wondered.

Kaia and her lopsided, lazy shrug tossed the ball to her other hand as he waited. "That—I'm bettin'...is a challenge."

But Kaia's eyes weren't set like decision; they were pressed into a question for Leti. *A—"you down?"*

And Leti's first instinct was to pull back—a little too much, a little too fast—but Kaia's grin was a dare on its own. The double dog kind of dare from the schoolyard. And there now—Leti looked around.

No baggage, no rules...*No reason not to.*

She threw Kaia's slack shrug back at her. An—"*I'm game,*" snagging the ball from Kaia's hand and taking the first step.

"Hell yeah!" the guy hollered.

The group—chatting shit in the distance—looked just a little older. Opened arms, chilled drinks pulled from coolers, and tongues as combative as Kaia's—dishing back exactly what her competitive streak gave. Simply just for the sake of existing.

It hung in the air like a language Leti didn't understand—this *ease* around each other—but Kaia slid in first, confident and safe with Leti at her back and drink in her hand. Her feet were inside the boundary lines of a game she's never played before anyone had to ask twice.

The confidence of a king; Leti smirked but kept to the outside of the game eyeing the group and noting the loudest cues.

Modest or wild; liquor or beer—and when Leti got bored, she felt herself adopt one at random and lean into the façade too. But eventually masks were forced to clear the way for muscle-deep, guttural laughter. That painful laugh you feel in your cheeks and your abs.

It wasn't intentional, but it made believing their sisterhood survived unscathed closer to real, and it didn't stop as the night got colder. Beer cans cracked on, the volleyball flattened more; no one had a watch, but they wouldn't have thought to check it if they did.

Especially not when the fire popped up and the people moved in, interacting with whoever was closest.

Kaia couldn't remember the last time she held deep conversations with anyone other than Leti and there she was having multiple.

Could vividly remember screaming at Millie; fighting with billing and funeral homes when Leti came back beat down; screaming at her dad's voice message—Kaia was no different than a feral cat. One which was just thrown into a colony to either make friends or fend. And maybe that's what drew her in.

The whole damn city was feral. You stop being noticeable and unique when everyone around is just as unique. And that is a beautiful thing to be lost in. Especially as herself.

Though now, she still tested the waters with half-truths and grin-curled lies and Leti stayed close. Sipping on a seltzer, pretending not to listen but doing so anyway.

Eight to fifteen people were left standing as the stars shifted and the moon waned. Some scurried behind dunes, others paced long, slow loops along the tide, but of those that stayed, most sat with the fire.

The guy—called him Kyle or Jason; or maybe it was Sam—hung around in their orbit a bit longer. Nothing big, just chatter.

He walked with them when they headed back up the beach to the car. Talked about the water and the cold; how the fog rolled in too fast and often stayed too long. But he didn't ask for Kaia's number at the end, or Leti's; didn't try and save face or save them.

He just made the silence feel a little less loud; the numb, a little less dull; and the city, a little more safe.

If the Boys Come Home

SOUTH SAN FRANCISCO
BRISBANE BARRIO | 2000S

|X|

The air tasted like copper and ash; sirens cut through the city, flashing red and blue across the wet asphalt; somebody yelled—sharp and panicked—

"Kayden!"

The blood rushed through their ears pounding the way their feet punched the ground, ducking behind storefronts and open businesses.

"Run!"   Run.

Shadows tore across cracked concrete and graffiti-streaked alleys as Cachí tried to make up ground from the back. Nervous and always coming in last; arms swinging shamelessly, forcing his body to move faster; almost close enough to grab Mick, which meant Matías and Dante weren't far at all.

Mikki's hair flying wild and her laugh in the air. Nothing would ever happen to her with Dante and Matías flanking her sides. Older, faster, holding back to be near should she or Cachí fall; always in reach to stop, catch, or push them.

Then at the front—running like he meant to rip the night open—Kayden. Racing the sirens that threatened to swallow the moon first; deafening, closing in as they tried to close out.

"Go, go, go, Mick—Turn, here!"

Feet sliding against the pavement, Dante's hand bracing the wall as they bounded the corner, out of sight for a second's time making Cachí's breath come short. Heart hammering against his ribs, but under his foot something unwanted twisted on the corner-slide.

The mask Cachí wore to fit in didn't keep the tremor from his voice when he hit cardboard on wet concrete and damn near flew.

But no scream, no yell—only a single, "whoa!" and held breath as he fell into a silent submission; sliding to the ground into the scent of lavender, rain, and rotten fish.

Matías was the first to react. Always. Beat of his feet into the pavement when he whipped around—Mikki, eyes wide, turning too.

"Cachí!"

Her voice cut through the madness while Cachí pulled his knee in, praying the ground would hold when Matías and Dante greeted him first—slapping a hand to his shoulders, dragging him up and sideways and nowhere right.

Then Kayden next—having looped back around—he popped Cachí in the head once, real good and hard.

A silent, "don't do it again, idiot."

But silence died with the look in his eyes as megaphone-voices bounced through the brick alley, homing in fast.

"Go!" Kayden hollered, looking at them all before listening for the sirens and counting the seconds.

Mikki listened—the boys hesitated—letting her take head of the charge now. Moving for her keys in a running frenzy.

Dropped them, scratched the ground to snap them back up, when she almost dropped them again. The pressure and nerve not her friend as the car came into view just up ahead.

Mick peeked behind her, tripping up when she didn't see Kayden any more and stumbling back.

"Kayden!" she hollered, popping up as quick as she went down. Rocks in teenage skin no bother when the threat of their mother lingered.

To hell with the sirens.

"Mick—start it up!" Dante bellowed with Cachí propped up against him.

She turned, hit the pavement in a dash before climbing into the front with rapid and chaotic repetition of, "come on, come on!" and "Kayden!?" breaking through the air.

The old volvo's back tires skid out when she ripped it around, aiming for Dante and Matías who stood in some kind of face off, intertwined and stuck—Cachí just stuck in the middle trying his damnedest not to cry from his aching knee.

"Kayden!" Matías hollered.

""¡Mati! ¡Muévete, güey!" Dante snapped

But Matías faced the opposite direction and Dante barely had the time to grab Matías's arm before his stride fully loaded, aimed for where ever Kayden went.

Cachí in one hand, Matías the other.

"Kade!" Matías shouted.

Dante then, too, "Kayden!" Steady and planted with a voice like a boom. But Kayden was gone. "Matí—we gotta'go!".

But Matí wouldn't turn.

"Kayden, vato!" Matí pleaded, yanking his arm from Dante and prepping to run again as the car slid in to a hot-stop; Cachí and Dante side-stepping—fumbling and desperate; and Mikki, sometimes the only sense.

Letters were yelled loud—letters, because they didn't form a word at first. Eventually they strung together for a name, "Matías!" But a scream like death that stopped them all cold—odds even Kayden stopped to look back.

Cachí. Dante. Breathing hard, eyes wide. And Matías—young, dumb, and crazy in love. The scream ripped through Mikki, the alley— everything. Didn't feel like there was a choice other than to turn back.

"Fuck!" he hollered, nearly tackling Dante and Cachí in a panic. Shoving at them now, telling them to, "turn, turn, turn!" as Cachí hobbled between the two, promising he broke his knee, but later only finding a bruise.

Matías didn't care— "We'll grab him on the corner!" Constantly thinking of Kayden. Logic knew better, but loyalty had to try.

Then on the opposite side of the block, Kayden finally slowed. His stride cracked like a racehorse letting go of the track; one last surge into asphalt before instincts started yelling different orders than his brain.

Every heartbeat was a hammer; every breath a ghost of every stupid decision he already knew he'd make again.

He bent, hands bruised on his knees, spit stringing from his lip as he sucked for air. Sirens closed in—one set, then two.

Then more.

Kayden straightened. Smirked, too. A little thrill, a little fear, and a little too late to choose which mattered more when the first cruiser rounded the corner, tires sliding out like he'd murdered someone instead of pulling some stupid prank.

The drama. For a window. A paint balloon.

A laugh.

Kayden didn't run. Not really. He stood in the middle of the road wide-legged, palms out like a goddamn cartoon.

First cop out his door, second gun already drawn but Kayden grinned—big, dumb, and young. Pup-eyed, breath still catching in his throat and "my bad man," sitting at the edge of his lips.

Hands higher, he said, "It was a jo—!" But he didn't finish.

Slammed from behind with no warning but full weight. The second hit a heartbeat later—a side angle. Sharp elbow to ribs, shin to hip, forearm to jaw—Kayden didn't see them coming. He barely remembered the sound he made when he went down; just the pavement, the breath knocked loose, and the laughter when he finally caught it back, calling, "foul!"

Because that's all it was. A game.

Just teenagers playing at life back when they believed they actually still stood a chance.

Kayden didn't speak when they pinned him; didn't flinch when the cuffs cut skin; didn't rat when they barked at him for names and threatened expulsion.

Face pressed to a curb still wet from morning sprinklers; eyes steady, breathing shallow. They took him away for two nights but let him go with Alice the third day.

And Kayden never blinked. He never even mentioned it again.

Sleeping Dragons of Pier 39

DOWNTOWN, DALY CITY
04:00:00:00

|IX|

The motel sat wedged between a shuttered liquor store and a corner lot where the air smelled like exhaust and spoiled groceries.Kaia and Leti had ended up further south than planned, following the coast down until the signs blurred. Smoke and industrial to the left; ocean further to the right; BART station nearby and bus stations even closer.

Neither Kaia or Leti wanted to drive around the city, fighting end of summer tourism, parallel parking, and tow zones, so they settled in the middle of all the transportation links. A motel with a promising picture of a Saguaro cacti and a western theme.

Though when they got there, the paint was flaking off the wall and the potted cacti were dead. They glanced at each other in silent mutual defeat, but desperate for a shower and exhausted, settled on going in.

"Not like we'll spend much time in there." Kaia reassured, gently letting off the breaks and rolling towards the center.

They'd checked in at a kiosk so bare it felt like a setup for a horror short—just a slab of a counter, a key on a hook, and a woman ducked behind it who barely looked up. She slid the paperwork across, traded cash for keys, then vanished into a side room like she'd clocked out the second they stopped talking.

The walls moaned with every shift in the wind and the first room had history. Recently. Upstairs and unclean, but not even a, "we'll handle tomorrow," unsanitary. But sheets unwashed and something unidentifiable on the mirror.

Kaia and Leti stood in the doorway, backpacks on, not looking at each other but playing.·

You ask, no you...Didn't matter who said what though.

Kaia's patience the size of a shot glass. She huffed and turned back for the counter. Dropped her bag hard first, not even bothering to take it back down to the car as she went.

The second room was further back, like punishment. Past a vending machine that buzzed as if it was a pissed roach; down a corridor that was colder than the rest, too.

"We should've done one night at a time," Leti muttered. "Down like four hundred bucks now."

Kaia didn't argue at first, but pulled the hoodie over head and cut to the shower. The water came on and her voice went up.

"It's just for a bed and a place to keep our shit. But—dear god let the water be hot…!"

Leti shimmied up the bed on hands and knees and collapsed onto a comforter that was no better than the sand, unfortunately. But it didn't really bother her—Leti's cheeks hurt more, from the laughter. And that alone was bittersweet: an evening she'll never forget, but the fight to get there something she *can't* forget.

Head heavy on the pillow, staring at the wall between them—Leti couldn't fall fully into the evening, because it asked her how much she missed who Kaia used to be. It dared her to see that the person Kaia is now—the one clawing to be seen and accepted, desperately needing to be wanted—might always be left wanting.

Leti couldn't explain it and wouldn't ever try because Kaia might never forgive—not Leti—*herself.* For changing in a way Kaia couldn't control. And besides, Leti just wanted more time to get to know this version of Kaia.

The more she got to know her, the more Leti believed she'd be able to understand. And if she could understand, then maybe she could keep up with Kaia long enough to pry the truth free.

The silence stretched as Leti ping-ponged possibilities in her brain; trying to push them out. Nothing but the water trickling, echoing, from old pipes—Leti counted the drops as Kaia moved like a ghost on the other side.

Leti thought about saying something then too, just to hear her voice, but she didn't. Told herself she didn't need to. She *shouldn't* need to.

At some point later, the water did shut off. Felt like hours, the constant, quiet dripping afterwards feeling even longer as Leti's eyelids twitched at each uncomfortable and irrationally loud *plop.*

She kept them closed though. Remembering the road down, the walk down the hallway in—replaying scenes since they'd left the house up until that first water drop *plopped.* But it felt wrong in memory.

Leti's eyes opened—it wasn't the memory that felt wrong, but the room. Drop still consistent and off beat.

Leti was so tired, she hadn't noticed the second bed in the room—was shocked actually. Moreso to see it empty and made, like Kaia was up and at it first thing. It made the room feel emptier if anything.

Air felt dry too, like Leti had been sealed shut for days and slept through the entire thing.

The way Kaia had.

The fear was real enough to make Leti's heart lurch. Real enough to jerk herself up, wonder for half a second if it was always her asleep; alone and dreaming.

Leti swung her feet to the ground, touching the damp hoodie around her. Not hot, not cold—just heavier. Like it was supposed to feel wet.

Neck, spine, collar, too. The air tasted like salt; nerves like salt in a wound. But no footsteps. No TV hum. No shower water—

Leti was at the door, just moving—unsure where, unsure why—and opening the door to reveal a dark cavern entrance waiting to swallow her down.

Crust encircling the rooms; Leti wasn't asleep—Leti was already six feet deep.

She pressed her back against the wall, shuffled past the dark, crumbling hole in the ground, pulling closer to the center when she approached a maid's cart—when she thought, *people*—stocked and untouched.

But the room beside it was locked tight. Leti only saw the curtains sway, like someone slid behind them fast. *Like someone avoided her.*

Another cart and curtain ten steps later.

Then another.

Leti passed them without stopping. Towels folded too tight; a bottle of cleaner tipped sideways, leaking onto the floor with the label peeled.

The front desk was dark too. No clerk, no chair. Just a taped sign on the glass and marker on the window that said:

Odd, Leti blinked.   ~~BACK IN FIVE~~ no wr not

And odder still, the hallway behind her had no end, only doors with holes in the wall where room numbers should have been.

A pit grew deep in her gut, deepening with every second, so she ran. Footsteps landing flat and hollow as though the air swallowed the sound and the cement her feet. Body not accellerating but damn near running in place.

Her throat ached to scream, but was arrested in silence.

She spun, breath jagged and fogging the air as words appeared in that fog, a voice too for below the cavern

—there's no one left to find, girl—

So Leti ran—faster now, against quick-sand concrete and hollow steps. Past the same things, ticking at the same time, thrumming behind locked doors.

Leti grabbed at doorknobs, rattling the hinges with no answer. She screamed for anyone, but nothing still. There weren't even shadows to hide in when she jerked up from the motel bed in a cold sweat and airless gasp.

Leti's fingers were in fists and her throat dry. The sweat on the back of her neck was cold this time as she breathed deep through her nose.

Real. And Kaia?

Neck cracked Leti jerked it so hard—but there she was. Not peaceful, but asleep. Looked almost smaller when she stopped moving long enough to be seen.

Kaia's eyebrows didn't twitch; her voice didn't call out to say what she wouldn't when awake. So Leti laid her head on the pillow beside her and watched for awhile.

Then quieter than a motel mouse, Leti breathed—"Kai," brushing the damp hair from Kaia's sleeping eye.

"I would take your every nightmare if I could," Leti nudged closer—closer enough to feel Kaia's breath and smell her familiar scent while they slept.

Then eyes closed, forehead to forehead, Leti pleaded:

"Just don't leave me this time."

Dear Alice,

| XI |

Mikki snagged food from her parents' favorite hide-away. Windows up, music low, as she passed through Colma on her way home; a city where the dead outnumbered the living.

She slowed past the army of statue angels with their goblets in hands, wings on their backs, and names at their feet. Grotesque, beautiful, and a place to pass when the world slowed long enough to allow

Mikki pulled into her old neighborhood, shuffling the food as she jostled out with a few groceries and things.

The shopping gave her a reason to pass by, but an excuse not to overstay.

On her way over she'd dragged an apology—and a date— out of Cachí for being so distant. Was able to slipped in the bonfire invite too while he was still clammy and apologetic.

Mikki smirked at herself. She loved that kid—but it was no wonder he rarely answered her. He'd do just about anything. Hell—they all would.

She slowly made her way into the house, driveway long and steep as she considered Cachí's long pause before the agreement.

The bonfire was one of those friends-of-friends things. Where the E-vite went buck wild and ten to twenty small groups, collected as one.

A clash of new blood and old. Mikki knew Cachí enjoyed venturing out of the circle, so his hesitance was unclear. Mikki always doing her best to encourage new friends and experiences all the while trying not to chase him away completely.

Distance-loving.

Mikki skipped up the stairs and nearly dropped everything as she jiggled the lock unsuccessfully. Arms full, key in pocket, eyes already rolling—

luckily Mikki's mom came in with the save having been eagerly waiting. The door swung open with a big grin waiting on the other side.

Just another dirty blonde but built in the east coast raising Mikki on the west. Her Mom helped her in and they fell into their usual step.

Mom asked about work, like she always did.

Her dad was at work, like he usually was.

But regarding Mikki's work, she couldn't have been happier. New job, telling her mom all about it highs. No longer the artist assistant, model, or errand girl, but curator.

Respected.

And it may have taken years, but name it and Mikki did it. Whatever it took to keep her foot in the door, because it never mattered how good a person was with art—realism, portraiture, surreal landscape—cities like New York and San Francisco were *saturated,* not only with people, but with talent.

And there's no permanence in art. No safety. After everything, Mikki needed safety. So it became a game of climbing to the top and stealing a name for herself in a place no one was willing to give her one.

Cachí used to come with back then—damn near better than her with half the practice. Drove her crazy but still—never more than friendly competition. To this day she still held her foot in the door for him. Not holding it open, necessarily. Just keeping it unlocked, in sight, and waiting. An option with no strings, because Mikki wanted nothing more than Cachí to be himself *without* feeling trapped between them and Kayden.

Mikki worried they both always would though. Her especially,between Kayden and Dante. She was simply better at working around it which was neither right nor wrong when there were no rules to loving someone who didn't believe they deserved it. No guidelines on how hard to hold or when to let go.

Mikki sighed because it hurt. Losing someone but in a slow, disgraceful burn where Kayden will swing for anybody in fear of having no one. A self-fulfilling prophecy with a different type of cruelness. Mikki's heart hurt, but her body remained useful, moving mechanically yet fluidly.

Plate for pops. Napkin folded hot dog style twice over, into the microwave to wait. Her brain fought harder, flickering like stop-motion pictures until her mom pulled her back.

Not out, but back.

"So—how's Kayden?" Though with simple questions that had loaded answers.

The two always gravitated towards the topic at some point. Probably hoped the other would come through.

Say, guess who came by—*guess who seemed like his old self?*

Having lived there, what—nearly eight or nine years old, up until twenty-two. Still—no one in the house could reach him after lockup.

No one anywhere could. Not Cachí, not Dante. And Dante—like breath. Easy and necessary to live after Matías.

Between the three of them, if they couldn't get through, then there probably wasn't anything left to get through to. Kayden died somewhere in that prison block and never came out.

And like a rock and a ripple, Mikki, her mom—they were learning how to live with his pain. Mikki wasn't sure how her mom coped yet, but Mikki found that she used a lot more black paint after that. And red. And then it kind of just—faded there. Disappeared as the paint dried and tears no longer fell. Still unresolved, unstitched, and unhealed.

Not because people didn't care, but because it made it impossible to go on when they did.

"Haven't heard from him much this year you know. Seems to be giving Dante a headache though. Just Kade, doing Kade things. You know..."

Next subject; one less raw.

"I'll be seeing Cachí this weekend though," Mikki said.

Her mother always loved Cachí. Sometimes more than the others because they ragged on him the most. Didn't stop Mikki or her mom from joining in sometimes too, but the love ran deep.

Another neighborhood mom with enough pizza bagels in the freezer to feed an army, and enough peroxide on tap for the bullshit that came rolling in bleeding. A village within the heart of the city, and she—a main artery.

"Oh that makes me so happy to hear."

Truth. Styrofoam squeaked.

The boys always made her smile. Toughened Mikki into a scrapper. Coming home with blood and a bruise—damn guaranteed it was either *because* of them or *for* them, because she can be big brother, too. Though less so with Kayden.

Always just Mouse.

They rolled through the house kicking each other's ass as teens—no where near blood, but bonded. Amazing how fast it all goes though. Ends. *Begins*.

The moment when a piece of you becomes a memory of the past and pride, shame, obligation, honor, failure—they become daily supplements.

Mikki made a plate for her dad. Gently cleared her throat from the pressure she was creating in her mind. Wrapped the plate in foil and set it by the back burner.

"Yeah, I got Cachí to agree to a date. And the bonfire. I'm calling Dante later too. You should come, Mom. Or at least dinner tonight."

"Oh no, I shouldn't. Can't keep up with you kids anymore. Could barely before..." finger pointing at one of her wild-kept squirrels outside. "I need to refill the feeders today..."

Mikki smiled. Damn army of the things. "Well, offer stands."

Back to tearing at the pita bread, "you said Dante, too? You guys have been running a lot too yeah? Lot of time together, is that—"

She cut her mom a look. Half warning; half willingness to engage if proceeding with caution.

Matí was five or so years ago. And it wasn't that she wasn't ready. She didn't think so anyway.

"I gotta call him when I leave. He's been on a lotta late shifts, but..."

Another side look and a cautious reach to the edge— "Yeah it feels like finding a little normalcy again. Can look at each other and see more than just...what happened. See good memories now, too. I don't know."

Her mother perked despite the chastising looks. "Almost the whole group together again."

"Mmhm," Mikki packed a couple bites for the road, "Almost." Leaned over her mother for a kiss on the cheek. "Love you—got to go though."

She didn't really—have to go. It just felt right.

The house locked up behind, door sealing despite the lean in the walls and the climb on the hills. Mom's head smiled through the curtains—*an* excited wave goodbye, and the city exhaled a breeze. And once the doors shut, Mikki finally felt like she could too.

The city squirmed, stomachs active with indigestion. People, trolleys, chaos. Even at night—city didn't sleep. So Dante didn't get to either as he sat hunched over his desk, coffee cold, spine tight.

His eyes tracked the glow of the screen in front of him, but his thoughts were chomping at memories and conclusions elsewhere. The knock came soft. Two fingers. A welcome relief, but...

Hesitation, Dante gathered.

Officer Rivas stepped in, file tucked under one arm like it bit him. "Wasn't sure who to give this to," he said, tossing a file down like it burned. "Fresh one," the guy grimaced.

Dante looked up like it was nothing and Rivas pulled a folded note from his belt, unkinking it awkwardly and sliding it against the corner of the desk.

Dante's brow dropped. "That necessary?"

And Rivas just shrugged. Grown, but green. Then, note in hand, he started chirping.

"Few kids found young male washed up between Candlestick and North SFO. Statements inside with contacts for all five."

Dante's arms crossed and he leaned back in the chair assessing Rivas. Dante'd bet he practiced between cold storage and here.

"I uh—keep going?"

Dante's mask cracked and he chuckled dryly. "Yeah, dude. What else on your note?"

"Cool. Cool—cool... So," big man cleared his throat now.

"Checked missing and alerted the neighboring—counties as well as pulled recent or even the—potential amber alerts. Looks young."

"Good job, thanks." Dante dropped back to expressionless when the kid held up the note and made a pained face, dropping the note.

Dante was both intrigued and terrified. So much so, he started to believe they're one in the same.

"Well," adjusting his belt, hands on his hips. "They uh...posted it."

"Beg your pardon?" Dante's eyebrow crept up slow and if a pen dropped, it'd echo.

"On TikTok, YouTube...Oh and uh—reddit. That's a good one."

Dante's cheeks darkened. "Are you *fucking* kidding me?" His voice was raised enough that officers outside the Detectives arena turned.

Rivas grimaced like it was his fault. Nodding first, then stopped and shook his head faster instead.

"TikTok yanked it down quick—working on contacting the others, but I mean...screen grabs and sick fucks, right?"

Absolutely infuriating. Rivas shifted uncomfortably when Dante didn't take the note. "I mean, can we like...arrest them for that or something? What if family see?"

Dante, head bent, elbows on table. Index and middle rubbing his temples, said, "Not unless they obstructed the scene or molested the corpse. Otherwise...Just morbid curiosity and protected speech I guess. And too many of 'em just want to shock each other for likes."

Dante shook his head and tossed himself back, leaning; toe against the desk, rocking gently. "Fuck man. Anything else to add?"

Rivas peeped the note. Looked ashamed when they locked eyes over it, but Dante was just thinking how he couldn't even remember Riva's first name. Anything but the dead kid.

"So, the uh...COD is pending full autopsy, but initial obs got us...uhh... oh—two GSWs—head, thigh, and uh..." He pulled his collar, arm went slack at his side and his face twisted.

Off script, he blurted: "Fish eat your fingertips? Eyes I get b—but..."

"Soft tissue."

Fear rubbed Dante's spine when he didn't flinch. *Way* too comfortable. Far too quick, and— *"soft tissue"*—was way too fuckin' cold.

He felt filthy now.

"Get to the end."

"Yeah sorry." Riva stood up straighter. "Finger and facial damage from aquatic activity delaying further details and identification. "

Dante stared. His eyes flicked to the note but he couldn't read anything, only see the blue-dyed ink.

Wondered if Riva knew the fish went for the lips first too. Wondered if asking him would get him out. That one, at least, did still bother Dante and he couldn't stomach repeating it as he began to picture it.

He nodded at Rivas once. Tried to get the thought out—opening the file like peeling wax.

"Goddamn." Dante tossed it back onto the desk. Black-and-white paper-clipped inside, a couple more still-shots behind the kid's distorted one from the morgue. It was amazing how cruel the ocean could be.

Annoyance pinged as Rivas watched Dante grab for the folder a second time. Dante thumbed the photos, spreading them as he read the summary once.

Then again.

But his jaw tightened on the third pass and he practically growled, "thanks, " twisting around in his chair so his back was to the door.

Dante didn't turn back until he heard the Rook slip out. Leaned over the folder hot with anxious anger and went for the other photos stacked behind the body one.

Black and white; street cameras from where he was last seen alive...

And of fucking course—Dante's stomach dropped. Because he knew that face. That stance. That goddamn shirt and guy who shared a stunningly notable resemblance to Cachíflin.

And Cachí had been there, at the station, randomly dropping by; the thought making Dante replay their conversation like Cachí had spelled out, '*catch me if you can*' in morse.

The silence stretched, and stillness too before Dante ran his tongue along his teeth and sucked in sharp.

Such a fucking knack for trouble. And Kayden all over again.

He debated calling Cachí to the station now, but that was rage. And fear. Which Dante swallowed back. And when he went for his phone, Mikki's sweet face came to mind first. Calming. Helped Dante remember: He'd be seeing Cachí very soon.

Would do his best not to spoil Mick's reunion, but it was a hell of a lot easier to catch a liar when they didn't know you were looking.

Dante looked through the glass divider to the rest of the station with a small pout; like he was a bad luck charm trying to play by the rules and everyone else was welcome to break them.

His hand slid from the desk then, knocking over the whole folder so Dante could scoop the shit up just as quick. Because one of those photos inside— a single black and white identifying image—never existed.

Fuck the rulebook.

Because it wasn't going to be Cachí. It wasn't going to be any of them ever again. But it was almost *always* the goddamn quiet shifts.

Medusa Was a Maiden First

SKYLINE DR., DALY CITY
03:00:00:⁰⁰

| XII |

Cachí glared at the texts over again, hour having past but nerves still tight, staring at the phone again and again. Too chicken to look away; too needy to say nothing at all.

> MIKKI
>
> IM EXCITED TO CU THIS WEEKEND <
> WHERE WE GOING TO DINNER? ♡ <

They hadn't spoken in a while. He wasn't sure what to say when she called after he ignored her again. He'd been ducking one too many attempts, and honestly? Wouldn't put it past her to show up on a doorstep at some point soon. Multiple door steps until found. *Or.…*

He could just cancel now that he got her off the phone. Talking sweet; asking how he'd been like she wasn't annoyed he was ignoring her. Cachí sighed heavily. Told himself to quit being an ass.

He was less concerned with lunch or dinner or whatever she wants to call tomorrow, but the Saturday thing? Kayden, Joey, all of them fucks would be there and Cachí was just too tired. Not today, just every day lately. Worse now, sitting here expecting Kayden at any minute.

Cachí was swallowed up inside the trap house, walls all but sagging in on him; air heavy with steam; house skirting the edge of the BART and the train lines just waiting for the owner to die to sell out. Turn it into a plant. Or a suburb; depends who sells out first.

Cachí heard a car pull in close; engine die out and a single door close.

He held his breath, listened further, and clocked Kayden's big ass steps and only his. He was alone.

Easy. No audience—no apologies or pride.

"So, fists or steel today, Kade…?"

Cachí was waiting, door at his back and kitchen ahead. Sunk into the leather lazily, but both boots planted down and calves tense. He played with an unlit cigarette between his fingers. Just something to do with his hands.

Kayden stepped onto the busted porch, through the door. Neither of them spoke as Kayden crossed his arms and leaned against the door frame; not amused, but not bothered either. *Yet.*

Bubbling beneath the surface—it wasn't tension between them. It was older than that. Like two wolves who'd forgotten why they kept circling—only that they couldn't stop.

"Didn't get lost then, *compa*?" Cachí finally said, voice dry enough to spark. "So why the displeasure today?"

Kayden rubbed a knuckle under his nose. Sniffed like he'd do something, but Cachí didn't bother. He knew Kayden—knew the kid who puffed his chest behind Matías back in the day. The kid who spent half his life defending Cachí only to beat him up himself. All—*I got your backs bro's*—no strings attached. Grimace as wicked as a fractured finger. Loyalty as reliable as a reflection in a mirror.Meaner now though.

Occasionally, Cachí peeped the outdated version of him banging on the inside of Kayden's skull—pleading to be seen. Then angry when he finally was seen.

"Cachí," Kayden eventually said, voice cracked and low. "Where the fuck is my bag bro? I ain't got the time today."

"Hm?" Cachí smiled, sweet as sugar glass. But calculated.

No *'have you seen;'* or, *'where's the kid.'* Only—where's the bag?

Interesting. "Didn't we just do this with a pistol?" Cachí smirked.

Proverbial stick in hand, target placed across Kayden's gut. "Where'd you leave it last?" *Poke.*

Kayden glanced at the mirror—then quick, back to Cachí. Cachí didn't like his own reflection anymore either. At least they still had that in common. Besides, the mirror was cracked straight through the center and only reflected fragments now.

Cachí heard a wisp in the air, movement from the side, and shot his arm up to block his face as an old, soggy magazine slapped his forearm like a wet kiss. Kayden said something through the haze, but Cachí could only hear the blood in his ears rising.

That wasn't a poke. That was a fucking swat. A foul.

Cachí stared through Kayden's skin to the twitching muscles underneath; maybe anger, maybe anxious when Cachí looked at the mag, then back to Kayden; slow and deliberate like there'd be a problem.

"You fuckin' listening to me, Cachíflin?"

"I'm trying not to," he growled back. One final look at the deflated magazine, half propped on the ground.

Kayden peeled off the doorframe and moved to the sink across the room tossing a dirty glass from the counter as he went. The lip cracked against the sink, but no one flinched. First one to flinch lost with them.

If either of them could even flinch anymore anyway.

"Fuck's sake, Cachí! Where's the goddamn bag?" Yelling now...

Because that'll make Cachí play nicer—*Right.*

Cachí raised his eyebrow—knows better, doesn't care—"Was it the pink one, sweetheart?"

Another step forward made Kayden look even taller. He looked at the door like he wanted to leave but was forced to stay and Cachí followed his gaze to the hall next.

"Hearing things again?" Cachí tried to look careless, but watched Kayden like it was his life. Listened to the wood under him for a shift in weight and tracked his shoulders in case he snapped or swung.

Not that Cachí thought he'd do something, but because—tumbling down this track—Cachí knew he could. *Anyone could.* Backed far enough up, no choices.

But betrayal? Brotherhood? Cachí wiped his nose the way Kayden had; head back and lifted with pride.

"I'm gonna beat your fuckin' ass, Cachíflin. Stop playing with me."

"Can't say I know what you're talking about, *perro.*" He flattened the last hump in the magazine with his toe. "Suga' momma might get you a new one though." Pause. "*If*...you're a good boy."

"The fuck, bro—you think this is funny?" Kayden's boot slammed the door frame, rattled the wall. His temper blazing deep enough the wood may have even cracked.

But Cachí just gave that single, boyish chuckle. "Yeah. Actually." Not cause it was funny, but because it pissed him off.

"That was a full fucking bag of scripts, Cachí! You think I won't hurt you for this?"

The fact that Kayden even said that—he wanted to stand up and say, *then do it.* See if he'd dare. 'Cause no way he was that fucking far out there. Cachí dragged the smoke that time. Slow.

Didn't choke, but sure as shit forgot it was tobacco. Just needed the time, because Cachí didn't know what the fuck to think.

"Kade...You think you scare me, bud?" Cachí's head tipped back, relaxed.

Kayden hated nothing more than disrespect. And the head tip—the relaxed nature—told Kayden he wasn't a threat. Not even an afterthought.

"You forget, *hermano... El barrio te crió.*" Cachí smirked. No heat. Just that same, old, and tired truth. And even so—Kayden's lip curled.

"Yeah? Did a shitty fuckin' job huh? Get the fuck up, Cachí—let's go."

Cachí stayed. Knees bent. Feet planted. Ass too. But stick still in hand, looking for what to jab next with a smirk pinned into a dimple.

Kayden only got more pissed. "Bro—you think I don't know you got your shadow in shit it don't belong? Walking a thin line, dude. I know everything around this goddamn neighborhood now—want to or not, come on!"

Instant—but zero regret: "Just not where some bag is, huh?"

Cachí considered standing now, but he didn't despite Kayden teetering the line of too close; Cachí was daring him to see if Kayden would push over making Cachí suicidal or curious. Questions he'll dig into later, honestly not even sure.

"Maybe you should chat with Jaylin."

To Cachí, they're brothers. But every now and again, Kayden talks like they were brothers *once.* And the longer Kayden avoided saying the kid's name—avoided asking, *'where the fuck is the runner'*—while acting different and threatening family, the deeper the dread tumbled.

Something was trying to change—Cachí could see that much, but maybe that just meant they still had something to fix. Cachí does his best to piss him off but under it, he believed there was an unmovable bound.

"I know you, Kayden," Cachí taunted again. But he didn't feel ease. Taunted himself with that one too. Because small voices whispered louder every day—*do you really though?*

Cachí's excuses for him, longer too. Harder to explain.

Would he have found Cody that quick? Would he really have looked? Would he have done something?

And then say he did—would Kayden beat him? Get Cody's boys to knock him around themselves? Name of the game—they've all had their ass handed to them a time or two; so maybe it wasn't as bad as Cachí was making it out to be. Maybe he just wanted reason to be angry and fight.

Cachí saw himself swing on that guy from earlier. *Because Kayden.* Cachí didn't even know his name, only that Kayden demanded the numbers. And it wasn't a battle Cachí was willing to fight against.

Man kinda deserved it anyway, right? But who made them judge and juror? Like Kayden for Cody. Cachí—sitting there, acting like he's so careful not to cross some line despite being on the opposite side of it.

The circle just came all the way around today. And Cachí was on the receiving end of the fist. Or at least, was about to be. Cachí opened his eyes. Shadows skittered. Ghosts that were his or Kayden's—though probably both.

"Ay yo, so who got the bag you're looking for?" Trying to lead a horse to water, Cachí nodded once.

Kade's jaw tightened enough that no answer was answer enough. Especially from Kayden. Just not the answer Cachí wants, and one he's not willing to accept. Not easily, anyway.

Cachí almost pulled from the cigarette again. Pretended to look at the burn when it was already halfway to his mouth and blew ash over the end of the chair—slow, low swings. Still. No one cared.

The proverbial stick felt heavier now though and he wasn't seeing Kayden—just a face pushed to the corner. A boy some days and beast the next. Both able to bite.

Cachí almost flinched when Kayden's phone buzzed and Kade jumped on it quick. Another buzz immediately after; another dodge from a situation that would have plummeted into the truth.

Somehow, despite Cachí being the antagonistic one, he was left feeling more unsatisfied than how Kayden had found him because Kade wasn't looking for Cody; he was asking questions, because he had to have already linked Cachí and Cody at the bus stop.

"Kade." Cachí didn't mean to say it, watching him approach the door, rapidly texting. But at the same time, the guy's not even out of the '*teens*.'

"What the fuck did you do to him?" Cachí's wall dared to crack down. Just once. Like if he peeked out first, Kayden could too. No stick. No poke. Just ugly truth and hurtful realizations as Kayden stared back. Empty. Because what else could he do?

Cachí wasn't asking what Kayden did, he was asking: *Who are you, really?* Least Kayden could do was take off the goddamn mask and own it. But another buzz instead. Kayden didn't look at Cachí again. He didn't flinch, but he wouldn't face him. And that counts, so Cachí let the smoke veil his face.

"Saved by the bell," he cooed, flat and cold. The boys behind both their eyes—gone.

"Something like that," Kayden muttered. Then he left with a lot of effort and zero result.

Shit doesn't look good, brother. Cachí watched him go. Feeling sorrowful. Angry. Mad he couldn't be stronger maybe. Mad *Kayden* couldn't be better. Because sometimes, the silence screamed loud and distracting it. But under it—*within it*—whispers of truth were there. You only have to listen for it.

Cachí thumped his head against the cushion twice. A third low and delayed, "come on." Reached for the phone, too. Pulled up his contacts.

> M I K K I *NEVER MIND.*

He didn't necessarily want to go to the bonfire, but he wanted even less to have her turning away disappointed in him. Dropping his shit the moment she shoved her little way back in.

Cachí erased the name and went back for another.

>D A N T E

Didn't want to be Kayden. Didn't want to be tied to this. But didn't want to give up too soon. And sometimes giving into Dante felt like giving up on Kade. Felt like leaving Kade the way Dante left them.

Cachí pictured the conversation and knocked his head back again as he corrected how it would go. Too many questions on Dante's part; too much disappointment too. He and Mikki worse than his damn parents.

Delete. Matías then.

Cachí hit speed dial, but it didn't even ring anymore. Went direct to that voice; bright and laughing. And in that narrow slice of tape—between, '*hey, it's Matí,*' and '*leave it at the beep*'—Cachí could lie to himself long enough to pretend he wasn't gone. Just out there, still meaning to call back.

At least until it reached the end. Cold, mechanical, and real:

This voicemail box is full.

If Black Holes & Supernovas Collide

SAN FRANCISCO, CALIFORNIA
04:00:00:00

| XIII |

Cachí spotted them before the door squeaked shut behind him. Dante in a sun-bleached booth, elbow on the backrest, half-smile already waiting; Mikki across from him, turning her water glass in slow circles that caught the dusty light.

The diner smelled of lime peel and charred tortillas and ceiling fans pushed warm air around, slow like a Sunday. Cachí paused at the threshold, hand in a pocket lazily letting the room settle and the knots to uncoil.

Dante lifted two fingers in a small salute, nothing showy, just sure and more relaxed than he had been the other day. Mikki's grin followed a beat later, softer, like she knew he needed the extra breath.

"About time you hauled your skinny ass in," Dante said when Cachí slid onto the vinyl bench. No accusation, just rhythm—an old song they all remembered the words too.

Mikki nudged a basket of still-steaming chips his way. No, *"why haven't you been answering me."* No, *"where've you been*s.*"* No weight. Only—*"Guess what I entered into?"* with her big, loving, familiar grin.

That was what reminded him. He avoided the calls because he missed this shit too much. Missed them.

Cachí forced a smile, but it was only a few before the real ones swept in like a bat for the right joke.

The clatter of plates and far-off traffic was only backdrop sounds, and this was the easy part; old jokes, new stories, catching up like they hadn't lost a damn minute. Laughing, leaning in, sunset slanting off the patio rails—it wasn't "good" or "great" or even "bad"; it was just different. It was the first time in a long time Cachí wasn't rehearsing a thousand ways to say *'don't look too close'* and *'I'm good'* in two different languages. Walking through coals between loyalty and survival. He loved Dante, always had. But that day, Cachí remembered he liked him too.

The conversation drifted—work, gossip, bullshit. It didn't tilt serious until Cachí tried to steer it. He leaned back and wiped a hand across his mouth like he wasn't thinking too hard, but all three knew he was. Dante in particular watching close.

"You hear anything about some kid named Cody?" Cachí tried to keep it light, like it wasn't pressing against his temples. *"Catrachito*-kid."

Dante didn't flinch or really react at first, but Cachí felt a shift from relaxed to calculated in the little-too-long of a pause.

"Nobody yet..."

The way Dante's eyes cut to Mikki after—quick, reflexive, like someone checking for a witness—then back in a blink.

Cachí didn't know what it meant, but he didn't like how it felt now. Not for himself and not for Cody. It was the *yet*. The slow, methodical nod of the detective while Mikki eyed from the sidelines—picking her battles carefully and letting others diffuse naturally.

"*Vale*—just wondering," Cachí played off his interest, because maybe it meant Cody was home. Nobody asking, "*what kid*" each time he asked... Because no one was *looking* for one.

...But it felt wrong, twisting in Cachí's stomach, stuck in the air between them. It didn't leave a silence but instead a weight in the air; like things that were supposed to be said lingered about around them. But Mikki, as usual, cut in with saving grace when the table cut a little too quiet.

Working the boys over about this or that; nothing they were bored of. Fascinating actually, the way she could thread her group together with topics and energy no matter the personalities. But Cachí was still distracted, looking to Dante a little too much. Wondering what kind of impression Cachí had left after so many months off and on; and even more acting like a pissed off girl Dante dumped.

The *yet* though. Dante said *yet*, and it scratched against Cachí's skin subtle, but deliberate. And they both knew it. Dante wanted him to; it was a subtle, *Im'ma see you later*. But no scene, no public outcry. *No effort.*

And it worked. Dante checking Cachí checking Dante after he said it...

Cachí rubbed the back of his neck. He was making himself look real stupid. Cracked his knuckles under the table and politely waved for the server when she had a second.

He was nervous, Dante was suspicious—talking less and observing more while Cachí scrambled to prove he wasn't all bad. Just an idiot.

But one that didn't have shit to do with anything. *Except Cody.*

The server made her way over. A smile, a *thanks for waiting*. He returned it, but when he felt Mick and Dante watching, he grinned like a ham and said, "Three shots please."

Most satisfying part is when no one objected.

"So," Cachí offered, rolling his fingers against the table for the small beats. "Running partners, huh?"

Dante stayed cool, unreadable, while Mikki chirped about new PRs and the difference a good pair of running shoes could make. Cachí chimed in with how he'd been running too after what felt like an appropriate amount of time. Then, "didn't need fancy sneakers though."

"You're running drugs?" Mikki gasped and Cachí frowned.

The joke landed like the right joke in the wrong room.

"No, Mick..." Cachí cooed, "I'm playin'." Just Cachí being a punk; trying to prove something whether strength, edge, or wit.

Dante was staring daggers though, and Cachí pretended he wasn't worried about it until Mikki picked up where it dropped off—pulling the air back into the room by her claws.

"Always with the jokes," continuing about some mud run Dante talked her in to doing but wasn't planning to join her. Couldn't tell if she was just sharing or trying to get Cachí to pipe in, but it took Dante a minute to come back down from his wall.

Dante eventually picked up the thread, pointed out something dumb across the patio—coaxed Mikki and Cachí into a hardy laugh from the gut in that way he always could.

They finished lunch a couple hours past, like it hadn't happened and let the late sun burn the concrete gold. Laughed more about stupid shit and shared their first *legal* round at the bar together with ages scattered between twenty-three and twenty-eight; Mick comfortable somewhere between. And so, a couple beers at the bar to lull the tequila starter.

They relaxed into each other in a corner spot near the outside patio pretending time didn't exist and history was only a bad dream. Dante eventually stood first—because someone had to—Mikki too enamored and Cachí with nowhere else to be.

But it was later than expected. Time flying between laughter. The other two got up following Dante and the city turned from evening to night.

"Later, 'manos," Dante clapped Cachí once on the back—solid. And *loving.*

Gave Mikki a peck on the forehead that didn't need translation, and then he was out. "See you Sunday, Mouse," eyes at Cachí next, "*Hermanito,* see you at the fire, I guess."

Leaving only a lazy peace sign as a wave goodbye.

Cachí's car was a few stops over; one too many wrong turns down one-way streets had him real selective about where he chose to drive. There was something unnerving about driving in the city, and something worse about parking here. So they walked a bit, and Mikki shared the trivial things with Cachí.

The pieces that never made headlines like how dates had gone, or how sometimes it was still weird for her. '*Not guilt,*' she'd said.

But weird because *no one compared to Matí.*

Words that made Cachí nostalgic in the perfect kind of way, hoping Matí was somewhere listening, too.

Her '*little*' promotion was next; dimming her shine so it wouldn't blind him or some shit, but he wanted her success; he wanted to *hear* about it, prying and asking more, hoping she'd one day let go of the guilt or restraint.

Cachí figured it was just her looking at him with pity because she got out while he stuck around dragging a chain. But even so, even if he never gets away, he still wanted the pieces of her success and wellness. Just to *know.*

"So, Sundays, huh?" Cachí eventually circled back around to running. Because maybe it wouldn't kill him. A new tradition with frantic feet, hungry diners, and a tapped beer after a hard run...?

It was unjust how real it felt, yet how far it was.

Cachí and Mikki hit the station entrance and slipped into the current of bodies, shoulder to shoulder like cattle. Mikki giggled, pretended her hips were a pinball and bumped Cachí sideways once, twice, and then a little too hard. Had him bumping against someone on the other side—

"*Disculpen!*" Cachí blurted out pardons to a couple girls on his other side while Mikki leaned in to flirt but choked on the pronunciation.

"*Gwa-pus...wah-pa....*"

"Quiet," Cachí shook his head and turned away as they turned to him and he elbowed Mick faster the opposite way.

"What?" She laughed, swerving her hips away while her arm was locked close around Cachí's.

"It's *guapa*," he whispered, feeling the people file in behind them with a loud-quietness. Almost every passenger on their phones with heads down save for a curious few. The woman he'd bumped was one of them with eyes up—her friend too— eyes wandering wide and close behind.

Cachí doubted they'd even noticed him when he'd shoulder checked the taller one; started to doubt they'd notice him now with big, beautiful eyes and a cropped 'I HEART SF' tee that screamed, *tourist.*

Cachí caught himself checking them out as they came into the same section of the tube with a swing in the walk that spelt eccentricity. And behind the first, like a moon to the sun, was a chick he hadn't gotten a good look on until now; blush sundress and soft eyes that skittered more than they wandered.

Cachí was trying not to blush when they shuffled into the same cart, but all hope went out the window and his face flushed when the tall one smiled, and said, "*guapas* "back to him and Mikki.

She looked like all gas no brakes until Mikki pointed at seats near them and said, "these are open."

The smaller one stepped on Mick's foot coming in past the pole and after a couple fun *sorrys* and *no worries,* chatter rolled into '*I love your this*'and '*oh, but your that*"—Mick and the taller one taking point.

Luna-girl wouldn't really look at him though, sitting quieter like him. It was in her subtle pauses or head tilts though—looking not *at* him, but *towards*—that told him she was paying attention.

Dark, thick hair spilled into braids that framed her face and when he leaned forward on his knees, he smirked when she leaned back.

"Hey..." he offered before immediately turning to Mikki for backup. Something to say or look at, or take off the quiet intensity on his side of things, but instead, Mick made it worse.

Mouthed, "wingman?" as if no one was paying attention when he was sure they were. Cachí's face was warm, reddening as he leaned on Mikkki, lightly knuckling her knee in a silent, "SOS, *before I beat your ass, sis.* "

But instead Cachí said, "too much."

Between the three women, he didn't know whose gaze was on him, just that he felt the weight of three beautiful women in silent agreement to not judge each other, but maybe pick at him. But when he looked back up—no one was paying attention, no one was looking. All just jokes and flirtatious laughs as the girls chat shit.

Mikki being Mikki—every face a new opportunity; no walls, no pause—just hellos, names, and easy small talk with bare foundations. But maybe it wasn't the worst thing. Easy, shallow conversations...

But Cachí never really got to start. Mikki and *Sol* over there—think she'd said her name was Kaia—kicking it off without much outside input.

Eventually Cachí was ripped in, the moon-girl, *Leti*, too.

Where you from? Where you headed?

Before he knew it some questions came out of his mouth, too. The kind of asks that have a rolodex of safe answers and no depth. They said they were besties, but he didn't believe it; too opposite, but too the same in the way only a sibling is.

Cachí sat up a little straighter at some point; face relaxed. They'd done the name exchanges—awkward moment wondering if they all shake hands—but didn't, and Kaia continued to sound like spitfire. Sometimes like Mikki—the cadence or word choice. Looked similar age too, but who really can tell.

But no matter how bold her and Mikki got, Leti was cautious. Kept drawing his attention into her. Something in her steady, calm...

Cachí didn't realize he was staring until Leti was too.

Tilted her head ever so slightly and really just looked at him back. She didn't flinch like he was danger; didn't flirt like it was performance. She just saw him. *And that—* scared the shit out of him.

Animated conversations even hushed the train when it hissed to slow and stop, but no one asked why or said weird when they all got off at the last stop on the line.

"Didn't know these things actually ended," Kaia admitted as the chatter went quicker and the steps slower, approaching the station-exit.

"Hey," Mikki perked back up when it started to settle for good. "We're doing a bonfire at the beach a couple nights from now. Saturday. Still on the south side too, you should come."

Public space. Wide open. Safe enough to feel spontaneous...Kaia and Leti exchanged a wordless glance that he knew was an entire conversation, but when they said yes, Cachí didn't really smile or make a fuss. Wouldn't have to perform; wouldn't have to relive old stories for the benefit of people who already knew how they ended. Cachí could ask questions with no stakes and maybe be seen as just him.

He smiled and quietly tucked the moment away under: *Things That Still Felt Good.*

Cachí and Mikki lingered near the parking lot watching the girls try to disappear into the fog after offering a ride and being declined. Leti had spoken up to say no—light, polite, but *no.* At least until they realized they misread the bus schedule.

Cachí and Mick heard a high-pitched, sheepish squawk from they way the girls had gone before they came back, tail tucked.

"What do you mean no more?" Quiet, but there, carried across the concrete like a secret in a sorority.

Cachí, forearms on the car roof, Mikki across from him, same position though more dainty, they both waited as the girls returned.

Kaia might as well have been having a blast with her arms out wide and hips swinging in the night. "We can walk, couple blocks."

Mikki called, "Just come on!" before Leti had a chance to finish the profanity at Kaia.

Cachí just, *there.* Holding the door. And probably looking a lot less entertained than he was. Sure as shit beat being at the Trap house having a pissing contest with Kayden.

Kaia walked with a grin while Leti was dragged close behind; reluctant, but along for the ride and when they reached them again, Kaia wore that, '*we're idiots, but we're charming*' smile while waiting for another invite.

Cachí just chuckled and hit the key fob twice. "Going home with strangers, huh? They say that's—"

"Cachí —shut up," Mikki groaned, apologizing to the girls.

But Kaia grinned wide, sliding in back and directly behind him while trying her own joke.

"Letting strangers into the car behind you. Huh? They say that's....ehem..."

She cleared her throat with a minor grab at Leti, but all eyes took a turn, waiting for the end of the sentence.

"Left me hanging," Kaia nudged Leti. "You were supposed to cut in."

"Kaia..." Leti shoved Kaia both in the car and towards the quiet, closing doors behind them. There were a few more last minute pleasantries, talk about the bonfire, some silliness, too, but nothing too deep.

Cachí pulled up to the motel kiosk in a slow roll when Kaia grabbed Cachí's seat and leaned forward.

"Cachí —real quick," she drew out with a seductive grin. "Kiss, marry, kill. Mikki, Leti, me—Go!"

He didn't say anything. *Not a chance.* So fucking random, too.

He didn't even use the rear view for this one. Cachí twisted in his seat, leveled her with a full-body look of mock judgment forehead to seatbelt— about as much of an up-and-down he could manage in that space—and said:

"So Kaia—real quick..." Equally sticky sweet and seductive.

She dropped back against the backrest, knowing he had something loaded and her cheeks got warm.

"You were worried about me being the creep? *Chica linda,*" he kissed his teeth with a sharp, *quick* sound. *"Por fa,"* and a glance at Leti. One that was just short enough for Leti to deny, but long enough for Kaia to clock.

Then, Cachí waved them off—" *Vete, chicas locas. "*

Mikki passed around chatter and goodbyes from the front and a '*see you Saturday!*' Told Leti and Kaia she and Cachí would pick them up and Kaia pushed Leti playfully to the opposite door, climbing out, bags of junk from the city in tow.

Cachí stuck his hand out the window—a half peace, half wave. Like Dante. But the sister's were already arm and arm on their way back to their little piece of ~~freedom~~ *forgotten.*

Cachí looped the kiosk, waved again and watched the saguaro grow distant while Mikki burned a hole into the side of his head with her smile. But not the Mikki smile he worked for and was happy to greet, the plotting one. The *strategic* one.

Cachí didn't look. "Uh-uh, don't." Not even sure what he was nuh-uh-ing but sensing something coming quick. But—*maybe if he just didn't look at her.* Habit more hassle than intent though.

Cachí pulled the car out, checked the rearview once, then glanced over at the sides. At Mikki. Who grinned a wicked one.

Dammit...

"So," sliding deeper into her seat, eyes half-closed. "Kiss, marry, or kill?" she reiterated. Cachí gave nothing but a tight-lipped smile and a shake of the head. He wouldn't say. *But*—he finally had something he wanted to paint when he got back. And that had to mean something.

Somewhere Between Broken & Belonging

SERRA MONTÉ COMPLEX
00:24:00:⁰⁰

|XIV|

Dante groaned when his phone buzzed on the nightstand. A violent, jittery whine against wood.

He stilled at first. Then just let it buzz. Eyes heavy. *Heavier.*

And another buzz. Another. Dante slapped the dresser then. Phone took the bigger blow, but the screen lit up and fought against the darkness of the room, the kitchen light bleeding under the door crack to help.

Dante, *alone*—with windows closed and doors shut—groaned. Louder and louder as he rolled his face into the pillow.

> 7:00PM—FIRE   ALARM 1 ALARM 1

"Goddamn it," he muttered swatting at the phone like it had insulted him personally.

Breathing out through the nose, matching the hum of the fridge—Dante sat up slower running a hand down his face. Rough and unshaven.

—maybe if he doesn't show…

His head hit the pillow again with a resigned bounce of the springs and jh groaned but pulled himself into momentum to roll into a frustratingly upright position. He had to at least show face.

For Mick.

Boots still by the bed; hoodie draped over the back of the chair. Wallet tucked beneath; no mirror, no performance, no mask. Just a guy, in a hoodie, by a fire, with a girl. And hopefully a cold beer, but lukewarm will do.

Leti crunched through the last of her vending machine chips cross-legged on a bed that still smelled like bleach and old smoke. Scratched too, right when you get comfortable. They'd half expected the blankets to thaw—relax when worn in—but they were just permanently allergic to skin.

Kaia had a foot propped against the sill. Small bottle of cheap polish in her hand; borderline mess on her toes. She gazed at them under the ugly yellow cast of dying streetlamps and sneered. At least it'll be dark.

"You think it'll be weird?" Leti asked, salt still on her fingers, crumbs still on her legs.

Kaia went to the bathroom side and tossed the polish like she hated it. Because she did. "What part?"

```
INCOMING CALL:      > CACHÍ
```

Leti's phone lit up next to her and a moment later, sound—sound that cut off immediately when Leti snatched it up quick.

"Hey!"

It was that second-nature, customer service tone that made Kaia's body turn and arms cross with a sly grin.

"Hey," Cachí said, low and lazy. "I'm outside. Mikki's meeting us there, hope that's cool."

"Totally cool," Leti smiled. Kaia's grin grew then.

"Do you liiiiiiiiikkkeee—"

"Cachí , give us a sec," Leti tossed a pillow at Kaia and turned her body away. "We'll be right out."

Cachí heard the echo of laughter through the receiver before it disconnected. He peeked through the windshield like he might catch the girls in motion—see the joke midair and get to laugh too—but no eyeline, no visual. All he saw was a kiosk and a lotta' closed blinds so Cachí let his head drop back against the seat with a huff.

Moments later, they came skipping out and about halfway over, Kaia stopped and turned to run back into the room leaving Leti standing in the center of the parking lot awkwardly. She didn't look at the car once; not until Kaia came trotting back out with jackets in hand and the same grin Cachí had left them with.

"Here," Kaia jogged towards the car tossing one of the jackets over her head to Leti, peeking to see if she caught it. "Let's go slow-poke!"

She jogged to the car, swung the back door open, and nodded at Cachí as she shimmied in.

"Hi there, *guapo.*"

Cachí laughed out but bit it back down. "Mikki said it, not me."

Kaia grinned and bumped the back of his chair as she leaned across to the opposite door, locking it as Leti reached for the handle.

"Whatcha doin'?" Cachí watched curiously, but she ignored him, shaking her head at Leti specifically.

"This ain't a taxi Lee," she called through the glass. "Get ya' ass to the front."

Cachí turned to the driver's side window just as the grin cracked across his face—bit down on that before it got too wide, too—like maybe the fog had caught his attention; or like Kaia and Leti didn't remind him of his people growing up; like they didn't give him a warm feeling in his chest.

When the passenger door up front finally opened, Cachí glanced back to Leti's spotty eye contact. Eyes illuminated by the courtesy lights showing a green haze blurred into yellow and brown like forests. A color that didn't quite settle on hazel but wasn't quite green either.

"Go on then," Cachí offered, hand turning over as if the seat was on display. He wasn't impatient, not annoyed; just present, and amused.

"Nice to see you," Leti slid in beside him quietly.

"Yeah. You too." Easing into gear when she buckled down.

The high beams cut through the street in patches, flickering where the low lights couldn't cut it. Cachí clicked on the radio to counter the silence as he slipped onto the highway where everything blurred fast and soft until it was all just dark.

"Sorry Mikki bailed on the ride," he said next, glancing at Leti in the mirror. "She got a better offer," he tempted.

"Hm."

She was dull and quiet, but when the streetlights caught her, her cheeks looked warmer and softened into pink. Cachí kept getting caught eyeing the mirror, tossing looks each time Leti'd check the back for Kaia—offputtingly quiet, watching the blocks fold into the next like dominoes.

Leti willed herself to say something casual. *Or cool.* She looked over at Cachí but he didn't look back at her that time. And Leti wasn't sure if it helped or hurt, but Kaia was the first to speak after what felt like forever—ears probably ringing with only the road to hear.

"So, weird one for ya'..." she announced, shuffling around in her seat until knees were out and legs crossed under her. "Alright! So is it true that bridge is like Japan's... shit... Aokih-*something*—the suicide Forest. But like... *here?*"

"Oh my God," barely sounded like words, but Leti stiffened and slunk towards the window; not a chance in hell she'd speak now.

Cachí made some kind of amused, bet hesitant sound. *Loading*, maybe. Then cautiously, and slow: "You a uh, murder podcast chick then, aye?"

Leti held her breath until it burned but Kaia was leaning into the rear view, applying pressure, throwing sultry eyes—fixed like she belonged in there and a look was an answer.

"Nice," he laughed. Eyes were on the road, but he still took a couple slick side checks on Leti who hadn't moved. Potentially hadn't breathed. Though on his second or third look it appeared her forehead sunk until it was held up by only the glass; eyes closed tight; shoulders taught with tension.

Then Kaia on the other end of it; curious and morbid—she tilted her head, waiting in the mirror and practically purred, "Sooo?"

"You asking about jumpers?" He sounded less sure, but she confirmed it quick with a nod. "Um, you know..."

He was split between Leti's energy and Kaia's eager reach. "I dunno actually, I guess like fifteen hundred I think. Or it was."

Another glance at Leti—still nothing—and then the road.

"Not something I regularly research, you know?"

Kaia turned back out the window as the bridge began to fade into the dark, but Leti stayed as she was, head rested on her own window. He couldn't see past the basics of the tension, but he caught the jest of it which is suicide is a boundary line for Leti.

Noted.

His hands gripped the wheel tighter, sweat beading in his palm, silence gaining weight. "So those nets underneath it," Cachí began softer, grasping for a *fix-it* line or joke. "Stick the landing, make it off, and you're in the Halfway to Hell club." Ended with a lazy shrug, because what else could he turn it into.

Kaia's eyes swerved across the mirror again. "Suicide support group?"

He shook his head, kept his eyes on the road. "Nah. Just accidents that turned into bar tales from the hard hats who maintain it."

"Halfway to Hell, huh?" she laughed, turning back to her window. "Nothings killed me yet—maybe I can give it a go."

He was going to ask if that was a drunken tale, but everyone flinched at how Leti's seatbelt locked with a crack. She'd never whipped around so fast—Kaia's eyes went wide. Cachí's too for a split when Leti's arm had bumped into his but she didn't seem to care.

"Great idea Kaia, let's do it together—!" Her voice caught, but her eyes screamed. And the vocab didn't match the meaning. Cachí had a few guesses, but he didn't ask. Just kept driving. Pretending he wasn't listening. Kaia trying to correct it. Leti's fake "it's fine, *we're fine.*"

It was never fine—it was like the word *yet.* With Dante. An intermission on a conversation that would continue later. But that time, it wasn't for Cachí. It wasn't from Dante. So he continued forward. Like the third wheel he was.

An awkward next fifteen minutes that felt like forty until concrete eventually surrendered to hills, and not far past those hills came the dunes.

Shadows and starlight shimmered at the mouth of the beach, bonfire light spilling like oil in the fog. They parked on a bluff where the road gave up and the sand took the lead; greens pushing through, adapting to the sand like soil.

Cachí was the first out; hood up against the wind, hands deep in his pockets, slouched and relaxed. The two followed in line with him, their jackets tucked around themselves tightly.

Kaia popped the collar up to protect her neck then brushed off the arm on Leti's. Now it was Kaia testing the water; seeking confirmation that it was ok—that her and Leti would be fine. Kaia gave a weak, reaching smile to Leti, one that didn't stand under the scrutiny well.

Though at the very least, she thought, they weren't stuck ignoring each other in a small space like the room or car with nothing to distract them.

Plenty to change the topic and keep their minds busy the way they were that night with Sam and his friends. It wasn't the same as the sand pit they found there. And it wasn't the cliffs falling off the highways on the PCH-1, but the small landslides of rock gave small pockets of beach to hide from the ripping winds.

Leti and Kaia continued looking at the crowd, finding something, and then looking at each other simultaneously. All tension evaporated for now.

Cachí stopped and turned when he reached the top of the dune. Long legs, head in the clouds, sand muffling the steps behind him—he hadn't gone far, just a little ahead. And when they caught up, out of breath, he was waiting with a gift: the view from the top. And this wasn't the friends' bonfire in the backyard or so small and far down the beach that no one cares...

This was organized; this was neighborhood, or city wide.

The beach below the dune was littered with bonfires, stone, and sand—ten to twelve fires down the cliffs edge, glowing like constellations scattered by hand.

Drumbeats rolled up the hill—tribal and low—from somewhere to the right; music box and speakers somewhere off to the left; laughter and chatter stitched between the two holding it all together.

"Holy—shit," Kaia laughed breathlessly.

Leti stared in awe too. Like films they dreamed of living once but knew they never would. Surreal, but beautiful. Leti was almost afraid to go in.

Almost afraid to let Kaia in. Fairy lights on driftwood. Fire, hoops, and poi in the sand. It wasn't a party. It was a ritual. Come one, come all.

Cachí's phone buzzed as his eyes searched the crowd from the higher ground. Leti and Kaia came up beside him, trailing him like a guide; one on the right, the other on the left. He didn't know whether he was surrounded or flanked.

Didn't matter if they followed or led the way; he'd still be responsible for leading the way in. *And out*, he reminded himself, noticing some of the shadier figures circling the flames below.

"Mikki texted..." he began when no one else spoke.

Kaia grabbed Leti's hand and pointed to something else in the distance and Cachí checked the phone.

```
MIKKI (2):
        HI HANDSOME<
   FIRE OFF JUDAH STR<
```

"Wanna find her?" He didn't open the message, but he saw the pop up, and when neither answered, Cachí took a few steps towards them when his phone buzzed again. And didn't stop buzzing.

```
                      HURRY! <
   BEFORE THEY BREAK OUT THE GUITAR. <
            AND SING KUMBAYA. <
```

Cachí chuckled under his breath and stuffed the phone back into his pocket.

Buzzed already huh, Mick?

But no answer for her from him; Cachí'd see her any second now anyway.

"Judah street it is..."

He waited behind Leti and Kaia, side by side, talking in a way no one else could join.

Comment. Immediate, instant response. Then retort.

No pause before they go again, straight back into the commentary, pouring into each other. Leti's spine even sat up a little straighter until Kaia threw a long arm around it and grinned.

"Now *this*—is cool," she gleamed; wandering eyes dilating, making space to take it all in.

But Cachí grew up doing this shit; he didn't see it the same way they might be seeing it now, but watching them fawn—*oh*-ing and *aw*-ing—he dared himself to try. At least for tonight.

"Come on then," he smiled, reaching out a hand and pointing towards Judah. "*Vamos pues, niñas.*"

Down the beach behind the shape of fire, smoke, and masks, Dante tipped his chin, slugged down another beer. Faster this time too because Mikki kept staring. Eyes slit playfully when she would until she made her way back over to him. Made his body come alive in the cool air—the warm flame—Mikki as beautiful as ever.

"Thirsty much?" She asked with playful surprise, but curiosity underneath.

Or maybe it was the beers.

Dante didn't speak, just tossed the beer in the pile and rubbed his hand against his jaw debating what he wanted to say.

Circling each other, always on a chase.

But Mikki was getting nervous. Arms crossed over her chest, because he—*him*?—was making...*her* nervous?

But something called butterflies an'shit was catching in *his* gut.

"What?" Mikki licked at her bottom lip, looking around.

He could've watched her until the buzz went numb. Music booming next to them, shadows dancing on her skin—he watched the firelight illuminate her face in waves, before he saw himself reaching out to touch her crossed forearm. Didn't feel like him, but he let it happen; let his touch slide against her arm to take her hand and pull her closer to him.

"Come dance with me," he whispered, scared she'd say no, but—for some reason, at that moment—more scared of having never asked.

The milliseconds felt like months before Mikki smiled like she didn't believe it.

Maybe he was feeling too bold. Maybe scared that someone'd ask her first. But really—Dante mostly just found himself wondering:

How much more of ourselves are we supposed to leave to the dead? And what's the time frame on '*too soon*'?

He couldn't say. Could only tell you Mikki was warm.

The Savage

swallow
fire long
enough...

and the
body
stops
asking
permission
to burn

the Flame

MUSSEL BEACH, DALY CITY
00:22:59:59

|XV|

"Vamos pues, niñas."

The words drifted behind him as Cachí made his way down the slope, steps loose and familiar into the night. Skies folded around them like a second skin; music got louder with every step.

The beat wasn't polished, but it pulsed. Thrummed the chest like someone hitting it—or maybe that was the drums down to the opposite end. Too far and too dark to see—but you could feel them.

Mikki's spot wasn't hard to find. A few heads turned as they approached. Curiosity mostly. And Mikki popped up seconds later. Right under them with hoodie drawn and grinning as she trotted forward.

"There you are!" she threw arms out to embrace Cachí. Reached for Leti and Kaia next. "And you found the chaos twins—wasn't sure you guys would come!"

Leti blushed but tried her hand: "Yeah, me neither."

Kaia smiled too but mostly swiveled her head around in awe. "Yeah, yeah... thanks for the invite." Leti's hand looser and looser with every step into the sand.

"Good, awesome!" Mikki half-heartedly pointed. "Drinks there, snacks wherever dropped," she sunk back into her seat, crossing her legs fireside. "Fire's hot, sand's cold. You know the rules."

The way she blended—it wasn't disappearing. It was becoming. Leti's heart skipped. Kaia's fluttered. And Mikki tugged at Cachí's pant leg when no one moved, pointing down shore. "Dante's around here somewhere too! Finally got that man to relax," she laughed and Cachí gave a knowing, but disbelieving, thankful grin.

"Didn't know he knew how!"

While wandering off to the coolers and pulling four of the coldest ones.

Kaia took another lap gaze down the beach, stalling on a bold figure in the tideline. They stared back under moonlight, over seashells, so Kaia smiled big. Even waved like everyone there was a potential friend.

And the way he stared back—maybe it was just how he stared, maybe just the fact he did at all without being a creep too—it did things to her stomach. Butterflies or something.

The strong shoulders, the confident lean. Kaia's skin sizzled. Worse when he tipped his head back at her. Watched her until she looked away like he had all the time in the world. Until their distant visibility to the other was blocked by flame. And not fire at their feet—the moving ones in the air.

Fire poi crossing through the sand. Laughter too—everywhere really. So much chatter you couldn't tell where it started, split, or ended.

And the fire trails chasing behind in the wind, moving with the wielder's bodies, was mesmerizing.

Cold drink from Cachí was sweatin' in Kaia's hand seconds later. She cracked it with a pop and took a swing, trying to keep eyes on everything, watching pieces shift like a board.

Exposed and then hid the tide line, peeped the next fire over on rotations. Doors all around them, and each leading to a new and unique experience.

Sensual, comfortable, tribal. Another sip—the fizz biting the back of her throat. People next to her tossed heads back laughing and Kaia loved her wooden earrings. And the ease.

She wanted it, taking another big swig.

Leti tracked the flicker of attention across the group. Cachí pulled in comfortably fireside near Mikki.

Which happened to be near Leti too. Mikki was thrilled when he sat down; began shuffling in her bag. "Look what I got!"

Pulled out a sketch book which just made Cachí roll eyes. Still smiled though. And took a pencil when she offered it.

Mikki held one to Leti next. "You draw at all?"

Leti was hesitant; wondering who all she'd be letting in, but it slipped like a test. "I paint." An offer to see what they do.

Kaia, off to the side, shaking her head and pacing. "She paints well." Not even looking but attuned to Leti's voice.

Kaia's head popped up at a new figure edging into the circle though.

Approaching like he owned it.

Leti eying the approaching pair too, while Mikki and Cachí were bit slower to notice. Heads bent in. Smiling like kids in a fort over something they weren't supposed to have.

"Wasn't looking, but look who I found, Jay. Here why don't you play with them?" A man; a pixie. Both dark hair that the night made darker.

"Hi Cachí -baby!" The Pixie—happy and eager. Sleek hair to her back and a too-young tone in her voice for the drink in her hand. Like her and Leti, maybe.

But Leti took her first sip. Not necessarily from want, but from blending in; give her a reason to stare without speaking. Particularly as the tension crept up.

Mikki spun her pencil. Met the pair with a welcoming smile and an ache in the eyes. Cachí gave the guy a chin lift after ignoring the other. Neutral. But kept eyes on him the way a man would watch a lit fuse. But it was the pencil toss that spoke the loudest.

Cachí's subtle, small, toss of the wood against the notebook, and silent roll into the sand. Again—like it never belonged to him.

Mikki caught it; a slight freeze in her smooth grace; maybe an angry glint in the eye? Her mask was up by the time she stood out for a hug. Reached out the way she had for Cachí, but stiffer.
Didn't bother greeting Jaylin.

Didn't even look at her and Leti tagged it. Focused on it because the way she edged closer to Kaia but away from them. Introduced herself to Kaia— voice syrupy, hand lingering tight a beat too long.

Could never tell if it was intuition or jealousy though. Worried about not only being left behind but left out. At least with Kaia. Couldn't hear what she giggled to the new girl about though—

Mikki's voice pulling Leti's focus. "I didn't know if I'd see you out here, mentioned to mom though." Mikki scanned the tide lines, then him again. "Don't think she's coming."

"I'll uh, have to give her a call maybe," he swallowed; that air of confidence wavering. "You look really good Mick... You uh, look like you're doing well." Pained, but the smile was real. For her anyway.

Leti tried to gauge Cachí while watching Kaia slip into the shadows with the weird pixie. Eyes delicate but over the can, Leti took another sip, lapping the circle again. The man's eyes crossed hers.

Maybe the first time he noticed; maybe the first time he cared to look elsewhere to Mikkie. Nodded at Leti mutually, and Cachí still stared—but at him now.

"What—no Dante?" Chuckled loud but he cut clean when she disagreed.

"He's around actually."

"Surprisingly," Cachí added quietly, nudging back onto the logs.

Leti took another sip;subconsciously relaxing some when he did. When *any* of them did.

Took another peek for Kaial, maybe to wind herself back up, but she was still close enough. Black-haired wispy girl had Kaia distracted and chatting close.

"You should call, mom," Mikki smiled but tugged on the hair strand over his jaw and loose. "But cut this shit if you turn on the camera."

Didn't need to be delicate between them, but it still sounded soft. She stilll dressed it up quickly, "But really, you look good, Kayden. You look like you're really good," hand on his bicep and back at her side.

Leti paused hearing them share the word, '*mom.*'

"Hey well, we all know looks are real deceiving, right?" Stretch joked.

There was an undercurrent that Leti could feel but couldn't name. Got distracted too when the Pixie tossed a hand up at Kaia and walked. Didn't seem like a fight—Kaia's a lot more obvious. But more like—bored now. Stories over.

Kaia waited, shocked? Confused? Standing, and Leti steamed watching Kaia wait in place, no longer in awe, as her confidence tried to reload.

 Eventually, looking at the floor first, she looked around and met Leti's stare with a smile. But Leti caught that little hurt feeling that she's usuaully to proud to admit.

Forced Leti away though, Kaia—tilting her head at the dancing-folk with her eyebrows raised. Leti scoffed, shaking her head once.

"Anyway," the guy said, "gotta find that little shit, drop her off with PJ or Matt..." Grumbling now. "Cachí Im'ma see you later. Mouse," a pause, and a gentle final aim. "Take care, ok?"

And like that, that rising tension, didn't pass, but it paused. Mikki promising, "always. Be good?" He laughed up another half a smirk, but it was the kind that hurt.

"Never."

And Cachí too, nodding at him once, mumbling, "*hasta luego.*"

Not angry but knowing. Sliding back down to lean against the driftwood. Sketchbook still untouched.

Mikki's eyes lingered after him before she took an audible breath—a restart—that Leti could name and shame. *Practiced control and masks.* Because there was a heavy story there.

A complex braid of time and history.

Leti did her Kaia check, who was already all but burning in the fire over. Surrounded by women barefoot in the sand, jewelry flashing.

Kaia watched like she was studying. Still danced—but slow uncertainty moved with more purpose and power the closer she got to the other dancers.

Leti kept eyes through catching small flashes through the spinning crowd. And when they both looked Kaia held her arms out, caught up somewhere between begging and inviting Leti to dance.

Mouthing, "Come here!"

A laugh sprung from Leti like popcorn—surprised her group, following her look to Kaia. Cachí, Mikki—two other regulars—didn't have to be on their wavelength to catch the drift. They smiled around her.

"Absolutely—*Not!*" Leti blurted, conversation twenty-something feet away.

Shuffling closer to Mikki like she was home-base; laughing, repairing the pencil into Cachí's hand and nudging the sketchpad back into focus. Ignoring the other two romanticizing tightly beside them.

Leti turned back to Kaia—didn't break her stride in the slightest and it lifted Leti.

No titles; no names; only breath and movement to set them free.

Volleyball in the sand; singing on the trolly; laughing until they died on the pier. Not knowing if she was helping or hurting by going along with it. But being rewarded with Kaia's lightness and ease.

It was conflicting. But for Leti—at least it was feeling at all.

Only half in the conversation about pasts and painting, mumbling about school—still watching for Kaia, arms swaying high. Flagging a ride down from the stars like they'd stop and take her home before the circle spun again, stealing Kaia from view.

Eventually Leti was in the chatter—picking it up like a language she didn't know she could speak. Easing in; the uncomfortably curt smile beginning to twist itself up.

Felt worse at first. Then transformed throughout the evening. Went from a performative stillness to a placated ease. And somewhere further into the night—the seltzers, smoke, and laughter—Leti stopped looking over her shoulder.

Fire at her back, maybe friends ahead. Placated even changed into 'present.'

Mikki noticed, too. Kept eyes on Kaia for Leti, giving them both a once over. Dante too, even Kayden once or twice. Eyes on her circle. A circle that was open for anyone true.

Mikkie handed the obscenely big, but emptying fast, bag of pretzels to Leti. Nodded towards the dancing-fire once with an assuring nod.

"She all good over there?" Mikki asked.

Returning the nod, "yeah," reaching for the pretzels—

Leti even smiled back with something earnest while settling against the driftwood. Looking over to Kaia once more before allowing herself this moment.

"Yeah, I think we'll be just fine."

the Flesh

MUSSEL BEACH
00:21:17:39

|XVI|

"Don't think we've met," he said, voice warm but too easy. "You were with Cachí, right? And Dante?"

Kaia sipped the seltzer and gave half a shrug with a full smile.

"You got a name, or should I make one up?" He reached over to her, joint between his fingers, offered like a greeting.

Kaia didn't answer right away. Didn't take it either but she stared for a minute. When he didn't waiver, she took it, and he smiled a coy thing like he won something. Stepped in closer on her exhale too.

Clocked Kaia eyeing him. Shoulders, arms. Not stalling... Kaia just liked the focus. It was magnetic. He wasn't anything unholy or perfect, but his height made her feel protected, and his eyes were so dark they reflected the flame. When he stepped in close it did this strange thing to Kaia's stomach.

He took the joint, puffed off it then stuck it back between hers with a sly grin. "You dance?" Nodding to the fireside.

Kaia paused. Not from doubt, from desire; fear of that recognized desire; the unknown maybe. Because there was something electric that made her skin crawl and her body thrum.

"I um," notably delayed, tensions tightening, man staring. *Smirking.* "Yeah. Sure."

Kaia didn't know what it was other than intense and alive, but she took his hand: Curious, reckless, and wanting,

Stretch spun her through the smoke a couple times. More show than rhythm to start. But on the next best song he anchored her hips to his and let the beat do the rest.

Hands hot on her skin. Steady and confident in their welcome.

Stretch gave her enough space to wind her body up so he could pull her down against him again.

His breath came hot on her neck, but Kaia would've bet lips grazed first. "You want another drink, doll?"

Her hands held onto his helplessly and she craned her neck to look up and back. Shouldn't have but did anyway. And stayed; body to body, eyes reflecting the night.

"Sure," nodding against his chest; tangling her hair with the smoke and sweat, too. Off-kilter and alive.

He nudged her with his head and when she shook hers embarrassed, cheeks flushing, his voice came through to smooth the nerves.

"I'm Kayden by the way."

Kaia took a step—maybe two—before both his hands found her hips again. Sucked her into him and held. The beat cracked deeper. Bass vibrating through the sand as he engulfed her.

"I like this song," grinding away with the fire dancers and the others.

He pressed even closer—rougher—and whichever direction he went with her, it was confidently, so Kaia leaned into it.

Heart beating faster, breath shallow. And a hand sliding against her chest—trailblazing—that put her knees at high risk.

Kaia had dated teens before. But she'd never felt this power and fragility between two people. Neither person the fragile one, but the space between them. She was scared he controlled it. Made her breath skip on command; lungs gasp sharp or slow—controlled every goosebump like they were rationed. The music faded out beneath them. Drifted into the pop of firewood and the talk of the night.

Kayden's hands traced the edge of her hips, then slipped lower, grasping her thighs tight before just letting off.

"Ready?"

Cold breeze on her sizes and back and soul. Hot to cold—unless dancing was allowed to feel that intimate.

Kaia looked around lost. Her body still shrieking things she may have experienced, but didn't fully understand.

Taunting, teasing, intimacy, love, fucking, safety—
what did any of it mean anyway?

Kaia turned again, tempting fate with his face this close. Her laugh, airy and small, sounded like a giggle. "Yeah."

Kaia turned back to the flames. The fire was getting too hot anyway, and she didn't mean the bonfire. Feeling him still hovering behind her; still grinning over something that got her nervous then and now.

Playing with how touch teased and tempted. Counting the shades of pink and tracking each twitch of her lips. How long it took before she looked away. Him refusing to break away first, let alone at all.

"Hey," his thumb dragged gently across her jaw. "Let me see your eyes."

She looked up but didn't mean to. Didn't want to this time, his breath hovering over her lips—humid, and *there.*

Older. Steady. Grounding, maybe. "Give me a kiss."

Kaia flushed brightly. Looked away quick and then back as if she heard wrong, but she didn't.

He smoldered confidently. Patiently waiting while her cheeks hurt and her head shook. Worse? The girlie facade knocked through with a hijacked *giggle* that both caught her off guard and disgusted herself.

Kaia dropped her sleeves over her knuckles and watched the sand—the way it moved under their feet. She Half expected him to swoop down and steal it anyways. Sweep her off her feet somehow. She braced for it like he would, but he just held the damn smirk and stare.

Didn't press, didn't push. And didn't take.

"Alright then," smiled all easy, breezy like. Not like she'd said no to something that wasn't technically a question.

Because it was a challenge. Not a rejection. Not yet anyway.

Kaia swallowed, watching him step just far enough back to let the air between them in again and the heat out.

"So how about a name?" he asked, nodding towards the cooler.

His hand brushed her lower back as they turned and stayed for a bit.

"Kaia," breath still shaky but returning. Something about that kiss-exchange had her feeling shorted. Like she changed her mind; wanted him to turn around and ask again.

Or take it, but nicely. But he didn't. He made boring talk about the people as they crossed the firelight and insisted on telling her stories with Cachí, Mikki, or the other one.

The beach had gone from warm chaos to a slow sprawl of bodies and blur. Movement thick with beer, sea salt and dusk. But the air around him felt sharper somehow. Like every other person in his orbit had something to do with him—good or bad.

Kaia clocked respect. Fear. Anger. *Want.* But the fear had her looking at his height differently. His hold.

—but maybe it was just the boys respecting the men.

And she was walking with the men. One who was charming. Quick, quiet wit she'd catch a mile away and banter rich with a similar humor. Just had to survive their heatwave first.

Her knees still weak until the absence of his attention braced them.

Kayden still tracked her, in a sense, but kept eyes on a small group a few feet back. Guys. Looked even younger than her and Leti. But they began to peel away at the sight of her and Kayden. Heads ducked and swerved.

The energy shifted and Kaia's shoulders leaned back from them all. Ensuring full vision of feet, hips, and hands, sensing a rigidity in Kayden and a strangeness from the others. One stood out particularly.

Young, jittery.

Locked eyes with Kayden but then immediately dropped his gaze.

That wasn't respect. Kaia watched Kayden watching the kid.

That was fear.

Kayden approached the cooler, standing taller too, as if the kid wasn't already two heads shorter. Showed a chink in Big Man's armor that he'd have everyone believe was bravado. Kaia scoffed, twisting to look back at the fires with her sister.

Cold bottle thudded against her arm and her jaw snapped shut surprised. Back teeth kissed too tight because Kayden didn't look at her. Just handed it off, already focused on something else.

"Jeremy—bud!" he whistled.

Jeremy, presumably the one with the hood on who visibly shrank. Sharp shoulders and skittish eyes looking up when Kayden approached.

"Kay-Kayden."

Slung an arm over Jeremy's shoulders. Clapped against the kid's bicep too hard. Squeezing like he could pop. Kaia's skin flared to the sound of skin slapping skin. The audio making her want to scream.

The fake-laugh, fake voice—it ripped at her ear drums. Then the silence among the group of "friends"? Salt in a shredded wound.

Kaia watched, judging. She should have stayed dancing in the firelight. The sounds of the party, the ocean, the traffic—

they were on the outside of it now.

"Where you been little man?" No longer in the world Kayden took her too when he didn't speak but moved against her. Now, the wrong-kind-of-touch energy.

Not grey. Not, wrong *but* pleasing. *Wrong.*

And the kid was scared. Jeremy shook his head rapidly. Shrinking. "Bro— I didn't have anything to do with it."

"Where is it?"

Jeremy tried to slide away, not hard enough to make a scene. Just enough to beg without making noise.

"Kayden—" Jeremy tried again. It cracked out like a whimper.

Kaia felt herself step back, like distance alone could melt her out of the scene. Not from fear, but for memory. And not ruining the one she just had, with the one he's currently creating. Glanced back to the fire again. Looked through the crowd for Leti but only found strangers.

"I wasn't with Cody that night, I swear—dude!" The last words came out tight and desperate.

Kayden squeezed down so hard his knuckles went white against the kid's skin. He nodded. Dropped his voice low. "You see Jeremy, that's my fucking point." He gave the kid one more sharp shake, then shoved him back into the cluster of kids.

Not friends, but audience. "You were supposed to. This shit lands on you now." Kayden returned to Kaia, casually.

Eyebrows furrowed at her sealed beer, before he plucked the bottle out of her loose grip. Jammed the neck between his teeth, cracked it open with a sharp wet pop, and spat the cap into the sand like it disgusted him.

More cold metal in a place that should be soft and inviting. Like sand.

He handed it back to her. But she didn't take it and someone pressed pause. No one there moved.

The party still did. Kaia did second. Eyebrows raised, planted themselves high. She looked at the boys, then Kayden up from down.

"Oh we just—roll right by that?"

He frowned. Considered it and took a long slow sip. His eyebrows went down.

Head cocked a little too. "You ever seen a knife fight before Kaia?"

Kaia didn't answer. Her body did. The slight upper lip raise, nose wrinkle and the tiniest recoil. *Disgust.* She was more afraid of him dancing and silent than when he stood over her insinuating—*what?*

"A real one, with men?" he lifted a brow. Another step closer.

Her body tilted. Her head too, forced to look further up the closer in he got. "No, but next time I see a man, I'll be sure to ask."

Kaia took the beer back. A bit too hard. He still smirked like he liked it. His body shifting, partially blocking the fire.

She hated bullies and top dogs. She wasn't always one of the underdogs, but now—? She didn't know what she was; but she wanted to.

"Switching over to hard to get then?" He grinned like he was playing. "It was getting a little too easy anyway."

Calm and cool to Kaia's icy-hot. It made her angry. Not the type of anger that she was used to. Not the tantrums, not the rage.

—it was getting a little too easy anyway—Doll.

Kaia sucked her teeth. Deliberately, tongue first, lips next. Pressed the bottle into her mouth and took a sip *slow.* Let the foam from the neck kiss her lip. And stay.

She wiped it eventually. Maybe even tugged her lip a little.

He licked his bottom lip back and smiled. Man still slide his foot back though—like he was preparing for a hit.

Because he knew it was coming, the two of them just playing a fuckin' game of dodge ball now. Shot for shot, gambling on who's got the most...*what?* Wit? Attitude? *Power.*

He reached out for her and she took another step back.

"Get over here." *—give me a kiss—*Not questions but demands.

Kaia checked the exits when she felt her tongue getting hot and a little technical. Her lips pursing. Ocean close enough to escape into; far enough she still had room to back. The churning in her chest.

She may have been putty, but she still had him pinned.

Holding, dominating. Posturing on teens about who knew what. Bopping the bottle on her arm one minute and smoldering her the next and stealing breath.

She saw a piece of her father. Of her ex. Of other emotionally stunted people in the world and flinched when her brain showed her herself.

Nah—*this was about him.* Another big boy in the world, with big feelings he never learned to play with and sort. Only other peoples.

Kaia smiled too, sweet like. Behaved, like. Head a bit down, shoulders a little tucked, eyelashes batting. One of the boys look back over their shoulder at them. Another underdog locked out in the cold too.

"I said come here." He took a step.

She wasn't going anywhere. She let her gaze drift down him and back up like he still wasn't worth hurrying for shit. That alone seemed to shift the energy between them. "So—" she began.

"You've got the gaze. Swag—sure. Pretty face, tall..." Her head tilted slowly, watching his do the same; calculating her response.

Kaia gave a sultry smile, eyes bat lovingly. "Guess if you don't have substance, and can't get respect, next best thing would just be being remembered, huh? Even if it's as a bitch."

Silence on that one was long.

Long enough for his knuckles to go white.

Long enough for them to relax. And then go white again.

The boys watched like a collision. Kayden, front and center of Kaia. Kaia, placed between the sea and the stone, chin too goddamn high.

Aware, but unable to stop while Kayden hovered over her, moved closer, didn't take eyes off her but sat in silence and made her wait with.

Knuckles relaxed, but he didn't blink until one of the kids pulled out a phone. Didn't make sound, but the movement got an immediate response from Kayden

Eyes never leaving Kaia—just cracked his arm out like a whip. Pointed not to the fire, but the fuck away.

"Get. Now."

Wasn't screamed. Wasn't growled. Just slow. And abundantly clear what he said.

The most nerve-wracking part wasn't him, or how it was said but the silence that followed. Kaia couldn't see if they still stood there, eyes rolling and scoffing.

Or if they split—cups spinning, hats landing. Cartoons in their wake because doing for others never guarantees they'd do for you. And she was stupid for forgetting.

"Run that by me one more time, doll face."

Kayden's tongue ran against the inside of his teeth; his chin lifted higher, so he looked down further.

Kaia couldn't even see her own "group." Only a long stretch of beach to the right, the south to the left, and then open water behind with a gas tanker leaking ahead. Face fired.

"I think you misspoke," he added coldly.

Kaia took another deliberate sip from the bottle but didn't blink either. —*Kaia don't*— She did think about it. Tried to remind herself she wasn't in a schoolyard. Real world, real people.

"Lemme try and be clearer then," still felt like an exciting tit-for-tat.

Little scary. Really sexy. But his undivided attention and emotion at her.

Kaia laughed hesitantly. Reconsidering what to say until the very end. "What I meant was..."

Another sip, running low, used to stall.

His weight shifted. The tide rolled and her feet got wet. Stepping back more before she realized.

He grabbed her wrist, not hard, but gently pulled her closer and from the wave.

The gentleness didn't match the ferocity in the eyes. But it gave her the last bit of confidence.

"So, I think what *you* think is charisma, *baby*," pulling from his hand, side stepping this time for him to step with again.

"Is a small man's compensation. And I don't mean in height."

Staring him down like they were post-fight, wondering maybe if this was actually only the face-off before. Fearful of that. Kaia's best shot taken first, unsure what he could say—but what she *would* say if he brought something back.

The tide surged hard somewhere behind them then, kissing her calves this time. And it wasn't enough to drag her under, but it was enough to remind her that it could.

the Fray

MUSSEL BEACH
00:21:05:⁰¹

| XVII |

Dante, eyes on no one in particular, stood near the edge of the sea. It was quieter there—or at least seemed so. He needed it. Heart thrumming from proximity panic. Dante wasn't sure it was because Mikki. At least told himself that.

Nerves—*body*—saying otherwise. How she didn't hesitate; didn't keep any distance between them. Made him both love and fear the moment but disappear into it regardless.

Until he saw Matí pacing the waterline. Waiting. *Fuck.*

Guilt. Anxiety. Moral affliction—maybe it wasn't Mikki at all but Dante. And who he was now, not by choice, but influence.

But what about Kayden then? Choice. *Influence.* Dante sighed heavily.

He'd heard Kayden was lurking around somewhere, too. Tried not to look, but he couldn't help it really. Dante would get lost in thought—find himself looking again until the sound of the waves devoured time.

Dante's heart slowed eventually, making his way to the group as it did. Rubbing his face like he was irritated.

He was hungry. Restless. Looked at his bottle deflated next—telling himself not to be a downer but seeing nothing but warm backwash, sand, and the lack of a point.

Couldn't focus on relaxing. Not even on Cachí. Mikki didn't help now, so instead, Leti had his attention.

There was another one somewhere around here, too. Happy and outgoing like Mick. Shiny distractions, in no better words.

Cachí kept gravitating towards the one that was here. Shorter, quieter one. Shifting between the open space and him like she wasn't clear on whether she wanted to stay or follow the other.

139

Cachí leaned one way though. A quiet, black hole pulling in towards her. Only made him suspicious because she was more than shy. She was careful. Wasn't sure if it was just how she was or if it switched when he got in and the other one left.

Maybe she smelled cop the way he smelt something just being *off.* And the other girl—the one he'd caught watching him—off and away as he came over. Didn't help feel off-putting.

Might have thought it was a coincidence, but the more he made himself look, the more he could find reasons to twist. Find himself deeper on an edge he'd never come off to begin.

The unknown faces from other places making empty spaces in the file. Didn't like it. Not with Cachí's reappearance, not with his questions or relation to a body—

Timing is interesting is all Dante was saying. Or, the distraction was at least. Trying to listen as she talked between the noise like she didn't speak at all. Didn't want to listen until he couldn't.

Mick leaning into her and coaxing out a personality otherwise hidden. Not taking up space; not being memorable with Cachí halfway to lust. Showing her shit on the phone, pulling her up on his socials—

Dante missed the username despite low-key listening for it. Kind of pissed him off but night wasn't over. Becoming a game now of how much he can learn through means other than her directly.

Leti unknowingly kicked it off with an official introduction that lacked the intro on her part. Dante had caved—spotted paying enough attention their way—and called over the noise:

"I'm Dante. Romero."

She was slow to reciprocate. Eyes flickered to the corner of his lips, his hands. Then back to his eyes.

"Leti." Said under another passing speaker box.

No last name or background before Mikki came in with the savior-from-silence—

"*Oh, my fault!*" Sharing the behind the scenes encounter on the BART.

"Yeah, right after you left actually."

"Busy day," he joked.joked, watching Leti coil back down into her cocoon. Search-and-swivel-eyes activated on her head again.

The small chatter continued around them, between them—Dante was part of it too, but found himself looking around every time Leti did. She looked disappointed; looked like she couldn't find her partner while tuning in and out of the conversations.

That almost became a game too—a find it first—when Dante looked around with her. Call it curiosity, call it a hero complex.

Call it a boredom.

Casually, and unbothered, he pushed himself up and Mikki's eyes were immediately following him. She touched his shin and even through jean she felt electric.

"You going again?"

His heart, her touch—he'd blame it all on the shots they'd taken on the passing bottles. Shrugged back at her like he was cool.

Not a yes, not a no. "Antsy, that's all."

And quick. Immediately spotting the other one. No longer dancing by flame but outside the firelight.

She jumped out the way Leti blended in. Could thank Kayden for that. Looking him over as he was over someone else. Small group around.

Dante couldn't remember last time he'd seen him outside the station. Lost his cool and was forced to step back for a conflict of interest. Pretended it was Dante's choice, but the whole fucking place knew better.

As if him and Kayden weren't on opposites sides of the world. Though now—together again. And then some.

But Dante didn't like the body language this time—not how the kid was looking, not how the girl was—felt poorly matched.

The friend, from here, she stepped back from them but kept eyes on. No smiles. No sips.

Didn't make sense—eight or nine teens drinking on the beach. Beautiful girl little older than them—no show-boatin'?

No shooting shots the way you do when young, dumb, and drunk?

Kayden stepped forward when she'd step back, or she stepped back because he went forward. Dante just stared. The idea of trouble making his anxiety whisper instead of yell.

So maybe Dante would go say hi. Feed into it. Since he missed out earlier—running eyes along Kayden again.

The fire snapped and popped, and when it simmered, the girl was looking his way now. Though not at them; not at the sparks. Just the group's general direction.

He'd seen it before. From Mikki. The side glance of "save me." Family reunions, social events—

Kayden over her like he'd do something.

Dante didn't want anything to happen necessarily, but a piece of him jumped at it. Like, let it be that easy—

Do something Kade. Give Dante—give them, give Mikki—a live show on what exactly he was capable of.

Dante didn't care why, he just knew he had to understand. Used to think it made sense before—justified even. But either experience or time whittled at reason, exposing excuse.

The girl looked back again. Looked like she started to turn when Kayden grabbed her wrist. Dante cocked his head. Took a step and paused when she ripped her arm back. Had a hand up and a finger on his chest then. Arguing at this point.

Pictured Kayden just laying her out with a hook and it made Dante flinch. Couldn't imagine why he would—couldn't picture it twice, but too vivid, too fucking real, that "*do something*" felt too karmically charged now.

Dante nodded towards them despite Mikki not being able to see.

"Need another drink," he fibbed. Before Kayden did something neither of them could undo. While Dante watched.

As he got closer, he heard more.

"*—you got nerve—*" "*Not my fault you got more body than brain—*"

The chick was spittin' back and leaving Kayden unusually quiet. Leaving Dante uncomfortable and quickly clearing his throat. Couldn't put a pin on the feeling it gave him, but his arms crossed and his feet planted.

Kayden whipped around to the sound, his angry expression morphing into a mask despite hers staying stubborn and true.

"Well I'll be damned—!" Grinning wide, like Kayden actually meant it.

Dante looked at her first, head to toe.

And she watched—not an ounce of insecurity. Looked Dante up from down right back. But no bruises, no split lip—Dante glared at Kayden next. Not sure what he'd expected him to do to her but couldn't imagine anything good. Explosive ass temper.

"Good to see you. Really." Kayden's voice was light and cautiously optimistic. "Havin' us a reunion with everyone huh?"

Dante's eyebrows lifted, eyes widened but just a flicker. Sarcasm without words—*cool story, bro.*

"*Hermosa,*" Dante all but purred at her instead, snagging her gaze so she ignored him too. She stared like she was aware though. "You mind handing me a drink?"

He asked closer to how he normally would, watching her walk when she turned while Kayden watched him. She gave no nod, no word, no spit like she had when he approached. Only eyes and gears turning and he wanted to know which way.

Kayden wiped his palms on his jeans while she bent into the cooler. "Still a cop, Dání—? Or still pretending?"

Dante nodded toward her and said simply, "Hands to yourself, ya?"

Nothing more than a look and Kayden nodded. Smothered a chuckle he forced to begin with and a tight smile. Wasn't the warm reception Kayden wanted, and Dante could see him adjusting to the scenario. Always so animated and easy to read.

Dante turned toward the chick when she came up the other side of Kayden; placing herself squarely between him and the fire. But not between him and Dante. Dante smiled. He liked critical thinkers. Taking the drink easy. "Thanks."

"Anytime." Looking back towards the group again—same way that dragged him over.

Dante tipped his head back toward that way, shifting a shoulder in front of Kayden and meeting her eyes again. "One of the girls was looking for you," he lied.

Because the body asks permission first, and she was asking to go back. Ego masking innocence, or naivete, or fear to say—something any grown man can sense. Kayden either choosing not to or with age came stupidity.

Dante looked over a shoulder once as she disappeared. *No goodbyes, no catch you later*—instead, Dante smiled back at Kayden, '*now what*' on Dante's face.

An offer to hover over someone his own size.

"New friends?" Kayden grumbled, hands to hips as if to expand.

Dante scoffed, cracking the beer while it was still cold.

"Adopted them this week," he joked, facing Kayden and really looking him over while it was just them there.

No mask, no front. "Sharing is caring, you know."

Dante didn't come for this, but he stayed for it.

Kaia walked back toward the fire with the bottle in her hand and heat on her skin that wasn't from the flames.

The voices behind her stayed low—edges of confrontation, not quite spilling over. She didn't turn at first. Didn't have to. She could feel them.

The stranger silent and unmoving. than Kayden: all shift and boil.

She slowed halfway back. Looked to the fires, then back again.

Something about their quiet swung harder than a fist. Didn't know what happened, but she liked the weight of it. The way the guy's voice cut through heat and ego like a blade. Kayden backing off but not backing down.

Kaia stalled again near the edge of the light, half-shadowed. The bottle in her hand was warm. Her mouth drier than before. Because she liked the way the random one looked at her.

Hadn't said a word, just—
looked her over. The look alone said, *I see every inch.*

Direct. She wasn't sure if it was fear, or want, or recognition. But something low in her stomach stirred when she thought about being watched.

It felt electric. But—*unsure.* But she wanted to run back to it.

Disappear, but be pulled closer all at once. So, she stood longer. Waited.

And she let herself wonder which man was going to move first. And what she wanted to do about it now.

Kayden's chin tilted like a shrug he never committed to, stepping in closer.

"What's with the hands-to-yourself shit, brotha?" Twitch in his mouth: half smile, half sneer. "I didn't know you liked to watch."

Dante cut a flat and unamused look and held it heavy. Left Kayden to shift under the weight—wait to see what comes to mind first—

Kayden hated it. Minute passed before his chest notably raised.

Once—twice, with a hard breath. He scoffed next and paced back a step as if giving himself space for the sudden anger.

"I didn't fucking touch her, not like that, *prick*."

Dante pulled his head back and his nose scrunched. "Wha—I..." Face showed surprise when he wanted to stay neutral so he bit the inside of his cheek. Went still again.

"Never said you did, Kayden." Dante shifted to face him and despite arms keeping crossed, they softened. "Something you wanna get off your chest?"

Kayden scoffed again—sharp enough to peel his throat—and looked at Dante like he was fucking stupid before swigging the beer.

Huffed and puffed so long Dante was trying to piece together what exactly did it. Reactions even quicker and hotter than before.

They both took another long sip of their beer. Moreso to buy each other time. The onus on the other in each of their book.

Kayden tried so hard to bury it all—*kill it*—but never could. Dante wasn't even sure how many things he was burying down now. This Cody shit, even if he's not involved: tied to Apollo, tied to a lot. Kayden *can't* keep it buried down.

Not sure if he knows it yet, but he was stuck in the hole he carved for the past, just waiting for the oxygen to run out now. Nothing keeping him company down there but the ripples and echoes he was trying to leave behind.

"You know what," Kayden finally said.

Dante' didn't know whether to expect an old friend or a fist, but the voice was neutral again. Calm even.

"I'm game, I got something to discuss wit'you," maybe even playful. "You and Matty's girl huh?" Kade thumbed vaguely toward the crowd.

Eyebrows dribbled twice with a grin. "The dance, the little mini skirt."

145

Should have stopped at, *'Matty's girl'*—because Dante was staring in a sort of, *awe.*

Speechless as to whether he was trying to be *funny*—or was fucking serious, and that lead Dante back to questioning if Kayden's stupid now. Grinning and open like they were still friends; feet planted like they would spar.

"I mean. She's not really my sister *so—*"

"Finish that sentence, Kayden." Quiet. Slow.

Expertly deliberate. Kayden paused. Stayed paused.

Likely weighing the next three possible outcomes because Dante was anything but unpredictable. Wasn't a question of *where* this was going if continued, but, *if* Kayden was taking it there.

Because he absolutely could get Dante to swing first. Night like tonight—already territorial and buzzed. *Abso-fucking-lutely.*

When Kayden didn't say anything—when he chuckled like he'd already won—Dante went on the offensive with the same dry, humorless chuckle.

Picked up where Kayden paused; "You lost the right to even say their names. Not to me."

Cut from both sides. Difference was Dante let it hurt, the way open wounds were supposed to, while Kayden ate it like fuel to hate.

"Damn bro alright...Fuckin' asshole."

The silence after wasn't silence, but heat. And pressure as another log cracked loud behind them. Heads snapped back—Dante's neck; Kayden's whole shoulders, knees, and face. Dante would have rather taken a punch then witness the flinch.

Turned back to the water, eyes closed to a deep breath and a thought. Kayden—them, *everyone*—shouldn't have had to fight at all, but still.

If he just fucking asked for help louder.

"*Look...*" Kayden. The word from him alone made Dante's jaw flex.

"Nah *vato.*"

Kayden was surprised, but *'Look'* wasn't an opening. It was an excuse wrapped in nostalgia.

"Not this time, man." Dante spun the bottle in his hand. "You always been good at talking circles, Imma stay here this time."

"Yo—I fuckin' piss you off? *Today* I mean. Like what the fuck, bro! Wicked ass attitude."

Kayden shuffled weight; palmed his jeans. Enough heat for them both. Dante didn't have to do or say anything.

"Girl yours? Not sure why else you're pissed, playing knight or taking fucking swings—not like I haven't seen you in months or whatever. Fucking *excuse me*—trying to fucking be polite."

"Sounding a little whiney there, brotha'."

The firelight didn't blink. Dante either—despite the wild ride between those sentences. Wasn't even sure what Kayden's baseline was anymore. Felt like trying to read an electric current.

Kayden licked his teeth. Nodding big, waiting for Dante to say something. *To bite.* Dante looked behind him instead.

Bored now. Or regretting. Maybe checking Mikki didn't sneak in ear shot.

"You know what your problem is, Dáni?" Kade smiled, because if he couldn't get engagement, he was going to get a fight.

"You act like you're above all this," waving a lazy hand across the beach, "like you ain't still circling the drain same as the rest of us."

Dante straightened. Tipped the last of the beer into the sand, nodding in agreement. "I am circling," he said seriously. "Difference is, I'm still trying to swim. You, *compa'*—you're at the bottom, pulling us down faster so you don't drown alone."

Kayden backed up a foot; his arms crossed tighter, and the air felt colder in Dante's chest. Sharp in his throat like he'd done wrong. But that ache moving to his chest where he let it get angry at the pain.

Kayden shifted back again. Smaller, but noticeable. "Didn't know that's how you felt," he said. "Finally gave up on the good memories then, huh?"

Paused—because it wasn't rhetorical, but they both were going to pretend it was. "Wasting time anyways, I guess."

This is where he was supposed to say, *'never been a waste; not too late,'* but he didn't want to lie. Could dream all day—*what if he asks to come home, what if he changes course even if we don't believe?*

Truth is right there in front of him.

Dante stepped back as the waves rolled over Kayden's feet and dared to reach for Dante's boots.

"Hey, you know what I do remember?" No matter how flat Dante said it, it couldn't stop the flash of hope across Kayden's face.

"Cody."

And the drop after; the micro wisp of air through Kayden's lips, the pause. Subtle enough to doubt, but plenty enough for Dante. For Dante with Kayden anyway, because they knew each other. Too well. Past selves choking Dante, begging him to tell Kayden, "*it's okay 'mano—it's over.*'

Make an excuse; say he had to. But protect him and—after everything—let them end in an embrace; no more space for no more graves. Not until the true end. And especially not graves they watched Kayden dig himself, blisters busting and no one stopping it.

"I um, who?" Blinked naturally. Sounded believable. But looked hollow.

The kid in Dante, the one who almost always lost to Kayden—but his size, not skill—took Kayden's shock as both guilt and victimhood.

Dante felt himself getting guilty despite knowing he shouldn't; feeling bad for noticing or knowing; hating his job; hating the political climate which he could tangent on too if only to distract himself.

But with Kayden in front of him—not sure distractions were good. Neither sorrow. But anger?

Dante booted the sand with his toe and chuckled. What a shit show. But confirmation if nothing else.

No matter how controlled, tonight confirmed Kayden—at the very least—was involved. Dante took the buzz in his gut and the fog in his head and dove into it.

"That first guy you—you—say for *familia*; for Matías. But maybe that was just the first time you got to show us who you really were."

Forehead scrunched and he didn't have a reaction at first. Processed it like he could change the definition the more he replayed it.

"That's low," eventually slipped free on weak breath with welled eyes.

Dante couldn't watch. Looked to the ocean instead but the pain was even in Kayden's voice. "Cold...Even for you."

And like he gave up—Kayden crossed between Dante and the water.

To leave. Calling, "sorry about Cody," over his shoulder. And maybe he was, but that helped light the anger up. Helped burn out the pain. Because Dante didn't want to be the one standing there like an asshole when he should have been the one to walk away.

Dante's tongue burned until he blurted it. "You involved Matty's boy, *pendejo.*"

Kayden whipped around, "who's fuckin' Matty's girl?"

"I—No—I—fuck you, bro." Might've swung were Kayden not ten paces out. "Say it to her face," knowing he wouldn't dare but also trying to compose himself.

"And Cachí involved him-damn-self. Can't blame me forever, kid's got his own mind, guilt....And gun."

Said it teasingly. But knew it had weight. Dante figured as much, peeling at the beer label. Still pissed him off to hear it. That confrontational attitude he'd come down with sourer now.

"Rattin' on Cachí now?"

"Bro there's nothing to rat on," walking away as he called back. "Not even sure what you're fuckin' talking about anymore. Oh—" turning back again, wave rolling his pant leg and making Dante uncomfortable.

"Since you got Mikki totally—*thoroughly*...covered, Im'ma continue where I was with lil'miss mkay?"

He was going to hold onto the Mikki digs like a dog and a fucking bone. Dante breathed slower. Deliberately. Reminding himself not to clench.

"You look like shit too, stop letting Mikki keep you up all night—get some sleep."

Dante flinched when someone looked but couldn't think of something to say. Feeding into it felt disrespectful, but resisting would only make Kayden dish more. And he could feel a brawl edging closer. Saying and doing nothing as Kayden went back to the fires.

"Sleep?" Dante smirked, watching him go; knowing any further would be a brawl. He tipped his head back to the sky and breathed in the cool air.

Mikki didn't bring them to a party tonight.

Brought him to a fucking funeral.

Silvana @ 28th Ave NW & HW532/Sunday Lake Rd, Arlington WA
→ 48.2063° N, -122.2495° W

Kalaloch, WA → 47.6130° N, -124.3717° W

Port Orford, OR → 42.7473° N, -124.5017° W

The Gorge, OR → 45.6643° N, -121.900° W

Hike 1 - Angel's Rest → 45.5607° N, -122.1717° W

Hike 2 - Multnomah Falls → 45.5757° N, -122.1155° W

Hike 3 - Dog Mountain → 45.7000° N, -121.7007° W

Yuba City, CA → 39.1407° N, -121.6169° W

Redwoods National Park → 41.2132° N, -124.0040° W

Eureka - Russian River Swim Hole Guerneville → 38.500° N, -122.9961° W

the Fallacy

| XVIII |

The crowd was a sea of firelit faces and a soft blur around the edges. Leti half-expected to catch Kaia swinging off someone's shoulders, racing toward the surf, or crashing a limbo contest just because she could. She half-hoped to catch Kaia doing *anything*.

So long as she could be in contact.

Kaia didn't have a reason to leave her behind. Not this time. Because Leti was playing by her rules. She was along for the ride.
And she was even relaxed. Main word—*was*.

Because Kaia had been there—dancing, teasing the tide, flirting with something other than death.

And now she wasn't.

Now the firelight looked too far away, the ocean looked rougher, and the men seemed meaner. Scanning too fast to see clearly, heart knocking harder than it should. No flicker of Kaia's hair, no laugh. And no footprint in the sand. Just gone. *Again.*

Leti swallowed back the swell in her throat pushing between strangers with a buzz that turned sour and floating that got heavier. Scarier. Moving towards the next bonfire, felt like a race.

Thought about calling Kaia's name, but something about that felt too desperate.

Too loud, too overbearing, or too much like she cared for someone who didn't care for her. They'd see her for the worst things about herself. Bordering on frantic turns and anxiety attacks. Leti caught something from the corner of her eye. Little further back, square building.

Motionless like reprieve. Public restrooms, state park type.

Not Kaia. But maybe a place to throw up. Or hide. Up until the night leaves her alone too, because nothing was worse than being surrounded by people, and feeling this empty.

She pushed the door open and stepped in. Smelled salt, and rust, and some version of regret as her body folded in on itself. One palm to the wall, the other covering her face when a stall door creaked, but she didn't care. Didn't think anyone would. She'd been left again and there was nothing she could do about it.

Leti's chest caved once, twice, three times—then, "*Leti?*"

Whole body went still.

Didn't breathe. *Didn't move.*

And when the moment didn't turn—when it didn't dissolve into someone else's voice or a trick of the buzz—Leti peeled her hands from her face to see mascara streaks like war paint and sand skid marks.

"You bitch." Leti meant every syllable with a sharp ache and hated how relieved she felt with Kaia there.

Smiling like she was drunk on moonlight, she cooed, "oh, Bitlet—come here."

Leti rooted down and hated the name now, but Kaia still stepped forward. Just not too fast, like she knew a storm was sitting behind Leti's eyes and wasn't sure if it would crack or clear. Waited instead. Leaning against the sink, hands gripping the edges.

Kaia looked like she'd been crying and laughing and spinning all at once, but Leti stayed by the door and like the hotel room, like the credit card—Kaia reached out of the silence first.

"So...You good?"

Settling, blinking, Leti looked up. "Yeah. I just, I don't. I got anxious. The drinks didn't help and—and—where's your phone?"

"The car. I hope." Playful, hair stuck to her temples too. until she splashed a little water to the face—buying time, cooling down.

"That guy. Kayden." Kaia slid onto the counter. "You met right, or saw him?" And off just as fast when the wall groaned and pipe squeaked.

Leti didn't answer but laughed. Kaia would bust the freaking thing. And Leti saw him alright. Not impressed.

"Yeah—we danced. Like totally normal, right? Kinda hot. Kinda hot," shaking her head and leaning on the stall.

"But like—I don't know. I know I have muscles and nerves and bones—but—I *felt them*. Like...man I don't know how to explain it."

"Not...*numb*," Leti offered. Couldn't relate on this one but *could*.

"Or angry! Heated as *Hell*, but...I don't feel angry. Or anxious. Right? But you? I mean..."

Leti's lip twitched and her chest ached, "I get it." Both of their smiles fading into something quiet. "I think. I just..." Leti trailed off, unsure.

"What?" twisting around, leaning against the wall Leti hogged, Kaia pressed in closer.

"Guess I'm just worried. Sometimes I think anger's the only thing keeping you—you know. Going. I guess."

"That's not true..."

"No?"

Kaia shrugged, "I don't know—I mean. Sometimes. Sometimes for me though, too. Or despite them..." Kaia moved away slowly. Arms crossed, but more doubt and coverage than resistance. "I mean, I don't *want* to be angry. And, I guess I kinda hoped you'd know—I'm going on for you. *Always*. You're my sister, Leti. I'm not here because anger...couldn't have left without you. And you're like, literally the only—we're *the same*. Four halves, two wholes. Come on!"

"I—well, yeah. I guess."

"No, not, *I guess*. This is how it's supposed to be. We're just—too *fucked* up to let it be. Right?" Grabbing onto Leti's biceps gently, bending neck to hook Leti's stubborn withdrawal. "*Right?* I mean...Leti...If we can't just—have this? If the swings keep coming, we might as well give up."

"Kaia—don't say that!" Voice cracked. "Goddamn, that's what I mean."

Kaia grabbed her, held her tight. Not like a bear, but like a sister who knows there's no fixing it. Only hoping it doesn't break again.

"I didn't mean it. I'm sorry." She shook her head. "I don't know. It's been a swing. Highs and lows."

Leti side-eyed her. She knew that already—just didn't know Kaia did.

"I'm talking too much shit, I know. I'll stop with the death jokes. I'll stop with the I'm-invincible thing."

"Promise?"

Kaia nodded, no hesitation. "*Promise*. I'm not trying to scare you. Just—kinda seemed funny to me."

Leti hugged her back—tight, then eased off like she needed air.

Trying to change the temperature, Kaia tried: "I swung past the fire on my way here..." Leti didn't return it. "You and Cachí—low key, kinda cute."

Leti laughed, safe inside with her sister. Door closed. Cheeks fully flushed. She could feel the looks. With him. They'd gotten longer.

Could feel the gravity of him too, every time he sat too close.

"Yeah. He's been good company since you ditched me." Kaia tried to interject; Leti kept on louder until she didn't.

"Doesn't matter though. I wouldn't even know where to begin. *How* to begin."

"Leti—come on. That just makes my next point. Mkay."

"Kaia, I don't have the—" "No-no," she cut in.

"You say something, and people look at *me*. I say something, and they look at *you*. Sure—we're the same. But we're not. Go flirt with him. Figure it out, figure you out. I know I'm dope, but two's too many."

"You have no idea how right you are..."

Kaia leaned in, eyes sharp for that, but soft. "Go let down the wall, Leti. We'll leave in like two days—if it goes horribly fuck it, we'll skip town tonight. Like—how cool is it to say that?"

Leti blinked hard. Looked down. Leti was the one who was supposed to be having the harder chats with Kaia. "Secondly, Miss *Oletta*—"

"Hey...We don't..." Actual pain. A word last said from their mother. Kaia's own left behind in the coma.

"Yeah. Sorry. Sorry. I didn't mean—but hey," gently put hands to Leti's cheeks. Sandy and rough. "Have the beer."
Leti pulling Kaia's hands down and holding them instead. Kaia shrugged. "Kiss the boy. Dance with me next time."

"Kaia...You know. There's stuff I want to talk about. With you, about..."

"I know." Barely a half smile, "I'm almost there, Lee."

"Really? Because...this isn't another '*deal with until we don't*,' Kai.

It's important, I just...am worried to send you into a freakin' melt down or—or—I don't know. I guess that's the problem."

"What, you don't want any more visiting rooms?"

Leti flicked her hands off Kaia's. Always shit talking. She went to splash her face too. Discard any swell before storming off. But stalling. "*No.*"

Kaia stole another hug from behind. Met Leti's eyes in the mirror. "I was gonna apologize, but looks like I've used a lot tonight, *sooo—*"

"Funny."

"You okay though? You hate this?" She let go and Leti turned.

Two more, like them but different, swooped in sloppily. Squeezed into the larger stall together—giggles and stumbles. "I mean—you having fun at least? You flirt with Cachí yet?"

"Who?"

"Leti... *Cam'onnnn*. What's it, god hows he say it, my *carino?*" Kaia widened her eyes. "You give him the time of day yet?"

Leti shrugged. "The time."

"Right... 'Kay then. I'll make you a deal, Bitlets."

"Here we go." Eyes rolling.

"You'll like it—maybe." Kaia's arms x'ed on her chest defiantly this time. Leti's eyes on the ceiling like there wasn't an offer in the world that'd amuse her now. "You want to talk about Dad? Coma? Mom? The Center?"

Leti's eyebrows dropped, neck turned, mouth loosened. "Ye—yeah, but—what—" "Right," arm snagged by Kaia. "So then lets take one of these huh," pinching the braided leather on Leti's wrists; plastic beads pretending to be gold; "Tomorrow. The beach. If... you, you know. Give him one."

Leti's eyes squinted, Kaia's smirk turned into grin but she went on before Leti's objections. "And I'll have a time limit, okay? Two hours?"

"Wait—where, are you going then?" Leti's chest got tight again.

"It's like the second or third fire down, dude. It's a beach—I can't get to the lot without passing you guys so—just don't leave me then, huh?"

Tactical responses. Because the decision was made. Kaia was just grasping for Leti to agree before she did it anyway.

"I mean, wanna come walk and dance then? Jaylin went that way, I dunno. Kinda bitchy but seems kinda tough and like she knows people. Maybe she'll invite us to something tomorrow—it's still the weekend, so?"

Leti searched her face, her tone, her posture. It seemed sincere. The issue was it always did. And it usually was. Until something else took over or came up. But what were the options?

Agree—fearful, but knowing? Or pitch a fit. Play hide and seek across the goddamn state? Go with—just to hear her tomorrow, *not talking about it since you didn't do it.*

Kaia wouldn't even have to disappoint Leti later, either, because that was happening now:

Even if she came back on the dot, Leti had to admit it to herself—she didn't trust Kaia. Not with this.

Eyes visibly pained, screaming, *I am trusting you!* Leti whispered, "two hours. *Okay?*" Resigning into it with no other real choice.

Kaia grinned and threw up two fingers before diving in for a hug. "Two hours. *Promise!*"

Pulled back like a confused racehorse that'd already heard the start.

"Okay—cool, so...?" Snapping and clapping in a rhythm that probably made sense to her.

"So..." Leti shrugged, holding her arm out to the door. "So go," like re-releasing an animal to the wild. Hoping to catch it again later.

Kaia grabbed her head for a big kiss, repeating *two hours* back like it'd make her more likely to abide; Leti rolled her eyes the whole time. Numb to it.

 All that anxiety and worry and it didn't climax, just sort of fell flat. Even ended up shuffling Kaia along as she stalled, worried about Leti, but both knowing she'd go anyway. Just deciding when.

So Leti decided for her before changing her own mind. Walking to the door with Kaia and parting ways when their toes returned to sand.

Leti was halfway back when she realized she hadn't looked behind her for Kaia. And not just that, but her chin—sat level with the earth.

Wasn't sure what the feeling was, but it wasn't numb. Felt maybe a little like relief. Planting roots and catching some rain.

the Foreplay

00:19:37:03

| XIX |

Behind the circle, Cachí tracked the firelight and the laughter, but his eyes kept drifting to Leti when she got back. Holding down the blanket when Mick left; fiddling awkwardly with bracelets probably bought on the pier. Some of those, twenty-five cents in a machine, fifteen bucks at the Wharf type-things. Braided leather and stamped metal.

Leti turned it over like it mattered. At least until she caught his gaze and flushed. Came back a little different—a little looser. Reaching into the cooler herself, pulling up a seat, and gettin' comfortable with them.
He liked it.

Leti turned to a sound behind her and smiled at someone. Forced it. But seemed like she was tryin' something out. Cachí couldn't decide if what he was feeling was him not wanting to go over, or him not wanting to be told to go away.

Looked behind himself casually—for Mikki; or a buffer. Caught Leti staring over at him too and he figured what the hell, stirring up the courage while he got up. Their eyes crossing awkwardly while coming closer.

"Vale, carino," he pulled up next to her and sat down a little sloppy; sitting before he changed his mind. "So I figured if we were gonna' throw eyes at each other all night...might as well come talk, yeah? Or...nah?"

That got it. The real one. Dimples exposed; lips weird and twisted from trying to bite it back. Couldn't tell if she blushed anymore though—her face held soft pink along her cheeks the rest of the night.

Cachí relaxed back, head against the driftwood, body stretched out; foot near the flame, other propped and bent. "So...How hard do I uh, need to work for a story out of you?" His voice was low. Slow and relaxed while she twisted and stretched the bracelets in her lap.

Kept her hands busy, all cute, cross-legged, and awkward. "Depends what kind you want."

Hadn't thought that far; just sounded like a good place to start. Cachí went for a second pass, nodding at her. "What'cha got?"

Fingers spread, revealing more of the bracelets as if he wasn't trying to use it as a topic. "Nice..." A second, aimless nod followed. Like maybe it'd shake up some shit to say. "You uh, warm enough?" Glancing toward the fire. "Or—Hungry?" But there wasn't any food, not sure what made him ask if not the butterflies. Cachí couldn't tell if they belonged more to her, or to him, only that he wanted to play in them a little longer.

"Yeah," separating the bracelets as she counted them. "Good. You?"

Cachí, hands behind his head now. Minor fidgeting. "Better today."

Minor weirdness. Looking through the corners of his eyes and leaving it there. Partially true confusion; partially stubbornness waiting for her to take a step to him. But he noticed her trying—breath like she'd speak and changing her mind.

Didn't think she wanted him to go. But she would look around, hesitate, like maybe she expected him to? Cachí shrugged despite nothing being said and he hunkered down deeper into the driftwood.

He didn't mind the quiet. Or the crackle of fire at his feet. Laughed when he caught her staring again, curiously. "You find your uh, Kaia? Earlier?"

"Oh...Yeah." Still there, toying with the bracelets.

If she didn't look like she wanted to say something he might have already dipped. But now it was worse—one eye squinting like she was arguing with herself.

Maybe even losing. "I uh," nervously laughing and redder than he thought she could turn. "It's—stupid—but I actually, have one. For you."

Cachí's eyebrows shot up, head cocked fast too. Recoiled himself, but not in disgust, not disdain. Just...*surprise*. And not much had surprised him nowadays, but *that* did.

The stuttering; avoidance in her eyes despite him shifting to face her more. Cachí's stomach twisted, her knee starting to bounce while her confidence began to drown—desperate for a hand that he wasn't sure how to reach.

Cachí opened his mouth like he had something but almost put a hand against her knee instead; the small of the back—
better with touch and tasks than the verbal shit but he wasn't confident with that just than either.

Kept thinking of doing anything but the simplest thing: *Taking the fucking bracelet.* Sat close but let her hand hang in the air like an idiot. Not entirely sure what his face was doing when she started up again, tripping the whole way.

"I mean—it's just...well, I don't know," struggling. Stumbling faster than she could stop the words and then quieter and quicker as if that didn't make it worse.

"We saw them. After—meeting you guys. We went—well fine, probably just an excuse to buy more crap, I don't know. Or couldn't pick, doesn't matter, they're cheap things. *Here*. Just take it," shoving it at him more forcefully than he expected. Back of her hand—not quit slapping his arm but announcing its presence. "Whatever..."

"I um..." One hand came out from behind his head and he grabbed her hand. Maybe for the bracelet, maybe for the Hell of it—noticing the way they both were extremely uncomfortable but not really sure why.

Compliments, gifts, words of affirmation—made him feel weird. And for whatever fucking reason she stepped on the ledge tonight. So Cachí tried too, delayed, but slid the bracelet from her grip. Couldn't help but feel something flutter when she got nervous at the touch.

Big, bad silent shield, but completely soft behind it. *Sentimental.* He turned the bracelet over in his hand then laid the back of his on her now. Left it there until she met his gaze, but didn't realize it probably looked like he was handing it back.

Leti looking at the bracelet in his hand like it betrayed her. Like she should have known, unsure how to move next.

"Well," he finally offered aid. "Double knot it good then, 'ight?"

Space between them paused as if she waited for the rug to pull or the joke to jab—Cachí nudged her again with the back of his hand to encourage something.

Reaching to his wrist, fingers careful not to graze him like she wanted to be all timid again. But he'd seen a crack in the mask—the pace in her nervous speak and the stubbornness when feeling on the outs.

Leti tied the bracelet loose, but twice, leaving him room to slide it off like she thought he wanted to. Cachí spun it twice and then tightened it for her with another encouraging look. "I like it." Decisive now. Leaning back against the log again and turning toward the fire.

No heavy looks, no sultry smiles—just a dare and a risk that didn't mean a lot, but it meant something to someone somewhere.

Kaia lingered at the edge of the firelight—half in, half out—watching a crowd of mostly older—mid-twenties, maybe a few closer to thirty—people, loose and golden under the burn of beer, bonfire, and smoke.

Too grown for her to fold into cleanly, too young to feel like adults.

Jaylin, nineteen to early twenties, but who knows. Like Kaia, past the age people pay attention to. Like we wake up and have the world fuckin' sorted. When really—itty, bitty turtles hatching on the beach.

Cute, easy pickings.

But maybe that—wasn't true for them both because Jaylin had a aura about her. A presence like quicksand—long bare legs, hoodie sleeves pushed to her elbows, laughing like she owned the city.

 Kaia moored to her for the night. Keeping where the air felt electric but still watching the clock. And still had another hour. Hopefully not spent listening to Jaylin speaking. Bit vapid and very much personal.

But maybe that was normal when you had friends.

Kaia's answers still shortened each question until there was nothing more than loose sounds. Losing herself in her own thoughts when the company got tedious.

Jaylin didn't need Kaia's participation to have a conversation. Just her attention. Started going on about the guys she liked—one in particular—but Kaia zoned in and out, wondering about her own. Tideline-guy. Not hers, but belonging nowhere else inside her head.

 The weird way she looked for Kayden too—adrenaline fueled tit-for-tat leaving her wanting more. Kept asking about the time though. At first.

Nervous edge disappearing the way that time did. Kaia couldn't remember a lot of what her worries even were anymore.

Already a sleeping section of her brain plotting an apology while the rest still wanted to party.

Blame not on Kaia, but on the beers. The weed. The vodka. *Lull of the strong waves and tides*—Time was simply fluid and invisible unless watching for it. Then it was stagnant.

Listening, watching—Kaia sighed and Jaylin whacked her with a bottle instantly. Texting with her other hand, maybe still telling stories—who fuckin' knows.

"Here," she said.

When Kaia scrunched her nose—the beginnings of an, '*I think I'm good* or '*not this round*—Jaylin looked insulted.

"Shy isn't cute. Not with this crowd. Have some fun," with another shove of the bottle. To which Kaia glared at but still took. Pretending she didn't want to go where the shadows didn't seem to reach. It was just fucking—*strong.*

Kaia took another cautious sip—fire down her throat—coughing before she could catch herself.

"You like it?" Jaylin asked, hand on her forearm like they were old friends and yanking it back. "It's homemade," she smirked wickedly.

Kaia nodded and the world moved like a floating table when she did. Feet stayed planted for a beat—arms low but air-planed to steady. Insides felt warm. Eyes sliding over the crowd and dancers blocking view with movements.

Except of Kayden; today's Sam. Lounging low in the sand across the fire. Golden and wrecked. Wasn't talking much and didn't seem to be listening to anyone either.

Just watching the flames like he could crawl inside and bury himself under the coals. A loose half-circle of people folding around him, but not with. Kind of pretty, but sad. Pretty in the way things are right before they die. Because it felt like rejection to Kaia.

Jaylin clambering and joking on about someone named Cody. Didn't seem like she was a fan.

But Kayden. Eyes warm and firelit again—didn't seem so scary now. Just a man and a game of tag, *which*—she was currently winning. And she had to give him a chance to catch up—right?

Jaylin caught Kaia looking and smirked. "Like that one?"

Kaia's stomach twisted. What would that mean to her if she did?

"Careful," Jaylin added, voice pitched low. "That one's been trouble since before he could spell it."

Kaia raised an unsteady eyebrow. Like the way she said no to the kiss earlier, and then wanted it after; she worried Jaylin would do something, and then, confused she wasn't. But Kaia was familiar with trouble. Hell of a lot more than anything else.

Doesn't make him off limits, makes him misunderstood. And she wasn't stupid—she wasn't calling him docile, wasn't saying he was safe.

Just damaged. Like her. She lolled her head to Jaylin. "You know him?"

"Everybody knows Kayden." Louder now and running her fingers through her sleek, black hair. Swayed against her lower back.

Disappeared into the night the way the ocean did the horizon.

Kaia's eyes flicked across the fire pit—Kayden already staring. Intense. In thought, but ears pricked like a dog called to dinner.

Jaylin blew him a kiss. He didn't acknowledge it once. Stared at Kaia. Unreadable and unmoving.

"We go way back," she grinned, thwapping Kaia with the warm, dry vodka bottle. "Here," and a quick look at Kaia, up from down.

Kaia shrank an inch. Went to say no again but couldn't even start this time. Not with double the eyes—Kayden half a smile and an eyebrow like he'd dared her.

She took smaller sips though. Like her outsides wanted to be wild, but her insides knew better. Handed it back. Same way Jaylin did to her. *Thwap.* Same way Kayden had with the beer.

Just a rough crowd is all. Kaia coughed. Shook her head to shake out the fuzz. Only made the ground uneven.

"He and my dad go way back actually," she went on. "Mentorship. Employer, employee type shit. You know."

But Kaia didn't, not really. He looked back at her from the flames. Sometimes even disappearing behind them—Kaia knew she was staring at times, just didn't know if it was a flirtatious glance or a lost lean.

Couldn't quite feel her face—and it made sense. The music. The song— she tried to even remember what they'd sung about—what her and Kayden fought about. *Fought.* Teased.

Tested the other's ability to catch swinging fists and not bend the wrist back. She had a way with words. And maybe he seemed more and more like the type that might be able to hang.

Spit back with her.

Not flinch when she's ugly and breaking from the cracks already here.

She was still staring. And he was too. Until that stupid giggle returned. Made Kaia look away first. She thought it was her own giggle honestly, but it was Jaylin.

Back against a pier leg. *Flagpole with no country.*

Left, broken, and forgotten. Storm ruined, and rising up from the sand. Kaia swayed with her gaze hit the top. Following it back down to Jay.

Small baggie in her hand, pouring into the bottle they'd shared.

Kaia still smiled, but mostly because she forgot how to turn it off.

"Told you. *Dangerous.*" She said it like a joke. But Kaia was wondering if she meant the pier or the bag. And… "*told her*"—told her—what?

"What is that?" Kaia's foot suck into the cool sand as she adjusted her body, turning to see better.

"I meant him." Jaylin toyed. Something feline behind it still.

Kaia watched the little powder slowly trickle through the vodka. Waves and sinkholes in the liquid as she swirled them together. Powder disappearing like it hadn't even been there. "Okay. What's that?" Kaia asked again, fighting imagination telling her something bad.

"What's what?" Jaylin laughed.

Kaia hesitated—she didn't even know where to start. Wasn't even sure what she thought it was the longer Jaylin pretended it wasn't real.

And it wasn't that Kaia believed her, it was just hazy. Staring and staring and soon enough, she was just annoyed at Jaylin but couldn't say why.

Just had this feeling, thought, of looking at someone—watching the mouth move, but words in red painted the sky. Lies, and lies.

But what about? Kaia fell into it. Watched the way the liquid swayed when she tipped it to her mouth again.

"You want some more?"

"Mmhm, I—I think I'm okay."

Another look of disgust, but no second chance this time: "Suit yourself, lightweight," and she was on her way. Slipped into the crowd again, swinging her bottle like a balloon in the wind.

Something about it stung. And Kaia stayed planted for a long breath.

Fire dancing in the corners of her eyes; a man and a face throbbing behind the flame, too. Propped against driftwood; haze blending him down just enough for her to fill in the missing details.

Kaia, empty-handed and alone. But not invisible—w*atched.* The pressure of his stare into her side was chewing her limbs raw.

She eventually looked, and he—mouthed, *finally.*' Looked down to the empty space next to him. And back to her.

It wasn't code. It was obvious and she shifted awkwardly. *Obviously.* Probably looked like a deer in headlights looking around and back the way she came. Because there was something she was forgetting. Something as blurred as the fire-dancers. And.the driftwood, the seat— it looked comfortable. He had one hand on a beer, other in the air. His finger pulling, *come here*; her mind whispering, *walk away.* Body screaming, but not violently. Pleasantly. Excitedly.

A cat and mouse. Smiling a little, rolling her eyes to keep it playful but unconsciously straightening her spine and popping a hip.

Must have walked, having found herself on the other side of the fire above him. Not a dream, not the past.

Just turned the lights off and said: *go.*

letting the body choose where. Kayden patted his hand down on the sand close to his lap. Kaia looked out to the crowd one final time.

Time. T-I-M-E. Or, E-M-I-T. Could also be M-I-T-E. Like *might.* Like *might* be okay. So she sat. Further back than where he'd told her—*asked her*—but she sat. Blurted immediately, "not mad at me?"

But could hear her own slur and it was wicked. Made her giggle. Moreso when he responded relaxed, comforting.

"For what, babydoll?" And when his slur mirrored hers. He stretched behind him—long, and solid and sexy—flipped a lid on a cooler and pulled out another bottle.

Kaia swallowed but it felt too dry when he mumbled, "hey, where were we?" Cracked it with his teeth. Again. Kaia just pictured his tooth snapping instead. Wasn't sure how she'd respond. And she wasn't sure whether he was fucking with her or not when he started to pour it out slow.

Stopped midway, reaching into his jean pockets—everyone but the right one first—groaning about it. Log whining under his bracing.

Eventually made his way to a small and familiar little baggie. Like the shows maybe. She'd seen it before. Kaia looked out again.

Crowds had definitely thinned, but still lively. So likely they spun. Maybe if she walked she could find Leti easier.

Maybe she couldn't get up. Maybe she'd get lost. Or maybe it was safest here until the fires went still and the beach cleared space.

And then what—? Back to the motel? Nothing for tomorrow yet, so just leave like it never was? Kaia turned back to Kayden, waiting with baggy in hand. Eyes slow and voice—not quiet sloppy but on its way.

"Hey Doll—? Pay attention to me. Now."

Entire brow lifted, "No misunderstandings, yeah?" Shoving into the baggie. Pulled a piece out and broke it under control.

Small, round thing. Pill. Moved casual but seemed intentional.

Consideration? She wasn't sure what to call it.

But maybe that's the natural order of things—natural way to experiment. Not in some stingy basement or dark concert hall.

But there, in town, surrounded by people. Surely hospitals nearby should the worst happen.

Kayden dropped it into the bottle and it fizzed slow when he lifted it for them both to watch.

Small, little moon thing in broken pieces too.

Took a slow, deliberate pull off the bottle next.

He was either very strategic, or a product of coincidence combined with circumstance. Mimicking her game from earlier; swallowing slow and heavy looks.

It wasn't attractive one way or the other, but the proximity had her body aching. Feeling the dance like an emotional replay. The heat, movement, euphoria—all new and experimental.

Kayden reached the bottle over to her. A gentle touch that time but it felt like a blaze. His smile a seduction. And his offer—a choice.

And he was leaving it to her. "What is it?"

Maybe surprised she asked, but no devilish grin, no pressure. Kayden seemed calmer. *Cooler.*

He tilted the bottle for show again. "Oxycodone IR—half of a 10mg," Factually. Like it wouldn't bother him one way or the other.

"I don't think I've tried that."

"Drinking with Jay?" He tilted his head sideways but she wasn't sure she understood. "Does that mean no?"

Shrugged. Stalling. Because she didn't know what it meant.

He scooted in an inch and leaned in. Not close enough she could feel him, but enough to talk over the kids behind them. "It's a pain pill. Doctors give them out like candy, Babydoll. But up to you." Sitting back then, "I'm just gonna vibe. Fuckin' day like today huh—? Join if ya want." He gently held the bottle again.

But did that mean she could only join through the bottle; or was she ok to sit there now? And does she ask about the day? Or—*Stupid.*

"What's it feel like?" she said instead. Equally stupid but already free.

His arm lowered, but wrist and bottle rested on her knee. Lazy like. "You'll feel drunker. I dunno, *good..*? Sleepy. Awake. Sad. Horny if I'm lucky, but why don't you relax a little and find out?"

She readjusted her clothes—baggy, swallowing her whole like she didn't quite belong.

He wasn't rushing her, but she felt rushed. And had he said it outright—*take this, do this,* she would've fought him harder than before. But to do what she wanted. To be what *he* wanted, where she wanted, just picking her trouble instead of trouble picking her...

Maybe he would get that kiss.

Kaia glanced back toward the bonfire she'd left her sister at. Toward the safer orbit, more visible as the crowds drifted out. And maybe she never really was lost.

Maybe that was just an excuse too.

Someone shifted and through the bodies Kaia caught a glimpse of Leti. Laughing, tucked close between Mikki, Cachí, and the damn Tideman.

Kaia almost got up. But she was wanted here, and maybe still invisible there. Firelight soft around Leti. Unburdened.

Kaia hesitated. Looked back to Kayden then, hand no longer resting, but holding her knee—head back, eyes closed.

And like he sensed her watching, a side peeked open and closed again. One side smiled. "Don't matter to me, babydoll. But what else you want?"

And that was it. Because she wants it to matter. It wasn't the drug she wanted. It was the permission she needed.

He offered it first. Nice and warm...

So she chose to reach back.

the Faux

MUSSEL BEACH
00:18:47:33

|XX|

Jaylin sauntered back into the circle like she owned it. A sensual, "*hi boys,*" as she closed the gap.
Stood there and blocked the flame—
neck of her bottle hooked between two fingers like it was an accessory.

"Seat still mine?" She flipped a sideways point toward Cachí and a side check to Leti. Cachí didn't grace her with an acknowledgement. Was sitting—arm strung over a bent knee, fencing her out on one side while facing in to Leti.

"Ignore this one," he mouthed. Both fighting back a smile when neither broke contact. An un-officiated stare down.

Leti didn't know why or what really—but felt herself settle back into the circle. Guards—not down, but lowering.

Mikki keeping peace, Dante at their backs. Somewhere between guarding and enjoying the view.

"Okay, rude." Jaylin put her free hand on her hip. Popped it sideways. "Cachí I need to talk to you—come, please."

Slurs blurring her tongue. Wave in her step not from the sand.

Leti clocked Dante shifting; cranking his neck back to get an unobstructed view of her before chuckling and settling back against his log.

Mikki was more like Leti in that moment than anyone else. But Mikki's hand rested on Dante's bicep when he postured harder. Muscles tense.

She pinched him as he laughed.

"You wanna go for a walk?" Cachí—still staring—and pulling Leti back to him like a magnet. Voice warm and tempting.

Leti opened her mouth to answer—Jaylin beat her to it.

"Sure are a rude bunch, aren't you? *Hi, Mikki*," with such venom. Voice climbing: "Get up Cachí I need to talk to you."

Dante tilted back again when Mick's hand slide from his arm. Crossing over her chest and her spine turning a little in.

Both her and Leti subtly turned out like they no longer wanted to be here, but defensive like they will if they have to be.

Forty seconds ago it was peace. Annd Dante *knew* Mikki hated fights.

And Jay was there looking for one.

Took him from slightly amused to formally done quick the moment the cold touched where Mick's hand had been.
Dante's eyes slide back to the water, body slack now. Relaxing into release over restraint. "Looking forward to your dad's trial coming up, Jay-Jay. Am I seeing you there?"

She took four steps around Cachí to be in front of Dante.

He smiled but wouldn't be moving. She's stupid —nah, *crazy*—enough to swing sure, but as small as she is, as drunk—the man could sigh and she'd stumble away.

"Oh. Now that's ballsy," she cooed.

Dante—strapped for the fight she wanted, just maybe didn't expect. But the whole picking on people your own size thing—using daddy's shadow, not sure where that puts her, but not with Mick.

Jay had the confidence of a chihuahua though. So, *why not*—Dante smirked, and said, "You remind me of a chihuahua."

And her silence made him feel accomplished. No cute voice or sweet smile. Just dead, hollow, *drunk* eyes. Memorizing every piece of sand as if Dante soiled it.

Eventually nodded like she'd only then convinced herself how she wanted to respond, but it was Leti who chimed in to everyone's' surprise.

"Trial—Dad thing explains, *a lot*," to Cachí quietly—though plenty loud.

"The fuck did she just say—to me?" Less docile dealing with another woman. Cachí smiled, but his shoulders shifted as if broadening the fence between Leti, the inner circle, and Jaylin.

Mikki sat up taller against her knees and as soft as possible, "Jaylin, you should go."

Leti knew who said it and why—but it still felt directed at herself. Jaylin snapped her neck toward Mikki with her words.

"Bitch was I—" Both the boys cuttin' in—

"*Ay—*"   "*Nu-uh*"

Voices sharp and louder, but otherwise unphased. Closer to taking bets than feeling threatened.

Leti knew better—but still felt like one of the sharp corrections was meant for her.

Neither she, or Jaylin moved much after the barking.

Jaylin glared at Leti a moment longer than she should have before she spit back against her teeth—a hard *tsk* sound.

The bottle lowered to her side and back to Cachí : "I guess I'll just see you when your boyfriend's not babysitting. Nights still early."

She took a long swing, turned her head down to Leti. "You must be new." Poured an even longer one into the sand beside her.

Pour was slow too—Cachí getting up annoyed. Mikki—realizing, reached for a log and tossed it on the flame behind Jay.

Knocked the wood into a shimmy and sparks in the air. Droplets for embers. *Bitch.*

The fire cracked.

The sand soaked the vodka, and Jaylin made her graceless exit, patting Cachí on the head before he was fully up.

No one really said anything until Dante just started laughing. Not hard. But plenty enough to make them turn and chuckle too.

"Well, that's always a pleasure." Mikki—shaking her head and leaning back into Dante some. Dante's foot shaking subtly the minute she did.

Leti tracked Jaylin as she slipped away—just enough of a disruption to make it stagnant; and the kind of person who left thumbprints on everything. And could be heading back to mark up her sister.

Leti didn't dislike her—didn't know her enough to. But she wanted to remember the face, and wanted to avoid it.

"So," Leti turned to Cachí.

Blocking the, '*I should have said this or that*' out and reclaiming the warmth between the circle. "Didn't you say something about s'mores?"

Laughter threaded their conversation with ease and warmth—Jaylin was long forgotten—and Mikki was making sounds of agreement as soon as someone uttered "*s'm—.*"

"Ah—she remembers," Cachí gleamed, stretching over and behind the driftwood before Dante eventually chucked him the JanSport.

Unchanged. Against the log. Partially for comfort—mostly to keep him up.

"You—"Cachí paused as he waved the bag over, caught it, and reached for skewers off to the side.

Soft shadow of a tattoo flashed under his shirt; kissing the edge of his hip and up his side—Leti looked away; too quickly to be casual but made eye contact with no one.

Couldn't be embarrassed that way.

"You can tell everything about someone," Cachí continued, voice half-dramatic, half-teasing, "by how they build a s'more."

Leti raised an eyebrow. "Oh yeah?"

"Yeah," Cachí shrugged, giving her a slow, deadpan glance.

"Do tell," Dante droned, eyes closed. Full beer in hand gone warm.

"Stackers are repressed. Burners have rage issues. Raw eaters are sociopaths."

She laughed—really laughed which he lit up at each time. Particularly when he caused it. "Okay so me then?" she nudged. Teasing—but not.

Cachí tilted his head, pretending to consider.

"Bets on a slow toaster," he said finally, voice dipping low and warm. "Still cooking, still figuring it out—but hot to the touch and sweet."

Leti flushed—not from flirtation, exactly... Hell maybe it was. But there was a kindness to it. He was just—simply, kind.

Like Sam. But better.

Leti's Sam. Not Kaia's. And there was a disarming weight to being seen without being judged.

Across from them, Mikki watched with a small, knowing smile—seeing something rare crack open in real time.

"You know," Mikki said after a beat, gaze slipping down to Dante. They couldn't get any closer if they tried. "Matí would've liked her," and it made Dante twist inside.

Not sure whether he agreed or not—not sure if he was right to. The fire shifted again. And something settled over the group. Not awkward—just heavier.

"Who was Matí?" Gently. Smile shrinking into something smaller because she didn't know the full weight of asking. But she respected it enough not to pretend.

"Matías," Cachí scraped his thumb through the sand. "He's—why—we are what we are. I guess," now like he was the one arguing himself.

Everyone waiting—letting him have the honor. *Curse.*

"He was my brother."

Was. Leti felt the pressure change—predicted the sad ending before it arrived. Mikki's admiration. Cachí's weight. Dante's silence with eyes now open. She didn't have to imagine; she thought Kaia was gone for eleven months.

But before she could ask how—or whatever was working its way out—as mouth opened, Cachí shrugged half a shoulder and shook his head.

"Anyway. Long time ago." Pulling at the marshmallow bag like they'd been on pause and someone hit fast forward.

That was pain there. An open wound trying to heal. And it was also someone with a door and a lock saying don't go in yet. The joke Kaia made about having there be two of her— felt a little funnier now.

"Alright, so," Cachí organized the troops, stabbing mallows with sticks and handing them out.

Sometimes people just need to speak it—taste how it sounds before they commit to more. And he didn't want to commit. Not to the past.

But, funny that—neither did Leti.

Cachí plucked a marshmallow from the bag, turned it in his palm like a worry stone, then held it out. "Leti, *cariño...*"

That word becoming one of her favorites now.

"Let's see who you are..."

the Fable

MUSSEL BEACH
00:18:03:15

|XXI|

The fire pulsed like breath against her skin, swaying with it.
Stitched between the sea and the sky—too loose to care.
Jaylin's grin blinked in and out of the firelight.
The sand slipping under her feet.
Smoke curling and sweet against her tongue.
The night folded around her like a stranger's hug—
felt, but unclear. There now as they sway.
Somewhere, someone called her name, too.
The music. The sensation.
Hands against the body as they danced.
Body didn't feel like hers. Skin felt alive.
The name—maybe hers too, calling.
Maybe Leti. Maybe memory or logic or time.
Time. Both too far away and too far gone.
Because Kaia was floating—back and forth.
Breath against her neck like wind under her wings.
And the tide, whispering beneath it all, reminding her—fly.
Because the tides coming in. And it won't only pull you back out.
It will pull you under.

They walked along the tide, shoes in their hands, the sand clinging cold between their toes.

The fires were thinning behind—music softer now, broken by the push and pull of the ocean.

They weren't talking much. Didn't need to. But every so often, Cachí would kick at the foam curling around his ankles, mouth twitching toward a smile he wasn't ready to let loose.

"You ever miss it?" Leti asked eventually. "Back then? When it was just...all of you?"

Cachí shrugged, glancing up at the stars swinging slow over them. "I don't know. Some of it."

He was quiet for a beat. "Matías was just..." drifting. Forehead wrinkled, fighting for the right words before an earnst huff of a laugh.

"So I missed my prom," he smiled, half turning to her. "Stupid thing, some girl too." Shrugged. "I had a date. Corsage. Rented the damn tux and she bailed the night of."

A ghost of a laugh. "Cried about it. Like an idiot. Matí heard me. I thought I was quiet." He didn't say it like he was embarrassed. Just—*true*.

Leti stayed silent, letting him steer the memory open slow:

Cachí, seventeen, curled up on his bed in a suit that didn't fit right. Corsage still in the plastic box like something already dead. Parents downstairs, TV buzzing through the walls; him upstairs, wrecked.

And Matí—twenty-one, already carrying the weight of the world. Didn't say a damn word. Just made a few calls.

Not even really Cachí's memory. Kayden told it best—the way he always did—painting their bad ideas in fire and grin.

Said Matí met him outside a busted Ross. Kayden already pacing like a caged thing, and Matí—*we need help*, Matí had said. *It's Cachí.*

Calm like asking for a lighter.

Kayden smiled—didn't even ask what. Dragged Mikki out of the house and said, *Drive. Matí and Cachí need us.* Eager.

Primed for anything, and prepped for war. No idea he was about to play dress up though he wouldn't have cared.

Just wanted to fuck up—or fuck with—anyone who tried to fuck up his. Not friends, not family, not anything—*but his.*

His to protect. His to keep safe. And his to make laugh.

It was chaos after that, Cachí had said.

Kayden picked a fight with an employee—loud and fearless—getting knocked around enough to turn heads while Matí slipped four tuxes under his arms and peeled out the back like he'd done it a hundred times.

And Kayden—blood in his mouth, fire in his laugh with every punch to his face. He wasn't trying to hurt the guy—but could of.

All still just a game. Giant taking punches like Hershey kisses. Then Matí, rallying the troops back together—*¡VAMOS, pendejada!*

Mikki in the car out front—mask on her face because it was exciting. But scary too.

Kayden rolled to his feet, sprinted—sirens already popping off in the distance. Fight, *disturbance.* Not three little shits, four cheap tuxedos, and a time of their life.

"It's one of the last couple memories I have of Matí. A favorite."

Cachí slid it in between Kayden's eyes and Matty's grin. Because by the time they hit the car, Kayden was howling; Matí barely breathing.

Mikki screaming at them behind a ski mask—*hurry hurry, get in, it's not funny!* But laughing regardless.

Just three best friends on the way to grab the fourth. Stealing what they thought was only time and laughs.

Because if it's not them picking on Cachí—not them giving the waterboarding in the pools, or the welts with the towels; not them with the wet willies, spitballs, and doggie piles; not them beating on him, then it was a problem.

They rolled through the city, windows down, stealing air. Liquor store run—*paid for that one though*—Cachí raised his eyebrow to Leti.

No reason.Just to look maybe, and then he went on:

Then even Dante—back before he changed—apparently quite the dancer. Didn't brag though..Just knew how to sweep them off the feet and wasn't shy about it. *Pre-military. Pre-leaving them.*

Leti tagged it but didn't pry. Another story for—hopefully—another night. A small moment of her own buried beneath his. *Hope.*

It'd been away awhile now.

Cachí had went on: *Mikki in the front—swapped as they grabbed Dáni.*

Dragged a stolen suit jacket over her tank like she'd been born to wear it. Pulled the slacks to her hips—found a safety pin and eventually jammed in like a damn hero.

Then she was calling every girl she knew: *I have someone I want you to meet.* Cachí would have thrown her phone out the window, he'd said, but didn't know at the time. Leti wasn't sure she believed it. Seemed gentle and shy so far.

Though anyway, he'd said. Somehow, someway. By midnight, half the senior class met them in Golden Gate Park. Tuxes stolen. Hearts hammered but loose.

A youthful buzz—silly, light—back when they drank to feel like adults. Not to avoid it. He remembered the knock. No—*the banging.* The other two waited, but Kayden and Matí—? Thundering through the house, past the parents—

　　　All good, don't worry about it—

Up the stairs like the goddamn cavalry charge. Cachí laughed. Leti could feel the warmth radiating from memory alone. She could picture it vividly too. Fun and—*familiar.* Sibling love and war.

"I didn't even have time to grab my Jordans."

She smiled. So Kayden slammed the door open, hauled his ass up; pulled him away from the closet when Cachí heard the noise, got up quick, and pretended to be doing something.

Sorting. Maybe. The bullshit you do to hide your weak. *Or whatever.* Next thing he knew—Carted down the stairs, and not carefully.

Another laugh from someplace safe, but Matí ran back for the damn sneakers—corsage too, which he threw at Mikki with a wink and a kiss.

Not like Cachí wanted the damn thing anymore, right? And so just like that, they were on their way.

Music quiet though trying. Busted up speakers blowing back at the commotion. Eventually someone used their car which killed it later, but it got the people through.

The longer the night went, the louder it got—other speakers, laughter, chatter—people spilling out of cars like they'd been waiting for someone to say it was okay.

Cachí remembered dancing with Mikki; remembered forgetting the girl who left—wasn't even really a girlfriend. *Just an embarrassment.*

A loss of trust in himself maybe. Because, again, *familiar.*

"Yeah I don't know anyone who could have pulled that out of thin air the way my brother did."

My brother—soft on the tongue, delicate to the ear. The word just sounded more vulnerable than the others.

"Ended better than if I'd gone to the stupid dance, at the stupid school," he nudged her shoulder with his elbow. Hands loose and relaxed in his pockets.

They'd reached the end of the bonfire stretch now. Just ocean and sky.

It left Leti with a pit in her gut, despite the warmth in her heart.

Cachí smiled small, almost to himself. "Anyway," he said, scuffing his toes deeper into the wet sand.

"More people came. Said it was better. And even more came."

Leti smiled too—not about the words. Just the weight of them being shared with her. And like the tide, the memory rolled in, and went back out; only a moment to remember.

She gulped, looking around. Caught in the moment, but tethered to reality—water swallowing sand until it disappeared behind wooden dividers and seafoam.

The night was getting colder; the heat of the fire, the warmth of the crowd—it leaked into the dark until only puddles were left.

Puddles they could see; laughter they could isolate and listen for.

Cachí straightened up, scanning the shadows ahead. Just enough of a shift to change the air. Leti was visibly more distressed in tiny movements.

The indent on the outside of her cheek when she chomped from inside.

The stretch in her sleeve with she hooked her fingers and opened-closed them while hiding. "Kaia got her phone?"

She couldn't even look at him now. Almost an entirely different face from the one who'd gleamed up to him moments ago. Longing for more memory and time, even daring to show him pictures of some art. Leti just shook her head at the sand now.

Hugging herself tight enough to hold her elbows.

"Ay—*cariño, todo bien*. Party always rolls on."

Words low and slow, but reassuring. "I'm pretty confident I know where they're at."

She felt his hand briefly on her shoulder. An awkward apology and even weirder stretch after, maybe pretending he didn't mean it.

Leti shaking her head, "no I'm sorry. My stupid sister." Her heart kicked, because *at least she's alive*— "I actually really loved that story..."

He put a gentle hand into the air; *don't even worry about it.* Eyes that said, *I know.* "Todo bien. Just a fireside story to keep your mind busy."

Scanning the area, a lot of other faces he knew were missing too. But not missing. Just not here.

"I got three places in mind," he added. "But betcha a dollar it's the first."

His feet stayed planted, sinking into the sand. Waiting on her warm eyes to come his way again.

No rush; no words in the meantime. Just waiting.

She peeked first. Busted looking, and then turned her face up. He was almost insulted by the mask she tossed on, almost as if it was too obvious.

"I'll bet ya' five she's not." Playful. *Light.*

And hoping to be anything but a burden. Just the tide, and the memory of music, corsages, and better times being washed out.

Because Kaia was gone. Again. Like always. And like every time before.

Three fucking hours; phone in the car. Sometimes it was amazing how something so beautiful, could be destroyed so fast.

Leti's jaw ticked—anger swelling where worry used to sit. Let her dance her way into the dark. And find her own damn way back. Because Leti had other places to be. Other things to do. At least—she wanted to.

But heart still ached. The panic Kaia put to ease earlier in the bathroom was knocking. But Cachí helped. Listened for her breath to quicken. Or stop. Would give her another memory when she did.

Cachí grazed her forearm, tipped his chin toward the dark. And they turned toward whichever way they came—or to whatever came next.

Leti breathed in his scent, and his calm. At least if nothing else would hold steady, the space between them did.

the Fervent

|XXII|

The car swayed under too many bodies. Kaia tried to sit up, but she dissolved; slumping sideways. Everything so bright. So fast.

Kaia couldn't tell who was talking.

Or what was funny. Just that everyone kept laughing like they were high on the same inside joke. Some small SUV maybe.

Or VUS—

SVU—*whatever they're called.*

She didn't want to try to remember. Like wearing a life jacket and trying to go down into the quiet. But it won't let you down—not when you're prepared. Because something kept yanking her back. Arms around her neck—not like threat, like affection. Squeezed and held.

"Leti?"

Heat made breath heavy. Noise made sound sharp. But she sank back into the softer, familiar bass. Like a heartbeat. Deep, through the hazy.

Guy to her right—she thinks. Unfamiliar. Only two voices familiar—maybe more, maybe music. *Maybe nothing.*

"My—mouth. Is dry." Humid breath—Cinnamon. *Vodka.*

Knew her smell and sound more than her face. Face made blue and hairy. *Jaylins. Bluejays.* Kaia reached up to the face on her shoulder. Made another sound when she nibbled onto her finger and laughed.

"Jaylin," A warning then from beside her. *Jaybird.*

Kaia's leg tensed under a burning hand. Relaxed just above her knee. Reminder: *Still here.*

Here where the breeze is warm and the birds kiss the collarbone. A brush of skin maybe.

"Jay—you're not cute. Back off." A pause.

The hand on her thigh came and went. "Quit being a fuckin' harlot."

Sounds like Kayden—*not our hands, not our words, not our realm*—

But they're so warm. Made sense. Kaia smiled.

The dance. The power. Her own hands skirting the top of her thigh to meet the hand there. She felt him look. So she didn't. But light, soft, and so playful—someone else looked for her.

A hand ran through Kaia's hair too. And she was pretty sure it wasn't her own. But she still had the other one—*only three?*

"If you don't cut the shit, I'm leaving you on the corner. Where you belong."

"What—?" A giggle. "Daddy Dante got you all worked up—hey, haha!" Something shifted around Kaia again. Quicker too.

She heard skin on skin. Tussling. But not her—nothing to do with it. Laughter—hissing, growling—angry animals.

Claustrophobic—white walled—late night, emergency psych evals. *Draw the animals—Mom & Dad & Leti too, signed at the bottom in red ink.* Who are you, who is he, she and she—

They're moving so fast.

Kaia's eyes widened to see through the window. Were they fast, or was she slow?

He—*he who, he him*—was a blur.

Spoke forward. Voice gone, because she didn't know that one. Didn't like hearing that one so close. Not when everything spun.

Spins. "I feel—sick."

Because Kaia could smell then cinnamon weave in and out of reach. The body next to her spinning to look and maybe even yell. Got so loud Kaia put it outside with the stray dogs. The unfamiliar—speaking, laughing. Another girl like her maybe—shot gun.

 Shot guns—bang—dead.

Kaia leaned back. Let her neck fade. "Nice try..." Then giggled.

She didn't like it still—normally caused such panic—but she just, didn't feel it right now.

Hiccups behind her, that liquid purge smell in the air. Vodka and toxicity. She could feel that still. In her throat.

Unhappy in her stomach, but unwelcome out through her mouth.

"D, hand me that—" *Kayden.*

Kaia's lips smacked together, crackling. She was so thirsty. Felt like petrified dust. On her tongue. Litter box.

Her eyes flicked between the vents on the roof. Then quick to the front. Reminder—*it's a car, not a room.* And there's more than just them three.

Because—back on the vents again—Kaia was a little concerned how much that intrusive thought scared her.

Being in a room alone with...*something.* And being the weakest one.

Her head shot up with a gasp. She didn't want to be weak anymore.

The thought of hands pulled behind her back alone almost leading her to hyperventilate. Eyes in the rear view on her like she's strange. Eyes cutting sideways from the right and left like she's dramatic.

Overkill.

"Sorry." Little bit of slur, lotta' bit regret. Wasn't shit to apologize for.

Crossed her arms with a embarrassing lean before righting again. *Always too much for everyone—*

Right side—he swigged back something clear. Almost choked laughing at something again—something from the front she didn't hear.

Couldn't see too far from view either. Heavy eyes. Sleep or booze. The little floating moon.

She grabbed his knee on accident, "give me that—please," leaning over Mr. Right for his right—the bottle at his feet. *Right-right-left?*

"Kayden," Jaylin again. "Don't be mad at me, wanna talk?"

Kaia tilted back—more vodka. *To push the old stuff back down.*

Probably a dream anyway—most of them fucking are. *Fly.*

Jaybird went on, whispering: "I'm a great listener." *Like the Evals, like the animals*—Mr. Right reached for Kaia's bottle and she bear hugged it.

Twisting towards the other two, still holding tight.

Kayden plucked it from her so hard and fast she spent a minute wondering if she'd apologized yet, and trying to remember what she did.

Just this—feeling like guilt. Or—something. Wanting even a stranger to say, '*you done good.*'

"Jaylin—one more time, girl." Slapping her hand from his bouncy bun. Kaia reached for it too then. Same slap to the hand she got.

Felt even worse than him snagging the bottle. She wanted to sink. No longer a passenger. Only a passenger seat. But he turned to her next: *A seat cover that's caught.*

"Enough," he warned. At her, to her, direct.

Is she bad though—ignoring it and letting the words slip and slide between the folds of her brain. Birdie watching from her perch, too. Kaia's head lifted off the backrest.

For a moment. Ears back off when the bird and the tree popped off arguing again. Vulgar and hateful like sport.

Kaia's head meant to tilt, but toppled onto her shoulder weak. Jay snagged the bottle from him now. Drank.

Tried to come over, and he'd turn—shoulder's seemed broader in here— holding her by her head. Wasn't effective, but honestly—Kaia thinks he might have thought it was funny.

Just a glisten in the eye.

Kaia still stared, eyes stuck open maybe. She felt them moving before registering that she saw them. Hands swatting at each other like a couple somewhere between fight and forgive.

Little tap, tap, tap sounds.
bird feet like rats, campsites, and crumbs—
Ava didn't like birds. *Mom just couldn't see the birds.*

But bird or mole—popped up behind her again and Kayden swung. *Whack-a-Miss.*

A Miss. A girl? Miss—"Blunder," Kaia started cackling again. "Down unda'." Covered her mouth and bit her tongue.

He wasn't her anchor—she felt more like his. Then vodka and cinnamon the flash flood—"Close to Kaia—close to your little D-boy?" Pulled on his ear. "That it, handsome?"

That was definitely it.

 Kayden's lungs turned off—Kaia froze. Like an eerie undertow just caught hold of the group.

"Jaylín, if you mention Dante or Cody or Cachí, Mikki—"

"How's about Matías then?" Jaylin cut in quick.

Scuffling again. But why is it always everybody else's name but them? Leti, her.

Didn't want to even picture Leti while Kaia was down—knowing how isolated they were together. Awkward introductions and lunch bullies at school—mean girls for means sake.

Just more inside things, reminding her she's out.

Head came up slow and struggling. Hand bumped his knee too. Watching, watching—*always watching.*

Kaia saw the bottle, reached again and he'd snagged it before she'd even leaned back up. "The fuck did I say, doll?" Face flat. Then he offered it with that same blankness. Kaia wasn't sure whether or not to reach, so she did— slow. *Tsk'ed* at her before holding her hand onto his thigh and drying the bottle from the inside.

Dropped it and slid his hand behind Kaia's neck to lean her in close. Every move, look, breath, a seduction—and she knew.

She just didn't know why she still wanted to run heady first into it willing. "Want some now?"

Yes. Close enough she *did* get some more. Almost. And she shook her head but still licked her lips—swarming with more then a buzz note even sure which was which. When he smiled, her stomach tightened and as much as she wanted to blame him and the temper—she'd pretty confident it was her shivering. Because trembling sounds too scared.

And Kaia isn't scared.

"I thought so," he chuckled. Hand coming off, but in a slow slide but was disturbed when her body crowded and hair pulled. Jay jumped like she'd climb back over.

"Hey—ow—" "Damn JL, chill," *The Stranger.*

"JL? I'm Kaia—no, *Mikki.* Just kidding," sneering and leaning forward into Kayden. "Matías? Dante. *Dante. Who else Kade wanna cry about?* Cachí " Someone, somewhere growled but she didn't stop.

"My new rendition of Duck, Duck, Goose. Just for us."

Kaia's eyes closed like they collapsed. She wasn't a passenger. She was a passenger seat. And the bluejays wanted her spot.

"Jaylin. Keep pushing me, baby. You're not gonna like what I do with you." The car went still. Silent like death. Except Kaia.

Reached over the stranger—reaching for a window.

"Get off her—" "Don't start, Kade." Stranger.

Kaia looked up, closer than she meant only wanting air. He tilted her chin— someone else tilted her spine.

Kayden reached under her hoodie for her waistline like a handle. Pulled her ass back to the middle seat closer to him.

Room—car—swung. Then the window rolled down. Kayden's side.

"I—shed." Kaia's own head cocked and she tried again. "I need water."

"Here." Mr. Right, Mr. Strange. She grabbled with it desperately. Fancy bottle with a snappy-pop straw. Drunken stupor. "All yours, we got more."

"Thanks." Stubbornly. But not Kaia. Kayden. *For Kaia.*

She looked at him curiously. His breath short and hot like dragons on a chain, watching her. Swatting Jay.

Tipped back the bottle and, straight into gulping it down. And y*eah*—

Nothing overtly violent or chargeable really. But gulp and a half maybe— tequila came hurling out like vomit. Collectively every person made a judgmental sound of distain before laughing their asses off like *bullies;* car ride rated E for evil. *Not* Everyone.

She was so embarrassed she tipped it back more to block it out, better prepared for the burn.

"What's your fucking problem, D—*are you fucking kidding me?*" Peeled her back by the hoodie when she laid on her thighs to trade with her stomach. Or something. Everything spun.

Birds chirping in the back— *"don't do this, she's that, wah wah."* "Don't give her shit—Don't touch her again."

Something cracked out, and someone hissed before cracking back across Kaia and at Kayden. Wasn't from the back though—quick one coming in from *Mr. Wrong.*

"Did you—just..." Movement. Recognition loading retribution.

Kaia. *Kaia toes.* Wondering where her shoes ran to without her. But under Kayden—sandy. Smoky. Jaylin laughing behind her, *"get him!"*

Both the boys and even the passenger, a mutual—though off beat—chorus of '*Shut up Jay—Shut the fuck up—Shut up already."*

"And Kayden—touch *me* again, and you bes'hope they don't ever put me on your back—you understand me?"

Kaia looked up to him and stared. Only still thing in the car right then.

Te-kill-yuh. Because he's mean.

"Fuck's the matter with you? Piece of shits." Kayden again; contrast scalding. "You not see her sitting with me? Fuck bro, back the fuck off."

"Wah, wah, wah—" birds chirping and antagonizing from the back.

Kaia shook her head and scrunched her face when Mr. Whoever massaged onto her knee.

His cheeks were less round and friendly—Kayden watching furiously like he'd swing with her there or not.

They were antagonizing—Mr. Right-Wrong looked at her like that to poke at Kade. Because no one wants her—he didn't earlier. Not the stranger anyways.

Kayden was interested since the jump. Kaia was touching his cheek and he pulled back. Surprise? For her too. But he had anger too, though the heat burned less the longer they soaked in it. Car otherwise whispering as his mouth tightened to a line. But he didn't swat her like Jaylin.

Kaia's other hand actually mirrored her first, his eyes squinting like she was hurting him until the Bluebirds popped off again. Then something really was hurting.

The sharp giggled. "Aww…" Jaylin. Kaia was out of it but she knew she did something wrong before anything even broke. "Good job, Kade. Finally someone who'll treat you like the bitch you are."

"Stop the car." Kaia braced as Kayden tensed. He grabbed her wrists and lowered. Real sadness behind it. Not because he'd ever say, but because she could taste that too. Behind the vodka.

Kayden slide under her and she jolted next. Only touched her long enough to pull her back onto his lap though, rolling the window as she was propped between it and himself. Only so he could lash out at the other two again.

Though Kaia was happy just not to be centered. Even if smooshed. Because even the front was taking shots too—arguing, cornering her and the wall in front of her. Yelling at Kayden for yelling at Jaylin. Only making Kayden aim his words to the front next.

Kaia tapped his shoulder like it was a meeting. "Hey…" Whispered under their curses and hiccupped in his ear. Smiled like a cheese ball when he looked. Wore surprise, annoyance, a lack of confidence. Her eyes closed, tin tilted up and she showed teeth in the grin. "You—have pretty eyes."

Because she and Kayden—they could leave everyone else out this time. Have their own inside jokes and exchanges to cool each other off, or rile the other up like command.

He blinked in slow motion but then kissed her fast. Kaia wasn't sure if it hurt or if she was being sensitive, but he pressed to her jaw and chin hard. Just a long peck.

"Thanks." He mouthed. Maybe for the distraction?

He flipped her hair over her shoulder and looked her up from down. Her illusive excitement churned into doubt but still, she pulled towards him. When he still looked unsure, still kept his arms locked at that close distance, Kaia couldn't help but withdraw back in.

Against the window, wanting to believe it was liquor and mixed signals, but reading it as lack of interest. A punch to her ego.

Kaia mumbled from her chest and laid her cheek against the window, watching the roads slip by and streetlights hang, but this wasn't the bar—this wasn't downtown. This was residential.

That should have raised more of an alarm. The shouting too. Flags up but only skies of red. Kaia was wearily aware but leaned into it like a wild ride. And the shouting beside her? The shouting was good.

Shouting shows where the aggressive ones are. And which way they'll go.

Kayden—his lap *under* her—the lead voice now, so loud. "Shut the fuck up and sleep on the goddamn porch."

"Yeah? Suck my dick bitch." The stranger, or bully, or Mr.

But Kayden wasn't gonna' hit Mr. Darcy, he was going to fuckin' stab him. Not even for words, but for disrespect.

Give him an extra for Cachí's, too. And fuckin' Dante. Literally—everyone else picking at the scabs like he did something wrong. Like he wasn't just trying to forget it all and breathe tonight, too. But maybe Jaylin had a point, as he watched Kaia drop her head against the window.

Kiss felt weird, but...*closer to her, closer to them?* If they're already going to think it, what would it mean to just let it be true?

Kayden's body tensed when bitch in the back started chirping again. But to Darcy. As if Kayden wasn't there. "You know what I think is super funny, D?"

It wasn't going to be funny. Grabbed onto Kaia a little tighter when Jay leaned her tits over like they had any fuckin' play. Reached across to run her hands on Kaia too, but Kayden popped her hand hard enough to make Darcy look.

"Come on now, Little Jay. Leave him alone, tell me what's funny."

Half tempted to push her back by her face and see what he does; ready for a fight so goddamn bad.

"I just think it's super cute how Kade things he's a good boy now." Sing song until she turned snottier on Kayden. "Five minutes. You let him get you all bundled tight after five, dude?"

"Jaylin," Kayden warned.

"Hey..." Darcy. Tapping her shoulder.

Talking to her sweet, like a man with an actual fucking brain. He grabbed her and she giggled; playful objections as he pulled her over the back seat. "Don't!"

"That what your crying about," lighter and friendlier than Kayden could stand him, wrapping her up on his lap. Jealous the one thing she couldn't buy was attention. Having to watch someone else like Kaia get it *asleep*.

Darcy tried to placate the brat. Made Kayden feel good making her feel small right about then.

Jaylin smirked at Kayden like he gave a fuck and Kayden nodded at Darcy in response. Mutual, unwritten respect that had everything close to calm. Damn close to the house.

Until Kayden turned to Kaia; Jaylin spit, ready for round ten: "Not my fault Dante crawled up his ass and got com—" "*Stop the car*" "—fortable."

The disrespect. The constant nagging. Climbing.

"Stop the fucking car before I throw them out the goddamn window!"

"Where—" Kaia stiffened but was silenced when she was *placed* onto the center console like an urn.

Kayden tapped the front-passenger—not kindly. "Hold this for me." Patting Kaia's hip.

"Kayden?" Darcy, with reasonable concern.

Kayden waited for the car—not to *stop*—but to slow. And just enough. Darcy was more tense then him and Kayden couldn't blame him, because not even Kayden knew what he was capable of. Especially not anymore.

"Oooo, scary."

"'Iighht—stupid—fucking cow," he shifted to face her, Kaia's knees too involved as she backed up anxiously.

Darcy's hand was forward, hanging in the middle like a white flag and Jay? "Kayden, don't start shit. Please."

Darcy had Jay in the worst seat of them all. Lapped on him and between them both. Kayden breathing like a bull and facing her down for a charge; shoulders front to back. Debating physical harm while the little thing played too goddamn much.

Smiling, "thinks he's a muh—hey!" Darcy shook Jay once.

Hard, stern warning under Kayden. Maybe the only one in the car who sees how dangerous Kayden felt. Only one who could recognize the fear Kade had of himself. Growling at Jay: *shut the fuck up*.

Made breathing less hostile. Like it wasn't the world against Kayden while trapped in the car. Reminding himself of Kaia—looking both terrified but dazed. Fighting not to fade into the high despite running out of time sober.

Kayden let his shoulders lower.

Hands slid down from the seats as he shrunk into himself again. Trying to be less. At least until home and he could walk.

Kaia swallowed, following his lead and dropping her shoulders too. Eyes followed and softened again, but time jumped funny then.

Kayden felt it off. Too quiet. Watching Kaia relax before her eyebrows shot back up, fear back on. Kayden was confused—audio processing slower. Last ditch effort to protect himself maybe. To keep from hearing and feeling hurt, because Kayden was going to lean back. Hold Kaia again. Play with kisses until it felt right.

"*Pussy*" sliced through. High pitched on a woman's voice and Kayden was activated. Not by the word but the persistent hounding tonight.

The stalking, flirting, fighting, unwelcomed fucking touches. Couldn't imagine any woman in the world pulling this same shit without retribution that people backed *him* on.

But Jay gets away with it. And Kayden was fuckin' done. Popped and whipped the door hard enough the bitch driving finally hit the breaks like he meant it.

Houses, complexes, streetlights—*whatever*. Kayden lunged forward at Jaylin. Kaia went back into the dashboard from Darcy pulling forward and trying to get Jay out of the center.

Kayden already had both biceps though, leaning over as she spit profanities. "You're gonna wanna let me go. Now, Kayden!" Him louder, snapping back, 'not scared huh—how about nows—at her futile objection. "I said let me go!" Darcy started swinging hard, too. Making contact but Kayden couldn't feel it. Started backing out as the pavement finally stopped rolling.

Too hyper-focused on making a point just wasn't sure what yet but let himself run the motions to see where they led. Bordering dangerously close—not to suicidal—but to not caring.

And Jay kicked. Kayden mocked, "*oooo.*" Yanked her out and lifted her by hoodie and jean like a damn bag when she was out. Stalled a moment then, hearing Darcy flying out of the car, the driver yelling something about being stupid.

"I will kill you myself!" Jaylin kept on saying shit, front driver telling her to shut the fuck up too—everyone thinking he was maybe ready to do so much more when he wasn't sure. Standing looking six feet down with a gym bag in his hands.

Kayden got excited and recharged when he saw the dumpster. When Jaylin noticed where he looked—*smart girl, just dumb*—Kayden went for it faster.

"Don't-you-dare!" She was *shrieking*. "Darcy! *Help!*"

Darcy stopped giving a fuck when he clocked the bin too. Halfway around the car like Kadeyn had lost his fucking mind when really—he was just establishing a new boundary with his fuckin' bestie.

Beastie. "*Darcy!!*"

Leaning against the SUV, supervising. "I'm here for your life, babes—not dignity. Hope nothing's wet, but Kayden couldn't hear the rest when he lifted her higher and her blood curdling scream sliced up his ears and threatened to wake the neighbors.

Kayden already caught nearest house watching when she started screaming shit about assault and sending him back.

Hit like an axe and was a lot less fuckin' fun then. Had him disgusted and caught in the realization he probably knew but never wanted to consider she could lie and he's already so close to the edge, no one would reach to help. No one would believe him. Everyone against him tonight already and for her.

That made him livid enough to drop her on the curb and turn. Other option was to deck her, but that was counterproductive.

Darcy chuckled as they essentially swapped places, clapping Kayden on the shoulder as he passed. "You kids done? I'm tired."

Kayden stood in his door, turned impatiently. "You riding or staying?"

"What?" Stupid look on his face as he un-gracefully yanked Jay up, who was sniffling like maybe he still made his point despite not feeling satisfied.

Kayden said it slower: "Riding, or walking?" Adding, "that's not getting in this car" when Darcy still stalled.

"*That?*" More sniffling from Jay which they ignored. Couldn't tell if she was hurt or angry but he didn't give a fuck. Hoped for both.

"Kayden, come on dude."

"Staying then," Kayden answered for him.

Darcy turned to pace once. "*You* fucking walk—ya'll can sort your shit, fucking tired bro."

Kayden slapped the roof, "Kaia. Reach over; shut that door. Now."

"For fucks sake, Kayden. Quit bein' a petty bitch, we gotta' deal with her."

"*Hey!*" But she still didn't matter. Because this was something between them now. Kayden refusing to see how it was still Jaylin, because he couldn't fight her. But Darcy? "You haven't seen petty bro."

Darcy cocked his head; "You got something to—" "Yeah!" Kayden was ready. "*Useless* piece of shit, I said *walk*. Since you are fucking incapable of handling shit!"

"What the fuck are you—" "Let's talk about Miles bro, you treacherous fuck! Cody. "

"The fuck you mean? I don't control the goddamn tide and you said you didn't want—""Careful," Jay warned. No one sure whether it was to the guys, or the passengers. Kayden assessed the three inside; front two occupied and down each other's throat, but Kaia—little curtain of hair swung into view when he turned. Like might have seen someone there were he a little faster.

"Darcy let's go. I don't want to rid with a whiney bitch anyway," fearless still, and walking to Kayden. So point not made.

 He didn't budge but she started screaming again. "My fucking bag, you— you *prick*!"

"Kaia!" Kayden roared, but at Jaylin. "Gimme the bag," sticking his hand through the door , and lower You ain't soiling my seats anymore lil-'girl."

"You're as dumb as you are big. Cant please anyone, waste of my dads time, no good, simple—"

"Jaylin!" Darcy barked now too, snagging her bicep, snagging her bag, and backing her up. One of us defending you *after* your hit won't take away the damage. Shut the fuck up; let's go."

 "Good to see you again, Jay. Nice looked weird on you." Slamming the door shut behind him With a smile ear to ear. And the hang loose out the window because Kayden *finally* caught breath that wasn't salt, sea, or fuckin' smoke.

He turned a little, all the space in the world back there now and reached to Kaia, now taking Darcy's seat.

"Come here, baby-doll," while he pulled her in close.

the Falcon

ITINERANT | DALY CITY
00:18:13:29

|XXIII|

Dante dropped Mikki off first—radio humming low, old soul barely breathing through hushed speakers.

She didn't say much about his disappearance tonight; didn't say anything about Kaia MIA. Assuming Mikki remembered.

She popped the door with half a marshmallow still stuck to the cuff of her hoodie. The cheery and buzzed wobble cuter than anything.

Mick turned back to him to lean in; tried to give sultry but just gave drunk. "You, Detective, don't get into any shit without me. Kay? And my forehead kiss," leaning closer to tip her head and point at it.

Couldn't get any closer with her hand on her seat keeping her up. Dante laughed warmly; hadn't seen her like that since college.

Wiped his thumb on another marshmallow spot and shook his head. Gave her a soft peck on the forehead.

Nothing any more or less than it'd ever been.

So why did he feel so guilty?

"Thank you, Officer," as she swung the door and sauntered off. Dante watched her climb the steps onto the porch and into whatever passed for peace. He waited for the doors to lock. Waited for the hallway light to flip on. And still—waited a moment more.

When all seemed calm, he swung the SUV wide and headed the opposite way, rolling over a mess of speed bumps.

There was a gas station about three blocks down he could use to stall. Because once he got home, he knew he'd be unreachable and asleep.

Bug-haloed light, half-dead neon sign humming above as he went in. Not much to see, but the coffee was surprisingly clean.

Dante leaned against the hood sipping it with his eyes on the stars; not because they would tell him anything, but at least they were pretty to look at.

Stuck in a circling train of thought. Longer the phone was neglected, the faster it went and the more sick Dante became. Anxiety about—*whatever*. Because his best friend's girl shouldn't be complex.

Though how fucked was it he still called her his best friend's girl and not his best friend? Soulmate even, because she shared the same shit.

What would she even say? To hear Dante call her 'Matty's.'

...Or 'mine.'

Panic scraping his heart, guilt his brain; desperately jumping topics to Kayden next; another stupid guy, with another puffed up chest. Dante was the same tonight though.

Arrogant and picking fights because—*because that was going to change Kayden?*

And say it did. Was Dante going to *forgive* or *accept* him had he wanted back in?

Couldn't say. Especially now with a file on his desk and Cachí and Kayden's name waiting within it.

Dante'd let everything go to his head tonight. Outcomes from the conversation with Kayden were vast—but none of them good. He knew that going in. Could sit there and lie and pretend he didn't, but he did. Making a bigger target on Cachí's back; an interest or small one on the sisters.

And worse? Because Dante was *"protecting her."*

That fucking stung, because he used her. *An excuse* to get over to Kayden. Keeps telling himself: *no, it was Kayden putting hands*, but he was on the look out for Kayden long before Kaia had anything to do with it. She was just the noblest excuse.

And Cody was worse enough Dante didn't want to think it. Made him a shit man and a bad cop, because if Kayden had any sense, anything left in his possession—*gone now*. Or would be soon.

Dante wanted to hate him. Might have even needed to. Shaking his head and giving up on the stars to head back in the car. Gave the tire a sad kick on his way in and then settled slow.

Coffee in the cup holder. Napkin and water where it spilled. Long, cold stare through the window: rhinos, metal gated doors and propane for sale. Open. Available.

Like the fuckin' trap house. On public street.

Dante tossed a moment longer but when the name 'Mikki' crossed his mind again, he decided.

If Cachí's gonna' ignore him, Dante's gonna' drive by Kayden's on the way home. Have a looksy.

Dante groaned, still feeling unsettled and pulling his cell.

CACHÍ
> LETTY FIND HER? LMK
> KDN too.

Cachí and his new friends were playing hide and seek but... *Mikki.*

So Dante dug through his emails. Then deeper still, deciding on something else and searching for the number to a very specific person. For hope. Answer. Distraction.

For: Akira
> HOW MUCH WOULD A FAVOR COST?
        DEPENDS WHOS ASKING <
> CALL ME. D.

Uneasy chaos to his controlled chaos, but she had a damn incredible mind for tech. Kind of turned into one of those great secrets everyone knows, but doesn't admit, starting as fixing things here and there. Adding coding to the rookie's computers which Dante or one of the others would catch but still made her the coolest in her group.

Code name slipped out of her drunk at a retirement sendoff: *Peppa the Pig*, thinking she was the funniest goddamn thing in town. And at that hour, Dante agreed. But it didn't stop him from giving her absolute hell, calling her Peppa for the next month.

When her number popped up, he exchanged their series of greetings, gave her a half hearted run down of not a lie and not everything, so not true.

Cachí was involved with some new people. Any information she can find on them would be great. She didn't care why; she wanted *what.* Longest part of the call was negotiating.

She has a friend—no. *There's this one ex that*—no.
Couple parking and speeding—*eh, depends.*

She laughed it off and eagerly took a hanging IOU before pressing for details to search. Asked the last names which—he hadn't considered. Hadn't thought through *at all*, making him second guess *it all.*

Doubt himself. Wonder about Mikki. Frazzle about life while backing down and out with "my bad" and owning it, but she only *hmm'd* and *ha'd*.

Didn't answer. So, he waited. Dreaded when she came back too fast but should have been thankful. "Hey, you said Flin's new friends?"

Mentally correcting, *Cachíflin*, but saying, "yeah?"

She just went quiet again. May have even muted him before swinging back on line for times louder singing, "Dante! Baby boy. My man!"

Sounded complimentary but he suspected it was for herself. Confirmed when she started singing, "who's your favorite?"

"Oh is it even a question, Ira-*cariño*." Flat, but not intentionally.

"That was pitiful, but points for the pet name."

He chuckled from her joy and confidence. High and positive energy.

"Anyway. Last name, *Taylore*. With an '*E*.' T-A-Y-L-O-R-E. Social media baby. Always social media. Though not looking super active. Other one must be...Sister? 'Nother *Lore*." He started to answer but she was on the hunt; spoke over and too fast for him to try. "Give me like 20 minutes 'kay? Might not find anything if they don't got nothing."

"Yeah I know. But hey...Ira?"

"Hmm?" *But barely.*

"I know you got some friends of friends around Kayden, too. I'm uh, looking for him. As a civ though, no badge."

"No gun?" Taunting, but typing away.

"Ain't like that..."

She laughed enough that his hair rose, but she also ended it as quick as she started it. "Yep, k. Chat soon boo-boo." *Click.* Call log flashed; only light around before his dark, but generic, home screen showed.

Dante pulled Cachí's number again, edging on impatient.

> NOT FAR. CAN LOOP AROUND

Not an offer for help, but a threat to answer the goddamn phone. Cachí would recognize the difference.

Dante dropped his head on the seat again, but the phone chimed before it settled. *For fucks sake*—No rest for the wicked. And not Cachí. Not Akira, but *Mick*. Butterflies. Frustration. Complexity.

Dante set the phone down without reading it and closed his eyes again. Not sure how long his silence counted as si

"*Idiot.*" Dante clicked into it. Simple, sweet, to the point:

```
THANKS FOR THE RIDE, GET HOME SAFE. XOXO <
```

A message he'd seen a million times that he was now trying to ruin.

Cachí was next. Came in while the phone was still in his hand thankfully. Dante read that at once. But—not at all the one he wanted.

Simple, plain, one worded, '*no.* "'Shit," he'd muttered.

Weekend traffic and shit. Maybe whole crew just hasn't gotten in. Or stopped for food. What was the worst Kayden would do anyway?

The thought was supposed to chill him out, but not only was he hands on tonight, he was in public. Shameless. Wouldn't have expected him to grab anyone. Unless he fuckin' meant it. And that made Dante wonder what else he's possibly gotten comfortable with.

Dante's phone buzzed again. Akira sent a link, warned to use the laptop versus the phone too. "Sounds like we got something then." He was intrigued now. Inner child antagonizing back in a battle she didn't even know she'd walked into. He might not have been able to read Leti well at the fire, but he'd be able to now.

Dante reached under the seat for the laptop, popped it open across his knees and cracked into his email once booted up.

Loaded slow; he was quick to blame the location, but as it loaded in, it definitely wasn't the location. It was the depth of the emails.

FIRST. SUBJECT: TAYLORE, OLETTA SKYE.

"*Oletta*—?" "*Oletta*—?" he scrolled, worried she grabbed the wrong one but settled after scanning further. "*Iight*...what's Kaia's then?" He nodded slow as he went through it. Second email reading, Kiraia.

Date of birth, alias he recognized—so far so good. So far so *normal.*

The body of the message was a decent dump of mostly CPS notes and welfare checks. '*Normal.*' People weren't guarded the way Leti seemed because of fun pasts. He wasn't surprised *something* popped up. He was surprised how much.

The weight in it, slowly pressing down the further he read. And a hell of a lot easier to weave together with the fuller picture. Couldn't even get a read on the sister—on the move all night and now...

Dante cleared his throat. He flicked back to his messages while he had

```
    > THANKS
  K @HOUSE OFF WALLABY LN<
         MANSION. NITE<
```

He looked at it. Almost let the *K* drop go over his head. Exhaustion.

Or something.

> CHAT ABOUT UR FRIEND TMRW. THANKS

Didn't want to. But didn't expect the amount she gave. And didn't expect to feel so mixed up about just— *everything.*

He went back to his phone. Pulled up Mikki's text again. Took his time deciding an appropriate response. It was self-sabotage. He knew it too. So he did what they all tend to do—phone to face, number still known by heart—*Matí.*

And he just stared at the name on the screen. Wrote a lot at first. Ended up deleting everything, rewriting, and deleting again, scared. Scared someone would read it. Use it.

Understand it. So he settled somewhere in the middle. Not pouring open, but not holding it all in.

MATÍ
> IM SORRY HERMANO. KAYDE. MICK..
> AÚN TE NECESITAMOS

Five years later and Dante missed him as much as the first. And he let it ooze there. Piece by piece, breath by breath. He let his eyes rest. Leaned into the sting. And when he felt his breath was rhythmic, holding without a fight, he pulled up Mikki.

> HOME

Nothing more, nothing less. Then greedily reaching for his laptop—still under old gas station light—eager to read about anyone else's shit than his own. Maybe no better than Kade, just better at hiding it.

Blocking it out, and extending the view:

> **>>AK-50//SECURE_TUNNEL:*

> >>>>>*HANDSHAKE COMPLETING....* 000.00.A554K.50.8308

> >>*PLEASE STAND BY*
> >>*AK50 LOGIN ERROR: PLEASE TRY AGAIN*
> >>
> >> *AK50 LO.. -- / -... .- -..*   **

"Is that fucking morse?" Dante squinted, the words gone as soon as they came—pages lapping his screen as Akira possessed it in a weirdly bad ass way. Kept seeing, AK-50 pop up. Texted when the screen kept scrolling.

>NO PEPPA?

D. ROMERO ID# 00097315 – DC DIS005 |

** >> ENCRYPTION: ACTIVE (AES-256)
>> PROXY CHAIN: ONLINE [4 NODES]
> ----- 3 ----21000000000000000000000000000-----
[OK] ENTRY PERMITTED — FILE ACCESS INITIATED...
[AK-50 // SECURELINK OVERRIDE]
> INITIATING PROTOCOL: GHOST-SPLICE_7.4...
> AUTH KEY...█*ACCEPTED*█
> TUNNELING NODE[WA] >> BRIDGE[PNW] >> MASKING
ORIGIN
> PING: 192.88.99.0 — 45MS LATENCY — STABLE
> ENCRYPTION LAYER — STRIPPED
> HOST FIREWALL — BYPASSED
> DEPLOYING WORM: NULLTHREAD V2.08...
> SCAVENGING ORPHANED FILES...
> - HASH MATCH FOUND: 1481-44-LT
> - HASH MATCH FOUND: 1481-44-KT
> RETRIEVING ARCHIVE...

> -- DECOMPRESSING // █ █ █
> -- DECRYPT PASS: **█
> -- VERIFYING CHECKSUM...OK
> STREAM INCOMING — 4.92MB/S
> WARNING: CONTENT FLAGGED — JUV / CPS CROSS-LINKED
> MORSE: .. -- / -... .- -.. // "IM BAD"
> TRANSFER LOCK — DO NOT INTERRUPT
> ----------------------------------- **
          >DOWNLOADIUNG USER TRANSFER NOW.... <

UR WELCOME <3 AK-50. THE NEW PIG.

**OOS [WA] DATABASE—CPS/PD/EDU LINKED CASE FILE
SUBJECT: TAYLORE, OLETTA SKYE [F]   DOB:
KNOWN ALIAS[ES]: SKYE, LETI, LEATI   (19Y) 02/13/2005
     JUV CLASSIFICATION: NA   CURRENT STATUS: CLOSED
                                        ID#: 1481-44-OT
FILE—NON-ACTIVE SUPERVISION ACCESS LEVEL: TIER II*
                                    CASE #CP-1294-OT 08/15/18
EMERGENCY REFERRAL FOLLOWING MOTOR VEHICLE FATALITY
▪ MOTHER (TAYLORE, AVA M.) DEAD ON ARRIVAL. TAYLORE, K. [AKA KRT]
EXTRACTED IN CRITICAL CONDITION, MEDICALLY INDUCED. STANDING BY. TAYLORE,
O. PRESENT W INJURY BUT STABLE. IMPACT TO AMT+KRT SIDE.
   ∴   SEMI V SEDAN, ROLL OVER. NO DWI/NO DRIVER FAULT; BRAKE FAILURES
       W AUTO CONFIRM. + USE OF R-RAMP POST SIDE SWIPE.
                                    CASE #CP-1294-OT 11/27/18
GUARDIAN 51-50, TEMP CARE TRANSX TO BEBO, MILDRED.
▪ UNDER DFS GUARDIANSHIP VIA MATERNAL AUNT. FATHER DRT ON EXTENDED HOLD
FOLLOWING TRAGEDY INVOLVING WIFE/DAUGHTER.
   ∴   BEBO, M. REPORTS CONCERNS OF SELECTIVE MUTISM. LOW PRIOR. **

"Wouldn't talk hmm?" He clicked through slowly, voice soft. A self sooth
as he reminisced. "I didn't either for a while there."

This was the shit that was easy to fall into. If he could detach from it. Not
picture the person he was trying to know that night, but see it for what it
is: words and screens and files. Because the weight of the dead and dying
broke his back years ago.

Dante sighed, scrolling. More in and out of foster in the eleven months Kaia
was—*apparently*—put up and away. His hand swept over his chin; the
earlier anger felt overdone now. Made sense why she was careful.

                              CASE #CP-1294-OT 07/15/19
▪ FULL GUARDIANSHIP RETURNED TO TAYLORE, D. OF OST & KRT FOLLOWING LRT
MEDICAL RELEASE. ~HIGHLY ENCOURAGE DFS TO MANDATE BEHAV. HEALTH & REG
FOLLOW UPS **

"Gonna' walk on the limb here and assume they didn't regularly check?"

                              CASE #CP-1492-OT 11/15/19
▪ NON SCHEDULE VISIT HOME+SCHOOL: ENVIRONMENTAL NEGLECT AND FIRE SETTING
/BEHAVIORAL RISK. SCHOOL REPORT: ABSENTEEISM, VOLATILE OUTBURSTS, PEER
ALTERCATIONS, SUSPENSIONS-SYMPATHETIC, BUT NEAR EXPLSN.
   ∴   GUARDIAN (FATHER) NOTED INTOXICATED DURING HOME CHECK. DISPLAYED
       VOLATILITY UPON QUESTION. TEMPORARY REMOVAL (7 DAYS) REUNIFIED
       UNDER SOBRIETY AGREEMENT. FLAGGED FOR CONTINUED

CASE #CP-1787-OT 01/13/20

▪ *REFERRAL: MINORS PLACED IN TEMP HOUSING. VOLATILITY & GUARDIAN PLACED ON 51-50 DUE TO GROWING SUICIDE IDEATION.*

∴ *REUNIFIED W MATERNAL AUNT 2 OF 4 WKS HOLD (BEBO, MILDRED) REMAINING 2 WEEKS → CPS-XFER GH-07 PURAVI IN CONTRA COSTA. (B, M. NO LONGER AVAIL. AS ALT CARETAKER)*

▪ *ADDITIONAL NOTES IN RP00WA2133 [CASE WORKER #ID-0998573-DJ]*

CASE #CP-1820-OT 02/26/20

• *COURT-MANDATED EVALUATION: CHRONIC ABSENTEEISM + SUSPECTED DEPRESSIVE EPISODE | SCHOOL SOCIAL WORKER REPORT: "SUSTAINED BEHAVIORAL WITHDRAWAL. FOOD INSECURITY. REPORTS OF SLEEPING AT MULTIPLE RESIDENCES." VOLUNTARY CPS INTERVIEW.*

NO IMMEDIATE ACTION TAKEN

• *MINOR DENIES INTENT / IDEATION BUT EXHIBITS PASSIVE SUICIDALITY REFERRED TO MISSION FAMILY SERVICES (OUTPATIENT YOUTH MENTAL HEALTH) WEEKLY CHECK-INS ASSIGNED (NONCOMPLIANT AFTER 5 WEEKS) KAIA TAYLORE (SIBLING) LISTED AS ALTERNATE CONTACT (ALSO NONCOMPLIANT)*

▪ *SCHOOL SOCIAL WORKER REPORT: "SUSTAINED BEHAVIORAL WITHDRAWAL, REPORTS OF SLEEPING AT MULTIPLE RESIDENCES." VOLUNTARY CPS INTERVIEW COMPLETED—NO IMMEDIATE ACTION TAKEN.*

• *CASE CLOSED: FAMILY REUNIFIED – FLAG REMAINS IN RECORD*

DATE: 10/05/21

→ *POLICE INTERVENTION – ON CAMPUS WITHOUT GUARDIAN*

• *PHYSICAL ALTERCATION INVOLVING FIVE MINORS*

• *EXPULSION RECOMMENDED FOR BOTH SISTERS*

• *CASE NOTES: "TAYLORE, K. INSTIGATED RETRIBUTION FIGHT"*

• *HOSPITAL DISCHARGE – ONE MINOR LEFT VIA AMBULANCE*

• *GUARDIAN UNAVAILABLE*

• *TEMPORARY RESIDENCE: W FERTZ#7398*

• *POLICE FILED SECOND REPORT FOR "MISSING MINORS (2)"*

• *FATHER LOCATED – INTOXICATED • REGAINED CUSTODY ON 101*

CASE OFFICER #ID-00002558

PNW HIGH (JEFFERSON CO., DISTRICT-5)

ATTENDANCE• DIPLOMA 2024 | TRUANCY CONCERNS – SELF-RESOLVED. MENTAL HEALTH FLAG – NOT SEALED LINKED SCHOOL COUNSELOR NOTES: DEPRESSION SCREENING (AGE 15): POSITIVE PEER CONCERN NOTE: "WITHDRAWN. ANTI-SOCIAL.→ VOLUNTARY SESSIONS: X2 REFUSED DIAGNOSIS. NO TREATMENT PLAN INITIATED NO ACTIVE CONCERN W SELECTIVE MUTISM OVER EXTENDED PERIODS OF TIME. SEEMS TO HAVE DISAPPEARED WITH KRT RETURN AND BECOMES SELECTIVE REGARDING PEOPLE. SUMMARY: "HIGH-FUNCTIONING DEPRESSIVE. AT-RISK: MODERATE LINKED DOMESTIC CALLS: X7 AT SHARED HOUSEHOLD ADDRESS

• *CALLER IDENTITY UNCLEAR. OFFICERS NOTED TENSION, NO THREAT OF VIOLENCE→ CASE NOT PURSUED.*

→ *NOTATION: "GOOD KID, BUT PRESSURE COOKER PROFILE. HIGH LIKELIHOOD ANY ISSUES RELATE TO KRT." ID#0003514-PD.* ⋆

"You carry it well kid. Tough."

Dante pulled out his phone. Still wasn't that little fucker. Akira sent more through. All the while continuing to replay when Kade, Kaia, and himself intersected. Because—could something else have been better?

But he saw her go back into the fire. Leti had mentioned seeing her too. And then *poof. Gone.* Everything wasn't his fault, but still somehow, everything *felt* like his fault. He clicked the second email.

Much slower then *Oletta's*—couldn't help himself but to smile—but the email came through like the first. but same thing.

That on its own was a story the files didn't tell.

SUBJECT: TAYLORE, KIRAIA RAYE

He played with the pronunciation but settled with Ki-*rye*-uh.

Occasionally read it as Ki-*ray*-uh or *ree*-uh. But however it's said, it loads up all the same. Same structure at the top as Leti's.

Same absolute dump of history. Just worded bit differently.

"Alright, Kiraia. Kiree. Kiwi..." Last one made him—*feel like an ass*—google the name. Didn't help when it gave multiple pronunciations. '*Rye*-uh seemed most common. Peeped her file next.

"What 'chu get yourself flagged on, *hermosa*?" Clicked back in, burning time, and losing purpose, but not interest. The contrary.

```
                    **SUBJECT: TAYLORE, KIRAIA RAYE [F] DOB:
    KNOWN ALIAS[ES]: TAYLORE, KAIA              08/11/2004
                                JUV CLASSIFICATION: FLAGGED
    CURRENT STATUS: CLOSED              ID#: 1481-44-KT
                FILE—NON-ACTIVE SUPERVISION ACCESS LEVEL: TIER II
```

CASE #CP-1294-KT 08/15/18

EMERGENCY REFERRAL FOLLOWING MOTOR VEHICLE FATALITY
- MOTHER (TAYLORE, AVA M.) DOA......TAYLORE, K. [AKA KRT] EXTRACTED IN CRITICAL CONDITION, MEDICALLY INDUCED. STANDING BY. SIBLING PRESENT W INJURY BUT STABLE. IMPACT TO AMT+KRT SIDE.
∴ SEMI V SEDAN, ROLL OVER. NO DWI/NO DRIVER FAULT; BRAKE FAILURES W AUTO CONFIRM. + USE OF R-RAMP POST SIDE SWIPE.

CASE #CP-1294-KT 07/15/19

- TEMPORARY CARE ASSIGNED TO #ID-0998573-DJ. HOSPITAL HOLD RELEASE INITIATED WK 2 POST REVIVE. BEGAN REHAB ON SITE PRIOR TO RELEASE; FOCUS MILD ATROPHY. BEHAVIORAL FLAGS PRESENT. ASSIGNED PSYCH, RESISTANT/NON VERBAL OUTSIDE OST. *HIGHLY ENCOURAGE DFS MANDATE POST DISCHARGE.
∴ SUBJECT DISPLAYS DELAYED-ONSET TRAUMA BEHAVIORS. MONITOR CLOSELY POST-RECOVERY 15/FRESHMAN >MED PAPERWORK PREPPED

CASE #CP-1492-KT 11/15/19

- NON SCHEDULE VISIT HOME+SCHOOL: ENVIRONMENTAL NEGLECT AND FIRE SETTING /BEHAVIORAL RISK. SCHOOL REPORT: ABSENTEEISM, VOLATILE OUTBURSTS, PEER

ALTERCATIONS, SUSPENSIONS-SYMPATHETIC, BUT NEAR EXPLSN.

∴ *GUARDIAN (FATHER) NOTED INTOXICATED DURING HOME CHECK. DISPLAYED VOLATILITY UPON QUESTION. TEMPORARY REMOVAL (7 DAYS) REUNIFIED UNDER SOBRIETY AGREEMENT. FLAGGED FOR CONTINUED MONITORING CASE WORKER #ID-0998573-DJ*

CASE #CP-1787-KT 01/13/20

▪ *REFERRAL: MINORS PLACED IN TEMP HOUSING. VOLATILITY & GUARDIAN PLACED ON 51-50.*

∴ *REUNIFIED W MATERNAL AUNT 2 OF 4 WKS HOLD (BEBO, MILDRED) REMAINING 2 WEEKS → CPS-XFER GH-07 PURAVI IN CONTRA COSTA. (B, M. NO LONGER AVAIL. AS ALT CARETAKER)*

▪ *ADDITIONAL NOTES IN RP00WA2133 [CASE WORKER #ID-0998573-DJ]*

CASE #CP-2450-KT 04/18/20

▪ *EXPULSION; ALTERCATION W TEACHER; FATHER UNREACHABLE.*

∴ *STANDING BY W CUSTODY OF TAYLORE K+O. SCHOOL VETO'D SUSPN. TAYLORE SISTERS EXPELLED-EVENTS UNCLEAR. BOTH TAKE FAULT. PEER FIGHT RESULTING IN INTERVENTION.*

CASE #CP-1896-KT 05/16/21

▪ *INCIDENT-TRIGGERED INTERVENTION | ARRESTED (NON-RESIDENTIAL) ARSON SUSPICION MINOR PROPERTY DAMAGE; >$1000 NO CHARGES FILED PSYCHIATRIC HOLD (72HR) FOLLOWING OUTBURST UPON ARREST: DISCHARGED AMA, AFTER EXTD*

"Damn...The—okay." scrolling through the colorful file. Leti's was a bite to ease into the spice. Most of the same events too, just shaded in the light of their personality.

51-50. PRESCRIBED ANTI-ANXIETY, REFUSED ADD. RECCS. REFERRAL TO OUTPATIENT THERAPY. MINOR MUST ATTEND PER RELEASE ** UPDATE; CASE REP #ID-0998573-DJ DECEASED. OVERLOADED FILES; CLASSIFIED AS LOW PRIORITY. MONITORING HALTED. 2022-2024.

CRISIS MANAGEMENT

CASE #CP-1992-KT 07/10/24

FATAL GUNSHOT:

"Wait, wait...." Mumbling to himself in the car. The dim, flickering lamp light almost too bright now.

▪ *KRT UNKNOWN/WITNESS/SUSPECT. VICTIM FATHER — GSW, IMPACT TO SKULL/F-TEMP LOBE. TAYLORE, D. [REFERENCE FILE#PP-DWT1990-DT]*

▪ *SIGNIFICANT HISTORY NOTATED-3+ PRIOR ATTEMPTS*

▪ *PD REQSTD CUSTODY OF KRT. DFS DECLINED-WANTED IT NOTATED THEY DO NOT BELIEVE KRT CAUSED. PROVIDED SIGNED NOTES & DATES OF TAYLORE, D PRIOR ATTEMPTS.*

▪ *SCENE DISTURBED; KRT PRESENTING W DEFENSIVE & OFFENSIVE WOUNDS. PHOTOS FILED. MINOR DAMAGE [L] ARM+HAND. SIGNIF. BRUISING TORSO/CHEST. MOD. DAMAGE TO HAND, POTENTIAL BREAK- [L] FINGER.*

▪ *KRT + OST PRESENT AT SCENE. [SEE #CP-OST021305-OT]*

▪ *NO STATEMENT RECEIVED VIA KRT. TRANSFERRED TO OLYMPIA FOR PSYCH*

-------STANDINGBYFOROPERATOR-------- D.vlMyCry ID# -..... -. / -- .00000000

INTERVX. OST DID NOT WITNESS IMPACT.
UNDETERMINED WHETHER SELF-INFLICTED | STANDING BY FOR UPDATES. TREATINNG
AS SUICIDE UNTIL FURTHER INFORM. BC HISTORY OF ATTEMPTS/INTERVENTIONS.
  - *KRT CONSCIOUS BUT UNRESPONSIVE/SUSPECTED SHOCK. STATEMENT VIA OST*
    [POST MEDICATION/NURSE #HGT879 WITNESSED/AGREED OST COHERENT.
  - *PER OST: AWOKE TO ALTRCN; ATTEMPTED ENTRY TO MSTR-BEDROOM, UNABLE.*
ALTERCATION PERSISTED-LOOSE SCRIPT PROVIDED IN FILE- ESSENTIALLY, 'LET
IT GO/NO/HELP" IF SISTER DISCLOSING. LIKELY TO COVER FOR KRT IF NOT.
CLAIMS TO ENTER VIA FORCE. BOTH VICTIM/SUSPECT UNRESPONSIVE AGAINST
DOOR. KAIA—FULLY CONSCIOUS + W PISTOL. REFUSED RELEASE. NEGOTIATOR
INTERVENTION UPON PD ARRIVAL
NON RESPONSIVE; NON COOPERATIVE.

"Well she can't cooperate if she's unresponsive now can she, genius."

Dante scrolled more. Full on fascinated now. Mostly because it's just the shit you don't see.

"Wait, what the fuck..." Re-checking the date, the year. Not sure the machine was right, showing less than a month ago. Wasn't sadness that rang through, or sympathy. Panic. Like if someone threw two explosives into a crowded room.

Normally this access felt cheeky at best, little invasive at worst, but he wasn't sure he was supposed to be reading this. At the same time of not being able to stop. Phone buzzed, but he didn't look.

- *DFS ARRIVED TO ASSIST, UNABLE. FORCIBLY SEPARATED AND REMOVED THREAT.*
  KRT TRANSFERRED TO OLYMPIA FOR PSYCH EVAL + TRTXW PD ESCORT. TRX FOR
  SHOCK.
    - *SECONDARY KEY WITN PRESENT > ALSO SUSPECTED UNTIL OTHERWISE NOTED*
  - *UPDATE: FORENSIC REPORT: GSR ON PALMS + LEFT FOREARM PARTIAL PRINTS ON*
  BARREL + GRIP. TXMENT 07/12 > REQUESTED TO BRING KRT IN FOR QUESTIONS.
    - *07/25 NO CHARGES FILED. COD DETERMINED: GSW, SELF-INFLICTED*
        - *CASE CLOSED 08/03/24FLAG REMAINS IN PLACE.*
  NOTES: SCREENING (AGE 16): POSITIVE PEER CONCERN DEFLECTION, RISK-
SEEKING, NON-COMPLIANT IN TREATMENT REFERRAL E DYSREGULATION UNDER STRESS;
AVOIDANT TRAUMA RESPONSE REFERRED TO THERAPY DECLINED
SUMMARY: HIGH FUNCTIONING — HIGH RISK.
JUVENILE RECORD CROSSMATCH (LINKED FILE)
$\longrightarrow$ *POSSESSION (DISMISSED)*
$\longrightarrow$ *OBSTRUCTION - JUV. COURT (NO CHARGES)*

→ CRIMINAL MISCHIEF | UNLAWFUL IGNITION
→ CRIMINAL MISCHIEF | UNLAWFUL IGNITION
→ CRIMINAL MISCHIEF | UNLAWFUL IGNITION
→ TRESPASSING | EX FOSTERS W OST. CHARGE NOT FILED
→ UNLAWFUL IGNITION ON SCHOOL GROUNDS
→ TRESPASSING | FEDERAL ARSON SUSPICION
(LACK OF EVIDENCE)
"SUBJECT PRESENTS WITH HIGH-RISK TRAUMA LOAD EMOTIONAL DYSREGULATION.
GRIEF RESPONSE MANIFESTS IN CONTROL-SEEKING AND ADRENALINE-CHASING.
REFUSAL OF THERAPEUTIC PATHWAYS RECOMMENDATION:
LONG-TERM TRAUMA STABILIZATION. NOT INITIATED. DELAYED ONSET TRAUMA
BEHAVIORS AND SOMETHING ABOUT RISK-TAKING"

INTERNAL OFFICER NOTES — VIEWABLE: RISK TO SELF AND OFFICERS. FLIGHT
BEFORE FIGHT BUT WILL RESIST. HAVE BACK UP IN POSITION. BRATS FAST TOO

But the way that just tied together neatly—was it actually? Had they ever brought her in about it?

Dante watched the clerk through the window, so bored of nothing he maybe decided productive wasn't worse.

Pictured the fires again.

After Mikki, but before Kayden. The strange lady staring at him on the beach. Smiling, waving—a moment of him thinking that's awfully cheerful and this be less than thirty days.

Couldn't land on whether it was strength or delusion. Dante had shot someone before. Seen even more shot before. Dante *was* shot. And it's not something you forget. Not easily anyway.

Not the first time. Whether justified or no, there is a sort of fragility to life you otherwise hadn't seen. How the animation works; inside the skin, and under the bone. Watching that leave is—life altering in the most subtle way possible.

Measuring your own worth, your own footstep in the world and what gets left behind. Start making noise, so you're not one of the things that's left.

Dante backtracked over the charges. *Ignition, ignition, arson, residue, involvement, arson—* "Baby Firebird then?"

Just enough heat to notice; not enough to bother pulling it out.

"*Te veo, niña.*"

But wasn't much else to see about their father's death. Reading '*suicide*' kept stinging in a weird way though.

Dante's people were taken. Kaia and Leti's left. Or—is Kaia's loud processing not being *left*, but being guilty? Might be worth a deeper look on a rainy day, but everything else—small, petty shit.

And pointless if she doesn't show face.

Couldn't find the exact words between the lines, but picture seemed clearer now. Despite their well-made efforts to conceal, maybe they did all belong together. Shit started five years ago for them, too.

Dante's laugh was bitter then.

Leti wasn't plotting or doing anything to Cachí—her "Mikki, Matí, Cachí" was MIA. Leti was probably just trying not to sink too, just on the other side of the wave.

And Cachí—may be keeping her head above the surface. Dante could have come in to both their faces in a folder Monday. If anyone even noticed.

He leaned back. That sucks.

And had Leti just dropped—or something—no one would even know to ask.

Kaia was with Kayden. No question. Just felt himself stringing together excuses—*Cody was different somehow*—

But Dante would've said the same about Cody had he been involved prior to finding him. So maybe fastest just to believe "danger" until he knows everyone's clear of it. Especially after tonight. Just the next in a long line down the drain. The song that never ends.

Going on and on my friends.

The corners of his mouth ticked up, but not enough for joy. Rolled his eyes back onto the screen, but the song would be stuck in his head for hours.

Shoved the key into the ignition and turned it over with a smooth growl. Radio didn't matter, just found something rough and cranked it loud.

Pulled out into the dark, texting Cachí one more goddamn time, jumping onto the freeway and heading west. The wild, wired west.

Find Me Where I Fall

SKYLINE DRIVE
00:17:27:37

|XXIV|

Cachí's car rattled up the cracked driveway—a couple of other cars already scattered half on the grass, half straddling the curb like the rules didn't apply anymore.

The house itself looked half-asleep—dark windows, a porch light blinking sickly, the low hum of voices leaking through the walls.

He killed the engine. Popped the keys loose.

The silence that followed felt heavier somehow.

Leti's chest tightened—a flicker of fear, quick and mean. The house. The endless horror stories from temporary homes and passing friends. Cachí caught it. Or caught something.

The way her hands gripped the seatbelt too tight, the way her body stayed wired even after the car stopped moving.

"Hey," he said low, turning toward her. "Want to stay here? I can run in real fast." It was an easy offer. No offense taken, no pressure laid down.

Leti unclipped her seatbelt, exhaling slow. "I appreciate it, but I'll come." Because Kaia bailed. And Leti wanted know if she even noticed.

Cachí nodded—no grin, no tease—and pushed open the driver's door. Leti following up the cracked walkway, shoes crunching on loose gravel. The porch light overhead buzzed and flickered.

At the door, Cachí hesitated, his hand resting on the knob—door already cracked open—house breathing smoke and laughter into the night.

"Just stay close," he mumbled under his breath, pushing the door wider. "And don't judge me."

Leti managed a ghost of a smile. Because if anything, she figured judgment was the last thing Cachí needed less of. Found herself judging elsewhere quickly though. Spotted Kaia first, immediately like a magnet.

Would bet she could find her anywhere in the world with enough time. Just would prefer not to, pointing her out to Cachí.

Spinning slow under a busted ceiling fan, arms carving loose, drunken circles in the smoke.

Leti was flushed with relief, panic, rage, affection, sympathy, jealousy—felt her heart climb into her throat, choking when she called out.

"Kaia!" Loud enough to be heard.

At least it used to be. Could have whispered before—but Kaia didn't turn. Just smiled a thin, glassy thing and kept moving, the static of the room dragging her under.

Cachí grumbling "watch outs" and something else she couldn't hear or understand. Squeezing through the room with her in tow. Had grabbed Leti's hand—interlocked it even—and didn't seem to notice when she stiffened and hesitated. Fourth or fifth time he'd reached out; first time he didn't play it off like an accident.

Leti couldn't tell what she liked more: the cheesy, squishy feeling it gave her, or the distraction from her damn sister.

Hair loose and kinked down her back swaying, too.

It wasn't a dance floor. It was kind of...everything.

Cachí reached for Kaia like they went way back and had done this before. Gave her an encouraging tug and flirtatious smile. Leti's head tilted, captivated. First time she wasn't the one sweeping together the pieces before making some great escape. *Silent* escape.

Cachí steered Kaia a few feet back, working Leti between with a confident ease. Or practiced. Leti noticed a lot of faces from the fire—all of them.

Tall shit head in particular, currently eyeing them, or tracking Kaia. His little Pixie-thing, eyeballing him as he watched them. And looking less steady by the minute: body and spirit. Everyone else? No names, no idea. Just a flash of familiarity and a shared experience.

"Hey now!" she giggled, swatting at Cachí's hands like they played; used Leti as a hiding pole.

Making Leti's anger take lead. "Come on dude, seriously. *Kaia!*"

"Hi baby-doll!"

"Don't—say that" Leti sighed, plucking hair from prescription glasses on Kaia's head like a bandana. Chuckled once and despite feeling real, Leti wasn't at all amused. Less so when the tall-fuck yelled from across the room.

"Kaia!" Like she was on a recall—

But Leti froze in a sort of awe when Kaia's head turned up at his voice through the music. Turned up to him the way she was supposed to when Leti called; when Cachí had to drag at her.

"Hey!" Leti meant to sound bitchy, slapping Kaia's arm, but it sounded immature and whiney enough to bother Leti more.

"Ay uh, should we..." Pointing—Leti wasn't sure where but—Cachí didn't look so "easy" anymore. Confidence and ease evaporating. Music—no, *bass* rising until it felt wrong.

"Kaia...Are you—okay?" She reached out, hands brushing Kaia's shoulder, grounding her best she could.

"Bitlet-baby," through an ugly grin. "You should—feel inside me—right now," breath airy and uneven. "I dunno to explain."

"Kai...Let's go home," Leti whispered, scrambling for Kaia's hand when she shook her head viciously, recoiling.

"Motel—I meant the fucking motel, Kaia. Stop—"

"Nope—Bitlet, come—" "Kaia! Doll ...Come here."

A snarl cracked Leti's mask and a gremlin emerged—hunched a bit, turning quick and flipping him off with a growl.

"Bro, fuck off," Cachí added, shifting to block her view of him antagonizing. "Try and ignore him, please." With very little fire left.

"Cachí, I'm sorry—"

"I—wanna go back," Kaia interjected. "I don't like this, right now."

Kaia, would you shut—" "*Oy*—Kayden's comin'," Kaia watched him speak like she just found something magical. The three of them ping ponging between each other rapidly.

Shifted stance, confirming Kayden was struttin' over to come play fourth point on a damn—bruised up and purple—triangle. Couldn't say he smiled big, because it never left his freaking face. Made it worse when she didn't think it could be—appraised Leti like making a decision then nodded approvingly.

"Kayden back—" "Can I help you?"

Leti put a low hand to Cachí's arm for a fraction of a second. Attempting to say, *'I got this,'* while not believing in herself.

"What?" Kayden bellowed. "Cute-lil-thing pissed the viper off, did ya?"

"Excuse me?" "Kayden, fuck off. It's late—we're tappin' out."

Kaia giggled. Tripped on her own stupidity and leaned onto the wall for support and Kayden winked at her like Cachí didn't speak.

"The fuck is everyone's fuckin' problem tonight. Showing appreciation 'cause it's funny, you prick. Relax." He stepped in closer to Leti. "Don't worry, you can stay too. But Im'ma need to borrow that ass for another dance," hand offered to Kaia, but blocked by a Cachí and a lazy lean.

"Try me, Cachí. Tonight—*try me.*"

Both Leti and Cachí were thrown by his sudden switch up. Cachí thought quickest— "Kaia...you uh, were just saying you're coming with. To Denny's, yeah? Where's ya' bag.

"Car," Leti added, Kaia leaning in, flushed red and whispering *"popular."*

Didn't need to say anything else. Leti knew. And at that moment, she knew there wasn't anything to fight. Not with her.

Leti turned back to Kayden. Neck tipped back, eyes damn near straight up. "I think it's weird you're pressing hard for a severely intoxicated—"

"I ain't pressin' shit," he laughed; hands up. "Not my fault she liked the attention," shaking his head as he walked away but stopping, full body pressed to whisper in Kaia's ear. Laughing like old friends.

Leti confused, buzzed, tired. And fucking over it. Watching while Kaia could barely stand but still stood there against Leti. Despite that she'd come. She'd *asked* someone to help and wasted his time—Leti's.

"Are you serious right now?" Eyes watering with rage. With ache and disappointment. And worse is the way it was a predicted let down.

"Fine!" Arms up, slapping her side. "Let's go then, Leti!"

"Jesus christ," Leti hissed as attention turned, but Kaia got bigger and bolder. Arms open, sweeping towards the exit, drenched in sarcasm.

Still good enough for Cachí though, helping her sweep until Leti gave hi a second quick—tap?—*notice....*

"Hold on." Pulling her hand back and protecting her heart with both arms. She couldn't help but see the bracelet on his wrist and want to cry. "Kaia—you just...don't care. About anyone. But you."

Wasn't planned or expected. Kaia's butt went to the wall. Both unsteady and aware, but trying. If that could only still be enough. "That's not...fair, Leti." Squeezing her head with her palms, eyes pressed tight. "I'm drunk. I know. *F-uhhhh-cked.*" She looked at Cachí as if he'd help.

"I won't judge, but I won't help." Not even teasing her.

"Thanks," Kaia scoffed. Or slurred. Trying again, "you're mad. I'm drunk. We'll talk—but tomorrow, k? So whatcha wanna do now—oh?"

Smiling; Cachí posturing taller. "Bro seriously."

Kayden shoulder checked him coming back through, more drinks in hand. It wasn't bad but it was enough to make a point. Scooped Kaia about a foot off her feet, too. Giggles and giggles and fucking real funny stuff apparently—Leti just wasn't in on it too. Leti was disgusted actually.

Kaia looking her way, *pretending* to put up a fight. *Pretending* she cared. But there was no, "stop" in her voice. Just chuckles and flirtations— '*tickles, stop*'—

Tee-hee-fucking-ha-ha. He was leaning over her whispering something again, hand somewhere between hip, thigh, ass. On the line but not over it, but *way* to comfortable on it.

Leti was waiting for something. Waiting for that hand to move an inch over. Or lips to her neck, some kind of grab other then playful fucking tackles like a teenage boy in his mid-to-late twenties.

Then poor Cachí. Patience of the dead.

Leti looked at him again and covered her face shaking her head. "I'm so sorry, I don't—"

"Nah, don't even worry about it. Honestly? Been there." He wasn't making eye contact despite all the waiting and watching.

Leti figured it was because the liquid fire in her eyes. Looked around the room to loose her pain in the crowd; yelled louder so she didn't have to look—"Bathroom?"

Cachí—chewing his bottom lip like there was something to say. He nodded sideways, having her follow him into the hall.

Leti was kinda bouncy on her feet. Spinning one of the rings on her finger like a fidget-toy. "You—I—if I'm like, cramping you're—"

"You're fine, Leti. Enjoying it." All eye rolls and honest smiles. He was turning around to walk away before she was finished, but it worked for them both.

Slipping inside before he could consider turning to look and the moment the door clicked, she reached for the counter. A friend to lean.

Music was—duller. Downside, the couple on the other side of the wall goin' at each other. Leti's cheeks flushed and she ran the sink like it'd hide the sound.

Felt like a child, and then mad at Kaia all over. Splashed her face for the second time that night and was beginning to wonder what was better.

A steady neutral, or low-lows in exchange for star-flying highs.

A few bodies peeled out over the next while. Laughing too loud, banging into door frames, leaving white crumbs along glass plates.

Music stayed on but dropped a few levels when someone came in yelling about neighbors, noise, and cops. Shut shit up, but didn't end a thing.

Leti tried to wait Kaia out, hoping she'd come back to earth enough to leave without a scene. Sat in a circle, drifting like a loose balloon between Jaylin and Kayden and a couple strangers she didn't even know.

And then...Leti. She even shooed Cachí off after awhile. Nicely. But—he clearly wasn't going to tell her he was bored. So she perched on the arm of a sagging couch, stiff as a fencepost, waiting. Counting the static in white noise, or the folds in her brain.

Offered a drink from some guy—so she pretended she was a mannequin.

Maybe it was a nap. Eyes wide to keep her and Kaia safe. Staring at her back for the last hour, thinking about promises at one point.

How easy they were to say. How easy they were to follow. But how terribly they can destroy something once so pure.

She sighed heavily. Maybe kind of waiting for Kaia to turn—see Leti pouting. Feel fucking bad like she should.

Instead—seems to be having a *grand* time. Gossiping with the black haired bitch who kept eyeing Leti like it was about her. Just mean girl behavior for mean girls sake.

Across the thinning crowd, Cachí caught sight of her. Kept tabs like he still wanted to come over but—maybe—didn't really like being told he was bored, busy, or too cool to be sittin' with her. Again. And again.

So he sat in a chair. Alone. And unintentionally made her regret shoving him off. Leti broke eye contact first. Maybe all she had to do was go over. Or wave him over.

Shoulders hunching like she could curl together and roll away instead. Cachí lingered for a minute longer—she could see him watching—like he was debating something.

By the time she looked up his back was turned too. Slipped out the front door without a word and...It hurt.

Didn't think it would, didn't expect it too—but after being seen all night, it caught her off guard. And those were the worst.

Dante nursed a black coffee and a burger as he coasted slow past the house. Headlights dim, elbow loose over the wheel, thumb tapping the lid like he could will the caffeine to hit faster.

Ugly ass house still looked the same; warped porch, slumped roofline, sagging under it's own weight. But still l, *movement* from his peripheral.

Jaylin. Spirit tough as a roach, loose hair hung over her shoulders, bottle resting loose between her knees. Dante eased off the gas slightly and let the car drift just slow enough to watch without catching attention.

Cachí cracked through the door few minutes after the engine cooled. Hood up, shoulders hunched. Moved with that casual steady gait—Jaylin pouting when he slipped by unnoticed.

Dante could catch the shit talk a block away. But Cachí Kept moving down the driveway until he reached his car parked a few houses down. Popped into the trunk first.

Looked to play with his shirt or belt—maybe both. Actions weren't atypical—deodorant, water hopefully, but tequila potentially—but the movements were bordering suspicious. Looking out and around like he was either guilty, or scared.

But Cachí had too much ego to show that much fear.

"Where is your little friend Cachí?" Or why hasn't he answered.

Dante shifted lower in his seat. Not hiding, but keeping his profile tucked as Cachí disappeared into the car. Dante's saw the lighter spark. *Figures.*

His phone buzzed in his pocket, A smirk on his face when he saw it was Cachí:

> FOUND HER <
> > WHERE AT?

Dante wrote back instantly but kept his eyes on him. Squinted through the mirror to see what he was doing. Cachí's face lit up after Dante sent his.

White light dimmed, red circle bloomed. And white light gone again.

Came back one more time a minute or so later and Dante chuckled. Seemed his boy was going back and forth on what to say.

"Been there, *compa.*"

A few more minutes passed. Cold creeping under the dashboard. Dante feeling suspicious, despite the block was lined with cars.

Cachí finally pulled back from the car, sack in his hand but more of a smile on his face than guilt now. Still no text message though. Phone either in the car or in his pocket when he headed back toward the house.

Didn't answer.

But didn't lie either. Dante took a deep breath in.

Won't admit it, but...Cachí, the dead kid. The t-shirt, bus station, fucking question at dinner—it was no wonder they grew up keeping his ass out of the trouble they created.

Kid would rat on himself when he didn't do it. But Cachí was better than Dante gave him credit for.

Just stupid. Walking a dangerous line.

Dante nodded and pursed his lips a little bit. Shrugged. "I'll take it."

Jaylin peeled herself off the step before he'd even rounded the garage. Intercepted him with a laugh. Too loud, too flirty, too drunk—

grabbing for his sleeve.

Grabbing for more if that didn't work. But Cachí tossed his hands up, easy and unbothered. A practiced *no,*before slipping back inside.

Definitely the right crowd. Just the wrong player.

He coasted another block, letting the car drift almost slow enough to stall, waiting.

Thought about when he, Kayden, and Matías were fifteen; driving nowhere, stealing smokes, daring each other to out-stupid the last mistake.

He coasted a little farther, the car picking up lazy traction under him, engine whispering low.

The house slipped behind him, just a sagging stain in the rearview; the dark swallowing it whole the further he got.

"I'll see you in a little bit..." Radio low, melting into the night.

Clocks & Bamboo Mandalas

SKYLINE DRIVE
00:16:41:07

|XXV|

Leti sat stiffly near the foot of the bed—down on the floor, against the wall, knees pulled close. Across from her, Cachí dropped onto the floor with a quiet grunt.

Maybe ten minutes after he left, maybe less—like shelter in a storm—he swung back through the front door. Old JanSport in hand. Crossed over to her with—not quiet a smile—a familiar ease, threading back into her orbit.

"Im'ma head up for the night. I'm not..." Paused and appraised her like he reconsidered something. "I'm not bein' funny. Bed, couch, separate sides of the room if you just wanted to crash. But I have some cards. Sketch book, if—you just want a break."

Music quiet enough they didn't have to yell.

Made it more uncomfortable in the hesitation after the offer, but Leti was just triple checking it over in her head. "Actually, that sounds—really good right now. She just wanted out of her head. And she couldn't with Kaia in the room. So maybe it'd be her turn to miss Leti.

Leti'd nodded more decidedly and Cachí—she almost took it back—looked like he hadn't expected her to say yes.

"Okay—cool." Shrugging along. Good. Because she wasn't taking it back though. Not this time. Done waiting for someone who already left the room. So she left too.

Still unsettled, but a little number again too. And closer to '*almost* bearable' when she didn't look back. Followed Cachí 's lead—who looked back multiple times. Not for anyone else, just down at Leti.

Now, he awkwardly crossed his legs like he was too long, figuring it out before setting down a beat deck of cards and sketchbook between them.

"Cards or drawing?" Voice low and easy.

Leti rubbed at her eyes. She was tired, but not the right kind of tired. Her body wanted to collapse; her mind wouldn't stop spinning. Kaia—glassy unreachable stare flickering behind her eyelid full of false promise and resentment.

That hadn't been Kaia. Not the Kaia Leti knew. Not the one that's been around. And not the one Leti wanted around. That had been something *less*. And it scared her more than she wanted to admit.

Leti dropped her hand and blinked at Cachí. "What card games do you know?" Voice a little rough.

He gave a lazy shrug, tilting his head back against the wall. "Poker. Rummy. Blackjack. Spades...*kinda*, that last one—not really." He paused, long enough to notice, then smirked faintly. "Strip Uno—if you're desperate."

Leti laughed. Tiredly, but genuinely. Mostly from the crack, but also the tension chipping away. Like something cracked loose. She didn't think he was serious either. The exhaustion wanted to tease back.

Say, *let's play*. See if she made him nervous—but it scared her more. Like it was too open—too casual. She twirled a lock of hair around her finger, hesitating. "Go Fish?"

This time, Cachí barked out a soft laugh. Genuinely surprised. He tipped his head to squint at her, like he couldn't tell if she was joking. Then—

"Oh, you're serious," with a boyish grin and scratch to the back of the head. "Yeah. Yeah—I know *Go Fish*."

She flushed, immediately embarrassed. "We lived near casinos. Doesn't meant we went in them... Never mind," Reaching for the notebook. "Let's just draw something."

He chuckled. Not necessarily with her, but definitely not at her. "Well if you ever want to, lemme know, *linda*." Cracked open the notebook to a blank page and scooted toward her across the floor. "Dealer's choice."

His eyes flicked to her hand, then back—like he wasn't sure she'd take the offer. Leti didn't reciprocate the long looks for awhile. But her shoulders stayed tilted his way and her comments more frequent.

She took the notebook. Smoothed it carefully. Thought about it.
"I like to do shapes. Like Mandalas right now," she said after a beat, almost apologetically. "I don't really draw though—just water color, straight to the page."

"I like that," Cachí said, settling back against the wall again. "Letting it tell you where it wants to go."

A smile. Just for him, from her. "Yeah...Started using these acrylic markers which...are kinda nice."

He cracked the deck open loosely in his hands, half-heartedly setting up a game of solitaire, but mostly just shuffling. Keeping the hands busy—mind slipping sideways with exhaustion.

Her foot slipped against his cards once—she gapped like she busted a window, apologized, trying to fix it.

Just a losing game he was hardly watching—*no need,* he'd said. Falsely fixing it back. And for a few minutes, they sat there like that.

The house creaked around them, voices muffled under the floorboards. But the room held something quieter—something almost safe. Leti worked on her mandala; the slow repetition of lines and circles pulling her mind into rhythm.

Cachí watched her through half-lidded eyes, behind cards laying without thought—red on black, Jack over King. Not really playing anymore, because he wasn't worried about the game. He wasn't watching the cards.

Just the edges of the room, the backs of eyelids. *Her.*

No, not the third. Not the second. Because if anything were to happen— how would he answer for himself?

Didn't think anything would happen there? Cachí lifted his head—heavy like stone—and gave it a small shake.

He wasn't going to make it much longer. And the place reeked of rot.

They weren't supposed to stay here. So who's fault then? Might as well have introduced the balloon and the porcupine. *Then Kaia.*

And Kayden primed ready to fight? Dante, Kayden earlier—Cachí was afraid to as; afraid to cause more suspicion, but Dante briefly mentioned seeing Kade. Came back from the bathroom in a mood Mick had to ease him down from.

Thinks she's subtle with a hand down the arm, friendly squeeze to the shoulders—she's not. Not subtle, but still appreciated. Dante—heavily.

But sometimes it tasted like something you knew was good for you, but didn't want. Cachí wanted them together, *sure.* But he wanted Mikki and Matí together more.

Couldn't help but wonder how he'd feel if they just let go and leaned in. He could see it in the way Dante's eyes guiltily flashed to Cachí at Mikki's touch. The way he checked Cachí's temperature when Mikki mentioned dancing together and wanting to go again. Everyone under their own type of fire tonight—and Kade?

Aware. Watching. Seeing them all burn together while he burned alone.

Glued to Leti's sister like a fucking pacifier. Like he was still sitting with them via her. As if—histories never happened because strangers didn't know. He didn't want to fall asleep yet.

Cachí felt—*responsible*. On edge. *Exhausted*.

For what exactly—he wasn't sure. Zoned out on Leti. Watching her curse softly under her breath—pen slipping wrong before she flipped to the next page frustrated. It was cute until it was *shock*.

He looked up quicker. Then felt his cheeks deepen. The sketch book. Pages no longer blank—but no longer hers. Figure emerging from a staircase, melted into color. Clock melting into in too—like time gave up trying to move forward, and where six steps up, meant six feet down.

Her mouth parted slightly, caught by it. A new detail the longer she looked.

When she flipped back, tearing out her page hastily he reached for her hand—half laughing, but fully serious. "Give that back," he said.

Because she was embarrassed. But he liked the squares and the shapes. And could already see a collaboration with it. The geometry in the background like a dance or a maze; portrait on the front. Maybe Leti, maybe her sister—*whatever*.

Because he wouldn't get the chance despite his lazy reach across. Leti's eyes stayed on the page, her hand pulled back to avoid him taking the drawing, but the rest of her—unphased and ignoring.

Like she drew nothing at all. "Did you draw this?" A whisper.

Cachí dropped hands back into his lap. Sat a little straighter too.

Sincerity suddenly uncomfortable. He rubbed at his eyes with the heel of his hand. Head tipped sideways onto his fist; elbow resting on his knee; and cards still fanned lazily between his fingers.

"Yeah..." He gave a half-interested shrug. "Finished couple weeks back." Then for ease—a sheepish grin. "Don't tell Mick."

There was something different in him now. Leti had ideas about Cachí before—sweet, sure. But unknown. Unpredictable.

But just then—felt like he'd just opened the door and showed her something valuable inside. And the bracelet loose on his wrist—she couldn't help but feel they both had that night.

"Cachí..." The breathless whisper almost made him tremble.

He looked at the cards again, listened to each one shuffle against another.

"You're *really* good," she nodded and he watched her. Thumb holding the edge of the notebook—sliding against the page like she could understand the ink through the touch alone. "I mean—this—you're extremely talented," breath, taking in more. "Do you do anything with it, or—do people know you draw like this?"

She cracked her head up, but when she caught him watching her silently, she looked back down to the notebook. He still caught the glisten though.

How she spoke faster and louder when something had her attention. And how she dulled herself down as soon as she realized she'd shown anything at all. Eyes still low, Cachí waiting—but not sure what for.

Another thumb swept across the page like braille. He would have sworn she brushed him and not the art.

"I'm sorry—you probably get that all the time. I don't—I don't know. Sorry," laughing awkwardly and settling from the awe.

"You're good *moy—perfecto.*" He shifted weight. Hand squeezed and released against the cards. Swallowed, and aimlessly added, "haven't drawn in years." Cards snapping together again. Few slipping from his unfocused grip.

"Haven't *completed* anything I guess. Scribbled here and there."

"Is there more?"

Cachí bundled the cards, starting flipping them same side up slowly. He thought about it. Eventually nodded his head.

Leti gave an extra couple seconds in case he changed his mind. Like maybe she wanted him to. Scared to say the wrong thing. Scared to be too complimentary. Not enough.

"What's most recent?"

Cachí smirked but not for long. It faded into the weariness. Layer by layer, wearing thinner. "Next page."

Next one wasn't titled or signed either, but it was beautiful earthy tones and a figure hidden within. Shadows and light work—nymph, maybe.

But full-body, turned just enough to be walking away. Wasn't even really there at all. Forest and thick lines of bamboo crossing over her limbs like she was caught between. Skin, hair, everything—flaked with browns and golden greens, but the rest pencil and incomplete.

"Did that just the other day." Cachí condensed the cards into a pile. Read Leti's face every so often.

"It's—" Shook her head. Shrugged softly and tried a light laugh again, but this one felt forced. And he didn't want it.

"Yeah I don't know what to say. Honestly. I'm...impressed. Like really."

The cards snapping under his hand again—bridging into each other.

Nervous tick at this point. "*Gracias, moy.*"

Room was feeling heavy. The word somehow softer than, *amore* but that same sentiment. Her body, feeling closer.

Leti peeked through her lashes; his hands stilled as she did and he just looked too. Caught his eyes rolling over her lips, neck. *Eyes*, just like he'd remembered in the drawing, but this time—

swollen and as exhausted as him.

He snapped the rubber band back around the deck, and when he looked back up, she had the same expression that it all might disappear too.

And for the first time all night, the weight between them shifted.

Histories, past, strangeness—it wasn't forgotten. It didn't disappear. But that calm stillness carried.

And not in the group—this one was uniquely there's. Hidden from worries that otherwise kept them on edge. Problems locked out with the music and the shit. Just safe, and still.

Even if just for a little while longer.

Cachí reached out his hand. Even then—elbow, weight, still all on his knee. "Now..." He bent his fingers in twice.

"Gimme back the mandala. I got an idea."

Glass Rocks & Stone Houses

SKYLINE DRIVE
00:15:25:11

| XXVI |

The walls creaked again. Closer this time. Cachí stirred first.

Pushed himself up on one elbow, head thick with sleep and the kind of exhaustion that made bones feel hollow.

Leti was slumped sideways against the wall, both of them still on the floor. The Mandala open over her legs and a pencil hugged in loose fingers.

Made him smile as he got closer. Fine lines on the drawing tight, neat, and controlled. Like she tries to be.

Cachí debated waking her—gently shaking her shoulder—but as she mumbled in her sleep, he couldn't bring himself to do it. Hovered—*lurked*—as if she'd say something revolutionary, but couple seconds pass—and when he felt like a creep, he kneeled down to her.

Intentions to slide her just up from the floor and onto the bed she leaned against, before making his way to the sofa. Breathed a little deeper when he smelt vanilla and firewood, easing his arms beneath her knees and back, lifting slow. His knees popping more than was fair for his twenties—and had he been just seconds faster, he might have been okay.

Regret, Leti—they woke like a bus into a brick wall. Sleeping fist came swinging from her far side and eyes peeled like they'd been skinned—it wasn't the fist that hurt. It was the recognition.

He couldn't agree with himself—he couldn't call it terror on her face. Because he caused it. And not just a small hiccup. A *jolt*—

"*Lo siento,* I—didn't mean..." *What?*

Unsure if what he thought she feared really was *what* she feared. Eyes open, fist landed solid on his breast bone. Other arm elbow deep, as if she was still trying to escape. Both settled high on his body. Rigid.

He picture how her thumb brushed along his art. Wallowed in that echo and felt ill. Not even the recognition washing onto her face—immediate, but not initial—eased his nausea. It was an aftertaste. Awkwardly there, loose grip but unsure whether to drop, stay, or go.

Her head swiveled around before coming back to him. Muscles behind her knees tight and twitching against his forearm. He kept an arm around her back, but let her feet down and backed a step before realizing she had a bundle of his hoodie like a blanket.

"Leti?" Stopped. Her eyes still wide, unchanged. And Cachí—angry almost. *Confused,* or maybe just impatient, but he felt her hand brushing his chest, twisting the fabric like a lifeline.

"I was just, trying to put you on the bed—you were on the floor. I...I was on the couch. I—should have just—woke you. It...uh..."

Slow, each word like boiling crab. Didn't seem to have her attention, and confirmed it when she didn't acknowledge that he spoke.

Cachí followed her vacant stare, but it only led to a closed door. His hand slid against her back once—slow, but not with intimacy, with hesitation.

"*Leti*? You're alright..."Slowly pulling his hand back.

Her fist opened against his chest—he looked at it but she'd closed it again. Fabric still in hand. Small, repetitive movements like habit. He stayed put, let her guide. Didn't even try to hide his jolt when she suddenly ripped her hands off like he'd bit.

"I'm sorry—I just got spooked." Looking around like he'd taken her somewhere new too. "I'm—" she looked back, but still not his eyes.

"I'm sorry. If I hurt your neck."

Cachí paused, but paid no mind to her small karate chop. Didn't like the apology though. Made it feel worse.

Him—confused. Her—*Lost.* For words, for familiarity, for sleep.
Cachí cocked his head, and the girl managed to get him to flinch. Had to stop himself from straight asking, *what the fuck*, when she peeled over laughed next.

Awkwardly, maybe fake to stary, but soon covering her face and rocking her shoulders from chasing down breath on a laugh. And still—it began to make sense. In one of those senseless kind of ways. Because it wasn't that anything was funny, really.

But the pressure too great, the walls too worn, and the room—*too safe.*

"Yeah, okay," she sighed, wiping her face but still at it. "I'm sorry."

His skin ticked. The apologies more than the baseless laughter.
And his neck too. Aching from the whiplash he'd blame on the hour.

Cachí wanted to loosen. Fall into a craze with her and laugh too, but he was edged. Felt coiled and unsure. And he could smell the rain through the walls—like he could see the storm clearer than the one who was currently brewing it.

He considered pulling Kaia in—him stepping out—because what the fuck was he even supposed to say? He didn't know her well enough to know what worked or wouldn't, and she was being a lil' weird.

Hell—they all were. But she was off base. Like holding two pieces of a face together with tape. A calm breath from her had him steal a careful and short look.

She muttered, "alright, sorry" as he looked away, but that forth apology snapped his head back up like he was angry and she was stupid.

Eyebrows pressed, nose scrunched and he twisted closer to her. "Jesus—*stop*, there's nothing to—" But the fucking flinch stopped him before the finished sentence did. The way she shifted back when he shifted up. Not even forward—just chest and head up, but sure—fast.

Not like he'd ever swing. Still took both their faces from apologetic and sorry to slate gray. Leti's third consecutive glitch in an otherwise very controlled, protected system. Covering it with a smile even as her eyebrows and eyes spelt out "liar." She didn't look like she felt so assured anymore.

And waking her up was one thing. Fine—he gets scary dreams. But awake—*looking straight at him*—having a conversation and a flinch. Cachí shifted weight. Cleared his throat.

"So...afraid of me now..." *Cariño, say cariño*—otherwise too defensive, too much ego.

"What?" Surprise—maybe she feigned it. Maybe she'd lie to his face. The flinch the most honest one in the room. "No." *Too late, too delayed.*

Door, four feet from Cachí's seven o'clock, throbbing for him to come back through. She watched him watching the door.

"Do I need to be?" Didn't yell, but held her voice steady and claimed the space between them.

Cachí shook his head, Realized his arms were crossed and tried to drop the tension and let his arms fall, too.

"Kay cool...didn't think I did."

But every time one thing seemed normal, he'd catch a signal elsewhere. Even then. She was a liar.

With cause, but didn't stop him from picking up on it and kind of feeling some type of way. And his arms were tight across his chest again. Not his own doing. But her.

Bed to the right—walls and Cachí filling in the other sides. It was in the way she gravitated closer to the wall now. Like there was more on the line than a disagreement between them.

She picked at her nails, as unsure as him, but also the one leading. Small looks toward the bed, door. Then nails again.

He wasn't trying to be cold. But he was ensuring he was ready. Waiting for the, "*get out, psycho*" or something. Feeling straight led into an upside down battle, hands tied, and lights off.

"You think I would do something?"

Didn't sound the way he meant it, but something had to know. Because why else would she have come if she didn't feel safe?

"What—Why—*No.*" Sharp. Like she knew how it sounded.

Cachí nodded slow—but already felt like he was losing having even asked. Having been more insulted by the insinuation than the fact that's an immediate, innate response for some. An asshole on top of hurt feelings.

He swallowed some of the anger down. Sparks for nothing. But the stillness that drew him in felt weaponized. Didn't want to be near it. But then—something in her distance itched too.

A careful placement of positioning. The worst though? He could taste the fight. As if he was cooking it himself. Meal or meds he didn't want, but couldn't stop. Simply self-fulfilling prophecies just to have a little magic somewhere.

"So..." Hands slapped her thighs, like an out of place penguin.

"That was fun."

Then. That there—he wanted to grab. Latch onto the sarcasm. But instead, only the flinch. On replay. Door thrumming louder behind him. Cachí took another small slide back.

Felt predatory even having the bed in his eyeline. Couch felt soiled. She didn't feel safe. He was acting like a bitch—but...Tried to imagine himself now kicking back asleep, while she anxiously kept up throughout the night.

He stared at his arms, biting the inside of his cheek, furiously unsure. His jaw only relaxing when her feet came into view—two small steps forward. Making an effort, because maybe she wasn't actually afraid.

Maybe he was. Leti smiled, graciously bridging that gap. Made the clench in his teeth unwind. "Like one big bad joke," he pouted. A gentle but confused offering for her to lead.

"Yeah," forced chuckle. When their eyes connected again, she gave a weak, principals office-smile, torn in half by a weary yawn.

Cachí's hands balled and released. But repeated for a bit longer. Just letting out the tension.

Leti had a couple more side pats before going towards the sketchbook and cards; collecting them from the ground. She let her hair shadow her face from him and set the shit on the plastic corner table thing.

When she kept her hands on the table and her back turned, Cachí's arms went back on his chest and his guard over his teeth.

"I— didn't mean to make it weird now, so, if you're mad at me, I *am* sorry."

Fourth time. He shook his head at her. "Leti—do you even know what you're apologizing for, or is it just some shit habit you've got?"

The green in her eyes hardened into grey. What felt like hours of unwinding—*gone. Idiot.*

His cheek bled under his tooth. "That wasn't what I meant—that's not *how* I meant it."

A glare like swallowing glass. "That's how you said it."

He shook his head instead, stepped to her. Froze when she mirrored it. Again. Like we'd walked into a second fist. Furious at himself now. Doubled steps the opposite way. Door three feet to his seven and a nasty mumble under his breath—"*not afraid?*"

Swallowing hurt. Chest felt heavy. This wasn't where this was supposed to end up. Pure intentions that ended with her looking down on him like the enemy. "Okay so…" *so what?* Cachí challenged himself.

The bracelet dragged sharper across his wrist. He had to swallow the urge to hand it back. To not be a child or the same apathetic fuck as usual.

"Yeah…I'm gonna go." He backed up, thumb on the door and eyes down. "Night Leti." an exasperated breath trying to mask as anything else. "The door uh, locks there." Couldn't have gone faster unless he ran. Door swinging behind him, an almost slam, but stopping short under her cry.

Voice soft as a bribe and quiet as shame— "That's unfair." A sniffle that made him half turn back, but be still instead. "I was sleeping—why do I feel like the bad guy here."

Handle fused to his palm like his life depended on it. Because maybe it did in a way. The loneliness, the reactivity, the walls—they had to end somewhere.

And this wasn't just because he was bored—he'd liked this one.

"Be–cause I apologized…?" she went again.

He heard movement in the house, but otherwise music at a lull and cityscapes mostly asleep. His throat was dry. And his anxiety reached for him like electricity. "No Leti. *Mierda*—you didn't do anything, okay? This is—me fucking steppin' in it like I do. I don't know."

He cleared his throat to cover his words when a restless straggler slid past in the hall. Cachí's Chin lifted higher despite feeling doused in mud. "You should get some sleep."

She scoffed like she was disgusted and he had to look. "*Thanks, dad.*"

Not cold, but straight dry fucking ice and sass. The way he bites at Kade sometime—disappointment, distain, ache.

He leaned up from the door to stare back at her; half shock, half *be so fucking for real right now*. Eyebrows and arms on the defensive, mouth going offensive.

"You don't need excuses to leave me too—just man up and do it already."

Cachí's hair rose like a dog in a fight. Muscles tensed, fist tightened on the knob, micro smile like he had shit to swing and a gaze that glared.

Mouth parted. Closed. Storms. Prophecy. And self destruction. Her foot tapped—bouncing. Could have taken it as aggression.

Took three breaths. Chose to see it as anxiety instead.

Another two. Picked his teeth with his tongue.

Anyone else—anyone he knew—punches were already stacked and would be flying. But the '*too*' spoke louder than the '*man up.*' Anger—felt weird, but when he peeked at the idea of settling, it just felt right.

She was swinging—him too—but not at each other. "*Primera, amor*—I'm not, '*leaving you too.*' Little Left field with that—"

"Oh, *right.*" It was the voice. Ten times over, it was the voice before the words. Dropped lower, spoke slower. *Drenched* in distain and sarcasm. "Halfway out the stupid door—tell 'em how you really stick around."

She wasn't loud. He didn't expect her to be, but she was bolder than he'd given credit for. Tagged it earlier with Jaylin but blamed the buzz.

His mouth twitched, but voice kept curious and kind. "So you want a fight then? I mean," He leaned his shoulder on the doorframe, head there too with body pointing in but feet still out.

"We talkin' play fightin' or piss—" " *What?*"

Bad joke."Leti, I think—If—" "You know what, this isn't even my place. Sorry for—I mean, I'm not *sorry,* but I should go."

Cachí's anger was draining as fast as it came; but seemed to only feed her. "Don't *not* say something because of me. I—" *Don't know.* Hand still welded to the knob. Not to pull it shut, but too scared to move forward while also fearful she'll kick it closed and vanish.

Watching her flicker through rage, fear, sadness, lust—maybe even as twisted as him. Something screaming, *shut up and stay.* For Mikki. Dante. Because Kaia didn't want to—because Cachí led them there—because maybe he was wrong, and maybe there was comfort in an expiration date should the vulnerabilities get too loud.

So he stayed. Not for anything other than standing there and letting her hit back because he took a swing first. Her pacing now. Tossing an occasionally, mean-girl, '*okay what*' sneer. He nervously let go of the door for a second—to rub the eyes quick. Returned her nasty shrug with a neutral one.

She dug around like her belongings weren't in a single small bag, organized and ready. Then grabbed it like he'd let her leave right then. *Let.* Whole other fucking conflict he didn't want to touch. Hoping she'd have enough sense to let him drive them where ever at least.

Dead man walking—or sleeping one.

"Leti...I didn't mean it. And I suck at this verbalizing shit. It's late..."

Her arms crossed. "Okay, thanks Cachí..." Voice losing strength though still dripping with irreverence. "I'll call a ride or something. I don't want to keep you or hold you up or whatever."

"Leti, *moy*—it's three in the fuckin' morning." Too irritated. But still the nice one.

He huffed and tried again. "I don't have anywhere else to be," much nicer though. And bordering on telling her he wanted to stay, he was into it. Not this exact moment necessarily—but the edge. *Jaylin.*

Stepping to Kayden, a head and a half shorter.

"...Yeah. Yeah, okay." Resigning, agonizingly slow and stubbornly.

He smirked then—trying not to think of it, trying not to show it. But finding it sexier than hell the more he did. Meant she wasn't just safe, but protective too.

She stopped pacing, but looked to the wall as if that'd called her. Watched her as he stepped back into the room and leaned on the inside wall. Still at the door.

"Hey, Leti? What do you need from me, right now? I promise you I'm not try'na make it worse."

"Yeah—promises," breath sucked in like she tried to take it back. Like she took a swing and everyone knew it wouldn't land, because they all knew exactly where it really came from. Then when it didn't come back—lips trembled, parted, closed, and then stuttered. "I—want...You to go..."

Weight shifted and arms held tighter. "I—Yeah."

Cachí pushed harder against the wall, rejecting instinct.

'Cause believing the words was too easy. Not running before she even finished? Less so. Convincing himself why he should stay before she unknowingly gave it to him as she went on. "You don't want to be here and you should go. So just do whatever you want, okay?"

He waited. Fires choke out when no air left in the room—turned, shutting the door with a light swing.

Her head whipped up to look, breath caught with tears down her face as if he really did, *'leave her, too.'*

"I can keep a promise." He shrugged, half a smile like an offering. Because that sharp, hopeless turn, was all the confirmation he needed. "I think we're swinging at the wrong ghosts, *cariño.*"

She watched him like he wasn't real and the distance felt heavier. But he was. And her too—someone he could reach and could help. Not sure how. But—the way Mikki sweeps him and Dante from a disagreement, he wanted to keep tonight's memories from behind disturbed.

And maybe he didn't know what to say, because there wasn't something to say. Shit just had to hurt sometimes. Least they could do was lay down. Sleep. Keep near so their own voices don't echo too far.

"Did you mean it just then?" he asked. "When you said do what you want? Cause Imma come over there if you're cool with it."

Sleeve over hand, hands bundled over her chest and mouth just protecting what's left too. Cachí crossed the room.

"*Cariño,*" it was an announcement, not a greeting. A gentle hand on the back when she turned and tried to bite it all back in.

Spine curved; forehead to wall. Arms holding her chest in while it was ripping itself out.

He might have been the catalyst tonight, but this was a long time coming.

Leti looked up at his touch surprised but still leaned into it. Edges still jagged and stiff, Kaia having sharpened them before she clocked out.

She leaked from her face silently. At first.

Tried to be hushed until she made a small sound Cachí didn't like. Slid his hand over her shoulder, and the other against her hip to turn her towards him. Eyes red, hiding behind sleeved fingers. He wasn't trying to watch or judge or whatever—just a fuckin' hug. Show there's more that could hold her then the damn walls. Even if her sister didn't.

"I'm—sorry—go. I don't—"

"Leti, stop. Never gotta' see me again if you don't wanna—we're already here, let it out, moy."

He twisted so he could lean now, then her into him and it triggered something heavy. She either let it out, or it freed itself, but fat tears and choked breath shook loose. He couldn't hold her in any tighter without hurting her but she kept leaning deeper into him.

Watching her with her sister—maybe it was just the first time someone let her break. Or fought to stay, not just stayed to fight. He laid his head on hers. Because it hurt. Because it was weird—because it was fate, destiny, coincidence, Hell. Seemed too convenient.

Someone who needed to save, stumbles along someone who needed to be saved. He squeezed onto her a little harder, breathing deep against her chest. Feeling them both fall in sync. Slowed. Until slower. And finally, slow. Individual breaths. Because sometimes all anyone needs is just someone to remind them how to rise and fall on their own.

"Leti?" Bed was right behind her; couch little further behind that. "Hey?"

"Mmm, all good," she chirped from deep under the sleeves. Customer service fake again. More training than sense. He delicately pulled a piece of hair weaved into the hidden mess.

Partially stared, partially zoned out until her hands slid down and dark lashes fluttered open. "Come on," he pressed, only stopping to yawn. "Go lay down....I'm going over there okay?" Losing his breath as she gained hers. Attraction, lust, logic, concern—.

"Stay...Please?" She rubbed her cheek against his chest.

Breath thinner now. Her hands still loosely around his waist; hoodie pinched in them and wet where her cheeks were.

Blinks tired, looks even more. Lasting longer, and falling deeper.

Everything screamed hold tight and let go. Face a little hot. Lips, hotter.

"Cachí?"

He couldn't bare the heat, the contact, the looks. He tipped his head back and against he wall. Not seeing her—but still feeling. And able to imagine but doing his best not to.

She shifted slightly in his arms, enough for her chin to rest on his chest; her gaze, lips, and soul looking up at him—he stared across the room.

Watched the shadows. Tried to listen for the twists in the floorboard. Because this growing flame, wasn't want. This was wanting to keep safe.

In every way. Grasping at any way.

"If I... if I asked you to kiss me right now...what would you say?"

He didn't answer fast. Looked at her—let her know he was thinking. Wondered what he should say, would say—what made her ask?

Didn't matter though—questions puddling into mud under pure physicality. Leti's hand—slow and cool—slid against his spine, touching his shoulder, and breathing blatant relief in front of him.

He thinks she was trembling but the likelihood it was him was high too.
      —*now or never*—

He meant to let go, but his body said kiss. Pretending they didn't both feel every hitch in breath and trip into it. He pulled back just enough to see her face, but didn't like the way they were still just rain on shattered window panes.

Told himself not too, but did it anyways. Hand to cheek, cradling hers when she tilted into it like she'd given up control. But hands trailing against his skin like she knew exactly what she wanted.

"I—think you know I would."

Thumb gently, barely, stroked against her bottom lip once. Soft. Plump. But torturing himself when he already said don't. Feverish curiosity chanting, *do*. Because a kiss—was allowed. PG shit.

And he—had plenty control here. Few interests since—shit went down. End the way they started. Little comfort, little healing, nothing more. Her chest rubbed against him when she toe'd up the smallest inch. Like her body wanted to take the lead, but her mind wouldn't let her fully.

And like he couldn't feel every thought.No longer a question of whether the other was interested. But only—*who moves first, how far is too far gone, and who's fault if it breaks?*

He lowered his head—still pretending he might listen to the part that said, '*no*'—and let his lip, jaw too, rub against her cheek moving to her ear.

"You're gonna' ask me though." Any semblance of control rattling.

She really only had to nod—starting with, "Then will you—" Thumb already under her chin tilting it up.

Leti offering parted lips, his other hand seeking out bare skin like her face and reaching under the hem of her shirt too, pulling her in. Fingers splayed against as much skin he could find.

Didn't realize how much he wanted a taste until she started dragging it in front of him. Honestly liked her though—didn't want this to change that.

And he'd never admit it, but—he wanted her to mean it too. At least a little. Wasn't entirely sure if she did. Not booze, not weed. Her sister. Though maybe it was worth it.

The chemistry and mutual hunger or need. They were identical there and she kissed him the way he considered kissing her. It wasn't practiced or clean or perfect, but it was wanting, and needing to *be* wanted. Enough to want to keep. And her scent—soft, like her skin. Vanilla, campfire, and bundled nerves.

He pulled his neck back. A small smile, a breath, or a break—but she touched his cheek and asked for more. Kissed him back like she hadn't been sure that he would want her until now. And now that he did, she didn't want it to stop. So maybe that was enough—maybe that would make it okay.

Her fingers dug a little deeper; ran against his arms. He tried to make space, but she used it against him; used it to move against him more so his hand found her jaw, the other her hip, holding her back a little.

Like if he could just help tow the line and hold it steady here, they could play longer. Forget longer and just stay right in the middle between walking away and too far.

He was good at the middle. But her fingers taunted at his side, tracing more than holding. He couldn't help but to lean into it and turn on. Only a few steps—only to hold. He guided her backwards, or she pulled.

Too few steps to tell which. Bed too close when it stopped them both, pressed against her calves and they went down slow. Her hands went to his chest from sitting below.

His knee touched the edge of the bed. Pressed forward, easing between her legs and laying her back. Middle ground. Staying here.

His entire body electric and alert from the way she felt on the outside. He all but quivered picturing reverse, grabbing her tighter pulling her thigh up to wrap him yet knowing better.

But maybe *better* didn't matter because she wasn't letting go first.
So why should he have to? Because.

Maybe it was the wet, tear ridden palms unconsciously weighing him down. But if he pulled his neck back, she'd push in. Couldn't tell if she was lustful or hiding for awhile.

Tilt his hips off, she'd threaten to come over, or arch up and at him begging to be pet in places that gave him the slightest pause but the greatest thirst.
  —now or never—

Her hands slid under his hoodie again. Quick and jerky at first, but it mattered less the more her touch warmed. Her hands, his chest.

Creaking in the hall and distraction knocking at his mind.

They subtly played with the hem of each others shirts—Leti trying to pull his, and then her own when he shook his head against the kiss.

Didn't stop for breath though—everything was climbing.

Someone made another objection; someone a response, and Cachí felt it. All of it.

He matched her for a second. Jaw tight, hand gliding along her ribs, thumb and hand stroking her chest and making her breath slow. Letting him explore her like maybe this was when they got to feel whole. Feeling her scoot deeper onto his knee—

He's had control. To this point. Breath cracked free like he'd been running—voice deepening the more his hands shook too. As though his voice could mask his nervous touch.

"Leti...Ah—" Sounded desperate. She grabbed him back; arched up off the bed. "Amor—*God.*"

Between breathless pants and desperate kisses. Her head shook *no*—weak words sprinkled between sloppy kisses that felt unsure.

"It—it's okay, you can." She kissed against his jaw, where the neck goes soft and he leaned into it to let her take more. He want to believe her.

Hesitantly—*barely*—kept her hip back down again, lifting his.

Despite it giving every obvious signal what he wanted to do. What he could be doing—couldn't stop long enough to start. Anxiety inside. On his tongue like spikes after each kiss and rot where it was wounded.

Pictured lips on her breasts, but felt her warm tears instead. Pictured his mouth crawling up her thigh but only saw her green eyes full of distain the next morning.

She never stopped kissing him though. Pulling against him—*she wasn't drunk,* so maybe they would—*but she wasn't okay.*

But so fucking hot and turned on. When she grazed his belt he pulled back enough to see her—really *see* her there under him, only to end wishing he hadn't.

Pulling away but pushing deeper in—her nails went into his chest again, angrier, and needier, but she hid her face within another kiss.

"*Vale, ya*—Leti." Couldn't blame her for not stopping when he wasn't.

Fingers trailed down his chest—he wasn't stupid, he was stalling. Somewhere between control and pleasure.

Holding her face, ignoring a second subtle bump at his belt.

Testing the way she would slow when he touched her greedily. Yet was unchained when he was reserved.

Nah, not it. He pulled her leg down, shifting himself up again slow. Like she wouldn't notice until she couldn't reach. His free hand claimed hers again, pulling it out from his waistline, before her other one very intentionally—very pointedly— slid over him.

Gentle enough to make him pause, but deep enough to make him stutter— his hips pressed into palm before he had the sense to take that hand, too.

Not sure he had the sense to hold them though—shaking, Screaming at himself in his head between fuck and don't.

"Hold on," He held them between themselves though; his other hand supporting him above her head. "*Espera*—damn."

Chin down, or neck turned. Eyes dashing. Being touched and edged because the mask wanted to but the girl didn't.

He was pretty positive she even began to mouth '*sorry*' before swallowing it back. And despite being frustratingly riled, he couldn't do it even if he wanted to right now.

Alarms ringing. Doubt too, about her. A *lot* about her. Age—if it was fucking honeest. Experience, society. *Training*. Like whether or not she was doing that shit because a sketch book and a quiet room. Or because she wanted to.

'Cause he caught a vibe it was an exchange of currency. His attention, her body. But—he wasn't here for the chump-change bullshit. He wanted to be wanted, too.

"Leti—" Stayed over her, keeping her hands pressed. Terrified the moment he let go, the Leti he'd been hanging out with would be gone.

He could sense it in her stillness Didn't say anything or make a sound. Steaming, burning hot to ice. He took the minute. Took advantage for real now. Closed his eyes, still slowing his breath.

"Leti," his hands loosened, his thumb circling slow against her hip. "I wanna ask you somethin'."

She stared at the wall. Other hand still on her wrists not only holding her down, but keeping him up—he tilted her head from the door carefully.

Like she'd bite. Knowing she might, but gentle curiosity asking anyway: "Have you—ever...?"

He wasn't holding her there but she still pulled her chin away like he was using force. Then was shocked he'd not held on. Nodded, but way too eagerly. "Yeah I—um..." Lips no longer trembling, but tripping.

"Yeah. Of course," she shifted under him. "Mind your business like what the fuck."

Cachí chuckled again. And though this one stung less, it was still more mask than man. "Leti. *Baby*....Your hand was on my junk." Abrupt call out.

But she deserved it. Flushed, turning her cheek further into the mattress.

"I'd say I am minding my business." But how does he ask someone to let him in, all the while telling them he wont be thrown out?

Either way—he'd never been so relieved to have stopped something. "Leti—we should sleep. You don't...Not *here*, not like that."

She squirming under him before he got the chance to move. And under her breath sassed off: "Don't blame it on me just 'cuz you don't want to fuck me."

He was more shocked than anything. Amazed too, at her stamina with a piss poor attitude and will to fight Laugh was a bit clipped, but it was real when he slide his knee back on the edge and took his same position over; back of his hand lightly pressing her arm but giving up when she wouldn't turn.

"You're kinda a fuckin brat huh?" whispered, smiled even. Knocking at the door *asking* how she'd prefer to let someone in and being damn patient. Still? No response.

His eyes hardened, mouth relaxed—but tone dropped cold. "Hey."

And her jaw was in his hand again. He didn't know what to say, but he was beginning to worry it was too handsy so the hold was extra light, but stern when she scoffed and he held on.

"Give me twenty seconds—okay? Cause you're bein' dumb, I'm not *blaming* anyone." He breathed deep, attempting to soften tone again.

"I don't want to 'fuck you.' Not gonna, *fuck you*. Say it like that, Leti..." Shook his head.

She swallowed, but fortunately for him, looked as unsure as he felt. Eyes watered and she jerked her arm as if she was trapped. Made him panic and bounce back quick, hands at his shoulders like a surrender.

"That mad—at me? *Enserio, moy*?" Arms crossed.

"No, we're fine. I'm not fuckable, got it."

"Leti." So utterly unamused.

"I—I'm gonna go." She sat up, back to him and facing the door and he shot her a look. But probably only because she couldn't see it. Pictured her not even leaving the house, just his room. Into another's just to make a point because who the fuck was he to her? *Nada*.

He didn't realize he was biting his lip until the skin pulled sharp.

"*Vale—quita tu ropa*," angrier than he meant it, but when she turned confused, he repeated less like a dick and more like a surrender.

"Clothes. Take 'em off." Turning back to an ass immediately when he thought she might actually do it "*Oy? Whatsa 'matter?* Whatever, I'm game. Quick *fuck* before bed ain't nothing, let's go."

She peeked over her shoulder like he wouldn't see.

He did. "Well?"

"*Well*," she snapped back quick.

"*Moy...*"

"I'm half tempted because you think I can't.

"Leti I don't know you well enough to decide what I think you're capable of or not," picking at his hands for something to do.

"But I would—like to. Know you... So you gonna' sit here and tell me you wouldn't see me differently if I picked up what you were putting down and took it there?" Sucked his teeth, leaning back on the wall, one foot on the bed. As close to a sleeping position as he could get. "And it's not even you, it's me."

"Didn't peg you for a cliché, Cachí."

"...Cute." He nodded. Thought about it—"I'll say it flat out then. I'm feelin' some type a way about fuckin' a virgin here. Fuckin anyone I res—"

"I'm not...I've—had a boyfriend, *Jesus* stop."

"Stop being embarrassed. Fresh off a panic attack then—*better*? Leti—? You really gonna treat me like I'm a bad guy here? The amount of filth in and out this house—baby, you don't want that—"

"*Baby* all of the sudden? You said it best earlier—you don't know me."

"God*damn*—thought you were shy, but you cut sharp, *loca*. Better?"

"I'm not—"

"Leti, *stop.*" Running his hands over his head as she curled onto her side into a fetal position.

"This is—fucking exhausting man, I—I'm not even mad. I honestly was just doing the right thing—and actually, I stand by it. So if you wanna be mad, then be mad. But don't be stupid. *Or*—a liar."

Head tipped back against the wall as he sighed. Found himself spinning the bracelet aimlessly. Felt like it scratched now. Room too. He wanted to grab on to something, but second stubborn little peek, he nudged her with his toe. "Leti?" He said soft.

"What?"

"Hey...what would you say, if I asked you to lay with me?" He spun the leather around again.

At least for the first thirty seconds. Zoned out at the door across the room for the second half of the minute. He could almost forget she was there, curled at the end like a cat.

Sighed heavily when she gave no sign of...not hating him? Maybe the benefit of wrappin' himself in shit he didn't understand, was he didn't have to think about it.

At least her chaos was internal—Cachí still *feeling some type of way* 'about a lot of things.

Unhooked his feet. "Here, come lay. I'll go." But as his feet swung for the floor, she unwound. Her hand touched his shin. She let go long enough to crawl to the top of the bed where he stayed on the edge, waiting.

"I um..." she looked around awkwardly. "I didn't..." She kind of just let it hang there, head down waiting for a save maybe.

Cachí pulled a pillow over, gave himself a wedge to lean on.

"You wanna just...sleep, *moy?* I want to—sleep..." But before he was even settled, she'd nuzzled in next to him.

When she looked up from his chest—sweet, soft, '*night*—there was a sort of release in his body, but up in his chest. He smiled and took what felt like the first breath since they left the beach.

It wasn't that same look from the BART, or maybe the feeling had changed. But it was the kind of look that asked: '*do you see me?*'

And the kind that answered: '*Not yet. But I'm trying.*'

be
careful
not to
confuse
the
rapture
for the
rescue

the Sandman & Calico Jack

|| ¿ ||

Kaia felt wrong. And it smelled like rot, dog, and a grave someone forgot to bury. Her body didn't feel like hers, a tight skin suit. On a ship.

Still until she lifted her head where it waved deep—slats in the door, windows maybe. Darkness around.

She filled like a balloon, movement rolling up, air helping, bile in her mouth too offering a hand. She slapped her own to her face. Burped.

A Closet? But open. Like a gally. Or the captains quarters and a big bed. Though not for the Kaia-bird. O*nly crackers, crumbs, and steel bars.*

There was light—soft and transparent trying to hide the darkness but too passive. Plain. And flat where the darkness sucks. *Still.*

Kaia jerked up again—on a swing. Reality when she pumped forward. Hell when hair and feet dragged back in the wind.

In the sails—"Hey—wanna—here?"

Voices outside—fragments. Nothing that made sense to track. Across the room—mirror or man. She hadn't recognized herself in ages. Couldn't find it.

"Oh—my god," she rolled. Little space left and her arm fell free; hit the ground and her body reacted like a button: heaved on impact.

The boat swayed. "Stop—spinning..." Grabbing her head. "I—why—"

"Come lay with me, baby, you're trippin'." *Already tried to fly—wings so cut.* Kaia squeezed her arms, her shoulders—anchoring down where the memories tried to wash her out; *but somebody said—something?*

Does it count if no one hears you—?

Cut out the tongue with the wings. She rolled to the other side.

Reached behind her back, scratching. Feeling for a zipper into her suit. Because the skin pulled too tight. Made an attempt at words that wouldn't come.

The voices came next. Real enough to tickle her spine and kick her in the back.

Let it go, someone screamed but she wouldn't. *But what'd she have?*

Leti screaming? No—*Kaia screaming.*

Because there is no Leti—Leti was Lies, *Lies*, *lies*—clamping her hands over her own eyes, pulling knees to chest, and melting into the ship.

Barnacle barbie. Scratchy face. Skin, too. But maybe if she held long enough the voices wouldn't find her. Or the ghosts would get bored.

Into the flames, into the rear view—but behind isn't the burning house. The golden gate. Center fallen through like the ocean took a single bite and they were swallowed down too. *Run. Go home—*

Kaia's spine tightened, breath held with every even beat.

She felt them grab her. *The horseman.* Something over her legs, fire ants chewing into the skin—she cried out.

This time they answered—deep: "Hey—*hey*—!" "—Get them off—!"

"It's a fuckin' blanket, fuck!" Someone grabbed her arms. Squeezed tight.

Big, warm, but no one here is steady. "Bad trip.. Fuckin' relax..."

He cut the sail, and fired the ants—right when the fire was making her warm. Quiet—and his springs collapsed under him like conditions breaking. But still for now. Only calm waters.

Alone. "*Leti—?*" Before the gun; before the blood; before the mistake. Before there were crying girls and open ears.

Because ears are more open with bullets inside. "I didn't mean it."

Black sails and black waters—dripping with silver glitter. Just floating in the space between sea and stars, where there is no middle, no past.

"I don't...know."

"*Shut. Up.* She's upstairs. Go." But clipped wings can't go up.

"I'm sorry..."

> So don't you dare come back down...

He wasn't surprised when a door somewhere in the house slammed—shook the floor, rattled the frame. Jolted Cachí like a punch under water. Leti made a sound from beside him.

Probably would have slept hours longer had she been somewhere of her own. Sun already up—heat through the blinds, peeling across his chest and her cheek.

Cachí could still vividly feel the way her finger traced along his spine last night. Hadn't expected her to stay—yet there she was still in his arms. Blanket twisted between them and her thigh hooked over his.

He swallowed. Blinked. Reminded himself to breathe, but nervous it'd be too deep. Her body feeling heavier—still warm where he hoped it wouldn't be. Cachí blinked again. Didn't trust the moment enough to breathe too loud.

Still. She began to stir at the sound of something else waking below them. But stirred slow—like she was dragging herself out of someplace she wanted to be; low mumbles, soft and closed-throat. Eyes slowly fluttering—open but not seeing. Until they did. Cachí blinked once.

Her head popped up—like caught somewhere she wasn't allowed to be. And when her leg snapped back—quick, almost rough—her shoulders hunched and she turned like she only meant to get up in the first place.

"I didn't mind." His side suddenly colder than he cared to admit.

Just rubbed his thumb against his jaw—didn't look up despite her glancing down. He sat up then too. Legs off the side, Leti at his back. Cracked his back and neck next.

Room felt muggy, and Leti shifted around it. He watched her over his shoulder then and her hands went to her hips. "What'd I do?"

A real and full smile then. Second breath. "No—you seen...my ex-sister?" Her voice cracked down the middle.

"Out there," yawning and nodding to the hall. "She's in Kade's space."

Leti stood up tall. "*What?*" Her spine was braced now. Breath locked.

He didn't have to ask. Opened his mouth, stumbled. And then confident, maybe too confidently: "Kayden wouldn't.... Nah —swear it.... She was too fucked up. Doors open."

Leti didn't look sold. And he—was feeling less so.

"Grew up with Mick, and.... hey, she was in the wall-nook thing."

He rubbed at his face.

"Saw 'em right before we—whatever, just go walk in if you want. Doors been open. Took a leak and it was open then too..."

Her discomfort made him doubt how stupid he was coming across right then. But there are lines people don't cross. People don't change that fast.

Coughing at the flashes of Cody through his head like if he could just be louder he wouldn't have to wonder. Eating her anxiety like he was starved. He pointed for his door. Encouraging.

Leti let out a breath like she'd been underwater. Shook her head. "No."

The tension didn't leave, just lowered. Looking over his shoulder again, one eyebrow up. "You need me to go—"

"What—? No, let her sleep, I don't care. I'm curious how long she'll go. Might even go move hotels." She shrugged.

Cachí reached under the bed for his stash of shit. Pulled two waters from a box, hesitating before he offered to help on that one. Handed a bottle off to Leti before demolishing the second.

She just about did the same. But slower. "What time is it anyway?"

"Almost eleven."

Groaning, "are you serious?"

"Sometimes the body just needs a restart," as he was getting up.

Neither of them said anything about the night. Not the kiss. Not the way she'd folded into him or cried. Not their want or ache—just water bottles and sore joints like nothing had cracked open at all.

"So...Bathroom?"

Cachí nodded toward the hall. "Straight back. First door."

She looked there, and then back more timid. Still pretending she didn't want to be seen. Or simply, not knowing how to be.

Cachí stood to stretch, but it was sharp. He couldn't put a name to it. Just a new uncomfortable creep to deepen the others already there. Cachí adjusted himself, scanning the ground for something clean.

Fear, excitement, admiration, lust, respect, anger, frisky, weird—he sighed, pulling his shirt over his head and turning for the stairs.

Might as well just call this one hers.

Feathers From the Cuckoo Nest

WESTLAKE MALL | ITINERANT
00:7:00:00

|XXVIII|

The parking lot gleamed under a thin coat of heat; pavement cracking at the seams. Somewhere off in the distance, skyscrapers knifed into the skyline—sharp and glassy. Just outside the city's real pulse.

Kaia followed Jaylin inside, blinking against the fluorescent burn. Air-conditioning slapped; fryer oil and sugar reeked. Jaylin stepped up first, mid-scroll.

"Get whatever," already peeling off to take a call. "Hey—yeah. I'm here now. What?" Whined, childlike.

Kaia was left at the counter. Alone. Cashier blinking at her—unimpressed. Kaia's mouth opened. Shut. Opened again. Someone behind her shifted. Another came through the shrill bell.

Kaia turned to Jaylin, eyes wider than they'd been since waking. Jaylin's voice was just out of reach, murmuring but sharp. She didn't know what to order. Didn't even want to. What she wanted was Leti. Just to see if Leti'd look at her.

Memory in fragments—but Kaia remembered. *I promise.* Kaia didn't say anything now. Slid a nasty look to Jaylin, but too chicken or ill to say shit.

Stepped a foot back from the counter and let the person behind go first. She leaned against the window to let the chill cool her back, but Jaylin was back up right when the curtains were closing.

"*Hey!*" she snapped at Kaia; dropping a card onto the counter instead the woman's hand "Hello, what the fuck you want?"

Kaia looked at Jaylin. Shook her head. "I—water."

"That it?"

"...Hashbrowns?" She looked at the cashier as if she'd help. She wouldn't.

"K. You heard her then. And gimme' a bacon sandwich, iced caramel swirl—oh, *extra swirl* and a dozen of whatever. *Surprise* me."

They'd shuffled to the side at some point and Jaylin was arguing again. Maybe about cops. Maybe code. Kaia watched the iced coffee churn slush over itself. Pictured herself inside, rewinding time.

Leti wasn't even going to kill her. She'd just never trust her. That was worse. Kaia rubbed her temples. Closed her eyes.

Bag crinkling behind her; the cashier dumping it and drinks on the counter. No smile, no thanks for coming. *Just go.*

Kaia grabbed it with a shaky hand and followed Jaylin out. "Eat, loser. You'll feel better." Hashbrown coming at Kaia's face. Doubted it.

Outside the city, traffic still lurched too and from at every corner light. Kaia's spit was rolling, gut begging to retch pulling up to the house.

It looked better at night.

Jaylin grabbed the bag and coffee, muttering, "You sure are boring." She stared at Kaia, assessing, and then shook her head with a heavy sigh. "I'm going home. I'll drop you off."

"Leti—?" Kaia croaked.

"Yep." Jaylin slid out, slamming the door and walking with a half march, half strut.

Kaia rolled her eyes; couldn't say why, just pressed her head against the cold window, counting seconds as she slowly pulled in air—burped something wicked that burned her throat. Looking around like the leather would snitch.

She turned back in time to see the door swing shut behind Jaylin— head tilted up the stairs but feet planted like she hadn't quite figured out where she wanted to start first.

Kaia groaned. Let her eyes stitch shut. And mentally prepared herself for the icy rage that was about to tip toe out of that house and take over the interior of that SUV.

"Just...don't puke..."

Inside the trap house, the walls breathed their usual heat. Blinds drawn, floorboards crooked, evenings heavy and ill.

Cachí rummaged through a half-clean laundry basket in the kitchen, looking for something that didn't reek of sweat, liquor, and weed.

He peeled off his wrinkled T-shirt, jeans low on his hips; weight that had abandoned his waist and taken up residence in his chest.

The ink on his side faded in and out of view as he moved; the skin and ink twisting with muscle as he turned.

He sniffed a hoodie. Hesitated then tossed it back.

'Cause it wasn't the hoodie.

He smelled her first: sharp-sweet, like a flower cut with gasoline and black cards with bloodstains. Then felt her next, running her eyes along his spine and in his head.Jay just fucking unnerved him.

Exhaling, he searched for a shirt a little faster. Steps growing even louder.

"Well hello there handsome." Coffee in one hand, bag in the other, eyes raking over him like she had a right to every inch.

Cachí didn't look up; just pulled the next shirt over his head. Didn't inhale; didn't want to know. "Lost, *Princesa*?"

She tossed the bag on the counter with an underhand. "Well no. I just didn't know laundry day came with a floor show," swinging her free arm and hip like a kid—voice masking as innocence, too.

"Little distracting. That's all." A wink. *A demon.*

Still not gonna' bite. Despite how she crawled under his skin better than anyone he knew. Cachí shook his head. Grabbed a hat from the graveyard shelf of sneakers, broken jackets, and worse left behind and saved for later.

"I don't even deserve respect anymore Cachí?"

Too easy. Still not biting. Just tossed a look instead both half entertained, and still half over it. 'Cause that was an intentional line up.

"Mmm," was all he managed. Sauntering to the crumpled bag and snatching it with half a smile and a head lift. "On Daddy?"

She looked a little less pleased with herself then. And that made it funnier. "You would call him that." Cachí peeked inside the bag shaking his head. Pulled two donuts from the twelve; one for himself, one with a napkin.

"For *Leti.*" Twisted the wrapped snack and bit into the other with slow, deliberate defiance. Tossed the bag back as he chewed slow.

She battered her eyelashes, put her palms back on the counter to lean. "Right. So not done with the new plaything either, I guess?"

Cachí's eyebrows flashed up and then down sarcastically. "Wouldn't matter either way now would it."

Took another bite as he turned, thoughts and wants upstairs with the other one. Less landmines and vultures.

"Okay then." she drawled. "I'll uh, let Kaiai know you two are sticking around then."

Immediately felt spikes under the skin. Didn't like the words, the tone, the girl. Cachí ran his tongue across his teeth. A second time for good measure. Looked, but said nothing. And she watched, twisting her hair and egging him on.

"She's with Kadem if you're curious."

Brushing her leg of lint. Or flourish. "Yeah I think Kayden's showing her around. Shouldn't be back until later, but probably will see her at the house."

Cachí's eyes closed. He almost walked—believed Kaia was actually gone.

But how stupid would he look if she was still asleep?

He all but stomped down the stairs. Almost let himself shoulder check her on passing—fuckin' hard too. Either chickened out or rose above last minute though.

Came back to her in the same spot. Eyes battin.' "Where'd they go Jaylin?"

That made her pause. That made her giddy. "I don't know. Mansion, lunch maybe," slight half shrug. "Or the Sub. Darcy's even—said he doesn't mind leftovers. *Filth.* I heard B's in town this week too."

She talked offhand like it was weather. Dropping heavy hitters as if Cachí was scared. But anything she picked up wasn't fear—it's *friction.*

Trying to be good but blocked at every turn. He couldn't hit her, but he could pay Kaia to maybe. *Wouldn't...* Yet..

But if it was Kaia—? Eyes narrowed; tongue whipped.

"*Enserio—donde va?*"

"You now I love it when you code switch, right?"

A door clicked upstairs. Maybe coming out of the bathroom, maybe going into the room. But they both looked up. And then back to each other.

Simplified him to nothing more than a mutt guarding a bone.

"Leti hear any of the sweet talk last night?"

She knew it stung—toxic red lips the most honest thing about her.

Whispering, she added: "Walls are pretty thin around here."

He laughed, but the ease dropped from his body. What settled instead was heat. He just prayed Leti wasn't tuning in if he was about to tune up.

"I wonder," she reached for his arm. Followed him when he yanked it away disgusted and went for the stairs. "Maybe I can get Leti to open up, too."

He hit the stairs hard with his foot.

"'Cuse me," Jay put her hand against his back just to prove she could.

Another test. Another corner. Another practice of control. He didn't lash despite but he fuckin' wanted to. Laughed instead somehow. Though cold, bitter, and scratchy. "Jaylin. I'm not Kayden. Cut the shit," he turned, hips and torso checking hers as he took a step down, forcing her down one too.

Stepped back up and spread over the step again. "This ain't your house girl—so *get*." Burning as much as possible and persistently trying for Cachí too. "If Kade isn't here—you aren't welcome or wanted."

"Rude." Flinging the neat twist she'd strangled into her locks. "I can bring her to Kaia," she tempted. "You think she'd rather be with you? *Honestly*," sucked her teeth back at him.

"I got it." Doubted himself as both man and monster—not sure what side was whispering: *just one swing*. Scarier though—the voice warning him: *she wants you to*. If only to send him to the cage with her pops like Kayden. Reduce, reuse, repeat until out and hardened to a little toy soldier, too.

Lips popped, hips cocked—posed like she was waiting for applause.

"So do you punish me if I admit I was up there last night? I can tell you what I heard if you want to reenact it."

She came up a step. Reached for his face resulting in a grab to the wrist. And as if they were dancing, he held her hand up and out—
half a turn, reaching over and guiding her down two steps.

Would have done all three if he could have reached. Because what else could he really fucking do. *Especially* when Jaylin kept on. Leaned against the wall kicking her foot up on his step like a leech he couldn't tear off.

Stared him down a long few seconds before shrugging like they'd compromised. "Yeah. Sweet girl..."

"You know Jaylin..." *Say it* Pounding in his ears like a pulse, body fighting to block blood from rushing his face.

Desperate to show no signs and give her no more buttons to break.

As if he wasn't already white-knuckling the banister and about to rage.

"Go on then, Cachíflin," she grabbed the hem of his t-shirt. Gently tugged him towards her but stepped up to him when he yanked it back.

Thought better of it still, turning sharp on his heel while he could.
"Get out Jay."

She grabbed at his hand with one of hers—reaching for his hip with the other. Far too comfortable with someone who had far too little control.

Spun sharp on adrenaline—already primed for a fight. Palms out. Didn't see Jay, just saw red. But pushed at her—and didn't let go. Pivoted towards the wall on a whim.

"¡*Ya basta*, Jaylin!" But asked himself why he didn't just let her roll.

"Close—but come on then, hot-shot. Probably be the only time you've been a man this week," pausing to add, "I'm sure Leti would agree."

His jaw flexed. *Coincidence*? *Eavesdropping*. And despite Cachí knowing *that* commentary there—*that* was what did it, he'd lie and say it's Leti's honor, or her privacy betrayed. *Whatever-whatever*.

"You know," He stepped down, closer to her but still a step above. —*talk like Kayden, in line like Kayden*—"What if I did Jaylin—? Swing, I mean."

Crossed her arms, but kept the grin. "Let's find out then." Want and can aren't even neighbors sometimes. He couldn't even fake it out.

Flinch forward with half a raise. Not like she wouldn't bounce back with a few blades and a smile.

She stayed down on the step they dropped. Mouth didn't though. "We both know you don't have it in you, sweetie."

"Yeah—maybe," he nodded. *Fuck it.* "Lemme ask you something though."

Her head slowly cocked to the side. Eyebrows up. An eager—*go on...*

Cachí's shoulder's broadened, chin lifted, and posture hovered. "You got a fire plan yet?" Voice went low. "*Tu papa*—prison again, right? Third times the charm?" Short whistle and a sharp smile. "Lotta' people die off that shit you deal, *niña*. Surely Pop's got himself some friends in there though, yeah?"

As she became more tense, arms crossing slow, he began to loosen. Tables shifting, mixing up a little offense and defense. A nod that didn't understand the whole meaning, but still got the message early.

Cachí looked up the stairs. Voice still hushed. Clocked it as guilt. Thought about leaving then. Wanted to make a better excuse for why he didn't, but really—he simply had it loaded with a match in hand. Didn't want to walk now.

"I was just thinking. You disappear real easy when no one gives a shit. And no one here likes you, Jaylin."

Gently pet a piece of hair from her face before she jerked her head back.

Cachi's hand dropped. He backed another step to appraise her. "Plus— not much of you to hide." Didn't look at her. Smiled at the donut—one finished in his mouth, one the other hand—and called back *"thanks."*

For the sparring match. Because he won that one. The silence following him up the stairs.

But hitting the second floor was like a cool cup to the face. Anger dropped and anxiety choked. Because what if he walked in—Leti across the room having heard it all—greeted with, *'I didn't know you threaten women'*

The bullshit—the way even his wins felt like a loss. The room he'd come from was closed, bathroom down the hall opened. He reached for the handle, taking a couple heavy breaths before twisting the knob.

But stepped in towards a smile that somehow made it worse.

Leti stepped closer—closest since they got up and he wanted to step back. Just feared that'd ripple something from last night.

"Kaia awake yet?"

His breath shallowed before it stilled. "So."

Shutting the door hesitantly. Turning with it just so she didn't have to look at his face, but turning back all too soon.

"About that..."

No Safe Passage Ahead

ITINERANT
00:6:33:05

|XXIX|

Kaia still had her forehead pressed to the passenger window, the glass warming with afternoon light. Jaylin might have been a minute, might have been thirty.

Drifted in and out, held warm in the car like a womb.

And Kaia chickened out on going in. Blamed it on feeling like shit. Worse then the coma, because at least then Leti was bedside.

Just run in, apologize. Grab Leti and go—forward, home—whatever.

But something nagged deep and said she couldn't. Terrified she might not be silent, but instead scream at her in front of people. At least Jaylin was just one.

Kaia wiped a tear, but the car jerked her awake, if it really even was real sleep. *Drift.*

Door swung open with a hard pull. Slammed shut even harder. And no Leti in tow. Only Jaylin, movements jerky, forehead wrinkled. Hair still long and sleek...

Still looked as miserable as Kaia felt. And that's not how she'd gone in.

Backpack slung over her shoulder, shit coming out the sides like a tongue. Half-zipped and packed quick. Kaia recognized it even like this.

Jaylin popped in—huffed and sighed until settled in her seat. Kaia smiled, but tucked her face. It was just kinda bratty. Kinda funny. Especially after seeing her as some Titan half the damn night.

Her and him both. Her Kaia's throat croaked. "You moving out? Leti?"

"Leti—*no.* Secondly, I don't live in this shit hole with those pigs." Key slid into the ignition.

Kaia glanced at her sideways. "Just party with—wait, where's Leti?"

Hand on the door, but Jaylin's on Kaia's arm just as fast. "She's not in there, you can't."

"Beg yer'problem?" Head cocked back like a gun but a mouth instead.

"Um. Kayden's roommate. No one's still in there. Older, mean fuck."

Arms relaxing one hair at a time. Kaia looked at the house. The windows. Stillness and sun-backed exposure on ugly things.

"I was texting Cachí—they're together. But no—that's why I got some of Kayden's stuff here. That guy. Friends of his later are even coming," smiling towards the end and turning back to the wheel.

Kaia wasn't sure what to say. Ignition cranked, gearshift dropped with unnecessary force, and she watched as it slid from the window and onto the next. Less decrepit each one they passed.

"Do you morning drink?" More judgement than anything else, but the backbone was missing from Kaia's tone.

"Suffering huh? Sucks to suck." Tasted—*playful*. But had a foul aftertaste.

"Dude I don't even have my phone," turning as if she'd run back now. Brain swiveling slower than neck.

"She's not in there. *Dude*."

Kaia made a new sound with her teeth—like a *tsk*, but lazier. Felt condescending and appropriate, but it aged her about ten years.

"She was actually a total bitch to me last night. You were with Kade by then a think."

"What'd you do?" But actually wondering whether the liquor made Jaylin nicer to Kaia, or just more *tolerable*.

"Cool—cool—cool," taking the turn a lot harder.

Their spat felt like running turned down *just* enough to count as a walk— lifeguard eyes on you, prepared to yell, *slow down*—except it's their attitude. Kaia didn't know when it started, only that she felt this pull saying, *compete* and this anger when she didn't. Stewing. Hungry, but proud.

Unbelievably miserable. Kaia sighed, unintentionally knocking the bag that'd gotten down there with her foot. Didn't look like clothes, looked like clothes wrapping something. "What's that?"

"Hm?" Looking over. "Oh, some folks should be dropping by later, *like I said*, so I snagged stuff for Kade. Low life's like to steal and shit,"

looked Kaia up from down and smiled something coy. "Still got your panties?"

"You're disgusting," rolling her eyes under her hand; Jaylin no better then the glaring sun. "But that a way to ask if I slept with your guy?"

Didn't expect the cackle. Whatever aggression scratched her up inside kept its claws in the jeep. "Please. As if." Looked Kaia up from down *again*. Kicking a dead fucking horse with her point. "No, sweetheart. He wouldn't. Not you."

They made Kaia write, '*I will not fight,*' five-hundred times a day for two weeks. And then again in cursive.

Sometimes it helped. Even now when she could still feel her hand cramping and the sharpener vibrating. Other times, she wanted to shake out the cramp.

Use the pencil like a shank and stir some shit right back.

"So, Leti?" Kaia asked instead.

"So Kayden?" Sunnies on her face—so oversized if Kaia squinted any more, Jay would look like a bug. *Squish.* Chuckling at herself quietly, but loud enough that Jaylin read it as insulting.

Tone got shaper, words faster. "Did you—actually, though. With Kayden...?" Looking a lot more self-conscious than she plays off.

But, '*I don't think so—I don't know,*' didn't make Kaia sound confident either. "I got mine, so...sounds like you're the one he doesn't want?"

Jaylin pulled her sunglasses down her face, staring far too fucking long as she drove through the fucking *city*.

"Stop," Kaia warned, gripping the door when she sped up.

"Understand something real quick babe," hitting the brakes hard enough to thrash Kaia against the belt. "Whoopsie," a giggle too. "But Kayden—is waitin' on me. Now, it'll be *longer*. Because—"

Eyes *up from fucking down,* and then, "Dirty."

The taunt bit Kaia in the ass faster than she expected leaving her wanting to defend herself but also not feeling remotely safe. Turns out she is low key crazy, so Kaia tried tuning her out. Tried to recognize it, too.

That anger, the wall. So familiar Kaia might as well call it home.

"Crying's for little girls who get left. I don't cry over things I can replace."

Blah, blah, blah—because, unlike home—Kaia just didn't care enough. Jaylin was an interesting time but wasn't actually a good one.

Besides, Kaia had to save for Leti's trench; she'd be digging out for a year.

"Mkay...*neat*. You have any more on Leti or should I stop asking."

"Both."

When Kaia didn't engage, Jaylin did, "They split. Went for lunch."

"Okay so..."

"*So?*" More annoyed than anything.

"I mean..." Kaia was attempting both conversation and leverage: something that'd appeal to Leti positively when she asked, "Cachí's alright, I guess?" Not like she wanted a conversation, though. Even less when the bitch next to her scoffed.

"Kaia, no one in that fucking house is '*alright.*' Bottom of the food chain, babe. I hope you enjoyed the fall."

That didn't sit right at all. Whether for Leti, herself, Mikki, Cachí, Kayden—she wouldn't call any of *them* bottom of the barrel.

"And you, seem to like them. Lots in common, huh?"

She felt the glare through her closed eyes but didn't open. Half expected to get thrown out but at that point—*fine.*

Superiority, classism, whatever it was—it was gross.

Jaylin reached for her phone. Scrolled with one hand, steering loose with the other. Kaia's breath choked out surprised when she slapped her stomach with the phone.

"Put in the address then, Jesus. Making people take care of you—maybe decline the invite next time. Not a light weight, you're a fuckin' feather."

Kaia hesitated in the burn. The bitch sliced—stole permission Kaia thought she had. A feeling she didn't know could be snagged.

"*Well?* Or walk," she added, pulling her arm back. "What's the name?"

Kaia peeped the sun coming over the sidewalk, the heat warming the windows—"Uh—Desert View. Desert.."

Jaylin squinted at the map. Flipped through satellite photos until she found the one with green shutters and a crooked neon sign.

Held it like it was trash.. "This one?"

"Yeah," Kaia mumbled.

Jaylin chuckled hard and it made Kaia worse in every way. "Well maybe Cachí is alright by your standards after all."

"Wow," Kaia was drained. And over it. Jaylin could win with the stupid fucking smirk and the little shoulder lift-cherry.

Kaia was silent the rest of the way, but Jaylin had stopped dragging her too. Ignored Kaia completely but bombed her phone with conversations in every media.

Kaia had audible relief when the little, hexagonal building came into view. Broken cactus loyally flagging down the stragglers and the sad, sun-faded signage. Kaia eagerly looked towards their room but froze. "Shit," feeling empty pockets along her cargos and slumping forward.
Staring at the hut—Jaylin staring at her.

"...I don't have my key."

"Tell them you got robbed." Didn't miss a beat. "You look like it."

Kaia yanked the door open as Jaylin scrolled her phone rapidly. "Thanks. For the ride."

Wasn't planning anything, but when her feet slapped the concrete—when she saw a little old woman in the hut—Kaia's spine lengthened and head lifted looking back.

"You know...I'd rather be likable than rich;" And then the sass dragged in— "Its really no wonder you're following around the newest person in the room."

Jaylin's head, turning. Locking on with her full attention.

"You said I'm uncool—or boring?" Kaia's turn to laugh. "Kayden had the right idea for you. Trash."

The door closed with a slam and a smirk.

But the devilish smile wasn't from Kaia's side. It sizzled through the tinted window and Kaia threw her hands up, looking around—

"What? Go!" Broiling under the stillness.

Jaylin's window rolled down, slick, and silent, but somehow still the loudest thing out there. Stopped at just about both their shoulders. Jaylin leaning over the passenger side to look out the window and at the building around them.

And then smiled.

"Have fun tonight. Mkay, babes?"

Leaving Kaia with only the sound of a window rolling back up; the tires rolling back out; and the stare of a cactus pretending to be a little old lady.

 —Fun night...

00:6:21:¹⁹ || XXIX || ITINERANT

Kayden had been circling for twenty minutes, not sure where he was headed. The coffee hadn't touched his hangover, and his stomach was already sour.

Every light seemed too long, every driver too slow, and every goddamn roach in his place right now.

The phone buzzed on the dash. Once. Twice. He peeked, but it proved his fucking point. Jaw flexing as he watched the street roll by.

> JAYLIN
>
> WAS LOOKING FOR U BUT WOKE YA GIRL INSTEAD <
>   MAYBE WE'LL GO PLAY WITH MIKKI. U LIKE? <

His grip on the wheel tightened until his knuckles showed. Kaia—if anyone's and if handing around—*was his*! Not hers.

The thought of her dragging Mikki into it too—when it was between Dante and him—made something coil in his gut and it wasn't the hangover. Another buzz from the bitch.

> JAYLIN
>
> WHEN IM DONE W HER ILL GIVE HER BACK <
>   I HAVE SOMETHING FOR U NE WAY <

He exhaled through his teeth, half-laughing without humor. *She's trying.*

Intentionally trying to piss him off—and it was working. Eyes kept drifting to corners, side streets. Not like he was looking for them—just if Jaylin's Ranger drove by.

If Kaia happened to be there, maybe she'd be up for lunch. Maybe she'd talk. Maybe Dante would have to see it.

> KAYDEN
>
> > FUCK OFF
> > WHERE ARE U 2?

He could see Jaylin's smirk. Lazy blink always makin' him wanna slam it. The kind of look that bragged she was winning, even when she wasn't.

The names jumped out first—than the words and what they meant.

> JAYLIN
>
>   ITS ABOUT KAIA <
> AND CODY A LIL BIT <

The hum through his chest felt like a growl too tired to try.

Jaylin had a fucking way with words and a man's spine. It twisted him up in odd places.

His phone buzzed again. And again.

And again—

```
JAYLIN
    AND THE DESERT <
SO GET TF OVER HERE<
        =) NOW <
```

He froze, but not fully—just that micro stillness before something goes bad. Like when a dog hears a sound you don't. That name—the *desert*— clung to the inside of his ribs, but he didn't get the reference. And he didn't think he would.

```
> COMING WHEN I FCKN FEEL LIKE IT
```

More she says, "*now,*" more it'll be later. He shook his head. Angry. *Intrigued.*

Goddammit Jaylin. Because that's all it took. And once you start, there's no walking off the board—not out here, not with her.

Because she's like the desert in a big way. More the more he pictured her burning between mirages. All heat and blur—tricks and taunts, but never a bluff. *Relentless.*

Kayden'd been under the sun too long. Trying not to admit the burn under his skin.

But that's the thing about heat. You can't really escape it—not even stripped down to nothing.

And he was cracked wide, just waiting for the smoke to clear to get an eye on what's left.

Where the Dollhouse Cracks

ITINERANT
00:05:053:01

| XXX |

Cachí pulled into the gas station, engine grumbling, still warming from the night. They'd just left the house and Leti couldn't feel her spine. She stared ahead when Cachí popped out.

The car jostling when he stuffed the nozzle into the tank. It was all too familiar—*close eyes and it'll be Kaia.* She didn't look until the routine drug on too long and became too still.

Her body gave little signal to her curiosity; eyes only flicked to the mirror. He'd probably gone off inside. Bathroom maybe.

Or left her completely maybe. She let her forehead slide to rest on the window, watching heat shiver off the asphalt.

How long did she sit here with him before parting ways? Phone dead. Money drying slow, split between both the bags at her feet.

She was too scared too count it near Cachí. And then too guilty when all he'd done is show respect. His head bobbed in the mirror, moved towards the cashier. She liked him, but he was still a stranger.

And she was—? *A burden.* Because what if Kaia isn't where he said she *might* be. What if not with that tall bastard she'd seen last night?

The motel then maybe? Realistically, Leti couldn't imagine her there *waiting.* No phone, no ID, *no key.*

Hopefully, she noticed. Or even cared.

But maybe Kaia was relieved. Too much nagging from Leti. Too much *of Leti.* Tears hovering near, but dried out and abrasive against her eyes.

She made jokes about Kaia leaving all the time, but she never expected to be left in a place like *this.*

With people she didn't know—dump Leti on the first people they find.

Just that needy—that fed up. To Cachí too—the night before. He wasn't coming back. Even ditched his car.

She hastily wiped her eyes, desperately palming one with her hand. *Because everything's fine!*

Kaia just took it a step too far again. They'd fight, Leti would cold shoulder her, they'd both feel terrible, and all would be right again.

Her body tightened then released to the sound of knuckles tapping the window. Cachí cracked the door, handing in a greasy napkin hugged pretzel and a cold water.

"Hope you like pretzels?" His eyebrows worn down, his eyes too.

She shook her head gently. Not trying to fight, just ill and eyes down. "Thanks, but I'm not hungry."

Cachí kissed his teeth and she peeked up, then back down. His voice was soft as silk. Please—? Didn't want the donut either..."

She fiddled with the sleeves. Sweat bead on her neck, and then her forehead. Car warming. Face too. Peeked back up—felt the warming air greet her in the door crack.

Met his eyes for a moment. She was normally the one doing this—*for Kaia.*

Now worried if she's eaten— or water, while Leti was onto the second. Leti peeled off a corner of the pretzel and ate a piece—even though it felt like chewing sand.

The gas pump clicked, done. Cachí replaced the nozzle, moved to uncap the tank, and swung back in next to Leti. She turned, watching him.

Seat belt pulling tight, jaw tighter, reaching forward and breathing life into the car. He caught her looking and smiled. "What?"

She shrugged, but stared—warmth coming into his cheeks, awkward and clipped looks tossed sideways... She was making him uneasy.

"Nothing," said neutrally, eyes sliding back to the dash board.

The sun hit full force when they slid out from the overhang and back onto the street.

"Nothing?" He asked it, but aired it like an easy offering. "I don't know," she laughed. Half real, half fake—but one-hundred percent desperate to be *easy. Light.* "I um...you can drop me off if you want."

Cachí didn't answer at first. He just sat in the words. Leti too, and they tasted saltier the longer they laid flat. Leti's eyes dropped, suddenly unsure.

"I appreciate the help. I just—you've been babysitting me all night," another painfully obvious fake laugh."She does this shit all the time—I'll be fine."

Fine is almost always fake. Cachí finally exhaled.

Turned his face just enough for her to catch the silhouette. "Don't insult me, *cariño*," soft but serious. "I'm not *babysitting*."

She blinked at that. But said nothing.He scratched the back of his head. Groaned under his breath, but not at her. At the weight of all of it.

Then quietly, when she didn't pipe up, he offered more. "I wouldn't feel better until I knew it was sorted anyway. And I know the neighborhood." He sounded annoyed, but when he stole a glance, he just looked tired.

Like he'd done this all before. "You want to keep looking or not?"

Leti nodded before she could stop herself and he knocked the gearshift, pulling out easy-like.

They spoke around the music, and maybe even made some of the same circles, but they didn't stop driving. There was concern, but not quiet panic for Kaia yet.

And for the two of them—Cachí and Leti—maybe it made it a lot easier to stand next to each other when they had something to look at ahead.

Like her goddamn sister, without her goddamn sense.

00:5:31:²⁴ || XXX || SOUTHSIDE

Leti watched the veins twist along his wrist, hand too, when he reached for the dash, desperate for background sound.

They weren't in the car much further from the gas station, but the minutes were definitely beginning to feel like hours together. Good and bad. Sun still high in the sky, stoplights like bumper cars the deeper into the city they went. Cachí's stomach twisted with regret as they got closer.

The Sub looked the same though. Never was. But *looked* it.

Sagging concrete. Rust dripping like old blood down the walls.

It was a hole cut into the ground, framed by concrete, and no better than a grave. What was once inside bristling with life and movement, now only bones and scrapes. And the quiet.

It crushed down where other silence left space. Smelled foul too. Cachí killed the engine and let it tick. Flicked the hazard lights on.

One slow breath. Then another.

He looked over at Leti. Quiet too, but safe. Clutching her backpack tighter in her lap like it was protecting her. Or maybe he just hoped it could.

"Stay here for me...?" Not a command. A request.

At least he thinks so. The idea of walking her down there—*Nah....*Because there's no music. No bathrooms. No self-respect. Even when the sun hit it; *rot.* Just warmer

But maybe it still counts as a choice if she says yes. Cachí didn't even come here. Not unless he had to.

There was no way Kaia would've followed someone down there. And if she had—Cachí wasn't sure how to finish that thought.

Leti adjusted her grip from the seat next to him. "I want to find my sister."

Of course she did. As annoyed as he wanted to be—as he was—he understood it. He would knowingly walk into death for Matí. He would have, anyways. Cachí cracked his neck. Stared through the windshield.

"You think Kaia would go down there? *Enserio?*" He ducked his head gazing through the window, eyes fighting the glare.

"Sometimes I don't even know who she is anymore." She mumbled, looking where he looked.

Someone always just watching someone. He didn't know whether she meant it, or she wanted comfort. But didn't know if he had any left.
Checked the rearview, side mirrors—stalling; *just leave. Gas it—*

"How would I go about convincing you to stay in the car?"

Leti didn't turn. Just rolled her head back. "What's down there?"

He shrugged but didn't look at her; kept his eyes on the street instead.. Watching them. *It.*

"Depends the day. But never anything good," he warned, nodding at the stairwell down. "That's not just our neighborhood down there. That's citywide rot."

No signal from her. No movement. Maybe she wasn't surprised. Maybe she just didn't want to give it the energy. Or maybe...She was like her sister. Reaching for the door handle ."Okay, okay—*espera, cariño!*"

Leti looked over, eyes flat. Door half popped.

"One second, yeah?" He reached for her waist like a seat belt. No strength behind it, just asking the best way he knew how. "Lemme just put something in the back okay?"

She just—swallowed. And nodded. Cachí popped out quick when she did, but moved slow. Twisted, then cranked the latch and dug through the gym bag like it wasn't urgent.

He knew he didn't want her to know. Maybe because he wasn't sure he could ever stomach using it. Or maybe because he didn't care if she got mad—it was coming. Backup lie already prepped if she asked—*pocket knife. Don't worry.*

As if she did. For herself. Ready to charge in blind already inching closer now. Cachí tucked a holster behind his back, between his belt and self.

Fixed the hem on the t-shirt and dropped the hood with a twist.

Then let the hood come down with a crash like he wasn't even there.

"Listo," he smiled. Double-tapped the fob and fell into step with her.

Feet were quiet, mouth managed as well—but the brain was far from. Jumped. Robbed. Harassed. See a body maybe—? Leti was determined.

Maybe she's already seen one—*maybe she's gonna become one*— He coughed like the air forcing out would somehow take the thoughts too and the stairwell hit fast. Piss, mildew, heat stacked on heat. Felt extra personal today. And Leti?

All but gone; steps small but quick. And like he wasn't shit. "*Oy,*" he whistled, sharp and short.

Leti looked around at the mouth of the entrance, then at him like they'd been doing this back and forth a lot longer than they had.

He gave her a stern look he couldn't help. "Leti don't wander off on me here, I can't take yo—" "*Take me*?" She cut in, shocked.

Round two. But there was no fight. Leti just turned, an*d walked*.

"Come on, Leti, *enserio*." Jogging to catch up from behind. Not that she'd gotten far, far...but it felt double the distance in the dark. Didn't grab her, didn't touch her that time. Because he was serious and getting frustrated.

"Hold up, *hold on*." He caught up, stood in front, side stepping until she was annoyed enough to stop. "I um," his hands dropped to his sides. "*Look*. You were honest with me yesterday. Imma be honest now..."

Her face softened but he wished it hadn't. Ultimatums loose in his mouth like broken teeth—"Leti if you keep taking off ahead...yeah-nah. I'm gonna have a panic attack, gonna physically haul you out before you even get in....sorry..."

He looked to the light behind them. A garage door, stuck open. Soon to be around the corner and gone.

"And I'm really not trying to pick a fight this time..." Covering ass as the silence ticked on. His hands went back up by shoulders; not like a fence, but a cop speed checking resolve when she said nothing—*did* nothing. "Yeah I know. But it's not just people, Leti, *come o*n. Theres holes— loading platforms missing a floor..."

She might have been glaring. Cachí might have been projecting. He went on, rambling at this point.

"Missing floors with rebar at the fuckin' bottom, Leti—I'm trying to help here." He paused to sigh. "I'm just asking you—"

"Okay," she interrupted. —*thank fuck*—

"...Okay?" His surprise thick in the voice.

"I said," she dropped the words slow, "Oh. *Kay*."

She tried to look annoyed but stepped closer. Maybe even relieved, too. "Lead the way then?"

He went forward without hesitation, but only because he worried she'd dip if he took a second longer than *fast*. Place was more unfamiliar than he remembered—shifting down the wrong corridor. Ones owned, or occupied.

Something wet glistened on the edge of the step. Dark enough to be blood, but better suited to be paint. He breathed in, pausing to listen for hers too.

Couple guys came down fast. Hoodies up. Heads low. Didn't make eye contact, didn't have a problem. Cachí nodded, *what's up*'d.

Not cause he cared, but because he was staring. And would continue to do so until out of sight—out of mind—both hands available, piece heavy on his back until so. But no issue. So far.

This was fear. But it wasn't for his life. He felt dropped in an ocean with people he had to protect, and left. Just vast space, and things that can happen that he can't control.

Might not even be able to defend *himself,* let alone her. His breath shook once. He still wasn't allowed to flinch.

Kayden, Matías—they could still see.

A small flame flickered off in the dark—bigger that a lighter, smaller than a campfire. Another Dweller howled deep in the tunnels. Another barked back and everything following echoed back feral.

Cachí had stopped. Nodded at the space beside him each time she got bold enough to wander. letting shadows soften her edges and blend her in. Not lost. Determined.

But Leti couldn't imagine Kaia going down here And at the third loading platform, Cachí extended his neck out, eyes down, checking the tracks. *That*—Leti watched.

Telling herself she misunderstood because that was more terrifying than the dark; then the barking, then the group of guys that'd shimmied by earlier with more numbers than them.

She looked at him. Looking down along the dirt, the tracks, and the tall stone walls, Leti may have looked terrified, because she felt it. Couldn't say it out loud, but it followed them in. Shadows chanting questions, asking if she looking for her sister, while Cachí looked for a body?

The words not even vocabulary she could process. One door creaked open. Smoke spilled out. Laughter too loud and someone coughing like their lungs were unraveling.

No Kaia. No Jaylin. No way. "I—" Leti didn't raise her voice. "I don't think she'd be here. "Then quieter, "I'm sorry...You were right."

She didn't look at him right away. Wasn't sure how she felt about any of this. But he didn't hover; didn't wait for a follow up. He just looked turned up at the corner of his mouth, eyes breathed out tension and in relief. But best of all—no time wasted; no '*I told you so*'s. Just a turn on his heels, a guiding hand at the small of her back, and a quick nod aimed the direction they'd come.

They walked side by side and didn't talk again until the street came into view. He bumped her shoulder softly. *Purposefully.*

"Hey—we good?."

She looked at him, surprised. Their steps together. "I mean..." she tossed around what she could say; meaningful, sharp, sad, funny...When he looked up to her quick, she couldn't help but feel butterflies against her heart.

He was worried. Her, *'I mean,'* her pause—the space between them a hair further. "I don't know," she went on
But did she even know how to be funny?"I thought we were really good but if you wanna drop back to ok—" "Yeah okay,"

Like his breath was held. "Get the fuck outta' here with that." Her chin held a little higher. His heart felt a little warmer and they reached the car quicker than they took to leave it.

Leti popped the door and slid in, Cachí followed, door thudding shut behind him but she caught him watching her like he didn't mean to.

Cranked up the ignition, "That was cute, Leti." Saying that—like he meant to? And for a moment, underneath all the static, Leti felt her own pulse. Just enough to remember it was still hers and only hers.

They stayed in the car after. Drove somewhere nearby. Sat again. Waiting. Stewing. Doors shut. Air thick. She eventually got hungry enough for lunch and they fought about who'd pay. Wasn't proud when she said she was paying or wasn't eating.

Leveled him with the gas he was putting in. The parking tolls. He caved. And she mentally promised to keep that one hour perfect. Didn't mention a single worry, but didn't suffer through her silence either. Lead the conversation until he figured what she was doing.

Talked about her art over a split pizza and a salad bar. Convinced him it really wasn't anything more than a side hobby when compared to his honors and selective classes towards it. He was vegan for awhile once too. Didn't last more than two years, but vegan was a hell of a lot stricter than vegetarian. Apparently that's where the extra weight went.

She was in gymnastics and ballet before—*before now*. He made a crack about twirls and tutus, and for what it was, it was good.

If only they held the corner pop-shop hostage with them and locked out the rest of the bullshit.

How to Boil Your Barbies

PEDRO POINT, PACIFICO
00:04:47:13
| XXXI |

Kayden checked the time. Same another impatient one from Jay he didn't bother with. He knew. But he couldn't turn down her street—looped the neighborhood for thirty minutes in that smoke of his.

Eventually, wheels turned. Kayden pulled up slow. Engine idling like it knew not to rest yet. The compound looked dipped in bleach and set under a heat lamp—too clean and too quiet for what it held inside. *Jay.*

Already waiting; perched on the stone wall lining the wide, winding steps. Smiling as he pulled in; sundress white, hair black as night and pinned back as if on her way to Sunday service.

Maybe it was the distance, or the legs crossed and the short hem—but from afar, it was the kind of pretty that had him forget he hated her. A memory and reason why with every step she took too him having sprung off the wall.

PJ's head popped up in the windows behind her—nodded once when he and Kayden locked eyes. Looking bored as hell—probably having already been chewed up and spit out by her.

None of them talked about it. Just vultures in bulletproof vests waiting for another carcass to drop.

She came straight through the window when she got to him—a small bag visible in her hand from his mirror—planted a small kiss on his cheek.

"What the fuck—Jay—don't." But she was already had hand through the window, bag in his lap. It was hot against his thigh. *Food.*

Jay prancing around the hood to the passenger—his hand already unlocking the car. A command she no longer had to even say.

She slid in next to him, caught a hot sandwich bag in her lap before she settled in too deep.

Her next to him, smiling. Always. Him, elbow on the window, hand on the roof, staring ahead. "It's a peace offering, Kade... Like, actually."

Could have insulted him a million ways, he wouldn't have looked. But he didn't know she knew the word *peace*.

And it worked for a second.

He looked at her, hand offering the bag back out to him. "It's one of those with like, meatballs...the guys eat them."

He couldn't help but to scoff at her. And he didn't take it. "I'm sure PJ's hungry," the urge to yell was at least calmed. "What do you want, Jaylin?"

"Kade. Take it." *There it is.* Not far from the surface at all.

He smiled, adjusting his shoulders. Getting comfortable to watch her boil. But humor flaked away slow. In big chunks.

Started with her red eyes. Not that he cared, but that he hadn't seen her upset before. Scratches along her arm like a cat—gripping too tight just to ground down. He adjusted again, but because he was uncomfortable. And unsure.

"Yeah cool, okay." He laughed when she leaned up, chucking the bag out the window with a calmness that wrapped his skin like wire.

"Whatever—I was just..." She pinched the bridge of her nose an Kayden wanted her out. He wanted out. Have the conversation standing, his back to the car—"Jaylin, what'd you do now?" He sounded concerned.

He was—"I—I didn't. You. *Stupid.*" All volume and heat, like a light switched and the breaker busted. "Seriously though—Kayden I love a good game but you went over the line with this one."

"Don't rile me up and get to the fucking point."

"The point?" She laughed, opposite her seat—body against the dash, knees coming his way. "Got some quality time with Kaia an hour ago—dropped her off, Kayden. Want to guess what she told me?"

"Not sure, kid—do I? Or you pissed I didn't take your fucking sandwich?"

"Go check the fucking call log, Kayden. Daddy's asking questions."

"Bluff—" "I'll wait."

His jaw clicked. Her face hardened. Endless fucking bullshit with someone who had nothing but time. "I'm already fucking waiting—tell me, or I'm gone and you and PJ can fucking handle it."

"Might be best since you can't handle your shit with the minor." His head snapped, nose twitched.

"What? Couldn't control yourself then either? Had to cry to Kaia—"

"What the fuck are you talking about?!" His voice boomed. Echoed. Didn't realize how much until another flash of PJ came—and didn't leave

His hand began to shake as she cracked the door again, gracefully pulling herself out of the firing zone. Neither would say it, but they both knew it—probably for the best.

She still came in reach though. Elbows dropped onto his window and his chest rose nearly four inches. Heavy, deep sighs. When she just stared his foot hit the break, hand on the gears—

"Kayden—you ran your mouth off to Kaia?"

Gears slid back. His head too with fire and weight in his tear-ducts. Playing with imaginary friends again.

He thought of Darcy last night all slick and shit. Kayden preferred the idea of trashing her, but instead:

"Do we have to do this today, girl? You want me begging—that it?"

"No," she barked out. Too heated. Edging on control.

"Really though—what the fuck did you say to her, Kayden? What the hell's the matter with you? She hurt your feelings at the bonfire?"

The words flared. Temper too, anxiously silent.

He knew he didn't say anything. At first.

"Decided to give her your soul when she didn't want your di—" Her torso came through the window. Face to face, her shirt damn near stolen from how tight he gripped it.

"Jay—" "Kayden!" They both looked.

PJ—far too young, and way to green—whistling from across the courtyard like he had a right to fucking say anything. Let alone whistle. At Kayden. Like a fucking dog.

"You're not my only one," she whispered, breath hot on his nose.

Despite her balance being shook—despite his fist was her support, or PJ popping into a light jog—he could see it in the eyes. She was having fun. Just innocent, good, *fun*.

"Jaylin...Tell him to go inside before I fucking shoot him," hand loosening. Tempted to recall that peace offer, but knew she'd toy with it too. "I can't with you today—I need you to stop. Before I do something, please. And tell me what the fuck your aiming for right now."

"One wasn't enough?" She peeled his fingers back.

PJ slowed to a trot. Getting a read. Not liking what it said. "Hey Kade..."

Shut ups—from them both, in their own exasperated way. "Jaylin, what the fuck you just say a second ago?"

PJ smiling nervously, edging in. Sixteen or seventeen, but the size of a line backer. Like Kayden was.

Awkwardly jamming his hands into his pocket, looking towards the house; the sky—walking the line between non confrontational and obedient.

"PJ," he looked attentively to her.

Kayden responded too—watching her now.

"I got you a meatball sandwich," with the audacity to point to the bag rolled twice in dirt. "Go take a lunch."

He awkwardly went for the bag—infuriating Kayden. He could shoot him. Put the dog down before they break his legs and retrain him how to walk.

PJ, shuffling the paper between both hands. "Miss Jay—you gonna be ok—"

Kayden's voice answered first; overpowered second.

"Are you fucking kidding me?

"Get the fuck out of her before I get out this mother fucking car kid. You know damn well who the fuck you're talking about right now, get—"

"Shh—baby, *shhhh*," she laughed. Hand on his bicep until he pulled it into the car. Her pointing and giggling toward the house. "PJ go away."

"Okay," leaning her back on the car and peeping Kayden through the mirror; both silently watching PJ go.

"You jealous?"

"You turn my dick inward if that says anything"

Gasp—laugh—*both*. Playing into her hands. Jay turned back to face him with her arms crossed. "That's a new one for me." Didn't look. Hand hovered on the gear. "I need you to go have a chat with your girl, and find out if she's already talked to Dante."

"What'd she say to you exactly? Bitch was high all fucking night, and passed out when you weren't there so really, Jay—dying to know what *our little stoner* had to say."

"Yeah, funny you say dying; why don't you ask—"

"Cause I'm fucking asking *you*!"

Her face blanched—as if power dropped but she scooped it before anyone knew. "You delete the body-text?" Voice she used rare enough he didn't recognize it. Clipped. More surgical.

And words that felt like the walls closing in. She wasn't as confident. But the problem was neither was he.

He swallowed—she smirked. Had him. And she almost hadn't.

"All I know is chatter in the station about some dead guy, a man named Kade, a pig named Dante, and a bitch named Kaia."

Cracking his knuckles against his hand.

"Why'd—where does Apollo come into this? You call him?" He cleared his throat when it came back through his ears trembling.

"*Please,*" he'd insulted her. "The hell would I do that for—no. He got a tip. Which—so did I, but that's good news for later."

He glared.

"I'm having the house cleaned. Yours. Don't worry about it." Stirring up fuck all. Just because. "Tell me what else she could have got on you, baby."

She leaned back to him, hand through the window against his chest, and a longing sigh. "You are my favorite, so...we'll figure it out if you don't 0know, but...you're going to have to figure it out Kayden. Ugly or not, you hear me? I'm not ready for you to go back to dad yet."

That landed. Full-body hit. His chin lifted to help swallow—like his throat forgot how that worked.

She was petting along his chest but he couldn't feel it. The air in the car had thickened into soup and he—fish out of water. His hand wrapped hers and moved it to the window, staring ahead.

"Don't be scare—"

"Shut the fuck up Jaylin. Whatever happened—however she knows— I have no doubt it'll circle back to you."

She went to laugh, but never made it. "Guess we'll see."

The next time she touched him he lashed. It wasn't that it was even cold. But hand dropped lazily into the car against his leg—like her whole being was a fucking trespass. Not because he couldn't stop it, but because he was scared he'd go too far; *permanently* stop it.

No matter how many times he chucked her at the wall, she'd bounce back at him twice as hard until one day she fucking won't. *Then what?*

Apollo'd have Kayden's skin peeled back slow. And so fucking much more—his skin chilled from the thought alone and it only gave her more.

The power lines invisible, but tied.

Her arm still, caught in the crossfire between him and the door.
A squeak of pain or surprise when he slapped her hand away from him.

PJ's head was floating around in the windows still—sandwich in hand like the good boys they're trained to be. "I don't think you have any idea what you've done..."

"Me? I bet I do, sweetheart."

A pause. Long enough to let the silence take shape, to hit back. "She was asking questions," Jaylin began again—broken records. The heat hit his throat. Tongue thick. Battery acid and shame.

"And Dad's guy saw her with Dante. At the *station*."

He smirked and turned with his eyes slit. "Oh yeah—when was that?"

Too quick to be convinced she lied—"like a couple hours ago dude. This all just happened. I got the call like...*whatever*.

I'm not playing twenty questions. You wanna go back to being a prison bitch—? *Be my guest. Or*...stop playing with your little childhood friends, and clean up the mess you made."

"I didn't—"

"Fine, *my* mess. Guess what Kade...I go down, you know who comes with?"

Kayden's grip on the wheel clenched. Tendons and knuckles flared white. "As if you'd ever take the fall for shit. That bullshit the other day, this whole reason we're talkin' right now—you did that on purpose, you fucking bitch."

"I'm not sure I have any idea what you're talking about."

"He's been wanting blood on my hands for months...And you—the fucking whore who made it happen in a day."

He had to choke it back down—else he'd break there in front of her and drown them both in that betrayal. There shouldn't be anything left to hurt—but it did.

"This how it always gonna' be? You forcing my fucking hand Jay? Fuck anyone in the way?"

"Kayden. Stop acting like a victim. You *have* victims."

He would have just preferred a real blade. Cut his fucking throat. *Please.* She stood, eyes closed to face the sun. Sickeningly angelic if he saw a picture alone. But press play and you'll see an angel of death.

He had to digest that one. But it was the embodiment of indigestion. And with broken wings, moves like a snake—she came back, leaning in two minutes later.

"Hey, look okay. Me, you—no bullshit, *one* minute." She pulled a pin from her hair just to toy with it and bend it out of shape.

"So. You clean this up and we'll take care of you Kade. Don't interrupt me," hand to his face—pin with it, against his nose and edging the eye. "I'm talking lawyer, shelter, job—dad knows you personally. He doesn't know these other guys like that. *You* do..."

She took her hand back, let her forehead rest on the window and twirled it again. "He always wanted a son—you know?" Eyes batted at him before tucking low again.

She backed up, kicking at a rock. And he believed it, he'd bet they would. If he listened. He didn't trust it. Other problem was he meant it when he says he hates her.

She rocked back while holding the door, letting her spine curl. Voice higher—childlike and playful. "And, I know how this sounds—but, I didn't deal the hand. Don't blame me."

She danced in the open space where his breath should have been.

"I mean honestly though, there wouldn't be something to force if you'd just...Kayden—I wanna eat, and fuck, and shop, and have a little fun. I think you'd agree my way isn't the worst thing ever—I'm not *that* bad."

She leaned closer to his mirror, hoping to force herself into his line of sight. He looked further to the passenger window opposite her.

"You think they'll still have love for you and visit once the truth about Connor's out?"

"*Cody*." "Was it?"

His blood slowed and boiled at her speed and confidence.

"Just go tie up this end and—the rest just, is the rest. But from this side of the cell, okay?" He would have preferred the violence. A direct threat. "Just think about it..." Offered like it was still a choice.

How many ways has he told her he hates her—how many ways has he been ignored. He couldn't find up from down here. And he wanted to curl up. *Disappear*.

Grabbed the note. Rougher than he should have; softer than he meant.

Conflicted.

"Where's the gun you shot him with?"

His eyes slid over—not even angry anymore. *Terminal.* Hopeless. But not stupid. "*What* gun, Jaylin?" Despite that he was so paranoid he had it on him now. No fuckin' way he'd leave it around; felt like everyone was asking for it.

She started pulling back from the car slow. A frown at first—that he could live with. But something in him said she was proud. And what the fuck did it mean if a person like her—wanted him close by?

"Actually think about it, okay? And come find me when it's handled."

She took five more steps back, but the moment he could see the end of her dress and the start of her skin, he kicked the car in reverse. Pulled out, dragging through the gravel. Aiming for the rocks to fire like bullets— knock a bitch in the head. But looking in the mirror—didn't see her, didn't see rocks.

Only space for a reflection that expected him to explain the difference between him and her after all. He didn't look back at the mansion—didn't slow while peeling out.

Gates nearly keying both sides of his car; a skinny miss, slicing through as they widened. But no matter the speed, no matter the clawing, or head punching—that sensation stayed in his chest, and in his head. And he couldn't name it. Only knew it had him heated. Excitable, but angry. Hysterical with tears and cackles. Violent. Physical, because physically *rattling.*

Because Jay was always going to be right in the end. Even when she wasn't. Kaia pulled his phone or spied like a fucking rat. Kaia knew something. *And now Apollo does* too. Spit caught in his throat at a sudden gasp. Memory black—nothing around but sensation. Out numbered, over powered—*darkness.*

He coughed viciously bur let tears mix as his eyes watered. Art and tragedy—*because it's never been real.* It stayed in his chest.

And at the next light, he opened the note.

Desert View—back left. Outside vending. Have fun while you can bby. & pick us…luv u (:

The light turned green and Kayden crushed the paper until his knuckles popped. Driving like maybe he could outrun whatever was coming next.

And if not—just pick up enough speed to take it out with him.

Love Languages

|XXXII|

Hours rolled by and later afternoon cracked into evening. Concern, edging on panic now. And hungry hang overs, plus a concern driver, found themselves in for one more bite. Maybe one more fight too. Leti ran to the "bathroom," and he'd already paid. Despite saying she could.

The chemistry was beginning to taste only like fighting and fucking, because she got mad-mad. Quiet on him as they drove through to Darcy's area. Only driving by. Not even sure Cachí was welcome.

Just running surveillance; checking for Kayden's ride. Or Jaylin's. Sun creeping sideways in the sky. They checked again an hour later, but still nothing. And he was getting anxious just from her. Failing.

"Where now?" she eventually asked, maybe pretending to be asleep, or maybe just actually tired. They didn't speak, but it felt less because of tempers and more just auto-pilot on two machines.

The once syrup-orange, shadows dragged long across the street. Heat too thick. Cachí cracked the window halfway. Lit a joint but stifled it out after 3 puffs and an offer. Leti shook her head. Said *thanks* a minute too late. She had been watching his knee bounce, small rapid jostles until he breathed in the fire. His body stilled.

Did it count as being better in the silence if he cheats?
Leti picked at her nail nervously. He was just going to let her be mad. *And* still help. She looked him from head to seat.
Eyes closed, car running but stalled in a loading zone. Traffic dense and nerve wracking beside them.

The further from lunch she got, the more she remembered the good conversations and the less she remembered about the anger. He opened his eye while she stared. Looked away quick, but he didn't fake it. Cleared his throat. "Sorry," he said to her, adjusting his seat further up.

"Some babe kept me up all night. Had to close 'em for a second."

"No, yeah," the laugh was small, but it didn't sound forced to either of them. "I—yeah...same"

The sun had shifted out, and the city had toot. Nine to fivers watering the families and closing their daily puzzle for the day. But the shadows and the crooks yawning, moonlight their morning.

Then turned the heat on low and turned like he was going to say something before his phone buzzed against his thigh.

"That can't be good," he grinned playfully.

But when he pulled the phone, his mouth twisted into something ugly. He stared into the cracked screen. "*Pinche pendejita,*" he muttered. Rejected the call for it to buzz again.

Rejected. Buzzed a third time and he snapped it up to his ear, voice sharp as a blade. "What?"

Leti shrank n her seat—not because of the volume, but because of the sharpness to it. The heat. Like being amputated and cauterized.

He didn't look, but she knew he noticed from how his shoulders shrunk.

On the other end, Jaylin's voice poured like syrup, drunk and playful. She said something filthy then laughed. Finished quick with,

"Don't hang up! I'm with Kaia," like it was an afterthought.

Cachí's hand whitened around the phone. Leti looked, then glared when he got out. Far enough to raise his voice, near enough tot say he wasn't trying to mute Leti out.

"Jaylin, I swear to god if—"

"Blah blah, big man, I know," she interrupted, laughing again. "Come find us, then." *Click.* Dead line.

Cachí slammed his palm against the roof of the Camry. Not hard, but enough for the echoes. Leti could see him standing there with tight shoulders, head bowed, contemplating. *Controlling.* Himself. Because he wasn't moving.

She stared forward, vision blurring. The spotlights coming down from the overhangs at the station blended together with some from the past.

Leti; her father; she couldn't remember how long. Maybe a month after the accident. Maybe a week. Time moved differently for a couple years after.

But that echo—that palm hitting metal on a car roof—bang *Bang.* One unsure, a second harder with confidence.

But Cachí wasn't him—she wasn't her. Father was though—out from the grave, cleaned and clothed. Screaming to the sky. Brake lights and white lights blew by in the street in front of her, but Leti saw police lights swirling red and blue.

You're alright now sweetheart. ' As if her father is the monster. As if his pain isn't warranted or allowed. *You're safe, its over.* The officer's voice: too soft to believe, too protective to understand. Remembers her self: too young to know such words, but tells her anyway:

This only just begun. '

Cachí groaned as he crumbled back into the seat. Maybe a way to speak when he didn't know the words? He reached over, and then leaned back, twisting the cap off her bottle and holding it to her the way you'd offer a bandage to someone too stubborn to admit they were bleeding.

She allowed herself a sly smile. "Not babysitting huh?"

He dropped the bottle into the holder between them, light water spitting through the open neck. Looked towards his window as he stuffed the phone back into his pocket.

Leti picked it up slow and drank from it. Let the seconds slide before she put her hand out for the lid. Couldn't really critique Kaia for rollercoasters when she still road them by herself.

Leti wet her lips. Almost apologized, but choked that back too.

"Lid please," she asked sweetly. *Apologetically.*

His fingers grazed, the lid dropping onto before he turned to the wheel, kicking the old thing to life once more.

"Alright," he said flatly. "Back to where we started."

She didn't answer. Just mentally sang, *and around, round we go.*

This would be scraped to both their exhaustion. Some kind of silent, mutual understanding under the tantrums and stubbornness.

She tucked her hands tighter around the bottle and let the car roll them back into the winding cityscape.

The drive stretched long and the sky sat somewhere between sun and moon. Just a glow across the sky that made you feel like time's running out without knowing why.

When Cachí finally pulled into the busted little neighborhood, he killed the engine but anchored down in the seat.

"Hey..." Cleared his throat again like it might clear the air. "Sorry. After the phone. Jaylin just. *No se*—she..." trailed off. Lost.

"I think I get it," Leti helped. "I got bad vibe at the bonfires."

"Yeah, vibes," he agreed softly.

"Anyways." Leti—picking her nails again. "Don't get mad but—uh," Tearing the nail; jerking her sleeves down to stop herself. "I'm sorry, too.

And I appreciate like, the ride...the friend. Last night. *Now*." The apology wasn't graceful or overdone, but he didn't look mad at it; looked like he needed it the way she needed him to ride it out.

Cachí nodded. Picked at the bottom of the steering wheel the way she did her nails. "*Vale*. Good," he said awkwardly before tearing at the door handle with a grin. Couldn't say if it was real or fake because he didn't left it long enough for Leti to judge. The metal door protested with a groan. Leti's followed, looking down through the window at the bags. "A—Are we staying here...?"

Cachí—head shaking—waiting near the hood, "you're not." Probably too quickly and too confident bur they exchanged thoughts in a look: he didn't mean it; she understood; he was surprised.

Leti moved towards him at the front and quietly sucked down the fresh air while they still had it. Cachí too. Stalling though. Worried Kaia wasn't inside. And wasn't sure where to check next.

Plus—Kayden's car MIA, and no sign of Jaylin slithering around—something didn't feel right. Just hiding on the other side of the fog, waiting for him to turn—metal pressing against his skin—intuition told him to go. *Now*.

Or at the very least, crawl back in the car; lock the doors, and wait there. Because he didn't think Kaia was dead or anything, but he didn't think she was here. Looking at the house again; shifting weight as Leti tugged at the locked door before rounding to the front of the hood too.

Cachí Scanned the tree line behind her—sounds lurking in the distance, dogs barking furiously like something was there. Streetlamps low.

"Let's just wait in the car, Kade's not here," she looked to the house and he stepped towards her, herding. "Hurry up, sorry."

"Cachí, are you...Cachí..." Tone dropped to fear, her poster straightened. And he blamed himself until she moved into him, eyes behind him, and screamed, "Watch out!"

His body tensed, spine braced, and arms spread as if he could hold the line and block them despite walking right there in the middle of something.

When Solar Flares Land

SKYLINE DRIVE
00:01:27:⁴⁷

|XXXIII|

Gravel scuffled behind him; voices came in closer.

"Freeze! Hands up!"

The trap house sank into the earth a foot. And then the floodlights hit. Voices rising—half command, half performance—Cachí was mid-step around the hood. Leti not far; one hand curled around her bag and the other hanging loose until they latched onto his damn hoodie.

Wrong time, wrong place, wrong company—Cachí swearing under his breath. Nostrils burning and control loosening—scent of Kelvar, pepper spray, and dog out past the lights.

"*FREEZE!*"   "Everyone out! S-F-P-D!"

Fists to the doors. More tires rolling in behind them, dog barking—a fucking bomb squad—*this wasn't routine.* This wasn't some bullshit flex to make a point at Kade.

This was Kayden getting swatted for pissing someone off.

Officers hiding within the lights to the left. More to the right casing the house—neighborhood lights slicing through blinds like judgement.

His eyes couldn't stop flickering, mouth couldn't close—only felt held to this earth by the trembling hand rattling against his spine.

Praying she doesn't go to the small of his back.

Eyes wide looking for Dante—unsure if he wanted to see him, or prayed he didn't. —*fuck!*— A barrel of a rifle caught the light and made him flinch—arm shooting behind him, pulling Leti into him, both drowning under the bellow of a megaphone blaring:

"Get your hands up! Do not reach—*GET 'EM UP!*"

Cachí's instincts weren't to resist, but she didn't do anything. And neither did he. But the metal cold on his back—was about to be colder and on his wrists.

That terrified him. Too late to toss it, too late to walk it back, too late for Leti to go.   —*are we staying here*—

Another barrel flashed in the light. He didn't like guns pointed at him.

Made him think about Matías. And Mikki—

screaming. Dante bleeding. Cachí's arms trembled too.

"What the fuck did I just say kid?"   *"Hey—what's your name...?!"*

      "Get down now!"   *"Hands up!"*

"You're gonna get tased!"   *"Open the door!"*

          "Dog will bite!"   *"Do it now!"*

He could taste the helplessness looming—feel the control pouring as his breath got deeper.

"Cachí..."

He pretended not to hear it. He couldn't—he didn't know how. Not there. Slowly, one hand came up. A pause too—yard felt quieter. Like maybe dull enough to claim innocence. "We're no—"

"I don't give a fuck—get *both* up now! Boutta get tased, brotha'!"

Leti's chest pushing into his back—voice only managing his name, like she couldn't complete a thought either until, "I don't—like the guns," like a fucking mirror. Always just a goddamn reflection—and he felt that deep, because neither did he. But how stupid will be look when she feels the one on his back. Or when the cops do; Cachí standing in the beginning of many ends.

He squeezed twice onto whatever part of Leti he was holding. "Stay behind me." He didn't ask. But he didn't have a choice. He let go. Raised both his hands, slow. Fluid and controlled. Breath steady despite deciphering what he saw.

Bullet—grinning through the muzzle and aimed between his fucking eyes— breath less steady then.

Everyone inside crowding outside. Some of the badges still running hot—some of them winding down like they were bored.

No bomb, no body. *Bullshit.*

Just angry they came and angrier to leave without something worth it. Guy in mesh shorts asking if this counted as community service; chick in smudged lashes clutching her heel like a toddler with a toy—*Cody.*

Cachí could hear that name from six feet down. It was a scream when he heard it across the yard.

Everyone always so— *"Haven't seen him."* Even before they were ever even asked. Maybe it wasn't a swat, maybe it wasn't Kayden cleaning house— *maybe it was Dante*. Dante.

The guns. *Matías*—but maybe it was Cachí that was shot. Maybe not then, but now—door slammed loud and he flinched like the gun ahead popped. Just saw the blood splatter.

Turned—Leti, down before he even got to say goodbye. For just a moment, lights flattened, and the men became shadows again—

Memories fact or fiction—?

Three seconds, maybe four—Cachí gasped, melted back. His body curved with relief when she pushed forward. Said something again, too.

Maybe even more than his name—but he didn't catch it.

Couldn't. Felt something like— *no fucking idea*, but maybe how a panic attack feels. Eyes squinting, scared of the dark now, like he'd be the only one in it.

Footsteps moving in though—he knew it was okay—but behind him, around him, the chaos before after Matí—more approaching on his flank—backside of the car, working their way behind him.

Not for him but teaming up for Leti. Frozen—more mumbles about the fucking gun, she's as bad as him but what the fuck for—

"Hey—*hey*," Cachí stammered, looking both to the ones over the car at the trunk, and the one coming straight ahead, out of the light like a ghost.

"She's just—careful!" Snatched his arm from the sky, but seemed relatively unalarmed. Stared at Cachí like his face was an exam, before calling back with a chuckle.

"Damn Rookie's right, man!" Confirming an object found—not a man. Under lights, pressure, and steel.

Copper walked him forward, cooperation within the chaos, and Cachí felt Leti's hand slip from his hoodie.

"Bro—" he tried a light tug back to Leti, and the grip on his arm got sharper. "I'm cooperative but I need—"

"Don't think about it man, just take it easy. We'll sort it out."

He couldn't look; he was furious.

At himself. At the cop—at Leti not getting back in the car quick enough when he gave her a single second—he was angry. *No*—he was scared.

Of everything. Leaving Leti in a limbo somewhere between the headlights and the concrete, all just a movie playing over the wrong soundtrack. Confused.

Officer in his ear talking over silence Cachí wanted to leave open for her. But *Dante this or that*—Cachí should have listened. *That* was the out.

But Leti's voice silently screamed. Sharp and too loud—they didn't earn her heat, they didn't deserve it. Just smashing through stone forcefully.

Plea's, small. Scared—behind him.

Knew the sound too well, just didn't want to know it from Leti. Wind-knocked-out, spine-pulled, fish-on-dock gasp that comes with someone throwing you face down against the hood.

His feet rooted into the grass, fists tightened at the sound of air squeaking through lungs like a mouse—*like Mouse.*

But the sound. The air, the room—*the control.*

Kayden, Mick, and Cachí jumping rooftops like an overlay. Leti's gasp on repeat, body-to-car too, when his foot missed the ledge.

Fingers grabbed the edge hopelessly—sliding, one at a time. Sweat, heat, excitement—knowing he was going to fall and wondering why he even held on anymore anyway.

He couldn't see Leti, but he could see it.

Hand on the shoulder, knee to the back of hers. Forcing her bent over, legs spread, angry metal cuffs on wrists meant for cheap bracelets and looping pens for mandalas.

No warning, no quiet pull or hot flush—only the storm. Where everything spun. Right before—it all went black.

00:01::22:18 || XXXIII || SKYLINE DRIVE

The hood of the Camry caught her like punishment. Not enough to break bone, but enough to knock the breath out of her, force a whimper before she bit it back down.

A cuff, latched down against her wrist almost immediately. It was too fast though—even faster than Kaia when Leti's mind pled for stillness.

She didn't even run—didn't *resist,* just didn't ask "how low" when they said *'down.'* Hesitated.

So many voices everywhere before she only heard her own gasp. Slammed down, a pause.

Another slam, and a third final one, only figuring out what the fuck was even happening when she was crashing down from the hood of the car.

Cachí was free from the guy that had him. *Free?* Because—maybe, now they weren't.

Both—*all of them*—coming straight towards her. Few feet away, and then tangled quick. Cement peeling back skin on her leg—space for the rocks.

She might have played dead. Might have just been searching for a familiar face. Because Cachí's slipped.

Thread snapping—everything in him lunging forward to either catch it or run from its explosion.

It wasn't fear she felt—it was too fast to settle and sit in fear. It was distance. It was *amusement.* When the man who'd slammed her hit the concrete harder than she the hood. Wasn't sorry about it. Half in the guys arms, half in his chest.

Cachí didn't swing—not yet. Just twisted in the mess together. Roars like animals. He took a hit to the face.

Then three blurs in blue colliding down with them too; Cachí beneath them—burying his anger in both English and Spanish until one knee came down on him.

Pressed hard on his shoulder, another across the back of his thigh and multiple hands shoving down. Pulling.

Leti's knees scrapped more, shuffling back. Mind didn't register fear, but her body still tried to. Sliding a foot beneath her once she got a couple feet between them, hand on the ground and her other on her knee—she doesn't run, but she stands. *Stood.*

Different officer, same force—kicked her foot, his ankle smashing against hers, dropping her another level. She got it now. *Kaia.*

She understood the need to move fast—because nothing was fast enough once caught. Not even the stillness kept her safe.

Unable to move, unsafe to freeze beside swinging fists and angry men. The Kicker came up like she was a rag doll too. Stole her arm out from under her; then the other.

Only contact when her chest pressed to the ground. "Cross your ankles!"

She didn't mean to, but the empty tears fell again. Feet didn't listen; eyes didn't.

She felt his hand over her shoe but against her heel before her leg dropped onto the other. "Stay down, and do not resist, or you will be tased," than louder, "You speak English?"

"*Do you!?*" She turned for that one—dialects only of violence—he didn't acknowledge that she spoke. Too busy salivating over the fight feet away.

Then dropped, cuffed, and handled. She watched him go. Chin against the cement. VIP not to a scene— a fucking burial.

Cachí–far from dead—centered ahead. Not even throwing fists, just shoving angrily and thrashing elbows like he just wanted the space.

Leti thought she tried. She must have—her voice was cracking and throat scratched.

Screamed for Cachí—*stop, please*. Or them. Just once. But no one heard—*no one cared*. So did she really say anything at all?

"Enough!" Eyes shifted, chin stayed. Cachí hadn't had enough.

"Shit—alright! That's one of the D's kids, get up."

"He fucking hit me I don't give a shit."

A fast spill of responses from Cachí straight into the ground. Twisted tongue and words sharp enough to slice clean despite the syllables breaking.

They pulled him back, arms pinned—but it was settling, she thinks.

The guy yelling shit walked by her face like she wasn't there either. Dust from his boot even kicked to her mouth. Somehow the boots were the loudest thing there. The sound of the rocks popping and crunching beneath them.

"Flin—you swingin' now?" skin must have slapped against skin, and a hearty chuckle from Boots. "Don't be a pussy, Jason. Get him up."

Kaia—Cachí, echoing between Leti's eyes. Leti's eyes were opened, but she'd gone digging for stillness in thought.

Finding only more chaotic memories she didn't need, but maybe wanted. Maybe the familiarity.

The way she could see Kaia slugging the school RO as if it wouldn't hurt. Started as a peer v peer scuffle that ended as teens expect it too. In house suspension—some missed events. Started feeling a little bold to the bullies when Kaia came back—wasn't even Kaia's fight. It was the way everyone assumed it was.

Leti's cheek twitched against an ant as she drooped further into gravel. Voices collided like a new band class.
She didn't lift her head for awhile after that. And couldn't wipe the ant from her cheek, so she didn't even try. Just fell deeper within her thoughts.

Not inside still memories. But memories that stilled reality. The sound though—more boots on the gravel near her head. She braced—arms back, unable to protect the vital parts; spine, cheeks, calves—anything exposed tightening like steel.

"Ay, get over here." Was she supposed to check if he was speaking to her? Was she planning on speaking to him if she was?

"Yeah?" Lady voice—but no—*she's wrong.*

Leti wasn't speaking to anyone. Because no one speaks to her.

"Why's this one bleeding—get her off the fucking ground and a napkin." Boots crunching away from her but closer to Cachí.

"Or some shit—come on guys. *Cachí*—quit it." Boots scuffed again—closer to Cachí, further from her.

But it didn't matter—didn't matter if she didn't lift her head to watch—her whole body came up.

Boots nodded once with an accomplished smile and a thumbs up. She hadn't moved or looked, and was glad she hadn't.
He didn't deserve her acknowledgement. But Cachí was motionless. She watched for his spine to lift, as if he no longer breathed. But he did. Slow. And noticeable. Face down, arms cuffed and pried back like a crowbar.

Boots slapped an officer's bicep—same sound, meant *again*. Rocked his head to the side, pointed opposite Cachí. "Get off, come on."

The three pinning him didn't challenge anyone—everyone looked unsure. Boots, too. Walking on limbs handing out vouches to angry things.

Cachí didn't really fight—not really. Sour ass attitude mostly, bodying the main guy backwards when they put him on his knees.

"My bad man—weak knees." Spitting to the side.

They all watched. Let boots handle him up annoyed. Bodied him back into the car and stood toe-to-toe.

"Cachíflin—*enough*!"

"Get fucked, Pig," less fire and more smoke.

"You made your point, boy. Stop thrashing like a goddamn toddler so I can talk to you like a man. Come on, get up."

Silence. Couple cruisers closing up, easy breeze. But the swearing stopped. The movement too. It took everyone surrounding Cachí a collective minute to ensure he meant it though.

"Alright," the older man tried again. "Last chance, kid."

Cachí came up ten times easier than he'd gone down. Spit blood that time. Maybe he did the first too—she didn't look, Leti didn't like red. Too much on her knee now that could *not* be there if she thought hard enough.

Leti looked at the moon. Silver. Forgot it was night with the floodlights. Never seen the bomb squad before.

Calling all clear and shit like it was real. Leti looked at the house. Maybe it was. Small slits in the blinds next door—many eyes peeking out—more entertained than disturbed. Cell phones in the window too.

Cachí looked when she shifted sideways. Wanting to be seen all this time—terrified her wishes will turn sour too. Give her exactly that, but exactly now. Make her rounds on the internet.

Leti was counting body cams—breath pacing faster, but still hers; still holding...But she sees bodycams online. Panicking about what she said, or how she fell. Tears. No. Silver. Moon.

The older man stepped in closer to Cachí. "You lash out again, and I can't write it off. You get me?"

They had him leaned against the trunk of his car.

Cachí's chest heaved under his hoodie, like his ribs were still trying to hold the last ten minutes in place. Shoulders sinking like that fought it the whole way, but arms locked so tight—didn't have a choice.

"You hear what I just said?" If he did, he didn't budge.

"Booyyy, you better fuckin' answer me. Put your ass right back where I found it and go my way."

Still, he only breathed. Another few minutes—though probably some kind of seconds. Slow moving and miserable. Cachí broke contact first.

Hands behind his back, he tipped his head over his shoulder.

Boots crossed his arms, rolled on the balls of his feet a moment and bounced heel to toe another one. "Got something you're trying to say, Cachíflin?"

Cachí watched the cracks in the ground. "Back pocket."

Boots was steady. *Stiff.* Tightened the way she braced like he already knew. Leti watched carefully now. Every silent exchange—

"Check his goddamn pockets, Officer. *Would ya?*" Less silent then.

The cop reached. And then swore and only then did Cachí cautiously turn to her—her gaze already ghosted the moment he breathed her way.

Then couldn't look back—too busy watching the hands on the silver body. Slick trigger. Less scary when not pointed, but terrible all the same. Accidental trigger fingers and twisted impulses people keep buried. She really didn't like it Shifting a bit, arms pulling against the cuffs.

Just wanted to cross her arms. Maybe she'd felt it. Maybe she didn't care so long as it didn't have a finger attached. "It was an emergency." Cachí grumbled. Stubborn. Guilty even.

Last gun she'd seen up close had chunks of her dad's head. She tried to match the two memories or mush them like a puzzle, but they didn't go.

So she stayed. Still. Scattered puzzle pieces in her hands with no place to go. No one said anything for a minute—at least not where she listened. Background noise was muted. Cachí stewing, but not heat.

Those nerves —*what do you need from me right now*—

She couldn't help but to watch. Boots looking disappointed.

Cachí rubbed his shoulder against his cheek, muttering. "I told you it was there, didn't I."

Rhetorical. But still calm, despite bordering on ruin. Boots gently squeezed Cachí's shoulder—head lower—and whispered:

"What would Matías think, kid?"

"That I should have hit him harder." All volume again, and spit to the feet of a specific Badge. "Matí didn't throw women. Or point pistols at them."

The last one cracked in his chest.

The older man, Boots—he rocked on his heels again and pursed his lips. "That's what this about? Freaked out?"

"Shut the fuck up, man. Not your goddamn business, *jodido puta.*"

The fury was false; and Boots—not sarcastic. The question and the venom poked at Leti's interest, too. Wondered what'd happen if she blurted it— *what are we talking about?*

Kaia probably would of. Scream it even if they ignore her. *Tried* to ignore her. Leti tries all the time. Thought amused her, but her brain skipped, then stomach dropped quick—Cachí stole a half glance towards her, but changed course and met the ground. Never made it.

The moment was tagged though—Leti'd come back to it. Somewhere safer. "Marcy—will you—deal with that?"

The lady-cop leaning on her car watching the show—leaned up, nodding to her name. Boots pointed around Leti's area again.

"The girl—will ya?." Boots pointed out Leti and Cachí was no longer shy about staring.

She burned under the glance but flinched when someone came up from behind. Settled back into the woman when she heard metal slide against metal and a lever release.

"You're good," the woman smiled. She reached around her belt—gun there too. Kleenex came her way next. "For your leg, hun. Little scratch."

Neither Leti or the woman ran away. Neither screamed. No one cried.

Leti swallowed, and watched her glide back to her car. Laughed in response to something another said. Not about Leti, she didn't think. Just—a joke. A laugh. A normal time. Everywhere as fucked as home.

Leti pulled her arms to her chest, hugging herself as if someone would come back to take them. Was she supposed to walk away now?

Did someone expect her to go inside—or was that not allowed? If her bag was in Cachí's car—could she ask for it.

Could she? Wasn't sure. And was she even free to go—or simply unrestrained? Commands as unclear as the start. "Alright, deal?" Boots.

Cachí had been watching her. Eyes felt like being pet by an urchin.

He looked—frustrated. Disappointed. Just not great, looking at her. Because would he even fucking be there right now if they weren't running around looking for Kaia?

"Cachíflin, dammit—" "*Ya*! Do what you gonna do but get on with it, *vato*."

"Yeah alright, go on then, tough guy." he swung his head toward the light. "I'll be sure Dante gets this. Hey—I think the boys will get him there best. Where the fuck did Todd go—" Suspicious smile, holding the gun up like an apple and waving it twice.

Cachí didn't resist when a young cop came up. Same age as Cachí, if not somewhere between him and her. Looked even younger in a baggy fitted badge. Nudged him forward before Cachí glared at him.

Boots gave another big thumbs up. "Go on 'den. Don't make Todd push."

The amazing part was—Leti smothered a laugh. And people seemed to acknowledge that. Not spoken word. "S—Sorry." He looked madder.

Nervous habit? Tension bubbling up. Watching her now, probably thinking next step was melt down.

Maybe that was why he was angry—messy night. *Needy.*

He shifted. One step, then another. And one final look back when Boots came up to Leti.

Jolly fuckin' guy. "Todd's excited is all. *Chatty.*"

And she waited. Looked the guy up from down—pretty average joe. Nothing was really ugly or attractive anymore.

At least until it spoke some. He looked—normal. Older. Like a dad.

Salt and pepper. Looked soft, but could have been the giddy grinning rounding out his cheeks. "Alrighty, be safe then, cutie." Saluting her and leaving. Felt oddly empty.

Eyes rolled back to Cachí, who—didn't toss her keys. Didn't say, *wait here please,* not even, *let's take a ride.*

He just...left. And didn't say anything at all.

00:01:19:³⁷ || XXXIII || SKYLINE DRIVE

The cruiser door opened ahead, hinges whining like a tired old man trying to stand. Cachí blinked once; let himself be turned. The officer guiding him didn't meet his eyes. Just walked through the motions.

Younger ones though—and familiar. Particularly the passenger side— but he couldn't place a name on the other one. But this one.

Grinning. Turned and staring though. Made Cachí's eyes slant. "*What?*"

"Nothing," he chirped. "Knew I recognized you."

Flat, head cocked five-degrees. "You want a fucking prize?"

Made the first settle back, but the second—driver seat—chimed in. "So, you allergic to walking or something?"

Cachí didn't blink. "I didn't do shit bro. You wasting time and money—*for what?*"

Rookie—*Todd*—slapped the driver's arm. Stupid fuckin' name, Todd. "Didn't do shit," mocking. Like Cachí wasn't going to see him on the other side of the door shortly.

The other one, piling on— "He's just passionate about hugging asphalt."

Cachí slumped back against the seat. Jaw clenched, breath fire—but sense present. "You're hilarious," he muttered. "So what then? Not telling me a charge, or—you just that shit at your job?"

"Aw, there goes the little girlfriend—op, *noooo*, not inside."

Cachí turned sharp. Other one: "Dante said if your name came up again— pull you in," scratching his head watching Cachí watch Leti.

"Bullshit," Cachí said—quieter now.

Eyes on his hands, breath quickening—face heating. House looming. Driver—droning on. Cachí didn't fucking care.

"You wanna argue with the big man," the passenger turned, smug again, "Do it somewhere with less zip ties my man."

Cachí didn't respond. But he ear marked it for later. Both their cruiser doors shut with a heavy thud. Air sealed in. World shut out.

And every other second he couldn't help but turn—counting the steps between Leti and the house. Even the street somehow better and worse. He could see it now. Engine grumbling under them. Kayden swooping by, Jaylin at his side, knights in shining fucking.

Come find us—Cachí's body slowed. Pieces clicked. Commentary, and silence. Knew it felt like a loss when he walked. "Fucking bitch..."

"Hey now," driver. "Not the girlfriend then?"

Through the back window, he could still see her. And he could see Jaylin. Not here, not what she could do—but how she *would* do it.

His neck nearly broke jerking around again, car coming off the E-brake.

He was going to thrash. He was going to break his fucking wrists and break the back fucking windows—Leti.

Still standing there, exposed and in the open. Her breath too shallow. Jaw set. Shoulders locked like she was holding something inside that wouldn't come out anyway.

Not fear. Not anger. Just weight. Her own weight. And no one else to help carry it. He clenched his jaw. Held still but clenched again. That's when it started. That slow twist in his chest. Not rage. Not even dread.

Just the sick, steady realization she was going to be left behind. And he wasn't going to break anything at all. He was going to take.

"Hey wait—"

The cruiser inched forward. A gravel scrape. A pause. They looked back through the mirror—four eyes and his own. "Weren't you asking about some kid—Cody?"

Front seats squeaked as Driver turned and passenger mimicked. "Flyn, you got something, or you going to make it worse on yourself?"

"I dunno," he muttered, down at his feet again. Fired up and confident, and then unsure like waves. "Cody....?"

Could fuck himself trying to un-fuck her and even crash down in Kayden's place. "He uh, was with someone before he uh...a girl, right?"

It tasted like undercooked regret. But their look changed from familiar neighborhood favors, to authentic. All jokes off.

"How, and what do you know?" Driver again. Passenger was a joke on his own.

Cachí cleared his throat, glancing towards the house again. "The girl you're assuming's mine—?"

Eager passenger turned. Cachí didn't want to look—leaned back instead.

Unintentionally letting the lie—the weight build, their pressure grow. Maybe it was intentional. Maybe he'd do it twice.

He turned again—Leti at his car door across the yard. Driver side; not trying to get in—just standing. Like a ghost, haunting someone on the other side. "That's the kids girlfriend."

A three-way of doubt and suspicious glanced around. Driver and passenger holding each others. Cachí still.

Passenger cracked a smile. More teen on caffeine then cop. Ducking his neck and searching his side mirror. *Sold.*

"Where is she—bro, they had female DN—"

"Shut the fuck up, Toad." Driver—weighing it out. Probably ensuring no obvious flaws in the logic. Else why not. Just taking her on a ride.

Cachí could feel their instant tension through the divider. Leaned back then. Nodding slow with a frown like he knew the rest. He didn't want to look—feared he'd look too angry when he should look more like a rat, but he had nothing to gauge the temperature with.

Couldn't see bodies, no words—cautiously, he looked up.

Passenger had typed something on his cell—shoving it at the Driver.

Driver's eyes slanted, watching Leti. Who was worse every time Cachí looked; leaned up against the garage now, knees to her chest on the ground.

Car almost hid her completely though, so, probably her point. But she didn't *disappear* completely. *Not yet.* Made what he did next more bearable.

"I—was told to watch her." Cachí stumbled to keep himself slow. Almost said *guard* to make it all the more tempting, but...imagined Dante leaving him out for kidnapping or something next.

Fucking gun didn't have numbers on it—fucking mess.

Those two up front too—subtle glances, tit-for-tats. But they were buying it. Jay would be so proud. Jay—would be. Proud. Of herself.

Call in a threat. Barely lift a figure but large odds dropping dynamite into a pond. Let just anyone in there get snagged on the drugs or the weapons charge. Too quiet when he left her on the stair.

Truly little fight when they clapped back at the bonfire.

Kaia—keeping Jay's obsession occupied.

Fire blazed against his chest then, because he absolutely hated her. Might even hate Kayden more for being *bought* though. *By them.*

Never did really understand what Apollo had. If it was for family—? Well Cachí thought it was enough. At the time.

He let the silence stretch. The lies—the truths—settle. Tired of not feeling safe. *Of not being it.*

Didn't even mean to go for the guy—didn't mean to take Leti with—but the cop kept firsthand her going down.

Cachí watched up front again when Driver fucking *finally* reached his radio clipped to his vest.

Didn't say another word. Didn't need to. And maybe they believed him. Maybe they didn't want to risk being wrong if it meant a life.

But all the ego, the jokes, the poking fun—? *Where at?* Cachí looked over his shoulder one last time.

Ball against the garage—Leti didn't react when the uniform came toward her. Didn't even look up at first, but he turned forward again. Didn't want to watch any more.

Cachí let the lie settle between his shoulders and the vinyl. Leti—safe at least.

Maybe it was finally safe enough to sleep. Dreams on a podium, debating himself and asking: Has he always felt unsafe?

Or does he just believe he deserves to?

Because the wrong sibling got tagged in for the long run and he's loosing them the race.

Omissions of the Kings

DALY CITY POLICE DEPARTMENT
00:00:49:⁵⁵

|XXXIV|

The station felt thin tonight. Officers worked slow. Paperwork stacked up. A stillness that made his skin feel tight. Like something underneath was trying to get out.

Dante wiped the back of his neck with his hoodie. He didn't join the raid. Easier that way. His badge got him access—his father's stars taught him when to vanish.

So he made his own coffee tonight.

Machine was still gross. Not sure how he ever came to like it in the first place. Shit machines, shit gas stations. Dante pouted at the cup before catching himself judgmentally.

Tossed the jacket over a chair when the fuel warmed his blood and—against all better judgement—went for his phone.

They had to be done by now.

```
> 1 MISSED CALL—AIREHART, J.
> 1 NEW VOICEMAIL.
```

He hit play. "Ay, guess who I found, mate! Say hi to you Pop-pop."

"You can still get fucked, pig—" Unmistakably Cachíflin. "Dante—you too." Felt a little bad that perked Dante up more than the coffee did. Died quick, someone else in the car with them bickering in the back now.

"At Lincoln again. But calling 'cause the girl he's...*escorting*, I guess. Says she the one hookin' up with the—guy. Person. Case.

Yeah, officer got some details, but otherwise told him to fuck off. Cute though.

T-A-Y-L-O-R-E, first initial 'O.'

Dante pulled a face and played it back but the voicemail didn't hesitate. Didn't rewind—just talked some more. "No priors, not resisting. Physically anyway," laughing, third player chatting in the back.

"Yeah, right…"

It was annoying. "Apparently RJ did ask if her tongue counts as a weapon though. Thought you'd want to know. Kid's carrying. Scratched up the only place it shouldn't be if you got me…Yeah, uh—LaMarco's got it."

Fuckin' pretty silent now. Dante stood still for a beat. Paperwork rattled in the air-con. He didn't touch it. Didn't trust his hands. Mouth. *Feet—*

Another step down the wrong street, kid.

The fluorescent lights buzzed louder than they should have and the laptop too, battery humming. He pulled the search and typed—TAYLORE, LETI.

Bit of a small file going at that point. For them both.

And this was a story he wanted to hear. Looking like fucking Swiss cheese already—he pulled Kaia's too. Tried to remember back to when Leti said they'd gotten into town. If he'd heard Cody's name even once at the fires…

Dante didn't like it. Didn't line up. And didn't have anyone else but Cachí's name all over it.

SISTER LISTED: TAYLORE, KAIA R.

Big eyes. Bigger file. Blank expression—just frozen mid-flight in arrest photos, school injury photos, evening of photos—hair stained red and bone like dust.

Medical, medical—he felt the spiral when his phone spooked him. Answered without thinking, eager for a run down.

"Hey, ya?" Dante pulled the phone back to check the name and his voice softened immediately. "You doing alright?"

Mikki came through warm and playful. "I am. Thought you might just have missed me—then saw the text."

Dante exhaled through a cracked smile. "Just wanted to see if we're still on for the run tomorrow," he rocked in his chair with a twist. "Or if you want to push it—I shoulda' called, sorry *amore.*"

Another pause. Mikki's voice gentled even more.

"You okay?" Dante hesitated counting the people around him. Station felt too big. All its old ghosts leaning closer.

"I think something's about to break loose. I'm good. Tired is all."

He pictured her stopped somewhere, biting back her lip struggling between pressing and privacy. Still working out the kinks again of what the other needs.

So he sat in the extra couple beats of quiet. Because it wasn't so unnerving with Mick. "Monday works, but we don't go far, I can make time. Just let me know, Dání. Get some rest, okay?"

"Yeah." Made him smile. Enough that he did a quick check for lurkers.

"Bye, babe."

He rocked the chair, "hey Mick?" *Idiot.* Couldn't say it now—*I do miss you*—wouldn't have said it then. "See you Monday," instead. And the line clicked off. Dante sat there a long moment, staring at the blank laptop screen. Another squeal as the chair came up.

The last time a missing girl hit his desk was also the last time he'd made a promise on the job. Mentor called it a hard lesson, but necessary. Woman came back. Just—not really.

Him fresh out of academy, and not far off from boot camp.

Learned every lady had a story then too—most just stop telling them in rooms not built to listen. Made Dante see Mick a little different. Protect her different. It'd piss her off hearing it plain, but it was obvious.

The job changed him. The bullshit before. *Life.* Nodding to himself.

Life just changes him. *People.* Time, the seasons, earth—

Dante closed the laptop with a hard snap and a snarl—and he had no doubt more would die and more would change the further down this road he ran. All he asks is the road is wide enough for three.

Outside, a siren split the night—long and low. Dante pressed the heels of his hands into his eyes, breathing deep.

Unsure whether it was the dread or duty keeping him upright, but he'd go until he dropped.

Run for now. *Again.* Or the range. This time, he just promised himself he'd be ready. *So—*

Guess he didn't learn his lesson after all.

The chair squealed as Cachí leaned back, arms slung casual over the frame's metal. Felt too casual when Dante closed the door behind him; no other officers.

Just him. And just Cachí. That was either a favor or punishment. But that evening—feels like punishment.

He dropped a file on the table but didn't sit; didn't even look like he wanted to. "Back pocket?"

That felt too calm. Tight muscles around Dante's eyes. A set up, is what that was. Eyebrows, unmoving. Masked. Cachí felt naked in an icebox. Silence drawn out. Then:

"Unregistered *tambien*?" Posture, tone, stayed relax. Mouth tightened.

Cachí kept his tone low like it changed the fact he thought he was in the right. "Your boys beat on—"

"Yeah I heard you body slammed her." Instant and flat but it sliced as deep as he could then. "Pistol taped to your spine? What happened to fists before steel?" Dante pressed.

That cut deeper actually. "Cachí…"

He'd never looked so grave. Not since Matí. Cachí's eyes hit the floor. Dante took a step closer, voice lower like they weren't listening *somewhere*. "Will this trace back to Cody's murder?"

Eyebrows furrowed, head shaking, expression shock first. "*No*."

Second was processing what that meant—if somehow, *someway* it did trace back to it? Like maybe Kayden took the gun from his trunk?

Put it back? He swallowed. Stared at the outside of the folder like it'd distract him. *It didn't.*

"Right. Just want to make sure I have the facts straight Cachíflin. Next on the list—*listo?*" Dante grabbed the back of the chair. Waited.

Then, "tell me what Cody had to do with Leti and Kaia," Dante dragged out the chair; screeched against concrete, "*Jodido idiota.*"

The folder was as unreadable as Dante.

"Let's have it, *hermono*. You think you're walking in some type of middle ground," he said, elbows on the table, hands together.

"Neutral territory died with the kid, '*compa*. And you find Kaia yet?"

Cachí didn't speak, and that was an answer. Dante nodded.

"You think Kayden won't sell you out if it's him on the line? Do you really still believe in him Cachíflin? Don't tell me, but ask yourself. Be honest for once."

Third cut. He had been trying to help her. But maybe even that was a lie he told himself. Even if Cachí could speak, if he had the energy too, he had nothing to say. He'd been asking himself that all month. Dante went on. Not loud. But full with intensity.

"You think Apollo's going to house you? And not ask Cachí—*demand* something back?"

Maybe it wasn't that it was intense. Maybe only that it was truth. Cachí's face didn't move. That stillness of his—dangerous in its own way.

"Do you think Cody's the first linked back to him?"

Dante shifted his head; told Cachí to look at him with movement.

"Fucking pattern, Cachí—youre walking into it with a smile."

Cachí's mouth was dry but his palms were wet.

Dante's elbows slacked; hands dropped with a thud. Tilted his head like he was lining up a shot—but something wicked.

Something that knew exactly where to poke and how hard.

"Should I be dragging the fucking Bay for Kaia too?"

Cachí's breath dropped.

Dante let it digest. Cachí mixing between imagination and reality—what would Kaia look like. What Cody must have looked like. Aggressive imagination of a visceral thinker.

"You were seen with Cody before the bus stop. Fine." Dante added, lower now. Slower. "Where, *and how*, do Leti and Kaia fit in?"

Cachí tapped his thumb against the chair leg. "I lied," he admitted.

Dante's wound. Even if Dante would never say it, even if he forgave it— Dante wouldn't forget it. Not why he lied; not how far.

Not at all. Dante waited. Not patient, but waited. "She didn't know anything. About Cody. I...don't think Kaia knows anything either, I—" Voice cracked at the end. "They were leaving her there."

"Interesting," Dante's eyebrow raised. "Trap house not a good place to be then huh?" Dante tapped his finger on the folder. Once. Sarcasm.

Then again—the tapping. A third time too. Dante sighed, position still relaxed; eyes still guarded. "Okay. Why the bus stop with Cody—?"

A long wait, a quiet whisper: "He was scared." It's not like you could rat out the dead.

Not really. *Right?* Give a little to Dante; leave a little out for Kayden. And not because he wanted to protect him.

"He was shot leg first. Then the head—close range. Kid had reason to feel afraid."Cachí didn't think he mean it like a jab, but it still felt like one.

"I'm asking *why*, Cachí." Dante met his eyes, leaned in on his crossed forearms. "And if you lie..."

Please don't— Cachí—*don't say it.* Dante—*don't do it.*

"You lie to me again Cachíflin, and you're on your own."

His name felt like a swear word. He wouldn't admit it stung, but his face did it for him.

Cachí met his eyes for a moment; a tug of war with his conscience and—not pain, but *ache*. The kind of ache that only a few people can inflict but you trust them not to anyway.

Dante felt it too; not that Cachí understood it fully but he saw it.

Bruises under Dante's eyes, frustration flat with no heat.

Dante recognized it, but didn't bend to help. Leaned back, further away, crossed his arms instead. Cachí would be another half-dead ghost to him;

Dante would take Mikki with him. Then Kayden and Cachí forever.

Chills crossed his arms. "I don't know," Cachí began, hand fisting then flexing. "But..."

Leg bouncing. This wasn't walking the line, it was slipping over but hanging on like hell. Faster now, like no one else in the world would here.

"He was running something I don't know what," Cachí spit it out like it was hot. "I mean...scripts, but not *what.*"

Truth in his eyes begging to be believed. Cachí couldn't handle any more ghosts—half-dead or not. And Cachí didn't want to be a ghost.

Anybody else, but not to Dante, and not to Mikki.

Dante waited. Hand relaxed, but thumb tapping. Small, with no rhythm. As if he was letting the chaos out in micro doses.

Looking at his hands now, "Dante... I don't want to get involv—"

"You already are." Not angry, only flat. Disappointed. *And done.*

The one rule he asked Mikki and Cachí for, kicked like a plaything. Cachí dropped back in his chair, shaking his head. Under his breath, "Going to get me killed mano."

Dante, same pitch he'd had before. No anger, only flat and exhausted. "I've done everything but brother."

Cachí opened his mouth—then closed it. What was there to say?

Dante turned his chair toward the wall. Looked at it instead of Cachí. "Pulled Cody from the water. Pretty hard to identify at that point."

Cachí didn't answer. He figured as much after the '*drag the bay for Kaia*' imagery. Fair eyes—bloated.   *Disintegrated.*

The silence spoke loud. Dante raked a hand across his face. The fatigue cemented into each laugh line and forehead wrinkle.

"Not gonna talk then." More taps to the table. "*Vale hombre.*"

Cachí tried to get a read off his face; Dante tried to get a statement off his conscious.

But who was he kidding—? Cachí made it clear. And Dante was stalling. He sighed. Nodded again. Always nodding; always resigning.

Because who had fight left for this anymore? He knocked on the table twice. No reason. More stalling he'd guess.

Dante pushed the chair back with his knees. "Well. At the very least—you know where you stand now."

He didn't look at Cachí. Only stopped when he gripped the bent in, keyed door handle—only for a second.

As if there was anything left to say.

Nine Millimeters to the Schoolyard

DCPD Interview R.E3
00:00:00:00

|XXXV|

The room smelled like metal and rain. And something heavy crawled beneath the skin in there. It left Leti rigid in the rigid seat, hands pressed flat against her knees.

Leti was counting voices on the other side of the door—
too many to catch, but enough that gave a layer of normalcy.

This was what she expected when she thought police. Not creatures coming out of the night, guns in your face, convincing you to disobey so they can fire.

Thats all it was. Haunted houses gone too far. Across from her, Dante again. They'd been there awhile already. Desperate to pull or bribe something useful. Might have been more willing to talk had the gross-one not come too.

Or maybe if her leg wasn't burning from the shredded skin. Dante's voice was calm.

"You know him?" But the edge was sharp. Much different than the fires. Downside of letting more people in maybe—hard to keep track of what face is the mask, and which is the man.

"Who?"

A little too clean around the edges. Because he already felt accusatory. Big man—*Jeb*—even his name sounded like snot. Elbowed Dante and talking some shit about taking her to the back...

Her and Kaia had looked up *Best Comebacks* once. Jeb had the punchline to one lining his head.

Tapped his thumb next to Dante.

Leti was busy sneering but caught a glimpse of a photo that looked more a drawing. A boy. Swollen round face on white paper. Large black eyes— *maybe*. She had a feeling it'd end up somewhere on a canvas.

"Leti-Leti, hunny." The round-one. She's never hated her name more.

He reached across, belly cutting into the table enough to move it were it not nailed down. Fiddled with the sets of dog-eared and paperclipped work.

"Yeah his parents couldn't identify him either," he went on.

Looked to Dante. Dante to him. When he found a secondary photo, he held it in front of her face.

"This better for you—? More PG, yeah."

That one at least looked like a body. A kid. Few years younger than her maybe. But sometimes good things just happen to bad people.

"Never seen him."

Dante didn't seem to waiver either. Watching her; waiting for something. He too had a way with making the stillness feel unsafe.

She gazed back, but the longer she looked, the more she felt his soul poking around looking for hers.

Cracks in the armor or a way in because—he wasn't watching. He was assessing. Her blink rate slower. Breathing too. They said nothing, only stared. Everyone mutually challenging each other in a *silence-off* of who gets uncomfortable first.

But this was nothing. Lonest stint was five months. *Bring it on.* Turned her chest to the wall. Shoulders high, chin neutral, arms crossed.

A shadow moved behind the mirror. She watched it for a moment.

Waited for another. Maybe Cachí—*or maybe Cachí's on his way to prison.*

"Is there a reason I'm here?" she asked politely. On principle alone.

The round one, legs spread—knee out one side of the table, other jostling under it—hacked. Leti shivered, and he—swallowed down whatever'd come up. Her chest hiccupped, but it was more bile than air. And Dante smirked at her like it was funny when sick.

"The boys dead," the loud one again. "*Executed.*"

Dante tapped on the file before pulling it in and swapping it for a thicker one. "You're not detained, Leti." He slid a different file forward.

"So I can go?" She didn't want to look—but her eyes moved faster than her brain. And her skin chilled.

"But maybe we can help each other." The writing on the side tab; the way he slid it too. The kind of movement you make when you're giving someone their own obituary.

Her name was on the tab. TAYLORE. More individual tags under that too.

Kaia's the most obvious. Size, not any flare. She didn't need to respond to this one either. She knew exactly what it was. What she didn't know, and would like to, was—"Where'd you get that."

Flat. *Stay flat.* "Lot of that should be redacted and sealed."

Dante still just watched. Not cruel. Not soft either—but a dog on a scent cleared only by hell or highwater. He smirked.

"You alright if Jeb steps out?"

Another cut through the stone. Neutral, and confused; her face flashed, mouth turned down. Eyebrows a little too. Not much—but enough.

She meant to say '*whatever*' but only nodded. Watched as he went, trying to take in the hallway as he disappeared into it.

Door slammed hard. She leaned a little further back in her chair; sole attention on Dante now. The only thing left to watch in the room; the only thing that was unpredictable.

Dante looked away first this time to dig into something else for something *soft* of Leti's. He thumbed open the folder. *Charades.* They both knew exactly what they were looking at.

"Hospital intake. Overdose. Minor possession. Truancy. Then Miss Kaia's... Yeah, little longer of a breath hold down. But redeemable." His voice didn't sharpen. Didn't press. But the words landed like gravel in a throat. "You know what I see when I look at this?"

Smelt an incoming pep talk somewhere in her near future. Didn't answer. Didn't nod. "I know you don't want to hear it Leti, but I'm going to tell you anyway," he said softly. "I see someone trying to survive a shitty hand. And I don't say that lightly."

He reached over to her, stop a few inches from her arm and tapped the table with his finger.

Small thuds. "I think there is a place to help each other here."

He was disarming when he wanted to be—she didn't have to look to know what he was doing. In the tone. In the slower movements. It wasn't an obvious switch. Might not have even been a malicious one. She looked. "You got an unbelievably shitty hand. I see it and its not fair, I know,"

Her head snapped away, eyebrows shrunk down. Arms hugged herself a little tighter too.   *—look up Leti—*

She lifted her chin. Swerved back to him. Shoulders locked.

"Go ahead and tell me about it." Deadpan.

Dante studied her. No clipboard. No notes. He nodded. "Yeah. Heard."

Looked to the mirrors too, wet lips, and back. He was as much apart of that room as the foundation. "When's the last time you saw Kaia?"
Leti blinked. Swallowed.

"Bonfire?" he prodded. "After?"

She winced. "I—I don't know. Cachí said he saw her sometime last night. Well, early this morning."

"*Cachí* saw her?"

She didn't expect the distrust in the name. Her numbness was swirling into anger. "I think you know that's a long time, Leti. Lot can happen to a body in fifteen hours," he exhaled.

Leti's back went straight like a shot and the stone cracked. "If this is your version of help, you can shove it back up your ass."

Dante rubbed a hand over his jaw. Next his eyes. "Yeah...too much," he admitted. "I'm sorry—I apologize. Seriously."

She was halfway out of the room now. Standing, but not stepping.

"Why would you say that?"

That hit harder than he'd meant it. The wall dropped real fear; someone afraid to lose someone they love. He hadn't really meant it at all.

One of those thoughts that slips. Not morbidity, just—*self preparation*. His own fears, maybe.

Dante stayed seated. Kept his tone surgical. "I don't have any reason to think Kaia's hurt. Other than who she's around. You're not detained. You can walk. No badge pressure." He paused.

Then offered the trap, plain and on the table: "I need—if she's at the mansion, I need a favor. Can pay something, too."

It was a great plan in his head. Felt less so out under Leti's appraisal.

"It's—a gun. That killed that kid. Someone else I suspect too—last year, but who fucking—sorry—I can't be sure."

She laughed once, then whispered, "Heard worse..."

Nodding slow, swallowing slower, Dante dared to continue. "I think we'd all benefit if she could take a casual look around—nothing to get her in trouble, forget it if not given the chance...*But...*"

Leti stared. Flat.

"If left alone, inside that house...?" A— *'catch my drift* type of ending.

Leti leaned up. Hands on the table. "So you want to use her?"

He'd practiced, and she knew. "I want the position she's in. That house." Because he served it neat and hot.

"Because...the kid; Kayden?"

He shrugged—lips copied the movement but upside down. "I mean... "Went quiet for a bit longer, rethinking through something. Leti hadn't moved and he hadn't either—picking up again.

"So, if he has the gun there—*this* particular one—I'd get access to the house. Which—firstly, Jaylin. Her dad."

Laughed then, like he'd impressed himself. "That would not benefit just us—that'd be the city."

Leti wasn't sure how she felt. Wasn't sold it was real the more she stared.

"Hey—might be nothing. But if you haven't seen her, *them*, anywhere else...I'd check there next."   —*if not dead*—

Leti waited—because wasn't sure what else to do. When he didn't add more—when the hallway got loud and quiet again— she participated. But barely. "You interrupted."

He and Cachí liked their smirks. Leti gave no expression. "None of it really matters if you can't find her. And I'm not...*not* going to look knowing Kayden's—potentially...I got ears out. Think about it though."

Nothing. Unless acknowledgement comes through a medusa-stare.

He slid the photo he'd hidden earlier, keeping it face down. Just fingertips on the edge.

"Kid was seventeen, Leti. I'm in a corner here. And I'm going to do anything to get out. And put him in."

A thread around her chest tugged. Floss between bloodied teeth.

"You trust that I'm not going to tell Kayden—? Are you letting me go?"

Didn't look at the photo. Didn't reach for anything but the heat she'd been gripping tight this whole time. Begging it to stay close.

"Leave now. As for Kayden—you gonna'?"

She wouldn't. She knew she wouldn't. She knew *he knew* she wouldn't.

"Doing it to *save* the city then?" She knew how it'd sound, and didn't stop it from sounding so. Only lost a slice of the anger as he looked through her with ease.

A person yelled in the hall. Door opened, *sorry*, then closed.

"I'm doing this for Cachí," he continued like it was only them. "Mikki. Kid's dad. *Shit*—for Kayden, from before it all...*Myself*."

Except he made the last one a punch line.

"Can I ask you something," her arms uncrossed. Lazily put her hands back in her lap. Face significantly softer. She couldn't resist.

And Dante—leaning back now—knew it was coming. And it was okay. Elbow still on the table—he held her folder up, then let it slap back down.

"Seems only fair."

Leti picked at her nails for the moment. Thought about wording but remembered his commentary on bodies and time. Arms back on the table, she leaned forward and spit it out. "How'd Matías die?"

He knew, but still paused. Still felt the mouth tightening. Still hurt under his ribs—scar tissue throbbed.

Dante leaned forward, forearms resting heavy and eye contact weaker than it had been. "Matías was shot."

He said it like it cost to say it plain.

"Tuesday morning; 9:50 AM." Cleared his throat. "There was a shooter at the Junior college....Seventeen of us were injured. And eleven died."

Leti didn't expect an answer—Leti didn't expect *that* answer. *Us*.
She opened her mouth. But closed it again.

Dante sunk back against the chair. Arms crossing over his chest.
Fidgeting too. Because it made him feel out of control talking about it. Like sometimes he couldn't force himself to breathe right.
Sometimes the rage, sometimes the survivor's guilt. Always the survivors guilt. The—   w*hat did I do to be more deserving*
        —*how do I make me worthy?*

"Cachí and Mikki were...Cachí a senior. Taking some—we dogged on him, but some specialty instructor led...art. Thing. With Mick. He's talented, you know?"

Having seen, that was an understatement. But now more then ever felt like a time to be still. It wasn't about the art.

"It's—was—at the campus. Other side."
He nodded towards something—agreeing with whispered regrets:
        could have done this; should have stayed there.

Leti blinked, but didn't interrupt. His fingers flexed. Thumb looked for lint to brush off, but only moved air. Anything to let that tension, anxiety, pain, injustice—bleed somewhere other than inside.

"Matías—we—Kayden, me, and Matí. We tried to cut across to reach them. Matí...the Idiot. So fucking worried."

Checking to the left like maybe Matty'd chime in at the bait. But from Dante's disappointment—it didn't seem like he did.

"Kayden—in front. The uh—guy," he hadn't practiced this part. "The shooter." But he'd never forget the name.

Never would forget his face—or the sound, the family, the manifesto, grades, socials—knowing it all. Except *why*.

"He walked out of a classroom between us. Stared right at each other—time, was weird. I don't know. But—I was first." Placed his hand over his side and let it relax against his leg.

"Matí—he knew, he saw. Him next." That broke the hard stare past Leti's shoulder. Face turned down to his hands—interlaced. Extended and tightened. Twice.

"It was quick though. I think he was gone before he hit the floor."

She remembered the sound. Kaia, her dad. It tracked in her mind like a scratch table. When he tagged the change—he didn't look away. Hard part's over—testing now; how its processed; where she might recoil.

If she recoils at all, or leans in like some sick fix. She's done it too; pressure tests, but on people. Because not everyone know how to handle the big scars.

"Long story short, Cachí and Mikki—everybody just trying to be a hero. I don't know. They both followed the chaos. And—found it. Us. I was out by then but...Kayden saved my life.

Mick, Cachí too. But—it was violent. Saw him come behind the guy. We'd never...Couldn't of imagined.

Fists, to the front—floor chewing the back of his head...Not sorry but— there's not a kinder way to put it, you know?

Shooter ended up in a bag and Kayden the cell..."

She could feel guilt stroking her skin wanting to come in. She opened her mouth again but still had nothing and he carried on when she wasn't able.

"...Didn't know the extent then, but—beginning of the end."

She tried again, "I—" Still couldn't.

Leti pursed her lips and then relaxed back in the chair. Mind a bit blown— which wasn't easy anymore. She hadn't realized she'd locked up.

He'd laid out— '*your turn*' with his silence though. And he was patient.

And in there—they were maybe safe.

"So uh," her chin moving up and then down slow. "Pretty shitty hand you were dealt yourself—huh, Detective?"

Didn't *sound* right—but *felt* right. And he smirked.

Because it was true. Truth without minimizing, without dismissing, without morbidity, and the usual fascination with pain when not their own. Simply recognition, and movement.

"You're trying to save Kayden?"

Tight lipped, he shook his head. "It's too late for Kayden. He knows it too."

"Cachí?" she followed up.

Dante gave a half shrug, arms still loosely crossed. Maybe not the mask, but the man. "You know Leti, someone told me, couple years back…"

She adjusted in her seat. *Incoming.*

"You can't drag someone out of hell if they're convinced it's home."

Leti didn't argue. Thought about saying something…Didn't really know what seeing how he'd eased her into that one. Showed bare skin. A lot.

Before returning to pick at hers more.

"Maybe that's where they live now. You know—not much difference between you and I. I've tried to save my brothers, too. I think I—know some people just can't be saved. And maybe you're mid-process, figuring it out." His voice was so even it hurt. The peephole in the wall slammed shut, locked down. Leti shook her head—gloves on.

"I know. I've *been* known," sloppy point to the folder. "Clearly cheated on the homework cause—go read it. I don't—have anyone left to save."

She reached over, keeping the folder with him but opening it like he never had. "No, the real difference between you and I?" Flipped another page, taking it in quickly.

"Difference is I'm willing to walk through hell for any sliver of her. I take what's left of her, and I say thank you."

Dante's face didn't change. But something behind the eyes flickered.

"So you save who you want, leave who you don't. This—" pointed around the room.

"I know Kaia would look—she'd try and serve them on a platter to you—how's it worded? Stop acting man—"

She tilted her head as if reading from the upside down paper, but knowing the lines by heart.

"Delayed onset trauma behaviors and something about risk-taking? Cat nip—right? Something you think you can either harness or fix?"

The file felt bigger there in front of him now. Dante's fingers tapped on the desk a little harder too, but still low.

Didn't imagine that would have triggered something—but very obviously stepped in it. And he didn't want to look at her—didn't want to make it worse but wouldn't walk wearing that accusation.

Just—"You're wrong Leti. And I hope you'd do more than only a, '*thank you*' if your sister hurt someone."

The round detective poked his head in but Leti's face didn't shift. Their gaze didn't part. Because—*would she?*

She nodded once. Not in agreement. Not thinking she'd let the train take ten of the world's, before her one. Because *that*—was their difference. She'd learned *plenty* already.

Dante turned. Craned his neck back at the intrusion. "Yeah?" Then back to Leti.

"Flin asked for you."

Dante's chuckle tried, but lost its way. Ended shaking his head. Not defeated. But well matched. "Cachí to the rescue again then huh?"

"Wasn't aware I'd been rescued," she bit back, jaw tighter.

He stood, the same fireside smirk creeping into his cheeks. Pushed his chair in with a lift, keeping it silent. "Yeah. Seems like you've got it." The tone wasn't angry or rude, but the eyes—they bugged her.

He stopped at the door, turned back.

"*Realemente, la diferencia*...I won't sacrifice myself for a piece of someone else. That's not heroic—that's tragic. And you're both dead then."

"...Doesn't count if you think of it walking away," Meant it nasty, but sounded more bratty than anything. Wasn't sure if be was smiling or growling but his head was shaking as the door was closing—

"Wait...What do I..I mean, am I allowed to go?"

Dante barely held the door open, shrugging, and being an antagonistic ass. "I'm sure you'll figure it out."

The engine had been off for almost twenty minutes, but Kayden hadn't moved. Sat in the dark, breathing through his teeth; one hand flexing against the steering wheel like pressure alone could snap it—like that might be enough to break himself free.

Tried to let it go. Did for a bit, but the more time there is to talk, the more anxious he was getting. His jaw clicked.

Jaylin, Kaia fucking mouths—bigger than the bitch, asking about the wrong things. Demanding the wrong things—*but how*—?She came and found him at the bonfire. And he'd laid some shit down with Jeremy. A little too loud, a little too loose.

But that was it. That's what she went and told Dante—after he *saved* her. "From the big fucking bad—"

The wheel moaned this time, small inner workings bending under the abuse of another hammer-fist.

Then she fucking found him again—actively sought him out. Dante told her he wanted more—it all was making sense now.

Ghosted this morning when he came back—had been nothing but nice, would have continued if she wanted it—but she didn't. She didn't want to be late. *Back to Dante.*

Who—on the attack out of no where—*just drive, leave*—His hands gripped tighter. His chest lurched. "Go dude, fucking go. Now."

Rip up the note. Or—go back. Beat everyone to the punch. Burn bright and hot and take Jaylin with. At least neg back at Apollo some how.

Kayden's vision blurred at the edges. He wasn't ready yet.

Not to go, not for real. Didn't believe in an afterlife, but maybe kind of also still did. And that was the problem.

Heat rising in his cheeks. The way it'll rise from the ground up. *Take him under*—but *Apollo will always have our back*—he screamed. Slammed his fist on the wheel.

The cells, the lights, the sterile facade when it reeked of piss, shit, and cum. And his vacant *shock* when it came down to it.

Breath was frantic.Boxed in—fighting like hell for what was left of his dignity, but pieces handed out like they weren't his.

But at least Apollo liked all the pieces. And Apollo didn't share. So maybe that was the mercy—*or maybe that was the leash.*

Windows nearly shattering from sound alone. "He—*killed*—Matí!"

Dante wouldn't have the air in his lungs to talk the shit that he did had Kayden not done what he had. Mikki too.

Definitely Cachí. Kayden scoffed so hard he might've tasted blood. And every one of them—despite all their fuck ups and their wrong doings—they somehow get to leave him feeling like less.

He was so goddamn tired of it. Go show Jaylin what he's really fuckin' capable of. Let her know? Maybe even let himself fucking know when whatever's done.

"Goddamn it..." His lips curled. Hand on his knee, his chest—replaying subservience like it'd look different the hundredth time around.

Wiped his face again—ring twisting in sweat. *Jaylin—Kaia*—Jaylin walked, not because she was smart, not because he forgave her or ever would. But because, he still wanted to live.

He's just done doing it on his knee. Besides—he and Kaia—they just needed a chat. Because she's chill. Like him too. No threats—no problems.

"It's chill. We're chill."

Just see how much she's already said, because hey—maybe even nothing at all. Kayden took good care of her, and only right she'd give him this slip.

He shoved the note into the ashtray, turned the key and the engine grumbled awake. Neck cracked, then knuckles.

And, Desert View wasn't even far. *We're fine.*

Everything is just—*fine.*

50/86'd 415

DCPD INTERVIEW R.E1
00:19:00:00

| XXXVI |

Dante kicked the door open with his foot, same damn folder in his hand. Traveling companion at this point. Shadow of a shadow.

"What?" *No hello, no patience*—Cachí bit his cheek.

"Leti still here?" Half tactic, half trap. Tossed like bait across the room.

Dante didn't bite. Didn't even square up. His body turned out. Like if Cachí said the wrong thing, he'd just keep walking. "Cachí ..."

A warning. Not light. Not loud. But loud enough.

Cachí stood at the back wall. Hands flexing. Fists. Fingers. Couldn't stop moving. Couldn't stop fidgeting. Up on his toes. Back down again. Leaned into the cold concrete like it might give him something back.

"I got a call from Cody. Said he fucked up." Breath. Half-laugh. Dry and dead at the edges. "I thought it was bullshit. Went to scoop him."

Dante finally turned. Full face now. Either warming up, or squaring up.

"Kid was in his fuckin' drawers at the bus stop. Shaking." Cachí blurted. "Gave him a hoodie, told him get in."

Small nod from Dante. The baggy t-shirt—rip along the collar under the hem; found on the dead kid—was on his couch for a week once. Cachí kept going.

"He was rambling. Said he hooked up with someone. Acting like it mattered."

"Leti?" Cachí jerked his head back, insulted.

Bordering defensive—brotherly conversation for later should they ever get the time. But here—care cost too much time. Time which people didn't have.

"*Jodido*—Jaylin. And...Jaylin." He chickened out. Dante's posture didn't relax. But it shifted.

"You saying Jaylin shot—"

"What? No! I mean...hell, *maybe*?"

Because that was a hell of a lot more tempting to believe. Dante didn't push. Just changed the question. "That's what you got?"

No, I'm not done. No, this isn't the worst of it—

Dante's ask—wasn't a question. It was an opening. He shifted the folder to his other hand. Tapped the edge.

"Shut the fuckin' door." Cachí. Stalling again. Dante pushed it closed without looking back while Cachí scuffed his sneaker on the cement.

"Am I gonna have—" "Quit fuckin' stalling, *hermanito*."

Cachí straightened and crossed his arms. Dropped them again pretty quick—too tired to hold the walls.

"I don't know what actually happened man—Jay. Cody. Kayden—Scripts. Cody was fuckin' with Jay, got out of his head I don't know—he took off."

Dante—scrunched face, gears not turning, but poking holes. "Jay—? To—stealing her own scripts, Cachíflin?"

The mistrust was tangible.

Cachí didn't even want to try now. "I don't fuckin' know."

"Then you need to try a lot fucking harder. *This isn't a game.*" Conditioned into believing maybe it was—Dante was getting heated again.

"Ask *her*, *carajo.*" Cachí bit his tongue and prayed Dante wouldn't. Really will get him killed.

"Dammit man, *no se!* Cody—they were fuckin' I guess—someone came in, he said she flipped script and told him to scat."

"Would he have gone back to the house, do you think they shot him—"

"*Hermano! No se! FUCK.*" Cachí's head dropped into his hands; chest moved like it'd been holding breath, heaving now.

"Please. *It's Jaylin.* I don't know, Dante—come on. I didn't take him back for it—I didn't want to be involved. Not with this—*I promise.*"

Cachí was begging, but didn't even care. Ego closed it's eyes because maybe it needed Dante, too.

So Dante let it beg. And break. Sifting through the flood water for the fish he wanted—Cachí went on.

"I—*I* told him to get the fuck out of here. *You saw him*—I'm not—she goes older bro, she wasn't fuckin him for fun—I'd bet my life. But *I didn't*. I kept out, please believe—"

"I do." No empathy, no warmth, but relief for them both. But Dante wasn't going to ease off Cachí yet—not since coming this close to the flame.

He almost wanted to give the kid a hug. The desperation, the sense to stay the fuck back. Maybe he would be okay—

"What else?" *Or maybe he was still straddling.*

Cachí back to talking to the table. Defeated. "Kade—*no se, pero*...he was diggin'. Found out I dropped Cody at the station. Thought I took the bag maybe. Pressed me." Eyed Dante for sympathy.

Only found stone. "He never asked about the kid; just the pills."

"Why would Jaylin take her own shit from her dad?"

Cachí made a face like Dante was aggressively stupid. Dante couldn't help but wonder if he was. For asking.

"She's been riding Kayden hard the last month. *Obsessively.* Coming at me a bit much too."

Another breath. Another ache. "I can't prove it. But I know it was him. *Them*, Dante."

Dante's face didn't shift. But something in his eyes softened. That almost-pride. That almost-grief. That almost—*something*. "Gracias, Cachí."

Cachí nodded once—barely. And then Dante stepped in again. Closer than Cachí was comfortable—closer than Dante would step.

And hovering. Weighing—Cachí's anxiety barked first.

"¿*Qué*?"

But Dante—as if he had a plan, as if he had it all under control: "I'm gonna ask you for something, and you won't like it. Remember—neither do I, okay?"

Turning him in—done. Cachí could see the end.

The tone wasn't familiar, but steady.

Like it'd been fake all along. No fight. No flight.

No Dante.

"I need a statement." Let the words breathe. Desperately holding onto the middle—holding onto Cachí. "I'm not telling you, *carnal...* "

That was Matty's word—and Dante's. Teased Cachí with it, but never let him hear it.

Cachí's eyes watered and he wiped them away.

Looked at Dante for judgement but got none.

He knew they had a brotherhood—but he needed the reminder. And that was the best way Dante knew how to drop it.

"I need a statement, and I'm asking. Because I need him off the street before someone else gets dragged under.

Apollo's trials coming up soon—this is already spiraling and we know it'll get worse."

Cachí stared at the table. "Yeah." A silent second.

"*Entiendo...*" Because he did understand. What Dante was asking for was the truth.

What he needed—*was a rat.* And what Cachí was— despite Dante—was no better.

Boiling Tides in Mojave

DESERT VIEW
00:19:17:⁰⁰

|XXXVII|

The water in the glass was warm and metallic, but Kaia drank it anyway. Scraped the roof of her mouth on the way down, settling hard in her gut; her fingers trembling too.

She rinsed the glass and filled it again. Trembling from thirst. From blood sugar maybe—*from poison...*

God—and still nothing from Leti.

Kaia understood anger and that she was going to be pissed—

but goddamn. She expected a phone call at the very least; a pulse check.

She fucking wanted one for Leti—but kept catching the fucking goddamn voicemail—and speaking, breathing—even thinking too loud made her sick. She just wanted—*a lot*, actually.

But water, icy water first. Angrily kicking on her sneakers, but kicking the door too. Shouldn't have hurt—everything did though.

Kaia snagged the ice bucket as she walked to the door. The air hit cooler and sharp, but her mouth wanted the ice more than her arms wanted warmth.

She flipped the lock so it wouldn't latch and left it cracked, as if fresh air could still save it now. Little hexagon building just up ahead. She hung a right—long way to the machine, swinging by the office. *Inspired.*

Kaia yanked on the office door, finding nothing but a dead bolt and absence. Put her hand and face to the glass—peeking through, eyes running along the desk.

The bulletin board, the papers. She didn't care about the lady. But she searched like maybe it'd been here the whole time—a message, missed call from Leti. Even—*I'm okay... but I still hate you.*

Because obviously Leti called when Kaia's cell didn't get shit. Old lady just didn't tell her. Simply—*laziness.*

Because everything's all good.

It had to be. Repeating it to every step as Kaia floated around the hall-square and came up on the backside again—left of the room. Somehow the motel felt more ghostly than her.

The vending alcove hummed all concrete breath and fluorescent stutter. Ice machine shrieked, Kaia muttered a curse to hear herself speak—maybe worried she couldn't anymore. Crunched a stolen cube.

Then took two more. Sneakers squeaking as she turned on the tile and headed back.

The door hadn't moved. Cool air coming in. Stale air dragging out. And still, no Leti. Becoming obsessed now—fear swirling into motion.

No keys. No backpack. No wallet. No ID. No cell—she tossed the bucket onto the old dresser and let ice pop out the top like popcorn. Maybe it'd melt into the room. Maybe the chill could melt into her.

Turning back, arm out to shut up and bolt down the room—Kaia eyed the bed for a nap. All the hope in the world to wake up to Leti's furious charm.

And skip through this little anxious part.

Find the pot in the bag—*move the foot from the door*—her arm whipped back, elbow popped. Feet taking frenzied steps back—spine cracked upwards—then recognition. Cruising in, fashionably late.

"*Kayden...?*" And a mixer with it—curiosity, and a familiar discomfort.

"Cut the act."

Kaia's face squished. Discomfort felt to light with Jaylin's voice singing in her head: *Oh I do hope you have a great night, Miss Kaia.* A wicked grin.

Felt something then. So discomfort definitely wasn't enough. Kaia's body went cold. But the mind—slowly ticking through reason. His entire being watching as she did.

The way Kayden held Kaia to him at the bonfire; the motel bed—one hand on the frame, one boot already inside. His body dwarfed the room. And his grasp on her body at the bonfire, their volatile tit for tat; yeah— didn't feel like foreplay anymore. Felt like warnings.

"Relax." He looked at her like she was pathetic; like he knew. Stepped in while she fret in silence.Kaia's eyes scanned the room once and then remained on him.

Panic wondering if it should head out. Metal lock up top, midway too—not secure, but bold and threatening now. And the bed—? Felt like a pistol. So panic—*stays*.

"We need to have a chat."

"Let's step outside then." Pride on her face—for the clarity. For the calm.

It made Kayden's nose twitch—the pride more than the comment. Made Kaia's skin crawl. Because something deep in the gut, deep in the mind, deep in the bone—screamed, *run*.

"Go sit down;" nodding at the bed.

"Steps outside are nice." She insisted.

He took a defiant step in and the wretched sound of metal swinging, clamoring together with its other half, confirmed it was real. Swing-latch slapped the door with sick satisfaction. Didn't lock the knob though. Didn't lock the deadbolt.

—*dead*. Kaia ran through the walk to the vending machine— windows, halls, people? Feet. She remembers watching her feet—*she was pathetic*.

"Not sure you should be here." She—as defiant as his step forward. His shoulders twitched.

She wasn't sure—she knew, but wouldn't believe— *she froze*. Eyes closed as he came closer, body tense when she could smell him.

Felt herself tossed onto the bed—she thought. Imagination, memory, fear—had everything running at full speed. Eyes opened— he simply body checked her like a goat. Passed her—stopped at the mirror, but turned to the bathroom. Motion jerky, and stiff. It was even more conflicting.

"I need to use the bathroom real quick," he muttered, standing outside it, six foot something, looking into a two-by-two. He didn't go in.

Looked at the walls. The roof. Then what Kaia assumed was the tub. Neutral profile, but hard to judge when they didn't move. Or breathe.

Kaia looked at the door behind her. Then back to the man—eyes now on her. She wanted the fire. But—*to that thought*—he'd had each and every opportunity to hurt her. And didn't— could she be so vain to think maybe he liked the time; maybe she wasn't the worst. "Kayden," but it just didn't fit. "Why are you here?"

He twisted and Kaia choked seeing his holster. T-shirt trying to hide it, but the bulge visible like a fresh grave. Kaia couldn't take her eyes off it. Wanted it away or wanted it against her, but the door was behind her with nothing was in the way.

And the man? Doing that thing where you're there but not. Too horrifyingly familiar. Dead bodies on a fallen battle field—she'd rather walk around them. Because at least then— we already know how it ends
     —*run Kaia-bird*—

Walls creaked and he snapped to her like she'd done it. —*bluejays and predators*—Door whispering, mind, sense, body—*go*.

"Go ahead," nodding once to the bathroom. She sounded meek.

"It's...I don't...I'm not fucking going in there, have you lost your fucking mind?" He focused on the door, and then her. And something in her chest sunk to her pelvises. Her entire gut and stomach twisted.

Feet twisting, despite the voice saying too late. His expanding, extending out. *Because birdies go in cages*— Kayden had her by the bicep. Didn't squeeze, but pulled until the door handle wasn't a tease.

"Nu-uh," he snapped, holding. "I told you I need to have a conversation."

 She leaned away from him. Skin pulling—caught between a gentle tug-o-war as he jerked a little harder to put himself back in the middle.

"Re-*lax*." he enunciated, "Fuck dude—everyone wanting a fucking problem with me." He shoved her at the bed and she avoided it like the plague—collapsing her seat and legs so she slide off the edge and hit the floor instead.

His legs wide, arms crossed. As much ready for a fight as she was. And normally—she actually believed she could win. Maybe it was the view from the floor, maybe it was the dreams—but it was different. Surprise not in her favor, neither size.

Kaia's brain split eight different ways, with eight different thoughts—because it was a new body. Before—fire, heat, air, evenings and outside. The size felt right.

The control—maybe even enough to manage her where no one could.

In that motel—man, built like a fucking compactor and that shit hole of a room the bag tightening. *Closing in*, with her inside.

Not to burn her—to *crush* her into *nothing*.

The power she so badly wanted to have, coming to give it to her.
     —*should the Reaper grow tired of failing*—

The bag getting fuller; the air flatter, oxygen thinner, and the cinch around the neck— "Kayden—you need to go."

"I—" she looked at the phone on the dresser behind her head. Standing up, reached for it like—a comfort, a weapon, a lifeline—?

"I'm not a cop caller man but," slapping dirt off her pants aggressively because she didn't want to finish. She didn't want to *have* to call.

Couldn't really then either—say, *a man is in my hotel room staring at me*? Doing nothing—*Yes.* But the nothingness—the still. *The stare;* a thousand yards gone. "Say what you need then ..." Too still for someone that needs to talk.

He blinked hard—a statue waking up in the twenty-first century. "What'd you just say about the cops?" Maybe he was high—*maybe he needed help.*

Familiarity. But—*Kaia-birds endangered; Kaia-birds extinct*—Kaia stayed back, shook her head. Shook the voices until they spun. But *stop.* Because even they were watching for him—noting the gap on the other side between wall and bed. Bathroom—*locks.* Downside is the door is a lean play thing. Neither seemed viable.

"I want to know about Cody, girl. Who said something?"

There wasn't any room to go back. His hand ran across his scalp once, pushed hair away, and it slapped. He was wet—sweating too much. "Jaylin right—?" Less clip, more rush.

"Or you and Darcy get close all the sudden? Yeah—you like him too? Or is it Dante that wants him?"

He had a sharp, unamused laugh that stopped like a pulled band aid. "What'd you tell him?"

"I don't—I said," Kaia tried again, firmer now, "you *need* to go."

His breath got weird—short and messy. Phone rattling in her hand, but as she looked down to it—flinched, eyes closed, he lunged.

Phone pulled from her hand same way it ripped from the wall. He shrugged innocently—just an everyday routine. This wasn't a familiar kind of danger. Not officers on her back or high school boys trying to fix the broken thing. This was realizing she's in the room with a grenade and the pin has long been pulled.

"I told you no, to go" he murmured to himself, because Kaia didn't make it out at first; or understand it when she did. "Didn't listen then either," he went again.

"*What—*" Maybe it was a word, maybe it was just breath. "Kayden—do you need me to call someone for you."

Ava's voice dropping, the motherly—*kill them with kindness.* Or maybe not whispered to her but begged to him. He reached—stopping when she backed again. Further from the door, closer to the bathroom and his face twisted up. "You think I'm gonna touch you? That it?"

His voice grated. "You think I want *you?*"

Kaia was immediately another two steps back. Running out of steps. Somehow that still stung—fraction of a second. "I don't know what to think—you're... scaring me. If—that's what you wanted—we're good..."

She swallowed because she felt weak. Like one more step and she'll beg. His eyes glassy like maybe he was on something. Mouth partially open— Kaia wasn't trying—wasn't *not* trying—but she saw herself. After every night terror, after every come down—triggered by horns blaring, but calm in chaos.

Maybe she was Leti and Kayden was Kaia. "Kayden I think you're making a mistake, I—I don't think you mean to be here."

He blinked at her, head lifted back high. "Why's that? Dante? You working for him or fucking him?" He stepped back this time—eyes to the mirror more than her.

Memory reached for him too—she could fucking see it—but tonight, hers stayed soft and silent. Edging in like a caress—and waiting at the gates, while instinct and focus flamed.

He took a heavy breath. Took back the steps he reversed, stopping where the bed ended and the bathroom began. Dividing themselves by invisible lines— "I want you to sit down. *Now*, Jay." He shook his head again like he balance.

"I'm not—" *"Sit down!"*

She vision shook—her head too, apparently. "No." He'd have to beat her down to lay her out—"This isn't funny..." Because maybe Leti was pranking her—so easy to believe.

She did in a way. Enough to try and convince her guts—telling her to run or die. Tell herself she deserved it if only a prank.

"Where's Cody, Jay?"

"What—No," she stammered. "I—Let's call her."

Playgrounds, and laughing, and games of freeze tag—neither moved. Kaia breathed. Quick and short—enough for them both. Counted the seconds between her and the outside—one step per second, harsh wind against the grain. Decaying light slipping under the door and calling out—ignoring the Reapers at her back. Because she didn't want to be asleep with the living again, or buried with the dead.

Somewhere in the middle, just not in the ground—and the middle was outside. So she looked at him deeper. Not at him, not around, but direct where she needed to go—straight through the fucking center.

'*—you're gonna want to let me go.*'

Kayden's body tensed taunting itself. Replaying the words.

Jaylin, haunted every room, and every place. Dante too—shadowing him through corners and halls while she tightens the collar. Sits back either laughing or leaving—Kayden stared back.

Was this face even real? Because why would they send him a new one? *They who?* '*Remember Cody*—?' '*Wasting time*—' '*I do*' *I die.* Soon.

Kayden hadn't realized he was holding his breath until the small gasp. The faceless in front of him—steadier than he'd ever managed to be. Yet nothing to stand for—*like them.*

She stared back. *He*—because it was Cody. Dante. Kaia—everything standing in his way of peace even if Jay promised. Forced to listen—*clean up, Cody*—

"Clean up yourself!" He snapped, shoving the kid back. Shout so feminine it made his molars grind. Could have sounded like Mikki—

'lost the right to talk about them—" *not to me*—

He shook his head.   A thing that is out of time.

Kayden gasped for his breath again—his muscles too weak to lift his chest. Body betraying him. Because he didn't take care of the body—*of the Cody.*

That's why he was there now, in the mirror. Not watching Kaia, but crying to Kayden. Begging to come out—not like a man, like a boy. In a cell.

Where Neverland met the Ice Age and Kayden—forever running, time ticking behind until pulled under and rolled.

She was still staring at him—eyes like glass shaped like shark teeth. His skin was boiling—"*I'm not going back, Jay*— "Everything he wanted to say to her a thousand times over again. *"I will not go back!"*

The way she stood there, the way she didn't run—*the way she knew.* He punched the wall near her; growled when she screamed to cover her head.

"What'd you tell her about Cody?" he screamed back. But even his roar trembled now. —*find me when it's handled'*

His mouth was dry and sweet like copper. His legs too long, too locked.

Hands itchy, like something lived inside them and wanted out.

Because Jaylin said. *Good boy.* His breath rasped.

That hiccupped, off-the-rails kind of inhale. He scratched the side of his scalp, hard. Then again with his other hand. Like he could claw the memory out before it fused permanently.

She knows. The fucking gun. The look on Cody's face.

"Say something," he barked, wet heat in his eyes. He watched her swallow. Counted the droplets of sweat.

She opened her mouth. Hesitated. Waited—*stalled?*

Wait-ing. Because police would be on there way—somehow Dante knows. Always fucking knows—always fucking looking—

"Say it goddamn it!"

"Okay," she yelped back, shoulders protecting her ears, hands steadying herself against the wall. Eyes peeled open like a scalped orange. Staring into his soul—*about to eat it out—*

"I want you to say—"

"Cachí right?!" she blurted. "Um, Mikki. 'Member—met you there. Pretty night right? I—I turn twenty this month. This—is my first trip, without the parents. You know? Um but, the other guy—you're friend, from that night?"

"....Jeremy?" mouthed because a whisper sounded too loud.

Her lip trembled, but her eyes kept biting towards him like teeth. "Older one—he interrupted us, 'member? Sounds like you know each other well.. Want to call one of them?"

"You mean...Dante?"

"Yeah—yeah okay. Got your cell? Mikki's a nice person, we're friends too. Don't—have many friends."

"Dante?" He repeated. Her face squished like it did when he came in—confused. "Sure?" He shook his head twice. Kayden didn't have anything.

Just what was given. What's been judged—*only God—*

Harm verse protect. And she—smaller packaging, but poisonous. *Venomous.* Like vipers and widows—who killed the jury house. And left it in Kayden's hands. He decides.

And she—was harm.

Might've taken an hour—might've been five minutes.

Time stopped and Cachí's hand still cramped from the pen. Really hadn't said much else. Silence and head nods the best comfort either could offer.

Dante eventually told Cachí Leti was actually still there. Curled into a cracked plastic chair, by the vending machines and a cordless wall plug.

He hadn't talked to her since their last exchange. Had considering getting her an uber, but—felt better looking the other way. Giving Cachí a chance to see her—despite crawling into his hood like a kid.

Her ankles uncrossed as they approached, but her arms did. Hugging tightly around her ribs like she could hold herself still enough to vanish.

Dante's boots hit the tile heavy. Each step like the end of something. "You good to walk?"

Leti blinked up. Cachí at his side. "Thought you were done talking to me." Cachí didn't look. Dante didn't sigh. Just ran a hand down his jaw like it weighed too much.

"So—you need a ride or not?" Nicer than he was going to be, but snippy enough for Cachí to glare.

A beat passed, slow and loud. Leti stood, still hugging herself but present in the circle. "I can walk, can I just—charge my phone?"

Cachí looked to that—but it wasn't anger. And that, made her—warmer. Not happy, not breathing easy, but a small light in the back room. Dante knew, even if he hadn't.

He motioned with his chin, arm followed, eyes rolled. "Get to steppin' girl— we'll drop you off."

She wasn't going to walk—he, *they*, weren't going to let her. Not in that neighborhood, not at that time, not up for debate. o they moved quiet down the hallway close to single file. Dante stopped just before the threshold. Looked between them.

"So where are we going?" She looked at him confused, picturing Cachí's car before Dante read her mind.

"You're not going back to that house." A hand up and direct at Cachí when he pipped up.

"You and I—have to chat. Your car, is going to wait. Don't trust you not to drive off, frankly."

He looked back to Leti.

"You—I mean, I'm not stopping. I don't recommend it though."

She tucked a strand of hair behind her ear; sweet on the surface and measured carefully. "Left in a hurry," eyes daring him to ask why. "And unless you're offering room and bored for me too, I need my keys. Wallet. Phone."

Dante had started to turn. Played with his keys, listening to them jingle in his hand, when he stopped. Faced her completely.

Head tilted. Eyes went down to her face.

The pause was him reminding himself of tone. Presence.

Power there in the station. Maybe not even his—Dante sighed like the inconvenience it was. "Five minutes," he clarified. "Get your shit and get out. No sightseeing. No errands. *No—Cachí.*"

Not a specific no—a general no. Covering all bases—but over her head and at Cachí. Made her scared he'd go so far as to leave her there.

Her words bit. "Bummer—damn Disney world in there."

Dante stared. Leti stared.

"My stuffs outside in his car. Relax boss man. You're in charge."

She felt like she won when Dante slid to Cachí—glared there instead. Leti turned then too, looking up at Cachí—bumper cards through expression.

Dante turned sharp on his heel. Shaking his head, he called back—

"*Ni los santos me tienen paciencia, Cachíflin.*" Pushing through the double door.

Late night city breeze pushing through the building lanes as Cachí and Leti fell in line silently. It felt bad—it felt like hot eyes and scratchy throat walking beside, saying nothing.

At least until she felt his hand brush against hers. His eyes trail her response. His smile—hidden in the hood, weak. But there. And hers.

The door slammed behind them. And for the first time in a long time, Dante didn't look back.

The folder stayed behind, and instead, every truth within it walked out beside them—here only to breathe life into the ghosts.

Unnatural Selection

| XXXVIII |

The air in the room changed. Her eyes never left him; not that there was anywhere else to go. Cornered like prey, but she couldn't call him a predator.

Predators were natural. Or ruthless. Kayden wasn't anything. But prey or predator didn't matter—this wasn't the wild.

The wild had rules. Harsh patterns. Survive, eat, fuck, reproduce, repeat. This *wasn't* wild. This was human.

"So, got his number?"

His eyes solidified in that hollow emptiness. She didn't feel herself walk back until the fake marble sink was pressing against her hips. His breath— short. Speeding.

She saw it before she thought it—mind blank, body moving, fate verse zero grace—Kaia hit the deck hard, not from him. From launching down and out. Scrambling on hands and knees—door was the goal, crack between the bed and wall—*the closest.*

Five or six or seven kicks made contact with something before hands were on her ankles like chains. Rug burned against her back sliding against it. Shouting, not screaming, not yet—because still somehow in denial even as it actively is happening it just couldn't be this. Every bad thing—it couldn't be this, not now, not like this.

"Wake up—!" Yanked a foot back and lost a shoe. Kept hollering too, voice losing shape. "Big fuckin'—get off!" Couple more in before that nabbed ankle was pulled. She got one final kick in as she slid—but knew she made contact that time. Knew it hurt.

Man hollered something wicked. Dragged her like a fucking rag doll. Off the ground—shouted over her. Screamed, maybe—"*Stop!*" But said— from *him* to *her.* As if he wasn't the one writing the scene.

Back against the wall. Panting. Wrists pinned between them. Kayden didn't seem with her. Door getting smaller, smaller. She kicked harder. Swung faster—*make it in time*, because gun, bullets, blood-names, and Reapers. And she didn't want to be friends.

He shouted something else but Kaia's brain was louder. Shushing her and going for his shin again. Or something. Backed against the wall only enough room to twist her quick and push her harder.

Arm locked up behind her like a straight jacket—like a bad dream. No control and can't get out—it doesn't feel good with your hands behind your back and your fight in your throat.

Kaia didn't stop fighting. But she stilled. Just the way Leti does.

Every intention to make it to the door—Kaia wasn't in the motel, she was cornered with Kayden in a deeper place. Someplace she didn't want to go.

"I don't want to do this—" Kayden flattened her against the wall until she couldn't move an inch. Grunting in her ear—*but crying*.

Room charged and alive. Something was off, something was worse. Something was in the room in a clock made of finality. She could feel deaths presence, knowing him so personally.

It went from thinking she'd be assaulted, to knowing she'd be buried. Because that sound he was making—that wasn't right.

That was different. Not tears—not close to tears. But pleas.

And desperation. Apologies for....*Forgiveness.* So later he may bow his head and say, *forgive me father I have sinned.* Worries whisked away on whispers. What justice there?

Pinned and forced still—she could feel every desperate twitch, and every heave at his demons. But she didn't want to.

"Please don't fight me—listen to me, I have to. Let's do it clean okay, easy Kaia. Please." Maybe wiped it in her hair.

Maybe just didn't have the distance between them. Pressure lightened, but held. Like maybe he pulled back to look at what he was about to do. And even without his weight—she wouldn't breathe. If not the last thing she controls.

Kayden leaned forehead to wall. "Listen to me," chin on her shoulder. That tension was gone—that warmth. Now let it be sex, let it be the room—don't let it be this ice age and will take both her and the truth and cover it like a blank start.

"See, yeah *Yeah*—that's good, Doll, we'll do it just like this." Muttering to himself and into the wall.

Hair along his jaw itchy and foul against Kaia's cheek. Twice more and he pressed into her like a machine. Kaia felt more fight and thrashing but didn't recall. Just this cold, white, vacant tundra.

Door to the room spidering with icicles and frost bite.

Soon—even if she makes it, will it be too late for anything alive to make it out? Or will only her shadows escape? They moved.

Maybe her—maybe him.

"Stop-stop-stop! It won't hurt, hey—we can do it together. I'll take two, and you'll just...More. Then easy, babydoll, some TV, chill. Me, or write something—your sister?"

The bridge. Leti. And—*let's do that together*—she got it now. Why Leti was so furious. "It's alright, babydoll, there you go."

Thought she laughed, but it felt more like a cry. Or a gasp. Like she was still fighting herself not to breathe, because maybe it's not funny. Maybe she dangled the edge, but she was watching—she wasn't going to trip.

Hanging on to the edge by the sand. Watching it crumble over the edge—slow motion fall. Where she gets to watch the show in reverse. Find some regret to wear on the way down—*now* she screamed.

Blood almost reached curdle but his shoulder—hand—something covered the sound. Muffled. "*Shh!* If you don't wanna be touched, maybe drive around? Can't find stars here, but see how far we get ...I'm not—we got time. "Still forehead to wall. He nodded to something only he saw. "Whatever you want. You—you—just can't wake up tomorrow."

Just a body. Gone not only still, but cold.

At least before, sleeping—they still kept her warm.

He let up only half an inch when she thought she'd choke first. Gasp, maybe it was a cry—even a scream that lost it's air.

"Wh—why—what are you going to do to me?" when she finally could say something. Not sure why it was that. But—it was Leti.

It was maybe even acceptance—like all that shit talk and challenge was dare for life to prove her right. One of those—hey no ones looking, maybe it'll work now.

But she never actually wanted it to. Because what if Leti walked in. Tip toeing, as if Kaia was sleeping peacefully. Temporarily. There aren't words.

He sniffled again. Bugs crackled and the lamp popped outside. "I don't know yet, got any requests," laughing like a joke. To crying.

"Don't think about it—don't go there—fuck what am I gonna do with you—" Head shaking rapidly now, pressure more push and pull, too.

Erratic. "I don't have to—you stay here, Leti can take you home and everything... No-no-shhhh," pulling her into a hug when the name broke another dam.

"I know—it's okay. You're just tired of fighting—right? They know."

Kaia made a sound. A choke, wheeze. *Whimper*. Not because it hurt, not because the fear—because it was her pain weaponized against her.

It was *hers* when she talked about quitting, or her story when she ran hard at the edge to see if the slide to base would send her over or stop in time— *her, her, her, hers!*

"And babydoll, hey-hey-look at me. You're safe with me—nothing you don't want, right? Let's lay down, okay? That's good..."

She couldn't speak. Couldn't breathe. Mouth open—the way someone leaves a building in a rush and forgets to lock up. Because Leti would think she killed herself.

He was psychotic. But *right*. No one would ask a thing. Wrapped up in box or fire—close the book, move on. Leti—somewhere still in the distance. No one left to make sure she was still following behind, moving forward. And that....that did something deep. Picturing him greeting Leti and Cachí with Kaia's blood under her nails.

Pictured him talking about her paintings, giving her special attention because he fucking could. No one would know.

"Say something?" He pushed into her. Then pulled back.

Squeezed like a sponge—another sound, gasp for breath. So he backed a bit. Arms still braced on her side. Watched her like a vulture watches the dying. Claimed. But waiting.

A mock-respect before the pick-apart. Kaia's vision tunneled to the door. She couldn't see anything else. Then—nothing at all.

'What I'd do, will it hurt, please don't— Didn't matter.

"Wrong place, wrong time kinda thing I think...I don't have a choice, hey...I'm not evil...I—I don't have a choice, please. You gotta understand, you're playing it too."

Plucked hair from her mouth. *Gentle*. Maybe not ill-intent by design, but it felt like a show of size.

Vision still black, except the door. Staring at it so hard she could practically see through. To the sidewalks, and the fence along the property—where she'll fall, what direction she can run—Kaia couldn't see him. Only the exits.

Corner of his mouth lifted. Not joy, or cruelty, or anything. Death in his eyes like he'd been the one chasing her half her life. The one trying to take her from Leti.

"You're eyes really are something, you know?" Loosening his grip only long enough to be interrupted.

Someone strange. Something inside was infuriated by that. By thinking about death while he enjoys the view.

Someone—thing—pushed through the other side of the wall—pushed through Kaia until she pushed him too. "Do it then—you big whiney, pathetic, fat-crying— "Moving—swinging—but not her choice.

"Bitch!" Screamed out with a stubborn, defiant battle cry before she met with the wall again—pulled back only far enough to slam down again, forehead bashed to wall.

"Best—you—fucking—*got!*" Because—when she goes—whether now, whether later—at the very least, it was going to be true. "Gonna have to kill me yourself—*bitch!*"

Maybe didn't expect a light switch, maybe expected a slow dim and an extra second. But she just met the wall and extra time—more coughs, but not pain. Just air leaving to make room for her ribs.

He called her "Jaylin" and said nothing else. Just savaged. Hand stretched across her throat, unsure if it wanted to grab tight to choke or hard to hold—shaking.

Door throbbing—closer and closer, it was coming to her. Backhand—twice—more? Pain stopped when something ripped across the skin like a nail or ring trying to take her cheek with.

Lip—split. Chin, under nose—warm. Fingers—blood, but not her own. Screams either. Her thumbs digging for the fucking gold flecks in his eyes until she screamed like a savage going for a kill. Voice cutting out only when and tightened down.

"*I can't clean it up! Fucking take the goddamn pills, bitch!*"

His other hand came down across her face again, but hit the wall in a mess of focus. Either wood or knuckle cracking under the smear of her hair. So she thrashed and he bore down.

Kaia clamped down on his arm. Just remembers that for awhile.

Eyes closed, heavy weights on her face, but she latched down like a dog and even felt herself lift when his arm did.

"I'll fuckin' kill you—think I fuckin' won't—*think I fuckin' can't take it?*"

Her hips bucked, foot planted against the wall—if it belonged to her, she was swinging it. It didn't matter how much it hurt.

It didn't matter how it wasn't fair. Didn't even matter how long it went on. Felt like an eternity, felt like a hot box filled with fiery waves.

Felt like a hell. But here. Squeezing tight—like maybe she didn't remember, because maybe this was her last kindness to herself.

"You stupid fucking nosey bitch, you did this!"

But how—how is that lie kindness? Would it be a lie now—her literally blood on his hands. Thought about giving in to sleep then. Thought about what a weak bitch that would make her. Because this wasn't about damage. It was about the body's survival. About doing it—or don't.

Scratching at his face and hands, but wrists like stumps and a body like the tree. His fingers even began to feel like bark against her neck.

Peeling one back but something harder underneath.

Slippery too—her hands falling each time she swung. Slower.

Mouth open, nothing coming out. Reminiscing over all the fights and all the wins. Even the ones that didn't feel like it at the time—but the small moments.

The tram. The caricature. The 'Sam,' and his existence in a place they could just—fucking—*reach!*

Phoenix on one shoulder, Hellhound on the other—one screaming goodbye one arguing, *I don't want to go!* But both just still trying to be *heard*—even at the very end—fighting each other. Wrapped so tight in the chains holding them down—the ones Kaia thought she could use like a leash, but really just showed them the world.

Acclimated them and bundled together wrestling—hands around her throat—the walls fading and falling the way the do in dreams.

Darkness climbing, strange things speaking—pulling, pulling, pulling against each other until finally, a pull together, because instinct wants to live more than trauma needs to die.

And—seconds on the clock, wrong end of the ice, too weak to meet in the middle—she was too weak to hold their chain.

Dropped it.

And something—didn't let go, but ripped violently from her control.

Criteria from the Cosmos

SKYLINE: DRIVE
00:19:49:00

|XXXIX|

The engine clicked as it cooled. Tires whispering against gravel somewhere down the block. Sirens long gone now—but the quiet they left behind was worse. Cachí flicked the keys between his fingers like a nervous tic.

"Deuces," he muttered, already moving to open the door.

"*Espera, 'mano.*" Dante just looked at him. Not mad. Just there. Present and bone-tired, like the rest of them. "We'll get your car later. Leti first."

Cachí stilled. Eyes flicked to him, then out the window. "You wanna chat or something?"

That made both men glance toward the front steps, then the car, as if she'd sneak back in. Had her body out of view though—mostly.

Catch a peep through the drivers window of her small frame, tired movements, and shuffling for belongings. She stook up, unsure. Looking to the house, them, the car—Cachí chuckled.

Relaxed on his window like they could finally just breathe.

"You good?" he asked, parked—*mostly*—clear of the street behind his own.

"Can—I...go in the trunk?" Leti asked like he'd say no but he smiled, nodded. Dante's head leaned in a little closer, watching her too. "Anymore pistols?"

Cachí didn't have to say anything. Wasn't that funny and the guilt was there. "Dragging me for more apologies then?" Not watching Dante, not checking for him. And not disrespect, but full trust. "No..." Dante sighed.

There wasn't anger between them, no frustration. Just words. Habit, history. Because, even when they denied it—that's not ignoring it—it's hiding the truths between them.

So Dante watched ahead, and behind. And Cachí—the center. Her. "Just... feel like we should. Talk. Or something."

Leti, still in it's shadow. Hand twisting restlessly in her sleeve as she popped the trunk. He could see it when she dropped her arms. Left one. Always. At least since he started noticing.

The same hand she can't distract with a pen. Her motions—hesitant, half-starts and pauses, checking over her shoulder, but not for them. Everywhere but them like—they blocked a side, but she still handled watching her own back.

"She moves like..." Cachí started, then stopped. Shrugged one shoulder.

"Like she doesn't—I don't know. Feel safe...I don't like it."

"Can't take it personally, Cachí. CPS, foster—don't make it worse being offended."

That made him look. Could only mimic though—"CPS?"

"Child protection. Family services, yeah-yeah." Took a minute—Dante maybe too relaxed. The confusion on Cachí's face not about the department, but about it's proximity to her. Waiting for more, eyes wide, breath—not how it was a minute ago.

Dante tilted his head, nodded towards her—no reason. Honestly, just knew it'd make Cachí look. Because Dante didn't mean to say it. Just kind of...came out. File probably still open if he checked back a few tabs.

Cachí blinked. "She was in the system?"

Dante winced. "I mean—I don't know the whole of it. Just caught a couple pieces doing some digging." He trailed off. Shook his head.

"Digging—for what?"

Curiosity. The hell of it. "Oh—*no se*, Cachíflin. Maybe—what she has to do with Cody came from left field.

Cachí still wasn't angry. He almost wanted to be. Whatever that turning in his chest was. Maybe just all of them—little Kayden's before he started acting like a bitch. "What happened?"

The trunk slamming shut. Dante looked at him disapprovingly, one shake to the head. "Not my story to tell."

"I know..." Maybe Cachí just—didn't want to care right then? Or maybe he felt weirder about feeling some type of way—Dante having a piece he didn't even get to see. Made him silent. Not a heavy one. But weighted.

Cachí's jaw shifted. His eyes still locked on her. Scrambling around the outside, checking all four doors in case maybe his fob didn't work. Didn't want it her fault.

Didn't feel comfortable apologizing to him. So she's making sure she never has to—even the trunk again as they whispered. Windows dangerously sure I'm getting any stories now. Not after tonight."

Dante sucked his teeth and chuckled. Cachí looked—surprised. "Quit feelin' sorry for yourself, *vato*. Think she's fragile?"

"I mean..." He did. But admitting it made him feel guilty too. Not guilty. Wrong, stupid—like it was obvious.

Misreading what it meant to be still. Or projecting his own apathy onto her because he didn't want to believe there was a middle ground on the bus forward. A way he didn't have to be complicit, but he didn't have to walk away either. Unwilling to break when she's needed. Aching, but not trying to hurt others.

Maybe the only traumatized one here that didn't ripple. Held inside herself like a steel box. Stillness—not from a calmness, not from a curiosity, but fight.

Cachí didn't answer. Felt like an ass. Dante's voice VIP in his head now—*sorry for yourself*—Maybe guilty not for what he did, but for how he felt. Wanting someone there sorry with him.

Tried to smile when she came to his window, both hands twisting in her sleeves now. Slack bags, one inside the other on a shoulder.

He didn't want to speak—didn't want to look. So when she reached to the window, he leaned the opposite way of himself. Let her drop the keys first then, "hey..." *Too late now.* So he sent it. Felt himself fucking fall and hated every second but grabbed her hand anyway. Not to pull, not to lead, but to just see.

She gave him an awkward little nod, like something was asked and she wasn't sure who was watching. but didn't pull. "You not...driving?"

Dante answered when Cachí didn't. "I wanted some extra time. Enjoying everyone's company."

Truly didn't matter *how* he said it. Would have sounded like sarcasm regardless after tonight. Turned away when he saw Cachí reach his other hand. Set it on her cheek. And while it looked the same as before, it felt different.

"You okay in there?" Quiet, but enough. Leti turned her hand in his. Even lightly held his wrist—staring at the entanglement before she smiled at him and gently slipped free. That's how he knew it wasn't a reflection, but her. Because he still wanted to hang on. Would have, too.

It stirred up Truth that wanted to be called, Anger. But was too weak to be called anything else but *Admission.* Only just starting to see how much he—maybe, *might*—be punishing himself not—necessarily for what he went through.

But because he survived it, when Matí didn't. Because his parent's didn't know who to blame, so he wanted to give them something.

And—because. Something out there, cracked him so bad it fundamentally changed him to his core. He didn't know how to feel, but maybe punished was the easiest.

And that was truth. So he let go. Not of this moment—but of her hand. Because words and shit—weren't it. He had to prove he wasn't going back—wasn't cowering in the middle—by taking the steps forward.

So maybe then they—*him*—can see he wants more than this somehow too. Leti climbed in behind Cachí without anymore fuss and once settled, she showed surprise catching Dante staring in the mirror. "We all good, then?"

"Just onto the next, right?" Unspoken, but screamed. *Kaia.*

They didn't say much, but something passed between them. That half-smile kind of thing people do when they've got too much on their chests and not enough left to say.

California-rolled the stop line before Cachí suddenly—but confidently and steadily—climbed from his seat. Dante tapping the breaks halfway into the four-way and Cachí looking less and less confident the further settled into the back he got.

Leti hesitated for half a breath. "Hi..."

Vulnerability lay bare in the seat next to her; no walls, no masks. "Hi.."

Dante started the heat before the gas, stealing a glance and watching Cachí and simply how he interacted. Stalling, too. Like maybe there'd be one more thing—*one more person.*

But the streets were empty. The house was silent And the heat rolled in slow while the conversation left fast. Cachí tilted his head to the window, but was really saying, "*to him.*"

Cachí leaned—and maybe it was Kaia's name; maybe he was terrified Leti'd breakdown. Or maybe he'd of done it just because—but his body calm in close to hers, taking up space to—*hopefully*—give her a soft place to land, and a shoulder to lean.

Kayden saw the words coming before she fully finished the sentence. Pulled her back, slammed her back to the wall. Can't talk shit when you can't breathe.

Her eyes were wild though; talking when she didn't say anything.

Open waters they wanted to drown him in—

he didn't think. Just slammed his fist to face like a boot to the spider.

Her torso hit the wall, her head behind it, and she yelled.

It went silent then. White, angry, unclean rage, like a beast in quicksand believing it could drink it all in before it drowned.

The sound echoed under the sink; the guttural cry twisted into Kayden's nerves. Made the hair on his arms, his neck, stand at attention.

He could have sworn he heard glass break, and kept jerking back to the mirror—kept seeing shadows crawl out of it like the TV—darkness lurk to pull him in with that boy. Face him.

And something inside him—it didn't let go, it snapped. Jagged pieces turned inward on himself like an enemy. Brain betraying body.

It wasn't a girl that fought under him. It was an enemy. It was memory.

It was everything he couldn't have or control in his fucking hands maybe? It wasn't excitement—it was edging some kind of sick release.

Inside him, low. One that laughed and roared and told him he was nothing, but also asked him—*what would happen if it felt good?*

Made him scream louder. Not scared of her—but himself.

Just more scared of Apollo. Of Dante—seeing him break, for Apollo.

Tell himself Dante would have had the same—calling himself a liar.

Everything did. The mirror, the ghosts, the walls—*Jaylin!*

"Could have been so easy..." Still crying. Because—that was good. He wanted to. Only thing he could use now to say, "*see, we're still good, we're still worth it.*"

Even when he could see through the condensation he made on the mirrors. They all came by to laugh at him.

They all watched him—like maybe he was the one in the box. In a mirror, or TV.

Maybe they all knew. Maybe they all replay that moment he stopped fighting. That moment he wanted this fucking bitch to, too. Half his size, bit younger—fighting harder than maybe he ever did. Thinks she can win. Because she see's it too.

How he's lost already. Squeezing out the power that tried to overcome him. "You did this I hate you!" He squeezed tighter. Then loosened.

Then tight again, a weep suffocating him. Telling himself just break it, but flinching—*shaking* that he even had the thought. He wasn't bad. He wasn't doing this—they were. His eyes burned. "I fucking hate you," his voice trembled between gritted teeth. Eyes closing. "I hate you, Jay..."

Seeing long black hair like that'd make it better. Like that'd make it Apollo. *Weakness.*

His hands loosened. Kissed her once and wanted to vomit. Both of them frozen for a half of second that held it's breath into ten more.

He bit his cheek until it bled. Staring into her like a fucking man would. Because he could handle his guilt. He could carry it all. He would.

"Last chance," he whispered. Eyes more red then turquoise now. Oxygen leaning itself out as if that'd help get through his grip. "Lemme lay down with you.

Bloodied like she'd been to war. Claws no longer scratching, but braced, one on his cheek the other his chest. Had to reply it nine times over in his head—couldn't believe this bitch.

As if Apollo had two.

Licked her lips—under her nose, and pulled in blood, eyes rolled— spit— Cackling echoes behind him—laughing at the disrespect. He looked at the spit. Pink and discolored, creep into the cotton near his cross.

Head move like he was hunting—slow, back on her. Unsure.

She couldn't run, she couldn't win. But somehow—those fucking eyes still dared him: *Your move.*

But what did that make him? Where was the line in the sand separating him from Apollo. Miles and miles away but getting closer.

This. Here. *Her.* In his hand a larger step there. But...*the spit.*

His skin raced with goosebumps when it was warm and moist and now stuck in the hoodie like a stain that everyone would see and no was him.

But—the disrespect. The way the world will make you a bitch when you let it slide...

He chuckled. Hand looser now because that was too quick. And still laughing, but not 'cause anything was funny—just a small break in his tension.

Tears and rage dangerously low—needed something from somewhere. His mouth moved more then him—wetting, trembling, biting the chapped skin. Pictured the way her mouth moved, tongue, jaw—

To. Spit.

On him. Like noting. And the bitch smiled. When he laughed. Like not even that was his.

"You just made this—a lot fucking easier, Doll…"

Her hands pressing against him. Him looking to the left—like there was something more he needed for this. Like there was more time.

Then to the left. The mirror.

Like he was guilty and waiting for the little Grudge-shaped nightmares to wrap arms over his back and ankles and wasit—pull him in—but something made him look down.

Movement first.

Shock maybe—second? Then pain. Bone to groin. Knee to tailbone.

Kaia screamed, but he didn't give her the air tightening—*trying to.* Something tightened. Like his entire body, but he didn't feel her warmth.

Couldn't see, but heard them both. Her desperate gasp, his agonized disbelief.

Heels had come up before his hands had dropped down. The rest of him after. He bent in—saw her feet land back to the ground as he did.

But then knees—His? Hers? *Both.*

Air too thin around them. They dropped. Together. Breathe for breath— an instant. Nausea. Black spots. Flash of the same war from the opposite side.

She'd started coughing air *out* chaotically—he even reached for it.

Trying to pull air *in*, but lungs, body, brain—airlocked.

Entire fucking gastric system choked.

Fed pieces of himself from the outside in and choking—how she should have been—*How she was.*

But her knee—packing him up for later. He roared but then something high pitched followed, watching her scrambling to her knees.

Vacuum still in his chest. He was going to kill her kindly, even when she acted up, he was going to get them pills down her throat. No mess.

No disrespect. Because—he's still fucking good.

And everything turns. On him. Watching her scrambling to her knees—crumbling for her, *towards her*, on his own.

Reaching, dizzy, for his gun, *but people will hear—and he will run—but he can't even reach—but she's going to try for Dante.*

Fast track to the box, he sucked like a fish on its last try. "Ssss—stop!"

Try harder. "I can't—" Gasping. Never hard enough.

Kaia's eyes popped open the second he just touched her.

Put a hand on her thigh to stop her—didn't even do anything—and she fucking scrambled faster. Stopped for him—hope, *we're good*—to kick. *Stopped to kick.* Head blurry, vision too.

If she even stopped at all. Used his face like kicking off the wall in the pool and he screamed out under it.

Growled so loud he didn't expect to hear the brass slap against the wall like a bell toll at the church.

Like the end of a class. Nah—*like the end of him.*

Paper Birds & Torn Wings

CITY SCAPE
00:20:03:00

|XL|

Kaia once asked her dad why the sun always looked better setting than rising. *'Because you lived through the day to see it'*
The sunrise came with uncertainty. You might've made it to another morning. But what if, by the end of it you wished you hadn't?
She hadn't understood it then, not really. Couldn't say the same now.

The city blurred around her as she flew. Wings beating— neon lights, cars snarling—somewhere behind her, a door slammed. One for anger, and again for defeat.

She knew—the shout that followed, raw and ownerless. Quieter the faster she flew. Aches heavy still—throbbing in beat with her feet on the pavement; head heavy, feet breathless.

One shoe. One bare foot—pavement chewing into her heel, keeping her from floating away for real. The burn in her side screamed, throat felt blocked, but she didn't stop. She couldn't.

Heartbeat—*too fast.* Feet—faster.

Legs cut through the wind like blades—*give her a cliff and she'll fly.* Only come down when she found what she was looking for.

Because the fight was gone and the air was hers. The sting in her heels and scream in the lung—the breath—*still hers.* The sting in her heels, the scream in her lungs—? *Still hers.*

Even as the world warped around her—the evening cold gnawing at her skin, blood drying under her nails. She clung to one thing.

He didn't win. And wasn't fucking done.

Su:20:03:⁰⁰ || XL || Desert View

Door handle crushed against the wall in a violent swing. Hand cuffs tightening, cells locking—he still choked for simply *breath*. Seconds felt like minutes of suffering—member and marbles jammed into one.

Couldn't pull enough air in to get up and stop her, enough to scream—until he did. A raw, animal howl that turned the room inside out, barreling into a ball and into an upright position again. Slammed the heel of his hand against the door frame so hard the wood leaned in.

Felt like he chased, but his legs—moved against himself and he feared his shit would crumble right off—hurt so fucking bad. As if he hadn't felt stuffed in prior. He leaned his head on the wood and just pictured chasing her into the traffic. Maybe it made him feel better about not running then. About feeling out of control.

Maybe it wasn't that bad before—and fucking maybe before he didn't feel like he was being played with by two *bitches*. Half his size like seven-years less experience—pissed him off. Burned him deep where he didn't think he could have more shame.

Not sure if for the spit, the kick, or the fucking foot to the face! She was no better—both on the ground together, using him like that. Equal. Respect—it was there.

He was fucking fair. And now he could only feel pain, see her smoke trails through the lot and into the architecture—disintegrating in front of him like a ghost in the fog.

"FUCK!" He let it hang in the air, long on the syllables. Hand still protecting himself. Down the hall, curtains cracked open. Owner or manager or wife. Apollo knew her. Apollo knew everyone. And Kayden knew Apollo.

He damn near snarled—his steam probably felt fifteen rooms down with her. Staring—debating if she wants to be another bitch who flirted with curiosity too long, too. *Tough thoughts like he did anything besides cry.*

Give her more reason to run to Dante. His fist hit the wall. The woman shut the curtain and he nodded rapidly, unsurely. Trying to tell himself, he's sure. Slammed the door so hard it shook paint off the walls. Pacing. Stood in the middle of the motel room like the walls were closing in.

The sink mirror now cracked, Kayden watched it. Feared Cody would twist himself out of the crevice and bring others along.

Reflection bent in, warped and hardly human. Kayden was heaving but it wasn't pain now. Splashed water on his face. Once, twice. But cold, pointless. —*can't escape*—

Not there. "But you're not there." He tried to breathe. Counted backward. Reached for Jaylin's name in his head and tried to reassign the hate to something he could grasp. Kaia again—*go get in the car.*

Might even be fun to chase. Breath heaving harder, but shorter. His panic making it worse—like he couldn't remember how to breath and when he finally does it'll be too late.

If not dead than at least the brain—*as if he's not already an inanimate tool? What brain?* Kayden thrashed—cried. Foot hit the wall. OtherS did too. Probably a hole, but he couldn't see.

The hold on his boot felt like hands keeping him still. Something ugly wanted out. Something hurt and not even this relinquishment to tears was hitting him where he needed.

"Never again," shredded. "I swear to God, never again."

The twitch in his temple pulsed. He crashed down onto the toilet. Room too small to have him earlier—now maybe just tight enough to hold the skin on his bones.

Something clinked behind him.

The gun slapped the back of the toilet still there and still loaded—couldn't reach it in time for her though, but the way it jumps for him—Kayden smashed that down too.

Freezing—maybe the last time he remembers he breathed—when Cody's blood cracked from it's broken handle. Not metal, but plastic. Like childhood teens and freedom—he slammed his chest with his fist shaking his head.

Coughing like he'd rather choke himself out than feel this weak.

Plastic gun not even an option—reality and dreams—blood on his feet, but it wasn't real, or was it water over flowing, "Oh god—"

Didn't know how he knew, just knew—Cody's blood. Body in the mirror if he dared go outside. Mirror coming for him too.

He should have used the gun, maybe the shower curtain—walls closing to hold him in place.

He wanted to be better. Pulled up his shirt too, everything was crawling.

If he didn't fix this, Apollo would kill him. If he ran, the cops would.

The court would—at least bodies couldn't talk—*but they were talking now.* He was trying so hard to make some kind of sense but he'd never felt this out of control or on a brink but not his life, his body.

Something else taking it over, choking him out too. Bodies of old selves buried in the back where he doesn't let anyone near.

But that fucking bitch—Jaylin—*we'll take care of you.*

So she has to. She said to go back. Call it a new home—get him out of the country—Kaia not even from here—he had to be like her though, now.

A ghost. Not even real. Leave Dante with only smoke and a memory that pissed him off—crouched forward, arms braced on his knees, rocking.

He could feel the tile under him but not the ground. Not the now. Didn't know if he was praying or just waiting for breath, repeating words and memories until they no longer sounded like words.

And more until even the voice didn't sound like his own. Because it wasn't. He was him. Crawling up the back of his teeth, he tried to count.

Breathes. *Not him.* Seconds. *Not him.* Sheep. *Anything. Anyone.*

Couldn't remember the numbers—call them—fine, take him to jail maybe, he was scared. There was so much of him and his vision was black—

body hitting the walls when he looked for the way out.

Stood—tried to remember the floor—but f*orgot his legs* and crashed down like the fat man in the chimney and the hands—were those shaking too? Because his head was—violently.

On his own or just his vision he didn't fucking no anymore—leaned over wherever he was and puked.

Came up scream, furious, and feeling *dirty*—even from prison Apollo had his fingers in Kayden's strings—but—

Kayden. How could even that feel foreign?

Because, *bang.* Breath held—only tears from the other side of the door and the sound of water running. So much water. Under his feet. Wet.

He wanted his shirt back. Door rattled hard again—it echoed—and then it cracked.

The ride back to the motel had been quiet, but not cold. Leti—stroking the key card like a pacifier; trapping it between her fingers despite desperately fighting sleep. Breathes breath was steady and slow.

Something soothing about how her head and shoulders went up when he breathed. *Moving stillness.* The best kind.

And even more—he looked asleep too. Backpack stuffed under her leg, his foot. Kaia's bag jammed in there too. And it was like Leti could sense her inside—eyes opening in time to see the motel coming into view. Somehow still standing too.

Outdated, and days numbered. Dante took the loop to the right...maybe on accident, maybe not, but when he wasn't looking, she gently pecked Cachí on the cheek.

His head—the smallest movement like he wanted to say bye, but dreams were sweeter. Tucked her head but had her chin back up before she had everything in her hand. "This you?" Dante didn't whispered, didn't have to. Low, calm, and gruff.

"Yeah, thanks. I—sorry if I was rude. I appreciate his and your help." Eye to eye—because it was only tenderness that terrified her.

"I'll reach out about—your sister. Try to get some rest."

Not sure if she had many heightened emotions left for Kaia outside anger. Leti quietly shut the door—more afraid of waking Cachí.

Dante's window rolled all the way down. "Hey, will you—let us, or him, know if she rolls in sometime tonight?"

"Yeah—absolutely." Words and hesitation hanging in the air. Him probably just waiting for her to turn, her—just—afraid how it'll feel once in there alone. "D—Do you think he's going to hurt her?"

The look on his face and the broken contact—the mask when he realized he looked guilty. Leti stumbled back a bit, shaking her head. "Never mind, sorry that..."

"Hey, honestly? I don't—I have no idea why he would. Non answer, non promise. "Kade and them—they have shitholes all over the place."

Another vague statement. Another work around. Leti spun the key card again, looking at Cachí's window like she could see."Try not to freak out. Yet. Okay? I'll be honest when it's time to start worrying..."

Brass bell painted red rang in her head. "With all due respect—bodies and bays?" As if they weren't together because he's concern with that man. She was just riling herself up more.

"You're right." Sighing into his seat. "I'm tied into this one. Some things are hard to read."

"Yeah…" She wished she hadn't even asked, walking to the door, key in hand, bags on shoulder. "Well…"

Beep access in. "I appreciate it. And I'm fine…reminding myself she's done this before. I'm just usually home—" spinning her index and hand like a fan—"*this place*, creepy." Slipping in and turning with a last minute smile, as fake as ever. "Also, her fault."

Dante gave her a final head nod. As she swung the door closed behind her, he mouthed: *Nice try.*

The room door clicked behind her. Lock slid into place with a bit of a jiggle. Same quiet, but different cold. The room sent chills down her skin, but the smell of Kaia's shampoo was there. Sunscreen, and scorched.

Her cargos too, tossed to the foot of the bed and a ratty tie-dye hoodie she only slept in there too. Still held the shape like Kaia'd just slipped out moments ago. Leti dropped both bags. "Kaia?"

Somewhere, someone was calling her name too. Maybe it was Kaia, maybe it was better sense. *"Kaia!?"* Sense that touched like condensation on the mirror and vanished like it never came. *Bang, bang—bang.*

"The fuck, dude— *where'd you go?!"* Yelling. But only the steam breathed.

"Kaia. Open the damn door." And again. No answer.

But someone was there.

Leti's skin burned, but not rage. Something fast, light. Like panic. Kaia's smell mixing with cigarettes and dirt of fruit trees—sweet and earthy. Her palms stung. But she knocked again.

Don't. Because something wasn't right. "Come on—answer me, I'm coming in! You can't just disappear like that!" Her forehead hit the door. "God, you asshole, I thought—I thought you were…"

She didn't finish it. Didn't know what she meant to say. And didn't want to say it out loud in case the walls repeated it back.

Thud-thud-thud…! "Kaia!" Pipes hummed. Something clinked. Shifted. But no voice. No cough. No curse. And when the door opened—*no Kaia.*

Jaws of a Hammerhead

SERRAMONTE COMPLEX
00:20:47:00

| XLI |

Cachí sat on the edge of Dante's battered leather couch, the old frame sighing beneath him like it didn't want to hold another body.

He hadn't moved much. Not since Dante shoved a plate of scrambled eggs and a half-assed bagel at him— cold, under-salted. The kind of dinner you make when the fridge was empty and your patience was gone.

Dante muttered something about a nap and a shower; had to swing back to the station after despite exhaustion leaking from the bones. You could hear it in the way his keys hit the counter, or the way he didn't wait for an answer.

The eggs were still there. Still untouched. Cachí's fingers drummed absently against the chipped coffee table, staring into the dark.

Everything about the place felt foreign. Warmth without expectation. Photos lined the walls; candid ones, messy, imperfect. Mikki mid-laugh; Matías with a surfboard. All caught in motion.

Alive in a way Cachí could barely remember being. It felt like standing inside someone else's memory; home stitched together out of scars that kept going anyway.

He hated how much it made him ache, but the framed prom photo drew him in. He smiled, jumped up for a picture of it with his phone.

Thought about texting it to Leti. Closed the phone, but opened it to look again. And second guessed himself for awhile letting in sit in his gallery.

Figured it *was* a better excuse to text versus some stupid shit.

Hi. What's up? Cool. Yeah—rinse and repeat.

But the picture? After he'd told her the story in as much detail as he could muster? *Just send it.* Not say anything with it.

The group of them, Golden Gate in the background; bottle in Kayden's hand, shit eating grins on their faces like they had forever.

Cachí leaned forward, elbows on his knees. But how the fuck had they gotten from there...*to here?*

To dead BART stations that reeked of mildew and rot; to dragging Leti into messes she didn't ask for, and taking partial credit on Kaia too. Losing a whole-ass person at the Trap house— more unnerving the more hours that passed.

Because Kayden wasn't slipping; he was gone. Cachí glanced at the phone.

Hadn't heard from her, but didn't expect to. Not that quick anyway. *Or maybe she's pissed.* Which, *rightfully so.* Whether it be the gun on his back, the raid in his presence, the drugs in his place, the rejection in his room— he swallowed.

She had reason. And he wasn't going to bug her again.

Dante had come back not long after he left, thankfully. Too many pictures and eyes, and not enough noise. Dante moved meticulously. Set up the coffee pot for the morning.

All his fancy additives—still looking as roughed up as Cachí busy worried about everyone else. Stood in the doorway after third or forth time passing. Morning prep probably complete. Apartment immaculate, meals prepped.

"What's the plan?" Predictable first words from Dante.

His voice didn't carry judgment but was what you'd expect.

That grounded weight Dante always wore.

Afraid to disrespect the dead for living a little too loud. Cachí shrugged, barely a breath.

"Don't die." His eyes didn't leave the photo.

Dante sipped a water, nodded like it was a decent strategy. "Solid."

Dry as ever. Nodding. "Shower. Eat. Sleep. You know the way around."

He didn't wait for a reply and turned on his heel towards the back bedroom. Stopped—whispered footsteps back.

"Leti say anything about Kaia at the house?"

Cachí shook his head. "Leti hasn't said anything about anything."

A pause.

"...*Right*..." Dante chuckled. "So. Leti. Interesting uh, woman."

Cachí looked, slight squint to the eyes. A, *tread lightly.*

Gave Dante a unsure smile—unwilling to agree until he could see the end. Dante sipped his water. Eyebrows animating his face. "Smarter than she lets on."

Cachí looked away, nodded slowly, and played with his fingernail. "Argumentative as hell, too...

Dante again—pulling teeth. Didn't get more from him with indirect nudges; eventually, tired and on a roll— "You two a—thing, a *fling*, a....?" Dragged it out as if he really expected an answer.

Cachí was quick with it though, "Ay yo, when'd you and Mick start gyratin' fireside?"

Dante huffed into the water: Maybe surprise, maybe laughter. Probably both. And Cachí glared, which only made Dante chuckle more. Laugh echoing the small hallway to his bed. The relief having that kid on his sofa right now—having the brotherhood he'd lost twice over. Heart hungry for what was.

"Hey..." Cachí peeped his phone again. Sighed as he waited—as Dante's head slunk around the wall slow.

Cachí—sitting up a little straighter now. "You going to look for her still...?"

Half of Dante rounded the corner, shoulder on the wall for support. "Why do you think I asked about Leti." Tone not sarcastic—but sympathetic.

Not apathetic.. Cachí rubbed his jaw few seconds after Dante brushed his nose.

"Almost don't want to even ask but—you gonna' stick around, or take the search upon yourself?"

Cachí went for his shoes. Lazily undid the laces. "Out of ideas. Else I'd be running them."

Dante nodded like that tracked, but it didn't sit right. Picking up what Dante'd dropped, Cachí added to it:

"I won't lie to you. And I'll let you know when I'm out." That seemed to help. Face looked lighter than it had five minutes ago. Dante nodded at him.

"Leti and I talked a bit. Telling you the same thing I told her, don't—I tell Mikki too. Don't let yourself drown to try an' save someone else."

Seems obvious until you're in the rapids with someone you'd save. Cachí nodded slow, upside-down smile and a jagged edge. Dante crossed his arms. Cachí tossed backwards into the couch, kicked his feet up too.

Dante didn't argue. Just rubbed his jaw, then his eyes. "I'll pull a couple favors tomorrow..." Arms dropped.

"What happens when Kaia's back?"

Cachí didn't answer. But noticed he said '*when*' instead of '*if*'.

Couldn't help wondering—was it really that easy? Was it Cachí?

The silence between them got sticky. Cachí shrugged. "They go back home. I guess." Let out the held breath.

He knew that the entire time. Still—saying it aloud, kinda actually sucked. In a way he didn't like, and then again in a way he felt dumb for liking someone after...? Twenty-four ish hours?

Did the space between the BART and bonfire count?

"So here when I wake up then?"

Clearly an active worry of his; Cachí rolled his eyes. "Imma shower too."

Tucked his head into his hood. Dante paced towards the room, than back for thirds. Cachí let his eyebrows up this time. "You know," arms crossed now, but thoughtful. "You're not stuck in this city, Cachí? Nothing is keeping you here."

Cachí's eyebrows shifted from up to inward and down. Nervous.

"I mean, you'll always—Mikki and I will always have your back. But, I don't know. Unknown's not off limits is all I'm trying to say I guess."

"What—" feet hit the floor as he leaned back up, but shoulders hunched. "Where the fucks that coming from?" Wasn't anger, or annoyance. But fear. Knowing it, but never admitting it—because, where would he even go. *Or what would he do?*

Doesn't even know what he *wants*. Distance from old influence may help. Or make him worse. Dante shrugged, playing back what he said himself.

"Maybe we all move the hell out of here." Hands pushed into the small of his back as he stretched it. Smiled a stupid grin with chunky cheeks. Said— "you wanna be me and Mick's boy? Dibs on playing Mom."

Cachí chucked a pillow across the room. "*Vete, pendejo.*"

And Dante slapped his hand on the wall twice as he walked away.

"*Te quiero, 'mano.*"

Back through the hallway, finally released from all duties, and sealed off in the back with a final *click* of the door.

Cachí kicked his feet back onto the couch. It was like old times.

Almost. But maybe close enough to rest.

Violins:

Last Refuge of the Incompetent

SU:20:50:⁰⁰

|XLII|

Leti felt it before she saw it. The wrongness in the air; the sound of a second breath where there should've been one—too close and too wrong. Her chest locked, spun for the door but her body went back instead. Skull cracked on something solid.

They were in the desert. But they hadn't made it yet. And she was so excited to go. Open. Empty. Still, and alive. Her eyes rolled for while. For a second. For a week. The sound of water leaking out. Shower? *Or blood.*

She was inside. Still felt cool air on her face, but warm and wet behind her head. "No," her mouth open wide, but she meant her eyes to.

Leti gurgled. When her eyes cracked open, she was inside. Not in a twisted up dream, but in reality, hugged and held down by six feet of dirt. Leti's gurgle cracked into a scream. Scream burned off the blur in her eyes like cold water to the face.

"Kaia!!" she screamed it—sloppy. "Cachí! *Dant—*" A hand clamped down. Springs creaked. Kayden was coming into frame; slow. Eyes opening under water. Under the blood in the brain—pressure lifted from her face.

"Kaia." Hand pulling away slow. But something harder coming down instead. A board from the ceiling maybe, a dropped phone. A fist sounded right—skin to skin—it just felt too cruel. Easier to believe the walls were coming in.

The room blinked. Didn't creak, but screamed. Harmonized with hers— each passing minute revealing a new detail.

Kayden hovering over; jaw slack, drool even. But breath sour.

"I told you to stop—" he slurred, voice sticky, consonants broken. Leti didn't freeze. Her body pulled for the door. She twisted, gasped. "Get off me!" Yelling at him like Kaia was the one sitting over her—bullying her like a sibling does.

"I told you—" Void. Of everything. "I'm not going back."

She fought. Repeated like ritual: *Fingers and toes bend easiest; eyes, ears, nose, mouth inside fastest; groin, knees, head, neck with enough of a swing*—but she couldn't wind back enough.

And when she did—nothing hurt him. Bounced like—*rubber, glue. Bounces from me—sticks to you—"Help!"*

But he wasn't even human then. Smelled only of sulfur and evil—no one ever fucking believed her—no one believed in *her*—but she had kicked Kaia's ass a time or three.

Might even have been more if Kaia didn't lead with surprise—reaching for his groin instead now—twisting apples from the fruit trees on one side, hooking a punch with the other—*anything*.

But only force. The right hand felt like a blade punching back every time she hit but—that had to mean she was doing something.

Left clipped the edge of his nose—already bloodied and eye torn at but unsure where or how she'd sliced him. Attention was on one thing and one alone: Exit.

"You will *never* touch me again!" Calloused hand slid across her waist, dug into her skin like a leech for blood. *But those were supposed to be her words*—not his.

"*Yea*—fuck you! *Kaia!*"

Him in the bathroom. Kaia's clothes on the floor. Him—scratched shirtless. "Kaia! *What the fuck did you do!*"

Because what if Kaia was still inside. What if she got a single second—had to choose. Freedom, Kaia? But she wanted both.

Instead the room just got smaller. The bed closer, his shadow darker—*maybe with everything so close, maybe then she could make it to both*—still talking to herself like she'd make it.

She twisted harder until his head cracked down against her nose. Leti cried out. She's cried before. Her brain.

Never had her *body* scream in pain like that before her mind knew what happened. Not even in the fights, not even in the temporary placements, not even when foster family's hands tried a little too hard but wanted her a little more docile.

But stillness was hers. *That*, they didn't take. They didn't stain.

Leti rolled when she felt her head—back, butt, thighs, *body everything*—hit the mattress. Skull a thousand pounds between the wall, his fist, and her own screaming—but she couldn't see.

Vision might have come back, but her hands were attached to her face. She wanted to swing. *Now.* But she gasped—she'd never broken something before—*that* felt broken.

Hand too when it screamed as loud as she did. Scream was shrill, but—Leti didn't hear the voices screaming, didn't have the support rooting her on inside. Only large, empty, echoing garage. Doors down, engine running, clock on. Him verse her.

It blurred again from there. Maybe from pain; maybe from fear—or maybe instincts kicking on to survive the only ways they know how. And she knew how. Her and Kaia used to fight a lot. Not argue. Spar. To be stronger.

Run. To be faster – "*Help!*"

It'd stopped being for the fun of it a long time ago. Never be caught off guard again. Today—not about to break a promise to herself. Just freeze.

Like the police told her—s*tay behind me*. Leti felt her body flip. Should have stayed—pretended to be asleep with Cachí longer. Froze then. Something asked if she wanted to survive and that's how it told her to. Unable to muscle out—she tasted the comforter as if she'd said the words aloud.

Shoulders—head, pushed so far into it, but elbows flailing back—*not* wildly—wickedly, with aim and determination.

But fists came down—not even as hard as the first, but quick, chaotic, and frantic. Twice as many for her one. Her shoulder, back of the head, lower back. Air was expensive now; hard to come by.

A hand slapped onto the back of her neck, the other wildly touching for her wrists.

Holding—rolling on top of them. Like handcuffs—she kneed him the moment she'd been forced to face him—*black eyes and all*—but was shocked into pain and surprise when he kneed back twice as hard.

Crying then, because what the fuck—completely restrained it didn't make sense. Asking why, watching him like it was a TV, but asking for her hands, saying she wanted this—she'd hold his neck, or go to knees, but he didn't stop fighting with his belt.

"You don't make these decisions anymore—" Kayden rasped, awkwardly weighted still holding arms back—Leti's shoulder's trembling trying to rip themselves free.

"Kayden—please," complimented more—called him strong, called him a man, handsome, offered not to fight if he promised not to hurt.

Lower half of her body came off the mattress only long enough for pants to follow. Then upper half next—jerky and rough when they had one final debate over her arms.

Then it was just—god so far from a release, but a free fall. Bottom made of spikes and shadows, there in sight, but the fall only deepening.

Speeding. Spinning.

None of that mattered—it was a bareness. A vulnerability that felt too exposed to move. Stripped her voice while his only went higher.

Because—when she looked at him, she didn't see because he wasn't there either. Not on her, not in himself. Screaming through hollowed hallways of her garage together.

Like a monster that can't see once things go still.

'It's too late for Kayden—he knows it too.'

Sweat and hair as he flattened down against her hard—she couldn't even convince herself it was okay.

Disgust louder than her, goosebumps now tattooed, but her leg—not even forced, only slack and defeated—bent up into his armpit before he tilted her, him—crashing in with surgical precision—Leti felt herself split, crushed under a silent man.

He wasn't drowning in the tide. He was already dead, but floating face up.

Couldn't find his way so he floods the space around until nothing is left standing, threatening to send those echoes back home.

The world tipped deeper on its axis at his first thrust. Mouth, eyes, everything pried open. Even mind—maybe the way a life flashes before death, relationships do. *Trust.*

Because this wasn't only a rape. It was a robbery.

First man, or hundredth—he robbed the past of a future feeling safe. And stole from a partner she didn't even yet know.

Because, maybe he'll leave her trust or maybe she'll find it back, but it'll never be that same beautiful glass trophy little-Leti kept safe for someone.

Only memories. And another hole in the ground that drops her out of her head from the smallest reminder or sensation. Like water drops.

Like a tempo. *Kaia's blood.* The lamp rocked but didn't fall.

The curtains fluttered once—slow motion. Like a crowd hushing before the exhibit. She whirled through the haze—curling, growing—But muted.

Leti's hand gripped the comforter behind her when her shoulder even felt like it'd break. It wasn't her sleeves, it wasn't Kaia's hand, it wasn't Cachí's hoodie—but she still held it the same.

Wouldn't let herself remember this part but maybe tried to lie to herself. Pretend it was someone else, pretend they agreed—candle lights and music on—just let the body trick the brain and deep the doors shut.

Because the bed wasn't a mattress. This moment was a secret, or a stage.

Every sound amplified inside an echo chamber with an orchestra. Textures touched; time slowed into a crawl yet rattled off the walls in a nonsensical cadence.

A frenzied *Kayden*. Her resistance, his punishment—*percussions*. Breath as bass. It was only a terrible concert.

"Fuck!" An angry audience. Deep—harsh objections with rough starts and false finishes where crescendo built but had no end.

Conductor angry against the walls like hands against drums.

The girls voice not a voice crying out at all, but the violins—the violins were shrill and sounded like screams.

Tempo clicked, conductor roared—the girl in the bed, taking it, may have even tried to speak, tell him *'it's okay.'*

But the string quartet snapped, and while the violence paused with the violins, the harps played. Because the shows—must always go on.

Leti held the blankets in her hand while the stage held their secret.

And laying down, looking up at herself—*enjoy the show...*

In the US,
1 in 5 women have experienced sexual assault and/or rape.
1 in 6 men have experienced sexual assault and/or rape.

Sexual assault occurs every 68 seconds.
But every 9 minutes—it's a child.

More than 90% of sexual assaults are never reported
97% of rapists never see the inside of a cell.

Media coverage and justice are even less accessible
to survivors from minoritized communities.

This isn't rare; this is ignored.

Gender, age, orientation, or race—
Sexual violence does not discriminate.
But the system does.

| UIHI.ORG | RAINN.ORG | UJIMACOMMUNITY.ORG | 1IN6.ORG |

THE VEIL

the
thing
about
seeing
clearly—

you
can't
unsee
it
after.

Stages With No Applause

|XLIII|

Leti didn't know how long it lasted. She'd tried to count the beats against the wall, the skin against skin, but she stopped around one-hundred seventy-three. Not because she couldn't go on—but because it didn't matter. Unsatisfied with the show, lighting the curtains on fire—*apologizing?*

Touch burned but made her look—like Kaia was maybe shaking her. Was here for her. Could tell her—*don't be ashamed.*

But Leti saw emptiness. She saw through him to the hollow insides where shame was bred. But he took her mask.

The hurt one, the panicked one.

And she—his. Numb now. Like he'd sucked her soul through himself. Took hers. Cause he didn't get one. *What's that make her now?*

"Leti!*?* Hey...wake up... Oh my god. "

Leti's not home right now.

Frantic footsteps pacing around her. Kicking through that locked mental prison like they had a chance to escape it.

Together, in that room, with that secret, *forever.*

Not even fear belonged to her anymore. Not even that quiet, still space. Black spots did though—Vision—

Didn't matter. Not until the door... Opened too nice; closed too neat.

She's never gotten out of here before, and he did? So easily, but why didn't he have to sit in it too? Why didn't he take any of it when he left?

Cages built for ninety-nine...And *him?* Why does he get to be the one percent that gets to walk free.

Seven wingbeats thrashed before it vanished, and only then did Leti's lungs remember how to move.

The motel curtains shifted once in the draft. A crow barked outside. Unsure if she was really back yet this time, but eyes opening slow like maybe the didn't want to be.

Maybe they'd change their mind.

Skin buzzing. Throat raw. No begin and no end to where pain started and ended. Expected it to hurt more inside; what he just did; fearing Kaia's dead in the tub....Leti's head rolled; water still dripping slow. Eternally.

Mirror shattered. Sirens ringing all around the city, but none for her—not even those were hers. Nothing left; not a woman—he took that and left her only a wound and a war. And the city wasn't going to help; they'd only tell her to fight quieter.

Should have never come to the city. Pastel houses hiding cold and sharp steel beams, airports, factories, and dense populations....they should have been in the woods.

Camping with the family—maybe they were, if she thinks hard enough. At the bottom of the mountain now. No where but up. Or just still.

She understood more about Kaia in the time away that the past few years, though it felt too late to matter. Kaia never existed—as if Leti never did.

But her wrists throbbed where she imagined him grabbing her, where she—pretended? Handcuffs bit her. They existed. Imprint there and down to the bone.

Not her fault—all she did was walk in, but still, the shame was so thick it suffocated the soul. Yeah—he's at fault, despite escaping so easily, but she can be too. Why that bonfire, why that group, why—

Does it even matter—Leti was so exhausted. And everyone dies; everyone stops existing—*let's do it together*—

Halfway to hell—Leti still didn't feel anything. Except *numb*.

"I—beat you....all the down, Kai..."

The fuck you did—get up, Bitlet. Not said aloud—not said at all, but it rang through her ribs like thunder.

"Kai...?" Like something not said but felt.

Leti, help me.... "Kaia.."

Pillow under her head warm, but wet with something thicker than sweat.

Legs were led. Lungs, paper. But the heart still beat. Slow, consistent beat. Not percussion—not headboard to wall—*heartbeat*. Thrumming. Alive, and maybe the only piece not torn. Beating.

One-hundred and seventy-four. Trying. One-seventy-*five*.

Communication from brain to limb and brain to self abnormally complex and slow. Overly focused on limbs—forgetting to tell itself, but up they went, gasping through the nausea. Air too thick.

And her head—worse upright—swollen unevenly and heavier to one side. The bridge between her eyes was demolished by swollen flesh.

She let herself roll off the bed, no other way seemed plausible. Grabbing the nightstand desperately and bringing it all down, too.

But no one was around to see her shame. Breeze on too many bare places, even wanting to hide her disgusting body from herself. Everything—arms, toes, too. Disgusted and betrayed by a body too weak to save itself.

You're not saved yet. Blood on the back of her skull. Hands red, dragging across the carpet, crawling to the nearest piece of clothing.

Still wouldn't cry though. So maybe Leti wasn't really ashamed at all—too proud to cry. Only feeling she *should* feel shame. Something about other people and their opinions on the matter.

> *Secret or stage, Leti?*

Curled on the floor hooking a pant let around her foot and resting for awhile repeated until she couldn't see her own skin anymore. Resting awhile more like surely time will tell. She won't have to do anything. Just say there, rest. Disappear, too.

Sound of a siren screeching nearby, keeping her from sleep. Or not a siren: Alarm, flashing 12:00 like it'd been reset too. Phone down with it. Leti dug for inspiration, but got heart break.

'*Didn't know I needed to be rescued.*'Challenging fate.

Cried at first. Hard. But it hurt too much. And she decided she meant it; didn't need a fuickin rescue. Pride not a deadly sin, but a living one; forcing her into a sickeningly long crawl. Hoodie bundled in both fists. Tan phone blending into the walls and the floors, but Leti locked onto the flashing red numbers beside it, hailing her in.

Didn't both with the hand held, just snagged the bottom, hit the top twice, and dialed three numbers stitched into the fabric of life.

"*911 what is you're emergency?*"

the Feast

PEDRO POINT, PACIFICO
SU:23:30:⁰⁰

|XLIV|

The water had gone cold. Kayden stood under the stream, back pressed against the tile. Eyes closed. He'd wait here until Cachí called him back. Or until the water wore him down like a stone. Kayden knocked his head against the wall—three times quick and hard, worse each time. Enough to make the room spin but still not enough to empty the house. *Coward—*

"Kaid...?" Jaylin's voice slid in with—*the others*—with a soft knock and Kayden stuck his face under the shower. Let the water steal any salty proof he was less of a man. Doorhandle twisted and swung slow. He didn't need to look.

"Hi, handsome." Sweet. And rotten. He didn't move. Didn't have the right to. Breath held, too. "All cleaned up then, babe?"

"Get out, Jay." She dropped her clothes like she was shedding old skin. "You seem—like you could use someone." Shower door peeked open next. Moving behind him slow, like she knew she was treading deep.

"What do y—" "To come in." Voice, poured slow and thick but tempered.

Different rules with bigger players. *Was he ever really any different than Cody?* Crossed one line; only brought himself closer to more.

But if they could just take him back. C*ompromise with him because—* because it wasn't his fault. *Leti.* He's sorry—*he'll see the doctor, the psych—* just have everyone forget and step three back.

Jolted from her hand on his side, pulling him back to a world he wasn't so sure about. Almost swung. Could blame it on another blackout. Start making shit up so none of them will believe him about the first. Voices loud in his head—*no one is going to anyway.*

"Kade?" When the shower door shut—he spun. Shoulders too broad and back too exposed.

"What the fuck, Jaylin? This how it gonna be until I'm out?"

Naked, bold, objectively attractive—looked her head to puss bored. She did nothing for him. Never had, never could, never sure why. Moved towards him faking some timid shit. Touch trying to pretend it was something intimate. Open hands tracing proof of the monster he was.

Evidence that maybe he really did deserve the cage too. What happened before then, or what happened after, ya—*Chicken or egg.*

Doesn't really matter—they're both fried. That fear, that disgust blurted from inside. "What did Kaia ever say? About...?"

"She didn't tell you?"

"Jaylin." He had to wear the weight, he should get to know why. Red flags and questions he *should've* asked in the dirt behind them both.

"About Cody?"sighed, bored maybe, but with an edge. Still— not the anger he knows, not the disgust he despises—just the flesh. Exposed. Honest. Even if she stood there and lied. "She was mean. Leti too. Crying all night about being left to Cachí, kinda started as a joke so she didn't know but—and actually, you too. You guys were so mean, I wasn't any different..."

Voice went down quieter when Kayden stood taller, but she didn't stop.

"And, hey, you talked about it in the car though, she could have put two and two with Dante, you know?"

His head didn't cock, but turned, to hear better. Turned back to speak better, but couldn't do either.

"I know. Kinda fucked up. I do know that."

"You...called Miles? On Cody, too? You didn't just bring...to me?" He was stunned, but she only batted eyes apologetically.

"I didn't call him, but I didn't like—omit details that...like might've... *helped.* I fucked up, I know! I was embarrassed and didn't know what Darcy would say, and then Miles was being mean and embarrassing and I just wanted it all to go away for a second. I didn't think they'd *bring* him back—" "The fuck you didn't..." he growled.

"Well, fine...but—I wasn't trying to lock you down. B—but ...Look I even yelled at Miles! And he yelled back, okay? But he made a good point—the dude left an entire bag after being told how serious this shit is, come on Kayden. I had nothing to do with that!"

Being in the shower might have saved her then. Cool water keeping him on ice; shifting horror keeping him numb. But Kayden didn't have breath for words, and that made her shifted uncomfortably. Maybe only used to his hate and fire; unsure what to do with him now that she hollowed him out.

"God can you imagine, if like—he'd taken it somewhere else, like what if I was some whore at some ho."

"You are." Turns out he had breath for that. Jay *tsked* at him and pulled her arms tight across her chest.

She wasn't damaged, she was another monster like Apollo. How funny that—there in the shower. And she was nervous, because he can see it now. And maybe she's sensing he's one now, too.

"My bad. Didn't expect love, but thought you'd fuck me. And I...well that never matters." With her slight pull away and higher pitch:

He scoffed. Moved in a step; tight little box.

'I'll go. Don't change your mind and beg later though." Tone had a bite, but she groomed more—adjusting hair, nails, crossing arms over herself..

Kayden pictured waking her up later. Then what "And, if I did?"

Causally checking for those cameras he'd heard about from Miles. Small piece reveling at the idea of fucking her on the banister to make the prick watch.

"Watch me leave and you don't." Acting powerful but, despite the million faces a day, that power's not in the shower with them. Trickery and long games is her protection, but now? Not a goddamn thing.

Looking a lot like her fuckin' father now. Soulmates even.

"Right...kay," she probably meant to sound sassy, but did. Tried to slide under his arm, too, but he pinned her shoulder to the wall and held sternly. No thoughts. Just two voices mirroring in a situation they're both too numb to know if they care enough to survive.

"I don't think...I ever realized," Kayden cleared his throat, weak and scratchy from screaming back at things. "You're no better than him..."

Her shoulders rose up to her ears and back down. "Never pretended I was."

Jay tried to gently push him from her shoulder but he gripped harder. "Tell me I'm gonna want to let you go, now. That's how you said it?"

"Kayden," started with an attitude, but lost it somewhere between him trying to cross her arms and him slapping them down.

"Cozy, aren't we Jay—" "Don't do this bullshit."

But that was fear, not fire. "Then, say—it." He pushed.

The hand he had on her shoulder stretched to her jaw. His body warming like maybe he did want this, so he kissed her. Soft—warm—*boring*. Not bad or good until he felt her excitement and it went south. He tasted her relief and felt hands on his cheeks and his skin crawled.

He held her back in her place and put that gap between them back too. "Don't—touch me. But *say it.*"

"Hey...?" face scrunched together. "You know I'm like—hella important for getting you out of country, right? Not gonna' lose it? On me, too?"

He chuckled at the words that really actually stung. Let go of her shoulder, rubbing his jaw, but when she took a step for the door he barked out real loud, '*Uh-uh.*' And Something twinged deep when she listened.

Or maybe not deep—just low.

"I don't—I don't care about any of that, I just need to hear it. Why don't you want to tell me what to do, Jaylin?"

"All right...*fuckin' weirdo*—" She flinched. Not because she meant to. "God, stop!" Because he made her. "Pissing you off was only way I got your attention. *Ever.*"

"You got it now, don't you." Gambling with card counters and bad luck, Kayden was beginning to see an end regardless. He didn't want this. He didn't think anyway. *No*—he wants out. Call Cachí for help, Dante too. Be done for good but it'll be more than promises this time.

Promise! Claim the game's been rigged.

Jaylin slipped back towards the door and his focus locked there, wet hand slapping the wall and holding to it. "I said, no." He rumbled low. Slithering in to confess her sins as if he had the room to carry them too. He needed a second. Give those secrets back, stuff them down her throat.

Or—? Turn her in. Trade. Fess up to manslaughter. A fight even—*but the bullets*—but, it didn't matter! *Brothers.* Dante could get him through it. Or if Cachí answered his goddamn phone. Mess of fucking voicemails on it, he needs a fucking reset. One final solid; maybe wit-pro even wasn't the worst and he could rat for Apollo too. Over here talking about the same fucking thing with a fraction of the country's manpower and eyes.

"Kayd—" "I said, shut up." *Picked the wrong side.*

"Shut the fuck up!" Because he didn't, he didn't even do wrong in most of these things people assume was his fault! He was so useful, he had so much leverage! He *was* worth saving and he could prove it. He's ready to talk now. Trial later this year. Fuckin' send Miles with him. Put Mick's ass in wit-pro, not like she'll ever speak with him. Not that he'll ever be able to sit in a room with her and not feel pure shame. Because... he was the worst of them all, and not even Jay truly knows.

Leti.

But really? Not even Kayden fully remembers. His memories have never been reliable before; why would he continue to believe them today? Though if he can adjust the memory, did he maybe adjust Cody's too? Was Miles ever really hear at all, just gone like a ghost? Like maybe it was him and Darcy all along. Asking, '*did I kill Cody and lie to myself?*' but pinching his nose because can't be, or can't matter now if he wants to survive—Leti's first. And Cachí, And she has to be good.

Bit of an altercation—he admits, he fucked up and was out of control, but these street thots and all, generally tough. And blackouts—they happen. They're fucking real—and he, them, they've been through it. Everything will be all fucking good. He turned away from her, face to the water. Because it felt like implosion.

Knowing he was lying to himself but having no other choice but to believe it. Because he can't live through the alternate. Because not even what Apollo did was as bad as what he did. Seeing her when he left—she didn't look human.

Apollo was persistent. Violent threat was there , but it was games of trust. Of pressure. *So much trust and so much pressure—*

"Get out," sniffling but hiding it under an aggressive sniff to huck up and spit between them. Kayden's chest was moving fast and short but he didn't understand. Just opened his mouth into the showerhead and wiped his face. Trying to ignore the hand against the small of his back before he breaks it.

That'd be biting the hand that feeds at this point, though. Her pet. His penance. But their proof—*everyones*—that maybe he never made it out in the first place. No home, no family anymore; maybe he's always been meant to be Apollo's.

"Kade, baby?" Twisting under his arm to creep between him and the wall. Hands sliding along his neck, holding him there.

"What do you fucking want, god—" "Are you—crying?"

"Get the fuck off me, girl god*damn!*" He didn't look down. He didn't move. He didn't know what he wanted to do, he just knew it felt like panic rooms. Hidden away, hollow.

"I mean—" Kissing his nipple, collar bone lightly. Like she was afraid but hands sneaking to his hips, regardless. "You want me to tell you exactly what I want?" she asked, back at her bullshit again. But he was too numb to feel even her. Thinking about them. Turning in Miles for what he did— but knowing, it couldn't be that easy. Fearing what they're going to say.

"Kayden?" Fucking refused to look down, but felt her inching in. Too far to whisper into his ear, but not for lack of effort. "I think I could be good for you. Couldn't hurt you even if I wanted, right?"

He smiled, hiding tears in the water that he would have normally put in rage. Not even wondering what she knows, or how. Not caring while she taunted him. Sliding against him, cupping him into her palm.

He felt no life; because he feared no more forgiveness now. Just demise; only thing left to choose is how, and who's coming. A good option in front; leaning against him not to speak quiet, but to touch around permission. He didn't say he was down, but he didn't stop her either. Hadn't been with anyone since it started happening. Hadn't let anyone try since it stopped. Though did this count? In his house; in his showers—still half of him there with Kayden now. Wrapping onto the only place that shocked Kayden into feeling both hopeful and hollow.

"Can't tell me you haven't thought about it?" Million different accents too, this one trying sultry. "Not *any* part of me?"

Kayden smirked at the ceiling, keeping water on his face to keep embarrassment away. But also just trying to hold his chin high while bundled in her hand like a fucking worm. Angry too, grumbling: "You should be thankful I don't act on all my thoughts." But she kept trying. Until he was too angry and disappointed, jerking himself away having proven himself right to himself.

"You don't think I'm pretty?"

Kayden thinks—about numbness, and if feeling comes back or if this is permanent. But looking at his dick, then her, he sighed: "Guess not."

Her eyes darted away—glossy, and Jay started twirling hair to block herself. Turned sideways too, nice soft curves along her back and down.

He reached for her ass and hip and she slapped his chest with a loud, wet slap. "I'll take my ugly ass, elsewhere."

"Or," he shifted in front of the door. "You stay right here until we're done," reaching again but surprised when she didn't react predictably, but instead let him spin her twice. Once to control it, make her stand there looking at her from behind. Then again to face him.

Wasn't entirely sure what they were supposed to be doing, and still figuring out what Kayden even *wanted* to do. But the one thing he did know, was he no longer just saw Jaylin. He saw a way to get to a man who got to him. And the color red.

The buzz came again. Not shrill, just persistent.

Dante didn't reach for it right away. Just lay there—still fully dressed, legs hung off the bed; eyes glassy and Cachí doing that same probably.

Buzzed again and his rage spiked but consciously checked himself. And as he woke up more so did his better attitude. Still wasn't full night's sleep, phone back in hand. Fourth voicemail waiting. Missed call had the light holding, telling him all that waited.

First three were Cody's. Left there for a reason. At least for tonight—his dad's pissed now. Denial, anger, something or other. It didn't bother Dante anymore. Not most things. Not disrespect on the precinct; curses; commentary on character flaws people knew nothing about though somedays he could agree.

But it was the, *you were supposed to care*—that was the heavy hitter.

Mikki said it twice. Wrote it once. After he went to boot camp, after the shooting. Probably still had the letter around there somewhere.

Phone rang again. Not the father though—*Jeb*. Dante grabbed the line immediately.

"What happened?" At that hour, that pair talking—couldn't be good. And greetings came when dawn did.

"The one from today—uh, Leti Taylore,"

Dante's spine straightened. Voice stayed even but heart dropped. He didn't want to ask, but his better half did anyway. "Something happen?"

"To say the least." He waited.

Dante, angrier by each fraction of a second guessing. Imagining. "*And?*"

"She came through the ER—got worked over bad. Rough shape. Not dead though."

"Start with that," he breathed. Voice low. "Where?"

"Some beat down motel," Jeb added. "Got the name somewhere."

"Desert View," Dante breathed quieter, eyes on his door, but not sure why until Jeb prodded.

"Uh, Cachí ...?"

Dante was silent. *Cachí*. He'd be pissed. Run through South Bay looking for an ass to kick. Jeb went on. "He get dropped off with her, cause—?"

"He's here," Dante's voice rose a decibel. "He's *been* here." More defensive than intended. Jeb sighed and Dante huffed back.

Not that it wasn't a decent place to start, but he could—feel the indifference radiating off the call. Because Jeb hated the way Dante and Lamarco kept Cachí floating just the outside of the system.

And it tasted bitter. *Especially* then.

"Know who?" Something said he didn't have to ask.

Jeb sighed. "Descriptions a bit loose, trying to debug a street cam and should know soon."

Dante nodded to no one. Jeb didn't sound finished; Dante's gut didn't feel settled.

"Off record, looks like ya' other one: Kayden. I'd say enough to bring him in to sweat. This and the kid. Did also get a blurry side profile, so we'll see what else they get."

"Right..." Didn't make sense. "She—hasn't ID'd him? She's seen him recently—knows the face if it's Kayden." Didn't sit right. "Where is she now?" He had to slow down.

"Seton Medical for initial triage. Doc said they'll send her over to Keller Center if she goes forward with the SAFE but she ain't conscious yet."

Blade to the heart. A lie. *Or it wasn't Kayden—*

"Eh—you got an emergency contact for her or anything? Sounds like you know her."

'SAFE' as a name didn't make it any easier to digest. Clean and brutal across the chest.

Sexual Assault Forensic Exams— might as well have just called it a rape kit. Might have well just said: *'Kayden raped someone.'* Kayden. Everything else, fucking *fine*—accepted. But of all people.

"You there?" Jeb went on when Dante acknowledged with a sound.

"Yeah well, not too much else. Looked to have put up a hell of a fight—called herself an ambulance too—listen when you get a chance—still saying please and thanks."

Jeb didn't *ha-ha* laugh, but. *The mimics*—the false normal—the roll past it like it was just another. Dante was quiet but, mixed as fuck.

Jeb continued on: "I'd bet she got DNA by the looks of it—broken hand, nose, overall shot to hell, but—good sign, huh?" If you have a realitive's contact, maybe they can come sit it out."

How long did she ward him off? How far were they in the parking lot before the first scream? What if he remembers hearing it now. But drove anyways—? How else could he make it his fault.

And Cachí—

Maybe Kayden wasn't there when they were. No way to know, no one to blame. But Dante still couldn't say anything. The only emotion he felt set on was fear. For opening his mouth.

Anxiety; rage; sorrow; regret; bile—they all fought to be first out. Then the ache for Cachí, too.

From delicately and nervously playing with sleeves to kissin' Cachí's cheek, holding hands and now... Broken fists and—*Rape.*

Didn't matter how many times he'd heard it. Sits different in the brain when someone you know gets hurt. No one should but—it's visceral when it's your community. Although now? Goddamn, fucking—Dickless Dictator of the states is a rapist. Might start to wonder who else creeps behind a mask. Who else looks at that tangerine-toupee-tyrant and thinks: Well he's doing alright. *Why can't I?'*

Fuckin spike in hate crimes and open season on anyone who doesn't look like the immoral dumpster fire himself.

Scary time to feel unseen right now. But worse than fear is the betrayal. Everyone already knew—*knows.* Equivalent to the outdated, *'they still got their whole lives ahead,'* whore-shit. Because so did the other "*they*." The assaulted. Ripples so big—we don't even pretend not to see them anymore. But hey—now we know what a traitor will sell a soul for. And how much they'll lie—feign ignorance—when someone turns around and sells theirs.

More vocal for the perpetrator's punishment than the survivors' truths.

Kind of should make you wonder what the point even is anymore. Badges not made of brass, but shades of green.

Baiting himself. As if being angrier would help. As though changing the topic and turning against something else—would help.

Kayden never told Dante anything—but Dante knew. Body talks. Tells the truth in flinches, glances, exits scanned too quick. You just have to know how to listen.

Dante listened, knew, but didn't imagine the long-term damage. Didn't ask. Didn't name it, because maybe Dante was fearful too. *Naming it*—as another man—what if it'd only split him further—faster?

He didn't say anything—but he waited for Kayden to. Never looked at him different. Never reached too far.

Not until he went too far. And now— what if that was the problem?

What if Leti was right?

What if he was supposed to take the parts and hold them still long enough to mend?

Not fix them himself, just to hold steady. Whoever holds stillest holds the scalpel. Cut them deep, or cut out the cancer—"Still there?" Jeb.

No. Because maybe he could have showed Kayden what to do with pain—instead of just passing it on. Can't take it back, so making someone else feel it to.

Age old cautionary tale—victimized becoming the victimizer in the sickest twist of probability. "Hey—" he blurted back. Late.

"Sorry. Processing," breathing. "Repeat that last thing back."

Jeb was talking three conversations around theirs anyway. Hospital or precinct, but didn't really sound like either. "Uh—shit—Oh! Emergency contacts, for the Taylore-tot. Something."

Dante nails went into his palm, fists bawled tight. It wasn't worth it. *It isn't worth it.*

"Sister. Somewhere nearby." At least he hopes she still does.

And Dante'd had Kayden. Fireside—under the influence. Dante fucking had him. Walked him back into it—he doesn't give a fuck, so long as Kayden gets the justice deserved.

And now—Dante had to be the one bringing him in.

"So—number on the sister then? I'm Gonna see if there's a Chaplin for the mean time I think."

"Oh—the fuck, almost forgot. My man—got something you should love."

The pauses—Dante was happy to be alone.

"Unregistered pistol. Back corner, bathroom. Kicked, tossed—gifts and horses mouths or something.

Size is a good match for the Berkeley-boy but Serial's torched and ballistics running. but we might have ya'boy for a lot more than just this."

Dante shook his head; eyes still closed.

"*This*—is plenty, amigo."

Night outside creeping through the edges of the curtains. It suited the mood. Dante took what felt like his first breath.

"Kaia," he said. "Sister."

"Got a number for her—I can reach out, try and get her here."

It was like a carousel; broken at high speeds and he couldn't get off.

Dante's brain threw static—he let it. Didn't fight it, but just rode it out until the flashing faded.

The anxiety was getting bad again. And Leti slumped in the doorway, Kaia bleeding—everywhere.

Wet like the sea; hair of kelp; motel room a sea of blood—Cody drowning in the window like a fishtank.

Jeb's voice helped the ghost pass quicker. "K. Well, like I said. Seton Med for now. I'll let ya know if I hear anything or if she moves."

No goodbyes, no comfort. Same as his no hellos. Just the flatline hush of a call that'd run out of things to say. Things that never wanted to be said to begin with.

Dante let the phone slide back to the nightstand. Didn't look at it again.

Stared through the cracked door, where low light bled into the dark and Cachí—probably getting the best sleep he's had in a month.

And she waved, door open. Alternate life on the other side.

This shit changed people. Permanently. Killed some, not from the action but the aftermath.

She wasn't safe yet.

Cachí mumbled happily in his sleep There was no question—

Dante wasn't telling him yet. Let him sleep. Let him dream. While he still lets himself have it.

Minutes ticked by, but the red glow had them all looking the same.

Dante was still long enough to feel the weight settle back in, but his breath still hadn't. Nerves strung like a tightline.

Natural response was to move. He went for his sweats, shoes, keys. Sure as hell wasn't going to sleep, and didn't even want to try.

The ghosts: Soft-footed, sharp-toothed. *Can't save any of us, can you, Dante?*

Maybe it was them. Maybe just himself.

Dante hesitated; glared at the phone. Glared at the speed dial that used to be Kade's, and now just kept empty.

Because none of it was fair. He blamed him but didn't want to have to.

Phone light dimmed; He turned it back on to rapid fired the first text because it'd make the second an easier burn.

And when he accepted he couldn't take back the first, he rationalized he might as well just send the second.

Even if the words looked week there in front of him.

He sent them anyway.

> I NEED HELP

The Famine

PEDRO POINT, PACIFICO
SU:23:45:⁰⁰

|XLV|

It was a false surprise when she let him turn her. Was still figuring out what he even wanted to do with her. Because in that moment, he couldn't see Jaylin.

He could only see the way to the man who got to him. And the color red. Darker like blood when she pushed back on his hand to face him and when he shoved back, she went low. Sunk to knees and tried to swallow him down whole.

It helped. Hand in the hair—pushing her to him. Didn't feel good enough, but it felt like the start of something disrespectful. And not even to her. To Apollo. In this house too.

Kayden pushed hips into it. Trying to psych himself up mentally. Take what's Apollo's—Kayden stopped when the entirety of him felt warmth and damp. Unsure what to call the twist he had watching her try to keep up. Struggling on him. But he liked it. He liked it a lot.

Tits like thumbtacks, legs sealed, water carving lines down. "Might've been wrong...you look pretty good from here."

Looked human.

But she took it like a joke, maybe not even aware how vulnerable. Kayden latched to her hair and hissed out like something had to break. She was making the sounds for him and doing the work, but—he felt tripped, pants around the fuckin' ankles. His own mouth opened, but only breath was loose—just swollen and uncomfortable.

Mirrors in the bathroom, mirror by the door—threatening to expose him from every side and making the vulnerability scratch. Maybe it wasn't just her who was exposed and threatened. He didn't even need to be in it. Ghosts inn the mirror taking up al the space.

Matí was there to replace the kid. He popped up over there when Kayden had pictured Mikki's mouth on his cock instead of Kaia, instead of Jay. Matty's face more real than his own. Damn near permanently deflated it. Voice echoing in the room—mostly words made by fantasy or desperate memory, but one phrase in particular.

Matty'd told him. After the shooting, during the cell. But before the showers. Brought him all the snacks and trading cigs he could ever need. Might have even been what caught their attention.

Feel that, Matí—Rage. Some bullshit back in the day—
    'rage isn't real—its armor built from memory and fear'

Fucking pussy. *It's okay to be afraid?* See, the thing is though—him dying, might have made him the luckiest one. That kid never tasted rage this deep or fear that deadly. Violation this dehumanizing—

He's not hypocritical, he just doesn't give a fuck. And guess what else? Matty's fucking gone. And Kayden? Done taking advice from the fucking grave, but wondering why he's caught up playing with dead things. Even the ghosts were to blame now.

The prison, Apollo. Leti—"fuck!" Waiting outside the fucking bathroom like some sick, twisted, fucking—he screamed. Thrusting so fucking hard. Water on her face maybe tears, hers or his, but it wouldn't have mattered— so fast and so fucking close to a fuckin bust, he even had to put his hand behind her head with the wall, but with logic went that edging. He had her on him still. His forehead to the wall. "I need you to be fucking quiet Jay." Apollo's fucking daughter.

Stroked her cheek, skin soaked and shivering,

"Take me to bed...Now." All the tone. None of the power.

There was a stillness for a moment. Rage at her voice. Their eyes burning into each other with something as strong as hate and as slutty as fear. Kayden snagged her by the bicep, kicked the shower door open and dragged her the six long strides to the bed.

Tossing her down onto the floor, back to it. "Easy Kayden. Jesus...." Scrambling her pieces together like some broken animal in the corner.

"Sorry sweetheart, this better?" Squatting down around her and boxing in again.

Her knees pulled tight over her breast. Center of gravity cracked and peaking open. Sucked on his bottom lip for a beat and then reached for her ankles slow. Slid them five more inches from each other.

Smiled at her and said, "stay?"

"This what you like? Really?" She reached up and grabbed the corner of the sheet, trying to hug it awkwardly when he shook his head and took it. Put it behind him.

"Kayden—I—we can be rough. But—let me...are you going to touch me too? Cause if not..."

He just looked her up from down slow. Trying to find where he felt the spark. Maybe try it the way he tried him.

Thought colorful things and crazy things and any time she moved—he'd tap her hand or take the pillow and hold his finger to his lips.

Like—how long would it take for her to give up and wait for command?

"Kayden." Her hand touched his cheek and when he felt it trembling he grabbed to look. Held it loosely. Didn't feel warm anymore.

But maybe that was him. "Never seen you afraid, Jay."

"I'm not." Hand snapped back mad. Answered first, and then looked like she thought about it after.

"Right." First time he loved on his woman, it was *him* shaking. Big, dumb, and clumsy; scared to hurt, break, or tear anything. Scared to be rough.

And now? Now it wasn't about women or men or pleasure. Now—even breath had motive. Stillness had capture; running had chase—the world no better than pack animals picking out the weak.

And he was weak. But still aware.

Enough to remember the before. The how it should have beens. Innocent butterflies from a kiss. Or a hand. Tight over your mouth.

Blanket and pillows not clouds and safety nets—something to grip and scream into when the pain hurts too much. "What do you see me doing to you?"

She bundled her soaked hair to one side. "...Killing me."

He feared release is to relive. "Killing you would be killing myself, Jaylin."

"Is that not the sales pitch?"

He laughed. Pinky trailing the inside of her shaking thighs. Eyes lower, but brows guilty, worried it could tell. Scared he stared too long. But then excited like maybe he should.

"So...?" she whispered.

Hopeful fear in them both, strung by different things. He stood up and over her to sit behind. Arms under hers to pull her between him on the edge of the bed.

She was stiff but relaxed into him the longer he weeded that trust. But the closer he got to what he wanted, the more fear he felt. Because she was physically—*plenty*. Attractive. And he still felt—*Nothing*.

And it wasn't even the '*how*'did things change so much. But how had he *been changed* so fucking much.

Her eyes and nose tucked into his neck, breath caught with his hand to her thighs and as much as he should have been looking down and helping her help herself—he kept his eyes across the way into the bathroom.

The shower ahead still damp. Kayden wanted to not just know, but experience when that moment goes from 'experimentation and pleasure to performance and shame.

Couldn't tell who was trembling and if it was fear, anticipation, or desire but when she put her hand over his between her—tried to guide him in with her fingers between his, he shook his head. Her body relaxing back into him, her legs leaning harder into his, begging from the soul and lifting her hips to their hands.

Whining *for him.* As if he wasn't even close to a boundary line.

"Kayden I want this. Like this. Do I have to beg you?" One hand holding his wrist other behind his neck.

"You can try."

"Please, just today. Right now." Mouth parting, slow nodding—breath deeper—Kayden stared into the wall. Eyes wet.

He didn't even care it was Jay anymore. He just wanted to want this—wanted to crawl onto his knees and be a fool in love. No taboo, no shame. No temptations baited by resistance. He let his fingers slide in. Wanted to feel himself twitch. Bit into her cheek too when she pushed against him desperately.

Her in the beginnings of a moaning fit. Him three deep letting her guide his participation. His other hand sliding under theirs. while he sucked hard on her neck. Hand becoming more patterned as she leaned back into him.

Patient right now with her melting in his grasp. He scooted forward, her gasp sharp in his ear with each thrust up until he had her on his lap over the edge. "Fuck me, please."

"Hold on—keep doing that," he leaned her back some, and let his other fingers trail. Softest touch until he felt a small muscle tighten behind the other one he worked. Pausing to rewind and hover just above. He just let it rest there some.

Then pressed at her—just enough to be known.

"E—Easy," her moaning. He nodded, kissing deeper into her neck. Causing her to relax further as if that was him agreeing, not *deciding*. Fingers circling her clit, he wanted to share this throb he had. This need of release.

"Kade...that's ..." lost to her loudest, slowest breath, before he pulled his fingers out slow enough she had the time to mourn. Grabbing his wrist like she could make him stay. Any pleasure gone with it, eyebrows dropping with more betrayal, turning back to him.

"Watch what you fucking say next," Kayden's voice was dark and intense "But...I—need to cum. The stress—I haven't—"

"I got you, baby, lay back."

"No fuck no. I—I want it rough." Like a silent admission.

"Rough? Like...more of the shower or...this—feels so good. Here."

"Not to me."

She pulled her legs closer like she was done, and he thought things he knew he shouldn't. Did it matter if he already did them though? Wondered how much consequence there would even be with Jay. Not to hurt her, just not to have to ask and explain everything

Would Apollo even care? Would be more upset his daughter was violated, his bitch—or his bitch violating his daughter. Kayden laughed bitterly.

She awkwardly shifted between him. "Okay..."

Hugged her. Teased that small bit of the neck behind the ear. "But make a decision, before I make it for us." Make her want to stay, strong handed squeeze onto her thighs. Not to hurt something, but to have something.

She turned, surprised. "Us, huh?"

"Well?" he pressed.

"Kayden...I mean, where are you hoping—"

"'Iight, out then." Patting her on the thighs and helping her off his lap.

She took a couple steps towards her clothes but turned. Arms awkwardly in a triangle as if she was subtle. Looking like she was debating where exactly all her little chalk boundary lines went in a storm.

Curious to him how the more he liked it the less she did. Phone buzzed which they both heard but neither cared. Mid-war. Mid-something, long time coming.

Buzzed again. Maybe it's Cachí. Maybe it's freedom. *Maybe this is the only release left.*

Battling his greatest opponent in front of a girl named Jaylin. Her eyes still on the floor, body closed up between his spread. Third buzz had him looking to the bathroom. Then the door.

"Who's here? Miles—where the fuck did he go?"

Jay, shook her head and he couldn't help but chuckle at this stranger between them both. "No one..." Voice repurposed too.

"Miles?"

"I...I think he's making a Vancouver run?"

Awe, bewilderment, excitement maybe—wandering thoughts egging him on, yet slow to rise and impossible to satisfy. "Just us then."

"What's this about?"

"Little bit of pleasure, little bit of pain?" Voice as plain as ever, but his own body knowing better. She went for her clothes slowly. Checking for his eyes almost every step.

"Kayden, I—I don't want *that*." Voice screaming just throw her down, but cock telling him to bleed it slow.

Get it out and end it today. "Wanna do something crazy?" Once—*Leti*—was an accident. Twice would have to mean monster. She looked at him like he *was* crazy. Most days—he saw himself the same.

"I dare you to trust me. Two minutes."

"To do what?"

"That'd be the trust part, Jaylin." Smiling.

"I—I don't wanna..."

"What—feel something?" Rubbed against himself and tried to toss it away like the fucking nuisance it was

"I—I'll stop, I wanna sit back down like you were doing."

He shook his head. "Nah. Got something else in mind."

"I'm actually trying for you...Doesn't that—mean something?"

He shook his head. "Not really...two minutes Jay. Try that." Waited. Waited more when she tightened like she'd walk. But she opened her stance and lowered her shoulders by half an inch.

"Well," biting her lip and setting the clothes against the desk. Couple more tit-for-tat exchanges as she inched her way back over.

"Hurry up then."

Eventually she stood between his legs again. Nervous or still an excellent actor. He brushed a strand from her shoulder so he could see the skin behind it.

"Trust me, 'ight?" Grabbing her hand as he stood. Stroked her sides before dropping onto a knee. Kissed her once, and before she tightened too stiffly, used her hips to spin her around.

"I—I..."

"Clock restarts every word." He massaged a cheek then kissed the other. That nude, two faced dancer weaving timid and wicked finally choked out with little to say.

Kayden watched her chew her lip looking over her shoulder to the door, back behind her at him and the bed behind him. Fighting herself on whether to stand, stall, or submit.

Like a door stop, his hand kept her pried open just enough to see it. Kiss where the thigh and ass crease. "I need you relaxed," he told her, guiding her around to face him now and looking up because this was going to have to be a long plan to be right.

"Where's the whiskey?"

"Dad's room.." she muttered unsure. And that was it. He could have almost bust from the idea alone—them there. Kill Apollo's innocence the same fucking way he coaxed out his.

"Come here baby," Kayden whispered, excited now. He lifted her thigh onto his shoulder, leaning in to clean her out. Thumb stroking her backside gently.

Just enough pressure to say he was there to stay, but not enough to tell her he wanted in.

Because *trust* first. Or something like it. But she had to choose to walk into that room with him.

And choose to take it in his bed. Else Kayden really is a monster. Every shove, every mess they made him clean—it all led here. Leti, Cody—it all had to happen.

All so he could be locked up, not with Apollo, but with the only thing that mattered to him. He pushed her to sit on the bed and kneeled between her. "Here's what's going to happen." *Pressure.*

"I don't want to, Kayden...not your—not fully."

"Did I stick my dick in your ass? The fucks the matter with you?" Pursed his lips then nodded at the door. "Go on then lil'girl. Go find you another runt then. Don't leave me a mess this time."

She stood like waters rising and looked more hurt or embarrassed than anything.

"Don't say that to me..." Letting her hair hide her face and collecting her little pile of clothes again.

"I—I didn't know you were this into as—" "

Shut the fuck up. I'm not." Stood up. Angry at the way she made him feel shame for curiosity about what'd been done to him. "Dammit, do you see this shit, bitch?" Pointing at the damn thing weighing him down. "Trying something new. Need to pop or I'll split in half. Happy?"

She shrugged with one shoulder and screamed short and sharp when his fist launched into the mirror near them.

"*Fuck bro*! you guys ever get fucking tired of seeing your self?" She held her clothes tighter and he stepped back once.

"It hurts." He growled, headed into the bathroom watching the blood pool in his hand.

"Tell you what," out hollered from out of view. "Come back if you decide you're ready to feel somethin' real, 'ight? But get the fuck out of here with this timid-whore-shit."

Silent, or silenced. He emerged with a towel in his hand as she slithered on back through that door.

"Hey Jay?" Stopped, but didn't turn.

"Don't come back for this after I'm asleep. Done before we even started." But she was gone before the sentence was finished.

Silent and unsure steps. Probably wondering is it him or is it herself—something told him it wasn't over. Let it be this, or something else, it was about time the Frankenstein's' started respecting their monsters.

Where Gargoyles Cry
& Angels Fall

|XLVI|

The street glared back. Not empty, but lonely. The disgraced building flickering ahead; new yellow tape on a door like a thin necklace, and a taunting glow casting shadow on the sidewalks, staining the pillars with red.

Dante stared, bull to a matador. His hand gripped the wheel, but he let go when he pictured hitting the gas. Driving through it not to hurt himself. But to break Leti and Cody and Kaia out of the fishbowl and rid the neighborhood of something stained.

His fists pulsed. The pillars lit up, flashed white. Cruiser was working drive arounds with the spotlight.

Dante hadn't meant to drive. Meant to run, but just sat in the car a while longer and left. Body actually left without him in it. Chasing to catch up and jump back into his skull.

Tip toing past Cachí. Angry at him even.

Stretched out on the couch like the world wasn't winding up to kick him in the teeth. Except the world didn't have to be the one to do it.

Dante almost grabbed him by the collar, threw him out. No reason other than guilt.

Make something his fault just to avoid having to be the one to tell him; because it might be more than just telling. It'll be breaking him.

Dante pictured Leti walking back through the door and he felt sick. Grabbed his head—breath rippled, sharp. Like his lungs hurt too much. They didn't care if his mind had it together; his system was done.

Cody, Leti; it wasn't even fully them, which only added guilt and shame on top the fury, the rage, and the unfairness of the whole thing.

They were right there. But he still couldn't stop thinking of his own: Kayden. Cachí. Mick.

That fucking middle ground everyone likes so much. Kaia too—Dante just knew he was gonna catch her in the Bay in the next three days.

Just something else to tell Leti; something else to tell Cachí too. If he doesn't burn himself burning everything first.

He wasn't going to fight someone, he was gonna' try and kill them.

Dante could tell Cachí liked her. They'd talked about her a little; not like he opened much, but was protective over the information.

It said plenty.

You were supposed to care.

Cody's fucking Dad in his ear; Kayden, sixteen and stupid as hell, grinning in his back seat. Dante's breath skipped—too fast and too shaky.

He hadn't felt this close to an edge in awhile. His head dropped back against the seat. Eyes closed. He pictured running.

Didn't feel well enough, but imagined sunny skies and patterned footsteps. In through the nose, holding. And out again.

Double-parked on the edge of some side street, a block up the street, direct from the motel. Ugly. And there, a new stain in the city.

Dante slapped his hand on the locks just in case more were out wandering about. Didn't open his eyes. Didn't want to see the dying painted cacti. The ghosts on those walls weren't his problem.

Except Leti's now. He should want to hit something. Didn't though. Just wanted to breathe right.

The sidewalk offered nothing when he looked. Just trash, wind, the flicker of another dead sign—liquor or smokes—the entire fucking city was full of ghosts. Surrounding him.

Pressing down. Seatbelt across his chest.

Dante ripped it off. Hand jerky and angry.

But the anger depleted before it even finished at times. Hands opening and closing—trembling like his breath; phone heavy on the passenger seat like it knew more than it said. Like it had already heard Cody's dad.

Already let Matías into the space next to him.

Don't let it be Cachí too.

Dante looked at the phone again.

Maybe it'd ring on its own. Like whatever he needed would come to him—
Dammit...

He turned to the window stubbornly. Reached back to the phone resistantly. Stared for a bit too, but once he pulled up messages—didn't give himself the time to think—the time to back out.

> MIKKI
> \> U AWAKE MICK?
> \> I NEED HELP

Because he needed someone else to hold it with him. And because his breath, though still ragged, softened when the message went through and he could put the phone down again.

It wasn't weighing in his passenger seat anymore.

Still—the *admission*.

He didn't want it to be real, but he couldn't change it. So maybe he wanted someone to look at it with him, before he put it fully on his back and carried it too.

> INCOMING CALL
> \> MOUSE

He pressed his forehead to the steering wheel, just for a second.

Tried to breathe through the last of the quakes so Mikki didn't carry that too. But something deep wasn't going to loosen; not tonight.

Dante answered the call as he leaned back again. Slumping into his seat.

"Dante?" Mikki's voice—sharp, braced already: "What's going on?"

He was going to apologize for the hour; work her into it.

Delicately get to Kayden…"I—*Kayden*, Mick, *fucking Kayden*."

Louder than he meant it, too. "Leti. He attacked…He *raped* Leti. Fuckin'…*jodido puta*! Probably killed this kid too…But I—I don't know why that's easier to wrap around—goddammit, I'm sorry I just. It's all—here. *Heavy*."

Dante checked all his windows again, voice shaking now. "I feel like—I don't know but can't fucking breathe right Mick."

Ah god vato, que pasa? His shoulder blades slightly arched; his head further back. The regret and need to go back physically ripped through his skin and felt toxic to his blood. Mikki was silent.

"I'm—" *Scared*. "Sorry," he breathed. Dante didn't expect anything, wake her up like it's something she had to know—

"Maybe we should meet tomorrow. Lunch? I didn't—I don't…"

"Dání baby—talk to me, please."

It wasn't pain that hit him then, but relief. He wanted—*needed* something. To do something.

Hear it, hold it—looking for anything that made it better, but he just didn't know what yet.

"Cachí and I dropped her off..." He was ashamed to admit it—wanted to take it back. And didn't want her to thinking he couldn't protect her either.

Dante dropped the phone to his leg. Covered his face—pressing into his forehead again. He didn't want to hold this. He didn't want this too. Not for him—*not for any of them.*

"Dante...don't cut out on me."

He was silent. Everything was. He didn't need her on speaker to hear. Still, grabbed it. Put her to his ear again. Opened his mouth, but choked.

"Dante...?" She knew he was there—he was breathing into the phone to be sure she did. He just didn't know where to start, where to end, where to even go.

"Mikki, I'm terrified. To tell Cachí...We're gonna lose him. Cachí's gonna kill something. *Himself.* Fuck, Kayden first."

"Don't say that, we don't know that. Is she—I—*Alive?* Will she be okay?"

"I guess—I don't know honestly. Guy said it's bad. And she's not conscious. No ones there, Mick. And fuckin'—*probably Kade again too!"*

She had small '*it's alright'* and bigger '*it'll be okays'*—asking where Leti was, gently prodding details, *feelings* he might want to share.

Helping him bleed it out, all the while laying under to bare the stain too.

"Mikki I'm...I don't know what I'm doing. I can't help anybody. She waved. She turned. She went in," mechanically, like structure would give it sense.

Then human, and hurting—

"I can't sleep, I'm just—I just keep seeing him. Like if she opened it an inch more, could have seen him *there. Sooner.* Could have jumped out—Or no, I *should* have at the bonfire—None of it would have—"

"Dante, stop. Absolutely not." Silence. Held breath. For him.

"You know you couldn't have known; it wasn't your fault—"

"¡Eso no me importa!—it was my fault, Mick!" Cracked out like a whip.

Too loud, too raw; and voice tearing at the seams—his chest *hurt.*

"No—"   "

No shut up—*it is,*" he felt his eyes well.

Wiped it shocked. Because the right wasn't his to have.

"I—I provoked him... at the bonfire. He and Kaia were there. He got handsy and I went over there."

"Because you're a good man, D—" "The fuck I am Mick, I was looking before. I went over jabbin' an old wound.

Y no se—started talking—he just—I told him he wasted everyone's time...

Puta. Did this because—getting even? Hates me now?" He adjusted in his seat. Tugging at his collar.

Mikki's voice was hard; she was persistent. "Dante, you don't need me to say Kayden had issues. We all know when it got worse, okay?"

The hood around his neck felt thicker. But smaller too. He never would have thought ghosts could rob the past. but thinking back now, on Kayden—the memories looked darker. Anything and everything with his face—

How long had they ignored it—? *What else did they miss*—Dante went cold. Not anger, not rage, not panic—just hollow, cold, and unsteady.

Teenage Mikki's ups and downs—maybe it was all there.

"Mick—has he—when he...you..." Dante didn't know how to ask, because what if she answered yes to something.

"Mikki..." A cracked plea over a question.

"He's never touched me Dante. Not even jokes."

Clear and slow for him. And then, "Not any I know either, I—I wouldn't have believed it if it wasn't coming from you."

He sighed. Didn't make anything better. Just didn't make it worse. Because then it wouldn't have been only Cachí to fear.

Mick hid it, but he could still hear her crying. "Hey—Dante?"

Paused. "I want you to hear me when I say this: Are you listening to me?"

He nodded weakly. Mumbled: "yeah."

"It is not your fault, what he did to Leti. God—if he'd done it..."

He listened to her breath—matched it.

"What Kayden does—is not on you. Like—am I being clear enough? It's not on us! Not mom, Matí, me, not Cachí, *not you*—not even on that fucking shooter or prison. He wasn't the only one carrying this."

And she wasn't only talking to Dante.

"Sometimes terrible shit just happens, babe... He doesn't get to do this and you wear it. We're all just trying to make it to the end. And—all he had to do was survive. Do it without hurting someone...Dante—not hurting someone should have been the easy part," she broke there, came in like a southern storm.

"He did that, not you, not us." She coughed. Dante gagged—ill.

"Mikki, I'm sorry...I know you love him."

"We all do...I know you *still* do. And that's okay—but this—*isn't.*"

He hadn't realized how badly he needed someone to tell him. Say it isn't his fault; he wasn't alone caring for someone who didn't deserve it.

He sunk into it—almost cried from the relief in her company alone.

His nerves began to settle. Breath held steadier. But more sounds from her end he registered as pain—key back in the ignition, waiting. But ready. Listening to her settle though barely.

"Mikki are you home?" He was going over. He didn't care anymore. He couldn't stand how deeply it hurt. Not himself, her. *Them.*

Leave him outside—let him in—with everything bad that's happened, he just wanted to see her breathe slow. Dry eyed.

He waited in the silence, eyes closed. She heard him. He knew she did. It was also just complex.

A sniffle. "I'm okay," tearless breath.

"I promise. It was coming. We knew it was coming," on a bitter laugh or excited breath, "maybe its relief too, I don't know, baby—"

"Mikki. I want to see you." Her voice just pulled it out of him, and it hurt to say. Because how true it was.

A figure entered his peripheral edging the shadows of the lot. Hoodie drawn. Shoulders caved. Just another bad thing lurking.

"I..." she stopped.

Plus the silence before it—Dante swallowed. Glared at the figure and used it as a reason to get territorial. Cover the ache. Get off the phone.

"It's okay," his tone stayed lifted, "Never mind, *amore.* You don't have to explain anything, okay. Just rewind a minute—"

"No," Face probably wet, but water main sealed. "Dante." Said it soft and left it alone.

His muscles contracted an inch. Didn't know what to say, but the weight was too heavy before she sighed and finished like there was never a pause.

"Dante I just. I don't know what it means for you—or. Well, never mind, let's talk about it. Here—how far are you?"

Dante shook his head, fingers in his eyes. Picturing the way she rolled against him at the fire.

The way he panicked—picked a fight. Suffocated the next song where her hips moved slow. *—what would it mean?—*

"You're right, I'm sorry," pages already chapters back. "I shouldn't—"

"Dante, don't. Not that. Come over—please?" *Please.* Feeling sicker.

"Mikki, cariño—you're right, we're both upset. It was stupid." Cleared his throat.

"Dante...I—want to see you..." Scared, walking herself on an edge.

He swallowed.

He could hear it. And what would be the worst? *Please—*

It wrote itself like a novella. And the worst is something irreversible. And maybe—it wouldn't happen.

But what if it did...?

Start as a conversation, end a tearful hug staring into each others' souls. Someone would break—tonight, someone would absolutely break.

She'd love on him, he'd forever worship her. Every night, tucking them into bed would be Matty's face and his bleeding heart.

Dante would see her face and feel unclean. Not warm, not Mikki.

Covered his mouth. Like it was time. He'd rather chase the taste forever, and never reach it, then watch it ruin. He took a slow breath, beating at the nausea.

"Mikki..." Her name alone was a breath. "You know I adore you, right?"

Eyes back on the figure—lurking closer to the motel. Watching the cruiser's spot light through every cut in the buildings. Waiting down low when it passed outside that fence; a fence—ending at a vending alcove.

Too close to the room. Dante leaned forward.

Yellow tape flimsy, but attached to both ends of a secured door. Phone closer to the steering wheel than his ear. Them—maybe fifty feet away.

"*Seriously*"— Mick getting angrier in the back.*—answer—*

Figure too small for Kayden, but perfectly sized for his boys. *Back for?* But then Jeb, earlier—

'*got something you should like.* 'Dante smirked and nodded.

"Missing something?" Smirk louder than the words—though Mick obviously still heard.

"*What?*" Cracked out like a whip.

He leaned back, rapidly blinking a few times. Neither of them liked this dance. One steps forward, the other leans back.

Rinse and repeat.

"Mick, *mi amor—*" watching the figure back themselves up. Cruiser lights closer to the room now on a slower swing. "I don't think you're going to believe—"

"Yep—here we go. Whatever Dante, it's fine." A scoff that made Dante's body recoil. Mick was shutting him out. Would ignore his next call—

"Have a good day tomorrow," *Time's up "Night D—"*

"Mikayla, don't hang up!"

He could see her pulling the phone away ready to disconnect on him. The only way she really *knows* how to rile Dante.

And in that moment—the exact thing that could make him implode.

"*Espera,* please. A minute..."

The figure looked around—like maybe they heard him. Thirty feet and faced his general direction.

He knew his windows were up but checked them again.

Shifted lower in his seat and kept eyes glued to the dark bush they were disappearing into, catching only glimpses of shadows. Waiting.

"Just wait..." he'd said.

Mikki gave no sign, not even breath. He had to check the call was still connected. Light touching his face until he locked it so it went black.

Couldn't grab eyes onto the figure after the screen fucked his sight. Even began to wonder if his anxiety made the person up. Or maybe they crawled through. Maybe that's home...

"Sorry," he admitted, whispering. "It's not us—this..."

"Dante—I'll talk with you—when—we talk next, okay?"

"Dammit, *stop*, Mouse. When we talk next? *Tsk—por fa.*"

"Bye Dante—"

"I'm outside their motel—somethings off. And someone is here, goddamn it. Please don't do this to me right now..."

He could hear her breath again—like she wasn't intentionally holding it or muting him anymore. "Okay..." Luke-warm.

His head snapped back to the bush—figure standing, taking two steps to the side. Staring. Still.

"So...?" Her voice gentle again, easing his blood.

But he unsettled more when the body moved. Tripped down from the curb to street. And stayed down. Like he hadn't just watched them catch the fall and sink into it. An oil stain.

Dante's eyebrows came together some. "I'm—gonna' call you back..."

Debating calling for the medics. But—felt that territorial edge bloat when they worked up to hands and knees.

Sat back. Head turning slow and cranking up towards the sky like shifting gears. Rested on the giant painted cactus now.

He'd be lying if he said it didn't creep him out. "Somethings not right," checking the glove box for his spare.

Holster nestled in there comfortably. He let it breathe. Hang open.

Spotlight swung. The person—delayed—but up and running after it did. *No*— cantering. With a heavy limp. Coming in closer while shapes and lines shook free from shadow.

Bare feet. Cargos.

Hood pulled high and heavy over their head, dark tangled hair helping them hide.

"I'm not sure what..." He was quieter as the words died out.

"Dante, I—. Be careful, okay?"

He nodded. "Uh-huh...Yeah..." Sort of.

"Call me back." She added. Firm. Louder. *Knowing* his ear was there but his mind was distant.

Figure slowing in the shadow of the shop next to him.

"Yeah," he whispered, eyes squinting for a look, but hood still doing its work. Pulling the phone from his ear, he mumbled "you too" and a *click.*

Figure keeps going the way they do, they'll pass right in front of him. Circling the block. Vulture sent to pick apart the room—he had to be there for the gun.

Likely can't go back without it. Scared of the yellow tape and the cruiser.

Especially now. Dante all but telling Kayden he was onto to him. Dante shook his head.

Came to a dead halt when he got a closer opportunity to peep the guys profile. Wanted to lean, but was nervous to move.

And even more out at a loss when it clocked long dark hair. And a body that just didn't look like a teenage boy—even under the rags.

But too much purpose to be homeless, too much secrecy to be innocent. And too much suspicion, to be let go. Dante's thumb impatiently tapped against his phone.

Other hand slowly slid his keys from the ignition and into his pocket. Even slower—he reached to the glovebox. Shutting it up good. Probably too confident but tired of the blood.

Wind rattled by, news paper picked into the air. Caught her attention and took her gaze up. Hood sliding a little, but not enough.

When the trash fell back to earth, her gaze didn't. Her, again— *motionless*.

So maybe not a dealer than—a receiver. Probably just high off her ass.

But maybe Kayden would come back. Because the gun. Would be far from the wildest idea.

So maybe Dante would stay. And supervise the shit show for the meantime.

Music of the Quetzalli

SENTON MEDICAL
MO:24:07:⁰⁰

|XLVII|

Leti thought she might be in a hospital. There were signs.

Beeping. Stiff cotton sheets. The sounds of metal rings crisping across metal rods overhead. Sharp. Voices and light that won't go off—a city that hates sleep.

The monsters here said she couldn't sleep. But reality is scarier than dreams—scarier than nightmares. She sees Kaia. Not in a hospital bed. The tub. Where "K" was.

Couldn't say it—even the initial hurt to think. Jamming Kaia through the drain. Acid probably. Happened on a podcast.

Maybe they were really the dream—tricked her the other way. Leti didn't mind the idea of sleep. Of quiet. Even if no one is there to wake her. Even when no one notices she's gone.

Just maybe if Leti could crawl to the light—turn it off, turn everything off. But abs squeezed and nothing moved.

Something sticky and hard biting into her elbow. Wires into her dress—down against her skin—machines panicked, screaming, when she started ripping wires from her. Room spinning. Skin foreign, clothes not hers—it was happening again. Nurses in; nurses out. Hushes and "it's okay's"—but they tasted foul.

She went for her elbow, but they wouldn't let her rip it out.

None of it was hers—everything. Pieces that were left—handed out to those more deserving.

Because she isn't a victim; she isn't a survivor.

She's just what was left.

Sounds rattled the alley; winds rattled the street. He'd only been watching two or three minutes before the weirdness faced his way.

Dante sighed and leaned back, but the lady's head snapped down to his car like electricity. He felt it through the air and into the car. Just feral energy staring into him like she didn't expect to see a person, let alone even know what one was.

And again—motionless, staring. His age—younger. *And bloodied.*

His hand went straight for the door but hesitated with it in hand.

Tired of the blood—He could stay out of it...

But something sharp tip toed up his spine. Faster when she noticed him. Backing up like he was the one who'd attack; arms at her side but not down. Holding out, making herself bigger and refusing to turn her back while walking that way. Hair sticking to parts of her face—bloodstained sea glass and tears—Dante's hand dropped against the door-rest with a thud.

"*Fuck,*" head cocked, body leaned.

Through the slash on her cheek; through the ripped neckline on her jacket, the split lip, bloody face, cracked skin—no start and no end—but familiar and wild.

"*Kaia—?*" He recognized her from the bonfire. Ten or so feet from the car. He so badly wanted to just tell himself it was Leti. Say there was only one— because there was no way.

But generally—lie to yourself or live with yourself. And that wasn't the one with Cachí. That was the one with Kade. The one going at it with him when he'd rolled up to stop it—deer with shark teeth.

Maybe Leti was collateral. And maybe this was the point.

"*Cálmate,* fire-bird." Dante slowly unclipped his seatbelt, hand back to the door. He looked to his phone on the seat and when he looked back—*dust.* She ran. And not like a someone running for help. A thing that had already been caught once and would rather die than be cornered again.

Every step screamed survival, every motion was chaos—undecided whether to fight, flee, or fold.

He needed more time to think—but had none—cranking open the door, sprinting until there was only a gap between them. Duty.

 Or a paced familiarity. Just catching up to Mikki—didn't have to hold back, didn't have to try hard—a distance runner following a sprinter in an eighty year Ultra.

Files were right though—girl's fast. She veered left.

Clipped a curb stumbling right—nearly went down but caught herself on the fall. Probably scuffed up palms and arms, but she didn't check—she didn't glance back once, not for him, not even for herself—because there was no back.

Hair whipping from under her hood—never mind 'firebird', this was catching mustangs with twine. He didn't call her—only followed. And already it was five times better than And this was still better than sitting in it helpless.

She took another turn in a slide and he clocked the alley as one of the many that curved to an end. He slowed at the entrance, still following in cautious, quiet steps. letting her out of sight with all the room to spin when she hit concrete walls, because there's reasons they used catch-poles for cornered things.

Chain-link rattle first. Then the desperate, raspy bursts: "No, no, no!" Vocal box fucked, like she'd over stressed it.

He came to a stop with her in site. Fingers twisted in the fencing like it might dissolve beneath if she wished it hard enough. "Hey..." he tested, tossing the word like wind.

She looked over her shoulder and turned in small increments as if scared to move too fast. Still looked feral.

"Kaia..." he tried again. Taking the smallest step forward.

She leaned into the fence, chest heaving for breath, eyes flicking across the alley—searching for tools. Escape routes. Looked toward the fire escape five feet above. Like she might actually try. Then the dumpster, like she might actually succeed.

Dante said her name twice more. Calm, not stressed, and fully intending to let her try and wait it out down here. But last ditch effort, as soft as the first."Ki—raia...?" Electricity. Her. At the name and him at the look. He had her full attention.

Dante's hands went up slow, palms out. Rooted himself into the pavement; no weapon, no badge—no *threat*.

"Hi...H—how are you? Im'ma stay her—or can move out'chya way?"

She didn't look like she'd even make it to him if she chose to. Instinct and adrenaline driving, but foot off the gas—*coasting* high speeds.

She began to slide from the fence catching hands to knees, hunched.

Didn't sit, didn't slide, didn't *breathe*—but she collapsed like strings letting marionettes go.

Elbows hugged her ribs to hold herself in. Gasping desperately like the air was too thin; slow at first but faster the lower down she crumbled.

Dante crouched down with her from where he was. Called out to her again. Shoulders slouched, toes bent, heels up.

"Hey—try and slow down, okay? Nothing will hurt you right now—I promise. Just breathe."

Because *'right now'* was a promise he could keep. He *would* keep. So long as her suffocating herself doesn't count against him.

She held her breath and let for seconds pass. Released and managed a real breath, though barely. Repeated that until it felt second nature again.

Dante watching the pavement near her.

Another hold, and a breath.

Her feet looked worse than her face. But that violent, defiant fear notably softened. Face changing as it curled in on itself.

Her body sagged against the ground. Eyes shifting, panic making space for shock maybe, but logical, human words.

"I didn't——know—where to go..." Coughing between the fight for both breath and words. "I—I don't know what—" Words disappearing into mumbles covered by her hands. Chest folded down next, arms around knees, and face buried. And, whether she meant it or not, it felt like trust. A chance to prove it may be a lot of us, but it's not everyone.

Duty. *Morality.*

So Dante leaned back; let his butt hit the pavement, and he stayed. Didn't say she'd be okay, just stayed how he was, where he was. Low. And level. And this time—he wanted to be more than only a witness. For all of them. And every single *'almost was'* or future *'going to be.'*

Not with Kayden. Not like this. Not anymore.

Kaia looked toward him about ten minutes later. Around, behind her too. His head tilted with a sad smile when she made it to him—up from down. And repeated rapidly. Still very much a wildness, but one that maybe wanted some roots.

Dante was getting comfortable, leaned on a wall, expecting to wait it out, but she didn't look away after he twisted back.

Scrutiny at first, but that hesitantly fell into—a mix, but familiarity in there somewhere, too.

Fingers interlaced, he offered a lazy shrug and a hand. "So...Rough night?" No sarcasm, no drama. Just recognition, respect, and presence.

Our Countdown Begins at One

SERRAMONTE COMPLEX
MO: 01:11:⁰⁰

|XLVIII|

Dante opened the apartment door like the hallway might hear him. Just the soft clink of keys, the lock sliding back, and Kaia trailing behind—surprised each time he checked. But maybe that only meant Cachí wouldn't be there still.

Held his breath. Door swung. And for once, it was relief—Cachí still planted on the couch where he'd left him. Plate cleaned and away. Bored, or troubled at most. And phone tossed at the entrance table like someone he wanted to hear from went quiet.

"Hey," Cachí nodded lazily. Likely waking from the key in the door.

Dante listened for the door to click shut. When it didn't, he had slight pause—turned to see her appraising the room from the outside.

Continued away from her, straight for the landline—an excuse—to slip by Cachí. Drop a warning disguised in greeting—

"Ey, what's up. *Despacio, hermano.*" Slow—steady, brother. "Por fa."

Then took a sharp left, settling in the kitchen at the third point of the triangle. Cachí's eyebrows, then head cocked. He and Dante sharing heavy glances first. Than Cachí sneering at the corner blocking the door.

To Dante again. Tempted by his subtle shake, 'no' and curiosity took over. Cachí's ass came few inches off the sofa, leaning forward to see who waited silently just inches out of view.

An awkward bend in his body and a blended mess of emotion when he saw the young, beat-up woman peeping from behind.

He sat back and looked at Dante for an explanation. Always been old school in that respect—*predictable too.*

When they told Dante he'd tackle a rookie, first words were '*what happened to the girl?*'

Because the dumbass had never fought the badge before. No matter what he was scooped or tagged with. But between hood, hair, and bruise—the way Cachí backed up like he'd walked in on someone he'd never met.

Dante counted seconds. Waited. Ass came off and all the way standing for the second round. It clicked. Thicker fury and faster breath—when he realized it wasn't a work project walking through. Rounding the corner to catch a full look—one foot half in this world, other half out; back against the frame for protection or support.

"Wha—" Stopped himself, turning back to Dante. It wasn't just anger looking back. Fear, betrayal, shock. Kaia, head tucked, melting deeper into the doorframe the longer Cachí built.

Dante, painful and forced, cut in. "You do anything while I was gone?" Both an obvious effort, and desperate plea, to regain control of the room before Cachí unintentionally ran her out—door still very wide open.

Eyebrows up: Dante in measured control, Cachí in unleashed surprise.

He knew he slept. They both knew he was fucking sleeping. Dante's neck pulsed from the strained glare and Cachí dropped ass back to seat. Staring across at Dante wide eyed and open mouth.

Still it was enough. Dante couldn't help it and added, *"gracias"* on a breath of relief. Wanted to add, *just fucking stay there*—no doubt there'd be more.

Kaia seemed aware too. Hyper alert, more accurately.

Watching their silent communication through slit eyes like she didn't trust it, but understood it.

Gaze skittering away from Dante and across the floor the way she had watched the city on the way back. Memorizing corners and turns like the motel was home base.

Coaxing her to the car was another thirty minutes of breathwork. Had to check the mirror—only place she'd sit was directly behind him. The apartment stairwell—those were a bit worse. Followed him up when he was a level and a half ahead.

Stopping every time he did. Watching each other through the center gap.

Dante moved a little closer but kept clear across the table. Pulling pockets—keys, wallet, gun, badge. Each set on the kitchen counter like offerings, but not habit. *Tactic.* Biding time for all three, each with their own needs.
Kaia—adjustment time.
Dante—thinking time. And Cachí— by the end—a bomb box.

Cachí popped up again, and turned right towards the window, sitting nicely at Dante's left, and direct ahead Kaia, who was on Dante's right. Perfect harmonized triangle of hell.

"You—want to sit?" Dante pointed at the chair. Turned when Kaia went to chew on her lip and winced when she did. Shared an awkward look of what he hoped she took as sympathy. Worried she took pity when she looked back down the hall like she was thinking about it.

But gaze shot to Cachí's phone. Silent, subtle, and short vibration against the table cloth. She stared there for awhile. The way she'd stared at him before she ran. Cachí either didn't hear, didn't care, or was smart enough to not prance over to her for it.

Kaia—no change. Hypnotized. But what really caught Dante's eye, was a change in expression. Didn't know what, but it was alive.

Dante's eyes squinted at the phone then too. Currently dark, undisturbed. But on his radar, so he could look on next alert. And it wasn't long at all.

"Kaia—?" Phone silent but bright—held her like an obsession.

He dared to take a step and she didn't budge, didn't look—which was a bigger alarm. Backlight dimmed a level, but man of the hour still lit on the screen.   *Kayden.*
Confirmed nothing he hasn't already guaranteed himself, but still gave Dante a lot to think. "Kiraia?" Nearly a whisper but her head snapped.

"Don't."

Cachí turned at her voice. Steady, just terrible.

"Won't do it again." Dante confirmed. Watching her head slowly drag back to the phone like it was her starting position. Cachí back to the couch silently before dropping deep into the center—elbow to knee, hands both wiping and covering his face.

Dante tried another approach. "You remember me? Bonfire?" His arms crossed but loosened enough to touch his chest. "I'm Dante."

She swallowed. Might have even nodded but it was subtle. He nodded to the couch. "You know Cachí." Paused. "You're safe here."

She pulled the hood curiously. Her way of joining the conversation. Attempting to flatten out her hair, but staring at her feet like she'd stain the floorboards.

Some kind of survivalist's tired attempt at performance. Dante's scratched his chin, but really covered his mouth.

Broken, chaotic *Vs* and *Ws* around her like a necklace, and more hidden under the neckline. Didn't know if he wanted to scream, cry, or fight knowing the likelihood this was Kayden.

"K-Kayden's friends?" She caught him off guard; name at the same time he thought it. But her voice. Somehow worse inside.

"Nuh—no." Dante, but louder on this one. Immediate. "You got that backwards, *hermosa.*"

She met his eyes there. "Tideman…" That second dose of recognition, but he wasn't sure what she recognized with that.

"From the beach, yeah.. And, well I won't speak for Cachí," Dante countered, faced pulled when Cachí started shaking his head in his hands. He was trying. So fucking hard, but Kayden's name might have been it.

Dante stepped forward like on ice. Juggling both comfort and calm, trying to dose them both the same. "I've got a case against him. I'm a detective."

Her feet shuffled. Not any closer or any further back, but shuffled. Doesn't surprise him—nice sized file, probably has a world of tales.

Cachí snagged their attention standing again, looking around the divider just enough to see. "Nah. Not friends…."

Dante should have said something then. Cachí's lips pressed and ruled in, looking to Dante. Didn't realize it was an SOS until the mouth opened again.

"Did Kayden fu—" Stopped himself when she physically resisted the words. Shoulders turned, arms wrapped to hug herself.

Dante grimaced like a premonition—he could see the leash trembling in Cachí's hand. First—a sharp breath like spit, and a laugh that turned bitter the moment words mixed with air.

Cachí swung around to Dante, hot. Eager for someone else to blame, because it was all going on himself.

"*Quién verga le hizo*?" Voice increasing in volume—dropping in tone.

Dante didn't blink. Just another small shake of the head.
The *'not now.'* A frustratingly calm and slow *'not now.'*

Because Dante got it. He understood. Pissed him off too, but he wanted to holler at the idiot—*time and place*. With some sense—Cachí clocked

Kaia's stiffening posture. Didn't sit down, but paced far enough he was blocked by the wall.

Not sure if not seeing him helped when the rage was still there.

"Oye—Dáni!"

Dante's gaze barked, but voice remained measured. "*Baja la voz, Cachíflin.*" Didn't need to be louder than that. "*Y siéntate, pendejito.*"

His eyes burned. Enough to make Cachí hesitate. Consider it.

Dante poured a glass of water. Pulled the first aid kit from the cabinet while Cachí huffed, thinking it over, but sneering as Dante went passed again. Been years since they brawled. And maybe it was time again.

Cachí held the glare but Dante didn't give him the time of day after that. Went back towards Kaia and slowed as he did.

Set the water on the table—close enough she couldn't ignore it, but far enough she wouldn't book it. "You should drink something if—"

"Where's Leti?" Finger bruises looking more like welts as they slid from her sleeves. Pulled back when she caught him counting marks.

But counting was easier than lying. Because he couldn't say it now. Leti— he wanted it off the chest, but it felt like it'd be lighting a fuse and destroying them all.
Cachí had eyes on him too. Like it'd only just then crossed his mind.

"We dropped her off at the motel."

"*When*?" she squeaked. Cachí's full attention his way—walking forward, breath held. Eyes almost as chaotic as Kaia's.

"I'm assuming after…It was—shit? Nine, ten?" *Truth.*

"We watched her go in. Waved at the door." *Truth still.* Because Kayden staying there in the room didn't make sense. Lying in wait. Planning even? Cachí's face softened, but Dante's battled hardening.

"She's good." Should have left it at, '*she waved.*'

With both hands on the first aid kit, he held it to his chest. Fingers tapped the sides like a desk. "This, in the bathroom. I have some of Mikki's things around—some sneakers. Sweats…"He planned to round out the end, but didn't. Didn't seem to matter that much anyway. He kept thinking about Kayden's name; the phone.

He wanted to ask. Because the lie burned his tongue and the idea of getting it over with sounded a whole hell of a lot better.

He bit his cheek. Hard. *Unless she already knew.* Like if she was there, too. He assessed how she looked; not that he'd fuckin' be able to tell, defensive wounds and rips from forehead to feet.

He couldn't wrap his head around the words. The nagging '*why?*' that was ripping him up, but the small step Kaia took towards them helped. Even let the door drop back a couple degrees, though she held it at an angle. Dante pointed to the bathroom with his hand. "Waters hot, towels inside… Door locks." Felt necessary. Or helpful. A lot closer to her now, torn feet busted, but pointed in. And her—too scared to look at him now, maybe scared it wasn't real. A trap.

For Leti… He was running out of time. Lie like a ticking time bomb

He waited beside the table; maybe five feet between them now. Close enough to see each pore and every clench in her jaw.

"You said...detective?"

Dante tried to predict where she was taking it—felt the silence weight and just blurted, "yeah."

"Are you gonna make me go to the police station?"

"Kaia," shaking his head. "You're not being forced to anything. This—"

"Why'd you come over at the bonfire? F-Found me now. Who...What..."

Dante paused; stupidly tried his hand at charming like that'd stop her from twisting up in paranoia next. "Little chance, little fate?" Her eyes narrowed though, so he backtracked to plain and honest. Always preferred that anyway.

"I've kept eyes on Kade a long time. When he was grabbing you—that *was* chance."

Cachí looked furious but kept feeding it to the window. Red flags firing in Dante's gut, red lights and sirens his head.

"And tonight?" Kaia grimaced on the last syllable.

Dante checked himself first, feeling some kind of defensive haze. "I think I know who—who did that to you. I'd like to help. I mean, even if it isn't him, will you let me help?" It felt prickly around the edges. And the room checked each other for reactions. The guys softened when she did.

She croaked, "How?" And it was a decent start. All things considered.

"Depends on you." Maybe only then realizing he'd run into this hoping to punish Kayden more than help Kaia. Easing. Almost seeming more unsure by the words than the people. "You don't need to decide now. You wanna use the kit? Get your feet cleaned and wrapped...Hey—might make running away easier, right?"

Cachí turned up, surprised; Kaia's chest puffed like it started to laugh, but ended in a tremble. Still better than numb, though. In theory.

After another long minute—time and patience shorter with Cachí kickin' up Dante's defenses. Tapping. Pacing. Being an overall pain in the ass while Kaia thousand yard-stared at Dante.

Sighing. "Kaia, look. I don't—this isn't okay. So the concern, offer, is real. I have my own desire to connect this to someone, yeah—but if it's not him, I'm also interested to nail who ever thinks that's gonna fly. That's my enttire motive; nothing malicious."

No words, just eyes; truth the only thing buying him her focus. Her arms twitched when she swallowed water. The room waited on her first; couldn't imagine how it felt. Could barely defend himself against Kayden

"Kayden?" Kaia pulled Cachí 's attention.

"If he's involved, yes." And to be clear, "*whoever.*"

She shifted uncomfortably. Cachí same—but angrily. Not really a one-size fits all lie, fix, or stitch for this.

"What...kind of questions?" Kaia went at her lip again and Dante winced with her. Pattern now.

"Well, I—" "*Cariño,* "Cachí cut in strong. "Say who beat—"

"I need a band aid—I—I...sorry." As she fled. Her words toppling Cachí's who'd done the same to Dante. Cachí knew better than to look at Dante. Left there grinding his teeth, fists shaking.

"I swear to God, *vato*. She just started to talk, you fuck." Tongue cleaning his teeth to keep his mouth shut after.

Cachí turned to him, Dante ready to swing—

But Cachí wasn't angry, not alarmed. Just unusually—sorrowful. Despite Dante had enough steam for them both, blowing it out slow.

Cachí stuttered on air before managing something. "It...it had to be him, right?" Multiple conversations with himself and scoffing.

"A band aid, D?"

The volume almost faded before reaching Dante, but Cachí didn't have to finish, Dante understood the point: a band aid—when she looked like she almost needed a Herse.

No one's been *accused*, pointedly anyways. But everyday something else feels like confirmation pointing at Kayden.

"Dante..." Cachí opened his mouth again but shut it quickly. Trudging back to the couch and staring at the photos on the wall. Defeated. Dante didn't say anything. Just told him to scoot with his hand and dropped onto the cushion beside him. Rage let go like a kite.

"Yeah, "Dante sighed. *"Yo se, 'mano. Yo se. "*

It needed more. But neither of them had something left to give it.

Daughters of Lilith

|XLIX|

Mikki stepped into the sterile hospital hallway, her sneakers whispering against tile. She moved like she owned the space. Approached the counter with the ease of someone who didn't need permission, smiling with a warmth that dissolved resistance.

"I'm here to see Leti Taylore," she said, voice light. "I'm an aunt."

The receptionist nodded, clicked through the computer, asked a side question to a secondary; Mikki wasn't worried. Waited. And when told where to go, left as she came.

Dante's call only an hour before. Tight voice, strained breath. Like he was trying to climb out of his own throat. He didn't ask. But his guilt did. And Mikki's too—knowing Kaia wasn't there. This was where Mikki could help. Hold something he and Cachí couldn't. Until Kaia returns.

And if a friendly lean helped Leti name the violence, then maybe it'd be best for them all. Just enough to confirm what they already knew.

Mikki checked if she was sleeping through the window, but the curtain was pulled. When Mikki saw her, she smiled. Said to herself it wasn't as bad as she expected. Despite having expected horrors and death.

Leti's face even softened under all the color and swell. Double take when Mikki rounded the corner. A surprise. "Hey, Leti." Crossing the space to sit in the chair beside the bed.

Leti didn't speak right away; they listened to machines hum and life be measured by an annoying beep. Arm splinted up to her fingertips, right eye swollen shut, eyes two different colors, nose split.

Maybe it was bad. Noting the morphine drip. Explaining the softer face.

Leti turned to Mikki. "Where's...Kaia?"

"She's..." Thought about it. "She's safe. She should be—okay."

"Look at you, sending back better than found," Leti picked at the blanket in her lap like an answer waited. "Kaia hasn't been okay in a long time. *Not okay*'s our normal."

Leti pulled a thread and kept pulling. Slurred, "I can't fix it, I can't fix any of it. I'm not even trying to be okay, I just want to be whole."

Mikki studied her. Let the pause land to piece her words carefully, too. "Leti, tell me to stop if I overstep. This is your space...But it doesn't have to be. You can be okay; you can even hope to be more than okay—you're not reaching for the stars with that one."

Mikki paused to read her; not wanting to be thrown out. Another beat of quiet, then leaning forward a hair, ventured further: "I know me saying this probably feels—empty, like I can't understand. But...I understand.

Believing it could never be okay; believing this is the best we get and carrying the dead with because they can't walk..."

Neither moved or looked at the other. Both at their hands—Leti still with fabric. Mikki at the band of her watch, loosening it.

"I can sit in the quiet with you. I can also help walk you back to reality, if you want. Because—and I hope this lands the way I mean it, babe—I just want you to know you're not alone. Even if it feels like you are, even if Kaia isn't here right now..."

Concrete weighed down Leti's bones; mind trying to drag them closer to what happened. Silence not resistance, but fear.

Mikki dared to go on. Walking through blindfolded—"This thing, what happened to you...Yours is your own story, your own ache. We start there; we end there. And you don't owe anyone your story or your silence. Full stop, 'kay?" Mikki watched for another full cycle of breath.

"I also want you to know this didn't just happen to you. You're surrounded by others who can feel this with you." She wanted to grab her hand, but thought better of it.

"Kaia doesn't have to be the only one able to hold the pain, you know? Especially if she can't hold her own...Because this—" looking at her own hands again,

"Worst part is too many women already know exactly how it feels. And too many others don't care about 'okay' either; they just want to be something that feels whole again."

Still didn't look at each other, but felt no change.

"If not me, that's fine, but if you need it—let me carry this weight with you." Mikki looked, but Leti couldn't.

Pressure growing—Mikki cut back in before it went too high.

"If you want to put the shame in the middle, Leti, throw it between us. Because it doesn't belong to you. Never should have touched you."

Shame belongs to Kayden but saying his name to Leti, right now, felt like an assault on its own. Leti had to say it first.

"Shame belongs to the one who did this. To the ones too broken to be fixed..."Reached forward, stopping short at the edge and resting there. "You don't have to break just because someone tried to break you. And you're already surviving. That's what matters.

When you're ready, Leti—let me know. Let others know. And remember, you don't have to carry this alone."

Leti didn't cry. Didn't speak either. Acknowledged it, though. A brief look. Might even count as a nod, depending who asked. But that's exactly as it was meant. Left hanging. Ambient noise far, but words close. Not to tempt reaction or debate—thought-provoke.

Activate something. Because it felt like the right thing.

Mikki's phone buzzed on the chair beside her, but she didn't glance or reach. The moment was alive, hoping to keep breathing, so she fanned the flame, waiting for Leti to direct what's next.

When the air cleared, when Leti's body loosened enough to speak again, it was barely a sound at all: "Are you...busy?"

Mikki shook her head, lips twitched downward—forced neutral. Leti, swollen and purple, glanced at Mikki but looked away, shy.

Her mouth opened, closed, stuttering. Eventually: "They want to do an exam..."

"Yeah?"

"It's somewhere else. They can't here..."

Mikki got it. Eagerly. Something she could do easily. "Leti, would you like me to ride and stay with you? For the SAFE?"

Heart slipped, lost count of the beats watching a tear roll down Leti's face while she nodded like something that'd just escaped after living sealed in stone. Frantically.

Unsure if the oxygen is real. Mikki smiled gently, rose slowly. "I'll be right back then, okay?" She crossed the threshold, phone already in her hand pressing CALL twice.

As it rang she leaned toward the nurses' desk. When the familiar face turned, her gentle smile turned knowing. Another time

"She's ready to arrange for a SAFE."

The nurse nodded once, curt. "We'll get pictures and clothes sent out from here. Bus over—probably a few hours to arrange." Mikki thanked her. Phone ringing. Nurse clicking away.

They knew each other in a way they both wished they didn't. Same hospital Matí and Dante were brought to. Same hospital Matí never walked out of.

Mikki blocked it, but was thankful when the line clicked.

Dante's voice came through tight, but still sent warmth down her soul.

Because—DNA test, Kayden, Kaia—it'd fall together. Only focus now was making sure Cachí didn't follow Kayden down.

Or kill him.

If the Reaper Were to Call

SERRAMONTE COMPLEX
MO:01:30 ⁰⁰

|L|

Inside, Kaia sat on the edge of the tub. Peeled off the old cargos like they'd grown teeth. Expecting to hiss when her feet hit water. She didn't though. Sat sideways. Drifted.

The hoodie came off next. Wet, sticky, clingy. Skin that didn't belong to her anymore. And her arms—shredded up, quiet lines from where panic met pavement. Everything hurt loud enough to drown each other out. Didn't know where to cry from first.

She chuckled out breathy puffs of pain, bending to wash her face in the tub. The lightest touches like rocks. Bashed, not scratched. So she wet the towel instead. Prodded at the wounds on the bottom half first.

Ventured as far as using the Neosporin tube. Felt like she could breathe again when she was finally sliding the sweatpants up, covering her legs from herself. Thick cotton.

Rinse and repeat the torso. Reattempting the face last. Just until she didn't feel crusty. Or until she could stomach the idea of facing herself in the mirror. Get the hoodie on first, in case she scares herself.

Matching set black on black; good enough to hide any of the missed mess. Only shame was it didn't cover her face. Kaia dried her feet carefully—even got socks. Bent—gauze in one hand, socks the other—ignoring the sharpness climbing her spine like a ladder, throwing hope through the mouth like a trash chute.

Wrapped her feet as if they were sprained when she could. Because maybe they were. Tucked them safely inside the long socks after. Gathering at the toes and sides of the foot. Those—man's, not Mikki's.

The gauze pressure—there to remind Kaia where her feet were when they felt detached. The fear didn't leave, but she turned. Out of body parts to stall with.

Didn't hit all at once, but she began to digest what she looked at. Like she'd thought, that girl wasn't her. Hollow eyes. Dried blood still inked under one nostril. Smeared across her face like a kid in Mom's makeup. Bruised chin. Hair pulled in uneven plumes from the tie. Sweat-slicked and stuck against her face.

She reached up. Touched the bruise, half-expecting it to wipe off but it didn't. Her fingers trailed down neck, collarbone—fingerprints like marks of a jaguar. Or spotted slug.

Compared her finger to the marks there—*the way he held her neck*—Gasped when she could feel it happening again; lungs locked up like it was real, but it wasn't real. Logic told her she was safe but adrenaline still sparked, something still fought.

What did safe mean anyways? Safe to who?

Physically. Mentally. Both? All? None.

Kaia pulled the sleeves down over her crusted knuckles. She went for the door—identical to the motel. Swing bar closed, bolt broken. And only that.

Her body jolted into the door desperately. Wept when the lock just rattled. Wept again at the madness when she recognized the trick; twisting the lock and yanking it open. Embarrassed.

Panting in the door frame, holding the knob with the same distrust as the front door. Saw no one. Heard, *"Quédate ahí"* between the two of them, but they sounded the same from there.

If not seconds later—out of the corner of her eye she saw Dante pass through, fiddling with something on the counter other end of the hall.

Brief. And pointed. He wasn't fiddling with anything, she knew exactly what that was. Sporadic checks people gave when they didn't trust you with yourself. And if she stood there long enough, sound or no sound, she knew there'd be another. She didn't want another.

Stared at the sneakers on the floor instead. Feet felt too dirty for shoes, but pavement too rough for wounds. The shoes didn't look big like the socks. They looked her size; like something she'd wear too.

Maybe even hers now, taken off when she'd walked in. But—couldn't have been. Because she remembers Kayden. Remembers his nails pulling down her leg, top layer of skin going with the shoe when he yanked her across the floor.

To die. Murder—Kaia took a ragged breath in. Was supposed to be deep, but lungs weren't ready for it yet. Reaper still missed.

Kaia bent for the shoes. She wasn't sure he had. Pain separating and individualizing. She winced but said nothing. And tied them too tight too. Because she'd never be able to wear them loose again.

Her fingers fumbled the laces, numb at first, then too sharp. Self-damage from open handed falls and unclenched her fists in a swing. Knuckles busted, wrists twisted. Not even a ghost anymore.

"Kaia?"

She flinched back. Dante was crouched down right in front of her. Hand on her forearm, but unsure when. She shocked him back by grabbing his forearm too. And tight. Because that time jump—that gap—felt scarier than he could ever be. Like a void. Stealing not a piece of her, but her entire being. Checked out.

How long? She heard Kayden's threats echo in the hall and Dante squeezed her forearm where he'd rested his hand.

Squeezed again some seconds later when her eyes started to glaze there in front of him. She looked at him, mouth open.

"I don't know—what just…"

Words disappeared into the confusion and Dante's knees popped as he stood. His grasp had gone slack, but she held on. Like she'd fall through the floor if she didn't.

"You're alright," he promised. "Come on, let's get you up." He grabbed her other forearm just as careful.

Like the left side might react differently than the right. He didn't pull her up though; not at first. Waited for her to pull up until the silent wincing. Assisted the lift then.

The energy around her drastically changed. Dante was already being hypervigilant, but if you could be more—*tag, he's it.*

Grip stayed light, prepared to back up at the first sign of whiplash. Because he wanted to let go in time. Wanted it to be the right time and not be too late again. Kaia kept her hood up after that. Didn't reach back out—not even sure she admits to the first time.

Dante pointed to the seat in front of Cachí loosely. An idea. Didn't care if she took it. And she didn't. Pretended she hadn't seen it despite holding his other arm.

She slipped away, hugging a chair top by the door and pulling it enough she could slide in sideways. The back of the chair creating a barrier between their two sides of the room.

Dante nodded, smiled softly. A day ago, battle with someone twice her size. Dancing with flames. Exploring, because she could. She was fearless. And now?

Now the caution radiated heavily.

"Can I get you anything?" Dante was getting paranoid. Wanted to check the scary places first, to ensure his promise could mean something.

Kaia shook her head.

Cachí fell into the couch; tension under the surface, still pouting, deciding what kind of person he wants to be in this story. Unconsciously practicing for Leti's drop.

The slow pacing when up, knee bouncing while down; hand over the mouth, arms over chest. Self containment. And within reach.

Kaia just watched. His gaze felt less intense. Almost casual, could the situation ever be such. He pointed at the chair across from her.

"Can I sit?"

"This place not yours?" She rasped.

It made him smile. "Alright," pulled out the chair. Curious. "So," he looked to Cachí too. Shaking an outstretched leg; fingers tapping invisible walls. Dante wanted to swat it like an itch. One on the calluses.

"Kaia," he said finally. Soft. She looked, but barely enough to clock his eyes. Not in the void quite yet but circling it. Head turned smooth and quick, mouth pacing it though quiet.

"This where—you make me tell you about—it?" He looked at his hands, fingers lazily interlaced. Moving.

"What'd I tell you earlier?"

Doubt made her forehead soften, but not much else.

"I said," slow, clear. "No one is going to force you to do anything, Kaia." Looking up to her now. "I meant that."

"So then..." she cleared her throat. Looked to regret it but wouldn't take the cup from him.

"I have sealed bottles if you'd pr—" "It's fine no," she grabbed the cup.

Stared at it before taking three small sips. "It's not the water."

Cachí—not sure he could hear, not sure it helped—dropped his head back on the backrest.

"Hurts to swallow."

"Yeah, okay," Dante nodded, but felt stupid. "Makes sense."

Moving on, she took another sip. Then, "what happens if I refuse to say anything? We sit here...jail? What?"

He couldn't see her—the real one—but he'd pretend until he did. Denying the way he only saw some poor thing beaten by someone he used to fight beside. *Fight for.*

Kaia's breath caught. Nowhere that made sense, like tripping over her own feet and he tried to hush the silence. "Kaia, I can say it eight different ways—you're leading this. If you want to be done, I'll take you to the hospital. To Leti—?"

Teetering truth, when it made the lies feel better. "There will be another way, because Kayden will hurt someone again," he yawned. He wasn't as careless as he was trying to make himself look. He didn't want her dropped off without something solid.

Or help him get something on Kayden from Leti if not Kaia. Because he didn't think he could face her. He didn't think, period. About it. Tried, anyway.

The phone blinked. Kaia didn't notice that time; eyes squinted, hands picking at themselves working out what he'd said.

"Guilt tactic?" she whispered.

"That's not at all what I meant," he remained steady. Someone had to.

Cachíflin from the couch—"Sounded like it."

"¿En serio, pendejo?" Dante rubbed the back of his neck, jaw locked. That fucker eager to pick a fight, blow off steam—and keep pushing. He was about to get one.

"Alright," Dante tossed exasperated. "I meant what I said. Where do you want to go?"

Motel? Kaia looked down. *Hospital?* She flinched.

Her voice was small. Stopped and started like it wasn't sure it belonged: "L–Leti's at the motel, you said?" The temperature dropped a degree. The room was about to speak again when Cachí's phone buzzed.

Five seconds, Cachí not bothered; Dante and Kaia reading the name but not addressing it. Then buzzed again. *Kayden.*

"Fuck's sake, 'mano. Check your goddamn phone."

Cachí lifted his head. Kaia watched him closely while he came in. She could have handed it to him. Didn't think about it until he was there. Dante's hands in his eyes.

Cachí headed over hot, slowed the way Dante had but snagged the phone off the table. He put it to his ear, saying nothing but pausing on the way to the couch. Intently listening. Like an old friend you hadn't heard from—or didn't expect to.

Dante didn't have to ask. Let it land how it'll land, but facades up. Just had to give it another minute. And on cue—Cachí turned to glare at Kaia before looking at the phone. Putting it back to his ear. Dante watching for a swing.

Kaia noticing neither for once. Because Kaia was standing in front of the motel, watching a piece of caution tape cross over their door. Bags inside. They didn't put the caution tape for her. No one knew about her. She appraised Dante again—eyes, mouth, face.

"The motel you said?"

He hesitated. Wasn't sure it mattered at that point. She was asking three different ways so when she calls it, says 'you lied'—it's deeper than omission. Deeper than a single lie. So it wasn't quite a question, but a dare.

Dante nodded—measured. "She was." Again, true.

Jaw tense, Kaia sensed it. "You said she was safe?"

Denial slowed her down, though. Still, neither of them moved. Something under the surface waiting to rupture. "She is safe. Yes."

She was staring through him again.

Testing every vowel, every pause—but it was Cachí. Whipped around so hard and aggressive, Kaia didn't flinch, she threw herself towards the fucking door. Violently.

Dante shot up too. Cachí recognized the fear, knew what he did. But didn't look like he could back down.

Fury and pleading—Dante didn't know whether he was going to hug him or hit him. No one to blame but himself—"*¿Qué pasa?*"

Dante didn't need to ask, but did. Merely a formality. And Cachí didn't answer, not right away. Just stood there, phone slack in one hand; the other twitching like it didn't know what to punch.

He looked at Kaia again. Then back to Dante.

"Tú dime." Cachí's voice sounded strained. "Hermano." Spit that one. Dante held his breath.

Kaia blinked slowly. Looked between them.

"Dante," Cachí pressed—pained. "Dónde. Está. Ella."

Kaia wasn't inside it anymore. Ostracized. Unable to understand but knowing it was hers to have. She just wanted to hear her name. For one of them to utter Leti.

Dante's jaw ticked with her watching him. "Atrás," he said, pointing to the back. "Vamos."

He moved first but Kaia shadowed him. Only a second behind—pressing into the edge of the room keeping Dante between her and Cachí, and no one between her and the door.

"Hey..." crackling. Weak. Kaia stepped forward, Cachí's shoulders squared at Dante. Body angry, eyes terrified. Kaia didn't exist.

"*¿No era así? Me mientes otra vez... y se acabó, ¿verdad?*" Cachí got into his face. "*¿Ah, Dání?*"

Dante didn't back down. Didn't escalate either. And Cachí was on him chest to chest. Cachí had a couple inches on Dante, but everything in Dante's build, his stance—everything in it said, 'I dare you to try.'

"Atrás." Dante again; harder.

"Wait..." No one looked at her.

Cachí's hand was shaking. She saw an arm raise and start to swing—eyes closed, arms to face—she heard contact, but didn't know with what. Void blinked. Glass broke. She couldn't see. Might've screamed.

But time skipped, right before it slowed. Picture frame crashing down from the wall. Ghostly and ghastlier—no one heard her.

And they kept erupting. Dante—not swinging, but slammed palms to Cachí's chest, shoving him back until he hit the door frame.

Again, saying: "¡Atrás!" Even Dante was getting loud. Another blink—another frame, the sound of glass.

They'd shifted. Dante's body at Cachí's back, arm around Cachí's neck—

Kayden's hands around her throat—"S—stop...!"

Cachí pulled forward, slamming back and trying for it again—Dante's foot almost putting holes in the wall, bracing against the one in front of them.

Unmovable. "Get the fuck off me, bitch!" "¡Tranquilo, Cachí!"

Dante released his throat, put his hand on his back, and shoved him towards the room.

Kaia's breath—rapid. Face might have been wet but she couldn't touch it. Partially because it hurt. Mostly because she didn't want to admit she was weak. Afraid.

Not men. Holstered guns. Different kinds, different shapes—they didn't have to touch her for her to feel fear. Bodies like pistols: loaded, cocked, and pointed her direction. Even when they weren't.

Dante holding the door open. Looked back once or twice. They yelled a few more things at each other—Dante turned, hand up like telling her to stop or stay—Hell if he even knew. His own eyes black, skin paler.

Opened his mouth, maybe got stuck, maybe Kaia was just faster—

"What—what did he say? Where's Leti?"

"I'm going to explain everything," he floundered; hand lightly defending himself from Cachí while blocking the door. "Please. Kaia—please just stay there, okay? I was working into telling you, espera."

"No!" Kaia's voice cracked. "Where is my sister?" Door already closed and rattling like someone was pushed against it. Everything but her breath. Faster and faster. Even pictured bursting in—what she'd say or ask but only imagined them both turning on her, and the hallway looked tiny. She wouldn't be able to fit if she tried.

But the fucking phone. Still there. Buzzing again. She watched it. Watched Cachí on replay. The call, the familiarity, the look—the anger.   —
Redacted—

Kaia was holding the phone again. Pulse throbbing. Call connected, and it was *him*.

He was on the line. He was talking to her now. Mumbled and fast—but she couldn't—she didn't want that voice in her ear again. Crying.

Panicked. But she could hear him either way. Voice getting louder as he was left unanswered.

"Cachíflin—I was cornered, I swear, please, I didn't mean to hurt her. It—it was someone else, I swear man, answer me. I—I don't know what to do, I need you to help me with Dante, please. This will destroy him, come on we don't—not after Matí. I need you to get something for me. Please. Please don't pick Leti over me—not after everything we've survived, right? Cachíflin, bro?" Sounds of fidgeting, pacing.

Kaia, motionless.

"I mean—Leti's going to be okay. Right? Yeah, we're gonna be okay. She was okay when I left man, something else...I—it's Apollo...please."

Kaia just stood there. Hands trembling. Rage wasn't the word, fury wasn't. It was an anger like death, because Kaia felt like she'd explode.

Speechless. Cornered. Remember how he'd barged in on her. Blaming others...Her head tilted.

The man yelling through the phone. The two yelling in the back; voices louder, angrier. And still in Spanish. Words that came down like blades on a guillotine—Leti. Kayden. Hospital. Same in either language.

Her chest went hollow.

"Cachí—please, say something! Where the fuck are you—I need you to get the gun bro. *Fuck!* I don't know how but I'll never bother you again if that's what you want—I can't, I can't go back."

Heard him crying and looked at the gun on the counter. Not sure it was the right gun, but it was a gun. *Felt* him crying again like he was on her again; fingers around the throat.

'You'll just take a few more than last night.'

Frozen between horrors—he didn't say anything. Kaia heard something bang—fist to wall maybe. Her body felt electric. Not excited. Sharp and unpredictable. Gaps of memory. Then hovering over Dante's spot in the kitchen.

Wallet. Keys. Gun. One of these doesn't belong.

"Fucking say something!" Kayden again.

She touched it, holstered still. On the counter. Voices in the back were still loud—less aggressive. Maybe they'd make it in time.

"Kayden..." Hers was softest.

He went quiet. She had to check he hadn't hung up. "L—Leti—?"

She almost said no. Didn't. And when he went in again, she couldn't.

"I didn't mean to touch you like that—trust me, I get it, you'll be fine. We're fine. This shouldn't destroy everyone, you can't tell. You'll be okay—we can work it out. What would I have to do. It was a mistake—you shouldn't sneak up on people. It was a bad week."

Kaia had to clock herself. Check reality.Because fury was taking her far from it. She opened the holster, somehow still listening. Slid the gun free. Nine by nineteen Austria. No obvious branding, small tags.

And not as big as her father's was. Compact. For traveling. A reaper and a scythe.

"Leti—look, we both, we'll get through this alright? Let's talk. I—you're gonna need to tell Cachí we're good though, alright?"

By the time she blinked she was back by the table. Something heavy and cold pulling at her sweats hard enough to need to tie them.

"Hey you get it, right? I mean, now that—you get it. So, Doll—beauty. Fucking talk to me!"

Kaia retied the sweats casually. Carefully. Slowly.

Dragged it. Until she heard the sobbing. The sound of it put her back in that room with him. And now—Leti. In there too. Drowned somewhere in sheets.

"I do forgive you, Kayden. But." Looked at the door. Heard nothing, but like she did. "I'm going to slit your throat." Not whispered. Not ashamed.

Not a threat.

For Leti. *Click.* Kaia turned the phone off. Tucked it away. Maybe they were waiting for her to leave before coming out. Like school.

Kaia looked at her hands, blood under her nails. Forever. She had to see Leti, so she would. Shadow first, then the sister.

And the silence behind her said they didn't even know she'd been there. And maybe they weren't even there either. She blinked again.

The wind was cool outside. The air crisp and the streets loud. Kaia disappeared into the in-betweens the way her head fell into the hood.

Black on black—she didn't have to hide though. No one will look—not for her. Kaia's body swayed then.

A bus suddenly under her feet, seats around her. Standing. Unsteady.

The wheels a distant hum beneath the weight pressing into her chest. Her eyes scanned the aisle. Met the driver's eyes in the mirror before quickly flittering away and slowly sinking into the seat. Feet and knees facing out.

The driver had the same look Dante had, peeking down the hall. When time escaped her. Checking if she hurt herself—

Kaia looked to the place she'd been outside. The void had only taken seconds.

The doors to the apartment—still nothing. Didn't bring her relief or pain, just nothing. Only the gun. Heavy, solid—resting in her pocket. And always there. In every reality. So maybe she was bound to reap herself.

Immortal and alone otherwise; she was a reaper. One of many. Because who else moved so fluidly between life and death, surviving what should have ended her? Third time wasn't the charm either. Not for Kaia. Leti.

Kaia jerked up from the seat, crossed to the other side as she breathlessly searched out the window for what she thought she saw. She'd seen it.

She swore she saw Leti there on the sidewalk. Face bloody, clothes drenched too, but not with her own. Puddling around her feet— fireworks in her hands, but gunshots in the air.

Kaia sank back down into the seat slow. Tucked her legs in when the driver's eyes slit in the mirror.

Those were real. But the rest—? It wasn't real. Her father's face flashing with each crack of the pistol. Twisted, enraged, and—gun raised. A chaotic struggle. Deafening final shot. Screaming as the door swung open behind her.

Bullet grazing past her cheek, blood splattering her temples. She never remembered these parts. She never could remember who pulled it. Who to blame, with four hands yanking on it violently. Like even if it was his finger, maybe it was because her arm.

The wrong nudge, an opposite pull. Three bodies hit the floor, not two. But only one screamed. Kaia as dead as their dad. As crimson cloaked.

Leti too in time to meet them before they hit the ground, but not in time to help Kaia stop it.

Kaia remembered laying there. Remembered wide eyes on the floor next to her—funny how dead eyes cloud like there is a soul turning around in there.

Everything forward blurred into softer corners and left holes for the weaker pieces. But staring at the black, plastic, embossed seat in front of her, she ignored the visions swirling around. Tried to read language from the sharpie scratch on the blue backseat.

Hands on her cheeks, warm and wet too. Not today, not painful, but when Leti was shaking her. When dad was bleeding out, Leti begged for Kaia to snap back, not leave her again— crying desperately while covered in red and defiance.

Refusing to look at him but refusing to let go. Leti had been there. She'd always been there.

Kaia straightened in her seat. The bus lurched again, lights outside blurring softly past her vision.

Reaper's gonna' swing by again later, but she promises it's not for her.

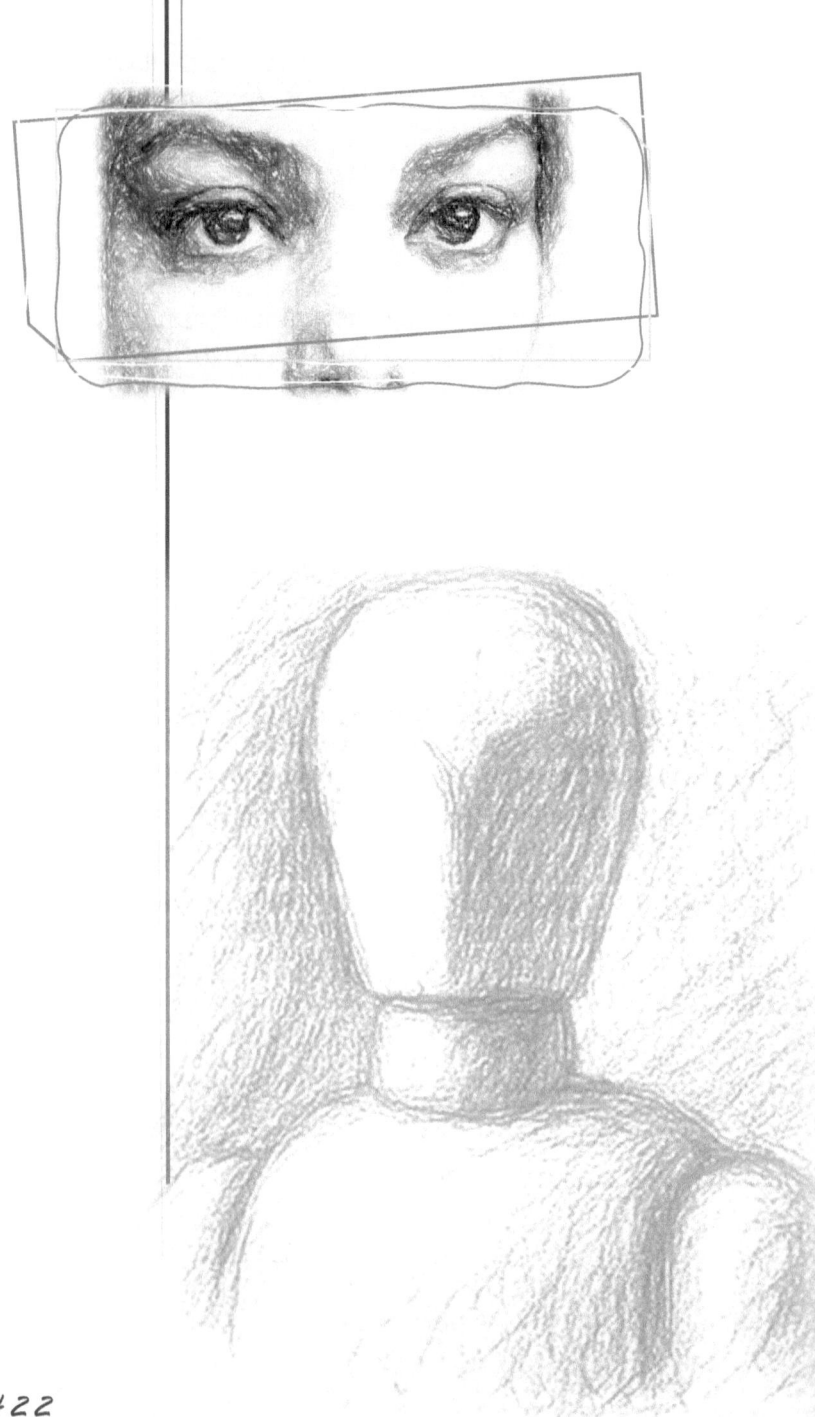

Water of the Womb

SETON MEDICAL
Mo:02:30:00

|LI|

Kaia didn't remember getting off the bus. But at some point she arrived. Stumbling through the hospital doors, her legs unsteady like the ground didn't want her and footsteps fast despite the ache.

The lobby smelled like antiseptic. Made her nostrils burn as she approached the counter; hollow-eyed, *pathetic*.

The receptionist gave her a long look. Kaia knows. Looks like she belongs in the hospital bed, not beside one.

Yet despite that, "I'm here to see Leti Taylore." Strings of the hoodie pulled as if the bunching the hood could fully cover the bruising.

Nurse stared too long. "Sweetie, do you—"

"I'm here for Leti. Can you help or not?" Kaia waited.

Only a second, and then not with her. She was looking for back up, so Kaia walked. Sliding through the halls floor by floor. Turning at locked doors.

Maybe it was one minute, maybe it was thirty, but it was Mikki Kaia saw first. On a double back from another dead end. Coffee in hand, phone in another.

Kaia couldn't gauge the expression but eyes were on each other. Mikki stepped to her—disappeared behind a nurse, and a wheel chair.

A girl in it—braid like Leti's but physique like grapes.

Chatter echoing. Machines thrumming. Gun should have gone off then. At Kaia. Because if she'd fought a little harder; stalled, somehow lasted longer—Leti wouldn't have gotten his rage.

"Leti..." Hand slapped over her mouth, ankles twisted to the wall.

Leti didn't hear or see Kaia until she felt her. The flatline. "Wait..."

The rain of pressure, of déjà vu, of something off. Leti turned neck achingly slow. Followed Mikki's, searching the hustle, pausing on a stilled, hunch in joggers, lurking the corner like Death.

Leti didn't want to go with the nurse anymore. Didn't want the kit or the evidence or the memory. *Didn't happen*—whispering instead, "*Kaia*."

The nurse watched Leti. Leti—Kaia. Back still turned. Made Leti's stomach tighten.

Still—the first spark of something real. Even if it was just anger, Leti wanted to be angry. It was warm.

Cautiously, stubbornly getting up. The nurse reached to grab her elbow. Leti bit back, snake like, and shoved against the nurse's shoulder.

Didn't look like she meant it. But didn't look sorry either. Because she wasn't.

There wasn't anything to feel if anger filled it first. "Kaia..."

Voice clipped, she started to her. Pictured hitting her. Throwing all the disgust she felt at herself—at the world—right at Kaia.

This stupid trip. Her stupid promise.

But dredging up every horror movie she'd seen, picturing Kaia squeezed into a drain, unsure what Kayden had fully done—anger wasn't only anger.

Leti choked out a single cry of relief but it physically hurt deep. Both moving towards the other. Nurse begrudgingly pushing the chair behind. Waiting for a collapse.

Neither of them wanted to be touched, but neither of them knew exactly what to say or how to stop when Kaia went for a hug.

Couldn't manage to let go, not even when they both gasped into the other— not from relief. From touch, crawling against skin and open wound.

Familiar, but tricking the mind and molesting every cell. Alien.

Vulgar.

Mikki drifted closer. Standing where she could pretend to study vending snacks but still listen. Kai," pushed out uncomfortably. "Come here..." Eyes sliding to a corner.

They went toward the end of the hallway, past the buzzing snack machines and empty chairs where the fluorescents didn't quite reach.

Kaia pushed one of the chairs into another, curled herself into it with Leti.

Both eyeballing the woman flying into of the bathroom four chairs from them in that same nook. It felt pocketed. When she was gone anyway.

Quiet hum of soda compressors and outer chatter to camouflage words. Finally a home-base in what felt like an endless game of tag.

Leti found a spot on the wall she liked. One spot in particular—where the beige paint was chipped from someone's shoe. Nike print either rest or rage against the wall.

She counted the beats between the machines' tones.

Beep. Pause. Beep. Her own pulse tried to sync with it, but couldn't. Kaia didn't know what to say, was trying to simply think.

Leti didn't help—wasn't expected too—but Kaia dropped deeper.

Wasn't ready. Didn't think Leti was.

"He raped me." But she didn't watch Kaia's face. She wanted the anger back, but just wanted to try the words. Maybe next time she'd put a name in it. Or maybe she'd never say it again. Silence long and full.

Until crying. Leti numb. Watching. Judging how quickly her eyes dried and then cried again. Never still. Never a mind made up.

Eventually, Leti spoke again. Maybe the drugs made it easiest. "Did he..."

Because it was her turn. Well past one-hundred miles and heavy things. And maybe Kaia didn't know how to start.

"I don't—he..." Kaia shook her head. Elbows on knees. She knew what she felt, but it still sounded dramatic aloud.

Unreal—like someone wouldn't believe her. To *murder*. "He—I...He—wanted me to OD. He didn't..."

It hurt less if she focused on the logistics. But also made less sense. Sneering at the floor, like the pattern was morse and offering an answer. "I thought he was gonna'...because the flirting...He mentioned Cody, and Dante, and *Jaylin—called me* Jaylin. I have no fucking idea. Honestly—I don't..." she hiccupped.

Or something. "I feel crazy—I don't know, *I don't know* what I did but he was so sure it was me."

Leti continued to stare at the paint. She didn't wish or want anything—but couldn't help replay the question.

Same one's Kaia was asking, just less visual. *Why then? Why* them.

Leti jumped back in the chair, heart racing when Kaia shot up. Lunging for the corner bin. Could have been heaving, could have been more— turned out the lights to the sound.

Waited for Kaia to flip them back on.

Chair slid back in inch, squealed out when Kaia did. Leg bouncing, staring. Sorrow and pain churning into anger. Leti's eyes slowly rolled over to her.

Felt like they slit when Kaia grimaced at Leti's face, but she probably couldn't tell the difference.

Kaia leaned forward quick, hissed when something ached, and put elbows back to knees. "Leti..."

Eyes slid to Kaia's—red-rimmed, bloodshot—*desperate*.

It was their father. In the jaw, the shake. Eyes identical. And it should have terrified Leti. And maybe it did. On the other side of the barrier. Somewhere she didn't think she could go anymore.

Kaia looked over her shoulder towards the hall, voice dropped, hands hid one side of her face, Leti the other. "I told him I was going to kill him..."

"Shouldn't make false promises," Quick with it. Because Kaia was more familiar with shit talk then proof.

"What if it wasn't false?" she challenged like she heard, saying: Defensive, not desperate. With more interest, Leti looked back at her. Stared until it hurt them both. Kaia started with fidgeting.

Wouldn't look at Leti—wouldn't because she'd flinch. And felt shame. Stifled a feral cry, when Leti didn't stop. Like she'd forgot where she was and chased the morphine through the clouds—

"I'm so serious," she promised.

"Are you—though? Words. Funny."

Wasn't sure she said it until Kaia answered. Not an ounce of insult, but bleeding with desperation for Leti's... Approval? Forgiveness?

Encouragement? *Didn't matter.* Leti didn't have any to give. Not even to lend. Kaia was still for awhile.

Eventually leaned back—was trying to point something out but had to clear her throat to get Leti looking. L-shape in her hand, under fabric.

Not quite an L, maybe right angle— "I mean...yeah. Don't you want me to be?"

Leti laughed—Mikki peeked. Kaia flinched. "I—don't know what to want right now, Kai."

Kaia leaned back. Nurse did a slow fly by. Lady never came out of the bathroom—Kaia watching the door imagining someone crying in the stall or fixing make up in the mirror.

School lunches in stalls and pain in privacy. Kayden by the fire—offering her candy, offering her acceptance—after another round of looks and privacy. Kaia poured salt.

"Does it bother you, picturing him smoking a blunt, watching the game. Blood washed off in the shower like it never happened."

Voice trembling between a scream and a whisper. "Doesn't bother you he'll either get away with it—or we'll be forced to repeat it a million times over?" Kaia didn't have to say it.

She had to get up. Like she was scared of herself. Backing up from Leti and keeping her spine against the wall. Fighting herself more than the world. "Because I'm fucking *livid*." Cracked out. Pulled looks. Mikki—distanced with more pain than curiosity.

Kaia looked at her hands in front of her like she'd already done it. Like she didn't recognize them. And maybe she didn't. Knuckles busted up and fingers purple.

Leti didn't grimace—she made a face of disgust. "Your fingers look like eggplants," she whispered.

"Your—" stopped herself with a smirk she didn't recognize. "Yeah. They—feel like..." Somehow proof she'd once felt light enough to dance and it wasn't nature that made her want to harm. It wasn't injury to herself—

"Leti I wanna hurt him. I don't want to kill him, I want to fucking *hurt* him and it's dark and it's heavy and I have to fix it. Seeing you—I—I hate him. I fucking hate him!"

Leti could say the same. Scream it twice as loud even. Felt it try to take over if she even allowed herself close enough to that internal flame.

But she let the ice spread.

Quiet stretched. Bathroom clicked again. They waited for the door, but nothing. Eventually Leti's back straightened without intent. Chin held a little higher. Maybe it felt like power and a weapon for a sister. Maybe it was morphine borrowing a random breath.

"I can do it Leti..."

Or maybe Leti could. A piece of her liked the idea. Be the one to crack the podium this time. Steal something back. "Let me check out," Leti nodded.

Nodded. She'd stopped trembling and it felt strange; feeling so steady now, after years of uneven ground.

Leti watched her quietly—reading Kaia like only she could. Tracing every bruise and scrape as if she might never see them again.

"Leti, you think you could?" Kaia finally whispered, voice hushed.

"I mean...you need to be here. And...you're—*Leti.* I—you think you'd pull the trigger with him there? He'll probably shoot back Leti, no."

She took a slow, careful breath, as if each word she spoke might fracture the air between them.

"*Was* Leti," she bit. But not so much to Kaia. To the wall.

But it bit them both back. Leti, at Kaia now. "What makes you think you can?"

"I dunno...because I already have..." She'd never said it.

It was what was waiting down the highway, or hiding into the horizon. The conversation. Moment Leti'd waited to have with Kaia. Where Kaia would let go and tell Leti, *it's my fault.*

And Leti could *prove* to her it wasn't. If they went home. If she'd just fucking be willing to talk about it. Pull out the notes, pull out the cause of death, shove the suicide note in her face again and again—because even if she did bump it.

He did it. And it was all there at the house. Millie brought it and maybe that's why Kaia hated her so much.

She couldn't know the truth; the anger kept her moving because the sadness held her still. And that, was more terrifying than violence.

And now—weapon at her waist—Leti couldn't predict what that information would make her do.

Argue, insist its her fault? Leti couldn't right now.

Believe she didn't do it, go at Kayden anyways? Freeze instead of fire.

"I've had a feeling," instead. "Lot to say there, Kaia. But I don't know if it matters anymore."

Leti just looked at her, really looked. "I don't see myself convincing you to wait for me, Kaia...Never was able to before."

Black hoodie, black sweats, black eyes—mouth open. Leti couldn't be sorry that it felt true.

"Lee...the coma wasn't my fault."

"But the promise was, Kai." Leti, walls, chairs, air—everything biting.

"I know. But I've never been a liar, so I'll earn it back. Or die trying."

"Yep," Leti's arm tried to swing up, tongue tried to be sarcastic, but wasn't sure either panned out. "Where'd you get the—thing...? Did you have it?"

"No." Firm, then eying for Mikki and whispering, "Dante's a cop."

"Yeah," Leti mouthed. Kaia thinks her eyebrows pressed, but couldn't tell behind the swelling. "What's that phrase you and people say...? Discounts, fingers," just whispers now—terminal stories from a past long passed.

"Five finger discount?"

"That. Back at it." Leti glared at the gun sagging against the fabric.

Kaia looked off-balance in body but her eyes never looked more sure. No longer a raging wildfire; but a pointed flamethrower. And maybe it wasn't morally right. Or legally.

Admittable.

But since when did that stop anyone? The billionaires, the kingpins, the Jaylin, and Kayden's— Cheats. Punishment equals a month, a year—but comfort and pleasure for life.

"I think—"

Mouths snapped closed as Mikki rounded the corner, shoes soft on the tile, hands half-raised like someone who walked into a room mid-confession.

"The nurse is ready for you," she said gently. Then following fast— "Kaia...I'm so glad you're okay." She meant it too.

But Kaia just gave a stern nod. She looked more behind Mikki than at her. Checking the space for shadows named Dante or monsters named Kayden.

"Kaia," Leti didn't look over. She just spoke, calm and neutral; eyes on the peeling paint. Like the nurse and Mikki didn't exist and it was no ones world but their own.

"You remember that dog we had—the retriever, Kai?

Really...loved that damn dog Remember?"

"The dog or love," she tried to joke but it landed rough on Kaia; but didn't land at all on Leti; didn't even acknowledge she spoke.

Kaia nodded like first answer never happened. "Yeah...the—the one who bit the neighbor?"

"Yeah," Leti said, pitch an octave higher; secret language one familiarity speaks. "The one they said had to be put down ."

Head tilting; concept foreign.

"You remember?" she asked again.

Kaia cocked her head with her; mirrored. "Who—bit the neighbor?"

"Yeah. And then got put down."

"Yeah..." Kaia understood as if she'd screamed it. Even Mikki picked up the draft. Kaia maybe even half expected, and waited, for Leti to say, *'wait, stop—don't go.'*

But that was her saying, *go*. Kaia blinked once.

Leti stepped up and in for another hesitant hug. Didn't brace for it, let it ache in the joints. And when they released—it was peeling something stuck to skin. "I love you, Kiraia."

"Trying to piss me off?"

"Maybe," Leti mumbled, looking down at both their hands, "hey Kaia...?" Leaning in to whisper, "don't miss. And come *back*."

Kaia's mouth twitched. Breathing, if only to stall. "I always do." letting go worse than the physical ache. "Love you."

Kaia wished he put it all into Kaia, every fist every inch. So long as he *left* when he was done.

Watching Leti crumble back into the chair, finally the one walking -away. And Kaia the one cleaning up.

"Leti..." Kaia called. Nurse looked first, then Mikki.

And last Leti— "I'll see you on the other side, Bitlet."

No longer only a childhood sentiment, but now, a battle cry.

Blood of the Covenant

|LII|

Mikki shifted weight, watched the space Leti and the nurse left through. Neither Kaia or Leti interested in speaking much to Mikki now—like it might echo a secret no one should know.

She turned to her anyways. Kaia, blinking heavily, snagged breaths. Stopped cold when she noticed Mikki assessing her—looking at Mikki like a stranger.

Mikki stepped forward anyway; reached without touching. Looking through the beating and the sweats to see the fire-brazen and blood girl in there with half-slept curls and boys jeans.

"Kaia—can I...*Help*? With anything?"

Kaia didn't answer. Didn't shift. Mikki wanted to believe Kaia was still in there. That maybe if she held eye contact long enough, the real girl would blink first. But the look Kaia gave back? *What look.*

"They're going to be sending her to a secondary hospital. For a rape kit," tilting, as if being more in Kaia's eyeline would help.

"Where?"

"I can get us the address." She knew it. The name too, but didn't say it. Unsure. But feeling *something*.

"Why don't we go check in with a nurse too? Your cheek," her phone buzzed and she paused. Moreso from Kaia's wall than the phone.

Fingers froze around the screen when she saw Dante's name. Hesitating like the floor had shifted underneath her. Pressure building—darkness shadowing Mikki's senses. "Kaia," unresponsive.

"*Kaia.* The exam is invasive as hell and takes a few *hours.*"

You need to be with your sister. Okay?" Nothing. "Just—hold on, I know where she's transferring. We'll—get you all up to date so you know where to go." Buying time, offering control.

Mikki had answered at one point, but held the phone against her chest. Adding more as she thought of it. But something told her not to go far, so she didn't.

Twisted around, standing near the vending machine like she'd forgotten what she was reaching for. "Dante—?"

"Is that Kaia?!"

"Alive and... Here. Yeah." Mikki dropped her voice to a whisper. Glanced back like Kaia might be standing right there. And though further back, there.

Mikki shifted, found another sliver of wall by the water fountain, facing the vending machine pocket.

"And Leti's starting the SAFE, so..."

"Yeah okay—but what's Kaia doing? Where is she now?" Dante's voice cracked somewhere in the middle. "Where's Kaia now?" he said faster.

"We were just talking, relax. Definitely a *weird* energy though, babe. She needs a doctor too. But something—I don't feel right, Dání."

"I'm twenty minutes out; *don't* lose her," he barked. Stopped. "And don't fucking—test her, Mikki. Okay?"

She checked the phone screen. Sounded like Dante, but, louder:

"Do you understand me?"

"I beg your—do *not* talk to me like that, Dání....*Understand.*" Mocking. Immature. She crossed her arms at herself mostly. Until—

"Mikki, not right now. Just do it dammit!"

The admission, '*I don't feel right*' felt like regret. He wasn't supposed to talk to her like that.

Not after this morning, not after that silence when she asked him to stay. After he'd asked to come.

"Mikki, tell me you're listening to—" *Click.*

"Tell you *that*, bubs." She stared at the phone after. Eyes welling from the weight of the place.

Picturing Dante coming in screaming.

Same way she had. For him and Matí. Dante was cracking at the seams. When they were supposed to keep each other solid.

She could taste it; hot and cold.

She gently wiped her eye; pinkie only, looking up. 'Cause it wasn't her day to cry. He called again. As if thirty seconds was enough to calm down.

Really—probably only enough to convince himself he'd been hung up on, get more angry about it. Yell at her. Regret it.

And use it to hate himself more later. She wanted to egg him on, but she wanted to protect him.

Mikki rejected it.
Got a little nervous—thought she didn't press end—because the speed at which the third came. *Rejected.*
Like he said about the other night—*they were both emotional.*
Best not.

Rejected again. Given enough time to wonder if another would ring. But a text came in hot instead. She could see him now—*seething.*

Worrying. Unbalanced. But not lashing out, not screaming. Pedal to the floor and a weave in his wheel.

> DANTE
> ANSWER THE GODDAMN PHONE <

She started to type back. Slow. Read it again. Slower.

> PLEASE <
> > FIX THE ATTITUDE
> > I CANT FIGHT W U HERE

Mikki posted up on the wall casually but, might have been only thing keeping her up. She knew Dante'd understand she was talking about him and Matí.

He may be in and out of that hospital for work, but Mikki hadn't been back much. If at all. Not this one.

Kaia didn't come out of the corner. For a heartbeat, Mikki almost believed things might settle. She turned the corner toward the alcove—and of course—not a bag.

Not a lean. Not even a footprint. Just blank space where a person used to be.

Her heart dropped before she could think and then the ideas or attempts at solutions came in like a flood. She just needed air, outside—smoker? Maybe.

Or maybe Mikki had already lost her and hadn't noticed until now. It wouldn't be the first time someone slipped past her because she was too busy trying to fix someone else.

She scanned fast. Nothing. Bathroom next to it though— *easy.* Obvious.

No panic. She pushed the door open with her shoulder.

"Kaia?" A little louder that time. But no answer. No sound.

Stepped in. Checked the stalls, glanced toward the mirror, then saw it. The other door.

Opposite wall. *Jack-and-Jill* entrances. Kaia was gone the moment Mikki turned her back.

Retriever—down—don't miss.   See you on the other side.

Mikki's jaw clenched and she hated Dante again. Kind of. Chin fighting to stay high. Pacing the bathroom—the smallest hope still alive.

"Shit..." She whined. She hadn't stood a chance.

Might have been Kaia who came in, but that wasn't who left.

That—Is a ghost. One deciding it no longer wanted to be seen.

Three Stones & One Dead Bird

|LIII|

The doors flung open too hard, caught air, and clapped shut behind him. Her eyes already on him the moment he hit the floor. Walking through like everyone there owed him an answer.

Nurses turned but didn't speak. They felt it too. Some kind of pressure change, something seismic.

Mikki leaned against the wall outside Leti's room; arms folded tight like she didn't trust her own weight. Not pacing. Not talking.

Just watching him like the air between them was bound to crack. Like she was unsure of him.

He avoided crossing into the window, but approached, shaking his head watching her well up like he'd be disappointed or come to fight.

Might have made him look angrier because she went to turn—he lunged forward hoping to catch her but hugging from behind when he didn't.

Hesitant, light kiss on her cheek.

"I'm sorry. That wasn't cool, that wasn't for you." He felt the release in her breath. Turning, arms going up over the neck and face hiding into his jacket. Tight like he was going to be sent away a second time.

"We're alright, Mick." Quiet.

He inhaled her scent, relaxing into it for the first time all week. Pulled his chin back to chat, but Mikki clung a little longer.

He dropped his chin onto her shoulder, nudging her head with his and whispered—"you're my favorite, *sabes*?"

A weak, tint of a smile—just couldn't quite make it up. Body touching ankle to neck. Dante gently peeled her off and held her out only far enough to catch her eyes.

"If you need—*want* to talk about it. Everything else waits."

She sniffled, hands on his chest just unsure where else to be. Hair swung, head saying '*no.*' "Why are you so angry? You never yell at me."

Dante set her back from him, crossing his arms stubbornly. Sucked his teeth, leaning on the wall and propped his foot there too. Debated not admitting it. Felt too guilty for yelling. For her being there.

"She took my gun," he mumbled. Mouth tight, words a shadow of a sentence. But her response wasn't his expectation.

Gave him a lump in his throat—even made him try and humiliate himself, say she's judging him, hates him. But Mikki only blinked slow.

"What?" he pressed.

She didn't answer at first. Her eyes focused past him, then a big breath. "Kaia's gone."

Dante stiffened. Paused. "How long ago?"

"Probably the minute you called, but between that and twenty minutes after." He seemed less apologetic then, but didn't say it. Stared ahead uncomfortably like he was doing everything he could not to just lose it.

And the only thing she knew to satisfy it was answers. "If it helps...Kaia said, 'I'll see you on the other side.'" Had his attention.

"Leti said *don't miss.* Hasn't said much else but her and Kaia definitely talked."

He felt it like a knock to the chest. That phrase—it didn't sound like surrender. It sounded like sacrifice. And it sounded like something he didn't want his weapon in.

"Mick. Don't give me riddles. What the fuck's going on?"

"Stop that," she groaned at his tone. "Leti said don't miss; Kaia said on the other side; you said she has your gun. One plus two equals three, *Dante.*" Small flourish on his name. He cut her a hard look.

Mikki threw it back. Eyes scanning his face to his mouth. "What happened to your lip?"

Dante leaned his head now too, as if the words had physical weight. "Kayden called Cachí before I had the chance to tell him. Little scuffle, but good now."

"What?" Hands on hips, to crossing—running through her hair or adjusting. Mikki wasn't sure what to do with the building energy.

Dante nodded. "Where all this started. Kade was blowing' Cachí's cell up.

Left a few voicemails, I didn't hear them yet. Heard him apologizing though, said one of the two cornered him—blacked out. I—don't know, amore."

"Did he admit to raping her?" she said quietly, then eagerly, "Dante, if that's on voicemail, might not have to put Leti through the exam."

"Mick. You know it should be done regardless."

"As if thousands aren't sitting in storage un—"

"Stop. I know this place surfaces some hard shit and I'm trying here. I can't with all the other bullshit wrong in the world—please, I'm sorry. Can we be on the same team again?"

When she didn't agree or argue, he cautiously continued.

"What were we...I—ya don't know the words used but, Cachí was set off. Immediately. Kaia—well you saw her—center stage of the fight. I figured she was spooked. Made a stupid call, maybe just grabbed it and ran. Feeling more planned *ahorita*."

"Why would you leave your gun out?"

He sighed heavily. *Guess not on the team thing.* "Shit I dunno—blindsided, distracted maybe? Overestimated sense—didn't expect him to swing with her screaming Leti under our goddamn feet. That *alright with you?*"

"Jesus...wait—*fought*. So he knows-knows? And y*ou left him?* Dante I could have stayed!" When she reached for her cell, he touched her arm, before crossing his.

"Didn't say that, did I?" Chin high. She wasn't going to like this one either but felt like a lose-lose. "He's got an escort outside. Already tested them a couple times," shrugging shamelessly. "Rookies are having a blast."

He cracked his knuckles. Didn't feel good about it. Deflected anyway.

"Cachí's not going to speak to you for a year Dante."

"Cachí won't be in prison for murdering Kayden, so I don't really give a fuck...Let Kaia get to him first then." He took a couple steps back at Mikki's recoil.

Wasn't sure if it was the tone, the words, or what, but he was still vehemently aware of his physicality after the caution with Kaia. "Dante, I can't believe you just said that."

His arms dropped. Face went blanket soft. "What?" She stared. Felt unnecessarily long. And his skin dirty. He knew he was in for a crack when she leaned in:

"When she's another ghost on the wall, I hope you enjoy the view."

He nearly growled; drunken secrets had always been off limits. And he confessed his ghosts to Mick and Jose one once upon a Wednesday.
His tongue ran across his teeth.

Felt like neither of them were going to speak to him for a year. "Mikki, I'm not sure—"

"Leti..." she whispered, a small nod to their nine o'clock, her hand gentle on his chest— relief she likely didn't even mean.

His weight shifted. Heart paused. Picturing Kayden and Dante's own brawls growing up. Fun or fights—the fists. And Leti.

Imagined his window down a little longer—rounding the office and hearing her in time. Both curious and terrified how far he'd go walking in on something like that. No different than Kayden in the hall for his friends— "I need to make a call."

Call him a fucking coward, he wasn't ready. Already defending himself to Mick in his head watching him go.

Mikki brushed hair from her shoulder and met Leti's chair in front of her room.

The bandages on her hands were fresh. Blood still crusted the occasional curve of her skin, but otherwise—cataloged and recorded. Mikki shifted off the wall to meet her, not happy, but welcoming.

"We alright?"

"Photos," the nurse replied, clipped. "I'll see if we have a SANE nurse that can discuss the rest of the process with you before we get you sent over, okay? Doing great, sweetheart."

Mikki nodded without meaning it, Leti chewed her lip.

Nurse left her wheels on lock and passed the torch onto Mikki.

"So," Mikki dropped into a squat beside the chair. Knees popped, hand on the wheel. Vinyl warm. "You okay?"

"I'm fine."

Mikki peeked behind her when she heard the bathroom open again. He took in the bruises. Watched her without flinch. Still stayed back though. Unsure if it was caring for his anger or her fear.

Felt more like he was afraid of scaring them himself. Leti's knuckles pulsed in the pause. Mikki watched them instead of her face.

"I wouldn't be surprised if you already knew," Mikki tried to thread it in gentle—but it edged. "Kaia's gone."

"No. He is." Looking down to her. Eyes not empty, but heated, "I appreciate your help, Mikki."

Too vulnerable under that look, under those words. Mikki stood, cautious like the air might crack. Leti too, but didn't wince and wouldn't take the help. The words didn't echo. They landed flat. Hollow. And too heavy to echo, or ripple. They just—*end.*

Leti used the handle, wall, bed frame—for support. Sucked a sharp breath after twisting her neck at Dante's voice. "Leti."

Mikki blocked the door with her arm. And wasn't subtle about it. He tensed under her palm, still a conversational distance away. And while it made sense, it hurt too. Regardless, he stayed where the boundary was set.

"What you just said—" "I'm tired," Leti interrupted him.

"Nuh uh," he went back at her. Surprising them all.

"Dante." Mikki grabbed a bundle of his hoodie, putting pressure for him to go back, but him keeping planted at the doorframe.

"Alright," Dante's hands flashed a quick surrender—looking between the two. Leti didn't look threatened. She looked as pissed as Cachí, Mikki—hell, Kaia along the fence. Wild.

He took a step back. Making space only so maybe she'd reach back. "I don't want her to die, Leti. Kayden's dangerous."

"Oh—Is it time to worry now?" Head tried to cock, but she stayed still.

Mikki's fingers loosened at Dante's flinch. Her hand slowly came down. Eyes flickered between Dante and Leti, focused on each other now. The recognition took him a minute; so many conversations and so many words lately—their last ones exchanged.

"This is some final mission, Leti. She's not okay."

Glared like he'd said something alien. "You don't know anything do you—you think someone who wants to die, fights that hard to live? *And* come find me."

"Let me help get her back to you then, Leti. Cachí's worried, too."

Another life, another memory, another touch. Leti's body clenched and her face wrinkled.

"Theres nothing to save here. Go play hero somewhere—"

"Leti, hey..." Mikki's posture shifted, edging in front of Dante now. "We'll—give you some space, but...come on, now. Just trying to help."

"Let me ask you something then," Leti sat on the edge of the bed, wincing until settled. "You helping to help her or hurt him?"

Dante's shoulders popped up. "Would it be so wrong to do both? Birds and stones and things." And down again.

"Then go hurt him, Detective." Her eyes glinted, sharp and terrible and on him. "If you can get there first."

Dante slowly nodded his head. He bit back the urge to repeat his part of their earlier dialog, too.

Yeah, looks like you're doing great.

Probably made her feel powerful to say it. He stood for a moment longer. Debating, digging. But this wasn't one he was going to win.

The worst was a piece inside that didn't even want to. Agreeing with them. Hurting for them.

"Ok," he muttered. Head up, but heel turning; mind stepping down through a checklist of possible access points to Kaia.

Hospital cameras would at least get him a direction. Motel had units on it. But Dante's best option, sure as shit wasn't going to cooperate. Leti or the other one.

Dante turned against the wall when he was out of eyeline from the window. All this—it didn't meant he was done. It just meant he had to be more creative.

"What now?"

Mikki asked. More wonder than sarcasm but a tinge of both.

"Going to ask Cachí," he admitted slowly. "Stalling. I don't know, Mick." Words flowing before thought and with minimal editing.

"How bad?" her eyes showed the sadness her face tried to hide. "You and Cachí fighting I mean?"

Dante breathlessly scoffed; leaned his head against the wall with the rest of him. "Well," his face pinched up awkwardly, his pause spoke volumes.

"Wasn't too bad, but that's before the Piglets in the hall."

Her arms crossed. Eyes said '*more*' but Dante shook his head; tried to call Cachí's cell first. Cause maybe if he's not mad, he won't have to admit it; or maybe Cachí just went to sleep....

One ring. Connection, straight to a cut call.

"Lot of you hanging up on me," he muttered; thumb on redial a wild amount today. This time it picked up—"*Vato!*"

Just long enough to get hung up on. A hiss through his teeth. "Really?" Each failed call felt less like a glitch and more like a middle finger. The third time didn't even ring.

Straight to voicemail. He stared at the phone for a beat, then hit the landline instead. It rang twice.

"Yeah?" Relatively tame; unsuspecting. "Oh, now you pick up?"

Mikki watched the tension wind up his spine like it was in control. It was about to get ugly before it got...helpful.

"You better have some good shit to say *'mano.* This little leash-shit! *No soy tu perrito, entiendes*? Not your watchdog, not your fucking friend only when its convenient, *jodido pendejo!*"

Dante let it roll over him like shrapnel—familiar, deserved, and still slicing. "*Ya, vamos, nino.* Let it out."

"Dante." Hopeless threats from Mick buried beneath real ones from Cachí.

"You put fucking cops on me, bro? You fucking kidding me right now? You thought I was gonna kill him huh? You think you can fuckin' keep my ass here long term, *jodido carajo*? You're lucky I don't trash the whole fuckin' yard!"

"Could use a redesign."

"*Y jodido* Rookies?" Kissed his teeth real sharp. "*Oy,* watch you miss me with that shit bitch—first mistake."

"Sounds like you're still there so, I don't know about mistake..."

"Dante," Mikki hissed louder. Maybe so Cachí could hear. Because it wasn't banter. It was two old injuries fighting to out-bleed each other. Both too quick to wear the fault.

"You should thank them, *flaco.* They didn't want you to get blood on your lil' nikes."

"Yeah? Lemme tell you somethin' you—you—"

"*Enough!*" Mikki shouted at the phone. Three staff turned.

"Ya, vale," Dante clearing his throat. "Where's your phone, *hermanito*?"

"Shut the fuck up pig—you're not my brother." Dante's head cocked back to that one, eyebrows up. Mouthing to Mikki: "Oh yeah, he's *pissed.*"

She pointed to her chest and put up two fingers. *Me too.* Stared down the hall, not looking at him once. Didn't do much, just made everything a bit worse. Book hitting the floor, probably folders too.

Paper shuffling through on Cachí's end. Dante rubbed his eye with his palm, yawned.

"No sé, you take the phone too? How long I fuckin' grounded for then?"

"Until you calm down and—"   "He raped Leti!!!"

Neighbors for sure heard that one. The walls echoed it back, and both he and Mikki as if Leti could potentially hear. Dante looked around him guilty. Turning into Kayden there, swinging at anyone in vicinity. One task, one focus, one feeling.

"Wow, wow, wow, wow," Mikki breathed—all kind of becoming one. "You know…I really thought this would be the thing. This would help him move on."

Mikki sighed heavily. Even had an aggressive tear that took bites of Dante's heart. She took concentrated breaths, pulled out her phone, and called what Dante could only assume was the apartment.

Cachí didn't say anything when he picked up.

"Hi babe," voice soft, but carrying like gauze over glass. "Dante's just angry because your girl's giving him hell, even now."

Another sniffle on his end. Breath. "She's not mine, Mikki…" She heard him moving things around, slower.

Said it like he'd practiced it, but it didn't land right.

"Is she, I—" something not shuffled, but thrown. "Mick, fuck, I don't even—how, what do I ask?"

"I know baby," her eyes closed, hand on her heart. Dante impatiently mouthed something from the side. She tossed her hand at him. "She's…okay. Gonna be a lot of healing though. Physically sure, but its the other side of it, you know? Gonna take some time."

"Mikki why would he do that, how could we have been friends with that? How can he honestly—like his fist and— I can't change it. How do I fix it, like what am I *supposed* to do?"

She bent at the waist like the pain physically dropped her as his voice broke—forehead to the glass, the other to her gut.

"I know—god I know, it's not fair. But…she's alive, Cachí. And she's lucky to be, he could have killed her without meaning to.

And Cachí, I love you babe, I am always here. I want to sit down with you and talk, but we need to get everyone safe first, okay?"

Dante's hand slowly rubbing her back despite his impatience. Not at Cachí—but at doing nothing.

"Talk with Dante so we can figure it out, okay? We're all struggling okay."

Silence. "He wants my phone—I can't find it."

"Thank you," Dante huffed. Phone to her ear, but volume like a speaker. He held his hand out, waved his fingers in for the phone. She flung her wrist, begrudgingly handing it over.

"*Lo siento, lo siento*, okay? So you're sure it's not there?" A sarcastic curse, and mumbled agreement. "I think Kaia snagged it then. When she took the…" cleared his throat.

"K. The fuck you want me to do about it?"

Dante pinched the bridge of his nose. This next one wasn't intentional. "Pull up the laptop. The phones on my account...have a lot backed up." Suddenly very aware of the heart behind his ribs. All very aware Cachí was on a plan with Dante.

"You really act a whole helluva lot more moral than you are, you know that? Don't even have shit to talk. What the fuck you want with it, where?"

That one sunk into Dante. Not because it wasn't fair—because it was. And because no part of him could argue with it and not sound like a liar. "Pull up your account," he said.

Another pause. Then the breathing shifted, resistance stirring. "What—"

"Check recent location hits, text history, anything she could've sent on the billing account. Or if she's searching locations. It's all bookmarked and logged in."

Cachí didn't say anything. "Cachí—pull the fuckin' thing up before he kills her, dammit. Or I—"

"*Ya ya*—find Nemo, *entiendo* man, fuck." Another pause. "You use this shit to spy on me man?"

Dante actually feared that tone. "If I promised I've used it once, would you believe me?" *Because it was true.*

Dante counted his three breaths, checked if Cachí hung up, and told himself that silence was his answer. "Just call me back."

That free fall feeling—hadn't felt that since he left for the Core. He didn't wait for the click. Just dropped the phone from his ear, hung it up, and turned it all off. But not the phone. Just himself.

Because what's done is done. And what's to come—on the way, in the Fastlane.

the Siren and the Siphon

|LIV|

His skin prickled with dried sweat, sour resentment, and forced patience. She came back. An hour and five minutes later—like she meant it. Not scared of him, but scared of what she was offering herself too. And halfway past drunk—if her sway could have anymore lean. Body— relaxed...

He opened the door slow. Didn't say a word. Just watched her take a step forward like a dare. When she asked to come in, he shook his head. "We doing it or what?"

She leaned to the wall, eyeing the bed behind him and he immediately started closing the door. Hollered out and slapped her hands against the wood crying, "*wait*," like a fucking teenage brat. "You must really hate me—"

"Grow up. Now."

She shifted weight nervously. His head tilted and she made an effort to stand a little taller, and a little wider. Decided maybe.

"Okay...rule though...*Rulez. Zuh. Suh.*" *Drawing an S in the air.* Kayden waited, quiet. She hiccupped. Waved the bottle like a trophy.

"Well," another hiccup—like she chugged it all at once. "Drunk, for onc."

"Kay," Kayden looked down the hall to Apollo's. Then her. "One more?"

"Two—three total. I already have it."

Kayden stepped wide leaning into the door, hips on hers with slight drag. "Let it go. What's last one?"

Her breath hitched. He took another swig—leaned himself forward but head back. "Zero."

"Gentle, Kade...and stay with me after," and after moments under his glare. "Gen—Gentle, then..."

So he kissed her. All gentle-like. Touched her hips—hands skating the curves. Than tapped the only piece of ass not on the wall.

"Let's go then, Jaylin." Jeans on, top off, sitting taller in himself with every willing step she took. Dark red slip covering her back up, but cheeks moving behind it like a silk package he got to reopen, but slower.

Giggling she pulled him to the wall with her. He went.

"Hallway maybe—instead?"   "Or later."

Every one of her giddy little pauses not making him impatient—but mentally stroking him out. He leaned into each and every one—just did the kissing shit. Not for any other reason than to think.

Maybe a little nervous the closer they got, too, but moving in regardless.

Shuffling her along, rubbing clit and sucking neck until she walked for him. One final stop at the door. Apollo's doors.

Kayden's heart slowed where he thought it'd speed. Didn't understand any part of himself anymore. Only—Need. *Obsession.*

Didn't even hate her—she wasn't the enemy—she just wasn't the point.

A siphon maybe—delivered and dangled in front of him, but prescribed to remove the toxins. *Put them right back where they belong.*

She hiccupped, swung too wide—shoulders on the door, hips on him this time. Kayden looked at the double door behind her.

Eyes running along the frame and brass knobs. He could see her under him staring while he did. Did any of it matter though. Kayden checked down the hall like he'd be there any minute.

Like Kayden had been there before. Knocking. Ordered in.

"You sure just us?" Staring down the long, bright lit hallway.

He saw he nodding below and to the side—Kayden's eye's scanning every inch like something might actually be watching.

She touched his crotch and he looked—mostly curious over the jean.

"Rules?" Still sounded so mousey. He cut her a hard look. Reached for her, but she grabbed his hand. Half brush off-half stalling. Eyeing him.

"One—drunk," yanking it and both sipping and feeding her it, too. "Two, Jaylin. You're mine for the next hour. Three. No rules."

He leaned down, lifting her as he gripped from thigh to hips and above.

He loved it—the resistant pull. Hands dragged the slip dress from hem to head and Kayden hung it neatly on Apollo's door knob like a brag.

Throb. Took the bottle back for his turn. Took a large fraction of the vodka too—four gulps. Then to her.

"You want to be drunk." Then he took another. "So. Are you?"

"Yeah, f—for gentle..."

"Open the fucking door, Jaylin."

"Am I gonna wanna be black ow—" He reached around her swatting at the handle like a cat. "Hey..."

"No. I wanna watch how you move."

"I just wanna wanna feel good..."

He scoffed—"Yeah funny that—me too." Kayden pushed her back. Just one step—not like she hadn't walked away, back, and then all the way there. She gave herself over to him for the night.

Kayden caught her waist when she stumbled over her own fucking feet. Yanked the bottle back and took five more this time while she righted herself, strolling quick to the nearest window.

Arguably bigger than him and Mick's first house together. Brisbane, maybe. Enough places and they blend. The smells though. Clover, peppermint. Shit people would never admit.

She stayed by the window, watching him like he might turn into something worse. Or maybe hoping he wouldn't.

He sat on the edge of the bed, running his fingers over the sheets like they held memory because maybe they did. Under. Into the mattress.

He'd been there before. Didn't remember it, but he's seen it. Somewhere. Maybe nightmares, maybe reality—Apollo wasn't always in prison.

Dark, simple, and dusty. Smelled like him though.

Primary bath, walk in. Suits, slacks. Kayden's eyes continued to roll.

Office chair. This big 'ol California King. *For a locked up California King.*

He stood, dropping his jeans before making a small circle around the room. Maybe touching—he didn't want to admit it. Didn't want to know.

Her voice broke through small, his eyes trailing book titles and CDs.

"Why here?" she asked, finally somewhat to serious. Tilts in her lean but acclimated. Probably noticing him stiffen too.

Despite making her work hard for an inch.

Kayden moved the needle on the record, played what was there low. Like a TV three condos down. He didn't look back, just shrugged.

"Dunno." He didn't have reasons anymore just impulses.

She teetered her way closer and he'd hardly paid her any mind. Old habits and dying slow—caught his eye once when she pushed down a vase.

Giggled again. "Because why not?"

Kade look from the desk, full strokes over it. "Exactly."

She playfully wrapped herself with the curtain. On that shy-girl shit again which maybe he did like. "Can I tell you something?" Peeked from them..

"Shouldn't." Shaking his head.

Eyes there, but slippery behind lids. "It's not—love confession," laughing long at that one. "I knew you first. I liked you before all this."

Went to and crawled across the bed like a cat. "Freshman year."

"I didn't fuckin' know any freshman."

She smiled; head cocked as she sat back on her heels nice and tall. "And Matías. A fight." His body tightened and she noticed.

"Okay...?"

"Busted up a big fight. All the kids on the bus. I think two flat tires."

Fifteen high school girls, nine little fucks rootin' them on, and one bus driver—spirit as broken as the damn tot-hauler cuttin' through the block.

Kayden laughed at that one. He did more laughing then too than any busting up.

The chuckle was a slow bleed though. Wasn't even that long ago.

And look where he was now. What he was excited to do, tucked away where no one would hear or see the shame.

"Yeah don't tell me that shit. Another life, another man."

"Okay," she touched. "Just saying. Wanted this for a long time."

"That's kinda sick, Jaylin.

She dropped back but still tried to please. Just didn't sit as tall like he'd embarrassed her.

But—to her credit. She did well. Offered without words, said little. Taunted him and let him figure out where he wanted to be while he watched for awhile.

Let him tell her what to do and that's when attention shifted from Apollo's objects to her.

Told her to turn around from the end, big large headboard braced at the top. Deep, dark rug beneath him. Thick blankets that looked like fur tangled around Jaylin—goddamn he hoisted until he had her ass up, face down, legs spread, and waiting at his disposal. "Never looked better," thinking maybe a good angle and a good fuck would satisfy his hyper fixated curiosity.

He held her hips to control the speed, just to getr things a little wet. "Slow-slow-slow," needing to watch; feeling a sense of godliness watching himself split through her lips with such ease. Something unholy about it too. Pulling her against him harder until her thighs were shaking and she was messy. Because turns out, looking wasn't enough. Pressure on his dick like it'll explode, the fuckin' record he actually knew—wanted to hear—skipping because Apollo probably predicted this! Broke away furiously.

Whipped it off its display and snapped it with the floor.

"Kayden!" more fear than anger. "Oh my god, that's not like—easily replaceable. Oh my god..."

Snagging the bottle as he came back. "Don't stiffen, not now," he warned, tossing it but glaring when he let it roll from her hand and onto herself.

He could see how that confidence of his made her nervous. And also wet. He pulled her closer to the edge and kneeled.

"Drink, *please*," kissing onto her every time she looked too unsure.

"No touching—I wanna look." Almost like he had to know how the throat worked too. "Wait—okay—just," laying his arm against her chest, hand loose around throat and jaw.

"That's all—drink?" He felt her swallow—not anything other than nerves. He mimicked but not on purpose. It just felt so—vivid—he wasn't ready for it. Nodded gently, nearly begging with no idea why.

Watching. While no one else was. And because she begged to be his experiment in every breath she took since he rolled in.

He slid back so he leaned on the wall and splayed across the bed. Opened up his legs to take a little more room and then just nodded at it.

She pouted but the way she leaned forward onto the bed and arched for him—said, *we're playing now.*

Grabbed her waist when she tried to climb over him, but straddled her down to ride reverse.

No one wanted to see either of their faces, honestly. Connecting with her—watching every starting second—then the way her spine moved.

It felt—*cinematic*. Not the moment, but the possibility.

The could've or should've been. A flash of a second. Not this girl, not his mind. But two bodies, two histories. And maybe somewhere, someplace on some alternate timeline—they were just two people experimenting and feeling intimacy in a world that maybe wasn't so grey and wasn't so mean.

Leaning back onto his chest, "Why—why is everyone *doll*? Not me?" Into his ear.

So quiet like she was afraid to know. But he wasn't afraid to inform. Wanted to just let her have it, let her be a damn doll but he couldn't make himself say it. Because....they weren't someplace else.

They weren't *someone* else.

"Dead things can't be dolls, Jaylin. And you and I—are already in Hell."

Drowning Sirens

Kaia paced the edge of the pier—wood groaning; lamps lining the drop off like they had anything left to give. City lights and sound on one side; ocean and depth, the other. It was late. Hours, maybe months even—who knew how long the void would swallow her whole. But she hadn't seen a sunrise yet.

Gun in her pocket. Like it knew where it was going or was excited to go.

She didn't sit. Couldn't. Sitting felt like stillness, and stillness was what they counted on. Still girls got erased—people get erased—and the world goes on. Her fingers twitched.

She pulled the gun out just to look at it. Just to make sure it was still real, but dropped it too. Swore out loud. One of those ugly laughs that tasted like too many sleepless nights. She shook her hand out, picked it back up like it had been lost. Barely heard it hit the deck under the sound of waves crashing into wood.

"This is what we wanted, right, disappear?" she muttered to no one. "*No*...but—"—*how else do we rectify it?* He hurt Leti. "Cody "apparently. Kaia, too. If she was honest. But she didn't survive three times to watch her sister bleed.

"S*oooo*...what do we say...?" She walked faster, one foot hitting harder than the next like she could stomp a hole in the whole goddamn world. Kayden hadn't killed her. Tried. Got close enough to think he would. And that pissed her off more than anything.

She should have been the one in that room. Not Leti. He had every opportunity, and it should have been her. And she should have found a way to kill him then. Broken mirror shard.

Kaia collapsing to the ground with him. She shook her head.

She wasn't prepared before. She was hopeful then. Wanted to be *helpful* then. Else maybe she could have won.

One way to find out—pulling the phone. Thumb hovered, dug around a bit for anything that could help, then tapped away before she could take it back. Before she dropped the gun for good or something. No flourish. No poetry. But *petty* maybe. And distain, in a text.

KAYDEN

> FORGOT SOMETHING? ROUND 2 U BIG BITCH

> COME N GET IT SOUTH EAST SF. PIER 96. <3 KAI 🖕

Took a deep breath, held:
She didn't wait to hear back. Didn't expect to. Knew she'd see him though. Unhinged man looking to offload a grenade. Something Kaia's mom would say.

She looked out at the black water; moon was lean. Made the water eerie, but the area safer. Eerier. Mechanical and cold.

The waves lapped against themselves and the foundation of the pier docks. She saw reflections and watched those long enough they turned into her parents—white wedding attire and petals floating.

"Come to watch then?" She thought about chucking the phone at her. See if she disappeared faster, but was going to wait on it. Little longer.

Scared herself back when the idea of shooting at it intruded. Riled her up, but she stayed in that position for a few seconds longer and then peeked back over. Watched the white vanish beneath the dark and tucked the phone back into the sweats.

Her mother's face lingered in the water longer than it should've. But it wasn't the face she remembered. It wasn't even hers. Not tonight.

It sat wrong. But Kaia let it sink anyway. She turned from the ocean and walked the perimeter—more concrete, containers, and construction than memory. The voices, the memories, the flashes—they dulled out the longer she was there. The dock she did find felt flimsy. Weak railings. Gaps wide enough to crawl under if she had to.

Counted steps. Measured how loud they landed on the concrete verse the wood. And asked the sea how quiet the ocean got when it listened back. Because it wasn't Kayden hunting her.

Kaia was haunting him.

"Cause you're not a doll, Jay, we're dead things."

Her head came off his chest, shoulders hunched when she twisted and he gave her the, *say something* face. *Prove me wrong*. Pretend she wasn't sitting on him acting offended but knowing the truth.

He gave her a mock pout—the new mask she's toting around—and pushed for her to lean back down and up for him but she resisted.

"Yo—do, really think that?" She slurred and his eyes rolled.

Bumped his hips at her too like he was going to lose the ride. "Come on, fuck. Later, Jaylin. What did I tell you I need?"

"Baby,"

"I'm not your baby," Kayden sucked his teeth but leaned up to lean her down. "Come on, Jay, use your arms. The fuck." Elbows to sheets, pressing her back down harder and fuckin her how she likes it until feelin' confident enough to switch.

Kayden hooked an arm under her leg, bending at the knee and tilting out before he laid over her. Like a weighted blanket.

He'd been hard before. Angry. Desperate. But this? This felt different. Animal. Curious.

He'd lie and say he thought this would be the most comfortable for her, when really it was identical to what played on repeat in his head. Following a script even—*something else to blame.*

And like a whisper in his ear, memory repeated into Jaylin's: "It'll only hurt at first," hand trembling, girl trying to question but unclear how, encircled by slurs that couldn't coordinate fast enough.

The only regret is he wanted to watch how it split her, too. How he had to hesitate at the entrance because she jerked in pain. Waiting, eager, but in complete and total control.

"Kayden—how much, I don't—"
"Hey shhhh, sweet girl. I can take care of you in here—relax. I'll get you through it.

Nodding feverishly and grabbing a pillow to tuck her face, and assumed she was sorted after that. Stopped checking; everything so round and corner free and...restricted.

Slow—like opening something sacred and wicked at the same time. He held the leg and kept her pressed between him and the bed, angled for access and counting how many twitches she had in a single breath.

"You're so fuckin' amazing, Jay, so good..." She didn't try to talk much, but they couldn't get her through a full sentence between the booze, the pillow, and him.

Asked if she wanted to sit on him—hoped to see something from her end—shoulders stayed tight, her head stayed down. He was careful though; probably even had her halfway to believing it felt okay before he finally got the tiniest bit of pressure relief. Leaking enough he got a smoother slide.

Even asked if he could really fuck her there when he was close, warned her he needed rough and she came back. Didn't tell him no. Same as the shower and her kisses.

"Always such a tough girl, huh?" Skin slapping skin but watching himself go straight through. "Jay come on, do something damn it I'm so fuckin' close, God, *fuck.*"

Litle back pop, arche, anything. But no response. Propped her hips where he could open his leg and get in good: clenching his jaw; wild eyes. Didn't say her name—didn't say anyone's—just fucked her fast, hard—only the sound of the bed. Expensive, sleek, and still creaking under the strength in his strain.

And when it went from leak to break, he'd pulled himself out, hand still tight and grip savage as he released.

Every intention was to fill her up, but in the heat of it—small voice said, *soil the place.* Years of boiled toxins spread staining his daughter to his pillows.

Only wish was to make Apollo watch from behind the cell. Which honestly—switches sides now, he might be able to mate that a reality. Snag a video with Jay some time soon.

"Goddamnm," he swallowed and laughed from the chaos. Pleasure, relief, adrenaline. "Who's fuckin' king now?"

Megalomania—which he'd evem agree to. But turns out that's the only way to win or get shit taken care of. Not believing in himself, worrying about cleaning up Kaia—gave me three more messes. Two?

Fuck it didn't matter. Just replaying how he stretched her on both sides; not an ounce of force only weak will and her attraction to him. His control over it—because he *did* have control. This proved it.

And the way they got away with Cody. Leti not yet, but he's going to chat with Cachí. Kaia, who he still needed to experience. Picturing twice the fight but wanting it more. Kayden groaned then, finally trusting his options and potential enough to let himself go.

Might even be worth looking for Kaia tonight while she's frenzied. While he's clear headed and alert.

"Jaylin?" He waited longer than he normally would. Gave her a chance, but she didn't move; hair over her face since they started. Not bothering to cover the rest of her.

Kayden went for her slip on the door handle. Walked back slow, but tall. Stomach, waist, balls—entire system lighter.

He stopped a few feet back noting scar tissue pattered high on her leg. Old wounds that didn't look as old as he'd expect. Demon battling her own demons. Kayden meant to set the slip on the bed. But tossed it gentle; covered those secrets for her since she—forgot.

She moved after, kind of. Still ignored him; her chest choking out held pain, recatching and holding its breath. Actively ruining something he's been needing. Something she helped him get and could be proud of.

"Hey…" Kayden tapped her foot gently with his knuckle. "You were right, you know. I mean that…That was—great for me," he backed towards the window not particularly feeling one way or another but wanting a response. An acknowledgement.

Outside: still pitch black, not even sure what day it is, only that it feels like it's been dark forever.

Not really sure what he was supposed to do now. Though maybe—at least—he could forgive Jaylin. For what she made him become. Because she may have helped build the cage and the monster, but she was also the only one able to set it free.

"Mkay," he sighed calm, but punched the limp.

She flinched for that. Alive. Aware.

"Imma go, but uh…you did great for me. Owe you one, I guess. You can— Im gonna shower. Welcome to do whatever yyou want."

He probably should have felt more. He just didn't know how he was supposed to care anymore.

Jaylin didn't move, not even to steal a coy look or tell him to '*fuck off*,' and he doesn't play. She wants to talk, she can speak.

Kayden backed out of the room and began the replays; analyzing where, what, and how, his new pleasure points will work. The power of the double doors clicking shut felt final and fucking revolutionary. Even messing up his hand on himself to wipe both Apollo's fuckin' door knobs. His girl somewhere inside and Kayden's cum marking his claims.

Clapping off his hands and feeling more pride that he's had in a long time.

Kayden's arms tossed in the air, dick hanging loose, spinning, searching for a camera. Too hyped to fuckin sleep. Find a quarter—tails for Kaia's little ass; heads for Cachí's smart mouth—figure out what problem to tackle next with this new motivation. Now on the hunt for his phone. Highly intrigued by wo was texting him when the and Jaylin were hangin a stand off.

Cachí was going to help him. He'd convince him same way he did Jaylin.

And he'd get what he needed. Went towards the dresser and plugged it in while pulling up the messages. And he had plenty.

"Mother—*fucker.*" Opening them.

FORGOT SOMETHING? <

Then another. Multiple more.
But that wasn't Cachí—Cachí knew better than to cross him like *this*. And who's the fool to catch him feeling this recharged and fired up.

Explains who Cachí just hadn't gotten back to him yet, too. Hadn't heard the messages or had the chance if this bitch had his phone.

Signed with a K and the middle finger—"You're timing—is fuckin' impeccable." She had the phone. She had the gun. And like Jay used to think, little Miss Kaia thinks she had him, too. Hate to repeat the same lesson twice in one day, but—rubbed at himself walking into the shower. "Or maybe hates too strong a word."

Moved rapidly after that. He didn't speak, didn't think. Went through the motions, ripped on some jeans again, and slammed the door.

Kayden had only a half second look to the room closed up at the end of the hall—only needed half a second for him to remember he didn't really care. Maybe one day. Tough, beautiful, wicked. She'll be there when he's ready. But today? Phone buzzing in his hand, thundering down the stairs through the lot, the gate, and the hood—*explosive.* Molding everything Jaylin ever did into everything Kaia has been. letting himself let it go and handle it just one final time.

Boundaries. Control. And a new mother fucking character for a new level. Apollo by proxy isn't enough. He wants his whole goddamn business.

Body rattling, pelvis tightening, gun loaded and tucked. But he planned to feel this one. Nothing better than an experiment with someone no one will miss, in a place no one will look.

Kayden punched the gas at the green and swerved like he was riding a high. He knew exactly where she was and nobody would hear if she were to scream.

xual coercion & abuse → when "choice" isn't real

agmented consent → yes, but not really | trauma bonding → love tangled up with fear

Duluth power & control wheel → every spoke a way to own you   L. Bancroft → he told on t

fore they'd admit it trauma literacy → learning the language of your own hurt

ycle of abuse →   the apology that resets the trap

issociation → not here, not now, not me | emotional labor → smiling while breaking insid

          coercive control → freedom shrinks one rule at a time

moral injury → they made me cross my own line   fragmented consent → pieces of "yes" that wer

whole pathological loyalty → staying when it's killing you

          cognitive dissonance → both can't be true, but both are   internalized oppression → ?

words in my own voice attachment injury → trust cracked where love once lived

maladaptive coping →

lief now, damage later | self-objectification → seeing me only through their eyes

          Transactional control → making help conditional on obedience

Minimization →

hrinking your own pain until it disappears

Survivor's logic → the bad choice that kept you alive   Trauma denial → it didn't hurt if I o

ook at it

          Learned helplessness → believing there's no way out

          Appeasement → safety bought with surrender

Self-betrayal → silencing yourself to keep the peace | Moral collapse → trading your own values for

lief Self-annihilation → erasing who you are to survive what's left

Identification with the aggressor → becoming what hurt you   Adaptive violence → striking first beca

          you expect to be struck

          When they outlawed softness,

          they planted the seeds for violence.

Called it misandry, but meant misogyny.

Wrote   rules   that   foiled   their   own

     sealed   their   truots   against   confesso

oolish enough to call it strength. But a body cannot hold forever,

o it festers. Hardens.   Seeks somewhere to break   And when it does—the blast spares no o

STATISTICS START TO SOUND THE SAME
AND FACTS ARE FELT, BUT OFTEN DISTANT

THIS **SHOULD** READ UNCOMFORTABLY.
NOT BECAUSE FETISH, BECAUSE—
A LACK IN SAFETY, CARE, AND RESPECT.
HOWEVER THE EXPERIENCE AROUND THAT MAY LOOK.

ABUSE IS NOT ALWAYS VIOLENT.
IT IS PATIENT. CHARMING. DEHUMANIZING.
AND RIGHT NEXT DOOR

THEHOTLINE.ORG | 800.799.SAFE [7233]
LOVEISRESPECT.ORG | 866.331.9474
RAINN.ORG

Masculinity is a mask built for war,

but the boys are just trying to survive the peace

The Bone Bird

MEMENTO MORI

Say Mercy

PIER 96 | SOUTHSIDE
MO:02:30:⁰⁰

|LVI|

The wind hit harder out here. It howled around the pier, sending Kaia's hair whipping across her face, stinging her skin. Bone white knuckling the gun. Last piece of control she had.

She stepped out of the shadows. Kayden's car screeched to a halt at the far end, headlights cutting through the fog like knives. The engine idled a second longer before it went silent. For a moment, everything did.

Forty paces, nothing but sky and open planks yawning between them.

He stepped out. And she saw it. Not rage. Not ego. *Fear.*
He was breathing too fast, his hand shaking as it hovered near his waistband, eyes scanning for her. Not the kind of fear that makes a man back down— but the kind that makes him dangerous. Back to the nights that still came for him when no one else could see. And Kaia?
Now one of those nights.

There to lurk and chew along his spine for what he thought he'd get away with. She moved without thinking. Sneakers quiet across the pier.

Her message was sent. Her trigger, primed.

There was no plan. Just the collision course. And half a hope to survive.

She hadn't always fit in, always felt sane, or always really *lived*— but she's always survived.

"Kaia," Kayden growled into the dark.

Voice echoing in the hollow corners. He read the text over again—light illuminating his face—jaw clenched. Kaia ducked behind cracked pylons, sliding across the slick wood.

Few stacked planks. Even fewer escapes. He was pacing now. Gripping the gun he didn't even look able to use anymore.

463

Hands rattling the way hers had before.

Not tonight though.

So for Kayden—fear or anger? They both made monsters sloppy. She pulled out Cachí's cell phone, smothering the light inside her jacket with her face. Just one, quick word.

Not a word. A kissy face.

His phone chimed. Closer now. Turned up Cachí's volume, stole a peek at the big beastie before slid the phone toward the pier's far end. Crawling like her life depended on it. Because it did.

Chilling laugh boomed along the dock. His voice next.

"The more you piss be off, Doll—the slower and rougher it's gonna go."

Light illuminating his face switched to his ear. Cachí's phone rang and he ran for it quick. Stopped short of three steps. Maybe expected commotion or rustling. Got nothing and moved toward it slower, but when there was no rustling to hide it, no quick movements to discard it, he got angrier. Figured it was a ploy before he reached it.

She was a step ahead, though a very tiny one—getting smaller, the bigger and angrier he got. Just a stupid, out-of-towner. Making him a fool in his own yard.

Kaia let him curse—mutter her name like a prayer he'd never believed in. Let the silence grow teeth. Let it bite. Because one wrong step would break it all open. And then, like a cold water to the face in an already terrible dream—the memory hit. Not grotesque. Not stretched out.
Just a flash.

A room. A carpet. Her face against it. His breath, thick with whiskey.
The steel of the gun, cold and alive between them.
        Let go, Kaia.

His voice, not angry, just broken. Big hands gripping hers, trembling. Not rage. But desperation. And a measure of madness. Falling apart—father that felt more left behind than needed her.
Neither trying to destroy or hurt them, just—*make it stop.*

Fighting over the gun—over control. Over who can stay—

        —what if it'd been her? Dead then, dead now.

A snap. Not even a bang. Just the weight of him crumpling like wet wood. A breath gone still because she never meant to let go. But it had gone anyway. And now—she needed it to go again.

Needed it to play out exactly as before. Her chest heaved once. Then steadied. Because Kayden was stepping forward. Not in memory—not in the in-between. But now. *Here.*

And this time, she wasn't fighting not to be left behind, wasn't fighting for someone to stay. She wanted to kick him out.

She rose from the shadows. Just out of reach like all the exits before. Kayden didn't see her for who she was, he never had—

he didn't *know* her." But not her body, not her power. *Not Leti.*

Just an animal, out for himself—practiced killer.

He lunged for her immediately—*instinctually* when he turned. No dramatic, cinematic pause. And Kaia—for once—thankful for every bad dream, for every night terror, or every sleep walk and panic attack.

Trigger like muscle memory. Shot cracked through the night.
First round not a bullet, but a knife slicing into his side. He staggered back, confusion flashing across his face.

Heat and blood—his side.

And then like a runner out of the gate before the next fire, he charged again. But another crack, seconds after he flinched—blown wide into something far off, unseen.

They didn't know, but he didn't stop so neither did she. Pulling it twice more, one into the railing busting the wood—distance between them rapidly tightening. Another two cracked out—and something grasped flesh and burrowed into blood. It wasn't silent the way her father had been though.

It wasn't numb, or still.

She didn't know whether the void stole time again, or she overestimated herself—his massive leaps, giant footsteps. Fast.

Hit, but still closing in on the last few feet. Hollered something she didn't catch—bracing when she should have stayed slack.

Hitting the boards like a dropped stone, force so fast and big it took three of her breaths away. His jacket unzipped, hanging around her like a trap. The smell of leather, sweat, and blood—swirling in the air between them.

His hand found her wrist. Yanked. *Pulled.* Another shot—upward into the skies—*at least not into a head—*

Though isn't that what she needed this time. But who's ever capable of doing things when His hand found her wrist. Yanked. *Pulled.* Another shot—upward into the skies like demons trying to break themselves in—her jaw cracked sideways when he swung. Fingers slackened and the cold metal skittered across the wood behind him.

> *Maybe it was okay to release it now.*

Something told her she wasn't going to win this one. Him hunched above her, staggering. One hand to his bleeding side, the other still hungry for something to hold.

Maybe it was okay to be still.

"Fuck," he spat, searching for the gun she'd had in her hand, hoping it was the one he'd needed. "Where's the fucking—"

> *Maybe not*—kicking against his knee as he got closer, scrambling for the gun. It was hard. Pushed her up while he swung his back. Might have popped, she didn't wait to see—she rolled.

Drug herself toward the edge.—*slower, rougher*—

She didn't know what she was trying for. Escape, the water, anything but him—but his boot slammed down on the small of her back. Ribs, lungs, arms, and everything buckled. Dropped her like a collapsed table.

He dragged her up again—lifted just enough to slammed her back down on the planks. letting her ribs curse the end, and her balance tease.

"Goddamn—fucking *bitch*!" he shoved Dante's gun into the waistband at his back while she fought for every breath.

Elbows nudged. Legs kicked maybe trying to pull herself back while arms dangled over the edge grasping desperately. *Though for what?*

The pier, the water, the Reaper.

The water below was like space. Dark and cold—though far from still. She trusted it more than this.

Kayden leaned in, hand fisting her hair to yank her into an arch.

"What'd I tell you, huh? You stupid cunt."

His boot pinned her thigh. Gun against her ribs. His body pressed her into the pier, into the blur between pain and nothing. He wasn't going to let her fall, but he wasn't going to let her free.

"What's it feel like, huh? Knowing you're just going to disappear?" Pressing his free hand into his side. Gapping at it.

"How's it feel—" crying out between words. "Being a pawn?"

His foot shifted—*intentionally*. Rocking her torso forward, dragging her toward the edge, splinters in her hips and belly.

"You think anyone's coming for you?" Kayden growled, his voice mean and dry, like rust cracking loose. "Another fuckin' street slut—I should have let the guys tear into you the other night."

Grotesque, painful, and broken. Voice split like skin flayed open. Whiplash tore through her spine the further he pulled her chest off the pier and into the air. Maybe he wanted to break her first. Fold in half.

She coughed, or maybe gasped—there was no air left to separate the two. She heard the words but refused to hold them. Meaningless.
Everything meaningless outside the hold on her and her options out.

His phone lit in his waistband. Just for a second. She couldn't read it, but maybe it would stop him. Maybe for a moment. Or maybe he would continue to hold her over, broken and breaking, taunting the waters and darkness below.

Blood oozing through fingers, hand still pressed against his side, elbow slumped on the rail barely able to hold the weight they brought down.

The other laced into her hair. Rotten to the core and on the edge of a snap.

She opened her mouth, but nothing came out. And he just held her there.

And bled.

Kayden stood above her, and he bled. He felt it on the inside, but also down his side. From his side. From his eyes. But maybe there was a future where he wasn't clawing through city shadows, where ghosts didn't wear Kaia's face, and didn't keep crawling up through Cody's skin.

Maybe he could outrun the graveyard he made and just turn it all off.

Just be the rook; the bodyguard; the bunkmate—*Jaylin*. He thought about how she felt—grounded himself down in the way her body gripped high tight. It'll take some work, but after today—that could work.

But not if he didn't get the gun he used to shoot Cody. Not if he left Kaia to retaliate—always against him. Not because he attacked her. But Leti.

He saw himself in Kaia. Willing to wage war for the ones we love. If it was him—he'd kill anyone who hurt his family. He'd already proven that. Kaia would have too, had she stood a fighting chance.

But they didn't have one. Never did. Squirming beneath his grasp—neck bent unnaturally. He could twist it. Make it quick. His blood soaking the pier beneath them. Maybe he let her fall. Fed her to the sharks like a secret too heavy to carry.

A second Cody; crawling back up through the city's throat. Jaylin first to know. To call him failure. *No.* "It'll be quick," he said.

She heard him—maybe felt him, felt herself shift as he did, reaching behind his back.

"I should say I'm sorry..." Whispered and mixed with a sigh. But he didn't feel it. And of her options—death by his hand still better than drowning or sharks. If he was quick.

But the sky didn't agree; the water wouldn't either as waves and wind howled. Sharp and sudden like they'd woke when the pistol cracked the clouds. Kaia's voice cried out with it; a collection of mourning in a song. The universe telling him it was okay, promising to cover his shame.

Kayden cocked the gun. Aimed it. "You'll be able to fly free now, Kaia." And it rang out. Lightning. Not from the sky, but through the air. A shot splitting the crying wind, and erupting under skin like a blanket pulled over a scream. Kaia felt her hair fall around her face; release. Not from him, from everything. The ground under her, the pressure on her—

Anchor was tossed, ropes around her wrists. And she fell.

Sons of the Harbor Master

|LVII|

Cachí paced the apartment, restless energy flooding his veins, unable to find any direction. His thoughts spun around Kaia—gone.

He hadn't realized how long he'd been staring at the computer screen until a new message finally appeared. His fingers hovered over the keys.

```
> ROUND 2 U BIG BITCH COME N GET IT
> SOUTHEAST SF. PIER 96
```

The pier. The texts.

His stomach dropped. It wasn't just a location. It was the point of no return. The gun, the phone—it was strategy, not chaos. Waiting, plotting. And provoking. Push just right and rage does the rest—sloppy, savage, and on display.

And now it was all in motion, slipping further out of control and deeper into the mess he couldn't untangle. Before he could even process it, another message popped up. Simple. Casual. Her signing off with signature and emoji. It twisted in his chest.

Anger should've been there, but it was buried too deep, worn too thin. Like a muscle that didn't hurt anymore—just an ache in the background, too familiar to notice.

Cachí ran a hand through his hair, snagged his jacket. His bag too. From his car the *jodido* rooks drove back. *Fuckers.* Slinging it over his shoulder and moved to the window instead of the front door. *Fuck Dante.*

And his fucking Rookies. Slipping onto the fire escape, boots careful but fast. Metal groaning soft under his weight. Dante covered the back too, but didn't seem like the one flying solo outside understood the severity.

Choking on a ciggie in his blues. Cachí smirked. Ducked into the alley off Dante's, eyes flicking toward the curb just in case Copper looked.

Kept moving, head down. Footsteps quick and quiet as he cut out into the dark and didn't turn back. His train of thought a blur on the ride—clattering tracks, the hum of the train car, the weight of the world pressing in. The weight of the *dead.* And Cachí was in fast forward with no plan.

Was she still alive? Would he be too late? Would Kayden actually do it—?

Then Leti—he could only imagine having seen Kaia. He pictured her antagonistic texts again and shook his head.

Suicidal, or absolutely wrecked.

The train rumbled beneath him, and he couldn't shake the feeling that he was already too far behind; that the damage had already been done. And what was he even trying to prove—*and to who?*

> *Dante? Leti? Himself and Matí?*

Cold air slapped his face. It didn't loosen the knot in his chest. Cachí ran through the dark, feet pounding against the uneven ground.

He had no phone, no way to track her outside the address she left an hour ago until—gunshot.

It rang out from somewhere up ahead. A sharp crack that echoed through the night. His heart raced, knowing exactly what it meant. Ran harder, faster, pushing his body until he risked a fall.

Another shot rang out. *What if it was Kaia who fired first—*

Dante's gun—? Then what? *Thank you? Fuck you?*

Then—*nothing.* He stopped dead in his tracks, breath ragged gasps.

And if she didn't, would the relief he felt be for Kayden's life—or for the chance to finish it himself. What would it take to excuse it, what he'd done? Could he even compare it to what he could have had—*Cody, or with Leti?*

What would it be like to have something built, something real, outside of this chaos? The thought hit like a punch to the gut.

Cold air filled his lungs and the world stopped. Like it seemed to do a lot now-a-days. It felt heavy. It felt like an end, and it felt near.

Kaia, Kayden, Dante, him?

A whimper echoed—faint. Like breath caught in a chest. But cutting in an otherwise silent place. *Kaia.*

His chest tightened, his feet moving again before his mind could catch up. He wasn't too late. And that—terrified him more than anything. The relief of hearing her wasn't enough to undo the anger in his gut, or the fear that he was slipping further into the dark for people already gone.

He ran, faster now, breath sharp in his lungs as his mind flared through everything—everything that had gotten him here. His pride, ego—pushed him to this moment. *What would Matías have said?*

Cachí couldn't say, because he didn't know. And that killed him a little.

He hadn't gotten to know the man Matías would've become. He knew he'd crack the world in half for Mikki, for Dante—but for strangers?

What if he couldn't save anyone? What if Matías would've told him to save himself?

He picked up speed again, rushing toward the sound, heart hammering in his chest, and as he neared—he saw them. Kaia, crumpled on the ground, twisted in a way that made his stomach turn—he couldn't just stand there. But Kayden...

Kayden had been there when they got the call. Matí, gone. Mikki in shock. Kayden silent. Cachí numb. They never spoke of it again—but they'd traded something that day. A piece of themselves. A promise to protect the ones left. *Familia.*

Cachí stepped forward slowly. Weakened and betrayed by the memory. He saw Kayden lean over Kaia, his face twisted in that same anger, that same madness. Nothing had changed. But at that same exact moment, everything had. The stakes changed. The expectations—

"*No one will ever find you,*" Kayden screamed at her.

Cachí's hands trembled, steel heavy in his bag. What was really worse?

To die in a cage, old and gray? Or take early access to the next round?

Shoes slapping against old-paved road. Imagined sunny skies and running with Dante and Mikki. Not being here, not choosing Kayden.

Cachí would rather be dead. But vengeance wearing mercy's mask, or vice versa. Cachí slowed. Flinched watching Kayden reach behind his back. Almost yelled to tell him to stop—*it's not to late.* But for the first time since Matí, it actually was.

His face clearer the closer he walked. Cachí mimicked him. A mirror to Kayden. "Kayden! *Stop, please!*"

—but that's not Kayden anymore—

Hasn't been for a long time. If he'd only admitted it sooner.

Cachí's feet planted, still moving with Kayden. Moving like Kayden and reaching for the piece. *Had Kayden done enough—?*

Or would Cachí freeze—only reacting to Kayden popping first. letting him take just one more? Have to face Leti and say his family took one more thing. Heavy and cool.

The irony of Matí being shot with the others. He tried to teach Cachí to play fair. But when the others didn't? Killing himself without having to actually pull the trigger. What he did to Leti—what he blamed on Leti—

'*I don't know—bro—cornered me—*'

The memory of the words; the way Kade convinced himself they were true. The way Cachí risked his friendships with Mick and Dante to keep Kade close—but seeing how real the marks were on Kaia and visualizing what he did to Leti. His hand shook.

Because they left her with him. Because she just walked in. Because Kade already told himself it was okay. And the gun fired. Shot rang through the air, loud and final, slicing through the tension and through his ear. Blistering, popped. He didn't even have the chance to look—wouldn't have happened if he had.

Paint balls. And paint. But thicker. Blood. Night sky, the ocean—it was all just shadows. Kayden falling in on himself. Cachí felt Kaia before he knew why, but he dove. Threw himself onto the wood so hard he wondered if he'd go through. Leaned as far out, down as he could without falling in. Felt her shoe graze between his fingers.

Felt Kayden's demon's crawling closer. Readying to stab Cachí in the back; let him know how it feels. Cold air collecting around them. Ice along his neck. *Death.*

Cachí hauled himself up, leaning over the rail. Watching the water; hoping he'll catch a glimpse. "Kaia!" He could still feel her slip through his hand— he had her. He screamed her name again, the sound tearing through him like it was ripping him open.

The sea, the night, the darkness—it swallowed her whole, and all he could do was watch. And after, rot slow.

Tears of Point Nemo

PIER 96 | SOUTHSIDE
MO:02:30:⁰⁰

|LVIII|

The water rose beneath her. A breath—then her body sank. The blood from her legs darkening the blue, blurring with the deep. For a breath, she saw him—a shadow, reaching—but too late. Desperate call swallowed by the sea. Water moving gently around her, like an old fire dance—but cold. Numb enough, it didn't hurt. Cradled her, pulling her down, its weight heavy and inviting.

And the world slowed—every ripple, every shimmer, suspended. Time curled around her in waves. Bubbles floating from her mouth, drifting like small ghosts, flickering toward the surface. Her legs floated above, blood unraveling into the dark like silk ribbon.

Black silk hair—*Miss Kaia bird—I do hope you have a great night.* Jaylin. Shadows, shape, and light—Kaia thought she saw the wedding dress. She thought of her mother. The pull.   The hush.

The cold—kissed her skin, pierced her ribs, and slid through her like memory. But there wasn't terror. Not here. There was release. Rest. Nightmares shallow and afraid of the deep.

Maybe the sea is the final Reaping. Not as a monster, but as a keeper. Maybe it was time to stop being anyone's savior, victim, or shadow. Maybe it was time to stop being anything at all.

The water swirled, and she tasted air—fleeting—before the weight took her again. The surface blurred, then vanished. Death held her in its hands. Tumbled her like stones. Asked if she wanted to stay.

And maybe now—she could.

Cachí stood at the railing, watching the water rise beneath him, its cold fingers reaching upward, pulling Kaia down. Bubbles trailing behind her, following her descent like some cruel final warning, some last breath swallowed by the ocean.

His heart skipped. The air thickened in his chest. This was it. She would disappear like so many others had—slip into the depths—

And even in death, Kayden would have won.

Cachí couldn't let her go. It would mean everything was for nothing.

It would mean he let himself go.

His mind began to taunt, flashing all the ways he could've done differently, all the ways he had failed the people around him.

What would Mikki think?

The past collided with the present, the weight of it all slamming into him like a crushing force.

Without thinking—

He threw himself over the railing.

The fall was slow, surreal, time feeling like it had stalled. His body twisted in the air, the cold night wrapping around him, and he was sinking— drowning in his regrets, in warnings, flags, and better options impossible to see until now.

You're not stuck here—
The weight of the black water came over him like a shroud, pulling him deeper and deeper. It felt like an end; a preview of death before it happened. Whether it was the sharks, the cold depths, or their self sabotaging panic.

His body floated. Ghost lost in the waves. Thrashing at the idea. Breaking the surface with a sharp gasp.
Air filled his lungs in jagged bursts. His eyes scanned frantically, but there was nothing. No Kaia.

Deeper blacks pulling him closer to beneath the pier. Waves crashing against pillars outlined in razor sharp barnacles—Cachí dropped his face in the water and swam out from it. Looking up to see where she'd fallen.

To his left, the shore. Everywhere else—depth. "Kaia!"

The emptiness was suffocating. The fear was real. What waited beneath.

His holler was lost to the vast, endless water. Couldn't tell if it was his voice or the sea itself, but it didn't matter. The ocean swallowed him whole—pushed him like a play thing.

And then, as if Poseidon himself took pity on his soul, he saw it—
a small, skinny limb tumbling in the curl of a wave. She was so close, but the shore still seemed so far away.

Rushing toward it, driven by the hope that maybe it was her. But cautious of loose fenders or buoys. But he couldn't wonder '*what if*,' only believe, '*it was*.' Because if she stood a chance, then maybe he did too.

Latched onto something angrily, ripping it through the water toward him. Maybe it would be purpose, maybe it would be forgiveness from Leti—just one glance that told him: *It wasn't your fault.*

So then maybe one day, he might forgive himself

Heavy cotton wanting to sink them down—he wasn't sure until he had her. Skin hidden, pulling her face from the water and slinging her arm over his neck. He swam.

Rough. Waves testing his resolve, cold temperature his will, and misleading distance his mind. Swimming sloppy, angry—begrudgingly, resentfully, ego and pride unleashed—whatever put in the work.

But Kaia's silence was like a weight belt. Her body like a sea creature pulling him down when ever he thought he felt or saw something in the dark. He wasn't walking the boundary line, or even the edge. He threw himself off it. As if the one extreme decision could excuse a past of passivity.

Now all he could hear was Dante's warnings, "*don't drown yourself.*"

—— Somewhere in the hush between crying and blood pressure cuffs—Leti sat. Not in crisis. not in control. Just there; with Mikki; letting her braid her hair. Body frightened but mind knowing.

And each twist in the braid deliberate, slow, and precise. Like maybe, if she got it tight enough, something inside would come back together.

"You wanna talk about anything?"

Leti's jaw twitched. She didn't speak much still.

Wasn't peaceful, but was there. Eyes locked on the far wall.

Mikki swung another strand over and under. Followed the pattern methodically. "Aye that's alright. I was thinking anyway. You ever notice how pain stacks?"

Another loop over. Another loop under. "Like, always starts small, you know? Then one day you just can't move."

Leti's leg began to bounce. Mikki picked out a small strand to frame her face and smoothed where it pulled. "No one thing breaks you, right? Not all at once. Just changes how you walk a little more every day.

Not even talking about the big things sometimes it's just the quiet that keeps silent as you rot. And it's like—worst part is, you don't always know when. When it's not just hurt anymore, but hate keeping someone alive."

Leti's jaw ticked again. Breath shifted. Maybe the hate kept her warm. *Still silent.*

"I guess I've tried to fix things that weren't mine," Mikki said, hands still working. "Thought if I just loved someone hard enough, it'd undo what broke them."She paused. Let the braid rest in her fingers. "Sometimes people don't want to be saved. Not yet, not ever. Depends... But sometimes pain's the only thing they know how to hold."

Leti didn't answer. But this time she did turn. Just enough to feel the presence beside her. Mikki shrugged while Leti watched her.

"I don't have all the answers," she said. "But I know this—pain doesn't get to own you. You don't have to run from it. You don't have to fight it every second either." She met Leti's glance and held it. "Just name it. Start there. And someone else will be there to check you're still breathing."

476

Games We Make
Toy Soldiers Play

PIER 96
MO:02:30 ⁰⁰
|LIX|

The streets were empty—no people, or things—just the weight of Dante's own thoughts pressing against his chest. The glow of old piers flickering; rusted boats with no stories left to tell.

Only the remnants of things that used to matter.

Dante sped through it all, the city moving, but not feeling alive., until he pulled in—dropped to a slow drag through rows of containers, shadows, and shambles.

Then he saw it—slumped figure on the docks. A body, lifeless in the darkness. His stomach twisted, gut churning with something cold and heavy. The scene was wrong. Dante slammed on the brakes, tires screeching as he jerked the car to a stop. His hand shot to the glove compartment, pulling out the spare gun with a swift, practiced motion. Fingers wrapped around it like an extension of himself—Cold steel grounding him.

Low. Alert. Bootcamp that never left his bones.He stepped out of the car, feet hitting the ground with a sharp slap. Body, too big for Kaia, but Cachí—?

Dante's eyes were locked, breaking away aggressively to keep eyes and tabs on his surroundings. When he went back—*Kayden.*

All the assumptions and logic in the world—still hit like a brick.

Eyes wide and blown open, like he saw it coming. Shot to the head. Dante's gun at his side—blood all over it and the pier. *Kaia.*

His chest tightened with the recognition, heart hammering harder with each step as he blindly went for his gun. Duty. Holding breath and refusing to look—he couldn't trust it. Disappearing now, getting away. It was too clean. Too still.

Dante moved slowly across the creaking wood of the pier, eyes out for Cachí's car but only seeing his own. Kept himself low. Every step echoed off the walls of his skull, the night pressing in from all sides. Scanning the shadows, instincts screaming.

Kayden's body was motionless. But the air was not—waves pounding trying to hide the night. Trying to eat them hole and the voices too.

Dante froze mid-step—*listening*. Tasted the panic in the plea before his blood went cold. That voice.

Matías—? He started scanning. Down the pier. Under it. Around—so *familiar*.

It was a holler, echoing in the night the way it echoed in the school. Not yelling for anything other than air. *Life.*

Heartbeat faltered, a stuttered mess of shock and disbelief, turning in fast circles. He heard it again and Dante's feet beat harder against the pier, closer to the edge—landed the rail so hard it might have cracked.

A desperate, angry roar from the black. Half drowned and familiar, dragging through the waters. Shapes clearer as Dante got closer—an emerging pair the sea refused to release—

creature in black on it's back threatening to drown him. Ocean swiping to take it back when it couldn't take him, but disappearing with them both.
    —*Cachí*

Every time his head went under, Dante buried him again. Mikki mourning, *screaming* first. Foolish man—angry enough to challenge Death and steal from his plate. Each drag of her body through the tide and sand holding onto something they were too scared to lose.

Not the girl, but the hope. That—*it'll change, it'll improve*. Because it's never been about anything other than fighting himself. The sound of planks cut out and concrete beat under boots. Dante was halfway to them. *But halfway to what really?*

Kaia didn't pull the trigger. He didn't see it, but he knew. Argued with himself—*murder-suicide; it was her*. But it didn't fit.

Didn't feel how he needed it to feel.

Boots slid into sand and Dante stumbled. Used the fall forward as a lean to run harder—*Go.* A sickening surge of panic. Kayden clapping from behind, challenging him: *faster, faster*—surrounded by ghosts, monsters, and death—*get him out of here, Dání.*

The voice wasn't loud. But it was his. Kayden's. Dante's breath hitched—ankle twisted—tossing himself over sandbags and rocks. His pace wasn't steady and it wasn't even. He didn't want to leave Kayden. Not alone, not like this.

But he didn't want to admit he loved a wicked man. Dante let himself trip up and slow. Physically pulled between the middle space. Aching. Sorry. *Stuck.*

Leti, Mikki. Knowing what caused every crack in Kayden's shield and how deep it went—Dante had gotten so numb to it. *Even now.* Trying to forget the bad he'd done to mourn in peace.

But would mourning a monster make him one, too?

He covered his face with both hands, as if he could wipe the last two minutes out of his mind. Swore into them, maybe even a second of prayer before Dante turned back to Cachí—already up the beach, fifty feet, oblivious and focused, dropping Kaia from his back and onto the grass as hard as he dropped himself.

He got her out.

Dante turned to the sounds of sirens. Kayden's ghost. Matías to his other side—watching. Trusting Dante would keep his word; keep safe—the ones he had to leave behind. He shook off his hands, blew out the nerves like candles, and ran the last few feet. Cachí laying her long. Frantically pumping her chest—*one, two...*

"Breathe!! *Por fa—loca...*"

Dante came up on his heels all but throwing himself into Cachí's back. He could hear the breathless, tired counts masked by fog. Blue lips.

A slide of hand right instead of left, a wild animal crossing at the wrong time, sky's a little wetter—Dante could have arrived to silence. To them all on the railing joking together, and an ocean that was fed. His heart twisted.

If Cachí had half the fight—Dante's breath caught too. *But it didn't happen.* Hands faltered and shook. Guilt flooded, fast and hot.

He looked at Kaia like maybe it was already too late. Like he already had to choose between Kayden and Cachí, and now here again—

Get him out of here.

As if he was ready to give up. Terrified. Walking the edge of loosing them both and choosing to give only *one*. And Matías—he'd take care of her where they failed to.

Dante—on Cachí's shoulders, shaking, but not heard—searched the silence for Kayden again because he could feel them both.

Maybe even a prayer on the wind, a—*send her back, please.*

Not for Leti, not for Kaia, not for Dante—*for Cachí.*

"Come on!" Dante screamed to the skies. Maybe at them, at Cachí, at himself. But tonight, their ghosts—more than light, shadows, or sound and Matí—beside Kade, arms on the rails actually there. Younger than when they left. And together. Matías promising Dante this time—

I got this one. Save what's left—

Buried between the echo of boys warm laughter and memories that held tight. Dante hesitated because the boy inside saw Neverland and might've wanted to go too. Stopped himself from reaching, from calling—watching Matías nod his goodbye. Kayden throwing a '*peace*'—before twisting into the wind together.

Not waiting for her *or* giving her back, but disappearing into lights of blue and white and red like warnings. Lights that swept the outside of the piers, working it's way through the street. Sweeping on a slow crawl.

Waiting for back up or a sign. But Cachí punching away off beat.

Dante's face flush. Hot. He was turning, swinging around and slamming into Cachí like the ghosts would get to him first.

"Let's go!" Dante grabbed his arm. Hard.

Cachí, on his knees—a sapling after the storm—tried to push him back but failed. Yanking his arm away from Dante, revolted when yanked halfway to standing.

"She isn't breathing, Dání, *ayudame por fa!*" Dropping back down to Kaia, pale faced, blue lipped, and still. Her file against his desk—another red stamp—DECEASED.

Dante's heart fractured more. For everyone. Cachí especially—begging, *help me.* But Dante was...

"One, two, three, four, five—"

"Cachí!" His voice a growl now. Rough and too raw. Working up the strength to not only walk away, but force his brother into it too.

Leaving not only Leti, but leaving her twice. *But if it were Mikki—Matí—*"Cachí!"

The water, the cold—only made the bruising worse. Salt, blood. Dante was halfway to convinced she was dead. And it was okay. He had to be convinced.

Jerking when Cachí shoved at Dante, whipping around and slamming his hand to the center of her chest. Dante couldn't swallow. Could hardly stand, only try to reason—

"Fuck, Cachí, let's go!"

Because the longer they waited there, the further Dante stitched into their future. Cachí to jail; bound to return in the mask Kayden left behind. Fast forward to the next kid, the next file, the next snake eating it's own tail until it combusts—one day numb enough he'd have to kill Cachí, too.

Dante, one knee into the grass, one ready to launch and run. Both hands fisted into Cachí's collar *making* him turn and stop—

He caught the first one to the face when Cachí thrashed twice. Popped Dante good and pissed him the fuck off between getting hit and hung up on. Kaia caught the second though. Intentional and centered—Cachí, if anything, a fighter. Shame Dante was too, holding Cachí's collar, fist cocked back, blood on his lip—

Kaia jostled. And they both froze.

A muscle in her neck constricted.. Dante's fist dropped. Hands stayed tight. And the girl gasped.

The only sounds following, waves crashing into rocks. Tires crunching slow on gravel, moving in. Creeping. Stillness—into danger when they needed speed. "Dání—what do we do?" He sounded so young.   *—just exhale—* Dante's heart—so loud.

No clocks, but he could hear it. Lurking. Until Kaia coughed.

Shoulders rounded and shook. She even made the smallest of sounds, more human than the first. And as if Kaia held their breath in her hand, their strings tangled around her life, the guys loosened.

Anger wiped like a slate and relief spread like morphine.

Cachí unsure it was real. Salt and water bubbling from her throat, breath trying to feed her life but ocean still fighting to take it.

Cachí didn't move. Fear, ignorance, panic—Dante shoved him sideways.

Reached for Kaia's body. Shoulder and thigh, sliding her leg towards him, bent at the knee. Braced against the grass like a kickstand. Cachí was quiet. "What—are you..."

Elbow bent too, wedging under her head but tilting her forward. "Keep her from choking."

Dante swept hair from her face. Leaned in like he needed a better look then a file to remember her by. And the world turned a little slower. Allowed a moment more of her breath. Three points on a triangle one final time.

Life, death, and somewhere in-between. Counterclockwise now. Outside Death's door, tempting fate. Dante couldn't explain it, but he still felt Matí and Kade with them. Distracting the Reapers and holding the door while she twirled through. Fire-bird too fast for even the dead.

She made another small and wet sound. Back heaved into it, and it was like permission. Dante hit overdrive. Snagged Cachí up, ignoring the hate he got back. Battle resumed—

"*Vamos carajo!*"

Cachí swinging and out of control quick. Though his edge through surprise vanished like his brother after the first contact with Dante's face.

Wouldn't happen twice. Dante snagged him by the back of the neck. Kicked out Cachí's foot. Dropped him to a knee and shoved his head and shoulders so far down— squeezed until Cachí admitted it hurt.

Flashbacks to teenage years and brotherly games of '*Mercy.*'

"She's breathing," Dante draggin' him back up. "You fucking saved her. Now save your fucking self." All fight—all street, taking another swing.

Kaia made a terrible sound from the back of the throat. Made Cachí freeze. His hands dropped as Dante was swinging—every intention of being blocked—slammed Cachí hard in the face, but Dante pulled the punch best he could. Still. Knocked him back down.

Cachí didn't care though. He braced one foot up, hand on the ground and watched Kaia. Body moving almost mechanically now. Water hacked out with force.

"Hear it Cachí? She's back—*let's go!* I'll come back!*"

Cachí went for her again, Dante blocked.

"I'm on your fucking side, '*mano*. But Kayden's got a hole in his head—*entiendes?* They won't look the other way, Cachíflin—they won't let me touch this."

Ghosts.

"*Oy—carnal!*" He shook Cachí's shoulders hard. "Doesn't matter what he did. You're both punishable. Separate crimes in the system.

You *want* to do this to us? To Mikki? Turn into—*¡Qué falta de respeto!*"

"*Eso es differente.*" Cachí's bloodshot eyes flickered up, finally meeting Dante's gaze as if to dare: "*Es mi culpa,* Dante."

"*Jesus Christ*—Cachí! Prison won't change that—it'll add to it, *vamos!*"

"*Dání* I— we just left her there." Dante could pick the exact syllable Cachí's voice cracked. The rest, a whimper in a whisper, finally giving the Fury a name. "I handed them to him—Leti—*¿Cómo voy a vivir con eso?*"

Dante sucked a sharp breath, hands shaking. On the verge of control. "She's breathing," Voice low but sharp enough to cut the air. "Leti's alive by sheer fucking will. Kaia too—*because you*. Alive! That's more than a lot of fucking people right now."

Cachí flinched. "No—"

"*Ahora!*" Dante forcing him back to the street.

Feet barely keeping themselves straight.

Cachí wanted to look away, but wanted another sign of movement more. Wanted to tell Leti he found her most. But instead, tell her he took that from her too. Through his proximity and apathy. Not stopped it then. Assigned Kaia a s'more too. But instead looked the other way while she lost herself with Kayden. *Jaylin.*

Cachí stumbled, backing up on a grassy hill. He was walking. Because—maybe he was lost, too. *Who else would be able to walk away twice?*

Made an effort to jerk away from Dante's grip, but not hard. Cachí didn't want to fight anymore. Still—something stabbed inside. Pain he didn't know how else to fight but physically.

Dante shoved him towards the street each and every time he turned to look. Wishing Dante could stop him from thinking, too. *Hoping.* Praying, if she could just sit up.

But he'd come back. *Cachí killed a man.*

The car moved quick, streets stretching like a dark blur.

They didn't say much. And Dante couldn't sit long in the quiet—not here and not tonight. He was tired of the time all the unsaid shit steals.

Cranked the heat as high as it'd go. Half turned his body, but had to actually turn the car. Less pressure going forward anyway.

"*Estoy aquí,* okay?" He wasn't here with any answers, but he was here. "I'm not going anywhere this time."

Cachí didn't acknowledge it, but he didn't need to. Eventually he dropped his head back on the headrest. Sounded like he was muffling pain, but Dante couldn't be sure. Took three laps around the hospital in case he wanted to really let it go and crack. Hell—might've been Dante who needed the laps. Maybe he wanted to let it go.

Maybe Kaia would take him on another run—

Grip tightening on the wheel, eyes fixed forward. Was going for another lap but guilt had him clip the curb turning into the parking lot.

Awkwardly met Cachí's eyes in the mirror before that deflated too.

The auto pilot, the hum of tires on freeways—Dante wanted it the way he wanted to know what joke Matí told Kayden before they left.

The way he wanted to know they'd still be there when it was his turn.

But he should be thinking about Kaia. Car moving forward—street fading into parking lot and pulling into a red lane at the side. Dark shadows holding their secret. Dante jerked open the door. Smelled like hot tar and copper. Sirens in the distance, coming and going.

Cachí's door cracked enough to put his legs out, lean against the metal while Dante popped the trunk. "What—are we doing here, Dante?"

"Put this on," he said, tossing a black zip up and pair of track pants onto Cachí's chest. Dante pointed. "Go in."

Cachí locked in place. "I can't."

"You can."

Cachí's jaw ticked. Any relief, Dante felt was instantly gone. "We put her here...I don't want—"

"*I don't give a fuck*—what you want, *entiendes?* I need you seen. With Mikki. In that waiting room," pointing again, "with cameras and nurses and cops all over the goddamn floor.

So dry the fuck off, put up your fucking hood, and go act like you always fucking do."

His eyes cut sharp in the dark, voice low but hot.

"I'm *not* losing another one, don't care how many times I have to fucking say it. Not this way, because you are not gonna be some ghost under the city or on some alley side chain gang."

Cachí shifted uncomfortably, squelching against the seat. Arms chilled in the open air. Dante softened, moved closed.

"Go in. Sit next to Mikki. Tell her you're working up the nerve—I don't know, but *wait* until I get back. And don't—fucking say a word on Kade."

Cachí looked at him betrayed.

"You nod. Breathe. And fucking be here—when I get back."

Cachí begrudgingly started peeling off the soaked shirt. "What if—what if she doesn't want to see me? How...bad?"

"Then don't go near and don't get mad at her—but all this—really not my point right now. Do you want to sit here asking obvious questions and arguing or can I try and rectify what I can?"

Confused. Glaring.

"Kaia." Dante barked, turning for driver's seat. Barely even allowing Cachí to close his door when he slid out. Half dry and half re-dressed. Watching Dante go. Just another ghost of a person in his rear view.

Pier Pressure at Three

PIER 96
MO:03:15:00

|LX|

The pier was still crawling with sirens and soaked shoeprints when Dante rolled up, headlights cutting through fog and tape. He parked crooked—didn't even kill the engine right away.

Just sat. Gripped the wheel, eyes locked on the spot where the water met the dock. The tide hadn't swallowed it whole, which meant it hadn't swallowed her either—right?

But he'd been wrong before.

He shoved the door open, boots hitting pavement hard, like grounding himself might keep him from slipping under. Scanned—faces, medics, a dead body, and a white sheet.

But no Kaia. Not in the ambulance. Not in cuffs. Not even in the fucking shadows.

He checked the cruiser logs like they might offer more than canned chaos. No name. No match. His fingers twitched over the keyboard—searched her anyway. Kaia Taylore. Tied it eight different ways. *Nothing.*

Searched again. Same key words like it'd change. "Fuck." he muttered, trying to keep cool head in the car. Windows not that thick and not that tinted.

He dialed Akira. No answer. Dialed again. When she picked up, he didn't even wait and would apologize later. "I need a pull on Kiraia R or S Taylore—possible sighting at the pier off Pier 96. Anything. I don't care how unofficial—street cams, foot patrol, the crazy corner drunk—I don't care."

A breath on his part. Silence on hers. Maybe she was mad.

Maybe he didn't care. "Check downtown if a girl matching her hit intake. If someone picked her up, if she got in a car, if she fucking vanished—I want eyes on it."

Akira made a noise—*hesitation.* He cut it off.

"I'll owe you," something between a snap and a plea. "You want vacation hours? A favor with Internal? You want cash? Pick something. I just—need this." He hung up before she answered. Before she argued.

He was out of reasons to argue with, and trampled by doubt. Back near the docks, his gaze crawled the high line of the beach again.

> *Could she have willingly gone back in?*
> *Did she kill Kayden, then herself—? Cachí didn't say it.*
> *Was anyone watching?*
> *Someone see her—?   Someone grab her?*

Every second was like lead dragged through his chest. Like if he stayed still long enough, maybe he'd hear her footsteps. Hear her say: *What took you so long?* But the only thing he heard was surf. And it was starting to sound like goodbye.

The drive back seemed a lot faster by himself. Maybe it was the lack of circling, or the anxiety of being pulled with a *murderer.* Fuck.

"*Jesus christ!*" He hollered. So he took two laps around the hospital like they'd done before, before he—regretfully—turned in.

Dante saw Cachí from across the lot. Slouched low, hoodie pulled deep, hands jammed into the sleeves like he was trying to disappear inside himself. At the very least, he changed. But he didn't budge.

Not when Dante pulled up. Not when the engine clicked off. And not when the door slammed shut behind him. Crossing the distance slow, Dante Called out, "You go in?"

Cachí kept his eyes on the pavement like it might tell him something new. Lights from the emergency bay cutting long, sharp angles across the asphalt though. Bit of a light show even. If you fade and let your vision blur enough.

"You been out here the whole time?"

Didn't look up. Barely even shrugged. Dante sighed crashing into the bench next to him. Elbow to knees, palms to head. Too familiar lately.

"I asked one fucking thing, '*mano.*"

Another shrug. Dante's arms dropped and hands clapped once. "Get up. *Ahora.*"

Slow and unimpressed. "I'm good."

Gust of wind kicked grit up from the pavement. The lights above buzzed, yellow and tired. Sometimes life felt like death by a thousand cuts. "Ass handed to you twice in one day—still ain't enough?"

"Yeah, *eso.* You're too comfortable treating me like a bitch, *perro.* Where's—"

"That's cause you've been acting like one," Dante barked a humorless laugh. And Cachí stood; quick too. Full of that twitchy, too-thin anger he never seemed to know what to do with. "Say it again, Dáni."

"*Carnal*, sit down. You can't beat me on your best day. Let alone after fuckin' with Poseidon, ay?" Dante shook his head but stood calmly, and an extra foot back. For tension. "We're not doing that. We're not fighting anymore."

Cachí's jaw flexed. His fists curled, but couldn't hold.

"You don't want to see Leti?" Dante pressed.

"I don't have the *right* to want to see her," breath hitching. "I'm too scared to even ask—but she's not with you, what does that even mean—*Kaia?* What do I tell Leti?"

"The truth. As much of it as she decides she wants—*if* she wants."

"What's the truth?" He laughed back. But it cut.

"I was thinking about asking you the same," Dante turned his back to him and just dug his hands into his face a bit. Ran them over his head and took a couple breaths. "Why didn't you wait for me?"

"*Enserio?!* Shut the fuck up, perro. He was—k..." bigger breaths, like he was trying to suck the atmosphere down. "Kayden—he didn't care—he was hurting—enjoying it...maybe. *Dante que pasado?*"

"She wasn't there."

"How do you sit there like it doesn't matter...How—did you make us leave? Why, Dante, *where* could she have gone—she was fucking blue!"

"Why don't you fucking hold it together then and maybe I can feel it. Ah? *Ya, vale,*" Dante went on. "I'm going to live with this—I don't know, maybe we should have brought her, maybe I fucked up—but I'm *going* to find her.

Because we're not behind fucking bars, *Cachíflin*. But I would rather die this time then to bury you both, I panicked. And now—Mick."

Cachí didn't react. Didn't speak. But his blood went cold and his breathing stopped. Because that admission felt foreign. And *Mick.*

"I don't want her to hear from someone else," Dante added, gentler. "She hasn't been here since…"

Cachí, sighed, staring up at the thing. "Yeah…Why do you think I'm still out here, *'mano*?" With a begrudgingly small step forward.

The lights felt too bright. Floors too clean. Time in hospitals didn't pass—it held its breath and crept. They'd made it halfway down the corridor, Dante pointing, "there, her room" before Cachí stopped.

Feet grabbed from under the surface. It wasn't that dramatic, but felt like it was then. Really, just a quiet freeze by the wall, eyes locked on the window ahead where Dante pointed while watching for Mikki. Five paces before Dante stopped, missing Cachí from next to him. Noticed. Doubled backed. "You good?"

Cachí took one step towards him. A second, and nodded slow. Steps slower with every inch closer. Blonde hair—back of Mikki's head just barely visible from the window. More so as they moved in, inch by inch. Mikki, few chairs deep, holding a cup in the center like she'd forgotten how to sit straight.

Only there for bad news and worse. Cachí shook his head once. "I'm not going closer."

"You're already close."   "I'm good here."

Dante turned to him—fist to chest, stopping them both out of view. Annoyance and stress lines in both their faces. Heat in the veins. Dante's eyes softened but worry lines deepened. "*Si no lo haces tú…* then who's gonna tell her? Rookies?"

Dante approached the window. Turned back. "Don't be a ghost, *vato*. Don't run off on her, too. See if she wants to talk."

Didn't want for Cachí's reaction—figuring it's more of the same. Tapped the window softly with his knuckle. Just enough to catch Mikki's attention. Cachí glared, stuck in it. But couldn't be mad. Too tired, too agreeable. Dante not saying anything he disagreed with.

Mikki emerged. Dark circles under eyes. Not the same energy bleeding into the people around her. Maybe only enough to circulate for herself. Fear took more of that energy. Quickly looking from them both. Taking in the their state, then their eyes.

Her face changed. The tension in her spine, the shift in weight. "Is everything okay?" Like it was pulled out and forced to ask.

Dante wanted to spare her. Bit his lip, cheek. Swallowed, "I need to talk to you." She didn't ask why. Just glanced once to Cachí off to the side and how he wouldn't look at her.

"Your head would be on the floor if it were any lower..." She wisped hopelessly. Made it worse when Cachí just nodded and then Dante looked away. Mikki wasn't sure she wanted to go forward. Leaning into Dante's arm and letting him guide her someplace. He debated privacy, but feared the stress would run Cachí out and Dante wanted eyes on him. Finish about Kayden and have her freak about Cachí next—? Dante couldn't handle much more. And he was scared he meant it this time. Found a corner. Present, but distant enough their words didn't belong to anyone else but them.

Other side of the hallway—Cachí. Feet unchanged, but body weight shifting aimlessly. Not guarding, though he may pretend too. It was stalling; Dante knows, because the way he did with Mikki now. Turned back to her, hands buried in his pockets. Didn't want to say it out loud. Didn't want it to be his voice that made it real. "It's bad... It's Kayden." But he had to. Else someone else would.

Mikki's head tilted. Eyes narrowing fast, like maybe she heard wrong. "What could possibly be...Dante...where...?"

He held her gaze, but took the band aid, and ripped. "He's gone." The words too sterile; too simple. Like the hospital walls swallowed the weight of it before it could fall. Dante was nodding. "He's—dead."

A beat passed. Then another. And so many more he lost count."...What?" After a few tries. But the voice kept brittle.

And she talked slow, gaining speed while rolling downhill together— "What do you mean, *dead*? Who—how—*what*—?"

Dante swallowed hard. The kind of swallow that scraped—*but he wouldn't let go*—

"Cachí—saved Kaia. But didn't make it in time for Kayden."

Too close to a lie. Omission. Making it up as he went.

Tell her everything at once—let her digest this—details later?

He wanted to protect her, too. "Cachí still hasn't told me— everything. But I saw Kade..."

"Hasn't—told you?" She recoiled back slow, but found herself against the wall and stayed. Like she trusted it more than him to hold her up.

"What—what do you mean?"

"What I know..." Hundred times over—*stalling*. Cleared his throat. Watching her suffer through his dragging. "Either Kaia did it, and jumped off the pier...Or she was thrown in, and Cachí—did it." Lips nearly on her ear at the end, unwilling to let the words go anywhere but direct to her.

Dante stopped long enough to breathe. To touch her arm and watch her recoil. Trying to convince himself it's shock. "Cachí almost drowned. He was pulling her out of the water when I found them," her eyes frantically searched the room. Cachí jerking his head away. Like he was guilty.

Like he shot her brother same way someone shot her lover.

"Mikki, *amor*—please. Breathe." Because that was the confirmation. "Cachí..."

Eyes down and quick-wit silenced. Shame masking his eyes from her completely. Mikki looked to Dante. Looked back to Cachí.

"Please, Mick." Not sure what he was asking. But not allowed to touch her, not able to walk away. Dante half turned, physically unable to watch. Started gently knocking the door stop with his toe. Eventually kicked it harder than he should have. Trying to let it sit. Not assigning blame. Not asking her to be mad at him.

But Mikki didn't react at first. He felt smaller under the pressure. Stared at each other begging the other move first.

Dante felt her eyes withdraw further and he reached to pull her back. "Mouse? Amore...Tell—me what I can do, please...?"

"Take it back—take it—I don't..." She stepped forward, pressing a flat hand into his chest. Not hard. Just weight while floating—

Finding a place she maybe can land. Balancing for the second wave. Whole body recoiling back, eyes instantly full. Any exposed skin he could see, covered in chills while her hair slipped loose from how much she shook her head.

"No. No—no—no, I don't want to hear this hear again!" Knuckles against his chest to hold him away. "I don't want to be here..."

Nearest nurses temperature checked them, one coming in closer and hanging around diddling files longer. Dante watched her for a minute—

neutral, not breaking his heart—and tried a smile but failed when she caught him looking.

"Dante, no—I—"mouth closing hard. Breath sharp and stolen back.

"He saved her life."

Trying her hardest. "No. Nope—that's not true I can't hear this—Matí..." About when the nurse cleared out. The shatter in her voice probably gutting her too. No one like s to feel pain. "*Cachi*?"

Fragile hands meant for art and soft touch hit his chest. Though not a punch, maybe a swing. Pain so great it turned physical. But he hadn't felt it. Fighting, hang ups, fists—he wasn't doing right by the ones he cared for most today and that stung deep, too. Losing his tempter, pressing Kayden at the beach...Last thing he said to him—Mikki's hand came down again, pulling him back this time. Slow overflow leaking out through the cracks. But breath held like she was forced under.

When she lifted her hand a third time, Dante caught it—not to stop her, just to keep her close. Like if she broke, he'd keep the pieces together.

"We're going to get through this, Micki, amore." He pulled her in. Her body gave out the second it touched his. Collapsed like she'd been balancing on nothing and only then just realized.

"*Te tengo,* my love—I gotchu." His voice may have even cracked, but he hid himself in her hair, same as she his chest and chin. Sound and breath breaking free in heavy cries and weighted '*whys*'.

He didn't say anything more. Just held tight. The same as Dante. That sharp, unforgiving love that doesn't know how to die with the body. Even if other's cant understand. They could. Cachí.

And in that corner of sterile tile and over lit grief, Dante promised her he wasn't leaving—really just whispered how sorry he was for leaving before. Wrecked by the same tragedies.

But Matí left them with the ability to find peace. Legacy. Kayden took every good moment and left them with '*what it's*' and '*should have beens*' like red ink mean girls yearbook photos.

Dante rested his forehead to hers, eyes shut, and sat with her until the pain stopped swinging. Everyone—just trying to breathe through the smoke and pick through the rubble for what had been stolen. Hoping there's maybe just a little relief and a little life on the way.

Distance Between

Goodbye & Don't Go

|LXI|

Leti didn't turn when she heard the tap at the glass, but she clocked the shift. Mikki did too—lifted her head like she'd been waiting for it, bracing. Dante stood outside the room, one hand still raised.

"Can I talk to you?" he asked, voice low but clear through the cracked door. Mikki searched his face, then Leti's. She set her cup down without drinking and stood—slow, like even simple movement took effort.

Leti watched her follow him into the hallway, past the corner where people took calls they didn't want overheard. Not hidden. Out of reach.

That was a death walk. She expected to be getting one herself later. Unless that was Dante asking Mikki to tell Leti. Leti hadn't noticed she was squeezing the blanket until her hands hurt.

In the convex mirror bolted high in the corner, she saw a flash of movement too—hood drawn up, back to the wall just out of view from the doorway. Seemed familiar. She didn't react. Just adjusted the blanket, kept watching the window. "Idiot."

And almost as if he'd heard, he moved. Not dramatic. Just slow, her way. Like he'd been working himself up to it. Stopped at the door, raised his hand, and knocked. Just once. She checked out the window—gave a quick flash to acknowledge him but otherwise, had a hard time making herself face him.

What would happen if she was the one asking: *Are you afraid of me?*

She braced for him to flinch at the sight of her.

She'd have to turn eventually. But Cachí stood with sleeves pulled over his hands, face down, hair damp. Didn't meet her eyes either.

Made it easier. "Can I come in?" he asked, already halfway turned away.

Leti nodded. Barely. Her gaze dragged down to her lap and breathed slow. Watching him awkwardly move a wall chair to sit in front of the doorway. Like stepping in fully might make things worse.

"...You wanna close it?" she asked. He hesitated, then stood—slow, quiet. Shut the door like he was afraid it might shatter. Rested his forehead against the wood.

Leti's eyes found the reflection again. Mikki's hand was raised, palm open. Grief, not fury. When she hit Dante again, he caught her wrist, pulled her in. Held her while her knees gave out. Let himself go down with her. Leti couldn't hear them. But she knew what he was saying.

'I know. I'm sorry. It's okay.'　　　　　*Same words, always.*

Kaia's name wasn't spoken, but it was everywhere. Leti didn't notice Cachí had turned until he was watching—not her face, but her shoulder, hands, the blanket clenched in her grip. "Cachí...who's dead?"

Because there's nothing worse than the imagination.

"Kayden," he said. Voice shredded. "I tried. I pulled her out."

Leti coughed once—shocked breath tangled up in relief. Bent forward, hands over her mouth. "And Kaia? Is she okay? Is she in trouble? I can't believe she actually..."

"...You knew?" Cachí blinked at her. Confused.

Leti's head snapped up. "What?"

"Did you know?" His voice cracked, rising. "Were you in on that shit too?"

"I don't know what you're talking about," Leti said quickly, defensive now. Turned to the window, pulled the blanket up. Skin too loud again.

Cachí was quiet. Tapping foot and heavy breath less so, but he was settling himself. Faster when he watched her. She accidently met his eyes, thinking he'd be looking elsewhere. "Your idea or hers?" he asked. But she was already looking away. And giving nothing back.

Cachí's voice cracked half way through, "I had to shoot my brother tonight."

She didn't react.

"I mean—I didn't have to. It just felt like I did." He sniffled.

"He had Kaia off the edge of the pier...Kade was reaching for his—the..." Didn't want to say the word; almost made a gesture, frazzled himself until his head was in his hands.

"I just—I remember running. I remember thinking about—stuff and then, she went in and I was so close I just...*No se*. I did CPR...and then Dante, and I just...was outside on the bench.

She stayed still, but her eyes were big now. Bracing again.

"Dante...came out of no where. He was yelling. Sirens coming. I thought—I thought I could get her back to you. Give you that." He buried deeper into the hoodie.

Leti wiped her face. "Where'd you leave her?"

Wincing, "up by the lot. She rolled. Coughed. Breathed...Cops were coming. Dante...H—he was worried they'd pick me up on—um, *ya*. Guess...that's not *self*-defense so...murder...then."

Breath shallow and then deep and choppy like waves. "I think—that makes me...that same."

Leti looked insulted and scoffed. Didn't make it around to explaining why and he shrunk a bit more. She gestured vaguely toward his mouth when he looked up long enough for her to slowly do so.

"Kayden bust your lip? Or Dante?" He gave her a weak smile. Nodded toward where Dante and Mikki were still on the floor. "You know..." Leti brushed the towel in her lap, once. "I'm sorry you killed your brother," she said. He tensed, waiting for the rest.

"I'm also thankful. Relieved even...Haven't felt much else but anger." it hung in the air silently. Cachí mulling it over—Leti debating: "What's that make me?"

"Justified," he muttered immediately.

"You weren't?" Shifting, but stopped when it hurt. "I...don't know how much—you actually know, but...um." She cleared her throat, voice smaller now. "I—don't know. Sorry..." Staring ahead again. Trapped inside. She doesn't want other people to know.

His breathy laugh inviting her back out, still stung. "Only what you tell me here, *moy*." Guess it's still called a lie, even if you're thankful for it? Clenching and releasing. Both of them.

She crossed her legs. "Right." Sounded angrier than intended. "So how do you know Kaia isn't dead?"
"Because," still didn't look at her.

"She was gone. Dante went back immediately—it's not far. Unless....you think she'd go back in? She wasn't there. No hospitals have her. No cops. Nobody."

"Because they're looking." Leti laughed. Real—but under the influence. A partial point. "Something I actually learned over this little—trip thing."

"She was hurt," he added slow.

"Isn't everyone?"

"Poetic, *cariño*. But not like—this. No."

"You just might not be looking close enough," reaching to her water and feeling her rib jab.

"...I saw you, didn't I?" Muted low; not hearing might have been the goal. She did though. And the more she sounded it out, the more it sounded like a reach for validation than a quip.

Regardless—she wasn't sure how she wanted to respond to...these feelings right now. It caused her heart to race in a way she didn't like. Edging close to herself instead of defaulting to Kaia.

But Leti's lips tightened into a smile, resettling with her blanket and thirst. He stood up hesitantly like he'd do something, and then sunk back down unsure.

"Need to go?" Leti tried to name his contained, cry-laugh. That bitter bite. He shook his head after one of those salty-things and stood back up. Moved slower than a slug—arguably worse—making moves to hand off the water cup; short, pink plastic and trembling. Water slipping from the top. She watched him thoughtlessly, then:

"...You okay...in there?" Wasn't sure what she was trying to do with the call back, but it felt lighter than anything else.

He tucked his face back into his sleeves once sunken into the seat again. "You know...in light of Kayden—bottling all his shit—I uh, I don't think I am. But, Dante, Mikki. Imma be alright. I just—I..." sighed angrily and leaned back on the wall.

"I feel so stupid; an apology just seems like a joke, and—I dunno what I can do to save it, but Leti, I—I didn't keep you safe, I said he was safe.. And just...just...there's nothing I—fuck, *no se. Lo siento.*"

"Oh. Ok." She nodded mechanically. Another day she would have brazenly twisted that apart; plucked at him having said '*all.*'
Not worth the bonfires, the bracelet—?

Today though—maybe he's right. Maybe that would have been best.

But—alternate routes didn't make the collision on this one his fault. At least, for right now, she didn't think so. She kept her voice soft. "Hey, Cachí." He didn't answer right away. So she waited. When he finally landed on her eyes, she leaned a little in. Not for him to fall into—but to prove the space was still there. And so was she.

"I don't hate you," she said. "And—I don't blame you."

That was the straw and the camel. Cracked the man wide and busted out something sharp and sudden. Not loud or messy, but tin folding under heat. Hands interlaced behind his head and he somehow sunk deeper into his elbows and knees. Falling from the sky like a plan crashing down.

Didn't say a thing. Eventually he unwound his fingers and just leaned there. His hand shifting under the sleeve of his hoodie, grounding over something beneath the fabric.

She knew what it was. And it wasn't the bracelet that broke her. It was the way he touched it—like a tether. Like a regret.

Wiped his face too fast, too hard—like he could erase it before it showed. Like grief was no better than shame. But the more he fought it, the more he lost himself into it. Hiding.

She didn't offer her hand, or reach to hold him. She just held the moment still. Because maybe that was all they had. So he tracked her and she let him. Held his eyes until it hurt and dropped first. She'd get there again.

He sighed slow and heavy. Mikki and Dante somewhere in the background coming back to a stand. Back down in chairs and the same embrace. "Are you and Mikki going to be okay?"

"God I hope so..." Cracked down to the voice that time. He nodded a little too long. "And Kaia? For real?"

"She'll be back. Just taking the long way home."

His eyes landed on her wrist—on the bracelet too. Still there, even through the bruises. He didn't reach for it, wouldn't even consider it now. "I know you need time," he said. "A day. A year, five—Doesn't matter...If you ever. I mean, if you need," hands to face and an exasperated rumble. "Maybe just...don't lose my number...Okay?"

Simply—*presence*. And that was an okay place to begin again.

VII

THE PERIPHERY

we don't
start over.

we start
again.

37.6664° N, −122.4943°

37.8087° N, −122.4098°

37.8080° N, −122.4157°

37.8109° N, −122.4098°

the Long Way Home

DALY CITY, CALIFORNIA

|∞|

The pier came into view, wood still creaking like it remembered what happened. Dante didn't stop.

Even steps, paced breaths.

He did glance sideways though. Like muscle memory.

Probably ran an extra mile for every second he looked, too. Came to a drag in the heart of it. Slushed drink, and a slow walk.

The gift shop lights were still on: tourist bait: saltwater taffy, postcards, overpriced glass jars full of beach sand and fake treasure maps. And in the window—familiar, but strange sea glass.
Greens. Ambers. White, and pieces of cobalt blue like it had been carved from the sky. Another—sharp, oval.

Storm-colored.

He saw movement behind the glass then—windows, silver trinkets, reflections twirling back in both—
Dante was moving, bell chiming overhead as he entered.

He looked out of place. Half a tank, gym shorts; cute slushie and covered in sweat. He also didn't care, slowly sliding past the rows of bottled shells and baskets of carved driftwood.

Not foolish enough to hope for anything, but curious enough to look.

Sea glass visible along the front window—chimes moving like she was watching for him too.

Another chase, another game. Dante wasn't sure if it was Kayden, Kaia, his imagination—
didn't want to believe he was losing it though. Not yet anyway.

Easier to look into a crowd of strangers and think they're hiding within them. If Dante only looked a little harder.

Dante picked up the storm-colored piece—felt the dull grind of polish beneath his thumb. Bins of it.

Artificial, mostly, smoothed not from the tide, but from trained systems and machines grinding together.

Movement like wind and the chimes made him whip around—tight grasp on the glass so it didn't vanish, too.

Wrong her, though. Clerk. Surprised, but still chipper: "You looking for anything in particular?" And young.

Dante shook his head once, glaring decidedly back at the storm shrouded glass.

"Nah. Just thought I saw an old friend."

Sometime in the nearly distant future....

What if I told you—
I spoke to the dead?
If I divulged what they say, and it's not death that we should fear, but it's here.

What would you say?

My name is Cachi, and this is my personal statement regarding the essay questions within the scholarship application.

The past few years, my work has been heavily influenced by survival, society, and what it means to be alive. You ask what my portfolio specifically speaks to in today's world, and after a lot of thinking—if I'm being honest—
I don't know.
Or, I didn't know. Maybe I'm only now listening?

Not only have I refused to allow my art a voice, but I think I feared what it wanted to say. About life and death; what's fair, what's not; how much I'm willing to endure to consider it worth it.
It began to scream so loud, my only choice was to let it bleed or let myself break. But it's hard to put to words without causing urgency.

And, pictures are worth a thousand, right? Words I mean.
I'm learning the worth in the way pictures speak to you in your own language, how you interpret what I'm

hoping to inspire, and how I can use that as a voice to speak in — or even against — a world I don't like, but maybe shouldn't leave. I'm hoping this school can better help me hone skill and aim to say how — it's not fate's fault. It's ours.

We make it possible to say, death isn't the scariest fate.
Death is — death. Nada mas. Worse is to run in a race built to consume. To refuse to question it; to insist you must be proud to be in it; and to shame those daring to walk the bounds of "acceptability". Rewarding — not integrity but breeding — the speed at which someone steals their way to the top.

A place where people aren't silent because incapacity, but because policy and preference. Where trauma is privatized; pain is profitable; and Lady Justice?
Justice is a ghost, until Vengeance is a solution.

So is it still considered choice, if it's the only option they leave?
Would they still call it a choice if we said, 'no thank you'?

Be honest. Because the system doesn't fail.
It functions exactly as intended. Crowds for a headline or a hashtag, but crickets for the truth —
Justice isn't blind; she's been bought, sold, and branded. And vengeance isn't

chosen. It's what's left. Red tag, half off. Maybe vendettas don't fix anything. But neither does silence. Neither does grief or time. Time distracts. But unjust memories sting just as bad no matter how distant. Just remind someone.

I don't glorify vengeance—not loudly anyway—but I think I paint it. It's origins and endings: the evolution of pain and how it all links to transform or implode. How grief sits heavy and changes your vision like age. And this world, this angry rush. No pause: no eulogy for innocence stolen in man-made storms; no funeral for the selves we bury in crowded rooms. Through the grief and weight, shaded at the edges of every mundane thing. Because survival isn't triumph, it's trying.

I let the ink dry and the brushes go brittle over my first ghost. And I thought I was done. But I kept hearing his echo. Eventually it made a ripple so big it rocked five years from the past. Reminded me that, while it may feel like a different time, it wasn't. It was still ours. And I began painting again. Mostly ghosts. Usually, they're the only ones who stay long enough for the paint to dry. But not the horror kind of ghosts—the familiar. Unseen, unrecognizable, and unheard.

But still here walking among us. Within us — waiting.

Somedays I paint like I could build them a way back in. Other days, I may paint how a road out may look. We'll always carry the ghosts of the people we can't save; or the people that receive no justice — that now get no rest — but the thing about ghosts is you can learn to live with them.

A boy in hand-me-downs, backwards cap, pushing swings in empty parks. Brothers, clambering down sleeping halls, laughing every time they say, "boo." Heavy chill on your spine — the loved whispering, "I got your back." People think ghosts haunt places, but they don't. They reflect us. And we haunt ourselves.

Included with my ~~portfolio~~ graveyard are my entry pieces for the 2026 scholarship; two compatible works I have chosen, titled The Hell Hound & The Phoenix. Somedays, we are the hellhound. Somedays, we are the phoenix. But we're here. And we come with fire. These are the ghosts I carry. The ones I witnessed and saw; The ones I hope to see again; And the one I hope still sees me.

I miss you Leti.

When the words finally hit, they did so quietly—like a weight pressing down through Leti's chest.

She stared at the note. The initials. Read it again, because it didn't sound like Cachí. Not the one she'd left at the hospital. Under the hood, balanced on a wire she was trying to cross back over—

Too afraid to ask her to stay but unwilling to say goodbye. And looking worse the longer he stayed. The longer she stayed as a reminder they were both frozen in it. Couldn't even say rape or murder to each other, let alone move in resistance.

And Leti was tired of stillness; one final "See you tomorrow."

Only—she didn't.

And she might have hated herself more for that than what happened. Torturing herself, imagining his face that day. The look when she wasn't there; the texts that came after...

"Just tell me you're okay." Left unread.

The others: charming, halfway teasing, halfway real: "*Gonna be pissed if I walk the bridge and see you and Kaia in the nets laughing.*"

"Just tell me you're okay." Left unread.

The others: charming, halfway teasing, halfway real: "*Gonna be pissed if I walk the bridge and see you and Kaia in the nets laughing.*"

He didn't try for a while after that one.

Closest he came to an answer was the angry texts that came later. Rage was the one thing Leti had plenty of, and his boldness tempted her to fight. Opened the threads, thumb hovering—until she saw he might've been drunk. Slurred spelling, sentences spiraling.

Hurt. Saying it was cruel to Dante or mean to Mikki. How it was affecting everyone—but him.

"*Not a crush anymore, its the principle.*"

She could hear the lie and the ache wrapped in it but still waited for him to attack her about Kayden one day.

He hadn't yet. Not even a shadow of a hint. She was beginning to wonder if he even blamed her.

He kept angry though. "Just the small, irritating questions keeping those two up at night." Kept blaming them.

Still unanswered.

She'd tried. Almost hit send more than once until he caught her typing and called.

Leti pressed a hand against her heart just thinking about it all again. Replaying where it went wrong first.

It didn't hurt then. Didn't even think twice.

Not of Kaia. Not of anything. Because once Leti unhooked from that hospital bed, it was her turn to run.

Questions, assumptions, follow ups, report—she didn't want any of it. Not alone. But she wasn't ready to talk to anyone but Kaia.

And most of all though, the way stillness betrayed her made her want to change. Leti needed to reorient, influence-free. Or she'd shatter.

Sighing, her eyes moved through the letter again.

Didn't sound like the kid who blamed himself like it was a job. Not the guy who didn't know if he wanted to exist. Not the man who fed on blame until it fed on him.

She peeled open the envelope. Pulled the photos out because the fire made her feel something deep and warm. She knew it was her, too, but kept telling herself it couldn't be. Too beautiful a photo, too stunning a piece. Wondered if it was framed or forgotten somewhere in a classroom.

Should've held that feeling longer though, because when she saw Kaia's— shark teeth and a reaper—she felt stone-cold and upset.

Leti shook her head. *Fucking Kaia.*

Maybe angry. Maybe annoyed. Maybe just in awe, but definitely still just trying to figure it all out.

A breeze swept through, dust and dirt moving with it. Soft push from the sky and fresh, open air.

Leti unlocked her phone, sneering at the stupid caricature grin screensaver of Kaia and her. Hesitated there a moment too before opening a new message field because maybe Kaia's been right and not even known it. Cool thing about being alive—even as a ghost—is picking when, where, and how she wants to come back.

Leti scrolled contacts, clicked, and then her thumb moved.

> STILL HERE

Thanks for staying.
Take care.
And don't forget to forgive yourself.